CONTENTS:

NOTE

When the first part of "Pelle Erobreren" (Pelle the Conqueror) appeared in 1906, its author, Martin Andersen Nexo, was practically unknown even in his native country, save to a few literary people who knew that he had written some volumes of stories and a book full of sunshiny reminiscences from Spain. And even now, after his great success with "Pelle, " very little is known about the writer. He was born in 1869 in one of the poorest quarters of Copenhagen, but spent his boyhood in his beloved island Bornholm, in the Baltic, in or near the town, Nexo, from which his final name is derived. There, too, he was a shoemaker's apprentice, like Pelle in the second part of the book, which resembles many great novels in being largely autobiographical. Later, he gained his livelihood as a bricklayer, until he somehow managed to get to one of the most renowned of our "people's high-schools, " where he studied so effectually that he was enabled to become a teacher, first at a provincial school, and later in Copenhagen.

"Pelle" consists of four parts, each, except perhaps the last, a complete story in itself. First we have the open-air life of the boy in country surroundings in Bornholm; then the lad's apprenticeship in a small provincial town not yet invaded by modern industrialism and still innocent of socialism; next the youth's struggles in Copenhagen against employers and authorities; and last the man's final victory in laying the foundation of a garden-city for the benefit of his fellow-workers. The background everywhere is the rapid growth of the labor movement; but social problems are never obtruded, except, again, in the last part, and the purely human interest is always kept well before the reader's eye through variety of situation and vividness of characterization. The great charm of the book seems to me to lie in the fact that the writer knows the poor from within; he has not studied them as an outsider may, but has lived with them and felt with them, at once a participant and a keen-eyed spectator. He is no sentimentalist, and so rich is his imagination that he passes on rapidly from one scene to the next, sketching often in a few pages what another novelist would be content to work out into long chapters or whole volumes. His sympathy is of the widest, and he makes us see tragedies behind the little comedies, and comedies behind the little tragedies, of the seemingly sordid lives of the working people whom he loves. "Pelle" has conquered the hearts of the reading public of Denmark; there is that in the book which should conquer also the hearts of a wider public than that of the little country in which its author was born.

OTTO JESPERSEN, Professor of English in the University of Copenhagen.

GENTOFTE, COPENHAGEN. April, 1913.

I. BOYHOOD

I

It was dawn on the first of May, 1877. From the sea the mist came sweeping in, in a gray trail that lay heavily on the water. Here and there there was a movement in it; it seemed about to lift, but closed in again, leaving only a strip of shore with two old boats lying keel uppermost upon it. The prow of a third boat and a bit of breakwater showed dimly in the mist a few paces off. At definite intervals a smooth, gray wave came gliding out of the mist up over the rustling shingle, and then withdrew again; it was as if some great animal lay hidden out there in the fog, and lapped at the land.

A couple of hungry crows were busy with a black, inflated object down there, probably the carcass of a dog. Each time a wave glided in, they rose and hovered a few feet up in the air with their legs extended straight down toward their booty, as if held by some invisible attachment. When the water retreated, they dropped down and buried their heads in the carrion, but kept their wings spread, ready to rise before the next advancing wave. This was repeated with the regularity of clock-work.

A shout came vibrating in from the harbor, and a little while after the heavy sound of oars working over the edge of a boat. The sound grew more distant and at last ceased; but then a bell began to ring— it must have been at the end of the mole—and out of the distance, into which the beat of the oars had disappeared, came the answering sound of a horn. They continued to answer one another for a couple of minutes.

The town was invisible, but now and then the silence there was broken by the iron tramp of a quarryman upon the stone paving. For a long time the regular beat of his footsteps could be heard, until it suddenly ceased as he turned some corner or other. Then a door was opened, followed by the sound of a loud morning yawn; and someone began to sweep the pavement. Windows were opened here and there, out of which floated various sounds to greet the gray day. A woman's sharp voice was heard scolding, then short, smart slaps and the crying of a child. A shoemaker began beating leather, and as he worked fell to singing a hymn—

"But One is worthy of our hymn, O brothers:
The Lamb on Whom the sins of all men lay. "

The tune was one of Mendelssohn's "Songs without Words. "

Upon the bench under the church wall sat a boat's crew with their gaze turned seaward. They were leaning forward and smoking, with hands clasped between their knees. All three wore ear-rings as a preventive of colds and other evils, and all sat in exactly the same position, as if the one were afraid of making himself in the very least different from the others.

A traveller came sauntering down from the hotel, and approached the fishermen. He had his coat-collar turned up, and shivered in the chill morning air. "Is anything the matter? " he asked civilly, raising his cap. His voice sounded gruff.

One of the fishermen moved his hand slightly in the direction of his head-gear. He was the head man of the boat's crew. The others gazed straight before them without moving a muscle.

"I mean, as the bell's ringing and the pilot-boat's out blowing her horn, " the traveller went on. "Are they expecting a ship? "

"May be. You never can tell! " answered the head man unapproachably.

The stranger looked as if he were deeply insulted, but restrained himself. It was only their usual secretiveness, their inveterate distrust of every one who did not speak their dialect and look exactly like themselves. They sat there inwardly uneasy in spite of their wooden exterior, stealing glances at him when he was not looking, and wishing him at Jericho. He felt tempted to tease them a little.

"Dear me! Perhaps it's a secret? " he said, laughing.

"Not that I know of, " answered the fisherman cautiously.

"Well, of course I don't expect anything for nothing! And besides it wears out your talking-apparatus to be continually opening and shutting it. How much do you generally get? " He took out his purse; it was his intention to insult them now.

2

The other fishermen threw stolen glances at their leader. If only he did not run them aground!

The head man took his pipe out of his mouth and turned to his companions: "No, as I was saying, there are some folks that have nothing to do but go about and be clever. " He warned them with his eyes, the expression of his face was wooden. His companions nodded. They enjoyed the situation, as the commercial traveller could see from their doltish looks.

He was enraged. Here he was, being treated as if he were air and made fun of! "Confound you fellows! Haven't you even learnt as much as to give a civil answer to a civil question? " he said angrily.

The fishermen looked backward and forward at one another, taking mute counsel.

"No, but I tell you what it is! She must come some time, " said the head man at last.

"What 'she'? "

"The steamer, of course. And she generally comes about this time. Now you've got it! "

"Naturally—of course! But isn't it a little unwise to speak so loud about it? " jeered the traveller.

The fishermen had turned their backs on him, and were scraping out their pipes.

"We're not quite so free with our speech here as some people, and yet we make our living, " said the head man to the others. They growled their approval.

As the stranger wandered on down the harbor hill, the fishermen looked after him with a feeling of relief. "What a talker! " said one. "He wanted to show off a bit, but you gave him what he won't forget in a hurry. "

"Yes, I think it touched him on the raw, all right, " answered the man, with pride. "It's these fine gentlemen you need to be most careful of. "

Half-way down the harbor hill, an inn-keeper stood at his door yawning. The morning stroller repeated his question to him, and received an immediate answer, the man being a Copenhagener.

"Well, you see we're expecting the steamer from Ystad today, with a big cargo of slaves—cheap Swedish laborers, that's to say, who live on black bread and salt herrings, and do the work of three. They ought to be flogged with red-hot icicles, that sort, and the brutes of farmers, too! You won't take a little early morning glass of something, I suppose? "

"No, thank you, I think not—so early. "

"Very well, please yourself. "

Down at the harbor a number of farmers' carts were already standing, and fresh ones arrived at full gallop every minute. The newcomers guided their teams as far to the front as possible, examined their neighbors' horses with a critical eye, and settled themselves into a half-doze, with their fur collars turned up about their ears. Custom-house men in uniform, and pilots, looking like monster penguins, wandered restlessly about, peering out to sea and listening. Every moment the bell at the end of the mole rang, and was answered by the pilot-boat's horn somewhere out in the fog over the sea, with a long, dreary hoot, like the howl of some suffering animal.

"What was that noise? " asked a farmer who had just come, catching up the reins in fear. His fear communicated itself to his horses, and they stood trembling with heads raised listening in the direction of the sea, with questioning terror in their eyes.

"It was only the sea-serpent, " answered a custom-house officer. "He always suffers from wind in this foggy weather. He's a wind-sucker, you see. " And the custom-house men put their heads together and grinned.

Merry sailors dressed in blue with white handkerchiefs round their necks went about patting the horses, or pricking their nostrils with a straw to make them rear. When the farmers woke up and scolded, they laughed with delight, and sang—

"A sailor he must go through
A deal more bad than good, good, good! "

A big pilot, in an Iceland vest and woollen gloves, was rushing anxiously about with a megaphone in his hand, growling like an uneasy bear. Now and then he climbed up on the molehead, put the megaphone to his mouth, and roared out over the water: "Do—you—hear—any—thing? " The roar went on for a long time out upon the long swells, up and down, leaving behind it an oppressive silence, until it suddenly returned from the town above, in the shape of a confused babble that made people laugh.

"N-o-o! " was heard a little while after in a thin and long-drawn-out cry from the sea; and again the horn was heard, a long, hoarse sound that came rocking in on the waves, and burst gurgling in the splash under the wharf and on the slips.

The farmers were out of it all. They dozed a little or sat flicking their whips to pass the time. But every one else was in a state of suspense. A number of people had gradually gathered about the harbor — fishermen, sailors waiting to be hired, and master-artisans who were too restless to stay in their workshop. They came down in their leather aprons, and began at once to discuss the situation; they used nautical expressions, most of them having been at sea in their youth. The coming of the steamer was always an event that brought people to the harbor; but to-day she had a great many people on board, and she was already an hour behind time. The dangerous fog kept the suspense at high pressure; but as the time passed, the excitement gave place to a feeling of dull oppression. Fog is the seaman's worst enemy, and there were many unpleasant possibilities. On the best supposition the ship had gone inshore too far north or south, and now lay somewhere out at sea hooting and heaving the lead, without daring to move. One could imagine the captain storming and the sailors hurrying here and there, lithe and agile as cats. Stop! —Half-speed ahead! Stop! —Half-speed astern! The first engineer would be at the engine himself, gray with nervous excitement. Down in the engine-room, where they knew nothing at all, they would strain their ears painfully for any sound, and all to no purpose. But up on deck every man would be on the alert for his life; the helmsman wet with the sweat of his anxiety to watch every movement of the captain's directing hand, and the look-out on the forecastle peering and listening into the fog until he could hear his own heart beat, while the suspense held every man on deck on tenterhooks, and the fog-horn hooted its warning. But perhaps the ship had already gone to the bottom!

Every one knew it all; every man had in some way or other been through this overcharged suspense—as cabin-boy, stoker, captain, cook—and felt something of it again now. Only the farmers were unaffected by it; they dozed, woke up with a jerk, and yawned audibly.

The seafarers and the peasants always had a difficulty in keeping on peaceable terms with one another; they were as different as land and sea. But to-day the indifferent attitude of the peasants made the sea-folk eye them with suppressed rage. The fat pilot had already had several altercations with them for being in his way; and when one of them laid himself open to criticism, he was down upon him in an instant. It was an elderly farmer, who woke from his nap with a start, as his head fell forward, and impatiently took out his watch and looked at it.

"It's getting rather late, " he said. "The captain can't find his stall to-day. "

"More likely he's dropped into an inn on the way! " said the pilot, his eyes gleaming with malice.

"Very likely, " answered the farmer, without for the moment realizing the nature of the paths of the sea. His auditors laughed exultingly, and passed the mistake on to their neighbors, and people crowded round the unfortunate man, while some one cried: "How many inns are there between this and Sweden? "

"Yes, it's too easy to get hold of liquids out there, that's the worst of it, " the pilot went on. "But for that any booby could manage a ship. He's only got to keep well to the right of Mads Hansen's farm, and he's got a straight road before him. And the deuce of a fine road! Telegraph-wires and ditches and a row of poplars on each side—just improved by the local board. You've just got to wipe the porridge off your mustache, kiss the old woman, and climb up on to the bridge, and there you are! Has the engine been oiled, Hans? Right away, then, off we go; hand me my best whip! " He imitated the peasants' manner of speech. "Be careful about the inns, Dad! " he added in a shrill falsetto. There were peals of laughter, that had an evil sound in the prevailing depression.

The farmer sat quite still under the deluge, only lowering his head a little. When the laughter had almost died away, he pointed at the pilot with his whip, and remarked to the bystanders—

"That's a wonderful clever kid for his age! Whose father art thou, my boy? " he went on, turning to the pilot.

This raised a laugh, and the thick-necked pilot swelled with rage. He seized hold of the body of the cart and shook it so that the farmer had a difficulty in keeping his seat. "You miserable old clodhopper, you pig-breeder, you dung-carter! " he roared. "What do you mean by coming here and saying 'thou' to grown-up people and calling them 'boy'? And giving your opinions on navigation into the bargain! Eh! you lousy old money-grubber! No, if you ever take off your greasy night-cap to anybody but your parish clerk, then take it off to the captain who can find his harbor in a fog like this. You can give him my kind regards and say I said so. " And he let go of the cart so suddenly that it swung over to the other side.

"I may as well take it off to you, as the other doesn't seem able to find us to-day, " said the farmer with a grin, and took off his fur cap, disclosing a large bald head.

"Cover up that great bald pumpkin, or upon my word I'll give it something! " cried the pilot, blind with rage, and beginning to clamber up into the cart.

At that moment, like the thin metallic voice of a telephone, there came faintly from the sea the words: "We—hear—a—steam—whistle! "

The pilot ran off on to the breakwater, hitting out as he passed at the farmer's horse, and making it rear. Men cleared a space round the mooring-posts, and dragged up the gangways with frantic speed. Carts that had hay in them, as if they were come to fetch cattle, began to move without having anywhere to drive to. Everything was in motion. Labor-hirers with red noses and cunning eyes, came hurrying down from the sailors' tavern where they had been keeping themselves warm.

Then as if a huge hand had been laid upon the movement, everything suddenly stood still again, in strained effort to hear. A far-off, tiny echo of a steam whistle whined somewhere a long way off. Men stole together into groups and stood motionless, listening and sending angry glances at the restless carts. Was it real, or was it a creation of the heart-felt wishes of so many?

Perhaps a warning to every one that at that moment the ship had gone to the bottom? The sea always sends word of its evil doings; when the bread-winner is taken his family hear a shutter creak, or three taps on the windows that look on to the sea—there are so many ways.

But now it sounded again, and this time the sound come in little waves over the water, the same vibrating, subdued whistle that long-tailed ducks make when they rise; it seemed alive. The fog-horn answered it out in the fairway, and the bell in at the mole-head; then the horn once more, and the steam-whistle in the distance. So it went on, a guiding line of sound being spun between the land and the indefinite gray out there, backward and forward. Here on terra firma one could distinctly feel how out there they were groping their way by the sound. The hoarse whistle slowly increased in volume, sounding now a little to the south, now to the north, but growing steadily louder. Then other sounds made themselves heard, the heavy scraping of iron against iron, the noise of the screw when it was reversed or went on again.

The pilot-boat glided slowly out of the fog, keeping to the middle of the fairway, and moving slowly inward hooting incessantly. It towed by the sound an invisible world behind it, in which hundreds of voices murmured thickly amidst shouting and clanging, and tramping of feet—a world that floated blindly in space close by. Then a shadow began to form in the fog where no one had expected it, and the little steamer made its appearance—looking enormous in the first moment of surprise—in the middle of the harbor entrance.

At this the last remnants of suspense burst and scattered, and every one had to do something or other to work off the oppression. They seized the heads of the farmers' horses and pushed them back, clapped their hands, attempted jokes, or only laughed noisily while they stamped on the stone paving.

"Good voyage? " asked a score of voices at once.

"All well! " answered the captain cheerfully.

And now he, too, has got rid of his incubus, and rolls forth words of command; the propeller churns up the water behind, hawsers fly through the air, and the steam winch starts with a ringing metallic clang, while the vessel works herself broadside in to the wharf.

Between the forecastle and the bridge, in under the upper deck and the after, there is a swarm of people, a curiously stupid swarm, like sheep that get up on to one another's backs and look foolish. "What a cargo of cattle! " cries the fat pilot up to the captain, tramping delightedly on the breakwater with his wooden-soled boots. There are sheepskin caps, old military caps, disreputable old rusty hats, and the women's tidy black handkerchiefs. The faces are as different as old, wrinkled pigskin and young, ripening fruit; but want, and expectancy, and a certain animal greed are visible in all of them. The unfamiliarity of the moment brings a touch of stupidity into them, as they press forward, or climb up to get a view over their neighbors' heads and stare open-mouthed at the land where the wages are said to be so high, and the brandy so uncommonly strong. They see the fat, fur-clad farmers and the men come down to engage laborers.

They do not know what to do with themselves, and are always getting in the way; and the sailors chase them with oaths from side to side of the vessel, or throw hatches and packages without warning at their feet. "Look out, you Swedish devil! " cries a sailor who has to open the iron doors. The Swede backs in bewilderment, but his hand involuntarily flies to his pocket and fingers nervously his big pocket-knife.

The gangway is down, and the two hundred and fifty passengers stream down it—stone-masons, navvies, maid-servants, male and female day-laborers, stablemen, herdsmen, here and there a solitary little cowherd, and tailors in smart clothes, who keep far away from the rest. There are young men straighter and better built than any that the island produces, and poor old men more worn with toil and want than they ever become here. There are also faces among them that bear an expression of malice, others sparkling with energy, and others disfigured with great scars.

Most of them are in working-clothes and only possess what they stand in. Here and there is a man with some tool upon his shoulder—a shovel or a crowbar. Those that have any luggage, get it turned inside out by the custom-house officers: woven goods are so cheap in Sweden. Now and then some girl with an inclination to plumpness has to put up with the officers' coarse witticisms. There, for instance, is Handsome Sara from Cimrishamn, whom everybody knows. Every autumn she goes home, and comes again every spring with a figure that at once makes her the butt of their wit; but Sara, who generally has a quick temper and a ready tongue, to-day drops her eyes in modest confusion: she has fourteen yards of cloth wrapped round her under her dress.

The farmers are wide awake now. Those who dare, leave their horses and go among the crowd; the others choose their laborers with their eyes, and call them up. Each one takes his man's measure—width of chest, modest manner, wretchedness; but they are afraid of the scarred and malicious faces, and leave them to the bailiffs on the large farms. Offers are made and conditions fixed, and every minute one or two Swedes climb up into the hay in the back of some cart, and are driven off.

A little on one side stood an elderly, bent little man with a sack upon his back, holding a boy of eight or nine by the hand; beside them lay a green chest. They eagerly watched the proceedings, and each time a cart drove off with some of their countrymen, the boy pulled impatiently at the hand of the old man, who answered by a reassuring word. The old man examined the farmers one by one with an anxious air, moving his lips as he did so: he was thinking. His red, lashless eyes kept watering with the prolonged staring, and he wiped them with the mouth of the coarse dirty sack.

"Do you see that one there? " he suddenly asked the boy, pointing to a fat little farmer with apple-cheeks. "I should think he'd be kind to children. Shall we try him, laddie? "

The boy nodded gravely, and they made straight for the farmer. But when he had heard that they were to go together, he would not take them; the boy was far too little to earn his keep. And it was the same thing every time.

It was Lasse Karlsson from Tommelilla in the Ystad district, and his son Pelle.

It was not altogether strange to Lasse, for he had been on the island once before, about ten years ago; but he had been younger then, in full vigor it might be said, and had no little boy by the hand, from whom he would not be separated for all the world; that was the difference. It was the year that the cow had been drowned in the marl-pit, and Bengta was preparing for her confinement. Things looked bad, but Lasse staked his all on one cast, and used the couple of krones he got for the hide of the cow to go to Bornholm. When he came back in the autumn, there were three mouths to fill; but then he had a hundred krones to meet the winter with.

At that time Lasse had been equal to the situation, and he would still straighten his bowed shoulders whenever he thought of that exploit. Afterward, whenever there were short commons, he would talk of selling the whole affair and going to Bornholm for good. But Bengta's health failed after her late child-bearing, and nothing came of it, until she died after eight years of suffering, this very spring. Then Lasse sold their bit of furniture, and made nearly a hundred krones on it; it went in paying the expenses of the long illness, and the house and land belonged to the landlord. A green chest, that had been part of Bengta's wedding outfit, was the only thing he kept. In it he packed their belongings and a few little things of Bengta's, and sent it on in advance to the port with a horse-dealer who was driving there. Some of the rubbish for which no one would bid he stuffed into a sack, and with it on his back and the boy's hand clasped in his, he set out to walk to Ystad, where the steamer for Ronne lay. The few coins he had would just pay their passage.

He had been so sure of himself on the way, and had talked in loud tones to Pelle about the country where the wages were so incomprehensibly high, and where in some places you got meat or cheese to eat with your bread, and always beer, so that the water-cart in the autumn did not come round for the laborers, but only for the cattle. And—why, if you liked you could drink gin like water, it was so cheap; but it was so strong that it knocked you down at the third pull. They made it from real grain, and not from diseased potatoes; and they drank it at every meal. And laddie would never feel cold there, for they wore wool next their skin, and not this poor linen that the wind blew right through; and a laborer who kept himself could easily make his two krones a day. That was something different from their master's miserable eighty ores and finding themselves in everything.

Pelle had heard the same thing often before—from his father, from Ole and Anders, from Karna and a hundred others who had been there. In the winter, when the air was thick with frost and snow and the needs of the poor, there was nothing else talked about in the little villages at home; and in the minds of those who had not been on the island themselves, but had only heard the tales about it, the ideas produced were as fantastic as the frost-tracery upon the window-panes. Pelle was perfectly well aware that even the poorest boys there always wore their best clothes, and ate bread-and-dripping with sugar on it as often as they liked. There money lay like dirt by the roadside, and the Bornholmers did not even take the trouble to stoop and pick it up; but Pelle meant to pick it up, so that Father Lasse would have to empty the odds and ends out of the sack and clear out the locked compartment in the green chest to make room for it; and even that would be hardly enough. If only they could begin! He shook his father's hand impatiently.

"Yes, yes, " said Lasse, almost in tears. "You mustn't be impatient. " He looked about him irresolutely. Here he was in the midst of all this splendor, and could not even find a humble situation for himself and the boy. He could not understand it. Had the whole world changed since his time? He trembled to his very finger-tips when the last cart drove off. For a few minutes he stood staring helplessly after it, and then he and the boy together carried the green chest up to a wall, and trudged hand in hand up toward the town.

Lasse's lips moved as he walked; he was thinking. In an ordinary way he thought best when he talked out loud to himself, but to-day all his faculties were alert, and it was enough only to move his lips.

As he trudged along, his mental excuses became audible. "Confound it! " he exclaimed, as he jerked the sack higher up his back. "It doesn't do to take the first thing that comes. Lasse's responsible for two, and he knows what he wants—so there! It isn't the first time he's been abroad! And the best always comes last, you know, laddie. "

Pelle was not paying much attention. He was already consoled, and his father's words about the best being in store for them, were to him only a feeble expression for a great truth, namely, that the whole world would become theirs, with all that it contained in the way of wonders. He was already engaged in taking possession of it, open-mouthed.

He looked as if he would like to swallow the harbor with all its ships and boats, and the great stacks of timber, where it looked as if there would be holes. This would be a fine place to play in, but there were no boys! He wondered whether the boys were like those at home; he had seen none yet. Perhaps they had quite a different way of fighting, but he would manage all right if only they would come one at a time. There was a big ship right up on land, and they were skinning it. So ships have ribs, just like cows!

At the wooden shed in the middle of the harbor square, Lasse put down the sack, and giving the boy a piece of bread and telling him to stay and mind the sack, he went farther up and disappeared. Pelle was very hungry, and holding the bread with both hands he munched at it greedily.

When he had picked the last crumbs off his jacket, he set himself to examine his surroundings. That black stuff in that big pot was tar. He knew it quite well, but had never seen so much at once. My word! If you fell into that while it was boiling, it would be worse even than the brimstone pit in hell. And there lay some enormous fish-hooks, just like those that were hanging on thick iron chains from the ships' nostrils. He wondered whether there still lived giants who could fish with such hooks. Strong John couldn't manage them!

He satisfied himself with his own eyes that the stacks of boards were really hollow, and that he could easily get down to the bottom of them, if only he had not had the sack to drag about. His father had said he was to mind the sack, and he never let it out of his hands for a moment; as it was too heavy to carry, he had to drag it after him from place to place.

He discovered a little ship, only just big enough for a man to lie down in, and full of holes bored in the bottom and sides. He investigated the ship-builders' big grind-stone, which was nearly as tall as a man. There were bent planks lying there, with nails in them as big as the parish constable's new tether-peg at home. And the thing that ship was tethered to—wasn't it a real cannon that they had planted?

Pelle saw everything, and examined every single object in the appropriate manner, now only spitting appraisingly upon it, now kicking it or scratching it with his penknife. If he came across some strange wonder or other, that he could not get into his little brain in any other way, he set himself astride on it.

This was a new world altogether, and Pelle was engaged in making it his own. Not a shred of it would he leave. If he had had his playfellows from Tommelilla here, he would have explained it all to them. My word, how they would stare! But when he went home to Sweden again, he would tell them about it, and then he hoped they would call him a liar.

He was sitting astride an enormous mast that lay along the timber-yard upon some oak trestles. He kicked his feet together under the mast, as he had heard of knights doing in olden days under their horses, and imagined himself seizing hold of a ring and lifting himself, horse and all. He sat on horseback in the midst of his newly discovered world, glowing with the pride of conquest, struck the horse's loins with the flat of his hand, and dug his heels into its sides, while he shouted a song at the top of his voice. He had been obliged to let go the sack to get up.

> "Far away in Smaaland the little imps were dancing
> With ready-loaded pistol and rifle-barrelled gun;
> All the little devils they played upon the fiddle,
> But for the grand piano Old Harry was the one. "

In the middle of his noisy joy, he looked up, and immediately burst into a roar of terror and dropped down on to the wood-shavings. On the top of the shed at the place where his father had left him stood a black man and two black, open-mouthed hell-hounds; the man leaned half out over the ridge of the roof in a menacing attitude. It was an old figure-head, but Pelle thought it was Old Harry himself, come to punish him for his bold song, and he set off at a run up the hill. A little way up he remembered the sack and stopped. He didn't care about the sack; and he wouldn't get a thrashing if he did leave it behind, for Father Lasse never beat him. And that horrid devil would eat him up at the very least, if he ventured down there again; he could distinctly see how red the nostrils shone, both the devil's and the dogs'.

But Pelle still hesitated. His father was so careful of that sack, that he would be sure to be sorry if he lost it—he might even cry as he did when he lost Mother Bengta. For perhaps the first time, the boy was being subjected to one of life's serious tests, and stood—as so many had stood before him—with the choice between sacrificing himself and sacrificing others. His love for his father, boyish pride, the sense of duty that is the social dower of the poor—the one thing with the other—determined his choice. He stood the test, but not bravely; he howled loudly the whole time, while, with his eyes fixed immovably

14

upon the Evil One and his hell-hounds, he crept back for the sack and then dragged it after him at a quick run up the street.

No one is perhaps a hero until the danger is over. But even then Pelle had no opportunity of shuddering at his own courage; for no sooner was he out of the reach of the black man, than his terror took a new form. What had become of his father? He had said he would be back again directly! Supposing he never came back at all! Perhaps he had gone away so as to get rid of his little boy, who was only a trouble and made it difficult for him to get a situation.

Pelle felt despairingly convinced that it must be so, as, crying, he went off with the sack. The same thing had happened to other children with whom he was well acquainted; but they came to the pancake cottage and were quite happy, and Pelle himself would be sure to—perhaps find the king and be taken in there and have the little princes for his playmates, and his own little palace to live in. But Father Lasse shouldn't have a thing, for now Pelle was angry and vindictive, although he was crying just as unrestrainedly. He would let him stand and knock at the door and beg to come in for three days, and only when he began to cry—no, he would have to let him in at once, for to see Father Lasse cry hurt him more than anything else in the world. But he shouldn't have a single one of the nails Pelle had filled his pockets with down in the timber-yard; and when the king's wife brought them coffee in the morning before they were up— —

But here both his tears and his happy imaginings ceased, for out of a tavern at the top of the street came Father Lasse's own living self. He looked in excellent spirits and held a bottle in his hand.

"Danish brandy, laddie! " he cried, waving the bottle. "Hats off to the Danish brandy! But what have you been crying for? Oh, you were afraid? And why were you afraid? Isn't your father's name Lasse—Lasse Karlsson from Kungstorp? And he's not one to quarrel with; he hits hard, he does, when he's provoked. To come and frighten good little boys! They'd better look out! Even if the whole wide world were full of naming devils, Lasse's here and you needn't be afraid! "

During all this fierce talk he was tenderly wiping the boy's tear-stained cheeks and nose with his rough hand, and taking the sack upon his back again. There was something touchingly feeble about his stooping figure, as, boasting and comforting, he trudged down again to the harbor holding the boy by the hand. He tottered along in his big waterproof boots, the tabs of which stuck out at the side and bore an astonishing resemblance to Pelle's ears; out of the gaping pockets of his old winter coat protruded on one side his red pocket-handkerchief, on the other the bottle. He had become a little looser in his knee-joints now, and the sack threatened momentarily to get the upper hand of him, pushing him forward and forcing him to go at a trot down the hill. He looked decrepit, and perhaps his boastful words helped to produce this effect; but his eyes beamed confidently, and he smiled down at the boy, who ran along beside him.

They drew near to the shed, and Pelle turned cold with fear, for the black man was still standing there. He went round to the other side of his father, and tried to pull him out in a wide curve over the harbor square. "There he is again, " he whimpered.

"So that's what was after you, is it? " said Lasse, laughing heartily; "and he's made of wood, too! Well, you really are the bravest laddie I ever knew! I should almost think you might be sent out to fight a trussed chicken, if you had a stick in your hand! " Lasse went on laughing, and shook the boy goodnaturedly. But Pelle was ready to sink into the ground with shame.

Down by the custom-house they met a bailiff who had come too late for the steamer and had engaged no laborers. He stopped his cart and asked Lasse if he was looking for a place.

"Yes, we both want one, " answered Lasse, briskly. "We want to be at the same farm—as the fox said to the goose. "

The bailiff was a big, strong man, and Pelle shuddered in admiration of his father who could dare to speak to him so boldly.

But the great man laughed good-humoredly. "Then I suppose he's to be foreman? " he said, flicking at Pelle with his whip.

"Yes, he certainly will be some day, " said Lasse, with conviction.

"He'll probably eat a few bushels of salt first. Well, I'm in want of a herdsman, and will give you a hundred krones for a year—although it'll be confounded hard for you to earn them from what I can see.

There'll always be a crust of bread for the boy, but of course he'll have to do what little he can. You're his grandfather, I suppose? "

"I'm his father—in the sight of God and man, " answered Lasse, proudly.

"Oh, indeed! Then you must still be fit for something, if you've come by him honestly. But climb up, if you know what's for your own good, for I haven't time to stand here. You won't get such an offer every day. "

Pelle thought a hundred krones was a fearful amount of money; Lasse, on the contrary, as the older and more sensible, had a feeling that it was far too little. But, though he was not aware of it yet, the experiences of the morning had considerably dimmed the brightness of his outlook on life. On the other hand, the dram had made him reckless and generously-minded.

"All right then, " he said with a wave of the hand. "But the master must understand that we won't have salt herring and porridge three times a day. We must have a proper bedroom too—and be free on Sundays. " He lifted the sack and the boy up into the cart, and then climbed up himself.

The bailiff laughed. "I see you've been here before, old man. But I think we shall be able to manage all that. You shall have roast pork stuffed with raisins and rhubarb jelly with pepper on it, just as often as you like to open your mouth. "

They drove down to the quay for the chest, and then out toward the country again. Lasse, who recognized one thing and another, explained it all in full to the boy, taking a pull at the bottle between whiles; but the bailiff must not see this. Pelle was cold and burrowed into the straw, where he crept close up to his father.

"You take a mouthful, " whispered Lasse, passing the bottle to him cautiously. "But take care that he doesn't see, for he's a sly one. He's a Jute. "

Pelle would not have a dram. "What's a Jute? " he asked in a whisper.

"A Jute? Good gracious me, laddie, don't you know that? It was the Jutes that crucified Christ. That's why they have to wander all over the world now, and sell flannel and needles, and such-like; and they always cheat wherever they go. Don't you remember the one that cheated Mother Bengta of her beautiful hair? Ah, no, that was before your time. That was a Jute too. He came one day when I wasn't at home, and unpacked all his fine wares—combs and pins with blue glass heads, and the finest head-kerchiefs. Women can't resist such trash; they're like what we others are when some one holds a brandy-bottle to our nose. Mother Bengta had no money, but that sly devil said he would give her the finest handkerchief if she would let him cut off just the end of her plait. And then he went and cut it off close up to her head. My goodness, but she was like flint and steel when she was angry! She chased him out of the house with a rake. But he took the plait with him, and the handkerchief was rubbish, as might have been expected. For the Jutes are cunning devils, who crucified——" Lasse began at the beginning again.

Pelle did not pay much attention to his father's soft murmuring. It was something about Mother Bengta, but she was dead now and lay in the black earth; she no longer buttoned his under-vest down the back, or warmed his hands when they were cold. So they put raisins into roast pork in this country, did they? Money must be as common as dirt! There was none lying about in the road, and the houses and farms were not so very fine either. But the strangest thing was that the earth here was of the same color as that at home, although it was a foreign country. He had seen a map in Tommelilla, in which each country had a different color. So that was a lie!

Lasse had long since talked himself out, and slept with his head upon the boy's back. He had forgotten to hide the bottle.

Pelle was just going to push it down into the straw when the bailiff —who as a matter of fact was not a Jute, but a Zeelander—happened to turn round and caught sight of it. He told the boy to throw it into the ditch.

By midday they reached their destination. Lasse awoke as they drove on to the stone paving of the large yard, and groped mechanically in the straw. But suddenly he recollected where he was, and was sober in an instant. So this was their new home, the only place they had to stay in and expect anything of on this earth! And as he looked out over the big yard, where the dinner-bell was just sounding and calling servants and day-laborers out of all the doors, all his self-confidence vanished. A despairing feeling of helplessness overwhelmed him, and made his face tremble with impotent concern for his son.

His hands shook as he clambered down from the wagon; he stood irresolute and at the mercy of all the inquiring glances from the steps down to the basement of the big house. They were talking about him and the boy, and laughing already. In his confusion he determined to make as favorable a first impression as possible, and began to take off his cap to each one separately; and the boy stood beside him and did the same. They were rather like the clowns at a fair, and the men round the basement steps laughed aloud and bowed in imitation, and then began to call to them; but the bailiff came out again to the cart, and they quickly disappeared down the steps. From the house itself there came a far-off, monotonous sound that never left off, and insensibly added to their feeling of depression.

"Don't stand there playing the fool! " said the bailiff sharply. "Be off down to the others and get something to eat! You'll have plenty of time to show off your monkey-tricks to them afterwards. "

At these encouraging words, the old man took the boy's hand and went across to the basement steps with despair in his heart, mourning inwardly for Tommelilla and Kungstorp. Pelle clung close to him in fear. The unknown had suddenly become an evil monster in the imagination of both of them.

Down in the basement passage the strange, persistent sound was louder, and they both knew that it was that of a woman weeping.

II

Stone Farm, which for the future was to be Lasse and Pelle's home, was one of the largest farms on the island. But old people knew that when their grandparents were children, it had been a crofter's cottage where only two horses were kept, and belonged to a certain Vevest Koller, a grandson of Jens Kofod, the liberator of Bornholm. During his time, the cottage became a farm. He worked himself to death on it, and grudged food both for himself and the others. And these two things—poor living and land-grabbing—became hereditary in that family.

The fields in this part of the island had been rock and heather not many generations since. Poor people had broken up the ground, and worn themselves out, one set after another, to keep it in cultivation. Round about Stone Farm lived only cottagers and men owning two horses, who had bought their land with toil and hunger, and would as soon have thought of selling their parents' grave as their little property; they stuck to it until they died or some misfortune overtook them.

But the Stone Farm family were always wanting to buy and extend their property, and their chance only came through their neighbors' misfortunes. Wherever a bad harvest or sickness or ill luck with his beasts hit a man hard enough to make him reel, the Kollers bought. Thus Stone Farm grew, and acquired numerous buildings and much importance; it became as hard a neighbor as the sea is, when it eats up the farmer's land, field by field, and nothing can be done to check it. First one was eaten up and then another. Every one knew that his turn would come sooner or later. No one goes to law with the sea; but all the ills and discomfort that brooded over the poor man's life came from Stone Farm. The powers of darkness dwelt there, and frightened souls pointed to it always. "That's well-manured land, " the people of the district would say, with a peculiar intonation that held a curse; but they ventured no further.

The Koller family was not sentimental; it throve capitally in the sinister light that fell upon the farm from so many frightened minds, and felt it as power. The men were hard drinkers and card-players; but they never drank so much as to lose sight and feeling; and if they played away a horse early in the evening, they very likely won two in the course of the night.

When Lasse and Pelle came to Stone Farm, the older cottagers still remembered the farmer of their childhood, Janus Koller, the one who did more to improve things than any one else. In his youth he once, at midnight, fought with the devil up in the church-tower, and overcame him; and after that everything succeeded with him. Whatever might or might not have been the reason, it is certain that in his time one after another of his neighbors was ruined, and Janus went round and took over their holdings. If he needed another horse, he played for and won it at loo; and it was the same with everything. His greatest pleasure was to break in wild horses, and those who happened to have been born at midnight on Christmas Eve could distinctly see the Evil One sitting on the box beside him and holding the reins. He came to a bad end, as might have been expected. One morning early, the horses came galloping home to the farm, and he was found lying by the roadside with his head smashed against a tree.

His son was the last master of Stone Farm of that family. He was a wild devil, with much that was good in him. If any one differed from him, he knocked him down; but he always helped those who got into trouble. In this way no one ever left house and home; and as he had the family fondness for adding to the farm, he bought land up among the rocks and heather. But he wisely let it lie as it was. He attached many to the farm by his assistance, and made them so dependent that they never became free again. His tenants had to leave their own work when he sent for them, and he was never at a loss for cheap labor. The food he provided was scarcely fit for human beings, but he always ate of the same dish himself. And the priest was with him at the last; so there was no fault to find with his departure from this life.

He had married twice, but his only child was a daughter by the second wife, and there was something not quite right about her. She was a woman at the age of eleven, and made up to any one she met; but no one dared so much as look at her, for they were afraid of the farmer's gun. Later on she went to the other extreme, and dressed herself up like a man, and went about out on the rocks instead of busying herself with something at home; and she let no one come near her.

Kongstrup, the present master of Stone Farm, had come to the island about twenty years before, and even now no one could quite make him out. When he first came he used to wander about on the heath and do nothing, just as she did; so it was hardly to be wondered at that he got into trouble and had to marry her. But it was dreadful!

He was a queer fellow; but perhaps that was what people were like where he came from? He first had one idea and then another, raised wages when no one had asked him to, and started stone-quarrying with contract work. And so he went on with his foolish tricks to begin with, and let his cottagers do as they liked about coming to work at the farm. He even went so far as to send them home in wet weather to get in their corn, and let his own stand and be ruined. But things went all wrong of course, as might well be imagined, and gradually he had to give in, and abandon all his foolish ideas.

The people of the district submitted to this condition of dependence without a murmur. They had been accustomed, from father to son, to go in and out of the gates of Stone Farm, and do what was required of them, as dutifully as if they had been serfs of the land. As a set-off they allowed all their leaning toward the tragic, all the terrors of life and gloomy mysticism, to center round Stone Farm. They let the devil roam about there, play loo with the men for their souls, and ravish the women; and they took off their caps more respectfully to the Stone Farm people than to any one else.

All this had changed a little as years went on; the sharp points of the superstition had been blunted a little. But the bad atmosphere that hangs over large estates—over all great accumulations of what should belong to the many—also hung heavy over Stone Farm. It was the judgment passed by the people, their only revenge for themselves and theirs.

Lasse and Pelle were quickly aware of the oppressive atmosphere, and began to see with the half-frightened eyes of the others, even before they themselves had heard very much. Lasse especially thought he could never be quite happy here, because of the heaviness that always seemed to surround them. And then that weeping that no one could quite account for!

All through the long, bright day, the sound of weeping came from the rooms of Stone Farm, like the refrain of some sad folk-song. Now at last it had stopped. Lasse was busying himself with little things in the lower yard, and he still seemed to have the sound in his ears. It was sad, so sad, with this continual sound of a woman weeping, as if a child were dead, or as if she were left alone with her shame. And what could there be to weep for, when you had a farm of several hundred acres, and lived in a high house with twenty windows!

> "Riches are nought but a gift from the Lord,
> But poverty, that is in truth a reward.
> They who wealth do possess
> Never know happiness,
> While the poor man's heart is ever contented! "

So sang Karna over in the dairy, and indeed it was true! If only Lasse knew where he was to get the money for a new smock-frock for the little lad, he would never envy any one on this earth; though it would be nice to have money for tobacco and a dram now and then, if it was not unfair to any one else.

Lasse was tidying up the dung-heap. He had finished his midday work in the stable, and was taking his time about it; it was only a job he did between whiles. Now and then he glanced furtively up at the high windows and put a little more energy into his work; but weariness had the upper hand. He would have liked to take a little afternoon nap, but did not dare. All was quiet on the farm. Pelle had been sent on an errand to the village shop for the kitchen-folk, and all the men were in the fields covering up the last spring corn. Stone Farm was late with this.

The agricultural pupil now came out of the stable, which he had entered from the other side, so as to come upon Lasse unexpectedly. The bailiff had sent him. "Is that you, you nasty spy! " muttered Lasse when he saw him. "Some day I'll kill you! " But he took off his cap with the deepest respect. The tall pupil went up the yard without looking at him, and began to talk nonsense with the maids down in the wash-house. He wouldn't do that if the men were at home, the scarecrow!

Kongstrup came out on to the steps, and stood for a little while looking at the weather; then he went down to the cow-stable. How big he was! He quite filled the stable doorway. Lasse put down his fork and hastened in in case he was wanted.

"Well, how are you getting on, old man? " asked the farmer kindly. "Can you manage the work? "

23

"Oh, yes, I get through it, " answered Lasse; "but that's about all. It's a lot of animals for one man. "

Kongstrup stood feeling the hind quarters of a cow. "You've got the boy to help you, Lasse. Where is he, by the by? I don't see him. "

"He's gone to the village shop for the women-folk. "

"Indeed? Who told him to go? "

"I think it was the mistress herself. "

"H'm. Is it long since he went? "

"Yes, some time. He ought soon to be back now. "

"Get hold of him when he comes, and send him up to me with the things, will you? "

Pelle was rather frightened at having to go up to the office, and besides the mistress had told him to keep the bottle well hidden under his smock. The room was very high, and on the walls hung splendid guns; and up upon a shelf stood cigar-boxes, one upon another, right up to the ceiling, just as if it were a tobacco-shop. But the strangest thing of all was that there was a fire in the stove, now, in the middle of May, and with the window open! It must be that they didn't know how to get rid of all their money. But wherever were the money-chests?

All this and much more Pelle observed while he stood just inside the door upon his bare feet, not daring from sheer nervousness to raise his eyes. Then the farmer turned round in his chair, and drew him toward him by the collar. "Now let's see what you've got there under your smock, my little man! " he said kindly.

"It's brandy, " said Pelle, drawing forth the bottle. "The mistress said I wasn't to let any one see it. "

"You're a clever boy, " said Kongstrup, patting him on the cheek. "You'll get on in the world one of these days. Now give me the bottle and I'll take it out to your mistress without letting any one see. " He laughed heartily.

Pelle handed him the bottle—*there* stood money in piles on the writing-table, thick round two-krone pieces one upon another! Then why didn't Father Lasse get the money in advance that he had begged for?

The mistress now came in, and the farmer at once went and shut the window. Pelle wanted to go, but she stopped him. "You've got some things for me, haven't you? " she said.

"I've received the *things,* " said Kongstrup. "You shall have them— when the boy's gone. "

But she remained at the door. She would keep the boy there to be a witness that her husband withheld from her things that were to be used in the kitchen; every one should know it.

Kongstrup walked up and down and said nothing. Pelle expected he would strike her, for she called him bad names—much worse than Mother Bengta when Lasse came home merry from Tommelilla. But he only laughed. "Now that'll do, " he said, leading her away from the door, and letting the boy out.

Lasse did not like it. He had thought the farmer was interfering to prevent them all from making use of the boy, when he so much needed his help with the cattle; and now it had taken this unfortunate turn!

"And so it was brandy! " he repeated. "Then I can understand it. But I wonder how she dares set upon him like that when it's with *her* the fault lies. He must be a good sort of fellow. "

"He's fond of drink himself, " said Pelle, who had heard a little about the farmer's doings.

"Yes, but a woman! That's quite another thing. Remember they're fine folk. Well, well, it doesn't become us to find fault with our betters; we have enough to do in looking after ourselves. But I only hope she won't send you on any more of her errands, or we may fall between two stools. "

Lasse went to his work. He sighed and shook his head while he dragged the fodder out. He was not at all happy.

III

There was something exhilarating in the wealth of sunshine that filled all space without the accompaniment of corresponding heat. The spring moisture was gone from the air, and the warm haze of summer had not yet come. There was only light—light over the green fields and the sea beyond, light that drew the landscape in clear lines against the blue atmosphere, and breathed a gentle, pleasant warmth.

It was a day in the beginning of June—the first real summer day; and it was Sunday.

Stone Farm lay bathed in sunshine. The clear golden light penetrated everywhere; and where it could not reach, dark colors trembled like a hot, secret breath out into the light. Open windows and doors looked like veiled eyes in the midst of the light, and where the roof lay in shadow, it had the appearance of velvet.

It was quiet up in the big house to-day; it was a day of rest from wrangling too.

The large yard was divided into two by a fence, the lower part consisting in the main of a large, steaming midden, crossed by planks in various directions, and at the top a few inverted wheelbarrows. A couple of pigs lay half buried in the manure, asleep, and a busy flock of hens were eagerly scattering the pile of horse-dung from the last morning clearance. A large cock stood in the middle of the flock, directing the work like a bailiff.

In the upper yard a flock of white pigeons were pecking corn off the clean stone paving. Outside the open coach-house door, a groom was examining the dog-cart, while inside stood another groom, polishing the best harness.

The man at the dog-cart was in shirt-sleeves and newly-polished top-boots; he had a youthful, elastic frame, which assumed graceful attitudes as he worked. He wore his cap on the back of his head, and whistled softly while he cleaned the wheels outside and in, and sent stolen glances down to the wash-house, where, below the window, one of the maids was going through her Sunday ablutions, with shoulders and arms bare, and her chemise pushed down below her bosom.

The big dairymaid, Karna, went past him to the pump with two large buckets. As she returned, she splashed some water on to one of his boots, and he looked up with an oath. She took this as an invitation to stop, and put down her pails with a cautious glance up at the windows of the big house.

"You've not had all the sleep you ought to have had, Gustav, " she said teasingly, and laughed.

"Then it isn't your fault, at any rate, " he answered roughly. "Can you patch my everyday trousers for me to-day? "

"No, thank you! I don't mend for another to get all the pleasant words! "

"Then you can leave it alone! There are plenty who'll mend for me without you! " And he bent again to his work.

"I'll see if I can get time, " said the big woman meekly. "But I've got all the work in the place to do by myself this afternoon; the others are all going out. "

"Yes, I see Bodil's washing herself, " said Gustav, sending a squirt of tobacco-juice out of his mouth in the direction of the wash-house window. "I suppose she's going to meeting, as she's doing it so, thoroughly. "

Karna looked cunning. "She asked to be free because she wanted to go to church. She go to church! I should just like to see her! No, she's going down to the tailor's in the village, and there I suppose she'll meet Malmberg, a townsman of hers. I wonder she isn't above having anything to do with a married man. "

"She can go on the spree with any one she likes, for all I care, " answered Gustav, kicking the last wheel into place with his foot, while Karna stood looking at him kindly. But the next moment she spied a face behind the curtains up in one of the windows, and hurried off with her pails. Gustav spat contemptuously between his teeth after her. She was really too old for his seventeen years; she must be at least forty; and casting another long look at Bodil, he went across to the coachhouse with oil-can and keys.

The high white house that closed the yard at its upper end, had not been built right among the other buildings, but stood proudly aloof, unconnected with them except by two strips of wooden paling. It had gables on both sides, and a high basement, in which were the servants' hall, the maids' bedrooms, the wash-house, the mangling-room, and the large storerooms. On the gable looking on to the yard was a clock that did not go. Pelle called the building the Palace, and was not a little proud of being allowed to enter the basement. The other people on the farm did not give it such a nice name.

He was the only one whose awe of the House had nothing sinister about it; others regarded it in the light of a hostile fortress. Every one who crossed the paved upper yard, glanced involuntarily up at the high veiled windows, behind which an eye might secretly be kept upon all that went on below. It was, a little like passing a row of cannons' mouths—it made one a little unsteady on one's feet; and no one crossed the clean pavement unless he was obliged. On the other hand they went freely about the other half of the yard, which was just as much overlooked by the House.

Down there two of the lads were playing. One of them had seized the other's cap and run off with it, and a wild chase ensued, in at one barn-door and out at another all round the yard, to the accompaniment of mischievous laughter and breathless exclamations. The yard-dog barked with delight and tumbled madly about on its chain in its desire to join in the game. Up by the fence the robber was overtaken and thrown to the ground; but he managed to toss the cap up into the air, and it descended right in front of the high stone steps of the House.

"Oh, you mean beast! " exclaimed the owner of the cap, in a voice of despairing reproach, belaboring the other with the toes of his boots. "Oh, you wretched bailiff's sneak! " He suddenly stopped and measured the distance with an appraising eye. "Will you stand me half a pint if I dare go up and fetch the cap? " he asked in a whisper. The other nodded and sat up quickly to see what would come of it. "Swear? You won't try and back out of it? " he said, lifting his hand adjuringly. His companion solemnly drew his finger across his throat, as if cutting it, and the oath was taken. The one who had lost the cap, hitched up his trousers and pulled himself together, his

whole figure stiffening with determination; then he put his hands
upon the fence, vaulted it, and walked with bent head and firm step
across the yard, looking like one who had staked his all upon one
card. When he had secured the cap, and turned his back upon the
House, he sent a horrible grimace down the yard.

Bodil now came up from the basement in her best Sunday clothes,
with a black silk handkerchief on her head and a hymn-book in her
hand. How pretty she was! And brave! She went along the whole
length of the House and out! But then she could get a kiss from the
farmer any day she liked.

Outside the farm proper lay a number of large and small
outbuildings — the calves' stable, the pigsties, the tool-shed, the cart-
shed and a smithy that was no longer used. They were all like so
many mysteries, with trap-doors that led down to pitch-dark,
underground beet and potato cellars, from which, of course, you
could get by secret passages to the strangest places underground,
and other trap-doors that led up to dark lofts, where the most
wonderful treasures were preserved in the form of old lumber.

But Pelle unfortunately had little time to go into all this. Every day
he had to help his father to look after the cattle, and with so large a
herd, the work was almost beyond their power. If he had a moment's
breathing-space, some one was sure to be after him. He had to fetch
water for the laundry girls, to grease the pupil's boots and run to the
village shop for spirits or chewing-tobacco for the men. There was
plenty to play with, but no one could bear to see him playing; they
were always whistling for him as if he were a dog.

He tried to make up for it by turning his work into a game, and in
many instances this was possible. Watering the cattle, for instance,
was more fun than any real game, when his father stood out in the
yard and pumped, and the boy only had to guide the water from
manger to manger. When thus occupied, he always felt something
like a great engineer. But on the other hand, much of the other work
was too hard to be amusing.

At this moment the boy was wandering about among the
outbuildings, where there was no one to hunt him about. The door to
the cow-stable stood open, and he could hear the continual
munching of the cows, now and then interrupted by a snuff of
contentment or the regular rattle of a chain up and down when a

cow rubbed its neck upon the post. There was a sense of security in the sound of his father's wooden shoes up and down the foddering-passage.

Out of the open half-doors of the smaller outbuildings there came a steamy warmth that smelt pleasantly of calves and pigs. The pigs were hard at work. All through the long sty there was munching and smacking. One old sow supped up the liquid through the corners of her mouth, another snuffed and bubbled with her snout along the bottom of the trough to find the rotten potatoes under the liquid. Here and there two pigs were fighting over the trough, and emitting piercing squeals. The calves put their slobbering noses out at the doors, gazing into the sunny air and lowing feelingly. One little fellow, after snuffing up air from the cow-stable in a peculiarly thorough way, turned up his lip in a foolish grin: it was a bull- calf. He laid his chin upon the half-door, and tried to jump over, but Pelle drove him down again. Then he kicked up his hind legs, looked at Pelle out of the corner of his eye, and stood with arched back, lifting his fore and hindquarters alternately with the action of a rocking-horse. He was light-headed with the sun.

Down on the pond, ducks and geese stood upon their heads in the water, flourishing their red legs in the air. And all at once the whole flock would have an attack of giddy delight in the sunshine, and splash screaming from bank to bank, the last part of the way sliding along the top of the water with a comical wagging of the tail.

Pelle had promised himself much from this couple of hours that were to be entirely his own, as his father had given him a holiday until the time came for the midday work. But now he stood in bewilderment, overwhelmed by the wealth of possibilities. Would it be the best fun to sail upon the pond on two tail-boards laid one across the other? There was a manure-cart lying there now to be washed. Or should he go in and have a game with the tiny calves? Or shoot with the old bellows in the smithy? If he filled the nozzle with wet earth, and blew hard, quite a nice shot could come out of it.

Pelle started and tried to make himself invisible. The farmer himself had come round the corner, and was now standing shading his eyes with his hand and looking down over the sloping land and the sea. When he caught sight of Pelle, he nodded without changing his expression, and said: "Good day, my boy! How are you getting on? " He gazed on, and probably hardly knew that he had said it and patted the boy on the shoulder with the end of his stick; the farmer often went about half asleep.

But Pelle felt it as a caress of a divine nature, and immediately ran across to the stable to tell his father what had happened to him. He had an elevating sensation in his shoulder as if he had been knighted; and he still felt the stick there. An intoxicating warmth flowed from the place through his little body, sent the adventure mounting to his head and made him swell with pride. His imagination rose and soared into the air with some vague, dizzy idea about the farmer adopting him as his son.

He soon came down again, for in the stable he ran straight into the arms of the Sunday scrubbing. The Sunday wash was the only great objection he had to make to life; everything else came and was forgotten again, but it was always coming again. He detested it, especially that part of it which had to do with the interior of his ears. But there was no kind mother to help; Lasse stood ready with a bucket of cold water, and some soft soap on a piece of broken pot, and the boy had to divest himself of his clothes. And as if the scrubbing were not enough, he afterwards had to put on a clean shirt—though, fortunately, only every other Sunday. The whole thing was nice enough to look back upon afterwards—like something gone through with, and not to happen again for a little while.

Pelle stood at the stable door into the yard with a consequential air, with bristling hair and clean shirt-sleeves, his hands buried in his trouser pockets. Over his forehead his hair waved in what is called a "cow's lick, " said to betoken good fortune; and his face, all screwed up as it turned towards the bright light, looked the oddest piece of topsy-turvydom, with not a single feature in its proper place. Pelle bent the calves of his legs out backwards, and stood gently rocking himself to and fro as he saw Gustav doing, up on the front-door steps, where he stood holding the reins, waiting for his master and mistress.

The mistress now appeared, with the farmer, and a maid ran down in front to the carriage with a little stepladder, and helped her in. The farmer stood at the top of the steps until she was seated: she had difficulty in walking. But what a pair of eyes she had! Pelle hastily looked away when she turned her face down towards the yard. It was whispered among the men that she could bring misfortune upon any one by looking at him if she liked. Now Gustav unchained the dog, which bounded about, barking, in front of the horses as they drove out of the courtyard.

Anyhow the sun did not shine like this on a week-day. It was quite dazzling when the white pigeons flew in one flock over the yard, turning as regularly as if they were a large white sheet flapping in the sunshine; the reflection from their wings flashed over the dung-heap and made the pigs lift their heads with an inquiring grunt. Above, in their rooms the men sat playing "Sixty-six, " or tipping wooden shoes, and Gustav began to play "Old Noah" on his concertina.

Pelle picked his way across the upper part of the yard to the big dog-kennel, which could be turned on a pivot according to the direction of the wind. He seated himself upon the angle of the roof, and made a merry-go-round of it by pushing off with his foot every time he passed the fence. Suddenly it occurred to him that he himself was everybody's dog, and had better hide himself; so he dropped down, crept into the kennel, and curled himself up on the straw with his head between his fore-paws. There he lay for a little while, staring at the fence and panting with his tongue hanging out of his mouth. Then an idea came into his head so suddenly as to make him forget all caution; and the next moment he was sliding full tilt down the railing of the front-door steps.

He had done this seventeen times and was deeply engrossed in the thought of reaching fifty, when he heard a sharp whistle from the big coach-house door. The farm pupil stood there beckoning him. Pelle, crestfallen, obeyed the call, bitterly regretting his thoughtlessness. He was most likely wanted now to grease boots again, perhaps for them all.

The pupil drew him inside the door, which he shut. It was dark, and the boy, coming in out of the bright daylight, could distinguish nothing; what he made out little by little assumed shapeless outlines to his frightened imagination. Voices laughed and growled confusedly in his ears, and hands that seemed to him enormous pulled him about. Terror seized him, and with it came crazy, disconnected recollections of stories of robbery and murder, and he began to scream with fright. A big hand covered the whole of his face, and in the silence that followed his stifled scream, he heard a voice out in the yard, calling to the maids to come and see something funny.

He was too paralyzed with terror to know what was being done with him, and only wondered faintly what there was funny out there in the sunshine. Would he ever see the sun again, he wondered?

As if in answer to his thought, the door was at that moment thrown open. The light poured in and he recognized the faces about him, and found himself standing half naked in the full daylight, his trousers down about his heels and his shirt tucked up under his waistcoat. The pupil stood at one side with a carriage-whip, with which he flicked at the boy's naked body, crying in a tone of command: "Run! " Pelle, wild with terror and confusion, dashed into the yard, but there stood the maids, and at sight of him they screamed with laughter, and he turned to fly back into the coach-house. But he was met by the whip, and forced to return into the daylight, leaping like a kangaroo and calling forth renewed shouts of laughter. Then he stood still, crying helplessly, under a shower of coarse remarks, especially from the maids. He no longer noticed the whip, but only crouched down, trying to hide himself, until at last he sank in a heap upon the stone paving, sobbing convulsively.

Karna, large of limb, came rushing up from the basement and forced her way through the crowd, crimson with rage and scolding as she went. On her freckled neck and arms were brown marks left by the cows' tails at the last milking, looking like a sort of clumsy tattooing. She flung her slipper in the pupil's face, and going up to Pelle, wrapped him in her coarse apron and carried him down to the basement.

When Lasse heard what had happened to the boy, he took a hammer and went round to kill the farm pupil; and the look in the old man's eyes was such that no one desired to get in his way. The pupil had thought his wisest course was to disappear; and when Lasse found no vent for his wrath, he fell into a fit of trembling and weeping, and became so really ill that the men had to administer a good mouthful of spirits to revive him. This took instant effect, and Lasse was himself again and able to nod consolingly to the frightened, sobbing Pelle.

"Never mind, laddie! " he said comfortingly. "Never mind! No one has ever yet got off without being punished, and Lasse'll break that long limb of Satan's head and make his brains spurt out of his nose; you take my word for it! "

Pelle's face brightened at the prospect of this forcible redress, and he crept up into the loft to throw down the hay for the cattle's midday meal. Lasse, who was not so fond of climbing, went down the long passage between the stalls distributing the hay. He was cogitating over something, and Pelle could hear him talking to himself all the time. When they had finished, Lasse went to the green chest and brought out a black silk handkerchief that had been Bengta's Sunday best. His expression was solemn as he called Pelle.

"Run over to Karna with this and ask her to accept it. We're not so poor that we should let kindness itself go from us empty-handed. But you mustn't let any one see it, in case they didn't like it. Mother Bengta in her grave won't be offended; she'd have proposed it herself, if she could have spoken; but her mouth's full of earth, poor thing! " Lasse sighed deeply.

Even then he stood for a little while with the handkerchief in his hand before giving it to Pelle to run with. He was by no means as sure of Bengta as his words made out; but the old man liked to beautify her memory, both in his own and in the boy's mind. It could not be denied that she had generally been a little difficult in a case of this kind, having been particularly jealous; and she might take it into her head to haunt them because of that handkerchief. Still she had had a heart for both him and the boy, and it was generally in the right place—they must say that of her! And for the rest, the Lord must judge her as kindly as He could.

During the afternoon it was quiet on the farm. Most of the men were out somewhere, either at the inn or with the quarry-men at the stone-quarry. The master and mistress were out too; the farmer had ordered the carriage directly after dinner and had driven to the town, and half an hour later his wife set off in the pony-carriage —to keep an eye on him, people said.

Old Lasse was sitting in an empty cow-stall, mending Pelle's clothes, while the boy played up and down the foddering passage. He had found in the herdsman's room an old boot-jack, which he placed under his knee, pretending it was a wooden leg, and all the time he was chattering happily, but not quite so loudly as usual, to his father. The morning's experience was still fresh in his mind, and had a subduing effect; it was as if he had performed some great deed, and was now nervous about it. There was another circumstance, too, that helped to make him serious. The bailiff had been over to say that the animals were to go out the next day. Pelle was to mind the young cattle, so this would be his last free day, perhaps for the whole summer.

He paused outside the stall where his father sat. "What are you going to kill him with, father? "

"With the hammer, I suppose. "

"Will you kill him quite dead, as dead as a dog? "

Lasse's nod boded ill to the pupil. "Yes, indeed I shall! "

"But who'll read the names for us then? "

The old man shook his head pensively. "That's true enough! " he exclaimed, scratching himself first in one place and then in another. The name of each cow was written in chalk above its stall, but neither Lasse nor Pelle could read. The bailiff had, indeed, gone through the names with them once, but it was impossible to remember half a hundred names after hearing them once—even for the boy, who had such an uncommon good memory. If Lasse now killed the pupil, then who *would* help them to make out the names? The bailiff would never stand their going to him and asking him a second time.

"I suppose we shall have to content ourselves with thrashing him, " said Lasse meditatively.

The boy went on playing for a little while, and then once more came up to Lasse.

"Don't you think the Swedes can thrash all the people in the world, father? "

The old man looked thoughtful. "Ye-es—yes, I should think so. "

"Yes, because Sweden's much bigger than the whole world, isn't it? "

"Yes, it's big, " said Lasse, trying to imagine its extent. There were twenty-four provinces, of which Malmohus was only one, and Ystad district a small part of that again; and then in one corner of Ystad district lay Tommelilla, and his holding that he had once thought so big with its five acres of land, was a tiny little piece of Tommelilla! Ah, yes, Sweden was big—not bigger than the whole world, of course, for that was only childish nonsense—but still bigger than all the rest of the world put together. "Yes, it's big! But what are you doing, laddie? "

"Why, can't you see I'm a soldier that's had one leg shot off? "

"Oh, you're an old crippled pensioner, are you? But you shouldn't do that, for God doesn't like things like that. You might become a real cripple, and that would be dreadful. "

"Oh, He doesn't see, because He's in the churches to-day! " answered the boy; but for safety's sake he thought it better to leave off. He stationed himself at the stable-door, whistling, but suddenly came running in with great eagerness: "Father, there's the Agricultural! Shall I run and fetch the whip? "

"No, I expect we'd better leave him alone. It might be the death of him; fine gentlemen scamps like that can't stand a licking. The fright alone might kill him. " Lasse glanced doubtfully at the boy.

Pelle looked very much disappointed. "But suppose he does it again? "

"Oh, no, we won't let him off without a good fright. I shall pick him up and hold him out at arm's length dangling in the air until he begs for mercy; and then I shall put him down again just as quietly. For Lasse doesn't like being angry. Lasse's a decent fellow. "

"Then you must pretend to let him go while you're holding him high up in the air; and then he'll scream and think he's going to die, and the others'll come and laugh at him. "

"No, no; you mustn't tempt your father! It might come into my mind to throw him down, and that would be murder and penal servitude for life, that would! No, I'll just give him a good scolding; that's what a classy scoundrel like that'll feel most. "

"Yes, and then you must call him a spindle-shanked clodhopper. That's what the bailiff calls him when he's angry with him. "

"No, I don't think that would do either; but I'll speak so seriously with him that he won't be likely to forget it in a hurry. "

Pelle was quite satisfied. There was no one like his father, and of course he would be as good at blowing people up as at everything else. He had never heard him do it, and he was looking forward to it immensely while he hobbled along with the boot-jack. He was not using it as a wooden leg now, for fear of tempting Providence; but he held it under his arm like a crutch, supporting it on the edge of the foundation wall, because it was too short. How splendid it would be to go on two crutches like the parson's son at home! He could jump over the very longest puddles.

There was a sudden movement of light and shadow up under the roof, and when Pelle turned round, he saw a strange boy standing in the doorway out to the field. He was of the same height as Pelle, but his head was almost as large as that of a grown man. At first sight it appeared to be bald all over; but when the boy moved in the sun, his bare head shone as if covered with silver scales. It was covered with fine, whitish hair, which was thinly and fairly evenly distributed over the face and everywhere else; and his skin was pink, as were the whites of his eyes. His face was all drawn into wrinkles in the strong light, and the back of his head projected unduly and looked as if it were much too heavy.

Pelle put his hands in his trouser pockets and went up to him. "What's your name? " he said, and tried to expectorate between his front teeth as Gustav was in the habit of doing. The attempt was a failure, unfortunately, and the saliva only ran down his chin. The strange boy grinned.

"Rud, " he said, indistinctly, as if his tongue were thick and unmanageable. He was staring enviously at Pelle's trouser pockets. "Is that your father? " he asked, pointing at Lasse.

"Of course! " said Pelle, consequentially. "And he can thrash everybody. "

"But my father can buy everybody, because he lives up there. " And Rud pointed toward the big house.

"Oh, does he really? " said Pelle, incredulously. "Why don't you live there with him, then? "

"Why, I'm a bastard-child; mother says so herself. "

"The deuce she does! " said Pelle, stealing a glance at his father on account of the little oath.

"Yes, when she's cross. And then she beats me, but then I run away from her. "

"Oh, you do, do you! " said a voice outside. The boys started and retreated farther into the stable, as a big, fat woman appeared in the doorway, and looked angrily round in the dim light. When she caught sight of Rud, she continued her scolding. Her accent was Swedish.

"So you run away, do you, you cabbage-head! If you'd only run so far that you couldn't find your way back again, a body wouldn't need to wear herself out thrashing a misbegotten imp like you! You'll go to the devil anyhow, so don't worry yourself about that! So that's the boy's father, is it? " she said, suddenly breaking off as she caught sight of Lasse.

"Yes, it is, " said Lasse, quietly. "And surely you must be schoolmaster Johan Pihl's Johanna from Tommelilla, who left the country nearly twenty years ago? "

"And surely you must be the smith's tom-cat from Sulitjelma, who had twins out of an old wooden shoe the year before last? " retorted the big woman, imitating his tone of voice.

"Very well; it doesn't matter to me who you are! " said the old man in an offended tone. "I'm not a police spy. "

"One would think you were from the way you question. Do you know when the cattle are to go out? "

"To-morrow, if all's well. Is it your little boy who's going to show Pelle how things go? The bailiff spoke of some one who'd go out with him and show him the grazing-ground. "

"Yes, it's that Tom Noddy there. Here, come out so that we can see you properly, you calf! Oh, the boy's gone. Very well. Does your boy often get a thrashing? "

"Oh yes, sometimes, " answered Lasse, who was ashamed to confess that he never chastised the boy.

"I don't spare mine either. It'll take something to make a man of such rubbish; punishment's half what he lives on. Then I'll send him up here first thing to-morrow morning; but take care he doesn't show himself in the yard, or there'll be no end of a row! "

"The mistress can't bear to see him, I suppose? " said Lasse.

"You're just about right. She's had nothing to do with the making of that scarecrow. Though you wouldn't think there was much there to be jealous about! But I might have been a farmer's wife at this moment and had a nice husband too, if that high and mighty peacock up there hadn't seduced me. Would you believe that, you cracked old piece of shoe-leather? " she asked with a laugh, slapping his knee with her hand.

"I can believe it very well, " said Lasse. "For you were as pretty a girl as might be when you left home. "

"Oh, you and your 'home', " she said, mimicking him.

"Well, I can see that you don't want to leave any footmarks behind you, and I can quite well pretend to be a stranger, even if I have held you upon my knee more than once when you were a little thing. But do you know that your mother's lying on her deathbed? "

"Oh no! Oh no! " she exclaimed, turning to him a face that was becoming more and more distorted.

"I went to say good-bye to her before I left home rather more than a month ago, and she was very ill. 'Good-bye, Lasse, ' she said, 'and thank you for your neighborliness all these years. And if you meet Johanna over there, ' she said, 'give her my love. Things have gone terribly badly with her, from what I've heard; but give her my love, all the same. Johanna child, little child! She was nearest her mother's heart, and so she happened to tread upon it. Perhaps it was our fault. You'll give her her mother's love, won't you, Lasse? ' Those were her

39

very words, and now she's most likely dead, so poorly as she was then. "

Johanna Pihl had no command over her feelings. It was evident that she was not accustomed to weep, for her sobs seemed to tear her to pieces. No tears came, but her agony was like the throes of childbirth. "Little mother! Poor little mother! " she said every now and again, as she sat rocking herself upon the edge of the manger.

"There, there, there! " said Lasse, patting her on the head. "I told them they had been too hard with you. But what did you want to creep through that window for—a child of sixteen and in the middle of the night? You can hardly wonder that they forgot themselves a little, all the more that he was earning no wages beyond his keep and clothes, and was a bad fellow at that, who was always losing his place. "

"I was fond of him, " said Johanna, weeping. "He's the only one I've ever cared for. And I was so stupid that I thought he was fond of me too, though he'd never seen me. "

"Ah, yes; you were only a child! I said so to your parents. But that you could think of doing anything so indecent! "

"I didn't mean to do anything wrong. I only thought that we two ought to be together as we loved one another. No, I didn't even think that then. I only crept in to him, without thinking about it at all. Would you believe that I was so innocent in those days? And nothing bad happened either. "

"And nothing happened even? " said Lasse. "But it's terribly sad to think how things have turned out. It was the death of your father. "

The big woman began to cry helplessly, and Lasse was almost in tears himself.

"Perhaps I ought never to have told you, " he said in despair. "But I thought you must have heard about it. I suppose he thought that he, as schoolmaster, bore the responsibility for so many, and that you'd thrown yourself at any one in that way, and a poor farm-servant into the bargain, cut him to the quick. It's true enough that he mixed with us poor folks as if we'd been his equals, but the honor was there all the same; and he took it hardly when the fine folk wouldn't look at him any more. And after all it was nothing at all—nothing happened? But why didn't you tell them so? "

Johanna had stopped crying, and now sat with tear-stained, quivering face, and eyes turned away.

"I did tell them, but they wouldn't listen. I was found there of course. I screamed for help when I found out he didn't even know me, but was only flattered at my coming, and wanted to take hold of me. And then the others came running in and found me there. They laughed and said that I'd screamed because I'd lost my innocence; and I could see that my parents thought the same. Even they wouldn't hear of nothing having happened, so what could the other rabble think? And then they paid him to come over here, and sent me away to relations. "

"Yes, and then you added to their sorrow by running away. "

"I went after him. I thought he'd get to be fond of me, if only I was near him. He'd taken service here at Stone Farm, and I took a place here as housemaid; but there was only one thing he wanted me for, and that I wouldn't have if he wasn't fond of me. So he went about boasting that I'd run away from home for his sake, and the other thing that was a lie; so they all thought they could do what they liked with me. Kongstrup was just married then, but he was no better than the others. I'd got the place quite by chance, because the other housemaid had had to go away somewhere to lie in; so I was awfully careful. He got her married afterwards to a quarryman at the quarries. "

"So that's the sort of man he is! " exclaimed Lasse. "I had my doubts about him. But what became of the other fellow? "

"He went to work in the quarry when we'd been at the farm a couple of years and he'd done me all the harm he could. While he was there, he drank and quarreled most of the time. I often went to see him, for I couldn't get him out of my head; but he was always drunk. At last he couldn't stay there any longer, and disappeared, and then we heard that he was in Nordland, playing Hell among the rocks at Blaaholt. He helped himself to whatever he wanted at the nearest place he could find it, and knocked people down for nothing at all. And one day they said that he'd been declared an outlaw, so that any one that liked could kill him. I had great confidence in the master, who, after all, was the only person that wished me well; and he comforted me by saying that it would be all right: Knut would know how to take care of himself. "

"Knut? Was it Knut Engstrom? " asked Lasse. "Well, then, I've heard about him. He was breaking out as wild as the devil the last time I was in this country, and assaulted people on the high-road in broad daylight. He killed one man with a hammer, and when they caught him, he'd made a long gash on his neck from the back right up to his eye. The other man had done that, he said; he'd only defended himself. So they couldn't do anything to him. So that was the man, was it! But who was it he was living with, then? They said he lived in a shed on the heath that summer, and had a woman with him. "

"I ran away from service, and pretended to the others that I was going home. I'd heard what a wretched state he was in. They said he was gashed all over his head. So I went up and took care of him. "

"Then you gave in at last, " said Lasse, with a roguish wink.

"He beat me every day, " she answered hoarsely. "And when he couldn't get his way, he drove me away at last. I'd set my mind on his being fond of me first. " Her voice had grown coarse and hard again.

"Then you deserved a good whipping for taking a fancy to such a ruffian! And you may be glad your mother didn't get to know anything about that, for she'd never have survived it. "

At the word "mother" Johanna started. "Every one must look after themselves, " she said in a hard voice. "I've had more to look to than mother, and see how fat I've grown. "

Lasse shook his head. "I shouldn't care to fight with you now. But what happened to you afterwards? "

"I came back to Stone Farm again at Martinmas, but the mistress wouldn't take me on again, for she preferred my room to my company. But Kongstrup got his way by making me dairymaid. He was as kind to me as ever, for all that I'd stood out against him for nine years. But at last the magistrate got tired of having Knut going about loose; he made too much disturbance. So they had a hunt for him up on the heath. They didn't catch him, but he must have come back to the quarry to hide himself, for one day when they were blasting there, his body came out among the bits of rock, all smashed up. They drove the pieces down here to the farm, and it made me so ill to see him come to me like that, that I had to go to bed. There I lay shivering day and night, for it seemed as if he'd come to me in his sorest need. Kongstrup sat with me and comforted me when the others were at work, and he took advantage of my misery to get his way.

"There was a younger brother of the farmer on the hill who liked me. He'd been in America in his early days, and had plenty of money. He didn't care a rap what people said, and every single year he proposed to me, always on New Year's Day. He came that year too, and now that Knut was dead, I couldn't have done better than have taken him and been mistress of a farm; but I had to refuse him after all, and I can tell you it was hard when I made the discovery. Kongstrup wanted to send me away when I told him about it; but that I would not have. I meant to stay and have my child born here on the farm to which it belonged. He didn't care a bit about me any longer, the mistress looked at me with her evil eyes every day, and there was no one that was kind to me. I wasn't so hard then as I am now, and it was all I could do to keep from crying always. I became hard then. When anything was the matter, I clenched my teeth so that no one should deride me. I was working in the field the very day it happened, too. The boy was born in the middle of a beet-field, and I carried him back to the farm myself in my apron. He was deformed even then: the mistress's evil eyes had done it. I said to myself that she should always have the changeling in her sight, and refused to go away. The farmer couldn't quite bring himself to turn me out by force, and so he put me into the house down by the shore. "

"Then perhaps you work on the farm here in the busy seasons? " asked Lasse.

She sniffed contemptuously. "Work! So you think I need do that? Kongstrup has to pay me for bringing up his son, and then there are friends that come to me, now one and now another, and bring a little with them—when they haven't spent it all in drink. You may come down and see me this evening. I'll be good to you too. "

"No, thank you! " said Lasse, gravely. "I am a human being too, but I won't go to one who's sat on my knee as if she'd been my own child. "

43

"Have you any gin, then? " she asked, giving him a sharp nudge.

Lasse thought there was some, and went to see. "No, not a drop, " he said, returning with the bottle. "But I've got something for you here that your mother asked me to give you as a keepsake. It was lucky I happened to remember it. " And he handed her a packet, and looked on happily while she opened it, feeling pleased on her account. It was a hymn-book. "Isn't it a beauty? " he said. "With a gold cross and clasp—and then, it's your mother's. "

"What's the good of that to me? " asked Johanna. "I don't sing hymns. "

"Don't you? " said Lasse, hurt. "But your mother has never known but that you've kept the faith you had as a child, so you must forgive her this once. "

"Is that all you've got for me? " she asked, pushing the book off her lap.

"Yes, it is, " said Lasse, his voice trembling; and he picked up the book.

"Who's going to have the rest, then? "

"Well, the house was leased, and there weren't many things left, for it's a long time since your father died, remember. Where you should have been, strangers have filled the daughter's place; and I suppose those who've looked after her will get what there is. But perhaps you'd still be in time, if you took the first steamer. "

"No, thank you! Go home and be stared at and play the penitent— no, thank you! I'd rather the strangers got what's left. And mother— well, if she's lived without my help, I suppose she can die without it too. Well, I must be getting home. I wonder what's become of the future master of Stone Farm? " She laughed loudly.

Lasse would have taken his oath that she had been quite sober, and yet she walked unsteadily as she went behind the calves' stables to look for her son. It was on his lips to ask whether she would not take the hymn-book with her, but he refrained. She was not in the mood for it now, and she might mock God; so he carefully wrapped up the book and put it away in the green chest.

* * * * *

At the far end of the cow-stable a space was divided off with boards. It had no door, and the boards were an inch apart, so that it resembled a crate. This was the herdsman's room. Most of the space was occupied by a wide legless bedstead made of rough boards knocked together, with nothing but the stone floor to rest on. Upon a deep layer of rye straw the bed-clothes lay in a disordered heap, and the thick striped blankets were stiff with dried cow-dung, to which feathers and bits of straw had adhered.

Pelle lay curled up in the middle of the bed with the down quilt up to his chin, while Lasse sat on the edge, turning over the things in the green chest and talking to himself. He was going through his Sunday devotions, taking out slowly, one after another, all the little things he had brought from the broken-up home. They were all purely useful things—balls of cotton, scraps of stuff, and such-like, that were to be used to keep his own and the boy's clothes in order; but to him each thing was a relic to be handled with care, and his heart bled every time one of them came to an end. With each article he laid down, he slowly repeated what Bengta had said it was for when she lay dying and was trying to arrange everything for him and the boy: "Wool for the boy's gray socks. Pieces to lengthen the sleeves of his Sunday jacket. Mind you don't wear your stockings too long before you mend them. " They were the last wishes of the dying woman, and they were followed in the smallest detail. Lasse remembered them word for word, in spite of his bad memory.

Then there were little things that had belonged to Bengta herself, cheap finery that all had its happy memory of fairs and holidays, which he recalled in his muttered reverie.

Pelle liked this subdued murmur that he did not need to listen to or answer, and that was so pleasant to doze off in. He lay looking out sleepily at the bright sky, tired and with a vague feeling of something unpleasant that was past.

Suddenly he started. He had heard the door of the cow-stable open, and steps upon the long foddering-passage. It was the pupil. He recognized the hated step at once.

He thrilled with delight. Now that fellow would be made to understand that he mustn't do anything to boys with fathers who

45

could hold a man out at arm's length and scold! oh, much worse than the bailiff. He sat up and looked eagerly at his father.

"Lasse! " came a voice from the end of the tables.

The old man growled sullenly, stirred uneasily, but did not rise.

"Las-se! " came again, after a little, impatiently and in a tone of command.

"Yes, " said Lasse slowly, rising and going out.

"Can't you answer when you're called, you old Swedish rascal? Are you deaf? "

"Oh, I can answer well enough, " said Lasse, in a trembling voice. "But Mr. Pupil oughtn't to—I'm a father, let me tell you—and a father's heart——"

"You may be a monthly nurse for all I care, but you've got to answer when you're called, or else I'll get the bailiff to give you a talking-to. Do you understand? "

"Yes, oh yes! —Mr. Pupil must excuse me, but I didn't hear. "

"Well, will you please remember that Aspasia's not to go out to pasture to-morrow. "

"Is she going to calve? "

"Yes, of course! Did you think she was going to foal? "

Lasse laughed, as in duty bound, and followed the pupil back through the stable. Now it would come, thought Pelle, and sat listening intently; but he only heard his father make another excuse, close the half-door, and come back with slow, tottering steps. Then he burst into tears, and crept far in under the quilt.

Lasse went about for some time, grumbling to himself, and at last came and gently drew the quilt down from the boy's head. But Pelle buried his face in the clothes, and when his father turned it up toward him, he met a despairing, uncomprehending gaze that made his own wander restlessly round the room.

"Yes, " he said, with an attempt at being cross. "It's all very well for you to cry! But when you don't know where Aspasia stands, you've got to be civil, I'm thinking. "

"I know Aspasia quite well, " sobbed the boy. "She's the third from the door here. "

Lasse was going to give a cross answer, but broke down, touched and disarmed by the boy's grief. He surrendered unconditionally, stooped down until his forehead touched the boy's, and said helplessly, "Yes, Lasse's a poor thing—old and poor! Any one can make a fool of him. He can't be angry any more, and there's no strength in his fist, so what's the good of clenching it! He has to put up with everything, and let himself be hustled about—and say thank you into the bargain—that's how it is with old Lasse. But you must remember that it's for your sake he lets himself be put upon. If it wasn't for you, he'd shoulder his pack and go—old though he is. But you can grow on where your father rusts. And now you must leave off crying! " And he dried the boy's wet eyes with the quilt.

Pelle did not understand his father's words, but they quieted him nevertheless, and he soon fell asleep; but for a long time he sobbed as he lay.

Lasse sat still upon the edge of the bed and watched the boy as he slept, and when he had become quieter, crept away through the stable and out. It had been a poor Sunday, and now he would go and see if any of the men were at home and had visitors, for then there would be spirits going round. Lasse could not find it in his heart to take any of his wages to buy a dram with; that money would have quite enough to do to buy bare necessaries.

On one of the beds lay a man asleep, fully dressed, and with his boots on. He was dead drunk. All the others were out, so Lasse had to give up all thoughts of a dram, and went across to the basement to see if there was any gaiety going among the maids. He was not at all averse to enjoyment of one sort or another, now that he was free and his own master as he had been in the days of his youth.

Up by the dairy stood the three farm-laborers' wives who used to do the milking for the girls on Sunday evening. They were thick-set, small, and bent with toil. They were all talking together and spoke of illnesses and other sad things in plaintive tones. Lasse at once felt a desire to join them, for the subject found an echo in his being like the tones of a well-known song, and he could join in the refrain with the experience of a lifetime. But he resisted the temptation, and went past them down the basement steps. "Ah, yes, death will come to us all! " said one of the women, and Lasse said the words after her to himself as he went down.

Down there Karna was sitting mending Gustav's moleskin trousers, while Gustav lay upon the bench asleep with his cap over his face. He had put his feet up on Karna's lap, without so much as taking off his shoes; and she had accommodated her lap, so that they should not slide off.

Lasse sat down beside her and tried to make himself agreeable. He wanted some one to be nice to him. But Karna was unapproachable; those dirty feet had quite turned her head. And either Lasse had forgotten how to do it, or he was wanting in assurance, for every time he attempted a pleasant speech, she turned it off.

"We might have such a comfortable time, we two elderly folk, " he said hopelessly.

"Yes, and I could contribute what was wanting, " said Gustav, peeping out from under his cap. Insolent puppy, lying there and boasting of his seventeen years! Lasse had a good mind to go for him then and there and chance yet one more trial of strength. But he contented himself with sitting and looking at him until his red, lashless eyes grew watery. Then he got up.

"Well, well, I see you want young people this evening! " he said bitterly to Karna. "But you can't get rid of your years, all the same! Perhaps you'll only get the spoon to lick after the others. "

He went across to the cow-stable and began to talk to the three farm-laborers' wives, who were still speaking of illness and misery and death, as if nothing else existed in the world. Lasse nodded and said: "Yes, yes, that's true. " He could heartily endorse it all, and could add much to what they said. It brought warmth to his old body, and made him feel quite comfortable—so easy in his joints.

But when he lay on his back in bed, all the sad thoughts came back and he could not sleep. Generally he slept like a log as soon as he lay down, but to-day was Sunday, and he was tormented with the thought that life had passed him by. He had promised himself so much from the island, and it was nothing but worry and toil and trouble —nothing else at all.

"Yes, Lasse's old! " he suddenly said aloud, and he kept on repeating the words with a little variation until he fell asleep: "He's old, poor man—and played out! Ah, so old! " Those words expressed it all.

He was awakened again by singing and shouting up on the high-road.

> "And now the boy you gave me
> With the black and curly hair,
> He is no longer little,
> No longer, no longer,
> But a fine, tall strapping youth. "

It was some of the men and girls of the farm on their way home from some entertainment. When they turned into the farm road they became silent. It was just beginning to grow light; it must have been about two o'clock.

IV

At four, Lasse and Pelle were dressed and were opening the cow-stable doors on the field side. The earth was rolling off its white covering of night mist, and the morning rose prophetically. Lasse stood still in the doorway, yawning, and making up his mind about the weather for the day; but Pelle let the soft tones of the wind and the song of the lark—all that was stirring—beat upon his little heart. With open mouth and doubtful eyes he gazed into the incomprehensible as represented by each new day with all its unimagined possibilities. "To-day you must take your coat with you, for we shall have rain about midday, " Lasse would then say; and Pelle peered into the sky to find out where his father got his knowledge from. For it generally came true.

They then set about cleaning out the dung in the cow-stable, Pelle scraping the floor under the cows and sweeping it up, Lasse filling the wheelbarrow and wheeling it out. At half-past five they ate their morning meal of salt herring and porridge.

After that Pelle set out with the young cattle, his dinner basket on his arm, and his whip wound several times round his neck. His father had made him a short, thick stick with rings on it, that he could rattle admonishingly and throw at the animals; but Pelle preferred the whip, because he was not yet strong enough to use it.

He was little, and at first he had some difficulty in making an impression upon the great forces over which he was placed. He could not get his voice to sound sufficiently terrifying, and on the way out from the farm he had hard work, especially up near the farm, where the corn stood high on both sides of the field-road. The animals were hungry in the morning, and the big bullocks did not trouble to move when once they had their noses buried in the corn and he stood belaboring them with the short handle of the cattle-whip. The twelve-foot lash, which, in a practised hand, left little triangular marks in the animal's hide, he could not manage at all; and if he kicked the bullock on the head with his wooden shoe, it only closed its eyes good-naturedly, and browsed on sedately with its back to him. Then he would break into a despairing roar, or into little fits of rage in which he attacked the animal blindly and tried to get at its eyes; but it was all equally useless. He could always make the calves move by twisting their tails, but the bullocks' tails were too strong.

He did not cry, however, for long at a time over the failure of his resources. One evening he got his father to put a spike into the toe of one of his wooden shoes, and after that his kick was respected. Partly by himself, and partly through Rud, he also learned where to find the places on the animals where it hurt most. The cow-calves and the two bull-calves all had their particular tender spot, and a well-directed blow upon a horn could make even the large bullocks bellow with pain.

The driving out was hard work, but the herding itself was easy. When once the cattle were quietly grazing, he felt like a general, and made his voice sound out incessantly over the meadow, while his little body swelled with pride and a sense of power.

Being away from his father was a trouble to him. He did not go home to dinner, and often in the middle of his play, despair would come over him and he would imagine that something had happened to his father, that the great bull had tossed him or something else; and he would leave everything, and start running homeward crying, but would remember in time the bailiff's whip, and trudge back again. He found a remedy for his longing by stationing himself so that he could keep a lookout on the fields up there, and see his father when he went out to move the dairy-cows.

He taught himself to whittle boats and little rakes and hoes and decorate sticks with patterns cut upon the bark. He was clever with his knife and made diligent use of it. He would also stand for hours on the top of a monolith—he thought it was a gate-post—and try to crack his cattle-whip like a pistol-shot. He had to climb to a height to get the lash off the ground at all.

When the animals lay down in the middle of the morning, he was often tired too, and then he would seat himself upon the head of one of the big bullocks, and hold on to the points of its horns; and while the animal lay chewing with a gentle vibration like a machine, he sat upon its head and shouted at the top of his voice songs about blighted affections and horrible massacres.

Toward midday Rud came running up, as hungry as a hunter. His mother sent him out of the house when the hour for a meal drew near. Pelle shared the contents of his basket with him, but required him to bring the animals together a certain number of times for every portion of food. The two boys could not exist apart for a whole day together. They tumbled about in the field like two puppies, fought and made it up again twenty times a day, swore the most fearful threats of vengeance that should come in the shape of this or that grown-up person, and the next moment had their arms round one another's necks.

About half-a-mile of sand-dunes separated the Stone Farm fields from the sea. Within this belt of sand the land was stony and afforded poor grazing; but on both sides of the brook a strip of green meadow-land ran down among the dunes, which were covered with dwarf firs and grass-wrack to bind the sand. The best grazing was on this meadow-land, but it was hard work minding both sides of it, as the brook ran between; and it had been impressed upon the boy with severe threats, that no animal must set its foot upon the dune-land, as the smallest opening might cause a sand-drift. Pelle took the matter quite literally, and all that summer imagined something like an explosion that would make everything fly into the air the instant an animal trod upon it; and this possibility hung like a fate at the back of everything when he herded down there. When Rud came and they wanted to play, he drove the cattle up on to the poor pasture where there was plenty of room for them.

When the sun shone the boys ran about naked. They dared not venture down to the sea for fear of the bailiff, who, they were sure, always stood up in the attic of the big house, and watched Pelle through his telescope; but they bathed in the brook—in and out of the water continually for hours together.

After heavy rain it became swollen, and was then quite milky from the china clay that it washed away from the banks farther up. The boys thought it was milk from an enormous farm far up in the island. At high water the sea ran up and filled the brook with decaying seaweed that colored the water crimson; and this was the blood of all the people drowned out in the sea.

Between their bathes they lay under the dunes and let the sun dry them. They made a minute examination of their bodies, and discussed the use and intention of the various parts. Upon this head Rud's knowledge was superior, and he took the part of instructor. They often quarrelled as to which of them was the best equipped in one way or another—in other words, had the largest. Pelle, for instance, envied Rud his disproportionately large head.

Pelle was a well-built little fellow, and had put on flesh since he had come to Stone Farm. His glossy skin was stretched smoothly over his body, and was of a warm, sunburnt color. Rud had a thin neck in proportion to his head, and his forehead was angular and covered with scars, the results of innumerable falls. He had not full command of all his limbs, and was always knocking and bruising himself; there were blue, livid patches all over him that were slow to disappear, for he had flesh that did not heal easily. But he was not so open in his envy as Pelle. He asserted himself by boasting of his defects until he made them out to be sheer achievements; so that Pelle ended by envying him everything from the bottom of his heart.

Rud had not Pelle's quick perception of things, but he had more instinct, and on certain points possessed quite a talent in anticipating what Pelle only learned by experience. He was already avaricious to a certain extent, and suspicious without connecting any definite thoughts with it. He ate the lion's share of the food, and had a variety of ways of getting out of doing the work.

Behind their play there lay, clothed in the most childish forms, a struggle for the supremacy, and for the present Pelle was the one who came off second best. In an emergency, Rud always knew how to appeal to his good qualities and turn them to his own advantage.

And through all this they were the best friends in the world, and were quite inseparable. Pelle was always looking toward "the Sow's" cottage when he was alone, and Rud ran off from home as soon as he saw his opportunity.

* * * * *

It had rained hard in the course of the morning, in spite of Lasse, and Pelle was wet through. Now the blue-black cloud was drawing away over the sea, and the boats lay in the middle of it with all their red sails set, and yet motionless. The sunlight flashed and glittered on wet surfaces, making everything look bright; and Pelle hung his clothes on a dwarf fir to dry.

He was cold, and crept close up to Peter, the biggest of the bullocks, as he lay chewing the cud. The animal was steaming, but Pelle could not bring warmth into his extremities, where the cold had taken hold. His teeth chattered, too, and he was shivering.

And even now there was one of the cows that would not let him have any peace. Every time he had snuggled right in under the bullock and was beginning to get a little warmer, the cow strayed away over the northern boundary. There was nothing but sand there, but when it was a calf there had been a patch of mixed crops, and it still remembered that.

It was one of two cows that had been turned out of the dairy-herd on account of their dryness. They were ill-tempered creatures, always discontented and doing some mischief or other; and Pelle detested them heartily. They were two regular termagants, upon which even thrashing made no impression. The one was a savage beast, that would suddenly begin stamping and bellowing like a mad bull in the middle of grazing, and, if Pelle went toward it, wanted to toss him; and when it saw its opportunity, it would eat up the cloth in which Pelle's dinner was wrapped. The other was old and had crumpled horns that pointed in toward its eyes, one of which had a white pupil.

It was the noisy one that was now at its tricks. Every other minute Pelle had to get up and shout: "Hi, Blakka, you villainous beast! Just you come back! " He was hoarse with anger, and at last his patience gave way, and he caught up a big stick and began to chase the cow. As soon as it saw his intention, it set off at a run up toward the farm, and Pelle had to make a wide circle to turn it down to the herd again. Then it ran at full gallop in and out among the other animals, the herd became confused and ran hither and thither, and Pelle had to relinquish his pursuit for a time while he gathered them together. But then he began again at once. He was boiling with rage, and leaped about like an indiarubber ball, his naked body flashing in loops and curves upon the green grass. He was only a few yards from the cow, but the distance remained the same; he could not catch her up to-day.

He stopped up by the rye-field, and the cow stood still almost at the same moment. It snapped at a few ears, and moved its head slowly to choose its direction. In a couple of leaps Pelle was up to it and had hold of its tail. He hit it over the nose with his cudgel, it turned quickly away from the rye, and set off at a flying pace down toward the others, while blows rained down upon its bony prominences.

Every stroke echoed back from the dunes like blows upon the trunk of a tree, and made Pelle swell with pride. The cow tried to shake Pelle off as it ran, but he was not to be got rid of; it crossed the brook in long bounds, backward and forward, with Pelle almost floating through the air; but the blows continued to rain down upon it. Then it grew tired and began to slacken its pace; and at last it came to a standstill, coughed, and resigned itself to the thrashing.

Pelle threw himself flat upon his face, and panted. Ha, ha! *That* had made him warm! Now that beast should—He rolled suddenly over on to his side with a start. The bailiff! But it was a strange man with a beard who stood over him, looking at him with serious eyes. The stranger went on gazing at him for a long time without saying anything, and Pelle grew more and more uneasy under his scrutiny; he had the sun right in his eyes too, if he tried to return the man's gaze, and the cow still stood there coughing.

"What do you think the bailiff will say? " asked the man at last, quietly.

"I don't think he's seen it, " whispered Pelle, looking timidly round.

"But God has seen it, for He sees everything. And He has led me here to stop the evil in you while there's still time. Wouldn't you like to be God's child? " The man sat down beside him and took his hand.

Pelle sat tugging at the grass and wishing he had had his clothes on.

"And you must never forget that God sees everything you do; even in the darkest night He sees. We are always walking in God's sight. But come now, it's unseemly to run about naked! " And the man took him by the hand and led him to his clothes, and then, going across to the north side, he gathered the herd together while Pelle dressed himself. The wicked cow was over there again already, and had drawn a few of the others after it. Pelle watched the man in surprise; he drove the animals back quite quietly, neither using stones nor shouting. Before he got back, Blakka had once more crossed the boundary; but he turned and brought her back again just as gently as before.

"That's not an easy cow to manage, " he said kindly, when he returned; "but you've got young legs. Shan't we agree to burn that? "

he asked, picking up the thick cudgel, "and do what we have to do with just our hands? God will always help you when you're in difficulties. And if you want to be a true child of God, you must tell the bailiff this evening what you did—and take your punishment. " He placed his hand upon Pelle's head, and looked at him with that unendurable gaze; and then he left him, taking the stick with him.

For a long time Pelle followed him with his eyes. So that was what a man looked like, who was sent by God to warn you! Now he knew, and it would be some time before he chased a cow like that again. But go to the bailiff, and tell of himself, and get the whip-lash on his bare legs? Not if he knew it! Rather than that, God would have to be angry—if it was really true that He could see everything? It couldn't be worse than the bailiff, anyhow.

All that morning he was very quiet. He felt the man's eyes upon him in everything he did, and it robbed him of his confidence. He silently tested things, and saw everything in a new light; it was best not to make a noise, if you were always walking in the sight of God. He did not go on cracking his cattle-whip, but meditated a little on whether he should burn that too.

But a little before midday Rud appeared, and the whole incident was forgotten. Rud was smoking a bit of cane that he had cut off the piece his mother used for cleaning the stove-pipes, and Pelle bartered some of his dinner for a few pulls at it. First they seated themselves astride the bullock Cupid, which was lying chewing the cud. It went on calmly chewing with closed eyes, until Rud put the glowing cane to the root of its tail, when it rose hastily, both boys rolling over its head. They laughed and boasted to one another of the somersault they had turned, as they went up on to the high ground to look for blackberries. Thence they went to some birds' nests in the small firs, and last of all they set about their best game—digging up mice-nests.

Pelle knew every mouse-hole in the meadow, and they lay down and examined them carefully. "Here's one that has mice in it, " said Rud. "Look, here's their dunghill! "

"Yes, that smells of mouse, " said Pelle, putting his nose to the hole. "And the blades of grass turn outward, so the old ones must be out. "

With Pelle's knife they cut away the turf, and set to work eagerly to dig with two pieces of pot. The soil flew about their heads as they talked and laughed.

"My word, how fast we're getting on! "

"Yes; Strom couldn't work as fast! " Strom was a famous worker who got twenty-five ores a day more than other autumn farm-hands, and his example was used as an incentive to coax work out of the laborers.

"We shall soon get right into the inside of the earth. "

"Well, but it's burning hot in there. "

"Oh, nonsense: is it? " Pelle paused doubtfully in his digging.

"Yes, the schoolmaster says so. "

The boys hesitated and put their hands down into the hole. Yes, it was warm at the bottom—so warm that Pelle found it necessary to pull out his hand and say: "Oh, my word! " They considered a little, and then went on scraping out the hole as carefully as if their lives depended on it. In a little while straw appeared in the passage, and in a moment the internal heat of the earth was forgotten. In less than a minute they had uncovered the nest, and laid the little pink, new-born mice out on the grass. They looked like half-hatched birds.

"They *are* ugly, " said Pelle, who did not quite like taking hold of them, but was ashamed not to do so. "They're much nastier to touch than toads. I believe they're poisonous. "

Rud lay pinching them between his fingers.

"Poisonous! Don't be silly! Why, they haven't any teeth! There are no bones in them at all; I'm sure you could eat them quite well. "

"Pah! Beastly! " Pelle spat on the ground.

"I shouldn't be at all afraid of biting one; would you? " Rud lifted a little mouse up toward his mouth.

"Afraid? Of course I'm not afraid—but—" Pelle hesitated.

"No, you're afraid, because you're a blue-bag! "

Now this nickname really only applied to boys who were afraid of water, but Pelle quickly seized one of the little mice, and held it up to his mouth, at exactly the same distance from his lips that Rud was from his. "You can see for yourself! " he cried, in an offended tone.

Rud went on talking, with many gestures.

"You're afraid, " he said, "and it's because you're Swedish. But when you're afraid, you should just shut your eyes—so—and open your mouth. Then you pretend to put the mouse right into your mouth, and then—" Rud had his mouth wide open, and held his hand close to his mouth; Pelle was under his influence, and imitated his movements—"and then—" Pelle received a blow that sent the little mouse halfway down his throat. He retched and spat; and then his hands fumbled in the grass and got hold of a stone. But by the time he was on his feet and was going to throw it, Rud was far away up the fields. "I must go home now! " he shouted innocently. "There's something I've got to help mother with. "

Pelle did not love solitude, and the prospect of a blockade determined him at once for negotiations. He dropped the stone to show his serious wish for a reconciliation, and had to swear solemnly that he would not bear malice. Then at last Rud came back, tittering.

"I was going to show you something funny with the mouse, " he said by way of diversion; "but you held on to it like an idiot. " He did not venture to come quite close up to Pelle, but stood watching his movements.

Pelle was acquainted with the little white lie when the danger of a thrashing was imminent, but the lie as an attack was still unknown to him. If Rud, now that the whole thing was over, said that he only wanted to have shown him something funny, it must be true. But then why was he mistrustful? Pelle tried, as he had so often done before, to bend his little brain round the possible tricks of his playmate, but failed.

"You may just as well come up close, " he said stoutly. "For if I wanted to, I could easily catch you up. "

Rud came. "Now we'll catch big mice. " he said. "That's better fun. "

They emptied Pelle's milk-bottle, and hunted up a mouse's nest that appeared to have only two exits, one up in the meadow, the other halfway down the bank of the stream. Here they pushed in the mouth of the bottle, and widened the hole in the meadow into a funnel; and they took it in turns to keep an eye on the bottle, and to carry water up to the other hole in their caps. It was not long before a mouse popped out into the bottle, which they then corked.

What should they do with it? Pelle proposed that they should tame it and train it to draw their little agricultural implements; but Rud, as usual, got his way—it was to go out sailing.

Where the stream turned, and had hollowed out its bed into a hole as big as a cauldron, they made an inclined plane and let the bottle slide down into the water head foremost, like a ship being launched. They could follow it as it curved under the water until it came up slantingly, and stood bobbing up and down on the water like a buoy, with its neck up. The mouse made the funniest leaps up toward the cork to get out; and the boys jumped up and down on the grass with delight.

"It knows the way it got in quite well! " They imitated its unsuccessful leaps, lay down again and rolled about in exuberant mirth. At last, however, the joke became stale.

"Let's take out the cork! " suggested Rud.

"Yes—oh, yes! " Pelle waded quickly in, and was going to set the mouse at liberty.

"Wait a minute, you donkey! " Rud snatched the bottle from him, and holding his hand over the mouth, put it back, into the water. "Now we'll see some fun! " he cried, hastening up the bank.

It was a little while before the mouse discovered that the way was open, but then it leaped. The leap was unsuccessful, and made the bottle rock, so that the second leap was slanting and rebounded sideways. But then followed with lightning rapidity a number of leaps—a perfect bombardment; and suddenly the mouse flew right out of the bottle, head foremost into the water.

"That was a leap and a half! " cried Pelle, jumping straight up and down in the grass, with his arms at his sides. "It could just squeeze its body through, just exactly! " And he jumped again, squeezing himself together.

The mouse swam to land, but Rud was there, and pushed it out again with his foot. "It swam well, " he said, laughing. It made for the opposite bank. "Look out for the fellow! " Rud roared, and Pelle sprang forward and turned it away from the shore with a good kick. It swam helplessly backward and forward in the middle of the pool, seeing one of the two dancing figures every time it approached a bank, and turning and turning endlessly. It sank deeper and deeper, its fur becoming wet and dragging it down, until at last it swam right under water. Suddenly it stretched out its body convulsively, and sank to the bottom, with all four legs outspread like a wide embrace.

Pelle had all at once comprehended the perplexity and helplessness —perhaps was familiar with it. At the animal's final struggle, he burst into tears with a little scream, and ran, crying loudly, up the meadow toward the fir-plantation. In a little while he came back again. "I really thought Cupid had run away, " he said repeatedly, and carefully avoided looking Rud in the face. Quietly he waded into the water, and fished up the dead mouse with his foot.

They laid it upon a stone in the sun, so that it might come to life again. When that failed, Pelle remembered a story about some people who were drowned in a lake at home, and who came to themselves again when cannons were fired over them. They clapped their hollowed hands over the mouse, and when that too brought about no result, they decided to bury it.

Rud happened to remember that his grandmother in Sweden was being buried just now, and this made them go about the matter with a certain amount of solemnity. They made a coffin out of a matchbox, and ornamented it with moss; and then they lay on their faces and lowered the coffin into the grave with twine, taking every possible care that it should not land upon its head. A rope might give way; such things did sometimes happen, and the illusion did not permit of their correcting the position of the coffin afterward with their hands. When this was done, Pelle looked down into his cap, while Rud prayed over the deceased and cast earth upon the coffin; and then they made up the grave.

"I only hope it's not in a trance and going to wake up again! " exclaimed Pelle suddenly. They had both heard many unpleasant stories of such cases, and went over all the possibilities—how they woke up and couldn't get any air, and knocked upon the lid, and began to eat their own hands—until Pelle could distinctly hear a knocking on the lid below. They had the coffin up in a trice, and examined the mouse. It had not eaten its forepaws, at any rate, but it had most decidedly turned over on its side. They buried it again, putting a dead beetle beside it in the coffin for safety's sake, and sticking a straw down into the grave to supply it with air. Then they ornamented the mound, and set up a memorial stone.

"It's dead now! " said Pelle, gravely and with conviction.

"Yes, I should just think so—dead as a herring. " Rud had put his ear to the straw and listened.

"And now it must be up with God in all His glory—right high, high up. "

Rud sniffed contemptuously. "Oh, you silly! Do you think it can crawl up there? "

"Well, can't mice crawl, I should like to know? " Pelle was cross.

"Yes; but not through the air. Only birds can do that. "

Pelle felt himself beaten off the field and wanted to be revenged.

"Then your grandmother isn't in heaven, either! " he declared emphatically. There was still a little rancor in his heart from the young mouse episode.

But this was more than Rud could stand. It had touched his family pride, and he gave Pelle a dig in the side with his elbow. The next moment they were rolling in the grass, holding one another by the hair, and making awkward attempts to hit one another on the nose with their clenched fists. They turned over and over like one lump, now one uppermost, now the other; they hissed hoarsely, groaned and made tremendous exertions. "I'll make you sneeze red, " said Pelle angrily, as he rose above his adversary; but the next moment he was down again, with Rud hanging over him and uttering the most fearful threats about black eyes and seeing stars. Their voices were thick with passion.

And suddenly they were sitting opposite one another on the grass wondering whether they should set up a howl. Rud put out his tongue, Pelle went a step further and began to laugh, and they were once more the best of friends. They set up the memorial stone, which had been overturned in the heat of battle, and then sat down hand in hand, to rest after the storm, a little quieter than usual.

It was not because there was more evil in Pelle, but because the question had acquired for him an importance of its own, and he must understand it, that a meditative expression came into his eyes, and he said thoughtfully:

"Well, but you've told me yourself that she was paralyzed in her legs! "

"Well, what if she was? "

"Why, then she couldn't crawl up into heaven. "

"Oh, you booby! It's her spirit, of course! "

"Then the mouse's spirit can very well be up there too. "

"No, it can't, for mice haven't got any spirit. "

"Haven't they? Then how is it they can breathe? " [Footnote: In Danish, spirit = aand, and to breathe = aande.]

That was one for Rud! And the tiresome part of it was that he attended Sunday-school. His fists would have come in handy again now, but his instinct told him that sooner or later Pelle would get the better of him in fighting. And anyhow his grandmother was saved.

"Yes, " he said, yielding; "and it certainly could breathe. Well, then, it was its spirit flying up that overturned the stone—that's what it was! "

A distant sound reached them, and far off near the cottage they could see the figure of a fat woman, beckoning threateningly.

"The Sow's calling you, " said Pelle. The two boys never called her anything but "the Sow" between themselves.

So Rud had to go. He was allowed to take the greater part of the contents of the dinner-basket with him, and ate as he ran. They had been too busy to eat.

Pelle sat down among the dunes and ate his dinner. As usual when Rud had been with him, he could not imagine what had become of the day. The birds had ceased singing, and not one of the cattle was still lying down, so it must be at least five o'clock.

Up at the farm they were busy driving in. It went at full gallop— out and in, out and in. The men stood up in the carts and thrashed away at the horses with the end of the reins, and the swaying loads were hurried along the field-roads, looking like little bristling, crawling things, that have been startled and are darting to their holes.

A one-horsed vehicle drove out from the farm, and took the high-road to the town at a quick trot. It was the farmer; he was driving so fast that he was evidently off to the town on the spree. So there was something gone wrong at home, and there would be crying at the farm that night.

Yes, there was Father Lasse driving out with the water-cart, so it was half-past five. He could tell that too by the birds beginning their pleasant evening twittering, that was soft and sparkling like the rays of the sun.

Far inland above the stone-quarry, where the cranes stood out against the sky, a cloud of smoke rose every now and then into the air, and burst in a fountain of pieces of rock. Long after came the explosion, bit by bit in a series of rattling reverberations. It sounded as if some one were running along and slapping his thigh with fingerless gloves.

The last few hours were always long—the sun was so slow about it. And there was nothing to fill up the time either. Pelle himself was tired, and the tranquillity of evening had the effect of subduing his voice. But now they were driving out for milking up there, and the cattle were beginning to graze along the edge of the meadow that turned toward the farm; so the time was drawing near.

At last the herd-boys began to jodel over at the neighboring farms, first one, and then several joining in:

> "Oh, drive home, o-ho, o-o-ho!
>> O-ho, o-ho!
>> O-ho, o-ho!
> Oh, drive home, o-o-ho!
>> O-ho! "

From all sides the soft tones vibrated over the sloping land, running out, like the sound of happy weeping, into the first glow of evening; and Pelle's animals began to move farther after each pause to graze. But he did not dare to drive them home yet, for it only meant a thrashing from the bailiff or the pupil if he arrived too early.

He stood at the upper end of the meadow, and called his homeward-drifting flock together; and when the last tones of the call had died away, he began it himself, and stepped on one side. The animals ran with a peculiar little trot and heads extended. The shadow of the grass lay in long thin stripes across the ground, and the shadows of the animals were endless. Now and then a calf lowed slowly and broke into a gallop. They were yearning for home, and Pelle was yearning too.

From behind a hollow the sun darted long rays out into space, as if it had called all its powers home for the night, and now poured them forth in one great longing, from west to east. Everything pointed in long thin lines, and the eager longing of the cattle seemed visible in the air.

To the mind of the child there was nothing left out of doors now; everything was being taken in, and he longed for his father with a longing that was almost a pain. And when at last he turned the corner with the herd, and saw old Lasse standing there, smiling happily with his red-rimmed eyes, and opening the gate to the fold, the boy gave way and threw himself weeping into his father's arms.

"What's the matter, laddie? What's the matter? " asked the old man, with concern in his voice, stroking the child's face with a trembling hand. "Has any one been unkind to you? No? Well, that's a good thing! They'd better take care, for happy children are in God's own keeping. And Lasse would be an awkward customer if it came to that. So you were longing for me, were you? Then it's good to be in your little heart, and it only makes Lasse happy. But go in now and get your supper, and don't cry any more. " And he wiped the boy's nose with his hard, crooked fingers, and pushed him gently away.

V

Pelle was not long in finding out all about the man who had been sent by God, and had the grave, reproachful eyes. He proved to be nothing but a little shoemaker down in the village, who spoke at the meeting-house on Sundays; and it was also said that his wife drank. Rud went to his Sunday-school, and he was poor; so he was nothing out of the ordinary.

Moreover, Gustav had got a cap which could turn out three different crowns—one of blue duffle, one of water-proof American cloth, and one of white canvas for use in sunny weather. It was an absorbingly interesting study that threw everything else into the background, and exercised Pelle's mind for many days; and he used this miraculous cap as a standard by which to measure everything great and desirable. But one day he gave Gustav a beautifully carved stick for permission to perform the trick of turning the crown inside out himself; and that set his mind at rest at last, and the cap had to take its place in his everyday world like everything else.

But what did it look like in Farmer Kongstrup's big rooms? Money lay upon the floor there, of course, the gold in one place and the silver in another; and in the middle of each heap stood a half-bushel measure. What did the word *"practical"* mean, which the bailiff used when he talked to the farmer? And why did the men call one another *"Swede"* as a term of abuse? Why, they were all Swedes! What was there away beyond the cliffs where the stone-quarry lay? The farm-lands extended as far as that on the one side. He had not been there yet, but was going with his father as soon as an opportunity presented itself. They had learnt quite by chance that Lasse had a brother who owned a house over there; so of course they knew the place comparatively well.

Down there lay the sea; he had sailed upon it himself! Ships both of iron and wood sailed upon it, though how iron could float when it was so heavy he did not know! The sea must be strong, for in the pond, iron went to the bottom at once. In the middle of the pond there was no bottom, so there you'd go on sinking forever! The old thatcher, when he was young, had had more than a hundred fathoms of rope down there with a drag, to fish up a bucket, but he never reached the bottom. And when he wanted to pull up the rope again, there was some one deep down who caught hold of the drag and tried to pull him down, so he had to let the whole thing go.

God... well, He had a long white beard like the farmer at Kaase Farm; but who kept house for Him now He was old? Saint Peter was His bailiff, of course!... How could the old, dry cows have just as young calves as the young ones? And so on, and so on.

There was one subject about which, as a matter of course, there could be no question, nor any thought at all in that sense, because it was the very foundation of all existence—Father Lasse. He was there, simply, he stood like a safe wall behind everything that one did. He was the real Providence, the last great refuge in good and ill; he could do whatever he liked—Father Lasse was almighty.

Then there was one natural centre in the world—Pelle himself. Everything grouped itself about him, everything existed for him— for him to play with, to shudder at, or to put on one side for a great future. Even distant trees, houses and rocks in the landscape, that he had never been up to, assumed an attitude toward him, either friendly or hostile; and the relation had to be carefully decided in the case of each new thing that appeared upon his horizon.

His world was small; he had only just begun to create it. For a good arm's-length on all sides of him, there was more or less *terra firma*; but beyond that floated raw matter, chaos. But Pelle already found his world immense, and was quite willing to make it infinite. He attacked everything with insatiable appetite; his ready perceptions laid hold of all that came within their reach; they were like the mouth of a machine, into which matter was incessantly rushing in small, whirling particles. And in the draught they raised, came others and again others; the entire universe was on its way toward him.

Pelle shaped and set aside twenty new things in the course of a second. The earth grew out under him into a world that was rich in excitement and grotesque forms, discomfort and the most everyday things. He went about in it uncertainly, for there was always something that became displaced and had to be revalued or made over again; the most matter-of-fact things would change and all at once become terrifying marvels, or *vice versa*. He went about in a state of continual wonderment, and assumed an expectant attitude even with regard to the most familiar things; for who could tell what surprises they might give one?

As an instance; he had all his life had opportunities of verifying the fact that trouser-buttons were made of bone and had five holes, one large one in the middle and four smaller ones round it. And then one day, one of the men comes home from the town with a pair of new trousers, the buttons of which are made of bright metal and are no larger than a sixpenny-piece! They have only four holes, and the thread is to lie across them, not from the middle outward, as in the old ones.

Or take the great eclipse of the sun, that he had wondered so much about all the summer, and that all the old people said would bring about the destruction of the world. He had looked forward to it, especially the destruction part of it; it would be something of an adventure, and somewhere within him there was a little bit of confident assurance that it would all come right as far as he was concerned. The eclipse did come too, as it was meant to; it grew dark too, as if it were the Last Day, and the birds became so quiet, and the cattle bellowed and wanted to run home. But then it grew light again and it all came to nothing.

Then there were fearful terrors that all at once revealed themselves as tiny, tiny things—thank goodness! But there were also anticipated pleasures that made your heart beat, and when you got up to them they were dullness itself.

Far out in the misty mass, invisible worlds floated by that had nothing to do with his own. A sound coming out of the unknown created them in a twinkling. They came into existence in the same way that the land had done that morning he had stood upon the deck of the steamer, and heard voices and noise through the fog, thick and big, with forms that looked like huge gloves without fingers.

And inside one there was blood and a heart and a soul. The heart Pelle had found out about himself; it was a little bird shut up in there. But the soul bored its way like a serpent to whatever part of the body desire occupied. Old thatcher Holm had once drawn the soul like a thin thread out of the thumb of a man who couldn't help stealing. Pelle's own soul was good; it lay in the pupils of his eyes, and reflected Father Lasse's image whenever he looked into them.

The blood was the worst, and so Father Lasse always let himself be bled when there was anything the matter with him; the bad humors had to be let out. Gustav thought a great deal about blood, and could tell the strangest things about it; and he cut his fingers only to see whether it was ripe. One evening he came over to the cow-stable and exhibited a bleeding finger. The blood was quite black. "Now I'm a man! " he said, and swore a great oath; but the maids only made fun of him, and said that he had not carried his four bushels of peas up into the loft yet.

Then there was hell and heaven, and the stone-quarry where they struck one another with heavy hammers when they were drunk. The men in the stone-quarry were the strongest men in the world. One of them had eaten ten poached eggs at one time without being ill; and there is nothing so strengthening as eggs.

Down in the meadow, will-o'-the-wisps hopped about looking for something in the deep summer nights. There was always one of them near the stream, and it stood and danced on the top of a little heap of stones that lay in the middle of the meadow. A couple of years ago a girl had one night given birth to a child out there among the dunes and as she did not know what to do about a father for it, she drowned it in one of the pools that the brook makes where it turns. Good people raised the little cairn, so that the place should not be forgotten; and over it the child's soul used to burn at dead of night at the time of year at which it was born. Pelle believed that the child itself was buried beneath the stones, and now and then ornamented the mound with a branch of fir; but he never played at that part of the stream. The girl was sent across the sea, sentenced to penal servitude for many years, and people wondered at the father. She had not named any one, but every one knew who it was all the same. He was a young, well-to-do fisherman down in the village, and the girl was one of the poorest, so there could never have been any question of their marrying. The girl must have preferred this to begging help of him for the child, and living in the village with an illegitimate child, an object of universal derision. And he had certainly put a bold face on the matter, where many another would have been ashamed and gone away on a long voyage.

This summer, two years after the girl went to prison, the fisherman was going home one night along the shore toward the village with some nets on his back. He was of a callous nature, and did not hesitate to take the shortest way across the meadow; but when he got in among the dunes, he saw a will-o'-the-wisp following in his steps, grew frightened, and began to run. It began to gain upon him, and when he leaped across the brook to put water between himself and the spirit, it seized hold of the nets. At this he shouted the name of God, and fled like one bereft of his senses. The next morning at sunrise he and his father went to fetch the nets. They had caught on the cairn, and lay right across the stream.

Then the young man joined the Revivalists, and his father abandoned his riotous life and followed him. Early and late the young fisherman was to be found at their meetings, and at other times he went about like a malefactor with his head hanging down, only waiting for the girl to come out of prison, so that he could marry her.

Pelle was up in it all. The girls talked shudderingly about it as they sat upon the men's knees in the long summer evenings, and a lovesick fellow from inland had made up a ballad about it, which Gustav sang to his concertina. Then all the girls on the farm wept, and even Lively Sara's eyes filled with tears, and she began to talk to Mons about engagement rings.

One day when Pelle was lying on his face in the grass, singing and clapping his naked feet together in the clear air, he saw a young man standing by the cairn and putting on it stones which he took out of his pocket; after which he knelt down. Pelle went up to him.

"What are you doing? " he asked boldly, feeling that he was in his own domain. "Are you saying your prayers? "

The man did not answer, but remained in a kneeling posture. At last he rose, and spat out tobacco-juice.

"I'm praying to Him Who is to judge us all, " he said, looking steadily at Pelle.

Pelle recognized that look. It was the same in expression as that of the man the other day—the one that had been sent by God. Only there was no reproach in it.

"Haven't you any bed to sleep in then? " asked Pelle. "I always say my prayers under the clothes. He hears them just as well! God knows everything. "

The young man nodded, and began moving about the stones on the cairn.

"You mustn't hurt that, " said Pelle firmly, "for there's a little baby buried there. "

The young man turned upon him a strange look.

"That's not true! " he said thickly; "for the child lies up in the churchyard in consecrated earth. "

"O—oh, inde—ed? " said Pelle, imitating his father's slow tones. "But I know it was the parents that drowned it—and buried it here. " He was too proud of his knowledge to relinquish it without a word.

The man looked as if he were about to strike him, and Pelle retreated a little, and then, having confidence in his legs, he laughed openly. But the other seemed no longer aware of his presence, and stood looking dully past the cairn. Pelle drew nearer again.

The man started at Pelle's shadow, and heaved a deep sigh. "Is that you? " he said apathetically, without looking at Pelle. "Why can't you leave me alone? "

"It's *my* field, " said Pelle, "because I herd here; but you may stay here if you won't hit me. And you mustn't touch the cairn, because there's a little baby buried there. "

The young man looked gravely at Pelle. "It's not true what you say! How dare you tell such a lie? God hates a lie. But you're a simple-hearted child, and I'll tell you all about it without hiding anything, as truly as I only want to walk wholly in God's sight. "

Pelle looked at him uncomprehendingly. "I should think I ought to know all about it, " he said, "considering I know the whole song by heart. I can sing it to you, if you like. It goes like this. " Pelle began to sing in a voice that was a little tremulous with shyness—

"So happy are we in our childhood's first years,
  Neither sorrow nor sin is our mead;
We play, and there's nought in our path to raise fears
  That it straight into prison doth lead.

Right many there are that with voice sorrowful
  Must oft for lost happiness long.
To make the time pass in this prison so dull,
  I now will write down all my song.

I played with my father, with mother I played,
  And childhood's days came to an end;
And when I had grown up into a young maid,
  I played still, but now with my friend.

I gave him my day and I gave him my night,
  And never once thought of deceit;
But when I him told of my sorrowful plight,
  My trust I had cause to regret.

'I never have loved you,' he quickly did say;
  'Begone! I'll ne'er see you again!'
He turned on his heel and went angry away.
  'Twas then I a murd'ress became."

Here Pelle paused in astonishment, for the grown-up man had sunk forward as he sat, and he was sobbing. "Yes, it was wicked, " he said. "For then she killed her child and had to go to prison. " He spoke with a certain amount of contempt; he did not like men that cried. "But it's nothing that you need cry about, " he added carelessly, after a little.

"Yes, it is; for she'd done nothing. It was the child's father that killed it; it was me that did the dreadful thing; yes, I confess that I'm a murderer! Haven't I openly enough acknowledged by wrongdoing? " He turned his face upward, as though he were speaking to God.

"Oh, was it you? " said Pelle, moving a little away from him. "Did you kill your own child? Father Lasse could never have done that! But then why aren't you in prison? Did you tell a lie, and say *she'd* done it? "

These words had a peculiar effect upon the fisherman. Pelle stood watching him for a little, and then exclaimed: "You do talk so queerly—'blop-blop-blop, ' just as if you were from another country. And what do you scrabble in the air with your fingers for, and cry? Will you get a thrashing when you get home? "

At the word "cry, " the man burst into a flood of tears. Pelle had never seen any one cry so unrestrainedly. His face seemed all blurred.

"Will you have a piece of my bread-and-butter? " he asked, by way of offering comfort. "I've got some with sausage on. "

The fisherman shook his head.

Pelle looked at the cairn. He was obstinate, and determined not to give in.

"It *is* buried there, " he said. "I've seen its soul myself, burning up on the top of the heap at night. That's because it can't get into heaven. "

A horrible sound came from the fisherman's lips, a hollow groan that brought Pelle's little heart into his mouth. He began to jump up and down in fear, and when he recovered his senses and stopped, he saw the fisherman running with head bent low across the meadow, until he disappeared among the dunes.

Pelle gazed after him in astonishment, and then moved slowly toward his dinner-basket. The result of the encounter was, as far as it had gone, a disappointment. He had sung to a perfect stranger, and there was no denying that that was an achievement, considering how difficult it often was only to answer "yes" or "no" to somebody you'd never seen before. But he had hardly more than begun the verses, and what made the performance remarkable was that he knew the entire ballad by heart. He sang it now for his own benefit from beginning to end, keeping count of the verses on his fingers; and he found the most intense satisfaction in shouting it out at the top of his voice.

In the evening he as usual discussed the events of the day with his father, and he then understood one or two things that filled his mind with uncomfortable thoughts. Father Lasse's was as yet the only human voice that the boy wholly understood; a mere sigh or shake of the head from the old man had a more convincing power than words from any one else.

"Alas! " he said again and again. "Evil, evil everywhere; sorrow and trouble wherever you turn! He'd willingly give his life to go to prison in her stead, now it's too late! So he ran away when you said that to him? Well, well, it's not easy to resist the Word of God even from the lips of a child, when the conscience is sore; and trading in the happiness of others is a bad way of earning a living. But now see about getting your feet washed, laddie. "

Life furnished enough to work at and struggle with, and a good deal to dread; but worse almost than all that would harm Pelle himself, were the glimpses he now and then had of the depths of humanity: in the face of these his child's brain was powerless. Why did the mistress cry so much and drink secretly? What went on behind the windows in the big house? He could not comprehend it, and every time he puzzled his little brain over it, the uncomfortable feeling only seemed to stare out at him from all the window-panes, and sometimes enveloped him in all the horror of the incomprehensible.

But the sun rode high in the heavens, and the nights were light. The darkness lay crouching under the earth and had no power. And he possessed the child's happy gift of forgetting instantly and completely.

VI

Pelle had a quick pulse and much energy, and there was always something that he was attempting to overtake in his restless onward rush—if nothing else, then time itself. Now the rye was all in, now the last stack disappeared from the field, the shadows grew longer every day. But one evening the darkness surprised him before his bedtime, and this made him serious. He no longer hastened on the time, but tried to hold it back by many small sun-signs.

One day the men's midday rest was taken off. They harnessed the horses again as soon as they had eaten their dinner, and the chaff-cutting was put off until the evening. The horse-way lay on the outer side of the stable, and none of the men cared to tramp round out there in the dark, driving for the chaff-cutter, so Pelle had to do it. Lasse protested and threatened to go to the farmer, but it was of no use; every evening Pelle had to be out there for a couple of hours. They were his nicest hours that they took from him, the hours when he and Father Lasse pottered about in the stable, and talked themselves happily through all the day's troubles into a common bright future; and Pelle cried. When the moon chased the clouds away and he could see everything round him distinctly, he allowed his tears to run freely; but on dark evenings he was quiet and held his breath. Sometimes when it rained it was so dark that the farm and everything disappeared; and then he saw hundreds of beings that at other times the light hid. They appeared out of the darkness, terribly big, or came sliding up to him upon their bellies. He grew rigid as he gazed, and could not take his eyes from them. He sought shelter under the wall, and encouraged the horse from there; and one evening he ran in. They chased him out again, and he submitted to be chased, for when it came to the point he was more afraid of the men inside than of the beings outside. But one pitch-dark evening he was in an unusually bad way, and when he discovered that the horse, his only comfort, was also afraid, he dropped everything and ran in for the second time. Threats were powerless to make him go out again, and blows equally so, and one of the men took him up and carried him out; but then Pelle forgot everything, and screamed till the house shook.

While they were struggling with him, the farmer came out. He was very angry when he heard what was the matter, and blew the foreman up sky high. Then he took Pelle by the hand, and went down with him to the cow-stable. "A man like you to be afraid of a little dark! " he said jokingly. "You must try to get the better of that. But if the men harm you, just you come to me. "

The plough went up and down the fields all day long, and made the earth dark in color, the foliage became variegated, and there was often sleet. The coats of the cattle grew thicker, their hair grew long and stood up on their backs. Pelle had much to put up with, and existence as a whole became a shade more serious. His clothing did not become thicker and warmer with the cold weather like that of the cattle; but he could crack his whip so that it sounded, in the most successful attempts, like little shots; he could thrash Rud when there was no unfairness, and jump across the stream at its narrowest part. All that brought warmth to the body.

The flock now grazed all over the farm-lands, wherever the cows had been tethered; the dairy-cows being now indoors; or they went inland on the fens, where all the farms had each a piece of grass-land. Here Pelle made acquaintance with herd-boys from the other farms, and looked into quite another world that was not ruled by bailiff and farm-pupil and thrashings, but where all ate at the same table, and the mistress herself sat and spun wool for the herd-boys' stockings. But he could never get in there, for they did not take Swedes at the small farms, nor would the people of the island take service together with them. He was sorry for this.

As soon as the autumn ploughing was started up on the fields, the boys, according to old custom, took down the boundary-fences and let all the animals graze together. The first few days it gave them more to do, for the animals fought until they got to know one another. They were never wholly mingled; they always grazed in patches, each farm's flock by itself. The dinner-baskets were also put together, and one boy was appointed in turn to mind the whole herd. The other boys played at robbers up among the rocks, or ran about in the woods or on the shore. When it was really cold they lighted bonfires, or built fireplaces of flat stones, where they roasted apples and eggs which they stole from the farms.

It was a glorious life, and Pelle was happy. It was true he was the smallest of them all, and his being a Swede was a drawback to him. In the midst of their play, the others would sometimes begin to mimic his way of talking, and when he grew angry asked why he did not draw his knife. But on the other hand he was from the biggest farm, and was the only one that had bullocks in his herd; he was not behind them in physical accomplishments, and none of them could carve as he could. And it was his intention, when he grew big, to thrash them all.

In the meantime he had to accommodate himself to circumstances, ingratiate himself with the big ones, wherever he discovered there was a flaw in their relations to one another, and be obliging. He had to take his turn oftener than the others, and came off badly at mealtimes. He submitted to it as something unavoidable, and directed all his efforts toward getting the best that it was possible to get out of the circumstances; but he promised himself, as has been said, the fullest reparation when he grew big.

Once or twice it became too hot for him, and he left the community and kept by himself; but he soon returned to the others again. His little body was bursting with courage to live the life, and would not let him shirk it; he must take his chance—eat his way through.

One day there came two new boys, who herded cattle from two farms on the other side of the stone-quarry. They were twins, and their names were Alfred and Albinus. They were tall, thin lads, who looked as if they might have been half-starved when they were little; their skin had a bluish tinge, and stood the cold badly. They were quick and active, they could overtake the quickest calf, they could walk on their hands and smoke at the same time, and not only vault but really jump obstacles. They were not much good at fighting; they were lacking in courage, and their ability forsook them in an emergency.

There was something comical about the two brothers. "Here are the twins, the twelvins! " cried the whole flock in greeting, the first morning they appeared. "Well, how many times have you had a baby in your house since last year? " They belonged to a family of twelve, and among these there had twice been twins, and this of itself was an inexhaustible source of raillery; and moreover they were half Swedish. They shared the disadvantage with Pelle.

But nothing seemed to have any effect upon them; they grinned at everything, and gave themselves away still more. From all he saw and heard, Pelle could understand that there was something ridiculous about their home in the eyes of the parish; but they did not mind that. It was the fecundity of their parents that was the special subject of derision, and the two boys quite happily exposed them to ridicule, and would tell all about the most private home matters. One day when the flock had been most persistent in calling "Twelvins! " they said, grinning, that their mother would soon be having a thirteenth. They were incapable of being wounded.

Every time they exposed their parents to ridicule, it hurt Pelle, for his own feelings on this point were the most sacred that he had. Try as he would, he could not understand them; he had to go to his father with the matter one evening.

"So they mock and make fun of their own parents? " said Lasse. "Then they'll never prosper in this world, for you're to honor your father and mother. Good parents who have brought them into the world with pain, and must toil hard, perhaps hunger and put up with much themselves, to get food and clothing for them! Oh, it's a shame! And you say their surname is Karlsson like ours, and that they live on the heath behind the stone-quarry? Then they must be brother Kalle's sons! Why, bless my soul, if I don't believe that's it! You ask them tomorrow if their father hasn't a notch in his right ear! I did it myself with a piece of a horse-shoe when we were little boys one day I was in a rage with him because he made fun of me before the others. He was just the same as those two, but he didn't mean anything by it, there was nothing ill-natured about him. "

The boys' father *had* a notch in his right ear. Pelle and they were thus cousins; and the way that both they and their parents were made fun of was a matter for both laughter and tears. In a way, Father Lasse too came in for a share of the ridicule, and that thought was hardly to be endured.

The other boys quickly discovered Pelle's vulnerable point, and used it for their own advantage; and Pelle had to give way and put up with things in order to keep his father out of their conversation. He did not always succeed, however. When they were in the mood, they said quite absurd things about one another's homes. They were not intended to be taken for more than they were worth, but Pelle did not understand jokes on that head. One day one of the biggest boys said to him: "Do you know, your father was the cause of his own mother's having a child! " Pelle did not understand the play of words in this coarse joke, but he heard the laughter of the others, and becoming blind with rage, he flew at the big boy, and kicked him so hard in the stomach, that he had to keep his bed for several days.

During those days, Pelle went about in fear and trembling. He dared not tell his father what had happened, for then he would be obliged to repeat the boy's ugly accusation, too; so he went about in dread of the fatal consequences. The other boys had withdrawn themselves from him, so as not to share the blame if anything came of it; the boy was a farmer's son—the only one in the company—and they had visions of the magistrate at the back of the affair, and perhaps a caning at the town-hall. So Pelle went by himself with his cattle, and had plenty of time to think about the event, which, by the force of his lively imagination, grew larger and larger in its consequences, until at last it almost suffocated him with terror. Every cart he saw driving along the high-road sent a thrill through him; and if it turned up toward Stone Farm, he could distinctly see the policemen—three of them—with large handcuffs, just as they had come to fetch Erik Erikson for ill-treating his wife. He hardly dared drive the cattle home in the evening.

One morning the boy came herding over there with his cattle, and there was a grown-up man with him, whom, from his clothes and everything else about him, Pelle judged to be a farmer—was it the boy's father? They stood over there for a little while, talking to the herd-boys, and then came across toward him, with the whole pack at their heels, the father holding his son by the hand.

The perspiration started from every pore of Pelle's body; his fear prompted him to run away, but he stood his ground. Together the father and son made a movement with their hand, and Pelle raised both elbows to ward off a double box-on-the-ears.

But they only extended their hands. "I beg your pardon, " said the boy, taking one of Pelle's hands; "I beg your pardon, " repeated the father, clasping his other hand in his. Pelle stood in bewilderment, looking from one to the other. At first he thought that the man was the same as the one sent by God; but it was only his eyes—those strange eyes. Then he suddenly burst into tears and forgot all else in the relief they brought from the terrible anxiety. The two spoke a few kind words to him, and quietly went away to let him be alone.

After this Pelle and Peter Kure became friends, and when Pelle learnt to know him better, he discovered that sometimes the boy had a little of the same look in his eyes as his father, and the young fisherman, and the man that was sent by God. The remarkable course that the event had taken occupied his mind for a long time. One day a chance comparison of his experiences brought him to the discovery of the connection between this mysterious expression in their eyes and their remarkable actions; the people who had looked at him with those eyes had all three done unexpected things. And another day it dawned upon him that these people were *religious*; the boys had quarrelled with Peter Kure that day, and had used the word as a term of abuse against his parents.

There was one thing that was apparent, and outweighed everything, even his victory. He had entered the lists with a boy who was bigger and stronger than he, and had held his own, because for the first time in his life he had struck out recklessly. If you wanted to fight, you had to kick wherever it hurt most. If you only did that, and had justice on your side, you might fight anybody, even a farmer's son. These were two satisfactory discoveries, which for the present nothing could disturb.

Then he had defended his father; that was something quite new and important in his life. He required more space now.

At Michaelmas, the cattle were taken in, and the last of the day-laborers left. During the summer, several changes had been made among the regular servants at the farm, but now, at term-day, none were changed; it was not the habit of Stone Farm to change servants at the regular term-times.

So Pelle again helped his father with the foddering indoors. By rights he should have begun to go to school, and a mild representation of this fact was made to the farmer by the school authorities; but the boy was very useful at home, as the care of the cattle was too much for one man; and nothing more was heard about the matter. Pelle was glad it was put off. He had thought much about school in the course of the summer, and had invested it with so much that was unfamiliar and great that he was now quite afraid of it.

VII

Christmas Eve was a great disappointment. It was the custom for the herd-boys to come out and spend Christmas at the farms where they served in the summer, and Pelle's companions had told him of all the delights of Christmas—roast meat and sweet drinks, Christmas games and ginger-nuts and cakes; it was one endless eating and drinking and playing of Christmas games, from the evening before Christmas Eve until "Saint Knut carried Christmas out, " on January 7th. That was what it was like at all the small farms, the only difference being that those who were religious did not play cards, but sang hymns instead. But what they had to eat was just as good.

The last few days before Christmas Pelle had to get up at two or half-past two to help the girls pluck poultry, and the old thatcher Holm to heat the oven. With this his connection with the delights of Christmas came to an end. There was dried cod and boiled rice on Christmas Eve, and it tasted good enough; but of all the rest there was nothing. There were a couple of bottles of brandy on the table for the men, that was all. The men were discontented and quarrelsome. They poured milk and boiled rice into the leg of the stocking that Karna was knitting, so that she was fuming the whole evening; and then sat each with his girl on his knee, and made ill-natured remarks about everything. The old farm-laborers and their wives, who had been invited to partake of the Christmas fare, talked about death and all the ills of the world.

Upstairs there was a large party. All the wife's relations were invited, and they were hard at work on the roast goose. The yard was full of conveyances, and the only one of the farm-servants who was in good spirits was the head man, who received all the tips. Gustav was in a thoroughly bad humor, for Bodil was upstairs helping to wait. He had brought his concertina over, and was playing love-songs. It was putting them into better spirits, and the evil expression was leaving their eyes; one after another they started singing, and it began to be quite comfortable down there. But just then a message came to say that they must make less noise, so the assembly broke up, the old people going home, and the young ones dispersing in couples according to the friendships of the moment.

Lasse and Pelle went to bed.

"What's Christmas really for? " asked Pelle.

Lasse rubbed his thigh reflectively.

"It has to be, " he answered hesitatingly. "Yes, and then it's the time when the year turns round and goes upward, you see! And of course it's the night when the Child Jesus was born, too! " It took him a long time to produce this last reason, but when it did come it was with perfect assurance. "Taking one thing with another, you see, " he added, after a short pause.

On the day after Christmas Day there was a kind of subscription merrymaking at an enterprising crofter's down in the village; it was to cost two and a half krones a couple for music, sandwiches, and spirits in the middle of the night, and coffee toward morning. Gustav and Bodil were going. Pelle at any rate saw a little of Christmas as it passed, and was as interested in it as if it concerned himself; and he gave Lasse no rest from his questions that day. So Bodil was still faithful to Gustav, after all!

When they got up the next morning, they found Gustav lying on the ground by the cow-stable door, quite helpless, and his good clothes in a sad state. Bodil was not with him. "Then she's deceived him, " said Lasse, as they helped him in. "Poor boy! Only seventeen, and a wounded heart already! The women'll be his ruin one of these days, you'll see! "

At midday, when the farm-laborers' wives came to do the milking, Lasso's supposition was confirmed: Bodil had attached herself to a tailor's apprentice from the village, and had left with him in the middle of the night. They laughed pityingly at Gustav, and for some time after he had to put up with their gibes at his ill-success; but there was only one opinion about Bodil. She was at liberty to come and go with whomsoever she liked, but as long as Gustav was paying for her amusements, she ought to have kept to him. Who but the neighbor would keep the hens that ate their grain at home and laid their eggs at the neighbor's?

There had as yet been no opportunity to visit Lasse's brother beyond the stone-quarry, but it was to be done on the second day of the new year. Between Christmas and the New Year the men did nothing after dark, and it was the custom everywhere to help the herdsman with his evening occupations. There was nothing of that here; Lasse was too old to assert himself, and Pelle too little. They might think themselves lucky they did not have to do the foddering for the men who went out as well as their own.

But to-day it was to come off; Gustav and Long Ole had undertaken to do the evening work. Pelle began to look forward to it as soon as he was up—he was up every day by half-past three. But as Lasse used to say, if you sing before breakfast you'll weep before night.

After dinner, Gustav and Ole were standing grinding chopping knives down in the lower yard. The trough leaked, and Pelle had to pour water on the grindstone out of an old kettle. His happiness could be seen on his face.

"What are you so pleased about? " asked Gustav. "Your eyes are shining like the cat's in the dark. "

Pelle told him.

"I'm afraid you won't get away! " said Ole, winking at Gustav. "We shan't get the chaff cut time enough to do the foddering. This grindstone's so confoundedly hard to turn, too. If only that handle-turner hadn't been broken! "

Pelle pricked up his ears. "Handle-turner? What's that? " he asked.

Gustav sprang round the grindstone, and slapped his thigh in enjoyment of the joke.

"My goodness, how stupid you are! Don't you even know what a handle-turner is? It's a thing you only need to put on to the grindstone, and it turns it by itself. They've got one by-the-way over at Kaase Farm, " he said, turning to Ole; "if only it wasn't so far away. "

"Is it heavy? " asked Pelle, in a low voice; everything depended upon the answer. "Can I lift it? " His voice trembled.

"Oh, no, not so awfully heavy. You could carry it quite well. But you'd have to be very careful. "

"I can run over and fetch it; I'll carry it very carefully. " Pelle looked at them with a face that could not but inspire confidence.

"Very well; but take a sack with you to put it in. And you'll have to be as careful as the very devil, for it's an expensive thing. "

Pelle found a sack and ran off across the fields. He was as delighted as a young kid, plucking at himself and everything as he ran, and jumping aside to frighten the crows. He was overflowing with happiness. He was saving the expedition for himself and Father Lasse. Gustav and Ole were good men! He would get back as quickly as possible, so that they should not have to toil any more at the grindstone. "What, are you back already? " they would say, and open their eyes. "Then you must have smashed that precious machine on the way! " And they would take it carefully out of the sack, and it would be quite safe and sound. "Well, you are a wonder of a boy! a perfect prince! " they would say.

When he got to Kaase Farm, they wanted him to go in to a Christmas meal while they were putting the machine into the sack; but Pelle said "No" and held to it: he had not time. So they gave him a piece of cold apple out on the steps, so that he should not carry Christmas away. They all looked so pleasant, and every one came out when he hoisted the sack on his back and set off home. They too recommended him to be very careful, and seemed anxious, as if he could hardly realize what he was carrying.

It was a good mile between the farms, but it was an hour and a half before Pelle reached home, and then he was ready to drop. He dared not put down the sack to rest, but stumbled on step by step, only resting once by leaning against a stone fence. When at last he staggered into the yard, every one came up to see the neighbor's new handle-turner; and Pelle was conscious of his own importance when Ole carefully lifted the sack from his back. He leaned for a moment over toward the wall before he regained his balance; the ground was so strange to tread upon now he was rid of his burden; it pushed him away. But his face was radiant.

Gustav opened the sack, which was securely closed, and shook out its contents upon the stone pavement. They were pieces of brick, a couple of old ploughshares, and other similar things. Pelle stared in bewilderment and fear at the rubbish, looking as if he had just dropped from another planet; but when laughter broke out on all sides, he understood what it all meant, and, crouching down, hid his face in his hands. He would not cry—not for the world; they should not have that satisfaction. He was sobbing in his heart, but he kept his lips tightly closed. His body tingled with rage. The beasts! The wicked devils! Suddenly he kicked Gustav on the leg.

"Aha, so he kicks, does he? " exclaimed Gustav, lifting him up into the air. "Do you want to see a little imp from Smaaland? " Pelle covered his face with his arms and kicked to be let down; and he also made an attempt to bite. "Eh, and he bites, too, the little devil! " Gustav had to hold him firmly so as to manage him. He held him by the collar, pressing his knuckles against the boy's throat and making him gasp, while he spoke with derisive gentleness. "A clever youngster, this! He's scarcely out of long clothes, and wants to fight already! " Gustav went on tormenting him; it looked as if he were making a display of his superior strength.

"Well, now we've seen that you're the strongest, " said the head man at last, "so let him go! " and when Gustav did not respond immediately, he received a blow from a clenched fist between his shoulder-blades. Then the boy was released, and went over to the stable to Lasse, who had seen the whole thing, but had not dared to approach. He could do nothing, and his presence would only have done harm.

"Yes, and then there's our outing, laddie, " he explained, by way of excuse, while he was comforting the boy. "I could very well thrash a puppy like Gustav, but if I did we shouldn't get away this evening, for he wouldn't do our work. And none of the others, either, for they all stick together like burrs. But you can do it yourself! I verily believe you'd kick the devil himself, right on his club-foot! Well, well, it was well done; but you must be careful not to waste your powder and shot. It doesn't pay! "

The boy was not so easily comforted now. Deep down in his heart the remembrance of his injury lay and pained him, because he had acted in such good faith, and they had wounded him in his ready, cheerful confidence. What had happened had also stung his pride; he had walked into a trap, made a fool of himself for them. The incident burnt into his soul, and greatly influenced his subsequent development. He had already found out that a person's word was not always to be relied upon, and he had made awkward attempts to get behind it. Now he would trust nobody straight away any more; and he had discovered how the secret was to be found out. You only had to look at people's eyes when they said anything. Both here and at Kaase Farm the people had looked so strange about the handle-turner, as if they were laughing inside. And the bailiff had laughed that time when he promised them roast pork and stewed rhubarb every day. They hardly ever got anything but herring and porridge. People talked with two tongues; Father Lasse was the only one who did not do it.

Pelle began to be observant of his own face. It was the face that spoke, and that was why it went badly with him when he tried to escape a thrashing by telling a white lie. And to-day's misfortune had been the fault of his face; if you felt happy, you mustn't show it. He had discovered the danger of letting his mind lie open, and his small organism set to work diligently to grow hard skin to draw over its vital parts.

After supper they set off across the fields, hand in hand as usual. As a rule, Pelle chattered unceasingly when they were by themselves; but this evening he was quieter. The event of the afternoon was still in his mind, and the coming visit gave him a feeling of solemnity.

Lasse carried a red bundle in his hand, in which was a bottle of black-currant rum, which they had got Per Olsen to buy in the town the day before, when he had been in to swear himself free. It had cost sixty-six ores, and Pelle was turning something over in his mind, but did not know whether it would do.

"Father! " he said at last. "Mayn't I carry that a little way? "

"Gracious! Are you crazy, boy? It's an expensive article! And you might drop it. "

"I wouldn't drop it. Well, only hold it for a little then? Mayn't I, father? Oh do, father! "

"Eh, what an idea! I don't know what you'll be like soon, if you aren't stopped! Upon my word, I think you must be ill, you're getting so tiresome! " And Lasse went on crossly for a little while, but then stopped and bent down over the boy.

"Hold it then, you little silly, but be very careful! And you mustn't move a single step while you've got it, mind! "

Pelle clasped the bottle to his body with his arms, for he dared not trust his hands, and pushed out his stomach as far as possible to support it. Lasse stood with his hands extended beneath the bottle, ready to catch it if it fell.

"There! That'll do! " he said anxiously, and took the bottle.

"It *is* heavy! " said Pelle, admiringly, and went on contentedly, holding his father's hand.

"But why had he to swear himself free? " he suddenly asked.

"Because he was accused by a girl of being the father of her child. Haven't you heard about it? "

Pelle nodded. "Isn't he, then? Everybody says he is. "

"I can hardly believe it; it would be certain damnation for Per Olsen. But, of course, the girl says it's him and no one else. Ah me! Girls are dangerous playthings! You must take care when your time comes, for they can bring misfortune upon the best of men. "

"How do you swear, then? Do you say 'Devil take me'? "

Lasse could not help laughing. "No, indeed! That wouldn't be very good for those that swear false. No, you see, in the court all God's highest ministers are sitting round a table that's exactly like a horseshoe, and beyond that again there's an altar with the crucified Christ Himself upon it. On the altar lies a big, big book that's fastened to the wall with an iron chain, so that the devil can't carry it off in the night, and that's God's Holy Word. When a man swears, he lays his left hand upon the book, and holds up his right hand with three fingers in the air; they're God the Father, Son and Holy Ghost. But if he swears false, the Governor can see it at once, because then there are red spots of blood on the leaves of the book. "

"And what then? " asked Pelle, with deep interest.

"Well, then his three fingers wither, and it goes on eating itself into his body. People like that suffer frightfully; they rot right away. "

"Don't they go to hell, then? "

"Yes, they do that too, except when they give themselves up and take their punishment, and then they escape in the next life; but they can't escape withering away. "

"Why doesn't the Governor take them himself and punish them, when he can see in that book that they swore false? "

"Why, because then they'd get off going to hell, and there's an agreement with Satan that he's to have all those that don't give themselves up, don't you see? "

Pelle shuddered, and for a little while walked on in silence beside his father; but when he next spoke, he had forgotten all about it.

"I suppose Uncle Kalle's rich, isn't he? " he asked.

"He can't be rich, but he's a land-owner, and that's not a little thing! " Lasse himself had never attained to more than renting land.

"When I grow up, I mean to have a great big farm, " said Pelle, with decision.

"Yes, I've no doubt you will, " said Lasse, laughing. Not that he also did not expect something great of the boy, if not exactly a large farmer. There was no saying, however. Perhaps some farmer's daughter might fall in love with him; the men of his family generally had an attraction for women. Several of them had given proof of it— his brother, for instance, who had taken the fancy of a parson's wife. Then Pelle would have to make the most of his opportunity so that the family would be ashamed to oppose the match. And Pelle was good enough. He had that "cow's-lick" on his forehead, fine hair at the back of his neck, and a birth-mark on his hip; and that all betokened luck. Lasse went on talking to himself as he walked, calculating the boy's future with large, round figures, that yielded a little for him too; for, however great his future might be, it would surely come in time to allow of Lasse's sharing and enjoying it in his very old age.

They went across country toward the stone-quarry, following stone dikes and snow-filled ditches, and working their way through the thicket of blackthorn and juniper, behind which lay the rocks and "the Heath. " They made their way right into the quarry, and tried in the darkness to find the place where the dross was thrown, for that would be where the stone-breaking went on.

A sound of hammering came from the upper end of the ground, and they discovered lights in several places. Beneath a sloping straw screen, from which hung a lantern, sat a little, broad man, hammering away at the fragments. He worked with peculiar vivacity—struck three blows and pushed the stones to one side, another three blows, and again to one side; and while with one hand he pushed the pieces away, with the other he placed a fresh fragment in position on the stone. It went as busily and evenly as the ticking of a watch.

"Why, if that isn't Brother Kalle sitting there! " said Lasse, in a voice of surprise as great as if the meeting were a miracle from heaven. "Good evening, Kalle Karlsson! How are you? "

The stone-breaker looked up.

"Oh, there you are, brother! " he said, rising with difficulty; and the two greeted one another as if they had met only the day before. Kalle collected his tools and laid the screen down upon them while they talked.

"So you break stones too? Does that bring in anything? " asked Lasse.

"Oh, not very much. We get twelve krones a 'fathom' and when I work with a lantern morning and evening, I can break half a fathom in a week. It doesn't pay for beer, but we live anyhow. But it's awfully cold work; you can't keep warm at it, and you get so stiff with sitting fifteen hours on the cold stone—as stiff as if you were the father of the whole world. " He was walking stiffly in front of the others across the heath toward a low, hump-backed cottage.

"Ah, there comes the moon, now there's no use for it! " said Kalle, whose spirits were beginning to rise. "And, my word, what a sight the old dormouse looks! He must have been at a New Year's feast in heaven. "

"You're the same merry devil that you were in the old days, " said Lasse.

"Well, good spirits'll soon be the only thing to be had without paying for. "

The wall of the house stuck out in a large round lump on one side, and Pelle had to go up to it to feel it all over. It was most mysterious what there might be on the other side—perhaps a secret chamber? He pulled his father's hand inquiringly.

"That? That's the oven where they bake their bread, " said Lasse. "It's put there to make more room. "

After inviting them to enter, Kalle put his head in at a door that led from the kitchen to the cowshed. "Hi, Maria! You must put your best foot foremost! " he called in a low voice. "The midwife's here! "

"What in the world does she want? It's a story, you old fool! " And the sound of milk squirting into the pail began again.

"A story, is it? No, but you must come in and go to bed; she says it's high time you did. You are keeping up much too long this year. Mind what you say, " he whispered into the cowshed, "for she is really here! And be quick! "

They went into the room, and Kalle went groping about to light a candle. Twice he took up the matches and dropped them again to light it at the fire, but the peat was burning badly. "Oh, bother! " he said, resolutely striking a match at last. "We don't have visitors every day. "

"Your wife's Danish, " said Lasse, admiringly. "And you've got a cow too? "

"Yes, it's a biggish place here, " said Kalle, drawing himself up. "There's a cat belonging to the establishment too, and as many rats as it cares to eat. "

His wife now appeared, breathless, and looking in astonishment at the visitors.

"Yes, the midwife's gone again, " said Kalle. "She hadn't time to-day; we must put it off till another time. But these are important strangers, so you must blow your nose with your fingers before you give them your hand! "

90

"Oh, you old humbug! You can't take me in. It's Lasse, of course, and Pelle! " And she held out her hand. She was short, like her husband, was always smiling, and had bowed arms and legs just as he had. Hard work and their cheerful temperament gave them both a rotund appearance.

"There are no end of children here, " said Lasse, looking about him. There were three in the turn-up bedstead under the window—two small ones at one end, and a long, twelve-year-old boy at the other, his black feet sticking out between the little girls' heads; and other beds were made up on chairs, in an old kneading-trough, and on the floor.

"Ye-es; we've managed to scrape together a few, " said Kalle, running about in vain to get something for his visitors to sit upon; everything was being used as beds. "You'll have to spit on the floor and sit down on that, " he said, laughing.

His wife came in, however, with a washing-bench and an empty beer-barrel.

"Sit you down and rest, " she said, placing the seats round the table. "And you must really excuse it, but the children must be somewhere. "

Kalle squeezed himself in and sat down upon the edge of the turn-up bedstead. "Yes, we've managed to scrape together a few, " he repeated. "You must provide for your old age while you have the strength. We've made up the dozen, and started on the next. It wasn't exactly our intention, but mother's gone and taken us in. " He scratched the back of his head, and looked the picture of despair.

His wife was standing in the middle of the room. "Let's hope it won't be twins this time too, " she said, laughing.

"Why, that would be a great saving, as we shall have to send for the midwife anyhow. People say of mother, " he went on, "that when she's put the children to bed she has to count them to make sure they're all there; but that's not true, because she can't count farther than ten. "

Here a baby in the alcove began to cry, and the mother took it up and seated herself on the edge of the turn-up bedstead to nurse it.

"And this is the smallest, " he said, holding it out toward Lasse, who put a crooked finger down its neck.

"What a little fatty! " he said softly; he was fond of children. "And what's its name? "

"She's called Dozena Endina, because when she came we thought that was to be the last; and she was the twelfth too. "

"Dozena Endina! That's a mighty fine name! " exclaimed Lasse. "It sounds exactly as if she might be a princess. "

"Yes, and the one before's called Ellen—from eleven, of course. That's her in the kneading-trough, " said Kalle. "The one before that again is Tentius, and then Nina, and Otto. The ones before that weren't named in that way, for we hadn't thought then that there'd be so many. But that's all mother's fault; if she only puts a patch on my working-trousers, things go wrong at once. "

"You ought to be ashamed of yourself, trying to get out of it like that, " said his wife, shaking her finger at him. "But as for that, " she went on, turning to Lasse, "I'm sure the others have nothing to complain of either, as far as their names are concerned. Albert, Anna, Alfred, Albinus, Anton, Alma and Alvilda—let me see, yes, that's the lot. None of them can say they've not been treated fairly. Father was all for A at that time; they were all to rhyme with A. Poetry's always come so easy to him. " She looked admiringly at her husband.

Kalle blinked his eyes in bashfulness. "No, but it's the first letter, you see, and it sounds pretty, " he said modestly.

"Isn't he clever to think of a thing like that? He ought to have been a student. Now *my* head would never have been any good for anything of that sort. He wanted, indeed, to have the names both begin and end with A, but that wouldn't do with the boys, so he had to give that up. But then he hasn't had any book-learning either. "

"Oh, that's too bad, mother! I didn't give it up. I'd made up a name for the first boy that had A at the end too; but then the priest and the clerk objected, and I had to let it go. They objected to Dozena Endina too, but I put my foot down; for I can be angry if I'm irritated too long. I've always liked to have some connection and meaning in everything; and it's not a bad idea to have something that those who look deeper can find out. Now, have you noticed anything special about two of these names? "

"No, " answered Lasse hesitatingly, "I don't know that I have. But I haven't got a head for that sort of thing either. "

"Well, look here! Anna and Otto are exactly the same, whether you read them forward or backward—exactly the same. I'll just show you. " He took down a child's slate that was hanging on the wall with a stump of slate-pencil, and began laboriously to write the names. "Now, look at this, brother! "

"I can't read, " said Lasse, shaking his head hopelessly. "Does it really give the same both ways? The deuce! That *is* remarkable! " He could not get over his astonishment.

"But now comes something that's still more remarkable, " said Kalle, looking over the top of the slate at his brother with the gaze of a thinker surveying the universe. "Otto, which can be read from both ends, means, of course, eight; but if I draw the figure 8, it can be turned upside down, and still be the same. Look here! " He wrote the figure eight.

Lasse turned the slate up and down, and peered at it.

"Yes, upon my word, it is the same! Just look here, Pelle! It's like the cat that always comes down upon its feet, no matter how you drop it. Lord bless my soul! how nice it must be to be able to spell! How did you learn it, brother? "

"Oh, " said Kalle, in a tone of superiority. "I've sat and looked on a little when mother's been teaching the children their ABC. It's nothing at all if your upper story's all right. "

"Pelle'll be going to school soon, " said Lasse reflectively. "And then perhaps *I* could—for it would be nice. But I don't suppose I've got the head for it, do you? No, I'm sure I haven't got the head for it, " he repeated in quite a despairing tone.

Kalle did not seem inclined to contradict him, but Pelle made up his mind that some day he would teach his father to read and write— much better than Uncle Kalle could.

"But we're quite forgetting that we brought a Christmas bottle with us! " said Lasse, untying the handkerchief.

"You *are* a fellow! " exclaimed Kalle, walking delightedly round the table on which the bottle stood. "You couldn't have given us anything better, brother; it'll come in handy for the christening-party. 'Black Currant Rum'—and with a gold border—how grand! " He held the label up toward the light, and looked round with pleasure in his eyes. Then he hesitatingly opened the cupboard in the wall.

"The visitors ought to taste what they brought, " said his wife.

"That's just what was bothering me! " said Kalle, turning round with a disconsolate laugh. "For they ought, of course. But if the cork's once drawn, you know how it disappears. " He reached out slowly for the corkscrew which hung on a nail.

But Lasse would not hear of it; he would not taste the beverage for the world. Was black-currant rum a thing for a poor beggar like him to begin drinking—and on a weekday, too? No, indeed!

"Yes, and you'll be coming to the christening-party, you two, of course, " said Kalle, relieved, putting the bottle into the cupboard. "But we'll have a 'cuckoo, ' for there's a drop of spirits left from Christmas Eve, and I expect mother'll give us coffee. "

"I've got the coffee on, " answered his wife cheerfully.

"Did you ever know such a wife! You can never wish for anything but what it's there already! "

Pelle wondered where his two herding-comrades, Alfred and Albinus, were. They were away at their summer places, taking their share of the good Christmas fare, and would not be back before "Knut. " "But this fellow here's not to be despised, " said Kalle, pointing to the long boy in the turn-up bed. "Shall we have a look at him? " And, pulling out a straw, he tickled the boy's nose with it. "Get up, my good Anton, and harness the horses to the wheelbarrow! We're going to drive out in state. "

The boy sat up and began to rub his eyes, to Kalle's great delight. At last he discovered that there were strangers present, and drew on his clothes, which had been doing duty as his pillow. Pelle and he became good friends at once, and began to play; and then Kalle hit upon the idea of letting the other children share in the merry-making, and he and the two boys went round and tickled them awake, all the six. His wife protested, but only faintly; she was laughing all the time, and herself helped them to dress, while she kept on saying: "Oh, what foolishness! Upon my word, I never knew the like of it! Then this one shan't be left out either! " she added suddenly, drawing the youngest out of the alcove.

"Then that's the eight, " said Kalle, pointing to the flock. "They fill the room well, don't they? Alma and Alvilda are twins, as you can see. And so are Alfred and Albinus, who are away now for Christmas. They're going to be confirmed next summer, so they'll be off my hands. "

"Then where are the two eldest? " asked Lasse.

"Anna's in service in the north, and Albert's at sea, out with a whaler just now. He's a fine fellow. He sent us his portrait in the autumn. Won't you show it us, Maria? "

His wife began slowly to look for it, but could not find it.

"I think I know where it is, mother, " said one of the little girls over and over again; but as no one heard what she said, she climbed up on to the bench, and took down an old Bible from the shelf. The photograph was in it.

"He is a fine fellow, and no mistake! " said Lasse. "There's a pair of shoulders! He's not like our family; it must be from yours, Maria, that he's got that carriage. "

"He's a Kongstrup, " said Kalle, in a low tone.

"Oh, indeed, is he? " said Lasse hesitatingly, recollecting Johanna Pihl's story.

"Maria was housemaid at the farm, and he talked her over as he has done with so many. It was before my time, and he did what he ought. "

Maria was standing looking from one to the other of them with a meaningless smile, but her forehead was flushed.

"There's gentle blood in that boy, " said Kalle admiringly. "He holds his head differently from the others. And he's good—so tremendously good. " Maria came slowly up to him, leaned her arm upon his shoulder, and looked at the picture with him. "He is good, isn't he, mother? " said Kalle, stroking her face.

"And so well-dressed he is too! " exclaimed Lasse.

"Yes, he takes care of his money. He's not dissipated, like his father; and he's not afraid of parting with a ten-krone note when he's at home here on a visit. "

There was a rustling at the inner door, and a little, wrinkled old woman crept out onto the threshold, feeling her way with her feet, and holding her hands before her face to protect it. "Is any one dead? " she asked as she faced the room.

"Why, there's grandmother! " said Kalle. "I thought you'd be in your bed. "

"And so I was, but then I heard there were strangers here, and one likes to hear the news. Have there been any deaths in the parish? "

"No, grandmother, there haven't. People have something better to do than to die. Here's some one come to court you, and that's much better. This is mother-in-law, " he said, turning to the others; "so you can guess what she's like. "

"Just you come here, and I'll mother-in-law you! " said the old lady, with a feeble attempt to enter into the gaiety. "Well, welcome to this house then, " she said, extending her hand.

Kalle stretched his out first, but as soon as she touched it, she pushed it aside, saying: "Do you think I don't know you, you fool? " She felt Lasse's and Pelle's hands for a long time with her soft fingers before she let them go. "No, I don't know you! " she said.

"It's Brother Lasse and his son down from Stone Farm, " Kalle informed her at last.

96

"Aye, is it really? Well, I never! And you've come over the sea too! Well, here am I, an old body, going about here quite alone; and I've lost my sight too. "

"But you're not *quite* alone, grandmother, " said Kalle, laughing. "There are two grown-ups and half a score of children about you all day long. "

"Ah yes, you can say what you like, but all those I was young with are dead now, and many others that I've seen grow up. Every week some one that I know dies, and here am I still living, only to be a burden to others. "

Kalle brought in the old lady's arm-chair from her room, and made her sit down. "What's all that nonsense about? " he said reproachfully. "Why, you pay for yourself! "

"Pay! Oh dear! They get twenty krones a year for keeping me, " said the old woman to the company in general.

The coffee came in, and Kalle poured brandy into the cups of all the elder people. "Now, grandmother, you must cheer up! " he said, touching her cup with his. "Where the pot boils for twelve, it boils for the thirteenth as well. Your health, grandmother, and may you still live many years to be a burden to us, as you call it! "

"Yes, I know it so well, I know it so well, " said the old woman, rocking backward and forward. "You mean so well by it all. But with so little wish to live, it's hard that I should take the food out of the others' mouths. The cow eats, and the cat eats, the children eat, we all eat; and where are you, poor things, to get it all from! "

"Say 'poor thing' to him who has no head, and pity him who has two, " said Kalle gaily.

"How much land have you? " asked Lasse.

"Five acres; but it's most of it rock. "

"Can you manage to feed the cow on it then? "

"Last year it was pretty bad. We had to pull the roof off the outhouse, and use it for fodder last winter; and it's thrown us back a

97

little. But dear me, it made the loft all the higher. " Kalle laughed. "And now there'll always be more and more of the children getting able to keep themselves. "

"Don't those who are grown up give a hand too? " asked Lasse.

"How can they? When you're young, you can use what you've got yourself. They must take their pleasures while there's time; they hadn't many while they were children, and once they're married and settled they'll have something else to think about. Albert is good enough when he's at home on a visit; last time he gave us ten krones and a krone to each of the children. But when they're out, you know how the money goes if they don't want to look mean beside their companions. Anna's one of those who can spend all they get on clothes. She's willing enough to do without, but she never has a farthing, and hardly a rag to her body, for all that she's for ever buying. "

"No, she's the strangest creature, " said her mother. "She never can make anything do. "

The turn-up bedstead was shut to give room to sit round the table, and an old pack of cards was produced. Every one was to play except the two smallest, who were really too little to grasp a card; Kalle wanted, indeed, to have them too, but it could not be managed. They played beggar-my-neighbor and Black Peter. Grandmother's cards had to be read out to her.

The conversation still went on among the elder people.

"How do you like working for the farmer at Stone Farm? " asked Kalle.

"We don't see much of the farmer himself; he's pretty nearly always out, or sleeping after a night on the loose. But he's nice enough in other ways; and it's a house where they feed you properly. "

"Well, there are places where the food's worse, " said Kalle, "but there can't be many. Most of them, certainly, are better. "

"Are they really? " asked Lasse, in surprise. "Well, I don't complain as far as the food's concerned; but there's a little too much for us two to do, and then it's so miserable to hear that woman crying nearly the whole time. I wonder if he ill-treats her; they say not. "

"I'm sure he doesn't, " said Kalle. "Even if he wanted to—as you can very well understand he might—he dursn't. He's afraid of her, for she's possessed by a devil, you know. "

"They say she's a were-wolf at night, " said Lasse, looking as if he expected to see a ghost in one of the corners.

"She's a poor body, who has her own troubles, " said Maria, "and every woman knows a little what that means. And the farmer's not all kindness either, even if he doesn't beat her. She feels his unfaithfulness more than she'd feel anything else. "

"Oh, you wives always take one another's part, " said Kalle, "but other people have eyes too. What do *you* say, grandmother? You know that better than any one else. "

"Well, I know something about it at any rate, " said the old woman. "I remember the time when Kongstrup came to the island as well as if it had been yesterday. He owned nothing more than the clothes he wore, but he was a fine gentleman for all that, and lived in Copenhagen. "

"What did he want over here? " asked Lasse.

"What did he want? To look for a young girl with money, I suppose. He wandered about on the heath here with his gun, but it wasn't foxes he was after. She was fooling about on the heath too, admiring the wild scenery, and nonsense like that, and behaving half like a man, instead of being kept at home and taught to spin and make porridge; but she was the only daughter, and was allowed to go on just as she liked. And then she meets this spark from the town, and they become friends. He was a curate or a pope, or something of the sort, so you can't wonder that the silly girl didn't know what she was doing. "

"No, indeed! " said Lasse.

"There's always been something all wrong with the women of that family, " the old woman continued. "They say one of them once gave herself to Satan, and since then he's had a claim upon them and ill-treats them whenever the moon's waning, whether they like it or not. He has no power over the pure, of course; but when these two had got to know one another, things went wrong with her too. He must have noticed it, and tried to get off, for they said that the old farmer of Stone Farm compelled him with his gun to take her for his wife; and he was a hard old dog, who'd have shot a man down as soon as look at him. But he was a peasant through and through, who wore home-woven clothes, and wasn't afraid of working from sunrise to sunset. It wasn't like what it is now, with debts and drinking and card-playing, so people had something then. "

"Well, now they'd like to thresh the corn while it's still standing, and they sell the calves before they're born, " said Kalle. "But I say, grandmother, you're Black Peter! "

"That comes of letting one's tongue run on and forgetting to look after one's self! " said the old lady.

"Grandmother's got to have her face blacked! " cried the children. She begged to be let off, as she was just washed for the night; but the children blacked a cork in the stove and surrounded her, and she was given a black streak down her nose. Every one laughed, both old and young, and grandmother laughed with them, saying it was a good thing she could not see it herself. "It's an ill wind, " she said, "that blows nobody any good. But I should like to have my sight again, " she went on, "if it's only for five minutes, before I die. It would be nice to see it all once more, now that the trees and everything have grown so, as Kalle says they have. The whole country must have changed. And I've never seen the youngest children at all. "

"They say that they can take blindness away over in Copenhagen, " said Kalle to his brother.

"It would cost a lot of money, wouldn't it? " asked Lasse.

"It would cost a hundred krones at the very least, " the grandmother remarked.

Kalle looked thoughtful. "If we were to sell the whole blooming thing, it would be funny if there wasn't a hundred krones over. And then grandmother could have her sight again. "

"Goodness gracious me! " exclaimed the old woman. "Sell your house and home! You must be out of your mind! Throw away a large capital upon an old, worn-out thing like me, that has one foot in the grave! I couldn't wish for anything better than what I have! " She had tears in her eyes. "Pray God I mayn't bring about such a misfortune in my old age! "

"Oh, rubbish! We're still young, " said Kalle. "We could very well begin something new, Maria and me. "

"Have none of you heard how Jacob Kristian's widow is? " asked the old lady by way of changing the subject. "I've got it into my head that she'll go first, and then me. I heard the crow calling over there last night. "

"That's our nearest neighbor on the heath, " explained Kalle. "Is she failing now? There's been nothing the matter with her this winter that I know of. "

"Well, you may be sure there's something, " said the old woman positively. "Let one of the children run over there in the morning. "

"Yes, if you've had warning. Jacob Kristian gave good enough warning himself when he went and died. But we were good friends for many years, he and me. "

"Did he show himself? " asked Lasse solemnly.

"No; but one night—nasty October weather it was—I was woke by a knocking at the outside door. That's a good three years ago. Maria heard it too, and we lay and talked about whether I should get up. We got no further than talking, and we were just dropping off again, when the knocking began again. I jumped up, put on a pair of trousers, and opened the door a crack, but there was no one there. 'That's strange! ' I said to Maria, and got into bed again; but I'd scarcely got the clothes over me, when there was a knocking for the third time.

"I was cross then, and lighted the lantern and went round the house; but there was nothing either to be seen or heard. But in the morning there came word to say that Jacob Kristian had died in the night just at that time. "

Pelle, who had sat and listened to the conversation, pressed close up to his father in fear; but Lasse himself did not look particularly valiant. "It's not always nice to have anything to do with the dead, " he said.

"Oh, nonsense! If you've done no harm to any one, and given everybody their due, what can they do to you? " said Kalle. The grandmother said nothing, but sat shaking her head very significantly.

Maria now placed upon the table a jar of dripping and a large loaf of rye-bread.

"That's the goose, " said Kalle, merrily sticking his sheath-knife into the loaf. "We haven't begun it yet. There are prunes inside. And that's goose-fat. Help yourselves! "

After that Lasse and Pelle had to think about getting home, and began to tie handkerchiefs round their necks; but the others did not want to let them go yet. They went on talking, and Kalle made jokes to keep them a little longer. But suddenly he turned as grave as a judge; there was a low sound of crying out in the little passage, and some one took hold of the handle of the door and let go of it again. "Upon my word, it's ghosts! " he exclaimed, looking fearfully from one to another.

The sound of crying was heard again, and Maria, clasping her hands together, exclaimed: "Why, it's Anna! " and quickly opened the door. Anna entered in tears, and was attacked on all sides with surprised inquiries, to which her sobs were her only answer.

"And you've been given a holiday to come and see us at Christmas time, and you come home crying! You are a nice one! " said Kalle, laughing. "You must give her something to suck, mother! "

"I've lost my place, " the girl at last got out between her sobs.

"No, surely not! " exclaimed Kalle, in changed tones. "But what for? Have you been stealing? Or been impudent? "

"No, but the master accused me of being too thick with his son. "

In a flash the mother's eyes darted from the girl's face to her figure, and she too burst into tears.

Kalle could see nothing, but he caught his wife's action and understood. "Oh! " he said quietly. "Is that it? " The little man was like a big child in the way the different expressions came and went upon his good-natured face. At last the smile triumphed again. "Well, well, that's capital! " he exclaimed, laughing. "Shouldn't good children take the work off their parents' shoulders as they grow up and are able to do it? Take off your things, Anna, and sit down. I expect you're hungry, aren't you? And it couldn't have happened at a better time, as we've got to have the midwife anyhow! "

Lasse and Pelle drew their neckerchiefs up over their mouths after taking leave of every one in the room, Kalle circling round them restlessly, and talking eagerly. "Come again soon, you two, and thanks for this visit and your present, Brother Lasse! Oh, yes! " he said suddenly at the outside door, and laughed delightedly; "it'll be something grand—brother-in-law to the farmer in a way! Oh, fie, Kalle Karlsson! You and I'll be giving ourselves airs now! " He went a little way along the path with them, talking all the time. Lasse was quite melancholy over it.

Pelle knew quite well that what had happened to Anna was looked upon as a great disgrace, and could not understand how Uncle Kalle could seem so happy. "Ah, yes, " said Lasse, as they stumbled along among the stones. "Kalle's just like what he always was! He laughs where others would cry. "

It was too dark to go across the fields, so they took the quarry road south to get down to the high-road. At the cross-roads, the fourth arm of which led down to the village, stood the country-shop, which was also a hedge-alehouse.

As they approached the alehouse, they heard a great noise inside. Then the door burst open, and some men poured out, rolling the figure of a man before them on the ground. "The police have taken them by surprise! " said Lasse, and drew the boy with him out into the ploughed field, so as to get past without being seen. But at that moment some one placed a lamp in the window, and they were discovered.

"There's the Stone Farm herdsman! " said a voice. "Hi, Lasse! Come here! " They went up and saw a man lying face downward on the ground, kicking; his hands were tied behind his back, and he could not keep his face out of the mud.

"Why, it's Per Olsen! " exclaimed Lasse.

"Yes, of course! " said the shopkeeper. "Can't you take him home with you? He's not right in his head. "

Lasse looked hesitatingly at the boy, and then back again. "A raving man? " he said. "We two can't alone. "

"Oh, his hands are tied. You've only got to hold the end of the rope and he'll go along quietly with you, " said one of the men. They were quarrymen from the stone-quarry. "You'll go with them quietly, won't you? " he asked, giving the man a kick in the side with the toe of his wooden shoe.

"Oh dear! Oh dear! " groaned Per Olsen.

"What's he done? " asked Lasse. "And why have you ill-used him so? "

"We had to thrash him a little, because he was going to chop off one of his thumbs. He tried it several times, the beast, and got it half off; and we had to beat him to make him stop. " And they showed Lasse the man's thumb, which was bleeding. "Such an animal to begin cutting and hacking at himself because he's drunk half a pint of gin! If he wanted to fight, there were men enough here without that! "

"It must be tied up, or he'll bleed to death, poor fellow! " said Lasse, slowly drawing out his red pocket-handkerchief. It was his best handkerchief, and it had just been washed. The shopkeeper came with a bottle and poured spirit over the thumb, so that the cold should not get into it. The wounded man screamed and beat his face upon the ground.

"Won't one of you come with us? " asked Lasse. But no one answered; they wanted to have nothing to do with it, in case it should come to the ears of the magistrate. "Well, then, we two must do it with God's help, " he said, in a trembling voice, turning to

104

Pelle. "But you can help him up at any rate, as you knocked him down. "

They lifted him up. His face was bruised and bleeding; in their eagerness to save his finger, they had handled him so roughly that he could scarcely stand.

"It's Lasse and Pelle, " said the old man, trying to wipe his face. "You know us, don't you, Per Olsen? We'll go home with you if you'll be good and not hurt us; we mean well by you, we two. "

Per Olsen stood and ground his teeth, trembling all over his body. "Oh dear, oh dear! " was all he said. There was white foam at the corners of his mouth.

Lasse gave Pelle the end of the rope to hold. "He's grinding his teeth; the devil's busy with him already, " he whispered. "But if he tries to do any harm, just you pull with all your might at the rope; and if the worst comes to the worst, we must jump over the ditch. "

They now set off homeward, Lasse holding Per Olsen under the arm, for he staggered and would have fallen at almost every step. He kept on murmuring to himself or grinding his teeth.

Pelle trudged behind, holding the rope. Cold shivers ran down his back, partly from fear, partly from secret satisfaction. He had now seen some one whom he knew to be doomed to perdition! So those who became devils in the next world looked like Per Olsen? But he wasn't unkind! He was the nicest of the farm men to Pelle, and he had bought that bottle for them—yes, and had advanced the money out of his own pocket until May-day!

VIII

Oh! what a pace she was driving at! The farmer whipped up the gray stallion, and sat looking steadily out over the fields, as if he had no suspicion that any one was following him; but his wife certainly did not mind. She whipped the bay as hard as she could, and did not care who saw her.

And it was in broad daylight that they were playing the fool like this on the high-road, instead of keeping their quarrels within four walls as decent people did! It was true enough that gentle folks had no feeling of shame in them!

Then she called out and stood up in the trap to beat the horse — with the handle even! Couldn't she let him drive out in peace to his fair charmer, whoever she was, and make it warm for him when he came home? How could she do the same thing over and over again for twenty years? Really women were persevering creatures!

And how *he* could be bothered! Having everlasting disturbances at home for the sake of some hotel landlady or some other woman, who could not be so very different to be with than his own wife! It would take a long-suffering nature to be a brute in that way; but that must be what they call love, properly speaking.

The threshing-machine had come to a standstill, and the people at Stone Farm were hanging out of the doors and windows, enjoying it royally. It was a race, and a sight for the gods to see the bay mare gaining upon the stallion; why, it was like having two Sundays in one week! Lasse had come round the corner, and was following the mad race, his hand shading his eyes. Never had he known such a woman; Bengta was a perfect lamb compared to her! The farmer at Kaase Farm, who was standing at his gate when they dashed past, was secretly of the same opinion; and the workers in the fields dropped their implements, stared and were scandalized at the sight.

At last, for very shame, he had to stop and turn round. She crawled over into his carriage, and the bay followed quietly with her empty vehicle. She put her arm about his shoulder, and looked happy and triumphant, exactly like the district policeman when he has had a successful chase; but he looked like a criminal of the worst kind. In this way they came driving back to the farm.

One day Kalle came to borrow ten krones and to invite Lasse and Pelle to the christening-party on the following Sunday. Lasse, with some difficulty, obtained the money from the bailiff up in the office, but to the invitation they had to say "No, thank you, " hard though it was; it was quite out of the question for them to get off again. Another day the head man had disappeared. He had gone in the night, and had taken his big chest with him, so some one must have helped him; but the other men in the room swore solemnly that they had noticed nothing, and the bailiff, fume as he might, was obliged to give up the attempt to solve the mystery.

One or two things of this kind happened that made a stir for a day or two, but with these exceptions the winter was hard to get through. Darkness ruled for the greater part of the twenty-four hours, and it was never quite light in the corners. The cold, too, was hard to bear, except when you were in the comfortable stable. In there it was always warm, and Pelle was not afraid of going about in the thickest darkness. In the servants' room they sat moping through the long evenings without anything to occupy themselves with. They took very little notice of the girls, but sat playing cards for gin, or telling horrible stories that made it a most venturesome thing to run across the yard down to the stable when you had to go to bed.

Per Olsen, on account of his good behavior, was raised to the position of head man when the other ran away. Lasse and Pelle were glad of this, for he took their part when they were put upon by any one. He had become a decent fellow in every respect, hardly ever touched spirits, and kept his clothes in good order. He was a little too quiet even for the old day-laborers of the farm and their wives; but they knew the reason of it and liked him because he took the part of the weak and because of the fate that hung over him. They said he was always listening; and when he seemed to be listening within to the unknown, they avoided as far as possible disturbing him.

"You'll see he'll free himself; the Evil One'll have no claim upon him, " was the opinion of both Lasse and the laborers' wives when they discussed Per Olsen's prospects at the Sunday milking. "There are some people that even the Almighty can't find anything to blame for. "

Pelle listened to this, and tried every day to peep at the scar on Per Olsen's thumb. It would surely disappear when God removed his judgment!

During most of the winter Pelle drove the horse for the threshing-machine. All day he trotted round upon the horse-way outside the farm, over his wooden shoes in trodden-down snow and manure. It was the most intolerable occupation that life had yet offered him. He could not even carve, it was too cold for his fingers; and he felt lonely. As a herd-boy he was his own master, and a thousand things called to him; but here he had to go round and round behind a bar, always round. His one diversion was to keep count of the times he drove round, but that was a fatiguing employment and made you even duller than the everlasting going round, and you could not leave off. Time held nothing of interest, and short as it was the day seemed endless.

As a rule, Pelle awoke happy, but now every morning when he woke he was weary of everything; it was to be that everlasting trudging round behind the bar. After a time doing this for about an hour used to make him fall into a state of half-sleep. The condition came of itself, and he longed for it before it came. It was a kind of vacuity, in which he wished for nothing and took no interest in anything, but only staggered along mechanically at the back of the bar. The machine buzzed unceasingly, and helped to maintain the condition; the dust kept pouring out at the window, and the time passed imperceptibly. Generally now dinner or evening surprised him, and sometimes it seemed to him that the horses had only just been harnessed when some one came out to help him in with them. He had arrived at the condition of torpor that is the only mercy that life vouchsafes to condemned prisoners and people who spend their lives beside a machine. But there was a sleepiness about him even in his free time; he was not so lively and eager to know about everything; Father Lasse missed his innumerable questions and little devices.

Now and again he was roused for a moment out of his condition by the appearance at the window of a black, perspiring face, that swore at him because he was not driving evenly. He knew then that Long Ole had taken the place of Per Olsen, whose business it was to feed the machine. It sometimes happened, too, that the lash of the whip caught on the axle and wound round it, so that the whole thing had to be stopped and drawn backward; and that day he did not fall into a doze again.

In March the larks appeared and brought a little life. Snow still lay in the hollows, but their singing reminded Pelle warmly of summer and grazing cattle. And one day he was wakened in his tramp round and round by seeing a starling on the roof of the house, whistling and preening its feathers in delight. On that day the sun shone brightly, and all heaviness was gone from the air; but the sea was still a pale gray down there.

Pelle began to be a human being again. It was spring, and then, too, in a couple of days the threshing would be finished. But after all, the chief thing was that waistcoat-pocket of his; that was enough to put life into its owner. He ran round in a trot behind the bar; he had to drive quickly now in order to get done, for every one else was in the middle of spring ploughing already. When he pressed his hand against his chest, he could distinctly feel the paper it was wrapped in. For it was still there, wasn't it? It would not do to open the paper and look; he must find out by squeezing.

Pelle had become the owner of fifty ores—a perfectly genuine fifty-ore piece. It was the first time he had ever possessed anything more than two and one ore pieces, and he had earned it by his own cleverness.

It was on Sunday, when the men had had a visit from some quarrymen, and one of them had hit upon the idea of sending for some birch-fat to have with their dram. Pelle was to run to the village shop for it, and he was given a half-krone and injunctions to go in the back way, as it was Sunday. Pelle had not forgotten his experience at Christmas, and kept watch upon their faces. They were all doing their best to smooth them out and busy themselves with one thing and another; and Gustav, who gave him the money, kept turning his face away and looking at something out in the yard.

When he stated his errand, the shopman's wife broke into a laugh. "I say, don't you know better than that? " she exclaimed. "Why, wasn't it you who fetched the handle-turner too? You've all found that very useful, haven't you? "

Pelle turned crimson. "I thought they were making fun of me, but I didn't dare say no, " he said in a low voice.

"No, one has to play the fool sometimes, whether one is it or not, " said the woman.

"What is birch-fat, then? " asked Pelle.

"Why, my gracious! You must have had it many a time, you little imp! But it shows how often you have to put up with things you don't know the name of. "

A light dawned upon Pelle. "Does it mean a thrashing with a birch-rod? "

"Didn't I say you knew it? "

"No, I've only had it with a whip—on my legs. "

"Well, well, you needn't mind that; the one may be just as good as the other. But now sit down and drink a cup of coffee while I wrap up the article for them. " She pushed a cup of coffee with brown sugar toward him, and began ladling out soft soap on to a piece of paper. "Here, " she said. "You give them that: it's the best birch-fat. And you can keep the money yourself. "

Pelle was not courageous enough for this arrangement.

"Very well, then, " she said. "I'll keep the money for you. They shan't make fools of us both. And then you can get it yourself. But now you must put on a bold face. "

Pelle did put on a bold face, but he was decidedly nervous. The men swore at the loss of the half-krone, and called him the "greatest idiot upon God's green earth"; but he had the satisfaction of knowing that that was because he had not been stupid enough. And the half-krone was his!

A hundred times a day he felt it without wearing it out. Here at last was something the possession of which did not rob it of its lustre. There was no end to the purchases he made with it, now for Lasse, now for himself. He bought the dearest things, and when he lingered long enough over one purchase and was satiated with the possession of it, he set about buying something else. And all the while he kept the coin. At times he would be suddenly seized with an insane fear that the money was gone; and then when he felt it, he was doubly happy.

Pelle had suddenly become a capitalist, and by his own cleverness; and he made the most of his capital. He had already obtained every desirable thing that he knew of—he had it all, at any rate, in hand;

and gradually as new things made their appearance in his world, he secured for himself the right to their purchase. Lasse was the only person who knew about his wealth, and he had reluctantly to allow himself to be drawn into the wildest of speculations.

He could hear by the sound that there was something wrong with the machine. The horses heard it too, and stopped even before some one cried "Stop! " Then one after another came the shouts: "Stop! Drive on! Stop! On again! Stop! Pull! " And Pelle pulled the bar back, drove on and pulled until the whole thing whizzed again. Then he knew that it was Long Ole feeding the machine while Per Olsen measured the grain: Ole was a duffer at feeding.

It was going smoothly again, and Pelle was keeping an eye on the corner by the cow-stable. When Lasse made his appearance there, and patted his stomach, it meant that it was nearly dinner-time.

Something stopped the bar, the horses had to pull hard, and with a jerk it cleared the invisible hindrance. There was a cry from the inside of the threshing-barn, and the sound of many voices shouting "Stop! " The horses stopped dead, and Pelle had to seize the bar to prevent it swinging forward against their legs. It was some time before any one came out and took the horses in, so that Pelle could go into the barn and see what was the matter.

He found Long Ole walking about and writhing over one of his hands. His blouse was wrapped about it, but the blood was dripping through on to the floor of the barn. He was bending forward and stumbling along, throwing his body from side to side and talking incoherently. The girls, pale and frightened, were standing gazing at him while the men were quarreling as to what was the best thing to do to stop the flow of blood, and one of them came sliding down from the loft with a handful of cobwebs.

Pelle went and peered into the machine to find out what there was so voracious about it. Between two of the teeth lay something like a peg, and when he moved the roller, the greater part of a finger dropped down on to the barn floor. He picked it up among some chaff, and took it to the others: it was a thumb! When Long Ole saw it, he fainted; it could hardly be wondered at, seeing that he was maimed for life. But Per Olsen had to own that he had left the machine at a fortunate moment.

There was no more threshing done that day. In the afternoon Pelle played in the stable, for he had nothing to do. While he played, he suggested plans for their future to his father: they were engrossed in it.

"Then we'll go to America, and dig for gold! "

"Ye-es, that wouldn't be a bad thing at all. But it would take a good many more half-krones to make that journey. "

"Then we can set up as stone-masons. "

Lasse stood still in the middle of the foddering-passage, and pondered with bent head. He was exceedingly dissatisfied with their position; there were two of them toiling to earn a hundred krones, and they could not make ends meet. There was never any liberty either; they were simply slaves. By himself he never got any farther than being discontented and disappointed with everything; he was too old. The mere search for ways to something new was insuperable labor, and everything looked so hopeless. But Pelle was restless, and whenever he was dissatisfied with anything, made plans by the score, some of the wildest, and some fairly sensible; and the old man was carried away by them.

"We might go to the town and work too, " said Lasse meditatively. "They earn one bright krone after another in there. But what's to be done with you? You're too little to use a tool. "

This stubborn fact put a stop for the moment to Pelle's plans; but then his courage rose again. "I can quite well go with you to the town, " he said. "For I shall— —" He nodded significantly.

"What? " asked Lasse, with interest.

"Well, perhaps I'll go down to the harbor and be doing nothing, and a little girl'll fall into the water and I shall save her. But the little girl will be a gentleman's daughter, and so— —" Pelle left the rest to Lasse's imagination.

"Then you'd have to learn to swim first, " said Lasse gravely. "Or you'd only be drowned. "

Screams were heard from the men's bedroom. It was Long Ole. The doctor had come and was busy with his maimed hand. "Just run across and find out what'll happen to it! " said Lasse. "Nobody'll pay any attention to you at such a time, if you make yourself small. "

In a little while Pelle came back and reported that three fingers were quite crushed and hanging in rags, and the doctor had cut them off.

"Was it these three? " asked Lasse, anxiously, holding up his thumb, forefinger, and middle finger. Truth to tell, Pelle had seen nothing, but his imagination ran away with him.

"Yes, it was his swearing-fingers, " he said, nodding emphatically.

"Then Per Olsen is set free, " said Lasse, heaving a deep sigh. "What a *good* thing it has been—quite providential! "

That was Pelle's opinion too.

The farmer himself drove the doctor home, and a little while after he had gone, Pelle was sent for, to go on an errand for the mistress to the village-shop.

IX

It was nothing for Pelle; if he were vanquished on one point, he rose again on two others: he was invincible. And he had the child's abundant capacity for forgiving; had he not he would have hated all grown-up people with the exception of Father Lasse. But disappointed he certainly was.

It was not easy to say who had expected most—the boy, whose childish imagination had built, unchecked, upon all that he had heard, or the old man, who had once been here himself.

But Pelle managed to fill his own existence with interest, and was so taken up on all sides that he only just had time to realize the disappointment in passing. His world was supersensual like that of the fakir; in the course of a few minutes a little seed could shoot up and grow into a huge tree that overshadowed everything else. Cause never answered to effect in it, and it was governed by another law of gravitation: events always bore him up.

However hard reality might press upon him, he always emerged from the tight place the richer in some way or other; and no danger could ever become overwhelmingly great as long as Father Lasse stood reassuringly over and behind everything.

But Lasse had failed him at the decisive moment more than once, and every time he used him as a threat, he was only laughed at. The old man's omnipotence could not continue to exist side by side with his increasing decrepitude; in the boy's eyes it crumbled away from day to day. Unwilling though he was, Pelle had to let go his providence, and seek the means of protection in himself. It was rather early, but he looked at circumstances in his own way. Distrust he had already acquired—and timidity! He daily made clumsy attempts to get behind what people said, and behind things. There was something more behind everything! It often led to confusion, but occasionally the result was conspicuously good.

There were some thrashings that you could run away from, because in the meantime the anger would pass away, and other thrashings where it answered best to shed as many tears as possible. Most people only beat until the tears came, but the bailiff could not endure a blubberer, so with him the thing was to set your teeth and make yourself hard. People said you should speak the truth, but most thrashings could be avoided by making up a white lie, if it was a good one and you took care of your face. If you told the truth, they thrashed you at once.

With regard to thrashing, the question had a subjective side as well as an objective one. He could beat Rud whenever he liked, but with bigger boys it was better to have right on his side, as, for instance, when his father was attacked. Then God helped him. This was a case in which the boy put the omnipotence quite aside, and felt himself to be the old man's protector.

Lasse and Pelle were walking through life hand in hand, and yet each was going his own way. Lasse felt it to be so. "We've each got hold of an end, " he sometimes said to himself despondently, when the difference was all too marked. "He's rising, the laddie! "

This was best seen in the others. In the long run they had to like the boy, it could not be otherwise. The men would sometimes give him things, and the girls were thoroughly kind to him. He was in the fairest period of budding youth; they would often take him on their knees as he passed, and kiss him.

"Ah, he'll be a lady's man, he will! " Lasse would say. "He's got that from his father. " But they would laugh at that.

There was always laughter when Lasse wanted to join the elders. Last time—yes, then he was good enough. It was always "Where's Lasse? " when gin was going round, or tricks were being played, or demonstrations made. "Call Lasse Karlsson! " He had no need to push himself forward; it was a matter of course that he was there. The girls were always on the look-out for him, married man though he was, and he had fun with them—all quite proper, of course, for Bengta was not good to quarrel with if she heard anything.

But now! Yes—well, yes—he might fetch the gin for the others and do their work for them when they had a holiday, without their doing anything in exchange! "Lasse! Where's Lasse? Can you feed the horses for me this evening? Can you take my place at the chaff-cutting to-morrow evening? "

There was a difference between then and now, and Lasse had found out the reason for himself: he was getting old. The very discovery brought further proof of its correctness, laid infirmity upon him, and removed the tension from his mind, and what was left of it from his body. The hardest blow of all was when he discovered that he was of no importance to the girls, had no place at all in their thoughts of men. In Lasse's world there was no word that carried such weight as the word "man"; and in the end it was the girls who decided whether you were one or not. Lasse was not one; he was not dangerous! He was only a few poor relics of a man, a comical remnant of some by-gone thing; they laughed at him when he tried to pay them attention.

Their laughter crushed him, and he withdrew into his old-man's world, and despondently adapted himself to it. The only thing that kept life in him was his concern for the boy, and he clung despairingly to his position as his providence. There was little he could do for him, and therefore he talked all the bigger; and when anything went against the boy, he uttered still greater threats against the world than before. He also felt that the boy was in process of making himself independent, and fought a desperate battle to preserve the last appearance of power.

But Pelle could not afford to give support to his fancy, nor had he the understanding to do it. He was growing fast, and had a use for all that he possessed himself. Now that his father no longer stood behind to shield him, he was like a small plant that has been moved out into the open, and is fighting hard to comprehend the nature of its surroundings, and adapt itself to them. For every root-fibre that felt its way into the soil, there fell to the ground one of the tender leaves, and two strong ones pushed forth. One after another the feelings of the child's defencelessness dropped and gave place to the harder ones of the individual.

The boy was engaged in building himself up, in accordance with invisible laws. He assumed an attitude toward his surroundings at all points, but he did not imitate them. The farm men, for instance, were not kind to the animals. They often lashed the horses only as a vent for their ill-humor, and the girls were just the same to the smaller animals and the dairy-cows. From these considerations, Pelle taught himself sympathy. He could not bear cruelty to animals, and thrashed Rud for the first time when the latter had one day robbed a bird's nest.

Pelle was like a kid that makes a plaything of everything. In his play he took up, without suspecting it, many of the serious phenomena of life, and gambolled with them in frolicsome bounds. He exercised his small mind as he exercised his body, twisted himself into everything and out of everything, imitated work and fun and shirking, and learned how to puff himself up into a very devil of a fellow where his surroundings were yielding, and to make himself almost invisible with modesty when they were hard. He was training himself to be that little Jack-of-all-trades, man.

And it became more and more difficult to catch him unprepared. The first time he had to set about a thing in earnest, he was generally handy at it; he was as difficult to take unawares as a cat.

* * * * *

It was summer again. The heat stood still and played over the ground, sparkling, with indolent voluptuousness and soft movements like the fish in the stream. Far inland it quivered above the rocks that bounded the view, in a restless flicker of bluish white; below lay the fields beneath the broiling sun, with the pollen from the rye drifting over them like smoke. Up above the clover-field stood the cows of Stone Farm in long rows, their heads hanging heavily down, and their tails swinging regularly. Lasse was moving between their ranks, looking for the mallet, and now and then gazing anxiously down towards the meadow by the dunes, and beginning to count the young cattle and the bullocks. Most of them were lying down, but a few of them were standing with their heads close together, and munching with closed eyes. The boys were nowhere to be seen.

Lasse stood wondering whether he should give Pelle a warning call; there would he no end of a row if the bailiff were to come now. But then the sound of voices came from among the young firs on the dunes, a naked boy appeared, and then another. Their bodies were like golden flashes in the air as they ran over the grass-wrack and across the meadow, each with his cap held closed in his hand.

They sat down upon the edge of the stream with their feet in the water, and carefully uncovered their captives; they were dragon-flies. As the insects one by one crawled out at the narrow opening, the boys decapitated them and laid them in a row on the grass. They had caught nine, and nine times thirty-five—well, it would be more than three krones. The stupendous amount made Pelle skeptical.

"Now isn't that only a lie? " he said, and licked his shoulder where he had been bitten by a mosquito. It was said that the chemist gave thirty-five ores apiece for dragon-flies.

"A lie? " exclaimed Rud. "Yes, perhaps it is, " he went on meekly. "It must be a lie, for anything like that always is. You might give me yours too! "

But Pelle would not do that.

"Then give me your half-krone, and I'll go to the town and sell them for you. They cost thirty-five ores, for Karl says so, and his mother washes the floor in the chemist's shop. "

Pelle got up, not to fetch the half-krone—he would not part with that for all the world—but to assure himself that it still lay in his waistcoat pocket.

When he had gone a little way, Rud hastily lifted a piece of turf at the edge of the stream, pushed something in under it, and jumped into the water; and when Pelle came back with slow, ominous steps, he climbed up the other side and set off at a run.

Pelle ran too, in short, quick leaps. He knew he was the quicker, and the knowledge made him frolicsome. He flapped at his naked body as he ran, as if he had no joints, swayed from side to side like a balloon, pranced and stamped on the ground, and then darted on again. Then the young firs closed round them again, only the movement of their tops showing where the boys ran, farther and farther, until all was still.

In the meadow the cattle were munching with closed eyes and attentive ears. The heat played over the ground, flickering, gasping, like a fish in water. There was a heavy, stupefying humming in the air; the sound came from everywhere and nowhere.

Down across the cornfields came a big, stout woman. She wore a skirt, a chemise, and a handkerchief on her head, and she shaded her eyes with her hand and looked about. She crossed the meadow obliquely, found Pelle's dinner-basket, took out its contents and put them in under her chemise upon her bare, perspiring bosom, and then turned in the direction of the sea.

There was a sudden break in the edge of the fir-plantation, and out came Rud with Pelle hanging upon his back. Rud's inordinately large head hung forward and his knees gave way; his forehead, which receded above the eyes and projected just below the line of the hair, was a mass of bruises and scars, which became very visible now with his exertions. Both the boys had marks all over their bodies from the poison of the pine-needles. Pelle dropped on to the grass, and lay there on his face, while Rud went slowly to fetch the half-krone, and handed it reluctantly to its owner. He stooped like one vanquished, but in his eye the thought of a new battle lay awaiting its opportunity.

Pelle gazed lovingly at the coin. He had had it now ever since April, from the time when he was sent to buy birch-fat. He had purchased with it everything that was desirable, and he had lost it twice: he loved that piece of money. It made his fingers itch, his whole body; it was always urging him on to spend it, now in one way and now in another. Roll, roll! That was what it was longing to do; and it was because it was round, Father Lasse said. But to become rich—that meant stopping the money as it rolled. Oh, Pelle meant to be rich! And then he was always itching to spend it—spend it in such a way that he got everything for it, or something he could have all his life.

They sat upon the bank of the stream and wrangled in a small way. Rud did his best to inspire awe, and bragged to create an impression. He bent his fingers backward and moved his ears; he could move them forward in a listening position like a horse. All this irritated Pelle intensely.

Suddenly he stopped. "Won't you give me the half-krone, then? You shall have ten krones when I grow up. " Rud collected money—he was avaricious already—and had a whole boxful of coins that he had stolen from his mother.

Pelle considered a little. "No, " he said. "Because you'll never grow up; you're a dwarf! " The tone of his voice was one of sheer envy.

"That's what the Sow says too! But then I'll show myself for money at the fairs and on Midsummer Eve on the common. Then I shall get frightfully rich. "

Pelle was inwardly troubled. Should he give him the whole fifty ores for nothing at all? He had never heard of any one doing such a thing. And perhaps some day, when Rud had become enormously rich, he would get half of it. "Will you have it? " he asked, but regretted it instantly.

Rud stretched out his hand eagerly, but Pelle spat into it. "It can wait until we've had our dinner anyhow, " he said, and went over to the basket. For a little while they stood gazing into the empty basket.

"The Sow's been here, " said Rud, putting out his tongue.

Pelle nodded. "She *is* a beast! "

"A thief, " said Rud.

They took the sun's measure. Rud declared that if you could see it when you bent down and looked between your legs, then it was five o'clock. Pelle began to put on his clothes.

Rud was circling about him. "I say! " he said suddenly. "If I may have it, I'll let you whip me with nettles. "

"On your bare body? " asked Pelle.

Rud nodded.

In a second Pelle was out of his trousers again, and running to a patch of nettles. He pulled them up with the assistance of a dock-leak, as many as he could hold, and came back again. Rud lay down, face downwards, on a little mound, and the whipping began.

The agreement was a hundred strokes, but when Rud had received ten, he got up and refused to have any more.

"Then you won't get the money, " said Pelle. "Will you or won't you? " He was red with excitement and the exertion, and the perspiration already stood in beads down his slender back, for he had worked with a will. "Will you or won't you? Seventy-five strokes then! " Pelle's voice quivered with eagerness, and he had to dilate his nostrils to get air enough; his limbs began to tremble.

"No—only sixty—you hit so hard! And I must have the money first, or you may cheat me. "

"I don't cheat, " said Pelle gloomily. But Rud held to his point.

Pelle's body writhed; he was like a ferret that has tasted blood. With a jerk he threw the coin at Rud, and grumbling, pushed him down. He wept inwardly because he had let him off forty strokes; but he made up his mind to lay into him all the harder for it.

Then he beat, slowly and with all his might, while Rud burrowed with his head in the grass and clasped the money tightly to keep up his strength. There was hatred in every stroke that Pelle struck, and they went like shocks through his playmate's body, but he never uttered a cry. No, there was no point in his crying, for the coin he held in his hand took away the pain. But about Pelle's body the air burnt like fire, his arms began to give way with fatigue, and his inclination diminished with every stroke. It was toil, nothing but hard toil. And the money—the beautiful half-krone—was slipping farther and farther away, and he would be poor once more; and Rud was not even crying! At the forty-sixth stroke he turned his face and put out his tongue, whereat Pelle burst into a roar, threw down the frayed nettle-stalks, and ran away to the fir-plantation.

There he sat for the rest of the day under a dune, grieving over his loss, while Rud lay under the bank of the stream, bathing his blistered body with wet earth.

X

After all, Per Olsen was not the sort of man they had thought him. Now that he had been set free in that way, the thing would have been for him to have given a helping hand to that poor fellow, Long Ole; for after all it was for his sake that Ole's misfortune had come upon him. But did he do it? No, he began to amuse himself. It was drinking and dissipation and petticoats all the summer through; and now at Martinmas he left and took work at the quarry, so as to be more his own master. There was not sufficient liberty for him at Stone Farm. What good there was left in him would find something to do up there.

Long Ole could not, of course, remain at Stone Farm, crippled as he was. Through kindness on the part of the farmer, he was paid his half-wage; that was more than he had any claim to, and enough at any rate to take him home and let him try something or other. There were many kinds of work that at a pinch could be performed with one hand; and now while he had the money he ought to have got an iron hook; it could be strapped to the wrist, and was not bad to hold tools with.

But Ole had grown weak and had great difficulty in making up his mind. He continued to hang about the farm, notwithstanding all that the bailiff did to get him away. At last they had to put his things out, to the west of the farm; and there they lay most of the summer, while he himself slept among the stacks, and begged food of the workers in the fields. But this could not go on when the cold set in.

But then one day in the autumn, his things were gone. Johanna Pihl —commonly called the Sow—had taken him in. She felt the cold, too, in spite of her fat, and as the proverb says: It's easier for two to keep warm than one; but whatever was her reason for doing it, Long Ole might thank his Maker for her. There was always bacon hanging in her chimney.

Lasse and Pelle looked forward to term-day with anxiety. What changes would it bring this time for people? So much depended on that. Besides the head man, they were to have new second and third men and some new maids. They were always changing at Stone Farm when they could. Karna, poor soul, was bound to stay, as she had set her mind upon youth, and would absolutely be where

Gustav was! Gustav stayed because Bodil stayed, so unnaturally fond was he of that girl, although she was not worth it. And Bodil herself knew well enough what she was doing! There must be more in it than met the eye when a girl dressed, as she did, in expensive, town-bought clothes.

Lasse and Pelle *remained*, simply because there was no other place in the world for them to go to. All through the year they made plans for making a change, but when the time for giving notice approached, Lasse became quiet and let it go past.

Of late he had given no little thought to the subject of marrying again. There was something God-forsaken about this solitary existence for a man of his age; you became old and worn out before your time, when you hadn't a wife and a house. On the heath near Brother Kalle's, there was a house that he could have without paying anything down. He often discussed it with Pelle, and the boy was ready for anything new.

It should be a wife who could look after everything and make the house comfortable; and above all she must be a hard-working woman. It would not come amiss either if she had a little of her own, but let that be as it might, if only she was good-natured. Karna would have suited in all respects, both Lasse and Pelle having always had a liking for her ever since the day she freed Pelle from the pupil's clutches; but it was nothing to offer her as long as she was so set upon Gustav. They must bide their time; perhaps she would come to her senses, or something else might turn up.

"Then there'd be coffee in bed on Sunday mornings! " said Pelle, with rapture.

"Yes, and perhaps we'd get a little horse, and invite Brother Kalle for a drive now and then, " added Lasse solemnly.

At last it was really to be! In the evening Lasse and Pelle had been to the shop and bought a slate and pencil, and Pelle was now standing at the stable-door with a beating heart and the slate under his arm. It was a frosty October morning, but the boy was quite hot after his wash. He had on his best jacket, and his hair had been combed with water.

Lasse hovered about him, brushing him here and there with his sleeve, and was even more nervous than the boy. Pelle had been born to poor circumstances, had been christened, and had had to earn his bread from the time he was a little boy—all exactly as he had done himself. So far there was no difference to be seen; it might very well have been Lasse himself over again, from the big ears and the "cow's-lick" on the forehead, to the way the boy walked and wore out the bottoms of his trouser-legs. But this was something strikingly new. Neither Lasse nor any of his family had ever gone to school; it was something new that had come within the reach of his family, a blessing from Heaven that had fallen upon the boy and himself. It felt like a push upward; the impossible was within reach; what might not happen to a person who had book-learning! You might become master of a workshop, a clerk, perhaps even a schoolmaster.

"Now do take care of the slate, and see that you don't break it! " he said admonishingly. "And keep out of the way of the big boys until you can hold your own with them. But if any of them simply won't let you alone, mind you manage to hit first! That takes the inclination out of most of them, especially if you hit hard; he who hits first hits twice, as the old proverb says. And then you must listen well, and keep in mind all that your teacher says; and if anyone tries to entice you into playing and larking behind his back, don't do it. And remember that you've got a pocket-handkerchief, and don't use your fingers, for that isn't polite. If there's no one to see you, you can save the handkerchief, of course, and then it'll last all the longer. And take care of your nice jacket. And if the teacher's lady invites you in to coffee, you mustn't take more than one piece of cake, mind. "

Lasse's hands trembled while he talked.

"She's sure not to do that, " said Pelle, with a superior air.

"Well, well, now go, so that you don't get there too late—the very first day, too. And if there's some tool or other wanting, you must say we'll get it at once, for we aren't altogether paupers! " And Lasse slapped his pocket; but it did not make much noise, and Pelle knew quite well that they had no money; they had got the slate and pencil on credit.

Lasse stood looking after the boy as long as he was in sight, and then went to his work of crushing oilcakes. He put them into a vessel to soak, and poured water on them, all the while talking softly to himself.

There was a knock at the outside stable-door, and Lasse went to open it. It was Brother Kalle.

"Good-day, brother! " he said, with his cheerful smile. "Here comes his Majesty from the quarries! " He waddled in upon his bow legs, and the two exchanged hearty greetings. Lasse was delighted at the visit.

"What a pleasant time we had with you the other evening! " said Lasse, taking his brother by the hand.

"That's a long time ago now. But you must look in again one evening soon. Grandmother looks upon both of you with a favorable eye! " Kalle's eyes twinkled mischievously.

"How is she, poor body? Has she at all got over the hurt to her eye? Pelle came home the other day and told me that the children had been so unfortunate as to put a stick into her eye. It quite upset me. You had to have the doctor, too! "

"Well, it wasn't quite like that, " said Kalle. "I had moved grandmother's spinning-wheel myself one morning when I was putting her room to rights, and then I forgot to put it back in its place. Then when she was going to stoop down to pick up something from the floor, the spindle went into her eye; of course she's used to have everything stand exactly in its place. So really the honor's due to me. " He smiled all over his face.

Lasse shook his head sympathetically. "And she got over it fairly well? " he asked.

"No; it went altogether wrong, and she lost the sight of that eye. "

Lasse looked at him with disapproval.

Kalle caught himself up, apparently very much horrified. "Eh, what nonsense I'm talking! She lost the *blindness* of that eye, I ought to have said. *Isn't* that all wrong, too? You put somebody's eye out, and she begins to see! Upon my word, I think I'll set up as an eye-doctor after this, for there's not much difficulty in it. "

"What do you say? She's begun to—? Now you're too merry! You oughtn't to joke about everything. "

"Well, well, joking apart, as the prophet said when his wife scratched him—she can really see with that eye now. "

Lasse looked suspiciously at him for a little while before he yielded. "Why, it's quite a miracle! " he then said.

"Yes, that's what the doctor said. The point of the spindle had acted as a kind of operation. But it might just as easily have taken the other direction. Yes, we had the doctor to her three times; it was no use being niggardly. " Kalle stood and tried to look important; he had stuck his thumbs into his waistcoat pockets.

"It cost a lot of money, I suppose? "

"That's what I thought, too, and I wasn't very happy when I asked the doctor how much it would be. Twenty-five krones, he said, and it didn't sound anything more than when any of us ask for a piece of bread-and-dripping. 'Will the doctor be so kind as to wait a few days so that I can get the cow property sold? ' I asked. 'What! ' he says, and glares at me over his spectacles. 'You don't mean to sell the cow so as to pay me? You mustn't do that on any account; I'll wait till times are better. ' 'We come off easily, even if we get rid of the cow, ' I said. 'How so? ' he asks, as we go out to the carriage —it was the farmer of Kaase Farm that was driving for me. So I told him that Maria and I had been thinking of selling everything so that grandmother might go over and be operated. He said nothing to that, but climbed up into the carriage; but while I was standing like this, buttoning up his foot-bag, he seizes me by the collar and says: 'Do you know, you little bow-legged creature! ' (Kalle imitated the doctor's town speech), 'You're the best man I've ever met, and you don't owe me a brass farthing! For that matter, it was you yourself that performed the operation. ' 'Then I ought almost to have had the money, ' I said. Then he laughed and gave me a box on the ears with his fur cap. He's a fine man, that doctor, and fearfully clever; they say that he has one kind of mixture that he cures all kinds of illness with. "

They were sitting in the herdsman's room upon the green chest, and Lasse had brought out a little gin. "Drink, brother! " he said again and again. "It takes something to keep out this October drizzle. "

"Many thanks, but you must drink! But I was going to say, you should see grandmother! She goes round peeping at everything with her one eye; if it's only a button, she keeps on staring at it. So that's what that looks like, and that! She's forgotten what the things look like, and when she sees a thing, she goes to it to feel it afterward —to find out what it is, she actually says. She would have nothing to do with us the first few days; when she didn't hear us talk or walk, she thought we were strangers, even though she saw us there before her eyes. "

"And the little ones? " asked Lasse.

"Thank you, Anna's is fat and well, but our own seems to have come to a standstill. After all, it's the young pigs you ought to breed with. By the bye" —Kalle took out his purse— "while we're at it, don't let me forget the ten krones I got from you for the christenings. "

Lasse pushed it away. "Never mind that, " he said. "You may have a lot to go through yet. How many mouths are there now? Fourteen or fifteen, I suppose? "

"Yes; but two take their mother's milk, like the parson's wife's chickens; so that's all saved. And if things became difficult, one's surely man enough to wring a few pence out of one's nose? " He seized his nose and gave it a rapid twist, and held out his hand. A folded ten-krone note lay in it.

Lasse laughed at the trick, but would not hear of taking the money; and for a time it passed backward and forward between them. "Well, well! " said Kalle at last, keeping the note; "thank you very much, then! And good-bye, brother! I must be going. " Lasse went out with him, and sent many greetings.

"We shall come and look you up very soon, " he called out after his brother.

When after a little while he returned to his room, the note lay upon the bed. Kalle must have seen his opportunity to put it there, conjurer that he was. Lasse put it aside to give to Kalle's wife, when an occasion presented itself.

Long before the time, Lasse was on the lookout for Pelle. He found the solitude wearisome, now that he was used to having the boy about him from morning till night. At last he came, out of breath with running, for he had longed to get home too.

Nothing either terrible or remarkable had happened at school. Pelle had to give a circumstantial account, point by point, "Well, what can you do? " the master had asked, taking him by the ear—quite kindly, of course. "I can pull the mad bull to the water without Father Lasse helping at all, " Pelle had answered, and then the whole class had laughed.

"Yes, yes, but can you read? "

No, Pelle could not do that—"or else I shouldn't have come here, " he was on the point of adding. "It was a good thing you didn't answer that, " said Lasse; "but what more then? " Well, then Pelle was put upon the lowest bench, and the boy next him was set to teach him his letters.

"Do you know them, then? "

No, Pelle did not know them that day, but when a couple of weeks had passed, he knew most of them, and wrote them with chalk on the posts. He had not learned to write, but his hand could imitate anything he had seen, and he drew the letters just as they stood in print in the spelling-book.

Lasse went and looked at them during his work, and had them repeated to him endlessly; but they would not stick properly. "What's that one there? " he was perpetually asking.

Pelle answered with a superior air: "That? Have you forgotten it already? I knew that after I'd only seen it once! That's M. "

"Yes, of course it is! I can't think where my head is to-day. M, yes— of course it's M! Now what can that be used for, eh? "

"It's the first letter in the word 'empty, ' of course! " said Pelle consequentially.

"Yes, of course! But you didn't find that out for yourself; the master told you. "

"No, I found it out by myself. "

"Did you, now? Well, you've become clever—if only you don't become as clever as seven fools. "

Lasse was out of spirits; but very soon he gave in, and fell into whole-hearted admiration of his son. And the instruction was continued while they worked. It was fortunate for Pelle that his father was so slow, for he did not get on very fast himself, when once he had mastered all that was capable of being picked up spontaneously by a quick intelligence. The boy who had to teach him—Sloppy, he was called—was the dunce of the class and had always been bottom until now Pelle had come and taken his place.

Two weeks of school had greatly changed Pelle's ideas on this subject. On the first few days he arrived in a state of anxious expectation, and all his courage forsook him as he crossed the threshold of the school. For the first time in his life he felt that he was good for nothing. Trembling with awe, he opened his perceptions to this new and unfamiliar thing that was to unveil for him all the mysteries of the world, if only he kept his ears open; and he did so. But there was no awe-inspiring man, who looked at them affectionately through gold-rimmed spectacles while he told them about the sun and the moon and all the wonders of the world. Up and down the middle passage walked a man in a dirty linen coat and with gray bristles projecting from his nostrils. As he walked he swung the cane and smoked his pipe; or he sat at the desk and read the newspaper. The children were noisy and restless, and when the noise broke out into open conflict, the man dashed down from his desk, and hit out indiscriminately with his cane. And Pelle himself, well he was coupled—for good, it appeared—to a dirty boy, covered with scrofulous sores, who pinched his arm every time he read his b-a—ba, b-e—be wrong. The only variation was an hour's daily examination in the tedious observations in the class-book, and the Saturday's uncouth hymn-repeating.

For a time Pelle swallowed everything whole, and passed it on faithfully to his father; but at last he tired of it. It was not his nature to remain long passive to his surroundings, and one fine day he had thrown aside all injunctions and intentions, and dived into the midst of the fun.

After this he had less information to impart, but on the other hand there were the thousands of knavish tricks to tell about. And father Lasse shook his head and comprehended nothing; but he could not help laughing.

XI

"A safe stronghold our God is still,
A trusty shield and wea—pon;
He'll help us clear from all the ill
That hath us now o'erta—ken.
  The ancient prince of hell
  Hath risen with purpose fell;
  Strong mail of craft and power
  He weareth in this hour;
On earth is not his fel—low."

The whole school sat swaying backward and forward in time to the rhythm, grinding out hymns in endless succession. Fris, the master, was walking up and down the middle passage, smoking his pipe; he was taking exercise after an hour's reading of the paper. He was using the cane to beat time with, now and then letting it descend upon the back of an offender, but always only at the end of a line— as a kind of note of admiration. Fris could not bear to have the rhythm broken. The children who did not know the hymn were carried along by the crowd, some of them contenting themselves with moving their lips, while others made up words of their own. When the latter were too dreadful, their neighbors laughed, and then the cane descended.

When one verse came to an end, Fris quickly started the next; for the mill was hard to set in motion again when once it had come to a standstill. "With for—! " and the half-hundred children carried it on—

"With force of arms we nothing can,
Full soon were we downrid—den; "

Then Fris had another breathing-space in which to enjoy his pipe and be lulled by this noise that spoke of great and industrious activity. When things went as they were now going, his exasperation calmed down for a time, and he could smile at his thoughts as he paced up and down, and, old though he was, look at the bright side of life. People in passing stopped to rejoice over the diligence displayed, and Fris beat more briskly with the cane, and felt a long-forgotten ideal stirring within him; he had this whole flock of

131

children to educate for life, he was engaged in creating the coming generation.

When the hymn came to an end, he got them, without a pause, turned on to "Who puts his trust in God alone, " and from that again to "We all, we all have faith in God. " They had had them all three the whole winter through, and now at last, after tremendous labor, he had brought them so far that they could say them more or less together.

The hymn-book was the business of Fris's life, and his forty years as parish-clerk had led to his knowing the whole of it by heart. In addition to this he had a natural gift. As a child Fris had been intended for the ministry, and his studies as a young man were in accordance with that intention. Bible words came with effect from his lips, and his prospects were of the best, when an ill-natured bird came all the way from the Faroe Islands to bring trouble upon him. Fris fell down two flights from spiritual guide to parish-clerk and child-whipper. The latter office he looked upon as almost too transparent a punishment from Heaven, and arranged his school as a miniature clerical charge.

The whole village bore traces of his work. There was not much knowledge of reading and writing, but when it was a question of hymns and Bible texts, these fishermen and little artisans were bad to beat. Fris took to himself the credit for the fairly good circumstances of the adults, and the receipt of proper wages by the young men. He followed each one of them with something of a father's eyes, and considered them all to be practically a success. And he was on friendly terms with them once they had left school. They would come to the old bachelor and have a chat, and relieve their minds of some difficulty or other.

But it was always another matter with the confounded brood that sat upon the school benches for the time being; it resisted learning with might and main, and Fris prophesied it no good in the future.

Fris hated the children. But he loved these squarely built hymns, which seemed to wear out the whole class, while he himself could give them without relaxing a muscle. And when it went as it was doing to-day, he could quite forget that there were such things as children, and give himself up to this endless procession, in which column after column filed past him, in the foot-fall of the rhythm. It was not hymns, either; it was a mighty march-past of the strong things of life, in which there stretched, in one endless tone, all that Fris himself had failed to attain. That was why he nodded so happily, and why the loud tramp of feet rose around him like the acclamations of armies, an *Ave Caesar*.

He was sitting with the third supplement of his newspaper before him, but was not reading; his eyes were closed, and his head moved gently to the rhythm.

The children babbled on ceaselessly, almost without stopping for breath; they were hypnotized by the monotonous flow of words. They were like the geese that had been given leave by the fox to say a prayer before they were eaten, and now went on praying and praying forever and ever. When they came to the end of the three hymns, they began again by themselves. The mill kept getting louder, they kept the time with their feet, and it was like the stroke of a mighty piston, a boom! Fris nodded with them, and a long tuft of hair flapped in his face; he fell into an ecstasy, and could not sit still upon his chair.

> "And were this world all devils o'er,
>   And watching to devour—us,
> We lay it not to heart so sore;
>   Not they can overpower us. "

It sounded like a stamping-mill; some were beating their slates upon the tables, and others thumping with their elbows. Fris did not hear it; he heard only the mighty tramp of advancing hosts.

> "And let the prince of ill
> Look grim as e'er he will, " —

Suddenly, at a preconcerted signal, the whole school stopped singing. Fris was brought to earth again with a shock. He opened his eyes, and saw that he had once more allowed himself to be taken by surprise. "You little devils! You confounded brats! " he roared, diving into their midst with his cane. In a moment the whole school was in a tumult, the boys fighting and the girls screaming. Fris began hitting about him.

He tried to bring them back to the patter. "Who puts his trust in God alone! " he shouted in a voice that drowned the clamor; but they did not take it up—the little devils! Then he hit indiscriminately. He knew quite well that one was just as good as another, and was not particular where the strokes fell. He took the long-haired ones by the hair and dragged them to the table, and thrashed them until the cane began to split. The boys had been waiting for this; they had themselves rubbed onion into the cane that morning, and the most defiant of them had on several pairs of trousers for the occasion.

When the cracked sound proclaimed that the cane was in process of disintegration, the whole school burst into deafening cheers. Fris had thrown up the game, and let them go on. He walked up and down the middle passage like a suffering animal, his gall rising. "You little devils! " he hissed; "You infernal brats! " And then, "Do sit still, children! " This last was so ridiculously touching in the midst of all the rest, that it had to be imitated.

Pelle sat farthest away, in the corner. He was fairly new at this sort of thing, but did his best. Suddenly he jumped on to the table, and danced there in his stockinged feet. Fris gazed at him so strangely, Pelle thought; he was like Father Lasse when everything went wrong; and he slid down, ashamed. Nobody had noticed his action, however; it was far too ordinary.

It was a deafening uproar, and now and then an ill-natured remark was hurled out of the seething tumult. Where they came from it was difficult to say; but every one of them hit Fris and made him cower. False steps made in his youth on the other side of the water fifty years ago, were brought up again here on the lips of these ignorant children, as well as some of his best actions, that had been so unselfish that the district put the very worst interpretation upon them. And as if that were not enough—but hush! He was sobbing.

"Sh—sh! Sh—sh! " It was Henry Bodker, the biggest boy in the school, and he was standing on a bench and sh—ing threateningly. The girls adored him, and became quiet directly; but some of the boys would not obey the order; but when Henry held his clenched fist up to one eye, they too became quiet.

Fris walked up and down the middle passage like a pardoned offender. He did not dare to raise his eyes, but they could all see that he was crying. "It's a shame! " said a voice in an undertone. All eyes were turned upon him, and there was perfect silence in the room.

"Play-time! " cried a boy's voice in a tone of command: it was Nilen's. Fris nodded feebly, and they rushed out.

Fris remained behind to collect himself. He walked up and down with his hands behind his back, swallowing hard. He was going to send in his resignation. Every time things went quite wrong, Fris sent in his resignation, and when he had come to himself a little, he put it off until the spring examinations were over. He would not leave in this way, as a kind of failure. This very winter he had worked as he had never done before, in order that his resignation might have somewhat the effect of a bomb, and that they might really feel it as a loss when he had gone. When the examination was held, he would take the hymn-book for repetition in chorus—right from the beginning. Some of the children would quickly drop behind, but there were some of them, into whom, in the course of time, he had hammered most of its contents. Long before they had run out, the clergyman would lift his hand to stop them, and say: "That's enough, my dear clerk! That's enough! " and would thank him in a voice of emotion; while the school committee and the parents would whisper together in awed admiration.

And then would be the time to resign!

The school lay on the outskirts of the fishing-village, and the playground was the shore. When the boys were let out after a few hours' lessons, they were like young cattle out for the first time after the long winter. They darted, like flitting swallows, in all directions, threw themselves upon the fresh rampart of sea-wrack and beat one another about the ears with the salt wet weeds. Pelle was not fond of this game; the sharp weed stung, and sometimes there were stones hanging to it, grown right in.

But he dared not hold himself aloof, for that would attract attention at once. The thing was to join in it and yet not be in it, to make himself little and big according to the requirements of the moment, so as to be at one time unseen, and at another to exert a terrifying effect. He had his work cut out in twisting and turning, and slipping in and out.

The girls always kept together in one corner of the playground, told tittle-tattle and ate their lunch, but the boys ran all over the place like swallows in aimless flight. A big boy was standing crouching close to the gymnastic apparatus, with his arm hiding his face, and munching. They whirled about him excitedly, now one and now another making the circle narrower and narrower. Peter Kofod — Howling Peter—looked as if the world were sailing under him; he clung to the climbing-pole and hid his face. When they came close up to him, they kicked up behind with a roar, and the boy screamed with terror, turned up his face and broke into a long-drawn howl. Afterward he was given all the food that the others could not eat.

Howling Peter was always eating and always howling. He was a pauper child and an orphan; he was big for his age, but had a strangely blue and frozen look. His frightened eyes stood half out of his head, and beneath them the flesh was swollen and puffy with crying. He started at the least sound, and there was always an expression of fear on his face. The boys never really did him any harm, but they screamed and crouched down whenever they passed him—they could not resist it. Then he would scream too, and cower with fear. The girls would sometimes run up and tap him on the back, and then he screamed in terror. Afterward all the children gave him some of their food. He ate it all, roared, and was as famished as ever.

No one could understand what was wrong with him. Twice he had made an attempt to hang himself, and nobody could give any reason for it, not even he himself. And yet he was not altogether stupid. Lasse believed that he was a visionary, and saw things that others could not see, so that the very fact of living and drawing breath frightened him. But however that might be, Pelle must on no account do anything to him, not for all the world.

The crowd of boys had retired to the shore, and there, with little Nilen at their head, suddenly threw themselves upon Henry Bodker. He was knocked down and buried beneath the swarm, which lay in a sprawling heap upon the top of him, pounding down with clenched fists wherever there was an opening. But then a pair of fists began to push upward, tchew, tchew, like steam punches, the boys rolled off on all sides with their hands to their faces, and Henry Bodker emerged from the heap, kicking at random. Nilen was still hanging like a leech to the back of his neck, and Henry tore his blouse in getting him thrown off. To Pelle he seemed to be tremendously big as he stood there, only breathing a little quickly. And now the girls came up, and fastened his blouse together with pins, and gave him sweets; and he, by way of thanking them, seized them by their pigtails and tied them together, four or five of them, so that they could not get away from one another. They stood still and bore it patiently, only gazing at him with eyes of devotion.

Pelle had ventured into the battle and had received a kick, but he bore no malice. If he had had a sweet, he, like the girls, would have given it to Henry Bodker, and would have put up with ungentle treatment too. He worshipped him. But he measured himself by Nilen —the little bloodthirsty Nilen, who had no knowledge of fear, and attacked so recklessly that the others got out of his way! He was always in the thickest of the crowd, jumped right into the worst of everything, and came safely out of it all. Pelle examined himself critically to find points of resemblance, and found them—in his defence of Father Lasse the first summer, when he kicked a big boy, and in his relations with the mad bull, of which he was not in the least afraid. But in other points it failed. He was afraid of the dark, and he could not stand a thrashing, while Nilen could take his with his hands in his pockets. It was Pelle's first attempt at obtaining a general survey of himself.

Fris had gone inland, probably to the church, so it would be a playtime of some hours. The boys began to look about for some more lasting ways of passing the time. The "bulls" went into the schoolroom, and began to play about on the tables and benches, but the "blennies" kept to the shore. "Bulls" and "blennies" were the land and the sea in conflict; the division came naturally on every more or less serious occasion, and sometimes gave rise to regular battles.

Pelle kept with the shore boys; Henry Bodker and Nilen were among them, and they were something new! They did not care about the land and animals, but the sea, of which he was afraid, was like a cradle to them. They played about on the water as they would in their mother's parlor, and had much of its easy movement. They were quicker than Pelle, but not so enduring; and they had a freer manner, and made less of the spot to which they belonged. They spoke of England in the most ordinary way and brought things to school that their fathers and brothers had brought home with them from the other side of the world, from Africa and China. They spent nights on the sea on an open boat, and when they played truant it was always to go fishing. The cleverest of them had their own fishing-tackle and little flat-bottomed prams, that they had built themselves and caulked with oakum. They fished on their own account and caught pike, eels, and tench, which they sold to the wealthier people in the district.

Pelle thought he knew the stream thoroughly, but now he was brought to see it from a new side. Here were boys who in March and April—in the holidays—were up at three in the morning, wading barefoot at the mouth of the stream to catch the pike and perch that went up into the fresh water to spawn. And nobody told the boys to do it; they did it because they liked it!

They had strange pleasures! Now they were standing "before the sea" —in a long, jubilant row. They ran out with the receding wave to the larger stones out in the water, and then stood on the stones and jumped when the water came up again, like a flock of sea birds. The art consisted in keeping yourself dryshod, and yet it was the quickest boys who got wettest. There was of course a limit to the time you could keep yourself hovering. When wave followed wave in quick succession, you had to come down in the middle of it, and then sometimes it went over your head. Or an unusually large wave would come and catch all the legs as they were drawn up in the middle of the jump, when the whole row turned beautifully, and fell splash into the water. Then with, a deafening noise they went up to the schoolroom to turn the "bulls" away from the stove.

Farther along the shore, there were generally some boys sitting with a hammer and a large nail, boring holes in the stones there. They were sons of stone-masons from beyond the quarries. Pelle's cousin Anton was among them. When the holes were deep enough, powder was pressed into them, and the whole school was present at the explosion.

In the morning, when they were waiting for the master, the big boys would stand up by the school wall with their hands in their pockets, discussing the amount of canvas and the home ports of vessels passing far out at sea. Pelle listened to them open-mouthed. It was always the sea and what belonged to the sea that they talked about, and most of it he did not understand. All these boys wanted the same thing when they were confirmed—to go to sea. But Pelle had had enough of it when he crossed from Sweden; he could not understand them.

How carefully he had always shut his eyes and put his fingers in his ears, so that his head should not get filled with water when he dived in the stream! But these boys swam down under the water like proper fish, and from what they said he understood that they could dive down in deep water and pick up stones from the bottom.

"Can you see down there, then? " he asked, in wonder.

"Yes, of course! How else would the fish be able to keep away from the nets? If it's only moonlight, they keep far outside, the whole shoal! "

"And the water doesn't run into your head when you take your fingers out of your ears? "

"Take your fingers out of your ears? "

"Yes, to pick up the stone. "

A burst of scornful laughter greeted this remark, and they began to question him craftily; he was splendid—a regular country bumpkin! He had the funniest ideas about everything, and it very soon came out that he had never bathed in the sea. He was afraid of the water —a "blue-bag"; the stream could not do away with that.

After that he was called Blue-bag, notwithstanding that he one day took the cattle-whip to school with him and showed them how he could cut three-cornered holes in a pair of trousers with the long lash, hit a small stone so that it disappeared into the air, and make those loud reports. It was all excellent, but the name stuck to him all the same; and all his little personality smarted under it.

In the course of the winter, some strong young men came home to the village in blue clothes and white neck-cloths. They had laid up, as it was called, and some of them drew wages all through the winter without doing anything. They always came over to the school to see the master; they came in the middle of lessons, but it did not matter; Fris was joy personified. They generally brought something or other for him—a cigar of such fine quality that it was enclosed in glass, or some other remarkable thing. And they talked to Fris as they would to a comrade, told him what they had gone through, so that the listening youngsters hugged themselves with delight, and quite unconcernedly smoked their clay pipes in the class—with the bowl turned nonchalantly downward without losing its tobacco. They had been engaged as cook's boys and ordinary seamen, on the

Spanish main and the Mediterranean and many other wonderful places. One of them had ridden up a fire-spouting mountain on a donkey. And they brought home with them lucifer matches that were as big, almost, as Pomeranian logs, and were to be struck on the teeth.

The boys worshipped them and talked of nothing else; it was a great honor to be seen in the company of such a man. For Pelle it was not to be thought of.

And then it came about that the village was awaiting the return of one such lad as this, and he did not come. And one day word came that bark so-and-so had gone to the bottom with all on board. It was the winter storms, said the boys, spitting like grown men. The brothers and sisters were kept away from school for a week, and when they came back Pelle eyed them curiously: it must be strange to have a brother lying at the bottom of the sea, quite young! "Then you won't want to go to sea? " he asked them. Oh, yes, they wanted to go to sea, too!

Another time Fris came back after an unusually long playtime in low spirits. He kept on blowing his nose hard, and now and then dried his eyes behind his spectacles. The boys nudged one another. He cleared his throat loudly, but could not make himself heard, and then beat a few strokes on his desk with the cane.

"Have you heard, children? " he asked, when they had become more or less quiet.

"No! Yes! What? " they cried in chorus; and one boy said: "That the sun's fallen into the sea and set it on fire! "

The master quietly took up his hymn-book. "Shall we sing 'How blessed are they'? " he said; and they knew that something must have happened, and sang the hymn seriously with him.

But at the fifth verse Fris stopped; he could not go on any longer. "Peter Funck is drowned! " he said, in a voice that broke on the last word. A horrified whisper passed through the class, and they looked at one another with uncomprehending eyes. Peter Funck was the most active boy in the village, the best swimmer, and the greatest scamp the school had ever had—and he was drowned!

Fris walked up and down, struggling to control himself. The children dropped into softly whispered conversation about Peter Funck, and all their faces had grown old with gravity. "Where did it happen? " asked a big boy.

Fris awoke with a sigh. He had been thinking about this boy, who had shirked everything, and had then become the best sailor in the village; about all the thrashings he had given him, and the pleasant hours they had spent together on winter evenings when the lad was home from a voyage and had looked in to see his old master. There had been much to correct, and things of grave importance that Fris had had to patch up for the lad in all secrecy, so that they should not affect his whole life, and —

"It was in the North Sea, " he said. "I think they'd been in England. "

"To Spain with dried fish, " said a boy. "And from there they went to England with oranges, and were bringing a cargo of coal home. "

"Yes, I think that was it, " said Fris. "They were in the North Sea, and were surprised by a storm; and Peter had to go aloft. "

"Yes, for the *Trokkadej* is such a crazy old hulk. As soon as there's a little wind, they have to go aloft and take in sail, " said another boy.

"And he fell down, " Fris went on, "and struck the rail and fell into the sea. There were the marks of his sea-boats on the rail. They braced—or whatever it's called—and managed to turn; but it took them half-an-hour to get up to the place. And just as they got there, he sank before their eyes. He had been struggling in the icy water for half-an-hour—with sea-boots and oilskins on—and yet—"

A long sigh passed through the class. "He was the best swimmer on the whole shore! " said Henry. "He dived backward off the gunwale of a bark that was lying in the roads here taking in water, and came up on the other side of the vessel. He got ten rye rusks from the captain himself for it. "

"He must have suffered terribly, " said Fris. "It would almost have been better for him if he hadn't been able to swim. "

"That's what my father says! " said a little boy. "He can't swim, for he says it's better for a sailor not to be able to; it only keeps you in torture. "

"My father can't swim, either! " exclaimed another. "Nor mine, either! " said a third. "He could easily learn, but he won't. " And they went on in this way, holding up their hands. They could all swim themselves, but it appeared that hardly any of their fathers could; they had a superstitious feeling against it. "Father says you oughtn't to tempt Providence if you're wrecked, " one boy added.

"Why, but then you'd not be doing your best! " objected a little faltering voice. Fris turned quickly toward the corner where Pelle sat blushing to the tips of his ears.

"Look at that little man! " said Fris, impressed. "And I declare if he isn't right and all the rest of us wrong! God helps those that help themselves! "

"Perhaps, " said a voice. It was Henry Bodker's.

"Well, well, I know He didn't help here, but still we ought always to do what we can in all the circumstances of life. Peter did his best— and he was the cleverest boy I ever had. "

The children smiled at one another, remembering various things. Peter Funck had once gone so far as to wrestle with the master himself, but they had not the heart to bring this up. One of the bigger boys, however, said, half for the purpose of teasing: "He never got any farther than the twenty-seventh hymn! "

"Didn't he, indeed? " snarled Fris. "Didn't he, indeed? And you think perhaps you're clever, do you? Let's see how far you've got, then! " And he took up the hymn-book with a trembling hand. He could not stand anything being said against boys that had left.

The name Blue-bag continued to stick to Pelle, and nothing had ever stung him so much; and there was no chance of his getting rid of it before the summer came, and that was a long way off.

One day the fisher-boys ran out on to the breakwater in playtime. A boat had just come in through the pack-ice with a gruesome cargo — five frozen men, one of whom was dead and lay in the fire-engine house, while the four others had been taken into various cottages, where they were being rubbed with ice to draw the frost out of them. The farmer-boys were allowed no share in all this excitement, for the fisher-boys, who went in and out and saw everything, drove them away if they approached—and sold meagre information at extortionate prices.

The boat had met a Finnish schooner drifting in the sea, covered with ice, and with frozen rudder. She was too heavily laden, so that the waves went right over her and froze; and the ice had made her sink still deeper. When she was found, her deck was just on a level with the water, ropes of the thickness of a finger had become as thick as an arm with ice, and the men who were lashed to the rigging were shapeless masses of ice. They were like knights in armor with closed visor when they were taken down, and their clothes had to be hacked off their bodies. Three boats had gone out now to try and save the vessel; there would be a large sum of money to divide if they were successful.

Pelle was determined not to be left out of all this, even if he got his shins kicked in, and so kept near and listened. The boys were talking gravely and looked gloomy. What those men had put up with! And perhaps their hands or feet would mortify and have to be cut off. Each boy behaved as if he were bearing his share of their sufferings, and they talked in a manly way and in gruff voices. "Be off with you, bull! " they called to Pelle. They were not fond of Blue-bags for the moment.

The tears came to Pelle's eyes, but he would not give in, and wandered away along the wharf.

"Be off with you! " they shouted again, picking up stones in a menacing way. "Be off to the other bumpkins, will you! " They came up and hit at him. "What are you standing there and staring into the water for? You might turn giddy and fall in head first! Be off to the other yokels, will you! Blue-bag! "

Pelle turned literally giddy, with the strength of the determination that seized upon his little brain. "I'm no more a blue-bag than you are! " he said. "Why, you wouldn't even dare to jump into the water! "

"Just listen to him! He thinks you jump into the water for fun in the middle of winter, and get cramp! "

Pelle just heard their exultant laughter as he sprang off the breakwater, and the water, thick with ground-up ice, closed above his head. The top of his head appeared again, he made two or three strokes with his arms like a dog, and sank.

The boys ran in confusion up and down and shouted, and one of them got hold of a boat-hook. Then Henry Bodker came running up, sprang in head first without stopping, and disappeared, while a piece of ice that he had struck with his forehead made ducks and drakes over the water. Twice his head appeared above the ice-filled water, to snatch a breath of air, and then he came up with Pelle. They got him hoisted up on to the breakwater, and Henry set to work to give him a good thrashing.

Pelle had lost consciousness, but the thrashing had the effect of bringing him to. He suddenly opened his eyes, was on his legs in a trice, and darted away like a sandpiper.

"Run home! " the boys roared after him. "Run as hard as ever you can, or you'll be ill! Only tell your father you fell in! " And Pelle ran. He needed no persuasion. When he reached Stone Farm, his clothes were frozen quite stiff, and his trousers could stand alone when he got out of them; but he himself was as warm as a toast.

He would not lie to his father, but told him just what had happened. Lasse was angry, angrier than the boy had ever seen him before.

Lasse knew how to treat a horse to keep it from catching cold, and began to rub Pelle's naked body with a wisp of straw, while the boy lay on the bed, tossing about under the rough handling. His father took no notice of his groans, but scolded him. "You mad little devil, to jump straight into the sea in the middle of winter like a lovesick woman! You ought to have a whipping, that's what you ought to have—a good sound whipping! But I'll let you off this time if you'll go to sleep and try to sweat so that we can get that nasty salt water out of your body. I wonder if it wouldn't be a good thing to bleed you. "

Pelle did not want to be bled; he was very comfortable lying there, now that he had been sick. But his thoughts were very serious. "Supposing I'd been drowned! " he said solemnly.

"If you had, I'd have thrashed you to within an inch of your life, " said Lasse angrily.

Pelle laughed.

"Oh, you may laugh, you word-catcher! " snapped Lasse. "But it's no joke being father to a little ne'er-do-weel of a cub like you! " Saying which he went angrily out into the stable. He kept on listening, however, and coming up to peep in and see whether fever or any other devilry had come of it.

But Pelle slept quietly with his head under the quilt, and dreamed that he was no less a person than Henry Bodker.

* * * * *

Pelle did not learn to read much that winter, but he learned twenty and odd hymns by heart only by using his ears, and he got the name Blue-bag, as applied to himself, completely banished. He had gained ground, and strengthened his position by several bold strokes; and the school began to take account of him as a brave boy. And Henry, who as a rule took no notice of anybody, took him several times under his wing.

Now and then he had a bad conscience, especially when his father in his newly-awakened thirst for knowledge, came to him for the solution of some problem or other, and he was at a loss for an answer.

"But it's you who ought to have the learning, " Lasse would then say reproachfully.

As the winter drew to an end, and the examination approached, Pelle became nervous. Many uncomfortable reports were current of the severity of the examination among the boys—of putting into lower classes and complete dismissal from the school.

Pelle had the misfortune not to be heard independently in a single hymn. He had to give an account of the Fall. The theft of the apple was easy to get through, but the curse—! "And God said unto the serpent: Upon thy belly shalt thou go, upon thy belly shalt thou go, upon thy belly shalt thou go! " He could get no further.

"Does it still do that, then? " asked the clergyman kindly.

"Yes—for it has no limbs. "

"And can you explain to me what a limb is? " The priest was known to be the best examiner on the island; he could begin in a gutter and end in heaven, people said.

"A limb is—is a hand. "

"Yes, that is one. But can't you tell me something that distinguishes all limbs from other parts of the body? A limb is—well? —a? —a part of the body that can move by itself, for instance? Well! "

"The ears! " said Pelle, perhaps because his own were burning.

"O-oh? Can you move your ears, then? "

"Yes. " By dint of great perseverance, Pelle had acquired that art in the course of the previous summer, so as not to be outdone by Rud.

"Then, upon my word, I should like to see it! " exclaimed the clergyman.

So Pelle worked his ears industriously backward and forward, and the priest and the school committee and the parents all laughed. Pelle got "excellent" in religion.

"So it was your ears after all that saved you, " said Lasse, delighted. "Didn't I tell you to use your ears well? Highest marks in religion only for moving your ears! Why, I should think you might become a parson if you liked! "

And he went on for a long time. But wasn't he the devil of a laddie to be able to answer like that!

XII

"Come, cubby, cubby, cubby! Come on, you silly little chicken, there's nothing to be afraid of! " Pelle was enticing his favorite calf with a wisp of green corn; but it was not quite sure of him to-day, for it had had a beating for bad behavior.

Pelle felt very much like a father whose child gives him sorrow and compels him to use severe measures. And now this misunderstanding —that the calf would have nothing to do with him, although it was for its own good that he had beaten it! But there was no help for it, and as long as Pelle had them to mind, he intended to be obeyed.

At last it let him come close up to it, so that he could stroke it. It stood still for a little and was sulky, but yielded at last, ate the green food and snuffed in his face by way of thanks.

"Will you be good, then? " said Pelle, shaking it by its stumps of horns. "Will you, eh? " It tossed its head mischievously. "Very well, then you shan't carry my coat to-day. "

The strange thing about this calf was that the first day it was let out, it would not stir, and at last the boy left it behind for Lasse to take in again. But no sooner was it behind him than it followed of its own accord, with its forehead close to his back; and always after that it walked behind him when they went out and came home, and it carried his overcoat on its back when it looked as if there would be rain.

Pelle's years were few in number, but to his animals he was a grown man. Formerly he had only been able to make them respect him sufficiently to obey him at close quarters; but this year he could hit a cow at a distance of a hundred paces with a stone, and that gave him power over the animals at a distance, especially when he thought of calling out the animal's name as he hit it. In this way they realized that the pain came from him, and learned to obey the mere call.

For punishment to be effectual, it must follow immediately upon the misdeed. There was therefore no longer any such thing as lying in wait for an animal that had offended, and coming up behind it when later on it was grazing peacefully. That only caused confusion. To run an animal until it was tired out, hanging on to its tail and beating it all round the meadow only to revenge one's self, was also stupid; it made the whole flock restless and difficult to manage for the rest of the day. Pelle weighed the end and the means against one another; he learned to quench his thirst for revenge with good practical reasons.

Pelle was a boy, and he was not an idle one. All day, from five in the morning until nine at night, he was busy with something or other, often most useless things. For hours he practiced walking on his hands, turning a somersault, and jumping the stream; he was always in motion. Hour after hour he would run unflaggingly round in a circle on the grass, like a tethered foal, leaning toward the center as he ran, so that his hand could pluck the grass, kicking up behind, and neighing and snorting. He was pouring forth energy from morning till night with open-handed profusion.

But minding the cattle was *work*, and here he husbanded his energy. Every step that could be saved here was like capital acquired; and Pelle took careful notice of everything, and was always improving his methods. He learned that punishment worked best when it only hung as a threat; for much beating made an animal callous. He also learned to see when it was absolutely necessary to interfere. If this could not be done in the very act, he controlled himself and endeavored upon the strength of his experience to bring about exactly the same situation once more, and then to be prepared. The little fellow, unknown to himself, was always engaged in adding cubits unto his stature.

He had obtained good results. The driving out and home again no longer gave him any difficulty; he had succeeded for a whole week in driving the flock along a narrow field road, with growing corn on both sides, without their having bitten off so much as a blade. And there was the still greater task of keeping them under control on a hot, close day—to hedge them in in full gallop, so that they stood in the middle of the meadow stamping on the ground with uplifted tails, in fear of the gad-flies. If he wanted to, he could make them tear home to the stable in wild flight, with their tails in the air, on the coldest October day, only by lying down in the grass and imitating the hum of gad-flies. But that was a tremendous secret, that even Father Lasse knew nothing about.

The amusing thing about the buzzing was that calves that were out for the first time, and had never made the acquaintance of a gad-fly, instantly set off running, with tail erect, when they heard its angry buzz.

Pelle had a remote ideal, which was to lie upon some elevated place and direct the whole flock by the sole means of his voice, and never need to resort to punishment. Father Lasse never beat either, no matter how wrong things went.

There were some days—well, what did become of them? Before he had any idea of it, it was time to drive home. Other days were long enough, but seemed to sing themselves away, in the ring of scythes, the lowing of cattle, and people's voices far away. Then the day itself went singing over the ground, and Pelle had to stop every now and then to listen. Hark! there was music! And he would run up on to the sandbanks and gaze out over the sea; but it was not there, and inland there was no merrymaking that he knew of, and there were no birds of passage flying through the air at this time of year. But hark! there was music again! far away in the distance, just such a sound of music as reaches the ear from so far off that one cannot distinguish the melody, or say what instruments are playing. Could it be the sun itself?

The song of light and life streamed through him, as though he were a fountain; and he would go about in a dreamy half-consciousness of melody and happiness.

When the rain poured down, he hung his coat over a briar and lay sheltered beneath it, carving or drawing with a lead button on paper—horses, and bulls lying down, but more often ships, ships that sailed across the sea upon their own soft melody, far away to foreign lands, to Negroland and China, for rare things. And when he was quite in the mood, he would bring out a broken knife and a piece of shale from a secret hiding-place, and set to work. There was a picture scratched on the stone, and he was now busy carving it in relief. He had worked at it on and off all through the summer, and now it was beginning to stand out. It was a bark in full sail, sailing over rippling water to Spain—yes, it was going to Spain, for grapes and oranges, and all the other delightful things that Pelle had never tasted yet.

On rainy days it was a difficult matter to keep count of the time, and required the utmost exertion. On other days it was easy enough, and Pelle could tell it best by the feeling. At certain times of the day there were signs at home on the farm that told him the time, and the cattle gave him other hours by their habits. At nine the first one lay down to chew the morning cud, and then all gradually lay down one by one; and there was always a moment at about ten when they all lay chewing. At eleven the last of them were upon their legs again. It was the same in the afternoon between three and five.

Midday was easy to determine when the sun was shining. Pelle could always feel it when it turned in its path. And there were a hundred other things in nature that gave him a connection with the times of day, such as the habits of the birds, and something about the fir-trees, and much besides that he could not lay his finger upon and say it was there, because it was only a feeling. The time to drive home was given by the cattle themselves. When it drew near, they grazed slowly around until their heads pointed in the direction of the farm; and there was a visible tension in their bodies, a homeward yearning.

* * * * *

Rud had not shown himself all the week, and no sooner had he come today than Pelle had to give him a blowing-up for some deceitfulness. Then he ran home, and Pelle lay down at the edge of the fir-plantation, on his face with the soles of his feet in the air, and sang. All round him there were marks of his knife on the tree-stems. On the earliest ships you saw the keel, the deck was perpendicular to the body. Those had been carved the first summer. There was also a collection of tiny fields here on the edge of the stream, properly ploughed, harrowed, and sown, each field about two feet square.

Pelle was resting now after the exertion with Rud, by making the air rock with his jubilant bawling. Up at the farm a man came out and went along the high-road with a bundle under his arm. It was Erik, who had to appear in court in answer to a summons for fighting. Then the farmer drove out at a good pace toward the town, so he was evidently off on the spree. Why couldn't the man have driven with him, as they were both going the same way? How quickly he drove, although she never followed him now. She consoled herself at home instead! Could it be true that he had spent five hundred krones in drinking and amusement in one evening?

"The war is raging, the red blood streams,
Among the mountains ring shouts and screams!
The Turk advances with cruel rage,
And sparing neither youth nor age.
They go—"

"Ho! " Pelle sprang to his feet and gazed up over the clover field. The dairy cows up there for the last quarter of an hour had been looking up at the farm every other moment, and now Aspasia lowed, so his father must soon be coming out to move them. There he came, waddling round the corner of the farm. It was not far to the lowest of the cows, so when his father was there, Pelle could seize the opportunity just to run across and say good-day to him.

He brought his animals nearer together and drove them slowly over to the other fence and up the fields. Lasse had moved the upper half, and was now crossing over diagonally to the bull, which stood a little apart from the others. The bull was growling and kicking up the earth; its tongue hung out at one side of its mouth, and it tossed its head quickly; it was angry. Then it advanced with short steps and all kinds of antics; and how it stamped! Pelle felt a desire to kick it on the nose as he had often done before; it had no business to threaten Lasse, even if it meant nothing by it.

Father Lasse took no notice of it, either. He stood hammering away at the big tether-peg, to loosen it. "Good-day! " shouted Pelle. Lasse turned his head and nodded, then bent down and hammered the peg into the ground. The bull was just behind him, stamping quickly, with open mouth and tongue hanging out; it looked as if it were vomiting, and the sound it made answered exactly to that. Pelle laughed as he slackened his pace. He was close by.

But suddenly Father Lasse turned a somersault, fell, and was in the air again, and then fell a little way off. Again the bull was about to toss him, but Pelle was at its head. He was not wearing wooden shoes, but he kicked it with his bare feet until he was giddy. The bull knew him and tried to go round him, but Pelle sprang at its head, shouting and kicking and almost beside himself, seized it by the horns. But it put him gently on one side and went forward toward Lasse, blowing along the ground so that the grass waved.

It took hold of him by the blouse and shook him a little, and then tried to get both his horns under him to send him up into the air; but Pelle was on his feet again, and as quick as lightning had drawn his knife and plunged it in between the bull's hind legs. The bull uttered a short roar, turned Lasse over on one side, and dashed off over the fields at a gallop, tossing its head as it ran, and bellowing. Down by the stream it began to tear up the bank, filling the air with earth and grass.

Lasse lay groaning with his eyes closed, and Pelle stood pulling in vain at his arm to help him up, crying: "Father, little Father Lasse! " At last Lasse sat up.

"Who's that singing? " he asked. "Oh, it's you, is it, laddie? And you're crying! Has any one done anything to you? Ah, yes, of course, it was the bull! It was just going to play fandango with me. But what did you do to it, that the devil took it so quickly? You saved your father's life, little though you are. Oh, hang it! I think I'm going to be sick! Ah me! " he went on, when the sickness was past, as he wiped the perspiration from his forehead. "If only I could have had a dram. Oh, yes, he knew me, the fellow, or I shouldn't have got off so easily. He only wanted to play with me a little, you know. He was a wee bit spiteful because I drove him away from a cow this morning; I'd noticed that. But who'd have thought he'd have turned on me? He wouldn't have done so, either, if I hadn't been so silly as to wear somebody else's clothes. This is Mons's blouse; I borrowed it of him while I washed my own. And Mr. Bull didn't like the strange smell about me. Well, we'll see what Mons'll say to this here slit. I'm afraid he won't be best pleased. "

Lasse talked on for a good while until he tried to rise, and stood up with Pelle's assistance. As he stood leaning on the boy's shoulder, he swayed backward and forward. "I should almost have said I was drunk, if it hadn't been for the pains! " he said, laughing feebly. "Well, well, I suppose I must thank God for you, laddie. You always gladden my heart, and now you've saved my life, too. "

Lasse then stumbled homeward, and Pelle moved the rest of the cows on the road down to join his own. He was both proud and affected, but most proud. He had saved Father Lasse's life, and from the big, angry bull that no one else on the farm dared have anything to do with. The next time Henry Bodker came out to see him, he should hear all about it.

He was a little vexed with himself for having drawn his knife. Every one here looked down upon that, and said it was Swedish. He wouldn't have needed to do it either if there'd been time, or if only he had had on his wooden shoes to kick the bull in the eyes with. He had very often gone at it with the toes of his wooden shoes, when it had to be driven into its stall again after a covering; and it always took good care not to do anything to him. Perhaps he would put his finger in its eye and make it blind, or take it by the horns and twist its head round, like the man in the story, until its neck was wrung.

Pelle grew and swelled up until he overshadowed everything. There was no limit to his strength while he ran about bringing his animals together again. He passed like a storm over everything, tossed strong Erik and the bailiff about, and lifted—yes, lifted the whole of Stone Farm merely by putting his hand under the beam. It was quite a fit of berserker rage!

In the very middle of it all, it occurred to him how awkward it would be if the bailiff got to know that the bull was loose. It might mean a thrashing both for him and Lasse. He must go and look for it; and for safety's sake he took his long whip with him and put on his wooden shoes.

The bull had made a terrible mess down on the bank of the stream, and had ploughed up a good piece of the meadow. It had left bloody traces along the bed of the stream and across the fields. Pelle followed these out toward the headland, where he found the bull. The huge animal had gone right in under the bushes, and was standing licking its wound. When it heard Pelle's voice, it came out. "Turn round! " he cried, flicking its nose with the whip. It put its head to the ground, bellowed, and moved heavily backward. Pelle continued flicking it on the nose while he advanced step by step, shouting determinedly: "Turn round! Will you turn round! " At last it turned and set off at a run, Pelle seizing the tether-peg and running after. He kept it going with the whip, so that it should have no time for evil thoughts.

When this was accomplished, he was ready to drop with fatigue, and lay crouched up at the edge of the fir-plantation, thinking sadly of Father Lasse, who must be going about up there ill and with nobody to give him a helping hand with his work. At last the situation became unbearable: he had to go home!

Zzzz! Zzzz! Lying flat on the ground, Pelle crept over the grass, imitating the maddening buzz of the gad-fly. He forced the sound out between his teeth, rising and falling, as if it were flying hither and thither over the grass. The cattle stopped grazing and stood perfectly still with attentive ears. Then they began to grow nervous, kicking up their legs under their bodies, turning their heads to one side in little curves, and starting; and then up went their tails. He made the sound more persistently angry, and the whole flock, infecting one another, turned and began to stamp round in wild panic. Two calves broke out of the tumult, and made a bee-line for the farm, and the whole flock followed, over stock and stone. All Pelle had to do now was to run after them, making plenty of fuss, and craftily keep the buzzing going, so that the mood should last till they reached home.

The bailiff himself came running to open the gate into the enclosure, and helped to get the animals in. Pelle expected a box on the ears, and stood still; but the bailiff only looked at him with a peculiar smile, and said: "They're beginning to get the upper hand of you, I think. Well, well, " he went on, "it's all right as long as you can manage the bull! " He was making fun of him, and Pelle blushed up to the roots of his hair.

Father Lasse had crept into bed. "What a good thing you came! " he said. "I was just lying here and wondering how I was going to get the cows moved. I can scarcely move at all, much less get up. "

It was a week before Lasse was on his feet again, and during that time the field-cattle remained in the enclosure, and Pelle stayed at home and did his father's work. He had his meals with the others, and slept his midday sleep in the barn as they did.

One day, in the middle of the day, the Sow came into the yard, drunk. She took her stand in the upper yard, where she was forbidden to go, and stood there calling for Kongstrup. The farmer was at home, but did not show himself, and not a soul was to be seen behind the high windows. "Kongstrup, Kongstrup! Come here for a little! " she called, with her eyes on the pavement, for she could not lift her head. The bailiff was not at home, and the men remained in hiding in the barn, hoping to see some fun. "I say, Kongstrup, come out a moment! I want to speak to you! " said the Sow indistinctly — and then went up the steps and tried to open the door. She hammered upon it a few times, and stood talking with her face close

154

to the door; and when nobody came, she reeled down the steps and went away talking to herself and not looking round.

A little while after the sound of weeping began up there, and just as the men were going out to the fields, the farmer came rushing out and gave orders that the horse should be harnessed to the chaise. While it was being done, he walked about nervously, and then set off at full speed. As he turned the corner of the house, a window opened and a voice called to him imploringly: "Kongstrup, Kongstrup! " But he drove quickly on, the window closed, and the weeping began afresh.

In the afternoon Pelle was busying himself about the lower yard when Karna came to him and told him to go up to mistress. Pelle went up hesitatingly. He was not sure of her and all the men were out in the fields.

Fru Kongstrup lay upon the sofa in her husband's study, which she always occupied, day or night, when her husband was out. She had a wet towel over her forehead, and her whole face was red with weeping.

"Come here! " she said, in a low voice. "You aren't afraid of me, are you? "

Pelle had to go up to her and sit on the chair beside her. He did not know what to do with his eyes; and his nose began to run with the excitement, and he had no pocket-handkerchief.

"Are you afraid of me? " she asked again, and a bitter smile crossed her lips.

He had to look at her to show that he was not afraid, and to tell the truth, she was not like a witch at all, but only like a human being who cried and was unhappy.

"Come here! " she said, and she wiped his nose with her own fine handkerchief, and stroked his hair. "You haven't even a mother, poor little thing! " And she smoothed down his clumsily mended blouse.

"It's three years now since Mother Bengta died, and she's lying in the west corner of the churchyard. "

"Do you miss her very much? "

"Oh, well, Father Lasse mends my clothes! "

"I'm sure she can't have been very good to you. "

"Oh, yes! " said Pelle, nodding earnestly. "But she was so fretful, she was always ailing; and it's better they should go when they get like that. But now we're soon going to get married again—when Father Lasse's found somebody that'll do. "

"And then I suppose you'll go away from here? I'm sure you aren't comfortable here, are you? "

Pelle had found his tongue, but now feared a trap, and became dumb. He only nodded. Nobody should come and accuse him afterward of having complained.

"No, you aren't comfortable, " she said, in a plaintive tone. "No one is comfortable at Stone Farm. Everything turns to misfortune here. "

"It's an old curse, that! " said Pelle.

"Do they say so? Yes, yes, I know they do! And they say of me that I'm a devil—only because I love a single man—and cannot put up with being trampled on. " She wept and pressed his hand against her quivering face.

"I've got to go out and move the cows, " said Pelle, wriggling about uneasily in an endeavor to get away.

"Now you're afraid of me again! " she said, and tried to smile. It was like a gleam of sunshine after rain.

"No—only I've got to go out and move the cows. "

"There's still a whole hour before that. But why aren't you herding to-day? Is your father ill? "

Then Pelle had to tell her about the bull.

"You're a good boy! " said the mistress, patting his head. "If I had a son, I should like him to be like you. But now you shall have some jam, and then you must run to the shop for a bottle of black-currant rum, so that we can make a hot drink for your father. If you hurry, you can be back before moving-time. "

Lasse had his hot drink, even before the boy returned; and every day while he kept his bed he had something strengthening—although there was no black-currant rum in it.

During this time Pelle went up to the mistress nearly every day. Kongstrup had gone on business to Copenhagen. She was kind to him and gave him nice things to eat; and while he ate, she talked without ceasing about Kongstrup, or asked him what people thought about her. Pelle had to tell her, and then she was upset and began to cry. There was no end to her talk about the farmer, but she contradicted herself, and Pelle gave up trying to make anything of it. Besides, the good things she gave him were quite enough for him to think about.

Down in their room he repeated everything word for word, and Lasse lay and listened, and wondered at this little fellow who had the run of high places, and was in the mistress's confidence. Still he did not quite like it.

"... She could scarcely stand, and had to hold on to the table when she was going to fetch me the biscuits, she was so ill. It was only because he'd treated her badly, she said. Do you know she hates him, and would like to kill him, she says; and yet she says that he's the handsomest man in the world, and asked me if I've seen any one handsomer in all Sweden. And then she cries as if she was mad. "

"Does she? " said Lasse thoughtfully. "I don't suppose she knows what she's saying, or else she says it for reasons of her own. But all the same, it's not true that he beats her! She's telling a lie, I'm sure. "

"And why should she lie? "

"Because she wants to do him harm, I suppose. But it's true he's a fine man—and cares for everybody except just her; and that's the misfortune. I don't like your being so much up there; I'm so afraid you may come to some harm. "

"How could I? She's so good, so very good. "

"How am I to know that? No, she isn't good—her eyes aren't good, at any rate. She's brought more than one person into misfortune by looking at them. But there's nothing to be done about it; the poor man has to risk things. "

Lasse was silent, and stumbled about for a little while. Then he came up to Pelle. "Now, see here! Here's a piece of steel I've found, and you must remember always to have it about you, especially when you go up *there*! And then—yes, then we must leave the rest in God's hand. He's the only one who perhaps looks after poor little boys. "

Lasse was up for a short while that day. He was getting on quickly, thank God, and in two days they might be back in their old ways again. And next winter they must try to get away from it all!

On the last day that Pelle stayed at home, he went up to the mistress as usual, and ran her errand for her. And that day he saw something unpleasant that made him glad that this was over. She took her teeth, palate, and everything out of her mouth, and laid them on the table in front of her!

So she *was* a witch!

XIII

Pelle was coming home with his young cattle. As he came near the farm he issued his commands in a loud voice, so that his father might hear. "Hi! Spasianna! where are you going to? Dannebrog, you confounded old ram, will you turn round! " But Lasse did not come to open the gate of the enclosure.

When he had got the animals in, he ran into the cow-stable. His father was neither there nor in their room, and his Sunday wooden shoes and his woollen cap were gone. Then Pelle remembered that it was Saturday, and that probably the old man had gone to the shop to fetch spirits for the men.

Pelle went down into the servants' room to get his supper. The men had come home late, and were still sitting at the table, which was covered with spilt milk and potato-skins. They were engrossed in a wager; Erik undertook to eat twenty salt herrings with potatoes after he had finished his meal. The stakes were a bottle of spirits, and the others were to peel the potatoes for him.

Pelle got out his pocket-knife and peeled himself a pile of potatoes. He left the skin on the herring, but scraped it carefully and cut off the head and tail; then he cut it in pieces and ate it without taking out the bones, with the potatoes and the sauce. While he did so, he looked at Erik—the giant Erik, who was so strong and was not afraid of anything between heaven and earth. Erik had children all over the place! Erik could put his finger into the barrel of a gun, and hold the gun straight out at arm's length! Erik could drink as much as three others!

And now Erik was sitting and eating twenty salt herrings after his hunger was satisfied. He took the herring by the head, drew it once between his legs, and then ate it as it was; and he ate potatoes to them, quite as quickly as the others could peel them. In between whiles he swore because the bailiff had refused him permission to go out that evening; there was going to be the devil to pay about that: he'd teach them to keep Erik at home when he wanted to go out!

Pelle quickly swallowed his herring and porridge, and set off again to run to meet his father; he was longing immensely to see him. Out at the pump the girls were busy scouring the milkpails and kitchen pans; and Gustav was standing in the lower yard with his arms on the fence, talking to them. He was really watching Bodil, whose eyes were always following the new pupil, who was strutting up and down and showing off his long boots with patent-leather tops.

Pelle was stopped as he ran past, and set to pump water. The men now came up and went across to the barn, perhaps to try their strength. Since Erik had come, they always tried their strength in their free time. There was nothing Pelle found so exciting as trials of strength, and he worked hard so as to get done and go over there.

Gustav, who was generally the most eager, continued to stand and vent his ill-nature upon the pupil.

"There must be money there! " said Bodil, thoughtfully.

"Yes, you should try him; perhaps you might become a farmer's wife. The bailiff won't anyhow; and the farmer—well, you saw the Sow the other day; it must be nice to have that in prospect. "

"Who told you that the bailiff won't? " answered Bodil sharply. "Don't imagine that we need you to hold the candle for us! Little children aren't allowed to see everything. "

Gustav turned red. "Oh, hold your jaw, you hussy! " he muttered, and sauntered down to the barn.

> "Oh, goodness gracious, my poor old mother,
> Who's up on deck and can't stand! "

sang Mons over at the stable door, where he was standing hammering at a cracked wooden shoe. Pelle and the girls were quarreling, and up in the attic the bailiff could be heard going about; he was busy putting pipes in order. Now and then a long-drawn sound came from the high house, like the distant howling of some animal, making the people shudder with dreariness.

A man dressed in his best clothes, and with a bundle under his arm, slipped out of the door from the men's rooms, and crept along by the building in the lower yard. It was Erik.

"Hi, there! Where the devil are you going? " thundered a voice from the bailiff's window. The man ducked his head a little and pretended not to hear. "Do you hear, you confounded Kabyle! *Erik*! " This time Erik turned and darted in at a barn-door.

Directly after the bailiff came down and went across the yard. In the chaff-cutting barn the men were standing laughing at Erik's bad luck. "He's a devil for keeping watch! " said Gustav. "You must be up early to get the better of *him*. "

"Oh, I'll manage to dish him! " said Erik. "I wasn't born yesterday. And if he doesn't mind his own business, we shall come to blows. "

There was a sudden silence as the bailiff's well-known step was heard upon the stone paving. Erik stole away.

The form of the bailiff filled the doorway. "Who sent Lasse for gin? " he asked sternly.

They looked at one another as if not understanding. "Is Lasse out? " asked Mons then, with the most innocent look in the world. "Ay, the old man's fond of spirits, " said Anders, in explanation.

"Oh, yes; you're good comrades! " said the bailiff. "First you make the old man go, and then you leave him in the lurch. You deserve a thrashing, all of you. "

"No, we don't deserve a thrashing, and don't mean to submit to one either, " said the head man, going a step forward. "Let me tell you—"

"Hold your tongue, man! " cried the bailiff, going close up to him, and Karl Johan drew back.

"Where's Erik? "

"He must be in his room. "

The bailiff went in through the horse-stable, something in his carriage showing that he was not altogether unprepared for an attack from behind. Erik was in bed, with the quilt drawn up to his eyes.

"What's the meaning of this? Are you ill? " asked the bailiff.

"Yes, I think I've caught cold, I'm shivering so. " He tried to make his teeth chatter.

"It isn't the rot, I hope? " said the bailiff sympathetically. "Let's look at you a little, poor fellow. " He whipped off the quilt. "Oho, so you're in bed with your best things on—and top-boots! It's your grave-clothes, perhaps? And I suppose you were going out to order a pauper's grave for yourself, weren't you? It's time we got you put underground, too; seems to me you're beginning to smell already! " He sniffed at him once or twice.

But Erik sprang out of bed as if shot by a spring, and stood erect close to him. "I'm not dead yet, and perhaps I don't smell any more than some other people! " he said, his eyes flashing and looking about for a weapon.

The bailiff felt his hot breath upon his face, and knew it would not do to draw back. He planted his fist in the man's stomach, so that he fell back upon the bed and gasped for breath; and then held him down with a hand upon his chest. He was burning with a desire to do more, to drive his fist into the face of this rascal, who grumbled whenever one's back was turned, and had to be driven to every little task. Here was all the servant-worry that embittered his existence — dissatisfaction with the fare, cantankerousness in work, threats of leaving when things were at their busiest—difficulties without end. Here was the slave of many years of worry and ignominy, and all he wanted was one little pretext—a blow from this big fellow who never used his strength for work, but only to take the lead in all disturbances.

But Erik lay quite still and looked at his enemy with watchful eye. "You may hit me, if you like. There is such a thing as a magistrate in the country, " he said, with irritating calm. The bailiff's muscles burned, but he was obliged to let the man go for fear of being summoned. "Then remember another time not to be fractious! " he said, letting go his hold, "or I'll show you that there is a magistrate. "

"When Lasse comes, send him up to me with the gin! " he said to the men as he passed through the barn.

"The devil we will! " said Mons, in an undertone.

Pelle had gone to meet his father. The old man had tasted the purchase, and was in good spirits. "There were seven men in the boat, and they were all called Ole except one, and he was called Ole Olsen! " he said solemnly, when he saw the boy. "Yes, wasn't it a strange thing, Pelle, boy, that they should every one of them be called Ole—except the one, of course; for his name was Ole Olsen. " Then he laughed, and nudged the boy mysteriously; and Pelle laughed too, for he liked to see his father in good spirits.

The men came up to them, and took the bottles from the herdsman. "He's been tasting it! " said Anders, holding the bottle up to the light. "Oh, the old drunkard! He's had a taste at the bottles. "

"No, the bottles must leak at the bottom! " said Lasse, whom the dram had made quite bold. "For I've done nothing but just smell. You've got to make sure, you know, that you get the genuine thing and not just water. "

They moved on down the enclosure, Gustav going in front and playing on his concertina. A kind of excited merriment reigned over the party. First one and then another would leap into the air as they went; they uttered short, shrill cries and disconnected oaths at random. The consciousness of the full bottles, Saturday evening with the day of rest in prospect, and above all the row with the bailiff, had roused their tempers.

They settled down below the cow-stable, in the grass close to the pond. The sun had long since gone down, but the evening sky was bright, and cast a flaming light upon their faces turned westward; while the white farms inland looked dazzling in the twilight.

Now the girls came sauntering over the grass, with their hands under their aprons, looking like silhouettes against the brilliant sky. They were humming a soft folk-song, and one by one sank on to the grass beside the men; the evening twilight was in their hearts, and made their figures and voices as soft as a caress. But the men's mood was not a gentle one, and they preferred the bottle.

Gustav walked about extemporizing on his concertina. He was looking for a place to sit down, and at last threw himself into Karna's lap, and began to play a dance. Erik was the first upon his feet. He led on account of his difference with the bailiff, and pulled Bengta up from the grass with a jerk. They danced a Swedish polka, and always at a certain place in the melody, he tossed her up into the air with a shout. She shrieked every time, and her heavy skirts stood out round her like the tail of a turkey-cock, so that every one could see how long it was till Sunday.

In the middle of a whirl he let go of her, so that she stumbled over the grass and fell. The bailiff's window was visible from where they sat, and a light patch had appeared at it. "He's staring! Lord, how he's staring! I say, can you see this? " Erik called out, holding up a gin-bottle. Then, as he drank: "Your health! Old Nick's health! He smells, the pig! Bah! " The others laughed, and the face at the window disappeared.

In between the dances they played, drank, and wrestled. Their actions became more and more wild, they uttered sudden yells that made the girls scream, threw themselves flat upon the ground in the middle of a dance, groaned as if they were dying, and sprang up again suddenly with wild gestures and kicked the legs of those nearest to them. Once or twice the bailiff sent the pupil to tell them to be quiet, but that only made the noise worse. "Tell him to go his own dog's errands! " Erik shouted after the pupil.

Lasse nudged Pelle and they gradually drew farther and farther away. "We'd better go to bed now, " Lasse said, when they had slipped away unnoticed. "One never knows what this may lead to. They all of them see red; I should think they'll soon begin to dance the dance of blood. Ah me, if I'd been young I wouldn't have stolen away like a thief; I'd have stayed and taken whatever might have come. There was a time when Lasse could put both hands on the ground and kick his man in the face with the heels of his boots so that he went down like a blade of grass; but that time's gone, and it's wisest to take care of one's self. This may end in the police and much more, not to mention the bailiff. They've been irritating him all the summer with that Erik at their head; but if once he gets downright angry, Erik may go home to his mother. "

Pelle wanted to stay up for a little and look at them. "If I creep along behind the fence and lie down—oh, do let me, father! " he begged.

"Eh, what a silly idea! They might treat you badly if they got hold of you. They're in the very worst of moods. Well, you must take the consequences, and for goodness' sake take care they don't see you! "

So Lasse went to bed, but Pelle crawled along on the ground behind the fence until he came close up to them and could see everything.

Gustav was still sitting on Karna's open lap and playing, and she was holding him fast in her arms. But Anders had put his arm around Bodil's waist. Gustav discovered it, and with an oath flung away his concertina, sending it rolling over the grass, and sprang up. The others threw themselves down in a circle on the grass, breathing hard. They expected something.

Gustav was like a savage dancing a war-dance. His mouth was open and his eyes bright and staring. He was the only man on the grass, and jumped up and down like a ball, hopped upon his heels, and kicked up his legs alternately to the height of his head, uttering a shrill cry with each kick. Then he shot up into the air, turning round as he did so, and came down on one heel and went on turning round like a top, making himself smaller and smaller as he turned, and then exploded in a leap and landed in the lap of Bodil, who threw her arms about him in delight.

In an instant Anders had both hands on his shoulders from behind, set his feet against his back, and sent him rolling over the grass. It all happened without a pause, and Gustav himself gave impetus to his course, rolling along in jolts like an uneven ball. But suddenly he stopped and rose to his feet with a bound, stared straight in front of him, turned round with a jerk, and moved slowly toward Anders. Anders rose quickly, pushed his cap on one side, clicked with his tongue, and advanced. Bodil spread herself out more comfortably on the ground, and looked proudly round the circle, eagerly noting the envy of the others.

The two antagonists stood face to face, feeling their way to a good grasp. They stroked one another affectionately, pinched one another in the side, and made little jesting remarks.

"My goodness me, how fat you are, brother! " This was Anders.

"And what breasts you've got! You might quite well be a woman, " answered Gustav, feeling Anders' chest. "Eeh, how soft you are! " Scorn gleamed in their faces, but their eyes followed every movement of their opponent. Each of them expected a sudden attack from the other.

The others lay stretched around them on the grass, and called out impatiently: "Have done with that and look sharp about it! "

The two men continued to stand and play as if they were afraid to really set to, or were spinning the thing out for its still greater enjoyment. But suddenly Gustav had seized Anders by the collar, thrown himself backward and flung Anders over his head. It was done so quickly that Anders got no hold of Gustav; but in swinging round he got a firm grasp of Gustav's hair, and they both fell on their backs with their heads together and their bodies stretched in opposite directions.

Anders had fallen heavily, and lay half unconscious, but without loosening his hold on Gustav's hair. Gustav twisted round and tried to get upon his feet, but could not free his head. Then he wriggled back into this position again as quickly as a cat, turned a backward somersault over his antagonist, and fell down upon him with his face toward the other's. Anders tried to raise his feet to receive him, but was too late.

Anders threw himself about in violent jerks, lay still and strained again with sudden strength to turn Gustav off, but Gustav held on. He let himself fall heavily upon his adversary, and sticking out his legs and arms to support him on the ground, raised himself suddenly and sat down again, catching Anders in the wind. All the time the thoughts of both were directed toward getting out their knives, and Anders, who had now fully recovered his senses, remembered distinctly that he had not got his. "Ah! " he said aloud. "What a fool I am! "

"You're whining, are you? " said Gustav, bending his face him. "Do you want to ask for mercy? "

At that moment Anders felt Gustav's knife pressing against his thigh, and in an instant had his hand down there and wrenched it free. Gustav tried to take it from him, but gave up the attempt for fear of being thrown off. He then confined himself to taking possession of one of Anders' hands, so that he could not open the knife, and began sitting upon him in the region of his stomach.

Anders lay in half surrender, and bore the blows without trying to defend himself, only gasping at each one. With his left hand he was working eagerly to get the knife opened against the ground, and suddenly plunged it into Gustav just as the latter had risen to let himself fall heavily upon his opponent's body.

Gustav seized Anders by the wrist, his face distorted. "What the devil are you up to now, you swine? " he said, spitting down into

Anders' face. "He's trying to sneak out by the back door! " he said, looking round the circle with a face wrinkled like that of a young bull.

They fought desperately for the knife, using hands and teeth and head; and when Gustav found that he could not get possession of the weapon, he set to work so to guide Anders' hand that he should plunge it into his own body. He succeeded, but the blow was not straight, and the blade closed upon Anders' fingers, making him throw the knife from him with an oath.

Meanwhile Erik was growing angry at no longer being the hero of the evening. "Will you soon be finished, you two cockerels, or must I have a bite too? " he said, trying to separate them. They took firm hold of one another, but then Erik grew angry, and did something for which he was ever after renowned. He took hold of them and set them both upon their feet.

Gustav looked as if he were going to throw himself into the battle again, and a sullen expression overspread his face; but then he began to sway like a tree chopped at the roots, and sank to the ground. Bodil was the first to come to his assistance. With a cry she ran to him and threw her arms about him.

He was carried in and laid upon his bed, Karl Johan poured spirit into the deep cut to clean it, and held it together while Bodil basted it with needle and thread from one of the men's lockers. Then they dispersed, in pairs, as friendship permitted, Bodil, however, remaining with Gustav. She was true to him after all.

* * * * *

Thus the summer passed, in continued war and friction with the bailiff, to whom, however, they dared do nothing when it came to the point. Then the disease struck inward, and they set upon one another. "It must come out somewhere, " said Lasse, who did not like this state of things, and vowed he would leave as soon as anything else offered, even if they had to run away from wages and clothes and everything.

"They're discontented with their wages, their working-hours are too long, and the food isn't good enough; they pitch it about and waste it until it makes one ill to see them, for anyhow it's God's gift, even if it might be better. And Erik's at the bottom of it all! He's forever boasting and bragging and stirring up the others the whole day long. But as soon as the bailiff is over him, he daren't do anything any more than the others; so they all creep into their holes. Father Lasse is not such a cowardly wind-bag as any of them, old though he is.

"I suppose a good conscience is the best support. If you have it and have done your duty, you can look both the bailiff and the farmer — and God the Father, too—in the face. For you must always remember, laddie, not to set yourself up against those that are placed over you. Some of us have to be servants and others masters; how would everything go on if we who work didn't do our duty? You can't expect the gentlefolk to scrape up the dung in the cow-stable. "

All this Lasse expounded after they had gone to bed, but Pelle had something better to do than to listen to it. He was sound asleep and dreaming that he was Erik himself, and was thrashing the bailiff with a big stick.

XIV

In Pelle's time, pickled herring was the Bronholmer's most important article of food. It was the regular breakfast dish in all classes of society, and in the lower classes it predominated at the supper- table too—and sometimes appeared at dinner in a slightly altered form. "It's a bad place for food, " people would say derisively of such-and-such a farm. "You only get herring there twenty-one times a week. "

When the elder was in flower, well-regulated people brought out their salt-boxes, according to old custom, and began to look out to sea; the herring is fattest then. From the sloping land, which nearly everywhere has a glimpse of the sea, people gazed out in the early summer mornings for the homeward-coming boats. The weather and the way the boats lay in the water were omens regarding the winter food. Then the report would come wandering up over the island, of large hauls and good bargains. The farmers drove to the town or the fishing-village with their largest wagons, and the herring-man worked his way up through the country from cottage to cottage with his horse, which was such a wretched animal that any one would have been legally justified in putting a bullet through its head.

In the morning, when Pelle opened the stable doors to the field, the mist lay in every hollow like a pale gray lake, and on the high land, where the smoke rose briskly from houses and farms, he saw men and women coming round the gable-ends, half-dressed, or in shirt or chemise only, gazing out to sea. He himself ran round the out-houses and peered out toward the sea which lay as white as silver and took its colors from the day. The red sails were hanging motionless, and looked like splashes of blood in the brightness of day; the boats lay deep in the water, and were slowly making their way homeward in response to the beat of the oars, dragging themselves along like cows that are near their time for bearing.

But all this had nothing to do with him and his. Stone Farm, like the poor of the parish, did not buy its herring until after the autumn, when it was as dry as sticks and cost almost nothing. At that time of year, herring was generally plentiful, and was sold for from twopence to twopence-halfpenny the fourscore as long as the demand continued. After that it was sold by the cartload as food for the pigs, or went on to the dungheap.

One Sunday morning late in the autumn, a messenger came running from the town to Stone Farm to say that now herring was to be had. The bailiff came down into the servants' room while they were at breakfast, and gave orders that all the working teams were to be harnessed. "Then you'll have to come too! " said Karl Johan to the two quarry drivers, who were married and lived up near the quarry, but came down for meals.

"No, our horses shan't come out of the stable for that! " said the drivers. "They and we drive only stone and nothing else. " They sat for a little while and indulged in sarcasms at the expense of certain people who had not even Sunday at their own disposal, and one of them, as he stretched himself in a particularly irritating way, said: "Well, I think I'll go home and have a nap. It's nice to be one's own master once a week, at any rate. " So they went home to wife and children, and kept Sunday holiday.

For a little while the men went about complaining; that was the regular thing. In itself they had no objection to make to the expedition, for it would naturally be something of a festivity. There were taverns enough in the town, and they would take care to arrange about that herring so that they did not get home much before evening. If the worst came to the worst, Erik could damage his cart in driving, and then they would be obliged to stay in town while it was being mended.

They stood out in the stable, and turned their purses inside out — big, solid, leather purses with steel locks that could only be opened by pressure on a secret mechanism; but they were empty.

"The deuce! " said Mons, peering disappointedly into his purse. "Not so much as the smell of a one-ore! There must be a leak! " He examined the seams, held it close up to his eyes, and at last put his ear to it. "Upon my word, I seem to hear a two-krone talking to itself. It must be witchcraft! " He sighed and put his purse into his pocket.

"You, you poor devil! " said Anders. "Have you ever spoken to a two-krone? No, I'm the man for you! " He hauled out a large purse. "I've still got the ten-krone that the bailiff cheated me out of on May Day, but I haven't the heart to use it; I'm going to keep it until I grow old. " He put his hand into the empty purse and pretended to take something out and show it. The others laughed and joked, and all were in good spirits with the thought of the trip to town.

"But Erik's sure to have some money at the bottom of his chest! " said one. "He works for good wages and has a rich aunt down below. "

"No, indeed! " whined Erik. "Why, I have to pay for half a score of young brats who can't father themselves upon any one else. But Karl Johan must get it, or what's the good of being head man? "

"That's no use, " said Karl Johan doubtfully. "If I ask the bailiff for an advance now when we're going to town, he'll say 'no' straight out. I wonder whether the girls haven't wages lying by. "

They were just coming up from the cow-stable with their milk-pails.

"I say, girls, " Erik called out to them. "Can't one of you lend us ten krones? She shall have twins for it next Easter; the sow farrows then anyhow. "

"You're a nice one to make promises! " said Bengta, standing still, and they all set down their milk-pails and talked it over. "I wonder whether Bodil hasn't? " said Karna. "No, " answered Maria, "for she sent the ten krones she had by her to her mother the other day. "

Mons dashed his cap to the floor and gave a leap. "I'll go up to the Old Gentleman himself, " he said.

"Then you'll come head first down the stairs, you may be sure! "

"The deuce I will, with my old mother lying seriously ill in the town, without a copper to pay for doctor or medicine! I'm as good a child as Bodil, I hope. " He turned and went toward the stone steps, and the others stood and watched him from the stable-door, until the bailiff came and they had to busy themselves with the carts. Gustav walked about in his Sunday clothes with a bundle under his arm, and looked on.

"Why don't you get to work? " asked the bailiff. "Get your horses put in. "

"You said yourself I might be free to-day, " said Gustav, making a grimace. He was going out with Bodil.

"Ah, so I did! But that'll be one cart less. You must have a holiday another day instead. "

"I can't do that. "

"What the dee—And why not, may I ask? "

"Well, because you gave me a holiday to-day. "

"Yes; but, confound it, man, when I now tell you you can take another day instead! "

"No, I can't do that. "

"But why not, man? Is there anything pressing you want to do? "

"No, but I have been given a holiday to-day. " It looked as if Gustav were grinning slyly, but it was only that he was turning the quid in his mouth. The bailiff stamped with anger.

"But I can go altogether if you don't care to see me, " said Gustav gently.

The bailiff did not hear, but turned quickly. Experience had taught him to be deaf to that kind of offer in the busy season. He looked up at his window as if he had suddenly thought of something, and sprang up the stairs. They could manage him when they touched upon that theme, but his turn came in the winter, and then they had to keep silence and put up with things, so as to keep a roof over their heads during the slack time.

Gustav went on strutting about with his bundle, without putting his hand to anything. The others laughed at him encouragingly.

The bailiff came down again and went up to him. "Then put in the horses before you go, " he said shortly, "and I'll drive yours. "

An angry growl passed from man to man. "We're to have the dog with us! " they said in undertones to one another, and then, so that the bailiff should hear: "Where's the dog? We're to have the dog with us. "

Matters were not improved by Mons coming down the steps with a beautifully pious expression, and holding a ten-krone note over his chest. "It's all one now, " said Erik; "for we've got to have the dog with us! " Mons' face underwent a sudden change, and he began to swear. They pulled the carts about without getting anything done, and their eyes gleamed with anger.

The bailiff came out upon the steps with his overcoat on. "Look sharp about getting the horses in! " he thundered.

The men of Stone Farm were just as strict about their order of precedence as the real inhabitants of the island, and it was just as complicated. The head man sat at the top of the table and helped himself first, he went first in mowing and reaping, and had the first girl to lay the load when the hay was taken in; he was the first man up, and went first when they set out for the fields, and no one might throw down his tools until he had done so. After him came the second man, the third, and so on, and lastly the day- laborers. When no great personal preference interfered, the head man was as a matter of course the sweetheart of the head girl, and so on downwards; and if one of them left, his successor took over the relation: it was a question of equilibrium. In this, however, the order of precedence was often broken, but never in the matter of the horses. Gustav's horses were the poorest, and no power in the world would have induced the head man or Erik to drive them, let alone the farmer himself.

The bailiff knew it, and saw how the men were enjoying themselves when Gustav's nags were put in. He concealed his irritation, but when they exultantly placed Gustav's cart hindmost in the row, it was too much for him, and he ordered it to be driven in front of the others.

"My horses aren't accustomed to go behind the tail-pullers! " said Karl Johan, throwing down his reins. It was the nickname for the last in the row. The others stood trying not to smile, and the bailiff was almost boiling over.

"If you're so bent upon being first, be it by all means, " he said quietly. "I can very well drive behind you. "

"No, my horses come after the head man's, not after the tail-puller's, " said Erik.

This was really a term of abuse in the way in which they used it, one after the other, with covert glances. If he was going to put up with this from the whole row, his position on the farm would be untenable.

"Yes, and mine go behind Erik's, " began Anders now, "not after— after Gustav's, " he corrected himself quickly, for the bailiff had fixed his eyes upon him, and taken a step forward to knock him down.

The bailiff stood silent for a moment as if listening, the muscles of his arms quivering. Then he sprang into the cart.

"You're all out of your senses to-day, " he said. "But now I'm going to drive first, and the man who dares to say a word against it shall have one between the eyes that will send him five days into next week! " So saying he swung out of the row, and Erik's horses, which wanted to turn, received a cut from his whip that made them rear. Erik stormed at them.

The men went about crestfallen, and gave the bailiff time to get well ahead. "Well, I suppose we'd better see about starting now, " said Karl Johan at length, as he got into his wagon. The bailiff was already some way ahead; Gustav's nags were doing their very best to-day, and seemed to like being in front. But Karl Johan's horses were displeased, and hurried on; they did not approve of the new arrangement.

At the village shop they made a halt, and consoled themselves a little. When they started again, Karl Johan's horses were refractory, and had to be quieted.

The report of the catch had spread through the country, and carts from other farms caught them up or crossed them on their way to the fishing-villages. Those who lived nearer the town were already on their way home with swaying loads. "Shall we Meet in the town for a drink? " cried one man to Karl Johan as he passed. "I'm coming in for another load. "

"No, we're driving for the master to-day! " answered Karl Johan, pointing to the bailiff in front.

"Yes, I see him. He's driving a fine pair to-day! I thought it was King Lazarus! "

An acquaintance of Karl Johan's came toward them with a swaying load of herring. He was the only man on one of the small farms. "So you've been to the town too for winter food, " said Karl Johan, reining in his horse.

"Yes, for the pigs! " answered the other. "It was laid in for the rest of us at the end of the summer. This isn't food for men! " And he took up a herring between his fingers, and pretended to break it in two.

"No, I suppose not for such fine gentlemen, " answered Karl Johan snappishly. "Of course, you're in such a high station that you eat at the same table as your master and mistress, I've heard. "

"Yes, that's the regular custom at our place, " answered the other. "We know nothing about masters and dogs. " And he drove on. The words rankled with Karl Johan, he could not help drawing comparisons.

They had caught up the bailiff, and now the horses became unruly. They kept trying to pass and took every unlooked-for opportunity of pushing on, so that Karl Johan nearly drove his team into the back of the bailiff's cart. At last he grew tired of holding them in, and gave them the rein, when they pushed out over the border of the ditch and on in front of Gustav's team, danced about a little on the high-road, and then became quiet. Now it was Erik's horses that were mad.

At the farm all the laborers' wives had been called in for the afternoon, the young cattle were in the enclosure, and Pelle ran from cottage to cottage with the message. He was to help the women together with Lasse, and was delighted with this break in the daily routine; it was a whole holiday for him.

At dinner-time the men came home with their heavy loads of herring, which were turned out upon the stone paving round the pump in the upper yard. There had been no opportunity for them to enjoy themselves in the town, and they were in a bad temper. Only Mons, the ape, went about grinning all over his face. He had been up to his sick mother with the money for the doctor and medicine, and came back at the last minute with a bundle under his arm in the best of spirits. "That was a medicine! " he said over and over again, smacking his lips, "a mighty strong medicine. "

He had had a hard time with the bailiff before he got leave to go on his errand. The bailiff was a suspicious man, but it was difficult to hold out against Mons' trembling voice when he urged that it would be too hard on a poor man to deny him the right to help his sick mother. "Besides, she lives close by here, and perhaps I shall never see her again in this life, " said Mons mournfully. "And then there's the money that the master advanced me for it. Shall I go and throw it away on drink, while she's lying there without enough to buy bread with? "

"Well, how was your mother? " asked the bailiff, when Mons came hurrying up at the last moment.

"Oh, she can't last much longer! " said Mons, with a quiver in his voice. But he was beaming all over his face.

The others threw him angry glances while they unloaded the herring. They would have liked to thrash him for his infernal good luck. But they recovered when they got into their room and he undid the bundle. "That's to you all from my sick mother! " he said, and drew forth a keg of spirits. "And I was to give you her best respects, and thank you for being so good to her little son. "

"Where did you go? " asked Erik.

"I sat in the tavern on the harbor hill all the time, so as to keep an eye on you; I couldn't resist looking at you, you looked so delightfully thirsty. I wonder you didn't lie down flat and drink out of the sea, every man Jack of you! "

In the afternoon the cottagers' wives and the farm-girls sat round the great heaps of herring by the pump, and cleaned the fish. Lasse and Pelle pumped water to rinse them in, and cleaned out the big salt-barrels that the men rolled up from the cellar; and two of the elder women were entrusted with the task of mixing. The bailiff walked up and down by the front steps and smoked his pipe.

As a general rule, the herring-pickling came under the category of pleasant work, but to-day there was dissatisfaction all along the line. The women chattered freely as they worked, but their talk was not quite innocuous—it was all carefully aimed; the men had made them malicious. When they laughed, there was the sound of a hidden meaning in their laughter. The men had to be called out and given orders about every single thing that had to be done; they went about it sullenly, and then at once withdrew to their rooms. But when there they were all the gayer, and sang and enjoyed themselves.

"They're doing themselves proud in there, " said Lasse, with a sigh to Pelle. "They've got a whole keg of spirits that Mons had hidden in his herring. They say it's so extra uncommon good. " Lasse had not tasted it himself.

The two kept out of the wrangling; they felt themselves too weak. The girls had not had the courage to refuse the extra Sunday work, but they were not afraid to pass little remarks, and tittered at nothing, to make the bailiff think it was at him. They kept on asking in a loud voice what the time was, or stopped working to listen to the ever-increasing gaiety in the men's rooms. Now and then a man was thrown out from there into the yard, and shuffled in again, shamefaced and grinning.

One by one the men came sauntering out. They had their caps on the back of their heads now, and their gaze was fixed. They took up a position in the lower yard, and hung over the fence, looking at the girls, every now and then bursting into a laugh and stopping suddenly, with a frightened glance at the bailiff.

The bailiff was walking up and down by the steps. He had laid aside his pipe and become calmer; and when the men came out, he was cracking a whip and exercising himself in self-restraint.

"If I liked I could bend him until both ends met! " he heard Erik say aloud in the middle of a conversation. The bailiff earnestly wished that Erik would make the attempt. His muscles were burning under this unsatisfied desire to let himself go; but his brain was reveling in visions of fights, he was grappling with the whole flock and going through all the details of the battle. He had gone through these battles so often, especially of late; he had thought out all the difficult situations, and there was not a place in all Stone Farm in which the things that would serve as weapons were not known to him.

"What's the time? " asked one of the girls aloud for at least the twentieth time.

"A little longer than your chemise, " answered Erik promptly.

The girls laughed. "Oh, nonsense! Tell us what it really is! " exclaimed another.

"A quarter to the miller's girl, " answered Anders.

"Oh, what fools you are! Can't you answer properly? You, Karl Johan! "

"It's short! " said Karl Johan gravely.

"No, seriously now, I'll tell you what it is, " exclaimed Mons innocently, drawing a great "turnip" out of his pocket. "It's—" he looked carefully at the watch, and moved his lips as if calculating. "The deuce! " he exclaimed, bringing down his hand in amazement on the fence. "Why, it's exactly the same time as it was this time yesterday. "

The jest was an old one, but the women screamed with laughter; for Mons was the jester.

"Never mind about the time, " said the bailiff, coming up. "But try and get through your work. "

"No, time's for tailors and shoemakers, not for honest people! " said Anders in an undertone.

The bailiff turned upon him as quick as a cat, and Anders' arm darted up above his head bent as if to ward off a blow. The bailiff merely expectorated with a scornful smile, and began his pacing up and down afresh, and Anders stood there, red to the roots of his hair, and not knowing what to do with his eyes. He scratched the back of his head once or twice, but that could not explain away that strange movement of his arm. The others were laughing at him, so he hitched up his trousers and sauntered down toward the men's rooms, while the women screamed with laughter, and the men laid their heads upon the fence and shook with merriment.

So the day passed, with endless ill-natured jesting and spitefulness. In the evening the men wandered out to indulge in horse-play on the high-road and annoy the passersby. Lasse and Pelle were tired, and went early to bed.

"Thank God we've got through this day! " said Lasse, when he had got into bed. "It's been a regular bad day. It's a miracle that no blood's been shed; there was a time when the bailiff looked as if he might do anything. But Erik must know far he can venture. "

Next morning everything seemed to be forgotten. The men attended to the horses as usual, and at six o'clock went out into the field for a third mowing of clover. They looked blear-eyed, heavy and dull. The keg lay outside the stable-door empty; and as they went past they kicked it.

Pelle helped with the herring to-day too, but he no longer found it amusing. He was longing already to be out in the open with his cattle; and here he had to be at everybody's beck and call. As often as he dared, he made some pretext for going outside the farm, for that helped to make the time pass.

Later in the morning, while the men were mowing the thin clover, Erik flung down his scythe so that it rebounded with a ringing sound from the swaths. The others stopped their work.

"What's the matter with you, Erik? " asked Karl Johan. "Have you got a bee in your bonnet? "

Erik stood with his knife in his hand, feeling its edge, and neither heard nor saw. Then he turned up his face and frowned at the sky; his eyes seemed to have sunk into his head and become blind, and his lips stood out thick. He muttered a few inarticulate sounds, and started up toward the farm.

The others stood still and followed him with staring eyes; then one after another they threw down their scythes and moved away, only Karl Johan remaining where he was.

Pelle had just come out to the enclosure to see that none of the young cattle had broken their way out. "When he saw the men coming up toward the farm in a straggling file like a herd of cattle on the move, he suspected something was wrong and ran in.

"The men are coming up as fast as they can, father! " he whispered.

"They're surely not going to do it? " said Lasse, beginning to tremble.

The bailiff was carrying things from his room down to the pony-carriage; he was going to drive to the town. He had his arms full when Erik appeared at the big, open gate below, with distorted face and a large, broad-bladed knife in his hand. "Where the devil is he? " he said aloud, and circled round once with bent head, like an angry bull, and then walked up through the fence straight toward the bailiff. The latter started when he saw him and, through the gate, the others coming up full speed behind him. He measured the distance to the steps, but changed his mind, and advanced toward Erik, keeping behind the wagon and watching every movement that Erik made, while he tried to find a weapon. Erik followed him round the wagon, grinding his teeth and turning his eyes obliquely up at his opponent.

The bailiff went round and round the wagon and made half movements; he could not decide what to do. But then the others came up and blocked his way. His face turned white with fear, and he tore a whiffletree from the wagon, which with a push he sent rolling into the thick of them, so that they fell back in confusion. This made an open space between him and Erik, and Erik sprang quickly over the pole, with his knife ready to strike; but as he sprang, the whiffletree descended upon his head. The knife-thrust fell upon the bailiff's shoulder, but it was feeble, and the knife just grazed his side as Erik sank to the ground. The others stood staring in bewilderment.

"Carry him down to the mangling-cellar! " cried the bailiff in a commanding tone, and the men dropped their knives and obeyed.

The battle had stirred Pelle's blood into a tumult, and he was standing by the pump, jumping up and down. Lasse had to take a firm hold of him, for it looked as if he would throw himself into the fight. Then when the great strong Erik sank to the ground insensible from a blow on the head, he began to jump as if he had St. Vitus's Dance. He jumped into the air with drooping head, and let himself fall heavily, all the time uttering short, shrill bursts of laughter. Lasse spoke to him angrily, thinking it was unnecessarily foolish behavior on his part; and then he picked him up and held him firmly in his hands, while the little fellow trembled all over his body in his efforts to free himself and go on with his jumping.

"What can be wrong with him? " said Lasse tearfully to the cottagers' wives. "Oh dear, what shall I do? " He carried him down to their room in a sad state of mind, because the moon was waning, and it would never pass off!

Down in the mangling-cellar they were busy with Erik, pouring brandy into his mouth and bathing his head with vinegar. Kongstrup was not at home, but the mistress herself was down there, wringing her hands and cursing Stone Farm—her own childhood's home! Stone Farm had become a hell with its murder and debauchery! she said, without caring that they were all standing round her and heard every word.

The bailiff had driven quickly off in the pony-carriage to fetch a doctor and to report what he had done in defence of his life. The women stood round the pump and gossiped, while the men and girls wandered about in confusion; there was no one to issue orders. But then the mistress came out on to the steps and looked at them for a little, and they all found something to do. Hers were piercing eyes! The old women shook themselves and went back to their work. It reminded them so pleasantly of old times, when the master of the Stone Farm of their youth rushed up with anger in his eyes when they were idling.

Down in their room, Lasse sat watching Pelle, who lay talking and laughing in delirium, so that his father hardly knew whether to laugh or to cry.

XV

"She must have had right on her side, for he never said a cross word when she started off with her complaints and reproaches, and them so loud that you could hear them right through the walls and down in the servants' room and all over the farm. But it was stupid of her all the same, for she only drove him distracted and sent him away. And how will it go with a farm in the long run, when the farmer spends all his time on the high-roads because he can't stay at home? It's a poor sort of affection that drives the man away from his home. "

Lasse was standing in the stable on Sunday evening talking to the women about it while they milked. Pelle was there too, busy with his own affairs, but listening to what was said.

"But she wasn't altogether stupid either, " said Thatcher Holm's wife. "For instance when she had Fair Maria in to do housemaid's work, so that he could have a pretty face to look at at home. She knew that if you have food at home you don't go out for it. But of course it all led to nothing when she couldn't leave off frightening him out of the house with her crying and her drinking. "

"I'm sure he drinks too! " said Pelle shortly.

"Yes, of course he gets drunk now and then, " said Lasse in a reproving tone. "But he's a man, you see, and may have his reasons besides. But it's ill when a woman takes to drinking. " Lasse was cross. The boy was beginning to have opinions of his own pretty well on everything, and was always joining in when grown people were talking.

"I maintain"—he went on, turning again to the women—"that he'd be a good husband, if only he wasn't worried with crying and a bad conscience. Things go very well too when he's away. He's at home pretty well every day, and looks after things himself, so that the bailiff's quite upset, for *he* likes to be king of the castle. To all of us, the master's like one of ourselves; he's even forgotten the grudge he had against Gustav. "

"There can't be very much to bear him a grudge for, unless it is that he'll get a wife with money. They say Bodil's saved more than a hundred krones from her two or three months as housemaid. Some people can—they get paid for what the rest of us have always had to do for nothing. " It was one of the old women who spoke.

"Well, we'll just see whether he ever gets her for a wife. I doubt it myself. One oughtn't to speak evil of one's fellow-servant, but Bodil's not a faithful girl. That matter with the master must go for what it was—as I once said to Gustav when he was raging about it; the master comes before his men! Bengta was a good wife to me in every way, but she too was very fond of laying herself out for the landlord at home. The greatest take first; that's the way of the world! But Bodil's never of the same mind for long together. Now she's carrying on with the pupil, though he's not sixteen yet, and takes presents from him. Gustav should get out of it in time; it always leads to misfortune when love gets into a person. We've got an example of that at the farm here. "

"I was talking to some one the other day who thought that the mistress hadn't gone to Copenhagen at all, but was with relations in the south. She's run away from him, you'll see! "

"That's the genteel thing to do nowadays, it seems! " said Lasse. "If only she'll stay away! Things are much better as they are. "

* * * * *

An altogether different atmosphere seemed to fill Stone Farm. The dismal feeling was gone; no wailing tones came from the house and settled upon one like horse flies and black care. The change was most apparent in the farmer. He looked ten or twenty years younger, and joked good-humoredly like one freed from chains and fetters. He took an interest in the work of the farm, drove to the quarry two or three times a day in his gig, was present whenever a new piece of work was started, and would often throw off his coat and take a hand in it. Fair Maria laid his table and made his bed, and he was not afraid of showing his kindness for her. His good humor was infectious and made everything pleasanter.

But it could not be denied that Lasse had his own burden to bear. His anxiety to get married grew greater with the arrival of very cold weather as early as December; he longed to have his feet under his own table, and have a woman to himself who should be everything to him. He had not entirely given up thoughts of Karna yet, but he had promised Thatcher Holm's wife ten krones down if she could find some one that would do for him.

He had really put the whole matter out of his head as an impossibility, and had passed into the land of old age; but what was the use of shutting yourself in, when you were all the time looking for doors through which to slip out again? Lasse looked out once more, and as usual it was Pelle who brought life and joy to the house.

Down in the outskirts of the fishing-village there lived a woman, whose husband had gone to sea and had not been heard of for a good many years. Two or three times on his way to and from school, Pelle had sought shelter from the weather in her porch, and they had gradually become good friends; he performed little services for her, and received a cup of hot coffee in return. When the cold was very bitter, she always called him in; and then she would tell him about the sea and about her good-for-nothing husband, who kept away and left her to toil for her living by mending nets for the fishermen. In return Pelle felt bound to tell her about Father Lasse, and Mother Bengta who lay at home in the churchyard at Tommelilla. The talk never came to much more, for she always returned to her husband who had gone away and left her a widow.

"I suppose he's drowned, " Pelle would say.

"No, he isn't, for I've had no warning, " she answered decidedly, always in the same words.

Pelle repeated it all to his father, who was very much interested. "Well, did you run in to Madam Olsen to-day? " was the first thing he said when the boy came in from school; and then Pelle had to tell him every detail several times over. It could never be too circumstantially told for Lasse.

"You've told her, I suppose, that Mother Bengta's dead? Yes, of course you have! Well, what did she ask about me to-day? Does she know about the legacy? " (Lasse had recently had twenty-five krones left him by an uncle.) "You might very well let fall a word or two about that, so that she shouldn't think we're quite paupers. "

Pelle was the bearer of ambiguous messages backward and forward. From Lasse he took little things in return for her kindness to himself, such as embroidered handkerchiefs and a fine silk kerchief, the last remnants of Mother Bengta's effects. It would be hard to lose them if this new chance failed, for then there would be no memories to fall back upon. But Lasse staked everything upon one card.

One day Pelle brought word that warning had come to Madam Olsen. She had been awakened in the night by a big black dog that stood gasping at the head of her bed. Its eyes shone in the darkness, and she heard the water dripping from its fur. She understood that it must be the ship's dog with a message for her, and went to the window; and out in the moonlight on the sea she saw a ship sailing with all sail set. She stood high, and you could see the sea and sky right through her. Over the bulwark hung her husband and the others, and they were transparent; and the salt water was dripping from their hair and beards and running down the side of the ship.

In the evening Lasse put on his best clothes.

"Are we going out this evening? " asked Pelle in glad surprise.

"No—well, that's to say I am, just a little errand. If any one asks after me, you must say that I've gone to the smith about a new nose-ring for the bull. "

"And mayn't I go with you? " asked Pelle on the verge of tears.

"No, you must be good and stay at home for this once. Lasse patted him on the head.

"Where are you going then? "

"I'm going—" Lasse was about to make up a lie about it, but had not the heart to do it. "You mustn't ask me! " he said.

"Shall I know another day, then, without asking? "

"Yes, you shall, for certain—sure! "

Lasse went out, but came back again. Pelle was sitting on the edge of the bed, crying; it was the first time Father Lasse had gone out without taking him with him.

"Now you must be a good boy and go to bed, " he said gravely. "Or else I shall stay at home with you; but if I do, it may spoil things for us both. "

So Pelle thought better of it and began to undress; and at last Lasse got off.

When Lasse reached Madam Olsen's house, it was shut up and in darkness. He recognized it easily from Pelle's descriptions, and walked round it two or three times to see how the walls stood. Both timber and plaster looked good, and there was a fair-sized piece of ground belonging to it, just big enough to allow of its being attended to on Sundays, so that one could work for a daily wage on weekdays.

Lasse knocked at the door, and a little while after a white form appeared at the window, and asked who was there.

"It's Pelle's father, Lasse Karlsson, " said Lasse, stepping out into the moonlight.

The door was unbolted, and a soft voice said: "Come inside! Don't stand out there in the cold! " and Lasse stepped over the threshold. There was a smell of sleep in the room, and Lasse had an idea where the alcove was, but could see nothing. He heard the breathing as of a stout person drawing on stockings. Then she struck a match and lighted the lamp.

They shook hands, and looked at one another as they did so. She wore a skirt of striped bed-ticking, which kept her night-jacket together, and had a blue night-cap on her head. She had strong-looking limbs and a good bust, and her face gave a good impression. She was the kind of woman that would not hurt a fly if she were not put upon; but she was not a toiler—she was too soft for that.

"So this is Pelle's father! " she said. "It's a young son you've got. But do sit down! "

Lasse blinked his eyes a little. He had been afraid that she would think him old.

"Yes, he's what you'd call a late-born child; but I'm still able to do a man's work in more ways than one. "

186

She laughed while she busied herself in placing on the table cold bacon and pork sausage, a dram, bread and a saucer of dripping. "But now you must eat! " she said. "That's what a man's known by. And you've come a long way. "

It only now occurred to Lasse that he must give some excuse for his visit. "I ought really to be going again at once. I only wanted to come down and thank you for your kindness to the boy. " He even got up as if to go.

"Oh, but what nonsense! " she exclaimed, pushing him down into his chair again. "It's very plain, but do take some. " She pressed the knife into his hand, and eagerly pushed the food in front of him. Her whole person radiated warmth and kind-heartedness as she stood close to him and attended to his wants; and Lasse enjoyed it all.

"You must have been a good wife to your husband, " he said.

"Yes, that's true enough! " she said, as she sat down and looked frankly at him. "He got all that he could want, and almost more, when he was on shore. He stayed in bed until dinner, and I looked after him like a little child; but he never gave me a hand's turn for it, and at last one gets tired. "

"That was wrong of him, " said Lasse; "for one good action deserves another. I don't think Bengta would have anything like that to say of me if she was asked. "

"Well, there's certainly plenty to do in a house, when there's a man that has the will to help. I've only one cow, of course, for I can't manage more; but two might very well be kept, and there's no debt on the place. "

"I'm only a poor devil compared to you! " said Lasse despondently. "Altogether I've got fifty krones, and we both have decent clothes to put on; but beyond that I've only got a pair of good hands. "

"And I'm sure that's worth a good deal! And I should fancy you're not afraid of fetching a pail of water or that sort of thing, are you? "

"No, I'm not. And I'm not afraid of a cup of coffee in bed on a Sunday morning, either. "

She laughed. "Then I suppose I ought to have a kiss! " she said.

"Yes, I suppose you ought, " said Lasse delighted, and kissed her. "And now we may hope for happiness and a blessing for all three of us. I know you're fond of the laddie. "

There still remained several things to discuss, there was coffee to be drunk, and Lasse had to see the cow and the way the house was arranged. In the meantime it had grown late.

"You'd better stay here for the night, " said Madam Olsen.

Lasse stood wavering. There was the boy sleeping alone, and he had to be at the farm by four o'clock; but it was cold outside, and here it was so warm and comfortable in every way.

"Yes, perhaps I'd better, " he said, laying down his hat and coat again.

* * * * *

When at about four he crept into the cow-stable from the back, the lantern was still burning in the herdsman's room. Lasse thought he was discovered, and began to tremble; it was a criminal and unjustifiable action to be away from the herd a whole night. But it was only Pelle, who lay huddled up upon the chest asleep, with his clothes on. His face was black and swollen with crying.

All that day there was something reserved, almost hostile, about Pelle's behavior, and Lasse suffered under it. There was nothing for it; he must speak out.

"It's all settled now, Pelle, " he said at last. "We're going to have a house and home, and a nice-looking mother into the bargain. It's Madam Olsen. Are you satisfied now? "

Pelle had nothing against it. "Then may I come with you next time? " he asked, still a little sullen.

"Yes, next time you shall go with me. I think it'll be on Sunday. We'll ask leave to go out early, and pay her a visit. " Lasse said this with a peculiar flourish; he had become more erect.

Pelle went with him on Sunday; they were free from the middle of the afternoon. But after that it would not have done to ask for leave very soon again. Pelle saw his future mother nearly every day, but it was more difficult for Lasse. When the longing to see his sweetheart came over him too strongly, he fussed over Pelle until the boy fell asleep, and then changed his clothes and stole out.

After a wakeful night such as one of these, he was not up to his work, and went about stumbling over his own feet; but his eyes shone with a youthful light, as if he had concluded a secret treaty with life's most powerful forces.

XVI

Erik was standing on the front steps, with stooping shoulders and face half turned toward the wall. He stationed himself there every morning at about four, and waited for the bailiff to come down. It was now six, and had just begun to grow light.

Lasse and Pelle had finished cleaning out the cow-stable and distributing the first feed, and they were hungry. They were standing at the door of the stable, waiting for the breakfast-bell to ring; and at the doors of the horse-stables, the men were doing the same. At a quarter-past the hour they went toward the basement, with Karl Johan at their head, and Lasse and Pelle also turned out and hurried to the servants' room, with every sign of a good appetite.

"Now, Erik, we're going down to breakfast! " shouted Karl Johan as they passed, and Erik came out of his corner by the steps, and shuffled along after them. There was nothing the matter with his digestive powers at any rate.

They ate their herring in silence; the food stopped their mouths completely. When they had finished, the head man knocked on the table with the handle of his knife, and Karna came in with two dishes of porridge and a pile of bread-and-dripping.

"Where's Bodil to-day? " asked Gustav.

"How should I know? Her bed was standing untouched this morning, " answered Karna, with an exulting look.

"It's a lie! " cried Gustav, bringing down his spoon with a bang upon the table.

"You can go into her room and see for yourself; you know the way! " said Karna tartly.

"And what's become of the pupil to-day, as he hasn't rung? " said Karl Johan. "Have any of you girls seen him? "

"No, I expect he's overslept himself, " cried Bengta from the wash-house. "And so he may! *I* don't want to run up and shake life into him every morning! "

"Don't you think you'd better go up and wake him, Gustav? " said Anders with a wink. "You might see something funny. " The others laughed a little.

"If I wake him, it'll be with this rabbit-skinner, " answered Gustav, exhibiting a large knife. "For then I think I should put him out of harm's way. "

At this point the farmer himself came down. He held a piece of paper in his hand, and appeared to be in high good humor. "Have you heard the latest news, good people? At dead of night Hans Peter has eloped with Bodil! "

"My word! Are the babes and sucklings beginning now? " exclaimed Lasse with self-assurance. "I shall have to look after Pelle there, and see that he doesn't run away with Karna. She's fond of young people. " Lasse felt himself to be the man of the company, and was not afraid of giving a hit at any one.

"Hans Peter is fifteen, " said Kongstrup reprovingly, "and passion rages in his heart. " He said this with such comical gravity that they all burst into laughter, except Gustav, who sat blinking his eyes and nodding his head like a drunken man.

"You shall hear what he says. This lay upon his bed. " Kongstrup held the paper out in a theatrical attitude and read:

"When you read this, I shall have gone forever. Bodil and I have agreed to run away to-night. My stern father will never give his consent to our union, and therefore we will enjoy the happiness of our love in a secret place where no one can find us. It will be doing a great wrong to look for us, for we have determined to die together rather than fall into the wicked hands of our enemies. I wet this paper with Bodil's and my own tears. But you must not condemn me for my last desperate step, as I can do nothing else for the sake of my great love.

"HANS PETER. "

"That fellow reads story-books, " said Karl Johan. "He'll do great things some day. "

"Yes, he knows exactly what's required for an elopement, " answered Kongstrup merrily. "Even to a ladder, which he's dragged up to the girl's window, although it's on a level with the ground. I wish he were only half as thorough in his agriculture. "

"What's to be done now? I suppose they must be searched for? " asked the head man.

"Well, I don't know. It's almost a shame to disturb their young happiness. They'll come of their own accord when they get hungry. What do you think, Gustav? Shall we organize a battue? "

Gustav made no answer, but rose abruptly and went across to the men's rooms. When the others followed him, they found him in bed.

All day he lay there and never uttered a syllable when any one came in to him. Meanwhile the work suffered, and the bailiff was angry. He did not at all like the new way Kongstrup was introducing—with liberty for every one to say and do exactly as they liked.

"Go in and pull Gustav out of bed! " he said, in the afternoon, when they were in the threshing-barn, winnowing grain. "And if he won't put his own clothes on, dress him by force. "

But Kongstrup, who was there himself, entering the weight, interfered. "No, if he's ill he must be allowed to keep his bed, " he said. "But it's our duty to do something to cure him. "

"How about a mustard-plaster? " suggested Mons, with a defiant glance at the bailiff.

Kongstrup rubbed his hands with delight. "Yes, that'll be splendid! " he said. "Go you across, Mons, and get the girls to make a mustard-plaster that we can stick on the pit of his stomach; that's where the pain is. "

When Mons came back with the plaster, they went up in a procession to put it on, the farmer himself leading. Kongstrup was well aware of the bailiff's angry looks, which plainly said, "Another waste of work for the sake of a foolish prank! " But he was inclined for a little fun, and the work would get done somehow.

Gustav had smelt a rat, for when they arrived he was dressed. For the rest of the day he did his work, but nothing could draw a smile out of him. He was like a man moonstruck.

A few days later a cart drove up to Stone Farm. In the driving-seat sat a broad-shouldered farmer in a fur coat, and beside him, wrapped up from head to foot, sat Hans Peter, while at the back, on the floor of the cart, lay the pretty Bodil on a little hay, shivering with cold. It was the pupil's father who had brought back the two fugitives, whom he had found in lodgings in the town.

Up in the office Hans Peter received a thrashing that could be heard, and was then let out into the yard, where he wandered about crying and ashamed, until he began to play with Pelle behind the cow-stable.

Bodil was treated more severely. It must have been the strange farmer who required that she should be instantly dismissed, for Kongstrup was not usually a hard man. She had to pack her things, and after dinner was driven away. She looked good and gentle as she always did; one would have thought she was a perfect angel—if one had not known better.

Next morning Gustav's bed was empty. He had vanished completely, with chest, wooden shoes and everything.

Lasse looked on at all this with a man's indulgent smile—children's tricks! All that was wanting now was that Karna should squeeze her fat body through the basement window one night, and she too disappear like smoke—on the hunt for Gustav.

This did not happen, however; and she became kindly disposed toward Lasse again, saw after his and Pelle's clothes, and tried to make them comfortable.

Lasse was not blind; he saw very well which way the wind blew, and enjoyed the consciousness of his power. There were now two that he could have whenever he pleased; he only had to stretch out his hand, and the women-folk snatched at it. He went about all day in a state of joyful intoxication, and there were days in which he was in such an elevated condition of mind that he had inward promptings to make use of his opportunity. He had always trodden his path in this world so sedately, done his duty and lived his life in such unwavering decency. Why should not he too for once let things go, and try to leap through the fiery hoops? There was a tempting development of power in the thought.

But the uprightness in him triumphed. He had always kept to the one, as the Scriptures commanded, and he would continue to do so. The other thing was only for the great—Abraham, of whom Pelle had begun to tell him, and Kongstrup. Pelle, too, must never be able to say anything against his father in that way; he must be clean in his child's eyes, and be able to look him in the face without shrinking. And then—well, the thought of how the two women would take it in the event of its being discovered, simply made Lasse blink his red eyes and hang his head.

* * * * *

Toward the middle of March, Fru Kongstrup returned unexpectedly. The farmer was getting along very comfortably without her, and her coming took him rather by surprise. Fair Maria was instantly turned out and sent down to the wash-house. Her not being sent away altogether was due to the fact that there was a shortage of maids at the farm now that Bodil had left. The mistress had brought a young relative with her, who was to keep her company and help her in the house.

They appeared to get on very well together. Kongstrup stayed at home upon the farm and was steady. The three drove out together, and the mistress was always hanging on his arm when they went about showing the place to the young lady. It was easy to see why she had come home; she could not live without him!

But Kongstrup did not seem to be nearly so pleased about it. He had put away his high spirits and retired into his shell once more. When he was going about like this, he often looked as if there was something invisible lying in ambush for him and he was afraid of being taken unawares.

This invisible something reached out after the others, too. Fru Kongstrup never interfered unkindly in anything, either directly or in a roundabout way; and yet everything became stricter. People no longer moved freely about the yard, but glanced up at the tall windows and hurried past. The atmosphere had once more that oppression about it that made one feel slack and upset and depressed.

Mystery once again hung heavy over the roof of Stone Farm. To many generations it had stood for prosperity or misfortune—these had been its foundations, and still it drew to itself the constant thoughts of many people. Dark things—terror, dreariness, vague suspicions of evil powers—gathered there naturally as in a churchyard.

And now it all centered round this woman, whose shadow was so heavy that everything brightened when she went away. Her unceasing, wailing protest against her wrongs spread darkness around and brought weariness with it. It was not even with the idea of submitting to the inevitable that she came back, but only to go on as before, with renewed strength. She could not do without him, but neither could she offer him anything good; she was like those beings who can live and breathe only in fire, and yet cry out when burnt. She writhed in the flames, and yet she herself fed them. Fair Maria was her own doing, and now she had brought this new relative into the house. Thus she herself made easy the path of his infidelity, and then shook the house above him with her complaining.

An affection such as this was not God's work; powers of evil had their abode in her.

XVII

Oh, how bitterly cold it was! Pelle was on his way to school, leaning, in a jog-trot, against the wind. At the big thorn Rud was standing waiting for him; he fell in, and they ran side by side like two blown nags, breathing hard and with heads hanging low. Their coat-collars were turned up about their ears, and their hands pushed into the tops of their trousers to share in the warmth of their bodies. The sleeves of Pelle's jacket were too short, and his wrists were blue with cold.

They said little, but only ran; the wind snatched the words from their mouths and filled them with hail. It was hard to get enough breath to run with, or to keep an eye open. Every other minute they had to stop and turn their back to the wind while they filled their lungs and breathed warm breath up over their faces to bring feeling into them. The worst part of it was the turning back, before they got quite up against the wind and into step again.

The four miles came to an end, and the boys turned into the village. Down here by the shore it was almost sheltered; the rough sea broke the wind. There was not much of the sea to be seen; what did appear here and there through the rifts in the squalls came on like a moving wall and broke with a roar into whitish green foam. The wind tore the top off the waves in ill-tempered snatches, and carried salt rain in over the land.

The master had not yet arrived. Up at his desk stood Nilen, busily picking its lock to get at a pipe that Fris had confiscated during lessons. "Here's your knife! " he cried, throwing a sheath-knife to Pelle, who quickly pocketed it. Some peasant boys were pouring coal into the stove, which was already red-hot; by the windows sat a crowd of girls, hearing one another in hymns. Outside the waves broke without ceasing, and when their roar sank for a moment, the shrill voices of boys rose into the air. All the boys of the village were on the beach, running in and out under the breakers that looked as if they would crush them, and pulling driftwood upon shore.

Pelle had hardly thawed himself when Nilen made him go out with him. Most of the boys were wet through, but they were laughing and panting with eagerness. One of them had brought in the name-board of a ship. *The Simplicity* was painted on it. They stood round it and wrangled about what kind of vessel it was and what was its home-port.

"Then the ship's gone down, " said Pelle gravely. The others did not answer; it was so self-evident.

"Well, " said a boy hesitatingly, "the name-board may have been torn away by the waves; it's only been nailed on. " They examined it carefully again; Pelle could not discover anything special about it.

"I rather think the crew have torn it off and thrown it into the sea. One of the nails has been pulled out, " said Nilen, nodding with an air of mystery.

"But why should they do that? " asked Pelle, with incredulity.

"Because they've killed the captain and taken over the command themselves, you ass! Then all they've got to do is to christen the ship again, and sail as pirates. " The other boys confirmed this with eyes that shone with the spirit of adventure; this one's father had told him about it, and that one's had even played a part in it. He did not want to, of course, but then he was tied to the mast while the mutiny was in progress.

On a day like this Pelle felt small in every way. The raging of the sea oppressed him and made him feel insecure, but the others were in their element. They possessed themselves of all the horror of the ocean, and represented it in an exaggerated form; they heaped up all the terrors of the sea in play upon the shore: ships went to the bottom with all on board or struck on the rocks; corpses lay rolling in the surf, and drowned men in sea-boots and sou'westers came up out of the sea at midnight, and walked right into the little cottages in the village to give warning of their departure. They dwelt upon it with a seriousness that was bright with inward joy, as though they were singing hymns of praise to the mighty ocean. But Pelle stood out side all this, and felt himself cowardly when listening to their tales. He kept behind the others, and wished he could bring down the big bull and let it loose among them. Then they would come to him for protection.

The boys had orders from their parents to take care of themselves, for Marta, the old skipper's widow, had three nights running heard the sea demand corpses with a short bark. They talked about that, too, and about when the fishermen would venture out again, while they ran about the beach. "A bottle, a bottle! " cried one of them suddenly, dashing off along the shore; he was quite sure he had seen a bottle bob up out of the surf a little way off, and disappear again. The whole swarm stood for a long time gazing eagerly out into the seething foam, and Kilen and another boy had thrown off their jackets to be ready to jump out when it appeared again.

The bottle did not appear again, but it had given a spur to the imagination, and every boy had his own solemn knowledge of such things. Just now, during the equinoctial storms, many a bottle went over a ship's side with a last message to those on land. Really and truly, of course, that was why you learned to write—so as to be able to write your messages when your hour came. Then perhaps the bottle would be swallowed by a shark, or perhaps it would be fished up by stupid peasants who took it home with them to their wives to put drink into—this last a good-natured hit at Pelle. But it sometimes happened that it drifted ashore just at the place it was meant for; and, if not, it was the finder's business to take it to the nearest magistrate, if he didn't want to lose his right hand.

Out in the harbor the waves broke over the mole; the fishermen had drawn their boats up on shore. They could not rest indoors in their warm cottages; the sea and bad weather kept them on the beach night and day. They stood in shelter behind their boats, yawning heavily and gazing out to sea, where now and then a sail fluttered past like a storm-beaten bird.

"In, in! " cried the girls from the schoolroom door, and the boys sauntered slowly up. Pris was walking backward and forward in front of his desk, smoking his pipe with the picture of the king on it, and with the newspaper sticking out of his pocket. "To your places! " he shouted, striking his desk with the cane.

"Is there any news? " asked a boy, when they had taken their places. Fris sometimes read aloud the Shipping News to them.

"I don't know, " answered Fris crossly. "You can get out your slates and arithmetics. "

"Oh, we're going to do sums, oh, that's fun! " The whole class was rejoicing audibly as they got out their things.

Fris did not share the children's delight over arithmetic; his gifts, he was accustomed to say, were of a purely historical nature. But he accommodated himself to their needs, because long experience had taught him that a pandemonium might easily arise on a stormy day such as this; the weather had a remarkable influence upon the children. His own knowledge extended only as far as Christian Hansen's Part I. ; but there were two peasant boys who had worked on by themselves into Part III., and they helped the others.

The children were deep in their work, their long, regular breathing rising and falling in the room like a deep sleep. There was a continual passing backward and forward to the two arithmeticians, and the industry was only now and then interrupted by some little piece of mischief that came over one or another of the children as a reminder; but they soon fell into order again.

At the bottom of the class there was a sound of sniffing, growing more and more distinct. Fris laid down his newspaper impatiently.

"Peter's crying, " said those nearest.

"Oh-o! " said Fris, peering over his spectacles. "What's the matter now? "

"He says he can't remember what twice two is. "

Fris forced the air through his nostrils and seized the cane, but thought better of it. "Twice two's five! " he said quietly, at which there was a laugh at Peter's expense, and work went on again.

For some time they worked diligently, and then Nilen rose. Fris saw it, but went on reading.

"Which is the lightest, a pound of feathers or a pound of lead? I can't find it in the answers. "

Fris's hands trembled as he held the paper up close to his face to see something or other better. It was his mediocrity as a teacher of arithmetic that the imps were always aiming at, but he would *not* be drawn into a discussion with them. Nilen repeated his question, while the others tittered; but Fris did not hear—he was too deep in his paper. So the whole thing dropped.

Fris looked at his watch; he could soon give them a quarter of an hour's play, a good long quarter of an hour. Then there would only be one little hour's worry left, and that school-day could be laid by as another trouble got through.

Pelle stood up in his place in the middle of the class. He had some trouble to keep his face in the proper folds, and had to pretend that his neighbors were disturbing him. At last he got out what he wanted to say, but his ears were a little red at the tips. "If a pound of flour costs twelve ores, what will half a quarter of coal cost? "

Fris sat for a little while and looked irresolutely at Pelle. It always hurt him more when Pelle was naughty than when it was one of the others, for he had an affection for the boy. "Very well! " he said bitterly, coming slowly down with the thick cane in his hand. "Very well! "

"Look out for yourself! " whispered the boys, preparing to put difficulties in the way of Fris's approach.

But Pelle did one of those things that were directly opposed to all recognized rules, and yet gained him respect. Instead of shielding himself from the thrashing, he stepped forward and held out both hands with the palms turned upward. His face was crimson.

Fris looked at him in surprise, and was inclined to do anything but beat him; the look in Pelle's eyes rejoiced his heart. He did not understand boys as boys, but with regard to human beings his perceptions were fine, and there was something human here; it would be wrong not to take it seriously. He gave Pelle a sharp stroke across his hands, and throwing down the cane, called shortly, "Playtime! " and turned away.

The spray was coming right up to the school wall. A little way out there was a vessel, looking very much battered and at the mercy of the storm; she moved quickly forward a little way, and stood still and staggered for a time before moving on again, like a drunken man. She was going in the direction of the southern reef.

The boys had collected behind the school to eat their dinner in shelter, but suddenly there was the hollow rattling sound of wooden-soled boots over on the shore side, and the coastguard and a couple of fishermen ran out. Then the life-saving apparatus came

200

dashing up, the horses' manes flying in the wind. There was something inspiriting in the pace, and the boys threw down everything and followed.

The vessel was now right down by the point. She lay tugging at her anchor, with her stern toward the reef, and the waves washing over her; she looked like an old horse kicking out viciously at some obstacle with its hind legs. The anchor was not holding, and she was drifting backward on to the reef.

There were a number of people on the shore, both from the coast and from inland. The country-people must have come down to see whether the water was wet! The vessel had gone aground and lay rolling on the reef; the people on board had managed her like asses, said the fishermen, but she was no Russian, but a Lap vessel. The waves went right over her from end to end, and the crew had climbed into the rigging, where they hung gesticulating with their arms. They must have been shouting something, but the noise of the waves drowned it.

Pelle's eyes and ears were taking in all the preparations. He was quivering with excitement, and had to fight against his infirmity, which returned whenever anything stirred his blood. The men on the beach were busy driving stakes into the sand to hold the apparatus, and arranging ropes and hawsers so that everything should go smoothly. Special care was bestowed upon the long, fine line that the rocket was to carry out to the vessel; alterations were made in it at least twenty times.

The foreman of the trained Rescue Party stood and took aim with the rocket-apparatus; his glance darted out and back again to measure the distance with the sharpness of a claw. "Ready! " said the others, moving to one side. "Ready! " he answered gravely. For a moment all was still, while he placed it in another position and then back again.

Whe-e-e-e-ew! The thin line stood like a quivering snake in the air, with its runaway head boring through the sodden atmosphere over the sea and its body flying shrieking from the drum and riding out with deep humming tones to cut its way far out through the storm. The rocket had cleared the distance capitally; it was a good way beyond the wreck, but too far to leeward. It had run itself out and now stood wavering in the air like the restless head of a snake while it dropped.

"It's going afore her, " said one fisherman. The others were silent, but from their looks it was evident that they were of the same opinion. "It may still get there, " said the foreman. The rocket had struck the water a good way to the north, but the line still stood in an arch in the air, held up by the stress. It dropped in long waves toward the south, made a couple of folds in the wind, and dropped gently across the fore part of the vessel. "That's it! It got there, all right! " shouted the boys, and sprang on to the sand. The fishermen stamped about with delight, made a sideways movement with their heads toward the foreman and nodded appreciatively at one another. Out on the vessel a man crawled about in the rigging until he got hold of the line, and then crept down into the shrouds to the others again. Their strength could not be up to much, for except for that they did not move.

On shore there was activity. The roller was fixed more firmly to the ground and the cradle made ready; the thin line was knotted to a thicker rope, which again was to draw the heavy hawser on board: it was important that everything should hold. To the hawser was attached a pulley as large as a man's head for the drawing-ropes to run in, for one could not know what appliances they would have on board such an old tub. For safety's sake a board was attached to the line, upon which were instructions, in English, to haul it until a hawser of such-and-such a thickness came on board. This was unnecessary for ordinary people, but one never knew how stupid such Finn-Lapps could be.

"They may haul away now as soon as they like, and let us get done with it, " said the foreman, beating his hands together.

"Perhaps they're too exhausted, " said a young fisherman. "They must have been through a hard time! "

"They must surely be able to haul in a three-quarter-inch rope! Fasten an additional line to the rope, so that we can give them a hand in getting the hawser on board—when they get so far. "

This was done. But out on the wreck they hung stupidly in the rigging without ever moving; what in the world were they thinking about? The line still lay, motionless on the sand, but it was not fast to the bottom, for it moved when it was tightened by the water; it must have been made fast to the rigging.

"They've made it fast, the blockheads, " said the foreman. "I suppose they're waiting for us to haul the vessel up on land for them — with that bit of thread! " He laughed in despair.

"I suppose they don't know any better, poor things! " said "the Mormon. "

No one spoke or moved. They were paralyzed by the incomprehensibility of it, and their eyes moved in dreadful suspense from the wreck down to the motionless line and back again. The dull horror that ensues when men have done their utmost and are beaten back by absolute stupidity, began to creep over them. The only thing the shipwrecked men did was to gesticulate with their arms. They must have thought that the men on shore could work miracles — in defiance of them.

"In an hour it'll be all up with them, " said the foreman sadly. "It's hard to stand still and look on. "

A young fisherman came forward. Pelle knew him well, for he had met him occasionally by the cairn where the baby's soul burned in the summer nights.

"If one of you'll go with me, I'll try to drift down upon them! " said Niels Koller quietly.

"It'll be certain death, Niels! " said the foreman, laying his hand upon the young man's shoulder. "You understand that, I suppose! I'm not one to be afraid, but I won't throw away my life. So you know what I think. "

The others took the same view. A boat would be dashed to pieces against the moles. It would be impossible to get it out of the harbor in this weather, let alone work down to the wreck with wind and waves athwart! It might be that the sea had made a demand upon the village — no one would try to sneak out of his allotted share; but this was downright madness! With Niels Koller himself it must pass; his position was a peculiar one — with the murder of a child almost on his conscience and his sweetheart in prison. He had his own account to settle with the Almighty; no one ought to dissuade him!

"Then will none of you? " asked Niels, and looked down at the ground. "Well, then I must try it alone. " He went slowly up the beach. How he was going to set about it no one knew, nor did he himself; but the spirit had evidently come over him.

They stood looking after him. Then a young sailor said slowly: "I suppose I'd better go with him and take the one oar. He can do nothing by himself. " It was Nilen's brother.

"It wouldn't sound right if I stopped you from going, my son, " said "the Mormon. " "But can two of you do more than one? "

"Niels and I were at school together and have always been friends, " answered the young man, looking into his father's face. Then he moved away, and a little farther off began to run to catch up Niels.

The fishermen looked after them in silence. "Youth and madness! " one of them then said. "One blessing is that they'll never be able to get the boat out of the harbor. "

"If I know anything of Karl, they will get the boat out! " said "the Mormon" gloomily.

Some time passed, and then a boat appeared on the south side of the harbor, where there was a little shelter. They must have dragged it in over land with the women's help. The harbor projected a little, so that the boat escaped the worst of the surf before emerging from its protection. They were working their way out; it was all they could do to keep the boat up against the wind, and they scarcely moved. Every other moment the whole of the inside of the boat was visible, as if it would take nothing to upset it; but that had one advantage, in that the water they shipped ran out again.

It was evident that they meant to work their way out so far that they could make use of the high sea and scud down upon the wreck—a desperate idea! But the whole thing was such sheer madness, one would never have thought they had been born and bred by the water. After half an hour's rowing, it seemed they could do no more; and they were not more than a couple of good cable-lengths out from the harbor. They lay still, one of them holding the boat up to the waves with the oars, while the other struggled with something— a bit of sail as big as a sack. Yes, yes, of course! Now if they took in the oars and left themselves at the mercy of the weather—with wind and waves abaft and beam! —they would fill with water at once!

But they did not take in the oars. One of them sat and kept a frenzied watch while they ran before the wind. It looked very awkward, but it was evident that it gave greater command of the boat. Then they suddenly dropped the sail and rowed the boat hard up against the wind—when a sea was about to break. None of the fishermen could recollect ever having seen such navigation before; it was young blood, and they knew what they were about. Every instant one felt one must say Now! But the boat was like a living thing that understood how to meet everything; it always rose above every caprice. The sight made one warm, so that for a time one forgot it was a sail for life or death. Even if they managed to get down to the wreck, what then? Why, they would be dashed against the side of the vessel!

Old Ole Koller, Niels's father, came down over the sandbanks. "Who's that out there throwing themselves away? " he asked. The question sounded harsh as it broke in upon the silence and suspense. No one looked at him—Ole was rather garrulous. He glanced round the flock, as though he were looking for some particular person. "Niels—have any of you seen Niels? " he asked quietly. One man nodded toward the sea, and he was silent and overcome.

The waves must have broken their oars or carried them away, for they dropped the bit of sail, the boat burrowed aimlessly with its prow, and settled down lazily with its broadside to the wind. Then a great wave took them and carried them in one long sweep toward the wreck, and they disappeared in the breaking billow.

When the water sank to rest, the boat lay bottom upward, rolling in the lee of the vessel.

A man was working his way from the deck up into the rigging. "Isn't that Niels? " said Ole, gazing until his eyes watered. "I wonder if that isn't Niels? "

"No; it's my brother Karl, " said Nilen.

"Then Niels is gone, " said Ole plaintively. "Then Niels is gone. "

The others had nothing to answer; it was a matter of course that Niels would be lost.

Ole stood for a little while shrinkingly, as if expecting that some one would say it was Niels. He dried his eyes, and tried to make it out for himself, but they only filled again. "Your eyes are young, " he said to Pelle, his head trembling. "Can't you see that it's Niels? "

"No, it's Karl, " said Pelle softly.

And Ole went with bowed head through the crowd, without looking at any one or turning aside for anything. He moved as though he were alone in the world, and walked slowly out along the south shore. He was going to meet the dead body.

There was no time to think. The line began to be alive, glided out into the sea, and drew the rope after it. Yard after yard it unrolled itself and glided slowly into the sea like an awakened sea-animal, and the thick hawser began to move.

Karl fastened it high up on the mast, and it took all the men—and boys, too—to haul it taut. Even then it hung in a heavy curve from its own weight, and the cradle dragged through the crests of the waves when it went out empty. It was more under than above the water as they pulled it back again with the first of the crew, a funny little dark man, dressed in mangy gray fur. He was almost choked in the crossing, but when once they had emptied the water out of him he quite recovered and chattered incessantly in a curious language that no one understood. Five little fur-clad beings, one by one, were brought over by the cradle, and last of all came Karl with a little squealing pig in his arms.

"They *were* a poor lot of seamen! " said Karl, in the intervals of disgorging water. "Upon my word, they understood nothing. They'd made the rocket-line fast to the shrouds, and tied the loose end round the captain's waist! And you should just have seen the muddle on board! " He talked loudly, but his glance seemed to veil something.

The men now went home to the village with the shipwrecked sailors; the vessel looked as if it would still keep out the water for some time.

Just as the school-children were starting to go home, Ole came staggering along with his son's dead body on his back. He walked with loose knees bending low and moaning under his burden. Fris stopped him and helped him to lay the dead body in the schoolroom. There was a deep wound in the forehead. When Pelle saw the dead body with its gaping wound, he began to jump up and down, jumping quickly up, and letting himself drop like a dead bird. The girls drew away from him, screaming, and Fris bent over him and looked sorrowfully at him.

"It isn't from naughtiness, " said the other boys. "He can't help it; he's taken that way sometimes. He got it once when he saw a man almost killed. " And they carried him off to the pump to bring him to himself again.

Fris and Ole busied themselves over the dead body, placed something under the head, and washed away the sand that had got rubbed into the skin of the face. "He was my best boy, " said Fris, stroking the dead man's head with a trembling hand. "Look well at him, children, and never forget him again; he was my best boy. "

He stood silent, looking straight before him, with dimmed spectacles and hands hanging loosely. Ole was crying; he had suddenly grown pitiably old and decrepit. "I suppose I ought to get him home? " he said plaintively, trying to raise his son's shoulders; but he had not the strength.

"Just let him lie! " said Fris. "He's had a hard day, and he's resting now. "

"Yes, he's had a hard day, " said Ole, raising his son's hand to his mouth to breathe upon it. "And look how he's used the oar! The blood's burst out at his finger-tips! " Ole laughed through his tears. "He was a good lad. He was food to me, and light and heat too. There never came an unkind word out of his mouth to me that was a burden on him. And now I've got no son, Fris! I'm childless now! And I'm not able to do anything! "

"You shall have enough to live upon, Ole, " said Fris.

"Without coming on the parish? I shouldn't like to come upon the parish. "

"Yes, without coming on the parish, Ole. "

"If only he can get peace now! He had so little peace in this world these last few years. There's been a song made about his misfortune, Fris, and every time he heard it he was like a new-born lamb in the cold. The children sing it, too. " Ole looked round at them imploringly. "It was only a piece of boyish heedlessness, and now he's taken his punishment. "

"Your son hasn't had any punishment, Ole, and neither has he deserved any, " said Fris, putting his arm about the old man's shoulder. "But he's given a great gift as he lies there and cannot say anything. He gave five men their lives and gave up his own in return for the one offense that he committed in thoughtlessness! It was a generous son you had, Ole! " Fris looked at him with a bright smile.

"Yes, " said Ole, with animation. "He saved five people—of course he did—yes, he did! " He had not thought of that before; it would probably never have occurred to him. But now some one else had given it form, and he clung to it. "He saved five lives, even if they were only Finn-Lapps; so perhaps God will not disown him. "

Fris shook his head until his gray hair fell over his eyes. "Never forget him, children! " he said; "and now go quietly home. " The children silently took up their things and went; at that moment they would have done anything that Fris told them: he had complete power over them.

Ole stood staring absently, and then took Fris by the sleeve and drew him up to the dead body. "He's rowed well! " he said. "The blood's come out at his finger-ends, look! " And he raised his son's hands to the light. "And there's a wrist, Fris! He could take up an old man like me and carry me like a little child. " Ole laughed feebly. "But I carried him; all the way from the south reef I carried him on my back. I'm too heavy for you, father! I could hear him say, for he was a good son; but I carried him, and now I can't do anything more. If only they see that! "—he was looking again at the blood-stained fingers. "He did do his best. If only God Himself would give him his discharge! "

"Yes, " said Fris. "God will give him his discharge Himself, and he sees everything, you know, Ole. "

Some fishermen entered the room. They took off their caps, and one by one went quietly up and shook hands with Ole, and then, each passing his hand over his face, turned questioningly to the schoolmaster. Fris nodded, and they raised the dead body between them, and passed with heavy, cautious steps out through the entry and on toward the village, Ole following them, bowed down and moaning to himself.

XVIII

It was Pelle who, one day in his first year at school, when he was being questioned in Religion, and Fris asked him whether he could give the names of the three greatest festivals in the year, amused every one by answering: "Midsummer Eve, Harvest-home and— and——" There was a third, too, but when it came to the point, he was shy of mentioning it—his birthday! In certain ways it was the greatest of them all, even though no one but Father Lasse knew about it—and the people who wrote the almanac, of course; they knew about simply everything!

It came on the twenty-sixth of June and was called Pelagius in the calendar. In the morning his father kissed him and said: "Happiness and a blessing to you, laddie! " and then there was always something in his pocket when he came to pull on his trousers. His father was just as excited as he was himself, and waited by him while he dressed, to share in the surprise. But it was Pelle's way to spin things out when something nice was coming; it made the pleasure all the greater. He purposely passed over the interesting pocket, while Father Lasse stood by fidgeting and not knowing what to do.

"I say, what's the matter with that pocket? It looks to me so fat! You surely haven't been out stealing hens' eggs in the night? "

Then Pelle had to take it out—a large bundle of paper—and undo it, layer after layer. And Lasse would be amazed.

"Pooh, it's nothing but paper! What rubbish to go and fill your pockets with! " But in the very inside of all there was a pocket- knife with two blades.

"Thank you! " whispered Pelle then, with tears in his eyes.

"Oh, nonsense! It's a poor present, that! " said Lasse, blinking his red, lashless eyelids.

Beyond this the boy did not come in for anything better on that day than usual, but all the same he had a solemn feeling all day. The sun never failed to shine—was even unusually bright; and the animals looked meaningly at him while they lay munching. "It's my birthday to-day! " he said, hanging with his arms round the neck of Nero, one of the bullocks. "Can you say 'A happy birthday'? " And Nero breathed warm breath down his back, together with green juice from his chewing; and Pelle went about happy, and stole green corn to give to him and to his favorite calf, kept the new knife—or whatever it might have been—in his hand the whole day long, and dwelt in a peculiarly solemn way upon everything he did. He could make the whole of the long day swell with a festive feeling; and when he went to bed he tried to keep awake so as to make the day longer still.

Nevertheless, Midsummer Eve was in its way a greater day; it had at any rate the glamour of the unattainable over it. On that day everything that could creek and walk went up to the Common; there was not a servant on the whole island so poor-spirited as to submit to the refusal of a holiday on that day—none except just Lasse and Pelle.

Every year they had seen the day come and go without sharing in its pleasure. "Some one must stay at home, confound it! " said the bailiff always. "Or perhaps you think I can do it all for you? " They had too little power to assert themselves. Lasse helped to pack appetizing food and beverages into the carts, and see the others off, and then went about despondently—one man to all the work. Pelle watched from the field their merry departure and the white stripe of dust far away behind the rocks. And for half a year afterward, at meals, they heard reminiscences of drinking and fighting and love-making—the whole festivity.

But this was at an end. Lasse was not the man to continue to let himself be trifled with. He possessed a woman's affection, and a house in the background. He could give notice any day he liked. The magistrate was presumably busy with the prescribed advertising for Madam Olsen's husband, and as soon as the lawful respite was over, they would come together.

Lasse no longer sought to avoid the risk of dismissal. As long ago as the winter, he had driven the bailiff into a corner, and only agreed to be taken on again upon the express condition that they both took part in the Midsummer Eve outing; and he had witnesses to it. On the Common, where all lovers held tryst that day, Lasse and she were to meet too, but of this Pelle knew nothing.

"To-day we can say the day after to-morrow, and to-morrow we can say to-morrow, " Pelle went about repeating to his father two evenings before the day. He had kept an account of the time ever since May Day, by making strokes for all the days on the inside of the lid of the chest, and crossing them out one by one.

"Yes, and the day after to-morrow we shall say to-day, " said Lasse, with a juvenile fling.

They opened their eyes upon an incomprehensibly brilliant world, and did not at first remember that this was the day. Lasse had anticipated his wages to the amount of five krones, and had got an old cottager to do his work—for half a krone and his meals. "It's not a big wage, " said the man; "but if I give you a hand, perhaps the Almighty'll give me one in return. "

"Well, we've no one but Him to hold to, we poor creatures, " answered Lasse. "But I shall thank you in my grave. "

The cottager arrived by four o'clock, and Lasse was able to begin his holiday from that hour. Whenever he was about to take a hand in the work, the other said: "No, leave it alone! I'm sure you've not often had a holiday. "

"No; this is the first real holiday since I came to the farm, " said Lasse, drawing himself up with a lordly air.

Pelle was in his best clothes from the first thing in the morning, and went about smiling in his shirt-sleeves and with his hair plastered down with water; his best cap and jacket were not to be put on until they were going to start. When the sun shone upon his face, it sparkled like dewy grass. There was nothing to trouble about; the animals were in the enclosure and the bailiff was going to look after them himself.

He kept near his father, who had brought this about. Father Lasse was powerful! "What a good thing you threatened to leave! " he kept on exclaiming. And Lasse always gave the same answer: "Ay, you must carry things with a high hand if you want to gain anything in this world! "—and nodded with a consciousness of power.

They were to have started at eight o'clock, but the girls could not get the provisions ready in time. There were jars of stewed gooseberries, huge piles of pancakes, a hard-boiled egg apiece, cold veal and an endless supply of bread and butter. The carriage boxes could not nearly hold it all, so large baskets were pushed in under the seats. In the front was a small cask of beer, covered with green oats to keep the sun from it; and there was a whole keg of spirits and three bottles of cold punch. Almost the entire bottom of the large spring-wagon was covered, so that it was difficult to find room for one's feet.

After all, Fru Kongstrup showed a proper feeling for her servants when she wanted to. She went about like a kind mistress and saw that everything was well packed and that nothing was wanting. She was not like Kongstrup, who always had to have a bailiff between himself and them. She even joked and did her best, and it was evident that whatever else there might be to say against her, she wanted them to have a merry day. That her face was a little sad was not to be wondered at, as the farmer had driven out that morning with her young relative.

At last the girls were ready, and every one got in—in high spirits. The men inadvertently sat upon the girls' laps and jumped up in alarm. "Oh, oh! I must have gone too near a stove! " cried the rogue Mons, rubbing himself behind. Even the mistress could not help laughing.

"Isn't Erik going with us? " asked his old sweetheart Bengta, who still had a warm spot in her heart for him.

The bailiff whistled shrilly twice, and Erik came slowly up from the barn, where he had been standing and keeping watch upon his master.

"Won't you go with them to the woods to-day, Erik man? " asked the bailiff kindly. Erik stood twisting his big body and murmuring something that no one could understand, and then made an unwilling movement with one shoulder.

"You'd better go with them, " said the bailiff, pretending he was going to take him and put him into the cart. "Then I shall have to see whether I can get over the loss. "

Those in the cart laughed, but Erik shuffled off down through the yard, with his dog-like glance directed backward at the bailiff's feet, and stationed himself at the corner of the stable, where he stood watching. He held his cap behind his back, as boys do when they play at "Robbers. "

"He's a queer customer! " said Mons. Then Karl Johan guided the horses carefully through the gate, and they set off with a crack of the whip.

Along all the roads, vehicles were making their way toward the highest part of the island, filled to overflowing with merry people, who sat on one another's laps and hung right over the sides. The dust rose behind the conveyances and hung white in the air in stripes miles in length, that showed how the roads lay like spokes in a wheel all pointing toward the middle of the island. The air hummed with merry voices and the strains of concertinas. They missed Gustav's playing now—yes, and Bodil's pretty face, that always shone so brightly on a day like this.

Pelle had the appetite of years of fasting for the great world, and devoured everything with his eyes. "Look there, father! Just look! " Nothing escaped him. It made the others cheerful to look at him—he was so rosy and pretty. He wore a newly-washed blue blouse under his waistcoat, which showed at the neck and wrists and did duty as collar and cuffs; but Fair Maria bent back from the box-seat, where she was sitting alone with Karl Johan, and tied a very white scarf round his neck, and Karna, who wanted to be motherly to him, went over his face with a corner of her pocket-handkerchief, which she moistened with her tongue. She was rather officious, but for that matter it was quite conceivable that the boy might have got dirty again since his thorough morning wash.

The side roads continued to pour their contents out on to the high-roads, and there was soon a whole river of conveyances, extending as far as the eye could see in both directions. One would hardly have believed that there were so many vehicles in the whole world! Karl Johan was a good driver to have; he was always pointing with his whip and telling them something. He knew all about every single house. They were beyond the farms and tillage by now; but on the heath, where self-sown birch and aspen trees stood fluttering restlessly in the summer air, there stood desolate new houses with bare, plastered walls, and not so much as a henbane in the window or a bit of curtain. The fields round them were as stony as a newly-mended road, and the crops were a sad sight; the corn was only two or three inches in height, and already in ear. The people here were all

Swedish servants who had saved a little—and had now become land-owners. Karl Johan knew a good many of them.

"It looks very miserable, " said Lasse, comparing in his own mind the stones here with Madam Olsen's fat land.

"Oh, well, " answered the head man, "it's not of the very best, of course; but the land yields something, anyhow. " And he pointed to the fine large heaps of road-metal and hewn stone that surrounded every cottage. "If it isn't exactly grain, it gives something to live on; and then it's the only land that'll suit poor people's purses. " He and Fair Maria were thinking of settling down here themselves. Kongstrup had promised to help them to a farm with two horses when they married.

In the wood the birds were in the middle of their morning song; they were later with it here than in the sandbanks plantation, it seemed. The air sparkled brightly, and something invisible seemed to rise from the undergrowth; it was like being in a church with the sun shining down through tall windows and the organ playing. They drove round the foot of a steep cliff with overhanging trees, and into the wood.

It was almost impossible to thread your way through the crowd of unharnessed horses and vehicles. You had to have all your wits about you to keep from damaging your own and other people's things. Karl Johan sat watching both his fore wheels, and felt his way on step by step; he was like a cat in a thunderstorm, he was so wary. "Hold your jaw! " he said sharply, when any one in the cart opened his lips. At last they found room to unharness, and a rope was tied from tree to tree to form a square in which the horses were secured. Then they got out the curry-combs—goodness, how dusty it had been! And at last—well, no one said anything, but they all stood expectant, half turned in the direction of the head man.

"Well, I suppose we ought to go into the wood and look at the view, " he said.

They turned it over as they wandered aimlessly round the cart, looking furtively at the provisions.

"If only it'll keep! " said Anders, lifting a basket.

"I don't know how it is, but I feel so strange in my inside to-day, " Mons began. "It can't be consumption, can it? "

"Perhaps we ought to taste the good things first, then? " said Karl Johan.

Yes—oh, yes—it came at last!

Last year they had eaten their dinner on the grass. It was Bodil who had thought of that; she was always a little fantastic. This year nobody would be the one to make such a suggestion. They looked at one another a little expectant; and they then climbed up into the cart and settled themselves there just like other decent people. After all, the food was the same.

The pancakes were as large and thick as a saucepan-lid. It reminded them of Erik, who last year had eaten ten of them.

"It's a pity he's not here this year! " said Karl Johan. "He was a merry devil. "

"He's not badly off, " said Mons. "Gets his food and clothes given him, and does nothing but follow at the bailiff's heels and copy him. And he's always contented now. I wouldn't a bit mind changing with him. "

"And run about like a dog with its nose to the ground sniffing at its master's footsteps? Oh no, not I! "

"Whatever you may say, you must remember that it's the Almighty Himself who's taken his wits into safekeeping, " said Lasse admonishingly; and for a little while they were quite serious at the thought.

But seriousness could not claim more than was its due. Anders wanted to rub his leg, but made a mistake and caught hold of Lively Sara's, and made her scream; and this so flustered his hand that it could not find its way up, but went on making mistakes, and there was much laughter and merriment.

Karl Johan was not taking much part in the hilarity; he looked as if he were pondering something. Suddenly he roused himself and drew out his purse. "Here goes! " he said stoutly. "I'll stand beer! Bavarian beer, of course. Who'll go and fetch it? "

Mons leaped quickly from the cart. "How many? "

"Four. " Karl Johan's eye ran calculating over the cart. "No; just bring five, will you? That'll be a half each, " he said easily. "But make sure that it's real Bavarian beer they give you. "

There was really no end to the things that Karl Johan knew about; and he said the name "Bavarian beer" with no more difficulty than others would have in turning a quid in their mouth. But of course he was a trusted man on the farm now and often drove on errands into the town.

This raised their spirits and awakened curiosity, for most of them had never tasted Bavarian beer before. Lasse and Pelle openly admitted their inexperience; but Anders pretended he had got drunk on it more than once, though every one knew it was untrue.

Mons returned, moving cautiously, with the beer in his arms; it was a precious commodity. They drank it out of the large dram-glasses that were meant for the punch. In the town, of course, they drank beer out of huge mugs, but Karl Johan considered that that was simply swilling. The girls refused to drink, but did it after all, and were delighted. "They're always like that, " said Mons, "when you offer them something really good. " They became flushed with the excitement of the occurrence, and thought they were drunk. Lasse took away the taste of his beer with a dram; he did not like it at all. "I'm too old, " he said, in excuse.

The provisions were packed up again, and they set out in a body to see the view. They had to make their way through a perfect forest of carts to reach the pavilion. Horses were neighing and flinging up their hind legs, so that the bark flew off the trees. Men hurled themselves in among them, and tugged at their mouths until they quieted down again, while the women screamed and ran hither and thither like frightened hens, with skirts lifted.

From the top they could form some idea of the number of people. On the sides of the hill and in the wood beyond the roads—everywhere carts covered the ground; and down at the triangle where the two wide high-roads met, new loads were continually turning in. "There must be far more than a thousand pairs of horses in the wood to-day, " said Karl Johan. Yes, far more! There were a million, if not more, thought Pelle. He was quite determined to get as much as possible out of everything to-day.

There stood the Bridge Farm cart, and there came the people from Hammersholm, right out at the extreme north of the island. Here were numbers of people from the shore farms at Dove Point and Ronne and Nekso—the whole island was there. But there was no time now to fall in with acquaintances. "We shall meet this afternoon! " was the general cry.

Karl Johan led the expedition; it was one of a head man's duties to know the way about the Common. Fair Maria kept faithfully by his side, and every one could see how proud she was of him. Mons walked hand in hand with Lively Sara, and they went swinging along like a couple of happy children. Bengta and Anders had some difficulty in agreeing; they quarrelled every other minute, but they did not mean much by it. And Karna made herself agreeable.

They descended into a swamp, and went up again by a steep ascent where the great trees stood with their feet in one another's necks. Pelle leaped about everywhere like a young kid. In under the firs there were anthills as big as haycocks, and the ants had broad trodden paths running like foothpaths between the trees, on and on endlessly; a multitude of hosts passed backward and forward upon those roads. Under some small fir-trees a hedgehog was busy attacking a wasps' nest; it poked its nose into the nest, drew it quickly back, and sneezed. It looked wonderfully funny, but Pelle had to go on after the others. And soon he was far ahead of them, lying on his face in a ditch where he had smelt wild strawberries.

Lasse could not keep pace with the younger people up the hill, and it was not much better with Karna. "We're getting old, we two, " she said, as they toiled up, panting.

"Oh, are we? " was Lasse's answer. He felt quite young in spirit; it was only breath that he was short of.

"I expect you think very much as I do; when you've worked for others for so many years, you feel you want something of your own. "

"Yes, perhaps, " said Lasse evasively.

"One wouldn't come to it quite empty-handed, either—if it should happen. "

"Oh, indeed! "

Karna continued in this way, but Lasse was always sparing with his words, until they arrived at the Rockingstone, where the others were standing waiting. That was a block and a half! Fifty tons it was said to weigh, and yet Mons and Anders could rock it by putting a stick under one end of it.

"And now we ought to go to the Robbers' Castle, " said Karl Johan, and they trudged on, always up and down. Lasse did his utmost to keep beside the others, for he did not feel very brave when he was alone with Karna. What a fearful quantity of trees there were! And not all of one sort, as in other parts of the world. There were birches and firs, beech and larch and mountain ash all mixed together, and ever so many cherry-trees. The head man lead them across a little, dark lake that lay at the foot of the rock, staring up like an evil eye. "It was here that Little Anna drowned her baby —she that was betrayed by her master, " he said lingeringly. They all knew the story, and stood silent over the lake; the girls had tears in their eyes.

As they stood there silent, thinking of Little Anna's sad fate, an unspeakably soft note came up to them, followed by a long, affecting sobbing. They moved nearer to one another. "Oh, Lord! " whispered Fair Maria, shivering. "That's the baby's soul crying! " Pelle stiffened as he listened, and cold waves seemed to flow down his back.

"Why, that's a nightingale, " said Karl Johan, "Don't you even know that? There are hundreds of them in these woods, and they sing in the middle of the day. " This was a relief to the older people, but Pelle's horror was not so easily thrown off. He had gazed into the depths of the other world, and every explanation glanced off him.

But then came the Robbers' Castle as a great disappointment. He had imagined it peopled with robbers, and it was only some old ruins that stood on a little hill in the middle of a bog. He went by himself all round the bottom of it to see if there were not a secret underground passage that led down to the water. If there were, he would get hold of his father without letting the others know, and make his way in and look for the chests of money; or else there would be too many to share in it. But this was forgotten as a peculiar

219

scent arrested his attention, and he came upon a piece of ground that was green with lily-of-the-valley plants that still bore a few flowers, and where there were wild strawberries. There were so many that he had to go and call the others.

But this was also forgotten as he made his way through the underwood to get up. He had lost the path and gone astray in the damp, chilly darkness under the cliff. Creeping plants and thorns wove themselves in among the overhanging branches, and made a thick, low roof. He could not see an opening anywhere, and a strange green light came through the matted branches, the ground was slippery with moisture and decaying substances; from the cliff hung quivering fern-fronds with their points downward, and water dripping from them like wet hair. Huge tree-roots, like the naked bodies of black goblins writhing to get free, lay stretched across the rocks. A little further on, the sun made a patch of burning fire in the darkness, and beyond it rose a bluish vapor and a sound as of a distant threshing-machine.

Pelle stood still, and his terror grew until his knees trembled; then he set off running as if he were possessed. A thousand shadow- hands stretched out after him as he ran; and he pushed his way through briars and creepers with a low cry. The daylight met him with the force of a blow, and something behind him had a firm grasp on his clothes; he had to shout for Father Lasse with all his might before it let go.

And there he stood right out in the bog, while high up above his head the others sat, upon a point of rock all among the trees. From up there it looked as if the world were all tree-tops, rising and falling endlessly; there was foliage far down beneath your feet and out as far as the eye could see, up and down. You were almost tempted to throw yourself into it, it looked so invitingly soft. As a warning to the others, Karl Johan had to tell them about the tailor's apprentice, who jumped out from a projecting rock here, just because the foliage looked so temptingly soft, Strange to say, he escaped with his life; but the high tree he fell through stripped him of every stitch of clothing.

Mons had been teasing Sara by saying that he was going to jump down, but now he drew back cautiously. "I don't want to risk my confirmation clothes, " he said, trying to look good.

After all, the most remarkable thing of all was the Horseman Hill with the royal monument. The tower alone! Not a bit of wood had been used in it, only granite; and you went round and round and round. "You're counting the steps, I suppose? " said Karl Johan admonishingly. Oh, yes, they were all counting to themselves.

It was clear weather, and the island lay spread out beneath them in all its luxuriance. The very first thing the men wanted to do was to try what it was like to spit down; but the girls were giddy and kept together in a cluster in the middle of the platform. The churches were counted under Karl Johan's able guidance, and all the well-known places pointed out. "There's Stone Farm, too, " said Anders, pointing to something far off toward the sea. It was not Stone Farm, but Karl Johan could say to a nicety behind which hill it ought to lie, and then they recognized the quarries.

Lasse took no part in this. He stood quite still, gazing at the blue line of the Swedish coast that stood out far away upon the shining water. The sight of his native land made him feel weak and old; he would probably never go home again, although he would have dearly liked to see Bengta's grave once more. Ah yes, and the best that could happen to one would be to be allowed to rest by her side, when everything else was ended. At this moment he regretted that he had gone into exile in his old age. He wondered what Kungstorp looked like now, whether the new people kept the land cultivated at all. And all the old acquaintances—how were they getting on? His old-man's reminiscences came over him so strongly that for a time he forgot Madam Olsen and everything about her. He allowed himself to be lulled by past memories, and wept in his heart like a little child. Ah! it was dreary to live away from one's native place and everything in one's old age; but if it only brought a blessing on the laddie in some way or other, it was all as it should be.

"I suppose that's the King's Copenhagen [Footnote: Country-people speak of Copenhagen as "the King's Copehagen. "] we see over there? " asked Anders.

"It's Sweden, " said Lasse quietly.

"Sweden, is it? But it lay on that side last year, if I remember rightly. "

"Yes, of course! What else should the world go round for? " exclaimed Mons.

Anders was just about to take this in all good faith when he caught a grimace that Mons made to the others. "Oh, you clever monkey! " he cried, and sprang at Mons, who dashed down the stone stairs; and the sound of their footsteps came up in a hollow rumble as out of a huge cask. The girls stood leaning against one another, rocking gently and gazing silently at the shining water that lay far away round the island. The giddiness had made them languid.

"Why, your eyes are quite dreamy! " said Karl Johan, trying to take them all into his embrace. "Aren't you coming down with us? "

They were all fairly tired now. No one said anything, for of course Karl Johan was leading; but the girls showed an inclination to sit down.

"Now there's only the Echo Valley left, " he said encouragingly, "and that's on our way back. We must do that, for it's well worth it. You'll hear an echo there that hasn't its equal anywhere. "

They went slowly, for their feet were tender with the leather boots and much aimless walking; but when they had come down the steep cliff into the valley and had drunk from the spring, they brightened up. Karl Johan stationed himself with legs astride, and called across to the cliff: "What's Karl Johan's greatest treat? " And the echo answered straight away: "Eat! " It was exceedingly funny, and they all had to try it, each with his or her name—even Pelle. When that was exhausted, Mons made up a question which made the echo give a rude answer.

"You mustn't teach it anything like that, " said Lasse. "Just suppose some fine ladies were to come here, and he started calling that out after them? " They almost killed themselves with laughing at the old man's joke, and he was so delighted at the applause that he went on repeating it to himself on the way back. Ha, ha! he wasn't quite fit for the scrap-heap yet.

When they got back to the cart they were ravenously hungry and settled down to another meal. "You must have something to keep you up when you're wandering about like this, " said Mons.

"Now then, " said Karl Johan, when they had finished, "every one may do what they like; but at nine sharp we meet here again and drive home. "

Up on the open ground, Lasse gave Pelle a secret nudge, and they began to do business with a cake-seller until the others had got well ahead. "It's not nice being third wheel in a carriage, " said Lasse. "We two'll go about by ourselves for a little now. "

Lasse was craning his neck. "Are you looking for any one? " asked Pelle.

"No, no one in particular; but I was wondering where all these people come from. There are people from all over the country, but I haven't seen any one from the village yet. "

"Don't you think Madam Olsen'll be here to-day? "

"Can't say, " said Lasse; "but it would be nice to see her, and there's something I want to say to her, too. Your eyes are young; you must keep a lookout. "

Pelle was given fifty ore to spend on whatever he liked. Round the ground sat the poor women of the Heath at little stalls, from which they sold colored sugar-sticks, gingerbread and two-ore cigars. In the meantime he went from woman to woman, and bought of each for one or two ore.

Away under the trees stood blind Hoyer, who had come straight from Copenhagen with new ballads. There was a crowd round him. He played the tune upon his concertina, his little withered wife sang to it, and the whole crowd sang carefully with her. Those who had learnt the tunes went away singing, and others pushed forward into their place and put down their five-ore piece.

Lasse and Pelle stood on the edge of the crowd listening. There was no use in paying money before you knew what you would get for it; and anyhow the songs would be all over the island by to-morrow, and going gratis from mouth to mouth. "A Man of Eighty—a new and pleasant ballad about how things go when a decrepit old man takes a young wife! " shouted Hoyer in a hoarse voice, before the song began. Lasse didn't care very much about that ballad; but then came a terribly sad one about the sailor George Semon, who took a most tender farewell of his sweetheart—

> "And said, When here I once more stand,
> We to the church will go hand in hand. "

But he never did come back, for the storm was over them for forty-five days, provisions ran short, and the girl's lover went mad. He drew his knife upon the captain, and demanded to be taken home to his bride; and the captain shot him down. Then the others threw themselves upon the corpse, carried it to the galley, and made soup of it.

> "The girl still waits for her own true love,
> Away from the shore she will not move.
> Poor maid, she's hoping she still may wed,
> And does not know that her lad is dead. "

"That's beautiful, " said Lasse, rummaging in his purse for a five-ore. "You must try to learn that; you've got an ear for that sort of thing. " They pushed through the crowd right up to the musician, and began cautiously to sing too, while the girls all round were sniffing.

They wandered up and down among the trees, Lasse rather fidgety. There was a whole street of dancing-booths, tents with conjurers and panorama-men, and drinking-booths. The criers were perspiring, the refreshment sellers were walking up and down in front of their tents like greedy beasts of prey. Things had not got into full swing yet, for most of the people were still out and about seeing the sights, or amusing themselves in all seemliness, exerting themselves in trials of strength or slipping in and out of the conjurers' tents. There was not a man unaccompanied by a woman. Many a one came to a stand at the refreshment-tents, but the woman pulled him past; then he would yawn and allow himself to be dragged up into a roundabout or a magic-lantern tent where the most beautiful pictures were shown of the way that cancer and other horrible things made havoc in people's insides.

"These are just the things for the women, " said Lasse, breathing forth a sigh at haphazard after Madam Olsen. On a horse on Madvig's roundabout sat Gustav with his arm round Bodil's waist. "Hey, old man! " he cried, as they whizzed past, and flapped Lasse on the ear with his cap, which had the white side out. They were as radiant as the day and the sun, those two.

Pelle wanted to have a turn on a roundabout. "Then blest if I won't have something too, that'll make things go round! " said Lasse, and went in and had a "cuckoo"—coffee with brandy in it. "There are some people, " he said, when he came out again, "that can go from one tavern to another without its making any difference in their purse. It would be nice to try—only for a year. Hush! " Over by Max Alexander's "Green House" stood Karna, quite alone and looking about her wistfully. Lasse drew Pelle round in a wide circle.

"There's Madam Olsen with a strange man! " said Pelle suddenly.

Lasse started. "Where? " Yes, there she stood, and had a man with her! And talking so busily! They went past her without stopping; she could choose for herself, then.

"Hi, can't you wait a little! " cried Madam Olsen, running after them so that her petticoats crackled round her. She was round and smiling as usual, and many layers of good home-woven material stood out about her; there was no scrimping anywhere.

They went on together, talking on indifferent matters and now and then exchanging glances about the boy who was in their way. They had to walk so sedately without venturing to touch one another. He did not like any nonsense.

It was black with people now up at the pavilion, and one could hardly move a step without meeting acquaintances. "It's even worse than a swarm of bees, " said Lasse. "It's not worth trying to get in there. " At one place the movement was outward, and by following it they found themselves in a valley, where a man stood shouting and beating his fists upon a platform. It was a missionary meeting. The audience lay encamped in small groups, up the slopes, and a man in long black clothes went quietly from group to group, selling leaflets. His face was white, and he had a very long, thin red beard.

"Do you see that man? " whispered Lasse, giving Pelle a nudge. "Upon my word, if it isn't Long Ole—and with a glove on his injured hand. It was him that had to take the sin upon him for Per Olsen's false swearing! " explained Lasse, turning to Madam Olsen. "He was standing at the machine at the time when Per Olsen ought to have paid the penalty with his three fingers, and so his went instead. He may be glad of the mistake after all, for they say he's risen to great things among the prayer-meeting folks. And his complexion's as fine as a young lady's—something different to what it was when he was carting manure at Stone Farm! It'll be fun to say good-day to him again. "

Lasse was quite proud of having served together with this man, and stationed himself in front of the others, intending to make an impression upon his lady friend by saying a hearty: "Good-day, Ole! " Long Ole was at the next group, and now he came on to them and was going to hold out his tracts, when a glance at Lasse made him drop both hand and eyes; and with a deep sigh he passed on with bowed head to the next group.

"Did you see how he turned his eyes up? " said Lasse derisively. "When beggars come to court, they don't know how to behave! He'd got a watch in his pocket, too, and long clothes; and before he hadn't even a shirt to his body. And an ungodly devil he was too! But the old gentleman looks after his own, as the saying is; I expect it's him that helped him on by changing places at the machine. The way they've cheated the Almighty's enough to make Him weep! "

Madam Olsen tried to hush Lasse, but the "cuckoo" rose within him together with his wrath, and he continued: "So *he's* above recognizing decent people who get what they have in an honorable way, and not by lying and humbug! They do say he makes love to all the farmers' wives wherever he goes; but there was a time when he had to put up with the Sow. "

People began to look at them, and Madam Olsen took Lasse firmly by the arm and drew him away.

The sun was now low in the sky. Up on the open ground the crowds tramped round and round as if in a tread-mill. Now and then a drunken man reeled along, making a broad path for himself through the crush. The noise came seething up from the tents—barrel-organs each grinding out a different tune, criers, the bands of the various dancing-booths, and the measured tread of a schottische or polka. The women wandered up and down in clusters, casting long looks into the refreshment-tents where their men were sitting; and some of them stopped at the tent-door and made coaxing signs to some one inside.

Under the trees stood a drunken man, pawing at a tree-trunk, and beside him stood a girl, crying with her black damask apron to her eyes. Pelle watched them for a long time. The man's clothes were disordered, and he lurched against the girl with a foolish grin when she, in the midst of her tears, tried to put them straight. When Pelle turned away, Lasse and Madam Olsen had disappeared in the crowd.

They must have gone on a little, and he went down to the very end of the street. Then he turned despondingly and went up, burrowing this way and that in the stream of people, with eyes everywhere. "Haven't you seen Father Lasse? " he asked pitifully, when he met any one he knew.

In the thickest of the crush, a tall man was moving along, holding forth blissfully at the top of his voice. He was a head taller than anybody else, and very broad; but he beamed with good-nature, and wanted to embrace everybody. People ran screaming out of his way, so that a broad path was left wherever he went. Pelle kept behind him, and thus succeeded in getting through the thickest crowds, where policemen and rangers were stationed with thick cudgels. Their eyes and ears were on the watch, but they did not interfere in anything. It was said that they had handcuffs in their pockets.

Pelle had reached the road in his despairing search. Cart after cart was carefully working its way out through the gloom under the trees, then rolling out into the dazzling evening light, and on to the high-road with much cracking of whips. They were the prayer-meeting people driving home.

He happened to think of the time, and asked a man what it was. Nine! Pelle had to run so as not to be too late in getting to the cart. In the cart sat Karl Johan and Fair Maria eating. "Get up and have something to eat! " they said, and as Pelle was ravenous, he forgot everything while he ate. But then Johan asked about Lasse, and his torment returned.

Karl Johan was cross; not one had returned to the cart, although it was the time agreed upon. "You'd better keep close to us now, " he said, as they went up, "or you might get killed. "

Up at the edge of the wood they met Gustav running. "Have none of you seen Bodil? " he asked, gasping. His clothes were torn and there was blood on the front of his shirt. He ran on groaning, and disappeared under the trees. It was quite dark there, but the open ground lay in a strange light that came from nowhere, but seemed to have been left behind by the day as it fled. Faces out there showed up, some in ghostly pallor, some black like holes in the light, until they suddenly burst forth, crimson with blood-red flame.

The people wandered about in confused groups, shouting and screaming at the top of their voices. Two men came along with arms twined affectionately round one another's necks, and the next moment lay rolling on the ground in a fight. Others joined the fray and took sides without troubling to discover what it was all about, and the contest became one large struggling heap. Then the police came up, and hit about them with their sticks; and those who did not run away were handcuffed and thrown into an empty stable.

Pelle was quite upset, and kept close to Karl Johan; he jumped every time a band approached, and kept on saying in a whimpering tone: "Where's Father Lasse? Let's go and find him. "

"Oh, hold your tongue! " exclaimed the head man, who was standing and trying to catch sight of his fellow-servants. He was angry at this untrustworthiness. "Don't stand there crying! You'd do much more good if you ran down to the cart and see whether any one's come. "

Pelle had to go, little though he cared to venture in under the trees. The branches hung silently listening, but the noise from the open ground came down in bursts, and in the darkness under the bushes living things rustled about and spoke in voices of joy or sorrow. A sudden scream rang through the wood, and made his knees knock together.

Karna sat at the back of the cart asleep, and Bengta stood leaning against the front seat, weeping. "They've locked Anders up, " she sobbed. "He got wild, so they put handcuffs on him and locked him up. " She went back with Pelle.

Lasse was with Karl Johan and Fair Maria; he looked defiantly at Pelle, and in his half-closed eyes there was a little mutinous gleam.

"Then now there's only Mons and Lively Sara, " said Karl Johan, as he ran his eye over them.

"But what about Anders? " sobbed Bengta. "You surely won't drive away without Anders? "

"There's nothing can he done about Anders! " said the head man. "He'll come of his own accord when once he's let out. "

They found out on inquiry that Mons and Lively Sara were down in one of the dancing-booths, and accordingly went down there. "Now you stay here! " said Karl Johan sternly, and went in to take a survey of the dancers. In there blood burnt hot, and faces were like balls of fire that made red circles in the blue mist of perspiring heat and dust. Dump! Dump! Dump! The measure fell booming like heavy blows; and in the middle of the floor stood a man and wrung the moisture out of his jacket.

Out of one of the dancing-tents pushed a big fellow with two girls. He had an arm about the neck of each, and they linked arms behind his back. His cap was on the back of his head, and his riotous mood would have found expression in leaping, if he had not felt himself too pleasantly encumbered; so he opened his mouth wide, and shouted joyfully, so that it rang again: "Devil take me! Deuce take me! Seven hundred devils take me! " and disappeared under the trees with his girls.

"That was Per Olsen himself, " said Lasse, looking after him. "What a man, to be sure! He certainly doesn't look as if he bore any debt of sin to the Almighty. "

"His time may still come, " was the opinion of Karl Johan.

Quite by chance they found Mons and Lively Sara sitting asleep in one another's arms upon a bench under the trees.

"Well, now, I suppose we ought to be getting home? " said Karl Johan slowly. He had been doing right for so long that his throat was quite dry. "I suppose none of you'll stand a farewell glass? "

"I will! " said Mons, "if you'll go up to the pavilion with me to drink it. " Mons had missed something by going to sleep and had a desire to go once round the ground. Every time a yell reached them he gave a leap as he walked beside Lively Sara, and answered with a long halloo. He tried to get away, but she clung to his arm; so he swung the heavy end of his loaded stick and shouted defiantly. Lasse kicked his old limbs and imitated Mons's shouts, for he too was for anything rather than going home; but Karl Johan was determined—

they *were* to go now! And in this he was supported by Pelle and the women.

Out on the open ground a roar made them stop, and the women got each behind her man. A man came running bareheaded and with a large wound in his temple, from which the blood flowed down over his face and collar. His features were distorted with fear. Behind him came a second, also bareheaded, and with a drawn knife. A ranger tried to bar his way, but received a wound in his shoulder and fell, and the pursuer ran on. As he passed them, Mons uttered a short yell and sprang straight up into the air, bringing down his loaded stick upon the back of the man's neck. The man sank to the ground with a grunt, and Mons slipped in among the groups of people and disappeared; and the others found him waiting for them at the edge of the wood. He did not answer any more yells.

Karl Johan had to lead the horses until they got out onto the road, and then they all got in. Behind them the noise had become lost, and only one long cry for help rang through the air and dropped again.

Down by a little lake, some forgotten girls had gathered on the grass and were playing by themselves. The white mist lay over the grass like a shining lake, and only the upper part of the girls' bodies rose above it. They were walking round in a ring, singing the mid-summer's-night song. Pure and clear rose the merry song, and yet was so strangely sad to listen to, because they who sang it had been left in the lurch by sots and brawlers.

> "We will dance upon hill and meadow,
> We will wear out our shoes and stockings.
> Heigh ho, my little sweetheart fair,
> We shall dance till the sun has risen high.
>   Heigh ho, my queen!
> Now we have danced upon the green. "

The tones fell so gently upon the ear and mind that memories and thoughts were purified of all that had been hideous, and the day itself could appear in its true colors as a joyful festival. For Lasse and Pelle, indeed, it had been a peerless day, making up for many years of neglect. The only pity was that it was over instead of about to begin.

The occupants of the cart were tired now, some nodding and all silent. Lasse sat working about in his pocket with one hand. He was trying to obtain an estimate of the money that remained. It was expensive to keep a sweetheart when you did not want to be outdone by younger men in any way. Pelle was asleep, and was slipping farther and farther down until Bengta took his head onto her lap. She herself was weeping bitterly about Anders.

The daylight was growing rapidly brighter as they drove in to Stone Farm.

XIX

The master and mistress of Stone Farm were almost always the subject of common talk, and were never quite out of the thoughts of the people. There was as much thought and said about Kongstrup and his wife as about all the rest of the parish put together; they were bread to so many, their Providence both in evil and good, that nothing that they did could be immaterial.

No one ever thought of weighing them by the same standards as they used for others; they were something apart, beings who were endowed with great possessions, and could do and be as they liked, disregarding all considerations and entertaining all passions. All that came from Stone Farm was too great for ordinary mortals to sit in judgment upon; it was difficult enough to explain what went on, even when at such close quarters with it all as were Lasse and Pelle. To them as to the others, the Stone Farm people were beings apart, who lived their life under greater conditions, beings, as it were, halfway between the human and the supernatural, in a world where such things as unquenchable passion and frenzied love wrought havoc.

What happened, therefore, at Stone Farm supplied more excitement than the other events of the parish. People listened with open-mouthed interest to the smallest utterance from the big house, and when the outbursts came, trembled and went about oppressed and uncomfortable. No matter how clearly Lasse, in the calm periods, might think he saw it all, the life up there would suddenly be dragged out of its ordinary recognized form again, and wrap itself around his and the boy's world like a misty sphere in which capricious powers warred—just above their heads.

It was now Jomfru Koller's second year at the farm, in spite of all evil prophecies; and indeed things had turned out in such a way that every one had to own that his prognostications had been wrong. She was always fonder of driving with Kongstrup to the town than of staying at home to cheer Fru Kongstrup up in her loneliness; but such is youth. She behaved properly enough otherwise, and it was well known that Kongstrup had returned to his old hotel-sweethearting in the town. Fru Kongstrup herself, moreover, showed no distrust of her young relative—if she had ever felt any. She was as kind to her as if she had been her own daughter; and very often it was she herself who got Jomfru Koller to go in the carriage to look after her husband.

Otherwise the days passed as usual, and Fru Kongstrup was continually giving herself up to little drinking-bouts and to grief. At such times she would weep over her wasted life; and if he were at home would follow him with her accusations from room to room, until he would order the carriage and take flight, even in the middle of the night. The walls were so saturated with her voice that it penetrated through everything like a sorrowful, dull droning. Those who happened to be up at night to look after animals or the like, could hear her talking incessantly up there, even if she were alone.

But then Jomfru Koller began to talk of going away. She suddenly got the idea that she wanted to go to Copenhagen and learn something, so that she could earn her own living. It sounded strange, as there was every prospect of her some day inheriting the farmer's property. Fru Kongstrup was quite upset at the thought of losing her, and altogether forgot her other troubles in continually talking to her about it. Even when everything was settled, and they were standing in the mangling-room with the maids, getting Jomfru Koller's things ready for her journey, she still kept on—to no earthly purpose. Like all the Stone Farm family, she could never let go anything she had once got hold of.

There was something strange about Jomfru Koller's obstinacy of purpose; she was not even quite sure what she was going to do over there. "I suppose she's going over to learn cooking, " said one and another with a covert smile.

Fru Kongstrup herself had no suspicion. She, who was always suspecting something, seemed to be blind here. It must have been because she had such complete trust in Jomfru Koller, and thought so much of her. She had not even time to sigh, so busy was she in putting everything into good order. Much need there was for it, too; Jomfru Koller must have had her head full of very different things, judging from the condition her clothes were in.

"I'm glad Kongstrup's going over with her, " said Fru Kongstrup to Fair Maria one evening when they were sitting round the big darning-basket, mending the young lady's stockings after the wash. "They say Copenhagen's a bad town for inexperienced young people to come to. But Sina'll get on all right, for she's got the good stock of the Kollers in her. " She said it all with such childish simplicity; you could tramp in and out of her heart with great wooden shoes on, suspicious though she was. "Perhaps we'll come over to see you at Christmas, Sina, " she added in the goodness of her heart.

Jomfru Koller opened her mouth and caught her breath in terror, but did not answer. She bent over her work and did not look at any one all the evening. She never looked frankly at any one now. "She's ashamed of her deceitfulness! " they said. The judgment would fall upon her; she ought to have known what she was doing, and not gone between the bark and the wood, especially here where one of them trusted her entirely.

In the upper yard the new man Paer was busy getting the closed carriage ready. Erik stood beside him idle. He looked unhappy and troubled, poor fellow, as he always did when he was not near the bailiff. Each time a wheel had to come off or be put on, he had to put his giant's back under the big carriage and lift it. Every now and then Lasse came to the stable-door to get an idea of what was going on. Pelle was at school, it being the first day of the new half-year.

She was going away to-day, the false wretch who had let herself be drawn into deceiving one who had been a mother to her! Fru Kongstrup must be going with them down to the steamer, as the closed carriage was going.

Lasse went into the bedroom to arrange one or two things so that he could slip out in the evening without Pelle noticing it. He had given Pelle a little paper of sweets for Madam Olsen, and on the paper he had drawn a cross with a lead button; and the cross meant in all secrecy that he would come to her that evening.

While he took out his best clothes and hid them under some hay close to the outer door, he hummed: —

> "Love's longing so strong
> It helped me along,
> And the way was made short with the nightingales' song. "

He was looking forward so immensely to the evening; he had not been alone with her now for nearly a quarter of a year. He was proud, moreover, of having taken writing into his service, and that a writing that Pelle, quick reader of writing though he was, would not be able to make out.

While the others were taking their after-dinner nap, Lasse went out and tidied up the dung-heap. The carriage was standing up there with one large trunk strapped on behind, and another standing on one edge on the box. Lasse wondered what such a girl would do when she was alone out in the wide world and had to pay the price of her sin. He supposed there must be places where they took in such girls in return for good payment; everything could be got over there!

Johanna Pihl came waddling in at the gate up there. Lasse started when he saw her; she never came for any good. When she boldly exhibited herself here, she was always drunk, and then she stopped at nothing. It was sad to see how low misfortune could drag a woman. Lasse could not help thinking what a pretty girl she had been in her youth. And now all she thought of was making money out of her shame! He cautiously withdrew into the stable, so as not to be an eye-witness to anything, and peered out from there.

The Sow went up and down in front of the windows, and called in a thick voice, over which she had not full command: "Kongstrup, Kongstrup! Come out and let me speak to you. You must let me have some money, for your son and I haven't had any food for three days. "

"That's a wicked lie! " said Lasse to himself indignantly, "for she has a good income. But she wastes God's gifts, and now she's out to do some evil. " He would have liked to take the fork and chase her out through the gate, but it was not well to expose one's self to her venomous tongue.

She had her foot upon the step, but did not dare to mount. Fuddled though she was, there was something that kept her in check. She stood there groping at the handrail and mumbling to herself, and every now and then lifting her fat face and calling Kongstrup.

Jomfru Koller came inadvertently up from the basement, and went toward the steps; her eyes were on the ground, and she did not see the Sow until it was too late, and then she turned quickly. Johanna Pihl stood grinning.

"Come here, miss, and let me wish you good-day! " she cried. "You're too grand, are you? But the one may be just as good as the other! Perhaps it's because you can drive away in a carriage and have yours on the other side of the sea, while I had mine in a beet-field! But is that anything to be proud of? I say, just go up and tell my fine gentleman that his eldest's starving! I daren't go myself because of the evil eye. "

Long before this Jomfru Koller was down in the basement again, but Johanna Pihl continued to stand and say the same thing over and over again, until the bailiff came dashing out toward her, when she retired, scolding, from the yard.

The men had been aroused before their time by her screaming, and stood drowsily watching behind the barn-doors. Lasse kept excited watch from the stable, and the girls had collected in the wash-house. What would happen now? They all expected some terrible outbreak.

But nothing happened. Now, when Fru Kongstrup had the right to shake heaven and earth—so faithlessly had they treated her—now she was silent. The farm was as peaceful as on the days when they had come to a sort of understanding, and Kongstrup kept himself quiet. Fru Kongstrup passed the windows up there, and looked just like anybody else. Nothing happened!

Something must have been said, however, for the young lady had a very tear-stained face when they got into the carriage, and Kongstrup wore his confused air. Then Karl Johan drove away with the two; and the mistress did not appear. She was probably ashamed for what concerned the others.

Nothing had happened to relieve the suspense; it oppressed every one. She must have accepted her unhappy lot, and given up standing out for her rights, now, just when every one would have supported her. This tranquillity was so unnatural, so unreasonable, that it made one melancholy and low-spirited. It was as though others were suffering on her behalf, and she herself had no heart.

But then it broke down, and the sound of weeping began to ooze out over the farm, quiet and regular like flowing heart's blood. All the evening it flowed; the weeping had never sounded so despairing; it went to the hearts of all. She had taken in the poor child and treated her as her own, and the poor child had deceived her. Every one felt how she must suffer.

During the night the weeping rose to cries so heart-rending that they awakened even Pelle—wet with perspiration. "It sounds like some one in the last agonies! " said Lasse, and hastily drew on his trousers with trembling, clumsy hands. "She surely hasn't laid hands upon herself? " He lighted the lantern and went out into the stable, Pelle following naked.

Then suddenly the cries ceased, as abruptly as if the sound had been cut off with an axe, and the silence that followed said dumbly that it was forever. The farm sank into the darkness of night like an extinguished world. "Our mistress is dead! " said Lasse, shivering and moving his fingers over his lips. "May God receive her kindly! " They crept fearfully into bed.

But when they got up the next morning, the farm looked as it always did, and the maids were chattering and making as much noise as usual in the wash-house. A little while after, the mistress's voice was heard up there, giving directions about the work. "I don't understand it, " said Lasse, shaking his head. "Nothing but death can stop anything so suddenly. She must have a tremendous power over herself! "

It now became apparent what a capable woman she was. She had not wasted anything in the long period of idleness; the maids became brisker and the fare better. One day she came to the cow-stable to see that the milking was done cleanly. She gave every one his due, too. One day they came from the quarry and complained that they had had no wages for three weeks. There was not enough money on the farm. "Then we must get some, " said the mistress, and they had to set about threshing at once. And one day when Karna raised too many objections she received a ringing box on the ear.

"It's a new nature she's got, " said Lasse. But the old workpeople recognized several things from their young days. "It's her family's nature, " they said. "She's a regular Koller. "

The time passed without any change; she was as constant in her tranquillity as she had before been constant in her misery. It was not the habit of the Kollers to change their minds once they had made them up about anything. Then Kongstrup came home from his journey. She did not drive out to meet him, but was on the steps to greet him, gentle and kind. Everybody could see how pleased and surprised he was. He must have expected a very different reception.

But during the night, when they were all sound asleep, Karna came knocking at the men's window. "Get up and fetch the doctor! " she cried, "and be quick! " The call sounded like one of life and death, and they turned out headlong. Lasse, who was in the habit of sleeping with one eye open, like the hens, was the first man on the spot, and had got the horses out of the stable; and in a few minutes Karl Johan was driving out at the gate. He had a man with him to hold the lantern. It was pitch-dark, but they could hear the carriage tearing along until the sound became very distant; then in another moment the sound changed, as the vehicle turned on to the metalled road a couple of miles off. Then it died away altogether.

On the farm they went about shaking themselves and unable to rest, wandering into their rooms and out again to gaze up at the tall windows, where people were running backward and forward with lights. What had happened? Some mishap to the farmer, evidently, for now and again the mistress's commanding voice could be heard down in the kitchen—but what? The wash-house and the servants' room were dark and locked.

Toward morning, when the doctor had come and had taken things into his own hands, a greater calm fell upon them all, and the maids took the opportunity of slipping out into the yard. They would not at once say what was the matter, but stood looking in an embarrassed way at one another, and laughing stupidly. At last they gradually got it out by first one telling a little and then another: in a fit of delirium or of madness Kongstrup had done violence to himself. Their faces were contorted with a mixture of fear and smothered laughter; and when Karl Johan said gravely to Fair Maria: "You're not telling a lie, are you? " she burst into tears. There she stood laughing and crying by turns; and it made no difference that Karl Johan scolded her sharply.

But it was true, although it sounded like the craziest nonsense that a man could do such a thing to himself. It was a truth that struck one dumb!

It was some time before they could make it out at all, but when they did there were one or two things about it that seemed a little unnatural. It could not have happened during intoxication, for the farmer never drank at home, did not drink at all, as far as any one knew, but only took a glass in good company. It was more likely to have been remorse and contrition; it was not impossible considering the life he had led, although it was strange that a man of his nature should behave in such a desperate fashion.

But it was not satisfactory! And gradually, without it being possible to point to any origin, all thoughts turned toward her. She had changed of late, and the Koller blood had come out in her; and in that family they had never let themselves be trodden down unrevenged!

XX

Out in the shelter of the gable-wall of the House sat Kongstrup, well wrapped up, and gazing straight before him with expressionless eyes. The winter sun shone full upon him; it had lured forth signs of spring, and the sparrows were hopping gaily about him. His wife went backward and forward, busying herself about him; she wrapped his feet up better, and came with a shawl to put round his shoulders. She touched his chest and arms affectionately as she spread the shawl over him from behind; and he slowly raised his head and passed his hand over hers. She stood thus for a little while, leaning against his shoulder and looking down upon him like a mother, with eyes that were tranquil with the joy of possession.

Pelle came bounding down across the yard, licking his lips. He had taken advantage of his mistress's preoccupation to steal down into the dairy and get a drink of sour cream from the girls, and tease them a little. He was glowing with health, and moved along as carelessly happy as if the whole world were his.

It was quite dreadful the way he grew and wore out his things; it was almost impossible to keep him in clothes! His arms and legs stuck far out of every article of clothing he put on, and he wore things out as fast as Lasse could procure them. Something new was always being got for him, and before you could turn round, his arms and legs were out of that too. He was as strong as an oak-tree; and when it was a question of lifting or anything that did not require perseverence, Lasse had to allow himself to be superseded.

The boy had acquired independence, too, and every day it became more difficult for the old man to assert his parental authority; but that would come as soon as Lasse was master of his own house and could bring his fist down on his own table. But when would that be? As matters now stood, it looked as if the magistrate did not want him and Madam Olsen to be decently married. Seaman Olsen had given plain warning of his decease, and Lasse thought there was nothing to do but put up the banns; but the authorities continued to raise difficulties and ferret about, in the true lawyers' way. Now there was one question that had to be examined into, and now another; there were periods of grace allowed, and summonses to be issued to the dead man to make his appearance within such and such a time, and what not besides! It was all a put-up job, so that the pettifoggers could make something out of it.

He was thoroughly tired of Stone Farm. Every day he made the same complaint to Pelle: "It's nothing but toil, toil, from morning till night—one day just like another all the year round, as if you were in a convict-prison! And what you get for it is hardly enough to keep your body decently covered. You can't put anything by, and one day when you're worn out and good for nothing more, you can just go on the parish. "

The worst of it all, however, was the desire to work once more for himself. He was always sighing for this, and his hands were sore with longing to feel what it was like to take hold of one's own. Of late he had meditated cutting the matter short and moving down to his sweetheart's, without regard to the law. She was quite willing, he knew; she badly needed a man's hand in the house. And they were being talked about, anyhow; it would not make much difference if he and the boy went as her lodgers, especially when they worked independently.

But the boy was not to be persuaded; he was jealous for his father's honor. Whenever Lasse touched upon the subject he became strangely sullen. Lasse pretended it was Madam Olsen's idea, and not his.

"I'm not particularly in favor of it, either, " he said. "People are sure to believe the worst at once. But we can't go on here wearing ourselves to a thread for nothing. And you can't breathe freely on this farm—always tied! "

Pelle made no answer to this; he was not strong in reasons, but knew what he wanted.

"If I ran away from here one night, I guess you'd come trotting after me. "

Pelle maintained a refractory silence.

"I think I'll do it, for this isn't to be borne. Now you've got to have new school-trousers, and where are they coming from? "

"Well, then, do it! Then you'll do what you say. "

"It's easy for you to pooh-pooh everything, " said Lasse despondingly, "for you've time and years before you. But I'm beginning to get old, and I've no one to trouble about me. "

"Why, don't I help you with everything? " asked Pelle reproachfully.

"Yes, yes, of course you do your very best to make things easier for me, and no one could say you didn't. But, you see—there are certain things you don't—there's something—" Lasse came to a standstill. What was the use of explaining the longings of a man to a boy? "You shouldn't be so obstinate, you know! " And Lasse stroked the boy's arm imploringly.

But Pelle *was* obstinate. He had already put up with plenty of sarcastic remarks from his schoolfellows, and fought a good many battles since it had become known that his father and Madam Olsen were sweethearts. If they now started living together openly, it would become quite unbearable. Pelle was not afraid of fighting, but he needed to have right on his side, if he was to kick out properly.

"Move down to her, then, and I'll go away! "

"Where'll you go to? "

"Out into the world and get rich! "

Lasse raised his head, like an old war-horse that hears a signal; but then it dropped again.

"Out into the world and get rich! Yes, yes, " he said slowly; "that's what I thought, too, when I was your age. But things don't happen like that—if you aren't born with a caul. "

Lasse was silent, and thoughtfully kicked the straw in under a cow. He was not altogether sure that the boy was not born with a caul, after all. He was a late-born child, and they were always meant for the worst or the best; and then he had that cow's-lick on his forehead, which meant good fortune. He was merry and always singing, and neat-handed at everything; and his nature made him generally liked. It was very possible that good fortune lay waiting for him somewhere out there.

"But the very first thing you need for that is to be properly confirmed. You'd better take your books and learn your lesson for the priest, so that you don't get refused! I'll do the rest of the foddering. "

Pelle took his books and seated himself in the foddering-passage just in front of the big bull. He read in an undertone, and Lasse passed up and down at his work. For some time each minded his own; but then Lasse came up, drawn by the new lesson-books Pelle had got for his confirmation-classes.

"Is that Bible history, that one there? "

"Yes. "

"Is that about the man who drank himself drunk in there? "

Lasse had long since given up learning to read; he had not the head for it. But he was always interested in what the boy was doing, and the books exerted a peculiar magic effect upon him. "Now what does that stand for? " he would ask wonderingly, pointing to something printed; or "What wonderful thing have you got in your lesson to-day? " Pelle had to keep him informed from day to day. And the same questions often came again, for Lasse had not a good memory.

"You know—the one whose sons pulled off his trousers and shamed their own father? " Lasse continued, when Pelle did not answer.

"Oh, Noah! "

"Yes, of course! Old Noah—the one that Gustav had that song about. I wonder what he made himself drunk on, the old man? "

"Wine. "

"Was it wine? " Lasse raised his eyebrows. "Then that Noah must have been a fine gentleman! The owner of the estate at home drank wine, too, on grand occasions. I've heard that it takes a lot of that to make a man tipsy—and it's expensive! Does the book tell you, too, about him that was such a terrible swindler? What was his name again? "

"Laban, do you mean? "

"Laban, yes of course! To think that I could forget it, too, for he was a regular Laban, [Footnote: An ordinary expression in Danish for a mean, deceitful person.] so the name suits him just right. It was him that let his son-in-law have both his daughters, and off their price on his daily wage too! If they'd been alive now, they'd have got hard labor, both him and his son-in-law; but in those days the police didn't look so close at people's papers. Now I should like to know whether a wife was allowed to have two husbands in those days. Does the book say anything about that? " Lasse moved his head inquisitively.

"No, I don't think it does, " answered Pelle absently.

"Oh, well, I oughtn't to disturb you, " said Lasse, and went to his work. But in a very short time he was back again. "Those two names have slipped my memory; I can't think where my head could have been at the moment. But I know the greater prophets well enough, if you like to hear me. "

"Say them, then! " said Pelle, without raising his eyes from his book.

"But you must stop reading while I say them, " said Lasse, "or you might go wrong. " He did not approve of Pelle's wanting to treat it as food for babes.

"Well, I don't suppose I could go wrong in the four greater! " said Pelle, with an air of superiority, but nevertheless shutting the book.

Lasse took the quid out from his lower lip with his forefinger, and threw it on the ground so as to have his mouth clear, and then hitched up his trousers and stood for a little while with closed eyes while he moved his lips in inward repetition.

"Are they coming soon? " asked Pelle.

"I must first make sure that they're there! " answered Lasse, in vexation at the interruption, and beginning to go over them again. "Isaiah, Jeremiah, Ezekiel, and Daniel! " he said, dashing them off hastily, so as not to lose any of them on the way.

"Shall we take Jacob's twelve sons, too? "

"No, not to-day. It might be too much for me all at once. At my age you must go forward gently; I'm not as young as you, you know. But you might go through the twelve lesser prophets with me. "

Pelle went through them slowly, and Lasse repeated them one by one. "What confounded names they did think of in those days! " he exclaimed, quite out of breath. "You can hardly get your tongue round them! But I shall manage them in time. "

"What do you want to know them for, father? " asked Pelle suddenly.

"What do I want to know them for? " Lasse scratched one ear. "Why, of course I—er—what a terrible stupid question! What do *you* want to know them for? Learning's as good for the one to have as for the other, and in my youth they wouldn't let me get at anything fine like that. Do you want to keep it all to yourself? "

"No, for I wouldn't care a hang about all this prophet business if I didn't *have* to. "

Lasse almost fainted with horror.

"Then you're the most wicked little cub I ever knew, and deserve never to have been born into the world! Is that all the respect you have for learning? You ought to be glad you were born in an age when the poor man's child shares in it all as well as the rich. It wasn't so in my time, or else—who knows—perhaps I shouldn't be going about here cleaning stables if I'd learned something when I was young. Take care you don't take pride in your own shame! "

Pelle half regretted his words now, and said, to clear himself: "I'm in the top form now! "

"Yes, I know that well enough, but that's no reason for your putting your hands in your trouser-pockets; while you're taking breath, the others eat the porridge. I hope you've not forgotten anything in the long Christmas holidays? "

"Oh, no, I'm sure I haven't! " said Pelle, with assurance.

Lasse did not doubt it either, but only made believe he did to take the boy in. He knew nothing more splendid than to listen to a rushing torrent of learning, but it was becoming more and more difficult to get the laddie to contribute it. "How can you be sure? " he went on. "Hadn't you better see? It would be such a comfort to know that you hadn't forgotten anything—so much as you must have in your head. "

Pelle felt flattered and yielded. He stretched out his legs, closed his eyes, and began to rock backward and forward. And the Ten Commandments, the Patriarchs, the Judges, Joseph and his brethren, the four major and the twelve minor prophets—the whole learning of the world poured from his lips in one long breath. To Lasse it seemed as if the universe itself were whizzing round the white-bearded countenance of the Almighty. He had to bend his head and cross himself in awe at the amount that the boy's little head could contain.

"I wonder what it costs to be a student? " said Lasse, when he once more felt earth beneath his feet.

"It must be expensive—a thousand krones, I suppose, at least, " Pelle thought. Neither of them connected any definite idea with the number; it merely meant the insurmountably great.

"I wonder if it would be so terrible dear, " said Lasse. "I've been thinking that when we have something of our own—I suppose it'll come to something some day—you might go to Fris and learn the trade of him fairly cheap, and have your meals at home. We ought to be able to manage it that way. "

Pelle did not answer; he felt no desire to be apprenticed to the clerk. He had taken out his knife, and was cutting something on a post of one of the stalls. It represented the big bull with his head down to the ground, and its tongue hanging out of one corner of its mouth. One hoof right forward at its mouth indicated that the animal was pawing up the ground in anger. Lasse could not help stopping, for now it was beginning to be like something. "That's meant to be a cow, isn't it? " he said. He had been wondering every day, as it gradually grew.

"It's Volmer that time he took you on his horns, " said Pelle.

Lasse could see at once that it was that, now that he had been told. "It's really very like, " he said; "but he wasn't so angry as you've

246

made him! Well, well, you'd better get to work again; that there fooling can't make a living for a man. "

Lasse did not like this defect in the boy—making drawings with chalk or his penknife all over; there would soon not be a beam or a wall in the place that did not bear marks of one or the other. It was useless nonsense, and the farmer would probably be angry if he came into the stable and happened to see them. Lasse had every now and then to throw cow-dung over the most conspicuous drawings, so that they should not catch the eye of people for whom they were not intended.

Up at the house, Kongstrup was just going in, leaning on his wife's arm. He looked pale but by no means thin. "He's still rather lame, " said Lasse, peeping out; "but it won't be long before we have him down here, so you'd better not quite destroy the post. "

Pelle went on cutting.

"If you don't leave off that silly nonsense, I'll throw dirt over it! " said Lasse angrily.

"Then I'll draw you and Madam Olsen on the big gate! " answered Pelle roguishly.

"You—you'd better! I should curse you before my face, and get the parson to send you away—if not something worse! " Lasse was quite upset, and went off down to the other end of the cow-stable and began the afternoon's cleaning, knocking and pulling his implements about. In his anger he loaded the wheelbarrow too full, and then could neither go one way nor the other, as his feet slipped.

Pelle came down with the gentlest of faces. "Mayn't I wheel the barrow out? " he said. "Your wooden shoes aren't so firm on the stones. "

Lasse growled some reply, and let him take it. For a very short time he was cross, but it was no good; the boy could be irresistible when he liked.

XXI

Pelle had been to confirmation-class, and was now sitting in the
servants' room eating his dinner—boiled herring and porridge. It
was Saturday, and the bailiff had driven into the town, so Erik was
sitting over the stove. He never said anything of his own accord, but
always sat and stared; and his eyes followed Pelle's movements
backward and forward between his mouth and his plate. He always
kept his eyebrows raised, as if everything were new to him; they had
almost grown into that position. In front of him stood a mug of beer
in a large pool, for he drank constantly and spilt some every time.

Fair Maria was washing up, and looked in every now and then to see
if Pelle were finished. When he licked his horn spoon clean and
threw it into the drawer, she came in with something on a plate: they
had had roast loin of pork for dinner upstairs.

"Here's a little taste for you, " she said. "I expect you're still hungry.
What'll you give me for it? " She kept the plate in her hand, and
looked at him with a coaxing smile.

Pelle was still very hungry—ravenous; and he looked at the titbit
until his mouth watered. Then he dutifully put up his lips and Maria
kissed him. She glanced involuntarily at Erik, and a gleam of
something passed over his foolish face, like a faint reminiscence.

"There sits that great gaby making a mess! " she said, scolding as she
seized the beer-mug from him, held it under the edge of the table,
and with her hand swept the spilt beer into it.

Pelle set to work upon the pork without troubling about anything
else; but when she had gone out, he carefully spat down between his
legs, and went through a small cleansing operation with the sleeve of
his blouse.

When he was finished he went into the stable and cleaned out the
mangers, while Lasse curried the cows; it was all to look nice for
Sunday. While they worked, Pelle gave a full account of the day's
happenings, and repeated all that the parson had said. Lasse listened
attentively, with occasional little exclamations. "Think of that! "
"Well, I never! " "So David was a buck like that, and yet he walked

in the sight of God all the same! Well, God's long-suffering is great—there's no mistake about that! "

There was a knock at the outer door. It was one of Kalle's children with the message that grandmother would like to bid them good-bye before she passed away.

"Then she can't have long to live, " exclaimed Lasse. "It'll be a great loss to them all, so happy as they've been together. But there'll be a little more food for the others, of course. "

They agreed to wait until they were quite finished, and then steal away; for if they asked to be let off early, they would not be likely to get leave for the funeral. "And that'll be a day's feasting, with plenty of food and drink, if I know anything of Brother Kalle! " said Lasse.

When they had finished their work and had their supper, they stole out through the outside door into the field. Lasse had heaped up the quilt, and put an old woolly cap just sticking out at the pillow-end; in a hurry it could easily be mistaken for the hair of a sleeper, if any one came to see. When they had got a little way, Lasse had to go back once more to take precautions against fire.

It was snowing gently and silently, and the ground was frozen so that they could go straight on over everything. Now that they knew the way, it seemed no distance at all; and before they knew where they were, the fields came to an end and the rock began.

There was a light in the cottage. Kalle was sitting up waiting for them. "Grandmother hasn't long to live, " he said, more seriously than Lasse ever remembered to have heard him speak before.

Kalle opened the door to grandmother's room, and whispered something, to which his wife answered softly out of the darkness.

"Oh, I'm awake, " said the old woman, in a slow, monotonous voice. "You can speak out, for I am awake. "

Lasse and Pelle took off their leather shoes and went in in their stockings. "Good evening, grandmother! " they both said solemnly, "and the peace of God! " Lasse added.

"Well, here I am, " said the old woman, feebly patting the quilt. She had big woollen gloves on. "I took the liberty of sending for you for I haven't long to live now. How are things going on in the parish? Have there been any deaths? "

"No, not that I know of, " answered Lasse. "But you look so well, grandmother, so fat and rosy! We shall see you going about again in two or three days. "

"Oh, I dare say! " said the old woman, smiling indulgently. "I suppose I look like a young bride after her first baby, eh? But thank you for coming; it's as if you belonged to me. Well, now I've been sent for, and I shall depart in peace. I've had a good time in this world, and haven't anything to complain of. I had a good husband and a good daughter, not forgetting Kalle there. And I got my sight back, so that I saw the world once more. "

"But you only saw it with one eye, like the birds, grandmother, " said Kalle, trying to laugh.

"Yes, yes, but that was quite good enough; there was so much that was new since I lost my sight. The wood had grown bigger, and a whole family had grown up without my quite knowing it. Ah! yes, it has been good to live in my old age and have them all about me — Kalle and Maria and the children. And all of my own age have gone before me; it's been nice to see what became of them all. "

"How old are you now, grandmother? " asked Lasse.

"Kalle has looked it up in the church-book, and from that I ought to be almost eighty; but that can scarcely be right. "

"Yes, it's right enough, " said Kalle, "for the parson looked it up for me himself. "

"Well, well, then the time's gone quickly, and I shouldn't at all mind living a little longer, if it was God's will. But the grave's giving warning; I notice it in my eyelids. " The old woman had a little difficulty in breathing, but kept on talking.

"You're talking far too much, mother! " said Maria.

"Yes, you ought to be resting and sleeping, " said Lasse. "Hadn't we better say good-bye to you? "

"No, I really must talk, for it'll be the last time I see you and I shall have plenty of time to rest. My eyes are so light thank God, and I don't feel the least bit sleepy. "

"Grandmother hasn't slept for a whole week, I think, " said Kalle doubtfully.

"And why should I sleep away the last of the time I shall have here, when I shall get plenty of time for that afterward? At night when you others are asleep, I lie and listen to your breathing, and feel glad that you're all so well. Or I look at the heather-broom, and think of Anders and all the fun we had together. "

She lay silent for a little while, getting her breath, while she gazed at a withered bunch of heather hanging from a beam.

"He gathered that for me the first time we lay in the flowering heather. He was so uncommonly fond of the heather, was Anders, and every year when it flowered, he took me out of my bed and carried me out there—every year until he was called away. I was always as new for him as on the first day, and so happiness and joy took up their abode in my heart. "

"Now, mother, you ought to be quiet and not talk so much! " said Maria, smoothing the old woman's pillow. But she would not be silenced, though her thoughts shifted a little.

"Yes, my teeth were hard to get and hard to lose, and I brought my children into the world with pain, and laid them in the grave with sorrow, one after another. But except for that, I've never been ill, and I've had a good husband. He had an eye for God's creations, and we got up with the birds every summer morning, and went out onto the heath and saw the sun rise out of the sea before we set about our days work. "

The old woman's slow voice died away, and it was as though a song ceased to sound in their ears. They sat up and sighed. "Ah, yes, " said Lasse, "the voice of memory is pleasant! "

"What about you, Lasse? " said the old woman suddenly, "I hear you're looking about for a wife! "

"Am I? " exclaimed Lasse, in alarm. Pelle saw Kalle wink at Maria, so they knew about it too.

"Aren't you soon coming to show us your sweetheart? " asked Kalle. "I hear it's a good match. "

"I don't in the least know what you're talking about, " said Lasse, quite confused.

"Well, well, you might do worse than that! " said the grandmother. "She's good enough—from what I know. I hope you'll suit one another like Anders and me. It was a happy time—the days when we went about and each did our best, and the nights when the wind blew. It was good then to be two to keep one another warm. "

"You've been very happy in everything, grandmother, " exclaimed Lasse.

"Yes, and I'm departing in peace and can lie quiet in my grave. I've not been treated unfairly in any way, and I've got nothing to haunt any one for. If only Kalle takes care to have me carried out feet first, I don't expect I shall trouble you. "

"Just you come and visit us now and then if you like! We shan't be afraid to welcome you, for we've been so happy together here, " said Kalle.

"No, you never know what your nature may be in the next life. You must promise to have me carried out feet first! I don't want to disturb your night's rest, so hard as you two have to work all day. And, besides, you've had to put up with me long enough, and it'll be nice for you to be by yourselves for once; and there'll be a bit more for you to eat after this. "

Maria began to cry.

"Now look here! " exclaimed Kalle testily. "I won't hear any more of that nonsense, for none of us have had to go short because of you. If you aren't good, I shall give a big party after you, for joy that you're gone! "

"No, you won't! " said the old woman quite sharply. "I won't hear of a three days' wake! Promise me now, Maria, that you won't go and ruin yourselves to make a fuss over a poor old soul like me! But you must ask the nearest neighbors in in the afternoon, with Lasse and Pelle, of course. And if you ask Hans Henrik, perhaps he'd bring his concertina with him, and you could have a dance in the barn. "

Kalle scratched the back of his head. "Then, hang it, you must wait until I've finished threshing, for I can't clear the floor now. Couldn't we borrow Jens Kure's horse, and take a little drive over the heath in the afternoon? "

"You might do that, too, but the children are to have a share in whatever you settle to do. It'll be a comfort to think they'll have a happy day out of it, for they don't have too many holidays; and there's money for it, you know. "

"Yes, would you believe it, Lasse—grandmother's got together fifty krones that none of us knew anything about, to go toward her funeral-party! "

"I've been putting by for it for twenty years now, for I'd like to leave the world in a decent way, and without pulling the clothes off my relations' backs. My grave-clothes are all ready, too, for I've got my wedding chemise lying by. It's only been used once, and more than that and my cap I don't want to have on. "

"But that's so little, " objected Maria. "Whatever will the neighbors say if we don't dress you properly? "

"I don't care! " answered the old woman decidedly. "That's how Anders liked me best, and it's all I've worn in bed these sixty years. So there! " And she turned her head to the wall.

"You shall have it all just as you like, mother! " said Maria.

The old woman turned round again, and felt for her daughter's hand on the quilt. "And you must make rather a soft pillow for my old head, for it's become so difficult to find rest for it. "

"We can take one of the babies' pillows and cover it with white, " said Maria.

"Thank you! And then I think you should send to Jacob Kristian's for the carpenter to-morrow—he's somewhere about, anyhow—and let him measure me for the coffin; then I could have my say as to what it's to be like. Kalle's so free with his money. "

The old woman closed her eyes. She had tired herself out, after all.

"Now I think we'll creep out into the other room, and let her be quiet, " whispered Kalle, getting up; but at that she opened her eyes.

"Are you going already? " she asked.

"We thought you were asleep, grandmother, " said Lasse.

"No, I don't suppose I shall sleep any more in this life; my eyes are so light, so light! Well, good-bye to you, Lasse and Pelle! May you be very, very happy, as happy as I've been. Maria was the only one death spared, but she's been a good daughter to me; and Kalle's been as good and kind to me as if I'd been his sweetheart. I had a good husband, too, who chopped firewood for me on Sundays, and got up in the night to look after the babies when I was lying-in. We were really well off—lead weights in the clock and plenty of firing; and he promised me a trip to Copenhagen. I churned my first butter in a bottle, for we had no churn to begin with; and I had to break the bottle to get it out, and then he laughed, for he always laughed when I did anything wrong. And how glad he was when each baby was born! Many a morning did he wake me up and we went out to see the sun come up out of the sea. 'Come and see, Anna, ' he would say, 'the heather's come into bloom in the night. ' But it was only the sun that shed its red over it! It was more than two miles to our nearest neighbor, but he didn't care for anything as long as he had me. He found his greatest pleasures in me, poor as I was; and the animals were fond of me too. Everything went well with us on the whole. "

She lay moving her head from side to side, and the tears were running down her cheeks. She no longer had difficulty in breathing, and one thing recalled another, and fell easily in one long tone from her lips. She probably did not now know what she was saying, but could not stop talking. She began at the beginning and repeated the words, evenly and monotonously, like one who is carried away and *must* talk.

"Mother! " said Maria anxiously, putting her hands on her mother's shaking head. "Recollect yourself, mother! "

The old woman stopped and looked at her wonderingly. "Ah, yes! " she said. "Memories came upon me so fast! I almost think I could sleep a little now. "

Lasse rose and went up to the bed. "Good-bye, grandmother! " he said, "and a pleasant journey, in case we shouldn't meet again! " Pelle followed him and repeated the words. The old woman looked at them inquiringly, but did not move. Then Lasse gently took her hand, and then Pelle, and they stole out into the other room.

"Her flame's burning clear to the end! " said Lasse, when the door was shut. Pelle noticed how freely their voices rang again.

"Yes, she'll be herself to the very end; there's been extra good timber in her. The people about here don't like our not having the doctor to her. What do you think? Shall we go to the expense? "

"I don't suppose there's anything more the matter with her than that she can't live any longer, " said Lasse thoughtfully.

"No, and she herself won't hear of it. If he could only keep life in her a little while longer! "

"Yes, times are hard! " said Lasse, and went round to look at the children. They were all asleep, and their room seemed heavy with their breathing. "The flock's getting much smaller. "

"Yes; one or two fly away from the nest pretty well every year, " answered Kalle, "and now I suppose we shan't have any more. It's an unfortunate figure we've stopped at—a horrid figure; but Maria's become deaf in that ear, and I can't do anything alone. " Kalle had got back his roguish look.

"I'm sure we can do very well with what we've got, " said Maria. "When we take Anna's too, it makes fourteen. "

"Oh, yes, count the others too, and you'll get off all the easier! " said Kalle teasingly.

Lasse was looking at Anna's child, which lay side by side with Kalle's thirteenth. "She looks healthier than her aunt, " he said. "You'd scarcely think they were the same age. She's just as red as the other's pale. "

"Yes, there is a difference, " Kalle admitted, looking affectionately at the children. "It must be that Anna's has come from young people, while *our* blood's beginning to get old. And then the ones that come the wrong side of the blanket always thrive best—like our Albert, for instance. He carries himself quite differently from the others. Did you know, by-the-by, that he's to get a ship of his own next spring? "

"No, surely not! Is he really going to be a captain? " said Lasse, in the utmost astonishment.

"It's Kongstrup that's at the back of that—that's between ourselves, of course! "

"Does the father of Anna's child still pay what he's bound to? " asked Lasse.

"Yes, he's honest enough! We get five krones a month for having the child, and that's a good help toward expenses. "

Maria had placed a dram, bread and a saucer of dripping on the table, and invited them to take their places at it.

"You're holding out a long time at Stone Farm, " said Kalle, when they were seated. "Are you going to stay there all your life? " he asked, with a mischievous wink.

"It's not such a simple matter to strike out into the deep! " said Lasse evasively.

"Oh, we shall soon be hearing news from you, shan't we? " asked Maria.

Lasse did not answer; he was struggling with a crust.

"Oh, but do cut off the crust if it's too much for your teeth! " said Maria. Every now and then she listened at her mother's door. "She's dropped off, after all, poor old soul! " she said.

Kalle pretended to discover the bottle for the first time. "What! Why, we've got gin on the table, too, and not one of us has smelt it! " he exclaimed, and filled their glasses for the third time. Then Maria corked the bottle. "Do you even grudge us our food? " he said, making great eyes at her—what a rogue he was! And Maria stared at him with eyes that were just as big, and said: "Yah! you want to fight, do you? " It quite warmed Lasse's heart to see their happiness.

"How's the farmer at Stone Farm? I suppose he's got over the worst now, hasn't he? " said Kalle.

"Well, I think he's as much a man as he'll ever be. A thing like that leaves its mark upon any one, " answered Lasse. Maria was smiling, and as soon as they looked at her, she looked away.

"Yes, you may grin! " said Lasse; "but I think it's sad! " Upon which Maria had to go out into the kitchen to have her laugh out.

"That's what all the women do at the mere mention of his name, " said Kalle. "It's a sad change. To-day red, to-morrow dead. Well, she's got her own way in one thing, and that is that she keeps him to herself—in a way. But to think that he can live with her after that! "

"They seem fonder of one another than they ever were before; he can't do without her for a single minute. But of course he wouldn't find any one else to love him now. What a queer sort of devilment love is! But we must see about getting home. "

"Well, I'll send you word when she's to be buried, " said Kalle, when they got outside the house.

"Yes, do! And if you should be in want of a ten-krone note for the funeral, let me know. Good-bye, then! "

XXII

Grandmother's funeral was still like a bright light behind everything that one thought and did. It was like certain kinds of food, that leave a pleasant taste in the mouth long after they have been eaten and done with. Kalle had certainly done everything to make it a festive day; there was an abundance of good things to eat and drink, and no end to his comical tricks. And, sly dog that he was, he had found an excuse for asking Madam Olsen; it was really a nice way of making the relation a legitimate one.

It gave Lasse and Pelle enough to talk about for a whole month, and after the subject was quite talked out and laid on one side for other things, it remained in the background as a sense of well-being of which no one quite knew the origin.

But now spring was advancing, and with it came troubles—not the daily trifles that could be bad enough, but great troubles that darkened everything, even when one was not thinking about them. Pelle was to be confirmed at Easter, and Lasse was at his wits' end to know how he was going to get him all that he would need—new clothes, new cap, new shoes! The boy often spoke about it; he must have been afraid of being put to shame before the others that day in church.

"It'll be all right, " said Lasse; but he himself saw no way at all out of the difficulty. At all the farms where the good old customs prevailed, the master and mistress provided it all; out here everything was so confoundedly new-fangled, with Prompt payments that slipped away between one's fingers. A hundred krones a year in wages seemed a tremendous amount when one thought of it all in one; but you only got them gradually, a few ores at a time, without your being able to put your finger anywhere and say: You got a good round sum there! "Yes, yes, it'll be all right! " said Lasse aloud, when he had got himself entangled in absurd speculations; and Pelle had to be satisfied with this. There was only one way out of the difficulty—to borrow the money from Madam Olsen; and that Lasse would have to come to in the end, loth as he was to do it. But Pelle must not know anything about it.

Lasse refrained as long as he possibly could, hoping that something or other would turn up to free him from the necessity of so disgraceful a proceeding as borrowing from his sweetheart. But nothing happened, and time was passing. One morning he cut the matter short; Pelle was just setting out for school. "Will you run in to Madam Olsen's and give her this? " he said, handing the boy a packet. "It's something she's promised to mend for us. " Inside on the paper, was the large cross that announced Lasse's coming in the evening.

From the hills Pelle saw that the ice had broken up in the night. It had filled the bay for nearly a month with a rough, compact mass, upon which you could play about as safely as on dry land. This was a new side of the sea, and Pelle had carefully felt his way forward with the tips of his wooden shoes, to the great amusement of the others. Afterward he learned to walk about freely on the ice without constantly shivering at the thought that the great fish of the sea were going about just under his wooden shoes, and perhaps were only waiting for him to drop through. Every day he went out to the high rampart of pack-ice that formed the boundary about a mile out, where the open water moved round in the sunshine like a green eye. He went out because he would do what the others did, but he never felt safe on the sea.

Now it was all broken up, and the bay was full of heaving ice-floes that rubbed against one another with a crackling sound; and the pieces farthest out, carrying bits of the rampart, were already on their way out to sea. Pelle had performed many exploits out there, but was really quite pleased that it was now packing up and taking its departure, so that it would once more be no crime to stay on dry land.

Old Fris was sitting in his place. He never left it now during a lesson, however badly things might go down in the class, but contented himself with beating on the desk with his cane. He was little more than a shadow of his former self, his head was always shaking, and his hands were often incapable of grasping an object. He still brought the newspaper with him, and opened it out at the beginning of the lesson, but he did not read. He would fall into a dream, sitting bolt upright, with his hands on the desk and his back against the wall. At such times the children could be as noisy as they liked, and he did not move; only a slight change in the expression of his eyes showed that he was alive at all.

It was quieter in school now. It was not worth while teasing the master, for he scarcely noticed it, and so the fun lost most of its attraction. A kind of court of justice had gradually formed among the bigger boys; they determined the order of the school-lessons, and disobedience and disputes as to authority were respectively punished and settled in the playground—with fists and tips of wooden shoes. The instruction was given as before, by the cleverer scholars teaching what they knew to the others; there was rather more arithmetic and reading than in Fris's time, but on the other hand the hymns suffered.

It still sometimes happened that Fris woke up and interfered in the instruction. "Hymns! " he would cry in his feeble voice, and strike the desk from habit; and the children would put aside what they were doing to please the old man, and begin repeating some hymn or other, taking their revenge by going through one verse over and over again for a whole hour. It was the only real trick they played the old man, and the joke was all on their side, for Fris noticed nothing.

Fris had so often talked of resigning his post, but now he did not even think of that. He shuffled to and from school at the regular times, probably without even knowing he did it. The authorities really had not the heart to dismiss him. Except in the hymns, which came off with rather short measure, there was nothing to say against him as teacher; for no one had ever yet left his school without being able both to write his name and to read a printed book—if it were in the old type. The new-fashioned printing with Latin letters Fris did not teach, although he had studied Latin in his youth.

Fris himself probably did not feel the change, for he had ceased to feel both for himself and for others. None now brought their human sorrows to him, and found comfort in a sympathetic mind; his mind was not there to consult. It floated outside him, half detached, as it were, like a bird that is unwilling to leave its old nest to set out on a flight to the unknown. It must have been the fluttering mind that his eyes were always following when they dully gazed about into vacancy. But the young men who came home to winter in the village, and went to Fris as to an old friend, felt the change. For them there was now an empty place at home; they missed the old growler, who, though he hated them all in the lump at school, loved them all afterward, and was always ready with his ridiculous "He was my best boy! " about each and all of them, good and bad alike.

The children took their playtime early, and rushed out before Pelle had given the signal; and Fris trotted off as usual into the village, where he would be absent the customary two hours. The girls gathered in a flock to eat their dinners, and the boys dashed about the playground like birds let loose from a cage.

Pelle was quite angry at the insubordination, and pondered over a way of making himself respected; for to-day he had had the other big boys against him. He dashed over the playground like a circling gull, his body inclined and his arms stretched out like a pair of wings. Most of them made room for him, and those who did not move willingly were made to do so. His position was threatened, and he kept moving incessantly, as if to keep the question undecided until a possibility of striking presented itself.

This went on for some time; he knocked some over and hit out at others in his flight, while his offended sense of power grew. He wanted to make enemies of them all. They began to gather up by the gymnastic apparatus, and suddenly he had the whole pack upon him. He tried to rise and shake them off, flinging them hither and thither, but all in vain; down through the heap came their remorseless knuckles and made him grin with pain. He worked away indefatigably but without effect until he lost patience and resorted to less scrupulous tactics—thrusting his fingers into eyes, or attacking noses, windpipes, and any vulnerable part he could get at. That thinned them out, and he was able to rise and fling a last little fellow across the playground.

Pelle was well bruised and quite out of breath, but contented. They all stood by, gaping, and let him brush himself down; he was the victor. He went across to the girls with his torn blouse, and they put it together with pins and gave him sweets; and in return he fastened two of them together by their plaits, and they screamed and let him pull them about without being cross; it was all just as it should be.

But he was not quite secure after his victory. He could not, like Henry Boker in his time, walk right through the whole flock with his hands in his pockets directly after a battle, and look as if they did not exist. He had to keep stealing glances at them while he strolled down to the beach, and tried with all his might to control his breathing; for next to crying, to be out of breath was the greatest disgrace that could happen to you.

Pelle walked along the beach, regretting that he had not leaped upon them again at once while the flush of victory was still upon him: it was too late now. If he had, it might perhaps have been said of him too that he could lick all the rest of the class together; and now he must be content with being the strongest boy in the school.

A wild war-whoop from the school made him start. The whole swarm of boys was coming round the end of the house with sticks and pieces of wood in their hands. Pelle knew what was at stake if he gave way, and therefore forced himself to stand quietly waiting although his legs twitched. But suddenly they made a wild rush at him, and with a spring he turned to fly. There lay the sea barring his way, closely packed with heaving ice. He ran out on to an ice-floe, leaped from it to the next, which was not large enough to bear him— had to go on.

The idea of flight possessed him and made the fear of what lay behind overpoweringly great. The lumps of ice gave way beneath him, and he had to leap from piece to piece; his feet moved as fast as fingers over the notes of a piano. He just noticed enough to take the direction toward the harbor breakwater. The others stood gaping on the beach while Pelle danced upon the water like a stone making ducks and drakes. The pieces of ice bobbed under as soon as he touched them, or turned up on edge; but Pelle came and slid by with a touch, flung himself to one side with lightning rapidity, and changed his aim in the middle of a leap like a cat. It was like a dance on red-hot iron, so quickly did he pick up his feet, and spring from one place to another. The water spurted up from the pieces of ice as he touched them, and behind him stretched a crooked track of disturbed ice and water right back to the place where the boys stood and held their breath. There was nobody like Pelle, not one of them could do what he had done there! When with a final leap he threw himself upon the breakwater, they cheered him. Pelle had triumphed in his flight!

He lay upon the breakwater, exhausted and gasping for breath, and gazed without interest at a brig that had cast anchor off the village. A boat was rowing in—perhaps with a sick man to be put in quarantine. The weather-beaten look of the vessel told of her having been out on a winter voyage, in ice and heavy seas.

Fishermen came down from the cottages and strolled out to the place where the boat would come in, and all the school-children followed.

In the stern of the boat sat an elderly, weather-beaten man with a fringe of beard round his face; he was dressed in blue, and in front of him stood a sea-chest. "Why, it's Boatswain Olsen! " Pelle heard one fisherman say. Then the man stepped ashore, and shook hands with them all; and the fisherman and the school-children closed round him in a dense circle.

Pelle made his way up, creeping along behind boats and sheds; and as soon as he was hidden by the school-building, he set off running straight across the fields to Stone Farm. His vexation burnt his throat, and a feeling of shame made him keep far away from houses and people. The parcel that he had had no opportunity of delivering in the morning was like a clear proof to everybody of his shame, and he threw it into a marl-pit as he ran.

He would not go through the farm, but thundered on the outside door to the stable. "Have you come home already? " exclaimed Lasse, pleased.

"Now—now Madam Olsen's husband's come home! " panted Pelle, and went past his father without looking at him.

To Lasse it was as if the world had burst and the falling fragments were piercing into his flesh. Everything was failing him. He moved about trembling and unable to grasp anything; he could not talk, everything in him seemed to have come to a standstill. He had picked up a piece of rope, and was going backward and forward, backward and forward, looking up.

Then Pelle went up to him. "What are you going to do with that? " he asked harshly.

Lasse let the rope fall from his hand and began to complain of the sadness and poverty of existence. One feather fell off here, and another there, until at last you stood trampling in the mud like a featherless bird—old and worn-out and robbed of every hope of a happy old age. He went on complaining in this way in an undertone, and it eased him.

Pelle made no response. He only thought of the wrong and the shame that had come upon them, and found no relief.

Next morning he took his dinner and went off as usual, but when he was halfway to school he lay down under a thorn. There he lay, fuming and half-frozen, until it was about the time when school would be over, when he went home. This he did for several days. Toward his father he was silent, almost angry. Lasse went about lamenting, and Pelle had enough with his own trouble; each moved in his own world, and there was no bridge between; neither of them had a kind word to say to the other.

But one day when Pelle came stealing home in this way, Lasse received him with a radiant face and weak knees. "What on earth's the good of fretting? " he said, screwing up his face and turning his blinking eyes upon Pelle—for the first time since the bad news had come. "Look here at the new sweetheart I've found! Kiss her, laddie! " And Lasse drew from the straw a bottle of gin, and held it out toward him.

Pelle pushed it angrily from him.

"Oh, you're too grand, are you? " exclaimed Lasse. "Well, well, it would be a sin and a shame to waste good things upon you. " He put the bottle to his lips and threw back his head.

"Father, you shan't do that! " exclaimed Pelle, bursting into tears and shaking his father's arm so that the liquid splashed out.

"Ho-ho! " said Lasse in astonishment, wiping his mouth with the back of his hand. "She's uncommonly lively, ho-ho! " He grasped the bottle with both hands and held it firmly, as if it had tried to get away from him. "So you're obstreperous, are you? " Then his eye fell upon Pelle. "And you're crying! Has any one hurt you? Don't you know that your father's called Lasse—Lasse Karlsson from Kungstorp? You needn't he afraid, for Lasse's here, and he'll make the whole world answer for it. "

Pelle saw that his father was quickly becoming more fuddled, and ought to be put to bed for fear some one should come and find him lying there. "Come now, father! " he begged.

"Yes, I'll go now. I'll make him pay for it, if it's old Beelzebub himself! You needn't cry! " Lasse was making for the yard.

Pelle stood in front of him. "Now you must come with me, father! There's no one to make pay for anything. "

"Isn't there? And yet you're crying! But the farmer shall answer to me for all these years. Yes, my fine landed gentleman, with your nose turned up at every one! "

This made Pelle afraid. "But father, father! " he cried. "Don't go up there! He'll be in such a rage, he'll turn us out! Remember you're drunk! "

"Yes, of course I'm drunk, but there's no harm in me. " He stood fumbling with the hook that fastened the lower half of the door.

It was wrong to lay a hand upon one's own father, but now Pelle was compelled to set aside all such scruples. He took a firm hold of the old man's collar. "Now you come with me! " he said, and drew him along toward their room.

Lasse laughed and hiccupped and struggled; clutched hold of everything that he could lay hands on—the posts and the animals' tails—while Pelle dragged him along. He had hold of him behind, and was half carrying him. In the doorway they stuck fast, as the old man held on with both hands; and Pelle had to leave go of him and knock his arms away so that he fell, and then drag him along and on to the bed.

Lasse laughed foolishly all the time, as if it were a game. Once or twice when Pelle's back was turned, he tried to get up; his eyes had almost disappeared, but there was a cunning expression about his mouth, and he was like a naughty child. Suddenly he fell back in a heavy sleep.

The next day was a school holiday, so there was no need for Pelle to hide himself. Lasse was ashamed and crept about with an air of humility. He must have had quite a clear idea of what had happened the day before, for suddenly he touched Pelle's arm. "You're like Noah's good son, that covered up his father's shame! " he said; "but Lasse's a beast. It's been a hard blow on me, as you may well believe! But I know quite well that it doesn't mend matters to drink one's self silly. It's a badly buried trouble that one has to lay with gin; and what's hidden in the snow comes up in the thaw, as the saying is. "

Pelle made no answer.

"How do people take it? " asked Lasse cautiously. He had now got so far as to have a thought for the shameful side of the matter. "I don't think they know about it yet here on the farm; but what do they say outside? "

"How should I know? " answered Pelle sulkily.

"Then you've heard nothing? "

"Do you suppose I'll go to school to be jeered at by them all? " Pelle was almost crying again.

"Then you've been wandering about and let your father believe that you'd gone to school? That wasn't right of you, but I won't find fault with you, considering all the disgrace I've brought upon you. But suppose you get into trouble for playing truant, even if you don't deserve it? Misfortunes go hand in hand, and evils multiply like lice in a fur coat. We must think what we're about, we two; we mustn't let things go all to pieces! "

Lasse walked quickly into their room and returned with the bottle, took out the cork, and let the gin run slowly out into the gutter. Pelle looked wonderingly at him. "God forgive me for abusing his gifts! " said Lasse; "but it's a bad tempter to have at hand when you've a sore heart. And now if I give you my word that you shall never again see me as I was yesterday, won't you have a try at school again to-morrow, and try and get over it gradually? We might get into trouble with the magistrate himself if you keep on staying away; for there's a heavy punishment for that sort of thing in this country. "

Pelle promised and kept his word; but he was prepared for the worst, and secretly slipped a knuckle-duster into his pocket that Erik had used in his palmy days when he went to open-air fetes and other places where one had to strike a blow for one's girl. It was not required, however, for the boys were entirely taken up with a ship that had had to be run aground to prevent her sinking, and now lay discharging her cargo of wheat into the boats of the village. The wheat already lay in the harbor in great piles, wet and swollen with the salt water.

And a few days later, when this had become stale, something happened which put a stop forever to Pelle's school attendance. The children were busy at arithmetic, chattering and clattering with their slates, and Fris was sitting as usual in his place, with his head against the wall and his hands resting on the desk. His dim eyes were somewhere out in space, and not a movement betrayed that he was alive. It was his usual position, and he had sat thus ever since playtime.

The children grew restless; it was nearly time for them to go home. A farmer's son who had a watch, held it up so that Pelle could see it, and said "Two" aloud. They noisily put away their slates and began to fight; but Fris, who generally awoke at this noise of departure, did not stir. Then they tramped out, and in passing, one of the girls out of mischief stroked the master's hand. She started back in fear. "He's quite cold! " she said, shuddering and drawing back behind the others.

They stood in a semicircle round the desk, and tried to see into Fris's half-closed eyes; and then Pelle went up the two steps and laid his hand upon his master's shoulder. "We're going home, " he said, in an unnatural voice. Fris's arm dropped stiffly down from the desk, and Pelle had to support his body. "He's dead! " the words passed like a shiver over the children's lips.

Fris was dead—dead at his post, as the honest folks of the parish expressed it. Pelle had finished his schooling for good, and could breathe freely.

He helped his father at home, and they were happy together and drew together again now that there was no third person to stand between them. The gibes from the others on the farm were not worth taking notice of; Lasse had been a long time on the farm, and knew too much about each of them, so that he could talk back. He sunned himself in Pelle's gently childlike nature, and kept up a continual chatter. One thing he was always coming back to. "I ought to be glad I had you, for if you hadn't held back that time when I was bent upon moving down to Madam Olsen's, we should have been in the wrong box. I should think he'd have killed us in his anger. You were my good angel as you always have been. "

Lasse's words had the pleasant effect of caresses on Pelle; he was happy in it all, and was more of a child than his years would have indicated.

But one Saturday he came home from the parson's altogether changed. He was as slow about everything as a dead herring, and did not go across to his dinner, but came straight in through the outer door, and threw himself face downward upon a bundle of hay.

"What's the matter now? " asked Lasse, coming up to him. "Has any one been unkind to you? "

Pelle did not answer, but lay plucking at the hay. Lasse was going to turn his face up to him, but Pelle buried it in the hay. "Won't you trust your own father? You know I've no other wish in the world but for your good! " Lasse's voice was sad.

"I'm to be turned out of the confirmation-class, " Pelle managed to say, and then burrowed into the hay to keep back his tears.

"Oh, no, surely not! " Lasse began to tremble. "Whatever have you done? "

"I've half killed the parson's son. "

"Oh, that's about the worst thing you could have done—lift your hand against the parson's son! I'm sure he must have deserved it, but—still you shouldn't have done it. Unless he's accused you of thieving, for no honest man need stand that from any one, not even the king himself. "

"He—he called you Madam Olsen's concubine. " Pelle had some difficulty in getting this out.

Lasse's mouth grew hard and he clenched his fists. "Oh, he did! Oh, did he! If I had him here, I'd kick his guts out, the young monkey! I hope you gave him something he'll remember for a long time? "

"Oh, no, it wasn't very much, for he wouldn't stand up to me—he threw himself down and screamed. And then the parson came! "

For a little while Lasse's face was disfigured with rage, and he kept uttering threats. Then he turned to Pelle. "And they've turned you out? Only because you stood up for your old father! I'm always to bring misfortune upon you, though I'm only thinking of your good! But what shall we do now? "

"I won't stay here any longer, " said Pelle decidedly.

"No, let's get away from here; nothing has ever grown on this farm for us two but wormwood. Perhaps there are new, happy days waiting for us out there; and there are parsons everywhere. If we two work together at some good work out there, we shall earn a peck of money. Then one day we'll go up to a parson, and throw down half a hundred krones in front of his face, and it 'u'd be funny if he didn't confirm you on the spot—and perhaps let himself be kicked into the bargain. Those kind of folk are very fond of money. "

Lasse had grown more erect in his anger, and had a keen look in his eyes. He walked quickly along the foddering passage, and threw the things about carelessly, for Pelle's adventurous proposal had infected him with youth. In the intervals of their work, they collected all their little things and packed the green chest. "What a surprise it'll be to-morrow morning when they come here and find the nest empty! " said Pelle gaily. Lasse chuckled.

Their plan was to take shelter with Kalle for a day or two, while they took a survey of what the world offered. When everything was done in the evening, they took the green chest between them, and stole out through the outside door into the field. The chest was heavy, and the darkness did not make walking easier. They moved on a little way, changed hands, and rested. "We've got the night before us! " said Lasse cheerfully.

He was quite animated, and while they sat resting upon the chest talked about everything that awaited them. When he came to a standstill Pelle began. Neither of them had made any distinct plans for their future; they simply expected a fairy-story itself with its inconceivable surprises. All the definite possibilities that they were capable of picturing to themselves fell so far short of that which must come, that they left it alone and abandoned themselves to what lay beyond their powers of foresight.

Lasse was not sure-footed in the dark, and had more and more frequently to put down his burden. He grew weary and breathless, and the cheerful words died away upon his lips. "Ah, how heavy it is! " he sighed. "What a lot of rubbish you do scrape together in the course of time! " Then he sat down upon the chest, quite out of breath. He could do no more. "If only we'd had something to pick us up a little! " he said faintly. "And it's so dark and gloomy to-night. "

"Help me to get it on my back, " said Pelle, "and I'll carry it a little way. "

Lasse would not at first, but gave in, and they went on again, he running on in front and giving warning of ditches and walls. "Suppose Brother Kalle can't take us in! " he said suddenly.

"He's sure to be able to. There's grandmother's bed; that's big enough for two. "

"But suppose we can't get anything to do, then we shall be a burden on him. "

"Oh, we shall get something to do. There's a scarcity of laborers everywhere. "

"Yes, they'll jump at you, but I'm really too old to offer myself out. " Lasse had lost all hope, and was undermining Pelle's too.

"I can't do any more! " said Pelle, letting the chest down. They stood with arms hanging, and stared into the darkness at nothing particular. Lasse showed no desire to take hold again, and Pelle was now tired out. The night lay dark around them, and its all-enveloping loneliness made it seem as if they two were floating alone in space.

"Well, we ought to be getting on, " exclaimed Pelle, taking a handle of the chest; but as Lasse did not move, he dropped it and sat down. They sat back to back, and neither could find the right words to utter, and the distance between them seemed to increase. Lasse shivered with the night cold. "If only we were at home in our good bed! " he sighed.

Pelle was almost wishing he had been alone, for then he would have gone on to the end. The old man was just as heavy to drag along as the chest.

"Do you know I think I'll go back again! " said Lasse at last in crestfallen tone. "I'm afraid I'm not able to tread uncertain paths. And you'll never be confirmed if we go on like this! Suppose we go back and get Kongstrup to put in a good word for us with the parson. " Lasse stood and held one handle of the chest.

Pelle sat on as if he had not heard, and then he silently took hold, and they toiled along on their weary way homeward across the fields. Every other minute Pelle was tired and had to rest; now that they were going home, Lasse was the more enduring. "I think I could carry it a little way alone, if you'd help me up with it, " he said; but Pelle would not hear of it.

"Pee-u-ah! " sighed Lasse with pleasure when they once more stood in the warmth of the cow-stable and heard the animals breathing in indolent well-being—"it's comfortable here. It's just like coming into one's old home. I think I should know this stable again by the air, if they led me into it blindfold anywhere in the world. "

And now they were home again, Pelle too could not help thinking that it really was pleasant.

XXIII

On Sunday morning, between watering and midday feed, Lasse and Pelle ascended the high stone steps. They took off their wooden shoes in the passage, and stood and shook themselves outside the door of the office; their gray stocking-feet were full of chaff and earth. Lasse raised his hand to knock, but drew it back. "Have you wiped your nose properly? " he asked in a whisper, with a look of anxiety on his face. Pelle performed the operation once more, and gave a final polish with the sleeve of his blouse.

Lasse lifted his hand again; he looked greatly oppressed. "You might keep quiet then! " he said irritably to Pelle, who was standing as still as a mouse. Lasse's knuckles were poised in the air two or three times before they fell upon the door; and then he stood with his forehead close to the panel and listened. "There's no one there, " he whispered irresolutely.

"Just go in! " exclaimed Pelle. "We can't stand here all day. "

"Then you can go first, if you think you know better how to behave! " said Lasse, offended.

Pelle quickly opened the door and went in. There was no one in the office, but the door was open into the drawing-room, and the sound of Kongstrup's comfortable breathing came thence.

"Who's there? " he asked.

"It's Lasse and Pelle, " answered Lasse in a voice that did not sound altogether brave.

"Will you come in here? "

Kongstrup was lying on the sofa reading a magazine, and on the table beside him stood a pile of old magazines and a plateful of little cakes. He did not raise his eyes from his book, not even while his hand went out to the plate for something to put in his mouth. He lay nibbling and swallowing while he read, and never looked at Lasse and Pelle, or asked them what they wanted, or said anything to give them a start. It was like being sent out to plough without knowing where. He must have been in the middle of something very exciting.

"Well, what do you want? " asked Kongstrup at last in slow tones.

"Well—well, the master must excuse us for coming like this about something that doesn't concern the farm; but as matters now stand, we've no one else to go to, and so I said to the laddie: 'Master won't be angry, I'm sure, for he's many a time been kind to us poor beggars—and that. ' Now it's so in this world that even if you're a poor soul that's only fit to do others' dirty work, the Almighty's nevertheless given you a father's heart, and it hurts you to see the father's sin standing in the son's way. "

Lasse came to a standstill. He had thought it all out beforehand, and so arranged it that it should lead up, in a shrewd, dignified way, to the matter itself. But now it was all in a muddle like a slattern's pocket-handkerchief, and the farmer did not look as if he had understood a single word of it. He lay there, taking a cake now and then, and looking helplessly toward the door.

"It sometimes happens too, that a man gets tired of the single state, " began Lasse once more, but at once gave up trying to go on. No matter how he began, he went round and round the thing and got no hold anywhere! And now Kongstrup began to read again. A tiny question from him might have led to the very middle of it; but he only filled his mouth full and began munching quite hard.

Lasse was outwardly disheartened and inwardly angry, as he stood there and prepared to go. Pelle was staring about at the pictures and the old mahogany furniture, making up his mind about each thing.

Suddenly energetic steps sounded through the rooms; the ear could follow their course right up from the kitchen. Kongstrup's eyes brightened, and Lasse straightened himself up.

"Is that you two? " said Fru Kongstrup in her decided way that indicated the manager. "But do sit down! Why didn't you offer them a seat, old man? "

Lasse and Pelle found seats, and the mistress seated herself beside her husband, with her arm leaning upon his pillow. "How are you getting on, Kongstrup? Have you been resting? " she asked sympathetically, patting his shoulder. Kongstrup gave a little grunt, that might have meant yes, or no, or nothing at all.

"And what about you two? Are you in need of money? "

"No, it's the lad. He's to be dismissed from the confirmation- class, " answered Lasse simply. With the mistress you couldn't help being decided.

"Are you to be dismissed? " she exclaimed, looking at Pelle as at an old acquaintance. "Then what have you been doing? "

"Oh, I kicked the parson's son. "

"And what did you do that for? "

"Because he wouldn't fight, but threw himself down. "

Fru Kongstrup laughed and nudged her husband. "Yes, of course. But what had he done to you? "

"He'd said bad things about Father Lasse. "

"What were the things? "

Pelle looked hard at her; she meant to get to the bottom of everything. "I won't tell you! " he said firmly.

"Oh, very well! But then we can't do anything about it either. "

"I may just as well tell you, " Lasse interrupted. "He called me Madam Olsen's concubine—from the Bible story, I suppose. "

Kongstrup tried to suppress a chuckle, as if some one had whispered a coarse joke in his ear, and he could not help it. The mistress herself was serious enough.

"I don't think I understand, " she said, and laid a repressing hand upon her husband's arm. "Lasse must explain. "

"It's because I was engaged to Madam Olsen in the village, who every one thought was a widow; and then her husband came home the other day. And so they've given me that nickname round about, I suppose. "

Kongstrup began his suppressed laughter again, and Lasse blinked in distress at it.

"Help yourselves to a cake! " said Fru Kongstrup in a very loud voice, pushing the plate toward them. This silenced Kongstrup, and he lay and watched their assault upon the cake-plate with an attentive eye.

Fru Kongstrup sat tapping the table with her middle finger while they ate. "So that good boy Pelle got angry and kicked out, did he? " she said suddenly, her eyes flashing.

"Yes, that's what he never ought to have done! " answered Lasse plaintively.

Fru Kongstrup fixed her eyes upon him.

"No, for all that the poorer birds are for is to be pecked at! Well, I prefer the bird that pecks back again and defends its nest, no matter how poor it is. Well, well, we shall see! And is that boy going to be confirmed? Why, of course! To think that I should be so forgetful! Then we must begin to think about his clothes. "

"That's two troubles got rid of! " said Lasse when they went down to the stable again. "And did you notice how nicely I let her know that you were going to be confirmed? It was almost as if she'd found it out for herself. Now you'll see, you'll be as fine as a shop-boy in your clothes; people like the master and mistress know what's needed when once they've opened their purse. Well, they got the whole truth straight, but confound it! they're no more than human beings. It's always best to speak out straight. " Lasse could not forget how well it had turned out.

Pelle let the old man boast. "Do you think I shall get leather shoes of them too? " he asked.

"Yes, of course you will! And I shouldn't wonder if they made a confirmation-party for you too. I say *they*, but it's her that's doing it all, and we may be thankful for that. Did you notice that she said *we—we* shall, and so on—always? It's nice of her, for he only lies there and eats and leaves everything to her. But what a good time he has! I think she'd go through fire to please him; but upon my word, she's master there. Well, well, I suppose we oughtn't to speak evil of any one; to you she's like your own mother! "

Fru Kongstrup said nothing about the result of her drive to the parson; it was not her way to talk about things afterward. But Lasse and Pelle once more trod the earth with a feeling of security; when she took up a matter, it was as good as arranged.

One morning later in the week, the tailor came limping in with his scissors, tape-measure, and pressing-iron, and Pelle had to go down to the servants' room, and was measured in every direction as if he had been a prize animal. Up to the present, he had always had his clothes made by guess-work. It was something new to have itinerant artisans at Stone Farm; since Kongstrup had come into power, neither shoemaker nor tailor had ever set foot in the servants' room. This was a return to the good old farm-customs, and placed Stone Farm once more on a footing with the other farms. The people enjoyed it, and as often as they could went down into the servants' room for a change of air and to hear one of the tailor's yarns. "It's the mistress who's at the head of things now! " they said to one another. There was good peasant blood in her hands, and she brought things back into the good old ways. Pelle walked into the servants' room like a gentleman; he was fitted several times a day.

He was fitted for two whole suits, one of which was for Rud, who was to be confirmed too. It would probably be the last thing that Rud and his mother would get at the farm, for Fru Kongstrup had carried her point, and they were to leave the cottage in May. They would never venture to set foot again in Stone Farm. Fru Kongstrup herself saw that they received what they were to have, but she did not give money if she could help it.

Pelle and Rud were never together now, and they seldom went to the parson together. It was Pelle who had drawn back, as he had grown tired of being on the watch for Rud's continual little lies and treacheries. Pelle was taller and stronger than Rud, and his nature — perhaps because of his physical superiority—had taken more open ways. In ability to master a task or learn it by heart, Rud was also the inferior; but on the other hand he could bewilder Pelle and the other boys, if he only got a hold with his practical common sense.

On the great day itself, Karl Johan drove Pelle and Lasse in the little one-horse carriage. "We're fine folk to-day! " said Lasse, with a beaming face. He was quite confused, although he had not tasted anything strong. There was a bottle of gin lying in the chest to treat the men with when the sacred ceremony was over; but Lasse was not the man to drink anything before he went to church. Pelle had not *touched* food; God's Word would take best effect in that condition.

Pelle was radiant too, in spite of his hunger. He was in brand-new twill, so new that it crackled every time he moved. On his feet he wore elastic-sided shoes that had once belonged to Kongstrup himself. They were too large, but "there's no difficulty with a sausage that's too long, " as Lasse said. He put in thick soles and paper in the toes, and Pelle put on two pairs of stockings; and then the shoes fitted as if they had been cast for his foot. On his head he wore a blue cap that he had chosen himself down at the shop. It allowed room for growing, and rested on his ears, which, for the occasion, were as red as two roses. Round the cap was a broad ribbon in which were woven rakes, scythes, and flails, interlaced with sheaves all the way round.

"It's a good thing you came, " said Pelle, as they drove up to the church, and found themselves among so many people. Lasse had almost had to give up thought of coming, for the man who was going to look after the animals while he was away had to go off at the last moment for the veterinary surgeon; but Karna came and offered to water and give the midday feed, although neither could truthfully say that they had behaved as they ought to have done to her.

"Have you got that thing now? " whispered Lasse, when they were inside the church. Pelle felt in his pocket and nodded; the little round piece of lignum-vitae that was to carry him over the difficulties of the day lay there. "Then just answer loud and straight out, " whispered Lasse, as he slipped into a pew in the background.

Pelle did answer straight out, and to Lasse his voice sounded really well through the spacious church. And the parson did absolutely nothing to revenge himself, but treated Pelle exactly as he did the others. At the most solemn part of the ceremony, Lasse thought of Karna, and how touching her devotion was. He scolded himself in an undertone, and made a solemn vow. She should not sigh any longer in vain.

For a whole month indeed, Lasse's thoughts had been occupied with Karna, now favorably, now unfavorably; but at this solemn moment when Pelle was just taking the great step into the future, and Lasse's feelings were touched in so many ways, the thought of Karna's devotion broke over him as something sad, like a song of slighted affection that at last, at last has justice done to it.

Lasse shook hands with Pelle. "Good luck and a blessing! " he said in a trembling voice. The wish also embraced his own vow and he had some difficulty in keeping silence respecting his determination, he was so moved. The words were heard on all sides, and Pelle went round and shook hands with his comrades. Then they drove home.

"It all went uncommonly well for you to-day, " said Lasse proudly; "and now you're a man, you know. "

"Yes, now you must begin to look about for a sweetheart, " said Karl Johan. Pelle only laughed.

In the afternoon they had a holiday. Pelle had first to go up to his master and mistress to thank them for his clothes and receive their congratulations. Fru Kongstrup gave him red-currant wine and cake, and the farmer gave him a two-krone piece.

Then they went up to Kalle's by the quarry. Pelle was to exhibit himself in his new clothes, and say good-bye to them; there was only a fortnight to May Day. Lasse was going to take the opportunity of secretly obtaining information concerning a house that was for sale on the heath.

XXIV

They still talked about it every day for the short time that was left. Lasse, who had always had the thought of leaving in his mind, and had only stayed on and on, year after year, because the boy's welfare demanded it—was slow to move now that there was nothing to hold him back. He was unwilling to lose Pelle, and did all he could to keep him; but nothing would induce him to go out into the world again.

"Stay here! " he said persuasively, "and we'll talk to the mistress and she'll take you on for a proper wage. You're both strong and handy, and she's always looked upon you with a friendly eye. "

But Pelle would not take service with the farmer; it gave no position and no prospects. He wanted to be something great, but there was no possibility of that in the country; he would be following cows all his days. He would go to the town—perhaps still farther, across the sea to Copenhagen.

"You'd better come too, " he said, "and then we shall get rich all the quicker and be able to buy a big farm. "

"Yes, yes, " said Lasse, slowly nodding his head; "that's one for me and two for yourself! But what the parson preaches doesn't always come to pass. We might become penniless. Who knows what the future may bring? "

"Oh, I shall manage! " said Pelle, nodding confidently. "Do you mean to say I can't turn my hand to anything I like? "

"And I didn't give notice in time either, " said Lasse to excuse himself.

"Then run away! "

But Lasse would not do that. "No, I'll stay and work toward getting something for myself about here, " he said, a little evasively. "It would be nice for you too, to have a home that you could visit now and then; and if you didn't get on out there, it wouldn't be bad to have something to fall back upon. You might fall ill, or something else might happen; the world's not to be relied upon. You have to have a hard skin all over out there. "

Pelle did not answer. That about the home sounded nice enough, and he understood quite well that it was Karna's person that weighed down the other end of the balance. Well, she'd put all his clothes in order for his going away, and she'd always been a good soul; he had nothing against that.

It would be hard to live apart from Father Lasse, but Pelle felt he must go. Away! The spring seemed to shout the word in his ears. He knew every rock in the landscape and every tree—yes, every twig on the trees as well; there was nothing more here that could fill his blue eyes and long ears, and satisfy his mind.

The day before May Day they packed Pelle's things. Lasse knelt before the green chest; every article was carefully folded and remarked upon, before it was placed in the canvas bag that was to serve Pelle as a traveling-trunk.

"Now remember not to wear your stockings too long before you mend them! " said Lasse, putting mending wool on one side. "He who mends his things in time, is spared half the work and all the disgrace. "

"I shan't forget that, " said Pelle quietly.

Lasse was holding a folded shirt in his hand. "The one you've got on's just been washed, " he said reflectively. "But one can't tell. Two shirts'll almost be too little if you're away, won't they? You must take one of mine; I can always manage to get another by the time I want a change. And remember, you must never go longer than a fortnight! You who are young and healthy might easily get vermin, and be jeered at by the whole town; such a thing would never be tolerated in any one who wants to get on. At the worst you can do a little washing or yourself; you could go down to the shore in the evening, if that was all! "

"Do they wear wooden shoes in the town? " asked Pelle.

"Not people who want to get on! I think you'd better let me keep the wooden shoes and you take my boots instead; they always look nice even if they're old. You'd better wear them when you go to-morrow, and save your good shoes. "

The new clothes were laid at the top of the bag, wrapped in an old blouse to keep them clean.

"Now I think we've got everything in, " said Lasse, with a searching glance into the green chest. There was not much left in it. "Very well, then we'll tie it up in God's name, and pray that, you may arrive safely—wherever you decide to go! " Lasse tied up the sack; he was anything but happy.

"You must say good-bye nicely to every one on the farm, so that they won't have anything to scratch my eyes out for afterward, " said Lasse after a little. "And I should like you to thank Karna nicely for having put everything in such good order. It isn't every one who'd have bothered. "

"Yes, I'll do that, " said Pelle in a low voice. He did not seem to be able to speak out properly to-day.

* * * * *

Pelle was up and dressed at daybreak. Mist lay over the sea, and prophesied well for the day. He went about well scrubbed and combed, and looked at everything with wide-open eyes, and with his hands in his pockets. The blue clothes which he had gone to his confirmation- classes in, had been washed and newly mangled, and he still looked very well in them; and the tabs of the old leather boots, which were a relic of Lasse's prosperous days, stuck out almost as much as his ears.

He had said his "Good-bye and thank-you for all your kindness! " to everybody on the farm—even Erik; and he had had a good meal of bacon. Now he was going about the stable, collecting himself, shaking the bull by the horns, and letting the calves suck his fingers; it was a sort of farewell too! The cows put their noses close up to him, and breathed a long, comfortable breath when he passed, and the bull playfully tossed its head at him. And close behind him went Lasse; he did not say very much but he always kept near the boy.

It was so good to be here, and the feeling sank gently over Pelle every time a cow licked herself, or the warm vapor rose from freshly- falling dung. Every sound was like a mother's caress, and every thing was a familiar toy, with which a bright world could be built. Upon the posts all round there were pictures that he had cut upon them; Lasse had smeared them over with dirt again, in case the farmer should come and say that they were spoiling everything.

Pelle was not thinking, but went about in a dreamy state; it all sank so warmly and heavily into his child's mind. He had taken out his knife, and took hold of the bull's horn, as if he were going to carve something on it. "He won't let you do that, " said Lasse, surprised. "Try one of the bullocks instead. "

But Pelle returned his knife to his pocket; he had not intended to do anything. He strolled along the foddering-passage without aim or object. Lasse came up and took his hand.

"You'd better stay here a little longer, " he said. "We're so comfortable. "

But this put life into Pelle. He fixed his big, faithful eyes upon his father, and then went down to their room.

Lasse followed him. "In God's name then, if it has to be! " he said huskily, and took hold of the sack to help Pelle get it onto his back.

Pelle held out his hand. "Good-bye and thank you, father—for all your kindness! " he added gently.

"Yes, yes; yes, yes! " said Lasse, shaking his head. It was all he was able to say.

He went out with Pelle past the out-houses, and there stopped, while Pelle went on along the dikes with his sack on his back, up toward the high-road. Two or three times he turned and nodded; Lasse, overcome, stood gazing, with his hand shading his eyes. He had never looked so old before.

Out in the fields they were driving the seed-harrow; Stone Farm was early with it this year. Kongstrup and his wife were strolling along arm-in-arm beside a ditch; every now and then they stopped and she pointed: they must have been talking about the crop. She leaned against him when they walked; she had really found rest in her affection now!

Now Lasse turned and went in. How forlorn he looked! Pelle felt a quick desire to throw down the sack and run back and say something nice to him; but before he could do so the impulse had disappeared upon the fresh morning breeze. His feet carried him on upon the straight way, away, away! Up on a ridge the bailiff was stepping out a field, and close behind him walked Erik, imitating him with foolish gestures.

On a level with the edge of the rocks, Pelle came to the wide high-road. Here, he knew, Stone Farm and its lands would be lost to sight, and he put down his sack. *There* were the sand-banks by the sea, with every tree-top visible; *there* was the fir-tree that the yellowhammer always built in; the stream ran milk-white after the heavy thaw, and the meadow was beginning to grow green. But the cairn was gone; good people had removed it secretly when Niels Koller was drowned and the girl was expected out of prison.

And the farm stood out clearly in the morning light, with its high white dwelling-house, the long range of barns, and all the out-houses. Every spot down there shone so familiarly toward him; the hardships he had suffered were forgotten, or only showed up the comforts in stronger relief.

Pelle's childhood had been happy by virtue of everything; it had been a song mingled with weeping. Weeping falls into tones as well as joy, and heard from a distance it becomes a song. And as Pelle gazed down upon his childhood's world, they were only pleasant memories that gleamed toward him through the bright air. Nothing else existed, or ever had done so.

He had seen enough of hardship and misfortune, but had come well out of everything; nothing had harmed him. With a child's voracity he had found nourishment in it all; and now he stood here, healthy and strong—equipped with the Prophets, the Judges, the Apostles, the Ten Commandments and one hundred and twenty hymns! and turned an open, perspiring, victor's brow toward the world.

Before him lay the land sloping richly toward the south, bounded by the sea. Far below stood two tall black chimneys against the sea as background, and still farther south lay the Town! Away from it ran the paths of the sea to Sweden and Copenhagen! This was the world— the great wide world itself!

Pelle became ravenously hungry at the sight of the great world, and the first thing he did was to sit down upon the ridge of the hill with a view both backward and forward, and eat all the food Karna had given him for the whole day. So his stomach would have nothing more to trouble about!

He rose refreshed, got the sack onto his back, and set off downward to conquer the world, pouring forth a song at the top of his voice into the bright air as he went: —

> "A stranger I must wander
> Among the Englishmen;
> With African black negroes
> My lot it may be thrown.
> And then upon this earth there
> Are Portuguese found too,
> And every kind of nation
> Under heaven's sky so blue. "

II. APPRENTICESHIP

I

On that windy May-morning when Pelle tumbled out of the nest, it so happened that old Klaus Hermann was clattering into town with his manure-cart, in order to fetch a load of dung. And this trifling circumstance decided the boy's position in life. There was no more pother than this about the question: What was Pelle to be?

He had never put that question to himself. He had simply gone onward at hazard, as the meaning of the radiant world unfolded itself. As to what he should make of himself when he was really out in the world —well, the matter was so incomprehensible that it was mere folly to think about it. So he just went on.

Now he had reached the further end of the ridge. He lay down in the ditch to recover his breath after his long walk; he was tired and hungry, but in excellent spirits. Down there at his feet, only half a mile distant, lay the town. There was a cheerful glitter about it; from its hundreds of fireplaces the smoke of midday fires curled upward into the blue sky, and the red roofs laughed roguishly into the beaming face of the day. Pelle immediately began to count the houses; not wishing to exaggerate, he had estimated them at a million only, and already he was well into the first hundred.

But in the midst of his counting he jumped up. What did the people down there get for dinner? They must surely live well there! And was it polite to go on eating until one was quite full, or should one lay down one's spoon when one had only half finished, like the landowners when they attended a dinner? For one who was always hungry this was a very important question.

There was a great deal of traffic on the high-road. People were coming and going; some had their boxes behind them in a cart, and others carried their sole worldly possessions in a bag slung over their shoulders, just as he did. Pelle knew some of these people, and nodded to them benevolently; he knew something about all of them. There were people who were going to the town—his town—and some were going farther, far over the sea, to America, or even farther still, to serve the King there; one could see that by their equipment and the frozen look on their faces. Others were merely going into the town to make a hole in their wages, and to celebrate May-day. These came along the road in whole parties, humming or whistling, with empty hands and overflowing spirits. But the most interesting people were those who had put their boxes on a wheelbarrow, or were carrying them by both handles. These had flushed faces, and were feverish in their movements; they were people who had torn themselves away from their own country-side, and their accustomed way of life, and had chosen the town, as he himself had done.

There was one man, a cottager, with a little green chest on his wheelbarrow; this latter was broad in the beam, and it was neatly adorned with flowers painted by his own hand. Beside him walked his daughter; her cheeks were red, and her eyes were gazing into the unknown future. The father was speaking to her, but she did not look as though she heard him. "Yes—now you must take it on you to look out for yourself; you must think about it, and not throw yourself away. The town is quite a good place for those who go right ahead and think of their own advantage, but it thinks nothing of who gets trodden underfoot. So don't be too trusting, for the people there are wonderful clever in all sorts of tricks to take you in and trip you up. At the same time you want to be soft-spoken and friendly. " She did not reply to this; she was apparently more taken up with the problem of putting down her feet in their new shoes so that the heels should not turn over.

There was a stream of people coming up from the town too. All the forenoon Pelle had been meeting Swedes who had come that morning in the steamer, and were now looking for a job on the land. There were old folk, worn out with labor, and little children; there were maidens as pretty as yellow-haired Marie, and young laborers who had the strength of the whole world in their loins and muscles. And this current of life was setting hither to fill up the gaps left by the swarms that were going away—but that did not concern Pelle. For seven years ago he had felt everything that made their faces look so troubled now; what they were just entering upon he had already put behind him. So there was no good in looking back.

Presently the old man from Neuendorf came along the road. He was got up quite like an American, with a portmanteau and a silk neckerchief, and the inside pockets of his open coat were stuffed full of papers. At last he had made up his mind, and was going out to his betrothed, who had already been three years away.

"Hullo! " cried Pelle, "so you are going away? "

The man came over to Pelle and set his portmanteau down by the side of the ditch.

"Well, yes; it's time to be going, " he said. "Laura won't wait for me any longer. So the old people must see how they can get along without a son; I've done everything for them now for three years. Provided they can manage all by themselves—"

"They can do that all right, " said Pelle, with an experienced air. "And they had to get help formerly. There is no future for young people at home. " He had heard his elders say this. He struck at the grass with his stick, assuming a superior air.

"No, " said the other, "and Laura refuses to be a cottager's wife. Well, good-bye! " He held out his hand to Pelle and tried to smile, but his features had it their own way; nothing but a rather twisted expression came over them. He stood there a minute, looking at his boots, his thumb groping over his face as though he wanted to wipe the tormented look away; then he picked up his portmanteau and went. He was evidently not very comfortable.

"I'll willingly take over the ticket and the bride, " shouted Pelle merrily. He felt in the deuce of a good humor.

Everybody to-day was treading the road along which Pelle's own young blood had called him—every young fellow with a little pluck, every good-looking wench. Not for a moment was the road free of traffic; it was like a vast exodus, an army of people escaping from places where everyone had the feeling that he was condemned to live and die on the very spot where he was born; an army of people who had chosen the excitement of the unknown. Those little brick houses which lay scattered over the green, or stood drawn up in two straight rows where the high-road ran into the town—those were the cottages of the peasant folk who had renounced the outdoor life, and dressed themselves in townified clothes, and had then adventured hither; and down on the sea-front the houses stood all squeezed and heaped together round the church, so close that there looked to be no room between them; there were the crowds who had gone wandering, driven far afield by the longing in their hearts—and then the sea had set a limit to their journey.

Pelle had no intention of allowing anything whatever to set a limit to his journeying. Perhaps, if he had no luck in the town, he would go to sea. And then one day he would come to some coast that interested him, and he would land, and go to the gold-diggings. Over there the girls went mother-naked, with nothing but some blue tattoo-work to hide their shame; but Pelle had his girl sitting at home, true to him, waiting for his return. She was more beautiful even than Bodil and yellow-haired Marie put together, and whole crowds followed her footsteps, but she sat at home and was faithful, and she would sing the old love-song:

> "I had a lad, but he went away
> All over the false, false sea,
> Three years they are gone, and now to-day
> He writes no more to me! "

And while she sang the letter came to the door. But out of every letter that his father Lasse received fell ten-kroner banknotes, and one day a letter came with steamer-tickets for the two of them. The song would not serve him any further, for in the song they perished during the voyage, and the poor young man spent the rest of his days on the sea-shore, gazing, through the shadow of insanity, upon every rising sail. She and Lasse arrived safely—after all sorts of difficulties, that went without saying—and Pelle stood on the shore and welcomed them. He had dressed himself up like a savage, and he carried on as though he meant to eat them before he made himself known.

Houp la! Pelle jumped to his feet. Up the road there was a rattling and a clanking as though a thousand scythes were clashing together: an old cart with loose plank sides came slowly jolting along, drawn by the two most miserable moorland horses he had ever seen. On the driver's seat was an old peasant, who was bobbing about as though he would every moment fall in pieces, like all the rest of his equipment. Pelle did not at first feel sure whether it was the cart itself or the two bags of bones between the shafts that made such a frightful din whenever they moved, but as the vehicle at last drew level with him, and the old peasant drew up, he could not resist the invitation to get up and have a lift. His shoulders were still aching from carrying his sack.

"So you are going to town, after all? " said old Klaus, pointing to his goods and chattels.

To town, yes indeed! Something seemed to grip hold of Pelle's bursting heart, and before he was aware of it he had delivered himself and his whole future into the old peasant's hands.

"Yes, yes—yes indeed—why, naturally! " said Klaus, nodding as Pelle came forward. "Yes, of course! A man can't do less. And what's your idea about what you are going to be in the long run—councillor or king? " He looked up slowly. "Yes, goin' to town; well, well, they all, take the road they feel something calling them to take.... Directly a young greyhound feels the marrow in his bones, or has got a shilling in his pocket, he's got to go to town and leave it there. And what do you think conies back out the town? Just manure and nothing else! What else have I ever in my life been able to pick up there? And now I'm sixty-five. But what's the good of talking? No more than if a man was to stick his tail out and blow against a gale. It comes over them just like the May-gripes takes the young calves— heigh-ho! and away they go, goin' to do something big. Afterward, then old Klaus Hermann can come and clean up after them! They've no situation there, and no kinsfolk what could put them up—but they always expect something big. Why, down in the town there are beds made up in the streets, and the gutters are running over with food and money! But what do you mean to do? Let's hear it now. "

Pelle turned crimson. He had not yet succeeded in making a beginning, and already he had been caught behaving like a blockhead.

"Well, well, well, " said Klaus, in a good-humored tone, "you are no bigger fool than all the rest. But if you'll take my advice, you'll go to shoemaker Jeppe Kofod as apprentice; I am going straight to his place to fetch manure, and I know he's looking for an apprentice. Then you needn't go floundering about uncertain-like, and you can drive right up to the door like the quality. "

Pelle winced all over. Never in his life had it entered his head that he could ever become a shoemaker. Even back there on the land, where people looked up to the handicrafts, they used always to say, if a boy had not turned out quite right: "Well, we can always make a cobbler or a tailor of him! " But Pelle was no cripple, that he must lead a sedentary life indoors in order to get on at all; he was strong and well-made. What he would be—well, that certainly lay in the hands of fortune; but he felt very strongly that it ought to be something active, something that needed courage and energy. And in any case he was quite sure as to what he did not want to be. But as they jolted through the town, and Pelle—so as to be beforehand with the great world—kept on taking off his cap to everybody, although no one returned his greeting, his spirits began to sink, and a sense of his own insignificance possessed him. The miserable cart, at which all the little town boys laughed and pointed with their fingers, had a great deal to do with this feeling.

"Take off your cap to a pack like that! " grumbled Klaus; "why, only look how puffed up they behave, and yet everything they've got they've stolen from us others. Or what do you suppose—can you see if they've got their summer seeds in the earth yet? " And he glared contemptuously down the street.

No, there was nothing growing on the stone pavements, and all these little houses, which stood so close that now and then they seemed to Pelle as if they must be squeezed out of the row—these gradually took his breath away. Here were thousands and thousands of people, if that made any difference; and all his blind confidence wavered at the question: where did all their food come from? For here he was once more at home in his needy, familiar world, where no amount of smoke will enable one to buy a pair of socks. All at once he felt thoroughly humble, and he decided that it would be all he could do here to hold his own, and find his daily bread among all these stones, for here people did not raise it naturally from the soil, but got it—well, how *did* they get it?

The streets were full of servants. The girls stood about in groups, their arms round one another's waists, staring with burning eyes at the cotton-stuffs displayed in the shops; they rocked themselves gently to and fro as though they were dreaming. A 'prentice boy of about Pelle's age, with a red, spotty face, was walking down the middle of the street, eating a great wheaten roll which he held with both hands; his ears were full of scabs and his hands swollen with the cold. Farm laborers went by, carrying red bundles in their hands, their overcoats flapping against their calves; they would stop suddenly at a turning, look cautiously round, and then hurry down a side street. In front of the shops the salesmen were walking up and down, bareheaded, and if any one stopped in front of their windows they would beg them, in the politest manner, to step nearer, and would secretly wink at one another across the street.

"The shopkeepers have arranged their things very neatly to-day, " said Pelle.

Klaus nodded. "Yes, yes; to-day they've brought out everything they couldn't get rid of sooner. To-day the block-heads have come to market—the easy purses. Those"—and he pointed to a side street, "those are the publicans. They are looking this way so longingly, but the procession don't come as far as them. But you wait till this evening, and then take a turn along here, and ask the different people how much they've got left of their year's wages. Yes, the town's a fine place—the very deuce of a fine place! " And he spat disgustedly.

Pelle had quite lost all his blind courage. He saw not a single person doing anything by which he himself might earn his bread. And gladly as he would have belonged to this new world, yet he could not venture into anything where, perhaps without knowing it, he would be an associate of people who would tear the rags off his old comrades' backs. All the courage had gone out of him, and with a miserable feeling that even his only riches, his hands, were here useless, he sat irresolute, and allowed himself to be driven, rattling and jangling, to Master Jeppe Kofod's workshop.

II

The workshop stood over an entry which opened off the street. People came and went along this entry: Madame Rasmussen and old Captain Elleby; the old maid-servant of a Comptroller, an aged pensioner who wore a white cap, drew her money from the Court, and expended it here, and a feeble, gouty old sailor who had bidden the sea farewell. Out in the street, on the sharp-edged cobble-stones, the sparrows were clamoring loudly, lying there with puffed-out feathers, feasting among the horse-droppings, tugging at them and scattering them about to the accompaniment of a storm of chirping and scolding.

Everything overlooking the yard stood open. In the workshop all four windows were opened wide, and the green light sifted into the room and fell on the faces of those present. But that was no help. Not a breath of wind was blowing; moreover, Pelle's heat came from within. He was sweating with sheer anxiety.

For the rest, he pulled industriously at his cobbler's wax, unless, indeed, something outside captured his harassed mind, so that it wandered out into the sunshine.

Everything out there was splashed with vivid sunlight; seen from the stuffy workshop the light was like a golden river, streaming down between the two rows of houses, and always in the same direction, down to the sea. Then a speck of white down came floating on the air, followed by whitish-gray thistle-seeds, and a whole swarm of gnats, and a big broad bumble-bee swung to and fro. All these eddied, gleaming, in the open doorway, and they went on circling as though there was something there which attracted them all—doubtless an accident, or perhaps a festival.

"Are you asleep, booby? " asked the journeyman sharply. Pelle shrank into his shell and continued to work at the wax; he kneaded away at it, holding it in hot water.

Inside the court, at the baker's—the baker was the old master's brother—they were hoisting sacks of meal. The windlass squeaked horribly, and in between the squeaking one could hear Master Jorgen Kofod, in a high falsetto, disputing with his son. "You're a noodle, a pitiful simpleton—whatever will become of you? Do you think we've nothing more to do than to go running out to prayer-meetings on a working day? Perhaps that will get us our daily bread? Now you just stay here, or, God's mercy, I'll break every bone in your body! " Then the wife chimed in, and then of a sudden all was silent. And after a while the son stole like a phantom along the wall of the opposite house, a hymn-book in his hand. He was not unlike Howling Peter. He squeezed himself against the wall, and his knees gave under him if any one looked sharply at him. He was twenty-five years old, and he took beatings from his father without a murmur. But when matters of religion were in question he defied public opinion, the stick, and his father's anger.

"Are you asleep, booby? I shall really have to come over and teach you to hurry! "

For a time no one spoke in the workshop—the journeyman was silent, so the others had to hold their tongues. Each bent over his work, and Pelle pulled the pitch out to as great a length as possible, kneaded some grease into it, and pulled again. Outside, in the sunshine, some street urchins were playing, running to and fro. When they saw Pelle, they held their clenched fist under their noses, nodded to him in a provocative manner, and sang—

> "The cobbler has a pitchy nose,
> The more he wipes it the blacker it grows! "

Pelle pretended not to see them, but he secretly ticked them all off in his mind. It was his sincere intention to wipe them all off the face of the earth.

Suddenly they all ran into the street, where a tremendous, monotonous voice lifted itself and flowed abroad. This was the crazy watchmaker; he was standing on his high steps, crying damnation on the world at large.

Pelle knew perfectly well that the man was crazy, and in the words which he so ponderously hurled at the town there was not the slightest meaning. But they sounded wonderfully fine notwithstanding, and the "ordeal by wax" was hanging over him like a sort of last judgment. Involuntarily, he began to turn cold at the sound of this warning voice, which uttered such solemn words and had so little meaning, just as he did at the strong language in the Bible. It was just the voice that frightened him; it was such a terrible voice, such a voice as one might hear speaking out of the clouds; the sort of voice, in short, that made the knees of Moses and Paul give under them; a portentous voice, such as Pelle himself used to hear coming out of the darkness at Stone Farm when a quarrel was going on.

Only the knee-strap of little Nikas, the journeyman, kept him from jumping up then and there and throwing himself down like Paul. This knee-strap was a piece of undeniable reality in the midst of all his imaginings; in two months it had taught him never quite to forget who and where he was. He pulled himself together, and satisfied himself that all his miseries arose from his labors over this wretched cobbler's wax; besides, there was such a temptation to compare his puddle of cobbler's wax with the hell in which he was told he would be tormented. But then he heard the cheerful voice of the young shoemaker in the yard outside, and the whole trouble disappeared. The "ordeal by wax" could not really be so terrible, since all the others had undergone it—he had certainly seen tougher fellows than these in his lifetime!

Jens sat down and ducked his head, as though he was expecting a box on the ears; —that was the curse of the house which continually hung over him. He was so slow at his work that already Pelle could overtake him; there was something inside him that seemed to hamper his movements like a sort of spell. But Peter and Emil were smart fellows—only they were always wanting to thrash him.

Among the apple trees in the yard it was early summer, and close under the workshop windows the pig stood smacking at his food. This sound was like a warm breeze that blew over Pelle's heart. Since the day when Klaus Hermann had shaken the squeaking little porker out of his sack, Pelle had begun to take root. It had squealed at first in a most desolate manner, and something of Pelle's own feeling of loneliness was taken away from him by its cries. Now it complained simply because it was badly fed, and it made Pelle quite furious to see the nasty trash that was thrown to it—a young pig must eat well, that is half the battle. They ought not to go running out every few minute to throw something or other to the pig; when once the heat really set in it would get acidity of the stomach. But there was no sense in these town folk.

"Are you really asleep, booby? Why, you are snoring, deuce take me!
"

The young master came limping in, took a drink, and buried himself in his book. As he read he whistled softly in time with the hammer-strokes of the others. Little Nikas began to whistle too, and the two older apprentices who were beating leather began to strike in time with the whistling, and they even kept double time, so that everything went like greased lightning. The journeyman's trills and quavers became more and more extraordinary, in order to catch up with the blows—the blows and the whistling seemed to be chasing one another—and Master Andres raised his head from his book to listen. He sat there staring into the far distance, as though the shadowy pictures evoked by his reading were hovering before his eyes. Then, with a start, he was present and among them all, his eyes running over them with a waggish expression; and then he stood up, placing his stick so that it supported his diseased hip. The master's hands danced loosely in the air, his head and his whole figure jerking crazily under the compulsion of the rhythm.

Swoop! —and the dancing hands fell upon the cutting-out knife, and the master fingered the notes on the sharp edge, his head on one side and his eyes closed—his whole appearance that of one absorbed in intent inward listening. But then suddenly his face beamed with felicity, his whole figure contracted in a frenzy of delight, one foot clutched at the air as though bewitched, as though he were playing a harp with his toes—Master Andres was all at once a musical idiot and a musical clown. And *smack!* the knife flew to the ground and he had the great tin cover in his hand— *chin-da-da-da chin-da-da-da!* Suddenly by a stroke of magic the flute had turned into a drum and cymbals!

Pelle was doubled up with laughter: then he looked in alarm at the knee-strap and again burst out laughing; but no one took any notice of him. The master's fingers and wrist were dancing a sort of devil's dance on the tin cover, and all of a sudden his elbows too were called into requisition, so that the cover banged against the master's left knee, bounced off again and quick as lightning struck against his wooden heel, which stuck out behind him; then against Pelle's head, and round about it went, striking the most improbable objects, *dum, dum, dum,* as though in wild, demoniacal obedience to the flute-like tones of the journeyman. There was no holding back. Emil, the oldest apprentice, began boldly to whistle too, cautiously at first, and then, as no one smacked his head, more forcefully. Then the next apprentice, Jens—the music-devil, as he was called, because anything would produce a note between his fingers—plucked so cleverly at his waxed-end that it straightway began to give out a buzzing undertone, rising and falling through two or three notes, as though an educated bumble-bee had been leading the whole orchestra. Out of doors the birds came hopping on to the apple-boughs; they twisted their heads inquisitively to one side, frantically fluffed out their feathers, and then they too joined in this orgy of jubilation, which was caused merely by a scrap of bright blue sky. But then the young master had an attack of coughing, and the whole business came to an end.

Pelle worked away at his cobbler's wax, kneading the pitch and mixing grease with it. When the black lump was on the point of stiffening, he had to plunge both hands into hot water, so that he got hangnails. Old Jeppe came tripping in from the yard, and Master Andres quickly laid the cutting-board over his book and diligently stropped his knife.

"That's right! " said Jeppe; "warm the wax, then it binds all the better. "

Pelle had rolled the wax into balls, and had put them in the soaking-tub, and now stood silent; for he had not the courage of his own accord to say, "I am ready. " The others had magnified the "ordeal by wax" into something positively terrible; all sorts of terrors lurked in the mystery that was now awaiting him; and if he himself had not known that he was a smart fellow—why—yes, he would have left them all in the lurch. But now he meant to submit to it, however bad it might be; he only wanted time to swallow first. Then at last he would have succeeded in shaking off the peasant, and the handicraft would be open to him, with its song and its wandering life and its smart journeyman's clothes. The workshop here was no better than a stuffy hole where one sat and slaved over smelly greasy boots, but he saw that one must go through with it in order to reach the great world, where journeymen wore patent-leather shoes on workdays and made footwear fit for kings. The little town had given Pelle a preliminary foreboding that the world was almost incredibly great, and this foreboding filled him with impatience. He meant to conquer it all!

"Now I am ready! " he said resolutely; now he would decide whether he and the handicraft were made for one another.

"Then you can pull a waxed end—but make it as long as a bad year!
" said the journeyman.

The old master was all on fire at the idea. He went over and watched
Pelle closely, his tongue hanging out of his mouth; he felt quite
young again, and began to descant upon his own apprenticeship in
Copenhagen, sixty years ago. Those were times! The apprentices
didn't lie in bed and snore in those days till six o'clock in the
morning, and throw down their work on the very stroke of eight,
simply to go out and run about. No; up they got at four, and stuck at
it as long as there was work to do. Then fellows *could* work—and
then they still learned something; they were told things just once,
and then—the knee-strap! Then, too, the manual crafts still enjoyed
some reputation; even the kings had to learn a handicraft. It was
very different to the present, with its bungling and cheap retailing
and pinching and paring everywhere.

The apprentices winked at one another. Master Andres and the
journeyman were silent. You might as well quarrel with the sewing-
machine because it purred. Jeppe was allowed to spin his yarn alone.

"Are you waxing it well? " said little Nikas. "It's for pigskin. "

The others laughed, but Pelle rubbed the thread with a feeling as
though he were building his own scaffold.

"Now I am ready! " he said, in a low voice.

The largest pair of men's lasts was taken down from the shelf, and
these were tied to one end of the waxed-end and were let right down
to the pavement. People collected in the street outside, and stood
there staring. Pelle had to lean right out of the window, and bend
over as far as he could, while Emil, as the oldest apprentice, laid the
waxed-end over his neck. They were all on their feet now, with the
exception of the young master; he took no part in this diversion.

"Pull, then! " ordered the journeyman, who was directing the solemn
business. "Pull them along till they're right under your feet! "

Pelle pulled, and the heavy lasts joggled over the pavement, but he
paused with a sigh; the waxed-end was slipping over his warm neck.
He stood there stamping, like an animal which stamps its feet on the

ground, without knowing why; he lifted them cautiously and looked at them in torment.

"Pull, pull! " ordered Jeppe. "You must keep the thing moving or it sticks! " But it was too late; the wax had hardened in the hairs of his nape—Father Lasse used to call them his "luck curls, " and prophesied a great future for him on their account—and there he stood, and could not remove the waxed-end, however hard he tried. He made droll grimaces, the pain was so bad, and the saliva ran out of his mouth.

"Huh! He can't even manage a pair of lasts! " said Jeppe jeeringly. "He'd better go back to the land again and wash down the cows' behinds! "

Then Pelle, boiling with rage, gave a jerk, closing his eyes and writhing as he loosed himself. Something sticky and slippery slipped through his fingers with the waxed-end; it was bloody hair, and across his neck the thread had bitten its way in a gutter of lymph and molten wax. But Pelle no longer felt the pain, his head was boiling so, and he felt a vague but tremendous longing to pick up a hammer and strike them all to the ground, and then to run through the street, banging at the skulls of all he met. But then the journeyman took the lasts off him, and the pain came back to him, and his whole miserable plight. He heard Jeppe's squeaky voice, and looked at the young master, who sat there submissively, without having the courage to express his opinion, and all at once he felt terribly sorry for himself.

"That was right, " buzzed old Jeppe, "a shoemaker mustn't be afraid to wax his hide a little. What? I believe it has actually brought the water to his eyes! No, when I was apprentice we had a real ordeal; we had to pass the waxed-end twice round our necks before we were allowed to pull. Our heads used to hang by a thread and dangle when we were done. Yes, those were times! "

Pelle stood there shuffling, in order to fight down his tears; but he had to snigger with mischievous delight at the idea of Jeppe's dangling head.

"Then we must see whether he can stand a buzzing head, " said the journeyman, getting ready to strike him.

"No, you can wait until he deserves it, " said Master Andres hastily. "You will soon find an occasion. "

"Well, he's done with the wax, " said Jeppe, "but the question is, can he sit? Because there are some who never learn the art of sitting. "

"That must be tested, too, before we can declare him to be useful, " said little Nikas, in deadly earnest.

"Are you done with your tomfoolery now? " said Master Andres angrily, and he went his way.

But Jeppe was altogether in his element; his head was full of the memories of his boyhood, a whole train of devilish tricks, which completed the ordination. "Then we used to brand them indelibly with their special branch, and they never took to their heels, but they considered it a great honor as long as they drew breath. But now these are weakly times and full of pretences; the one can't do this and the other can't do that; and there's leather colic and sore behinds and God knows what. Every other day they come with certificates that they're suffering from boils from sitting down, and then you can begin all over again. No, in my time we behaved very different—the booby got held naked over a three-legged stool and a couple of men used to go at him with knee-straps! That was leather on leather, and like that they learned, damn and blast it all! how to put up with sitting on a stool! "

The journeyman made a sign.

"Now, is the seat of the stool ready consecrated, and prayed over? Yes, then you can go over there and sit down. "

Pelle went stupidly across the room and sat down—it was all the same to him. But he leaped into the air with a yell of pain, looked malevolently about him, and in a moment he had a hammer in his hand. But he dropped it again, and now he cried—wept buckets of tears.

"What the devil are you doing to him now? "

The young master came out of the cutting-out room. "What dirty tricks are you hatching now? " He ran his hand over the seat of the stool; it was studded with broken awl-points. "You are barbarous devils; any one would think he was among a lot of savages!"

"What a weakling!" sneered Jeppe. "In these days a man can't take a boy as apprentice and inoculate him a bit against boils! One ought to anoint the boobies back and front with honey, perhaps, like the kings of Israel? But you are a freethinker!"

"You get out of this, father!" shouted Master Andres, quite beside himself. "You get out of this, father!" He trembled, and his face was quite gray. And then he pushed the old man out of the room before he had struck Pelle on the shoulder and received him properly into the handicraft.

Pelle sat there and reflected. He was altogether disillusioned. All the covert allusions had evoked something terrifying, but at the same time impressive. In his imagination the ordeal had grown into something that constituted the great barrier of his life, so that one passed over to the other side as quite a different being; it was something after the fashion of the mysterious circumcision in the Bible, a consecration to new things. And now the whole thing was just a spitefully devised torture!

The young master threw him a pair of children's shoes, which had to be soled. So he was admitted to that department, and need no longer submit to preparing waxed-ends for the others! But the fact did not give him any pleasure. He sat there struggling with something irrational that seemed to keep on rising deep within him; when no one was looking he licked his fingers and drew them over his neck. He seemed to himself like a half-stupefied cat which had freed itself from the snare and sat there drying its fur.

Out of doors, under the apple-trees, the sunlight lay green and golden, and a long way off, in the skipper's garden, three brightly dressed girls were walking and playing; they seemed to Pelle like beings out of another world. "Fortune's children on the sunbright shore," as the song had it. From time to time a rat made its appearance behind the pigsty, and went clattering over the great heap of broken glass that lay there. The pig stood there gobbling down its spoiled potatoes with that despairing noise that put an end to all Pelle's proud dreams of the future, while it filled him with longing—oh, such a mad longing!

And everything that possibly could do so made its assault upon him at this moment when he was feeling particularly victorious; the miseries of his probation here in the workshop, the street urchins, the apprentices, who would not accept him as one of themselves, and all the sharp edges and corners which he was continually running up against in this unfamiliar world. And then the smelly workshop itself, where never a ray of sunlight entered. And no one here seemed to respect anything.

When the master was not present, little Nikas would sometimes indulge in tittle-tattle with the older apprentices. Remarks were made at such times which opened new spheres of thought to Pelle, and he had to ask questions; or they would talk of the country, which Pelle knew better than all of them put together, and he would chime in with some correction. *Smack!* came a box on his ears that would send him rolling into the corner; he was to hold his tongue until he was spoken to. But Pelle, who was all eyes and ears, and had been accustomed to discuss everything in heaven or earth with Father Lasse, could not learn to hold his tongue.

Each exacted with a strong hand his quantum of respect, from the apprentices to the old master, who was nearly bursting with professional pride in his handicraft; only Pelle had no claim to any respect whatever, but must pay tribute to all. The young master was the only one who did not press like a yoke on the youngster's neck. Easygoing as he was, he would disregard the journeyman and the rest, and at times he would plump himself down beside Pelle, who sat there feeling dreadfully small.

Outside, when the sun was shining through the trees in a particular way, and a peculiar note came into the twittering of the birds, Pelle knew it was about the time when the cows began to get on their feet after their midday chewing of the cud. And then a youngster would come out from among the little fir-trees, lustily cracking his whip; he was the general of the whole lot—Pelle, the youngster—who had no one set over him. And the figure that came stumbling across the arable yonder, in order to drive the cows home—why, that was Lasse!

Father Lasse!

He did not know why, but it wrung a sob from him; it took him so unawares. "Hold your row! " cried the journeyman threateningly.

301

Pelle was greatly concerned; he had not once made the attempt to go over and see Lasse.

The young master came to get something off the shelf above his head, and leaned confidentially on Pelle's shoulder, his weak leg hanging free and dangling. He stood there loitering for a time, staring at the sky outside, and this warm hand on Pelle's shoulder quieted him.

But there could be no talk of enjoyment when he thought where good Father Lasse was. He had not seen his father since that sunny morning when he himself had gone away and left the old man to his loneliness. He had not heard of him; he had scarcely given a thought to him. He had to get through the day with a whole skin, and to adapt himself to the new life; a whole new world was before him, in which he had to find his feet. Pelle had simply had no time; the town had swallowed him.

But at this moment his conduct confronted him as the worst example of unfaithfulness the world had ever known. And his neck continued to hurt him—he must go somewhere or other where no one would look at him. He made a pretence of having to do something in the yard outside; he went behind the washhouse, and he crouched down by the woodpile beside the well.

There he lay, shrinking into himself, in the blackest despair at having left Father Lasse so shamelessly in the lurch, just for the sake of all these new strange surroundings. Yes, and then, when they used to work together, he had been neither as good nor as heedful as he should have been. It was really Lasse who, old as he was, had sacrificed himself for Pelle, in order to lighten his work and take the worst of the burden off him, although Pelle had the younger shoulders. And he had been a little hard at times, as over that business between his father and Madame Olsen; and he had not always been very patient with his good-humored elderly tittle-tattle, although if he could hear it now he would give his life to listen. He could remember only too plainly occasions when he had snapped at Lasse, so unkindly that Lasse had given a sigh and made off; for Lasse never snapped back—he was only silent and very sad.

But how dreadful that was! Pelle threw all his high-and-mighty airs to the winds and gave himself up to despair. What was he doing here, with Father Lasse wandering among strangers, and perhaps unable to find shelter? There was nothing with which he could console himself, no evasion or excuse was possible; Pelle howled at the thought of his faithlessness. And as he lay there despairing, worrying over the whole business and crying himself into a state of exhaustion, quite a manful resolve began to form within him; he must give up everything of his own—the future, and the great world, and all, and devote his days to making the old man's life happy. He must go back to Stone Farm! He forgot that he was only a child who could just earn his own keep. To protect the infirm old man at every point and make his life easy—that was just what he wanted. And Pelle was by no means disposed to doubt that he could do it. In the midst of his childish collapse he took upon himself all the duties of a strong man.

As he lay there, woe-begone, playing with a couple of bits of firewood, the elder-boughs behind the well parted, and a pair of big eyes stared at him wonderingly. It was only Manna.

"Did they beat you—or why are you crying? " she asked earnestly.

Pelle turned his face away.

Manna shook her hair back and looked at him fixedly. "Did they beat you? What? If they did, I shall go in and scold them hard! "

"What is it to you? "

"People who don't answer aren't well-behaved. "

"Oh, hold your row! "

Then he was left in peace; over at the back of the garden Manna and her two younger sisters were scrambling about the trellis, hanging on it and gazing steadfastly across the yard at him. But that was nothing to him; he wanted to know nothing about them; he didn't want petticoats to pity him or intercede for him. They were saucy jades, even if their father had sailed on the wide ocean and earned a lot of money. If he had them here they would get the stick from him! Now he must content himself with putting out his tongue at them.

He heard their horrified outcry—but what then? He didn't want to go scrambling about with them any more, or to play with the great conch-shells and lumps of coral in their garden! He would go back to the land and look after his old father! Afterward, when that was done, he would go out into the world himself, and bring such things home with him—whole shiploads of them!

They were calling him from the workshop window. "Where in the world has that little blighter got to? " he heard them say. He started, shrinking; he had quite forgotten that he was serving his apprenticeship. He got on his feet and ran quickly indoors.

Pelle had soon tidied up after leaving off work. The others had run out in search of amusement; he was alone upstairs in the garret. He put his worldly possessions into his sack. There was a whole collection of wonderful things—tin steamboats, railway-trains, and horses that were hollow inside—as much of the irresistible wonders of the town as he had been able to obtain for five white krone pieces. They went in among the washing, so that they should not get damaged, and then he threw the bag out of the gable-window into the little alley. Now the question was how he himself should slip through the kitchen without arousing the suspicions of Jeppe's old woman; she had eyes like a witch, and Pelle had a feeling that every one who saw him would know what he was about.

But he went. He controlled himself, and sauntered along, so that the people should think he was taking washing to the laundrywoman; but he could only keep it up as far as the first turning; then he started off as fast as he could go. He was homesick. A few street-boys yelled and threw stones after him, but that didn't matter, so long as he only got away; he was insensible to everything but the remorse and homesickness that filled his heart.

It was past midnight when he at last reached the outbuildings of Stone Farm. He was breathless, and had a stitch in his side. He leaned against the ruined forge, and closed his eyes, the better to recover himself. As soon as he had recovered his breath, he entered the cowshed from the back and made for the herdsman's room. The floor of the cowshed felt familiar to his feet, and now he came in the darkness to the place where the big bull lay. He breathed in the scent of the creature's body and blew it out again—ah, didn't he remember it! But the scent of the cowherd's room was strange to him. "Father Lasse is neglecting himself, " he thought, and he pulled the feather-bed from under the sleeper's head. A strange voice began to upbraid him. "Then isn't this Lasse? " said Pelle. His knees were shaking under him.

"Lasse? " cried the new cowherd, as he sat upright. "Do you say Lasse? Have you come to fetch that child of God, Mr. Devil? They've been here already from Hell and taken him with them—in the living body they've taken him there with them—he was too good for this world, d'ye see? Old Satan was here himself in the form of a woman and took him away. You'd better go there and look for him. Go straight on till you come to the devil's great-grandmother, and then you've only got to ask your way to the hairy one. "

Pelle stood for a while in the yard below and considered. So Father Lasse had gone away! And wanted to marry, or was perhaps already married. And to Karna, of course. He stood bolt-upright, sunk in intimate memories. The great farm lay hushed in moonlight, in deepest slumber, and all about him rose memories from their sleep, speaking to him caressingly, with a voice like that contented purring, remembered from childhood, when the little kittens used to sleep upon his pillow, and he would lay his cheek against their soft, quivering bodies.

Pelle's memory had deep roots. Once, at Uncle Kalle's, he had laid himself in the big twins' cradle and had let the other children rock him—he was then fully nine years old—and as they rocked him a while the surroundings began to take hold of him, and he saw a smoky, raftered ceiling, which did not belong to Kalle's house, swaying high over his head, and he had a feeling that a muffled-up old woman, wrapped in a shawl, sat like a shadow at the head of the cradle, and rocked it with her foot. The cradle jolted with the over-vigorous rocking, and every time the rocking foot slipped from the footboard it struck on the floor with the sound of a sprung wooden shoe. Pelle jumped up—"she bumped so, " he said, bewildered. "What? No, you certainly dreamed that! " Kalle looked, smiling, under the rockers. "Bumped! " said Lasse. "That ought to suit you first-rate! At one time, when you were little, you couldn't sleep if the cradle didn't bump, so we had to make the rockers all uneven. It was almost impossible to rock it. Bengta cracked many a good wooden shoe in trying to give you your fancy. "

The farmyard here was like a great cradle, which swayed and swayed in the uncertain moonlight, and now that Pelle had once quite surrendered himself to the past, there was no end to the memories of childhood that rose within him. His whole existence passed before him, swaying above his head as before, and the earth itself seemed like a dark speck in the abysm of space.

And then the crying broke out from the house—big with destiny, to be heard all over the place, so that Kongstrup slunk away shamefaced, and the other grew angry and ungovernable.... And Lasse... yes, where was Father Lasse?

With one leap, Pelle was in the brew-house, knocking on the door of the maid's room.

"Is that you, Anders? " whispered a voice from within, and then the door opened, and a pair of arms fastened themselves about him and drew him in. Pelle felt about him, and his hands sank into a naked bosom—why, it was yellow-haired Marie!

"Is Karna still here? " he asked. "Can't I speak to Karna a moment? "

They were glad to see him again; and yellow-haired Marie patted his cheeks quite affectionately, and just before that she kissed him too. Karna could scarcely recover from her surprise; he had acquired such a townsman's air. "And now you are a shoemaker too, in the biggest workshop in the town! Yes, we've heard; Butcher Jensen heard about it on the market. And you have grown tall and townified. You do hold yourself well! " Karna was dressing herself.

"Where is Father Lasse? " said Pelle; he had a lump in his throat only from speaking of him.

"Give me time, and I'll come out with you. How fine you dress now! I should hardly have known you. Would you, Marie? "

"He's a darling boy—he always was, " said Marie, and she pushed at him with her arched foot—she was now in bed again.

"It's the same suit as I always had, " said Pelle.

"Yes, yes; but then you held yourself different—there in town they all look like lords. Well, shall we go? "

Pelle said good-by to Marie affectionately; it occurred to him that he had much to thank her for. She looked at him in a very odd way, and tried to draw his hand under the coverlet.

"What's the matter with father? " said Pelle impatiently, as soon as they were outside.

Well, Lasse had taken to his heels too! He couldn't stand it when Pelle had gone. And the work was too heavy for one. Where he was just at the moment Karna could not say. "He's now here, now there, considering farms and houses, " she said proudly. "Some fine day he'll be able to take you in on his visit to town. "

"And how are things going here? " inquired Pelle.

"Well, Erik has got his speech back and is beginning to be a man again—he can make himself understood. And Kongstrup and his wife, they drink one against the other. "

"They drink together, do they, like the wooden shoemaker and his old woman? "

"Yes, and so much that they often lie in the room upstairs soaking, and can't see one another for the drink, they're that foggy. Everything goes crooked here, as you may suppose, with no master. 'Masterless, defenceless, ' as the old proverb says. But what can you say about it—they haven't anything else in common! But it's all the same to me—as soon as Lasse finds something I'm off! "

Pelle could well believe that, and had nothing to say against it. Karna looked at him from head to foot in surprise as they walked on. "They feed you devilish well in the town there, don't they? "

"Yes—vinegary soup and rotten greaves. We were much better fed here. "

She would not believe it—it sounded too foolish. "But where are all the things they have in the shop windows—all the meats and cakes and sweet things? What becomes of all them? "

"That I don't know, " said Pelle grumpily; he himself had racked his brains over this very question. "I get all I can eat, but washing and clothes I have to see to myself. "

Karna could scarcely conceal her amazement; she had supposed that Pelle had been, so to speak, caught up to Heaven while yet living. "But how do you manage? " she said anxiously. "You must find that difficult. Yes, yes, directly we set out feet under our own table we'll help you all we can. "

They parted up on the high-road, and Pelle, tired and defeated, set out on his way back. It was broad daylight when he got back, and he crawled into bed without any one noticing anything of his attempted flight.

III

Little Nikas had washed the blacking from his face and had put on his best clothes; he wanted to go to the market with a bundle of washing, which the butcher from Aaker was to take home to his mother, and Pelle walked behind him, carrying the bundle. Little Nikas saluted many friendly maidservants in the houses of the neighborhood, and Pelle found it more amusing to walk beside him than to follow; two people who are together ought to walk abreast. But every time he walked beside the journeyman the latter pushed him into the gutter, and finally Pelle fell over a curbstone; then he gave it up.

Up the street the crazy watchmaker was standing on the edge of his high steps, swinging a weight; it was attached to the end of a long cord, and he followed the swinging of the pendulum with his fingers, as though he were timing the beats. This was very interesting, and Pelle feared it would escape the journeyman.

"The watchmaker's making an experiment, " he said cheerfully.

"Stop your jaw! " said the journeyman sharply. Then it occurred to Pelle that he was not allowed to speak, so he closed his mouth tight.

He felt the bundle, in order to picture to himself what the contents were like. His eyes swept all the windows and the side streets, and every moment he carried his free hand to his mouth, as though he were yawning, and introduced a crumb of black bread, which he had picked up in the kitchen. His braces were broken, so he had continually to puff out his belly; there were hundreds of things to look at, and the coal-merchant's dog to be kicked while, in all good faith, he snuffed at a curbstone.

A funeral procession came toward them, and the journeyman passed it with his head bared, so Pelle did the same. Eight at the back of the procession came Tailor Bjerregrav with his crutch; he always followed every funeral, and always walked light at the back because his method of progression called for plenty of room. He would stand still and look on the ground until the last of the other followers had gone a few steps in advance, then he would set his crutch in front of him, swing himself forward for a space, and then stand still again. Then he would swing forward again on his lame legs, and again stand still and watch the others, and again take a few paces, looking like a slowly wandering pair of compasses which was tracing the path followed by the procession.

But the funniest thing was that the tailor had forgotten to button up the flap of his black mourning-breeches, so that it hung over his knees like an apron. Pelle was not quite sure that the journeyman had noticed this.

"Bjerregrav has forgotten—"

"Hold your jaw. " Little Nikas made a movement backward, and Pelle ducked his head and pressed his hand tightly to his mouth.

Over in Staal Street there was a great uproar; an enormously fat woman was standing there quarrelling with two seamen. She was in her nightcap and petticoat, and Pelle knew her.

"That's the Sow! " he began. "She's a dreadful woman; up at Stone Farm——"

Smack! Little Nikas gave him such a box on the ear that he had to sit down on the woodcarver's steps. "One, two, three, four— that's it; now come on! " He counted ten steps forward and set off again. "But God help you if you don't keep your distance! "

Pelle kept his distance religiously, but he instantly discovered that little Nikas, like old Jeppe, had too large a posterior. That certainly came of sitting too much—and it twisted one's loins. He protruded his own buttocks as far as he could, smoothed down a crease in his jacket over his hips, raised himself elegantly upon the balls of his feet and marched proudly forward, one hand thrust into the breast of his coat. If the journeyman scratched himself, Pelle did the same—and he swayed his body in the same buoyant manner; his cheeks were burning, but he was highly pleased with himself.

Directly he was his own master he went the round of the country butchers, questioning them, in the hope of hearing some news of Lasse, but no one could tell him anything. He went from cart to cart, asking his questions. "Lasse Karlson? " said one. "Ah, he was cowherd up at Stone Farm! " Then he called to another, asking him about Lasse —the old cowherd at Stone Farm—and he again called to a third, and they all gathered about the carts, in order to talk the matter over. There were men here who travelled all over the island [Bornholm] in order to buy cattle; they knew everything and everybody, but they could tell him nothing of Lasse. "Then he's not in the island, " said one, very decidedly. "You must get another father, my lad! "

Pelle did not feel inclined for chaff, so he slipped away. Besides, he must go back and get to work; the young master, who was busily going from cart to cart, ordering meat, had called to him. They hung together like the halves of a pea-pod when it was a question of keeping the apprentices on the curb, although otherwise they were jealous enough of one another.

Bjerregrav's crutch stood behind the door, and he himself sat in stiff funereal state by the window; he held a folded white handkerchief in his folded hands, and was diligently mopping his eyes.

"Was he perhaps a relation of yours? " said the young master slyly.

"No; but it is so sad for those who are left—a wife and children. There is always some one to mourn and regret the dead. Man's life is a strange thing, Andres. "

"Ah, and potatoes are bad this year, Bjerregrav! "

Neighbor Jorgen filled up the whole doorway. "Lord, here we have that blessed Bjerregrav! " he shouted; "and in state, too! What's on to-day then—going courting, are you? "

"I've been following! " answered Bjerregrav, in a hushed voice.

The big baker made an involuntary movement; he did not like being unexpectedly reminded of death. "You, Bjerregrav, you ought to be a hearse-driver; then at least you wouldn't work to no purpose! "

"It isn't to no purpose when they are dead, " stammered Bjerregrav. "I am not so poor that I need much, and there is no one who stands near to me. No living person loses anything because I follow those who die. And then I know them all, and I've followed them all in thought since they were born, " he added apologetically.

"If only you got invited to the funeral feast and got something of all the good things they have to eat, " continued the baker, "I could understand it better. "

"The poor widow, who sits there with her four little ones and doesn't know how she's to feed them—to take food from her—no, I couldn't do it! She's had to borrow three hundred kroner so that her man could have a respectable funeral party. "

"That ought to be forbidden by law, " said Master Andres; "any one with little children hasn't the right to throw away money on the dead. "

"She is giving her husband the last honors, " said Jeppe reprovingly. "That is the duty of every good wife. "

"Of course, " rejoined Master Andres. "God knows, something must be done. It's like the performances on the other side of the earth, where the widow throws herself on the funeral pyre when the husband dies, and has to be burned to death. "

Baker Jorgen scratched his thighs and grimaced. "You are trying to get us to swallow one of your stinking lies, Andres. You'd never get a woman to do that, if I know anything of womankind. "

But Bjerregrav knew that the shoemaker was not lying, and fluttered his thin hands in the air, as though he were trying to keep something invisible from touching his body. "God be thanked that we came into the world on this island here, " he said, in a low voice. "Here only ordinary things happen, however wrongheaded they may be. "

"What puzzles me is where she got all that money! " said the baker.

"She's borrowed it, of course, " said Bjerregrav, in a tone of voice that made it clear that he wanted to terminate the conversation.

Jeppe retorted contemptuously, "Who's going to lend a poor mate's widow three hundred kroner? He might as well throw it into the sea right away. "

But Baker Jorgen gave Bjerregrav a great smack on the back. "You've given her the money, it's you has done it; nobody else would be such a silly sheep! " he said threateningly.

"You let me be! " stammered Bjerregrav. "I've done nothing to you! And she has had one happy day in the midst of all her sorrow. " His hands were trembling.

"You're a goat! " said Jeppe shortly.

"What is Bjerregrav really thinking about when he stands like this looking down into the grave? " asked the young master, in order to divert the conversation.

"I am thinking: Now you are lying there, where you are better off than here, " said the old tailor simply.

"Yes, because Bjerregrav follows only poor people, " said Jeppe, rather contemptuously.

"I can't help it, but I'm always thinking, " continued Master Andres; "just supposing it were all a take-in! Suppose he follows them and enjoys the whole thing—and then there's nothing! That's why I never like to see a funeral. "

"Ah, you see, that's the question—supposing there's nothing. " Baker Jorgen turned his thick body. "Here we go about imagining a whole lot of things; but what if it's all just lies? "

"That's the mind of an unbeliever! " said Jeppe, and stamped violently on the floor.

"God preserve my mind from unbelief! " retorted brother Jorgen, and he stroked his face gravely. "But a man can't very well help thinking. And what does a man see round about him? Sickness and death and halleluiah! We live, and we live, I tell you, Brother Jeppe—and we live in order to live! But, good heavens! all the poor things that aren't born yet! "

He sank into thought again, as was usual with him when he thought of Little Jorgen, who refused to come into the world and assume his name and likeness, and carry on after him.... There lay his belief; there was nothing to be done about it. And the others began to speak in hushed voices, in order not to disturb his memories.

Pelle, who concerned himself with everything in heaven and earth, had been absorbing every word that was spoken with his protruding ears, but when the conversation turned upon death he yawned. He himself had never been seriously ill, and since Mother Bengta died, death had never encroached upon his world. And that was lucky for him, as it would have been a case of all or nothing, for he had only Father Lasse. For Pelle the cruel hands of death hardly existed, and he could not understand how people could lay themselves down with their noses in the air; there was so much to observe here below — the town alone kept one busy.

On the very first evening he had run out to look for the other boys, just where the crowd was thickest. There was no use in waiting; Pelle was accustomed to take the bull by the horns, and he longed to be taken into favor.

"What sort of brat is that? " they said, flocking round him.

"I'm Pelle, " he said, standing confidently in the midst of the group, and looking at them all. "I have been at Stone Farm since I was eight, and that is the biggest farm in the north country. " He had put his hands in his pockets, and spat coolly in front of him, for that was nothing to what he had in reserve.

"Oh, so you're a farmer chap, then! " said one, and the others laughed. Rud was among them.

"Yes, " said Pelle; "and I've done a bit of ploughing, and mowing fodder for the calves. "

They winked at one another. "Are you really a farmer chap? "

"Yes, truly, " replied Pelle, perplexed; they had spoken the word in a tone which he now remarked.

They all burst out laughing: "He confesses it himself. And he comes from the biggest farm in the country. Then he's the biggest farmer in the country! "

"No, the farmer was called Kongstrup, " said Pelle emphatically. "I was only the herd-boy. "

They roared with laughter. "He doesn't see it now! Why, Lord, that's the biggest farmer's lout! "

314

Pelle had not yet lost his head, for he had heavier ammunition, and now he was about to play a trump. "And there at the farm there was a man called Erik, who was so strong that he could thrash three men, but the bailiff was stronger still; and he gave Erik such a blow that he lost his senses. "

"Oh, indeed! How did he manage that? Can you hit a farmer chap so that he loses his senses? Who was it hit you like that? " The questions rained upon him.

Pelle pushed the boy who had asked the last question, and fixed his eyes upon his. But the rascal let fly at him again. "Take care of your best clothes, " he said, laughing. "Don't crumple your cuffs! "

Pelle had put on a clean blue shirt, of which the neckband and wristbands had to serve as collar and cuffs. He knew well enough that he was clean and neat, and now they were being smart at his expense on that very account.

"And what sort of a pair of Elbe barges has he got on? Good Lord! Why, they'd fill half the harbor! " This was in reference to Kongstrup's shoes. Pelle had debated with himself as to whether he should wear them on a week-day. "When did you celebrate hiring-day? " asked a third. This was in reference to his fat red cheeks.

Now he was ready to jump out of his skin, and cast his eyes around to see if there was nothing with which he could lay about him, for this would infallibly end in an attack upon the whole party. Pelle already had them all against him.

But just then a long, thin lad came forward. "Have you a pretty sister? " he asked.

"I have no sisters at all, " answered Pelle shortly.

"That's a shame. Well, can you play hide-and-seek? "

Of course Pelle could!

"Well, then, play! " The thin boy pushed Pelle's cap over his eyes, and turned him with his face against the plank fence. "Count to a hundred—and no cheating, I tell you! "

No, Pelle would not cheat—he would neither look nor count short—
so much depended on this beginning. But he solemnly promised
himself to use his legs to some purpose; they should all be caught,
one after another! He finished his counting and took his cap from his
eyes. No one was to be seen. "Say 'peep'! " he cried; but no one
answered. For half an hour Pelle searched among timbers and
warehouses, and at last he slipped away home and to bed. But he
dreamed, that night, that he caught them all, and they elected him as
their leader for all future time.

The town did not meet him with open arms, into which he could fall,
with his childlike confidence, and be carried up the ladder. Here,
apparently, one did not talk about the heroic deeds which elsewhere
gave a man foothold; here such things merely aroused scornful
laughter. He tried it again and again, always with something new,
but the answer was always the same—"Farmer! " His whole little
person was overflowing with good-will, and he became deplorably
dejected.

Pelle soon perceived that his whole store of ammunition was
crumbling between his hands, and any respect he had won at home,
on the farm or in the village, by his courage and good nature, went
for nothing here. Here other qualities counted; there was a different
jargon, the clothes were different, and people went about things in a
different way. Everything he had valued was turned to ridicule, even
down to his pretty cap with its ear-flaps and its ribbon adorned with
representations of harvest implements. He had come to town so
calmly confident in himself—to make the painful discovery that he
was a laughable object! Every time he tried to make one of a party,
he was pushed to one side; he had no right to speak to others; he
must take the hindmost rank!

Nothing remained to him but to sound the retreat all along the line
until he had reached the lowest place of all. And hard as this was for
a smart youngster who was burning to set his mark on everything,
Pelle did it, and confidently prepared to scramble up again.
However sore his defeat, he always retained an obstinate feeling of
his own worth, which no one could take away from him. He was
persuaded that the trouble lay not with himself but with all sorts of
things about him, and he set himself restlessly to find out the new
values and to conduct a war of elimination against himself. After
every defeat he took himself unweariedly to task, and the next
evening he would go forth once more, enriched by so many

experiences, and would suffer defeat at a new point. He wanted to conquer—but what must he not sacrifice first? He knew of nothing more splendid than to march resoundingly through the streets, his legs thrust into Lasse's old boots—this was the essence of manliness. But he was man enough to abstain from so doing—for here such conduct would be regarded as boorish. It was harder for him to suppress his past; it was so inseparable from Father Lasse that he was obsessed by a sense of unfaithfulness. But there was no alternative; if he wanted to get on he must adapt himself in everything, in prejudices and opinions alike. But he promised himself to flout the lot of them so soon as he felt sufficiently high-spirited.

What distressed him most was the fact that his handicraft was so little regarded. However accomplished he might become, the cobbler was, and remained, a poor creature with a pitchy snout and a big behind! Personal performance counted for nothing; it was obvious that he must as soon as possible escape into some other walk of life.

But at least he was in the town, and as one of its inhabitants— there was no getting over that. And the town seemed still as great and as splendid, although it had lost the look of enchantment it once had, when Lasse and he had passed through it on their way to the country. Most of the people wore their Sunday clothes, and many sat still and earned lots of money, but no one knew how. All roads came hither, and the town swallowed everything: pigs and corn and men—everything sooner or later found its harbor here! The Sow lived here with Rud, who was now apprenticed to a painter, and the twins were here! And one day Pelle saw a tall boy leaning against a door and bellowing at the top of his voice, his arms over his face, while a couple of smaller boys were thrashing him; it was Howling Peter, who was cook's boy on a vessel. Everything flowed into the town!

But Father Lasse—he was not here!

317

IV

There was something about the town that made it hard to go to bed and hard to get up. In the town there was no sunrise shining over the earth and waking everybody. The open face of morning could not be seen indoors. And the dying day poured no evening weariness into one's limbs, driving them to repose; life seemed here to flow in the reverse direction, for here people grew lively at night!

About half-past six in the morning the master, who slept downstairs, would strike the ceiling with his stick. Pelle, whose business it was to reply, would mechanically sit up and strike the side of the bedstead with his clenched fist. Then, still sleeping, he would fall back again. After a while the process was repeated. But then the master grew impatient. "Devil take it! aren't you going to get up to-day? " he would bellow. "Is this to end in my bringing you your coffee in bed? " Drunken with sleep, Pelle would tumble out of bed. "Get up, get up! " he would cry, shaking the others. Jens got nimbly on his feet; he always awoke with a cry of terror, guarding his head; but Emil and Peter, who were in the hobbledehoy stage, were terribly difficult to wake.

Pelle would hasten downstairs, and begin to set everything in order, filling the soaking-tub and laying a sand-heap by the window-bench for the master to spit into. He bothered no further about the others; he was in a morning temper himself. On the days when he had to settle right away into the cobbler's hunch, without first running a few early errands or doing a few odd tasks, it took hours to thaw him.

He used to look round to see whether on the preceding evening he had made a chalk-mark in any conspicuous place; for then there must be something that he had to remember. Memory was not his strong point, hence this ingenious device. Then it was only a matter of not forgetting what the mark stood for; if he forgot, he was no better off than before.

When the workshop was tidy, he would hurry downstairs and run out for Madame, to fetch morning rolls "for themselves. " He himself was given a wheaten biscuit with his coffee, which he drank out in the kitchen, while the old woman went grumbling to and fro. She was dry as a mummy and moved about bent double, and when she was not using her hands she carried one forearm pressed against her midriff. She was discontented with everything, and was always talking of the grave. "My two eldest are overseas, in America and Australia; I shall never see them again. And here at home two menfolk go strutting about doing nothing and expecting to be waited on. Andres, poor fellow, isn't strong, and Jeppe's no use any longer; he can't even keep himself warm in bed nowadays. But they know how to ask for things, that they do, and they let me go running all over the place without any help; I have to do everything myself. I shall truly thank God when at last I lie in my grave. What are you standing there for with your mouth and your eyes wide open? Get away with you! " Thereupon Pelle would finish his coffee—it was sweetened with brown sugar—out of doors, by the workshop window.

In the mornings, before the master appeared, there was no great eagerness to work; they were all sleepy still, looking forward to a long, dreary day. The journeyman did not encourage them to work; he had a difficulty in finding enough for himself. So they sat there wool-gathering, striking a few blows with the hammer now and then for appearance's sake, and one or another would fall asleep again over the table. They all started when three blows were struck on the wall as a signal for Pelle.

"What are you doing? It seems to me you are very idle in there! " the master would say, staring suspiciously at Pelle. But Pelle had remarked what work each was supposed to have in hand, and would run over it all. "What day's this—Thursday? Damnation take it! Tell that Jens he's to put aside Manna's uppers and begin on the pilot's boots this moment—they were promised for last Monday. " The master would struggle miserably to get his breath: "Ah, I've had a bad night, Pelle, a horrible night; I was so hot, with such a ringing in my ears. New blood is so devilishly unruly; it's all the time boiling in my head like soda-water. But it's a good thing I'm making it, God knows; I used to be so soon done up. Do you believe in Hell? Heaven, now, that's sheer nonsense; what happiness can we expect elsewhere if we can't be properly happy here? But do you believe in Hell? I dreamed I'd spat up the last bit of my lungs and that I went to Hell. 'What the devil d'you want here, Andres? ' they asked me; 'your heart is still whole! ' And they wouldn't have me. But what does that signify? I can't breathe with my heart, so I'm dying. And what becomes of me then? Will you tell me that?

"There's something that bids a man enter again into his mother's womb; now if only a man could do that, and come into the world again with two sound legs, you'd see me disappear oversea double-quick, whoop! I wouldn't stay messing about here any longer.... Well, have you seen your navel yet to-day? Yes, you ragamuffin, you laugh; but I'm in earnest. It would pay you well if you always began the day by contemplating your navel. "

The master was half serious, half jesting. "Well, now, you can fetch me my port wine; it's on the shelf, behind the box with the laces in it. I'm deadly cold. "

Pelle came back and announced that the bottle was empty. The master looked at him mildly.

"Then run along and get me another. I've no money—you must say— well, think it out for yourself; you've got a head. " The master looked at him with an expression which went to Pelle's heart, so that he often felt like bursting into tears. Hitherto Pelle's life had been spent on the straight highway; he did not understand this combination of wit and misery, roguishness and deadly affliction. But he felt something of the presence of the good God, and trembled inwardly; he would have died for the young master.

When the weather was wet it was difficult for the sick man to get about; the cold pulled him down. If he came into the workshop, freshly washed and with his hair still wet, he would go over to the cold stove, and stand there, stamping his feet. His cheeks had quite fallen in. "I've so little blood for the moment, " he said at such times, "but the new blood is on the way; it sings in my ears every night. " Then he would be silent a while. "There, by my soul, we've got a piece of lung again, " he said, and showed Pelle, who stood at the stove brushing shoes, a gelatinous lump. "But they grow again afterward! "

"The master will soon be in his thirtieth year, " said the journeyman; "then the dangerous time is over. "

"Yes, deuce take it—if only I can hang together so long—only another six months, " said the master eagerly, and he looked at Pelle, as though Pelle had it in his power to help him; "only another six months! Then the whole body renews itself—new lungs—everything new. But new legs, God knows, I shall never get. "

A peculiar, secret understanding grew up between Pelle and the master; it did not manifest itself in words, but in glances, in tones of the voice, and in the whole conduct of each. When Pelle stood behind him, it was as though even the master's leather jacket emitted a feeling of warmth, and Pelle followed him with his eyes whenever and wherever he could, and the master's behavior to Pelle was different from his behavior to the others.

When, on his return from running errands in the town, he came to the corner, he was delighted to see the young master standing in the doorway, tightly grasping his stick, with his lame leg in an easy position. He stood there, sweeping his eyes from side to side, gazing longingly into the distance. This was his place when he was not indoors, sitting over some book of adventure. But Pelle liked him to stand there, and as he slipped past he would hang his head shyly, for it often happened that the master would clutch his shoulder, so hard that it hurt, and shake him to and fro, and would say affectionately: "Oh, you limb of Satan! " This was the only endearment that life had vouchsafed Pelle, and he sunned himself in it.

Pelle could not understand the master, nor did he understand his sighs and groans. The master never went out, save as an exception, when he was feeling well; then he would hobble across to the beerhouse and make up a party, but as a rule his travels ended at the house door. There he would stand, looking about him a little, and then he would hobble indoors again, with that infectious good humor which transformed the dark workshop into a grove full of the twittering of birds. He had never been abroad, and he felt no craving to go; but in spite of this his mind and his speech roamed over the whole wide world, so that Pelle at times felt like falling sick from sheer longing. He demanded nothing more than health of the future, and adventures hovered all about him; one received the impression that happiness itself had fluttered to earth and settled upon him. Pelle idolized him, but did not understand him. The master, who at one moment would make sport of his lame leg and the next moment forget that he had one, or jest about his poverty as though he were flinging good gold pieces about him—this was a man Pelle could not fathom. He was no wiser when he secretly looked into the books which Master Andres read so breathlessly; he would have been content with a much more modest adventure than a journey to the North Pole or the center of the earth, if only he himself could have been of the party.

He had no opportunity to sit still and indulge in fancies. Every moment it was, "Pelle, run and do something or other! " Everything was purchased in small quantities, although it was obtained on credit. "Then it doesn't run up so, " Jeppe used to say; it was all the same to Master Andres. The foreman's young woman came running in; she absolutely must have her young lady's shoes; they were promised for Monday. The master had quite forgotten them. "They are in hand now, " he said, undaunted. "To the devil with you, Jens! " And Jens had hastily thrust a pair of lasts into the shoes, while Master Andres went outside with the girl, and joked with her on the landing, in order to smooth her down. "Just a few nails, so that they'll hang together, " said the master to Jens. And then, "Pelle, out you go, as quick as your legs will carry you! Say we'll send for them early to-morrow morning and finish them properly! But run as though the devil were at your heels! "

Pelle ran, and when he returned, just as he was slipping into his leather apron, he had to go out again. "Pelle, run out and borrow a few brass nails—then we needn't buy any to-day. Go to Klausen— no, go to Blom, rather; you've been to Klausen already this morning. "

"Blom's are angry about the screw-block! " said Pelle.

"Death and all the devils! We must see about putting it in repair and returning it; remember that, and take it with you to the smith's. Well, what in the world shall we do? " The young master stared helplessly from one to another.

"Shoemaker Marker, " suggested little Nikas.

"We don't borrow from Marker, " and the master wrinkled his forehead. "Marker's a louse! " Marker had succeeded in stealing one of the oldest customers of the workshop.

"There isn't salt to eat an egg! "

"Well, what *shall* I do? " asked Pelle, somewhat impatiently.

The master sat for a while in silence. "Well, take it, then! " he cried, and threw a krone toward Pelle; "I have no peace from you so long as I've got a farthing in my pocket, you demon! Buy a packet and pay back Klausen and Blom what we've borrowed. "

"But then they'd see we've got a whole packet, " said Pelle.

"Besides, they owe us lots of other things that they've borrowed of us. " Pelle showed circumspection in his dealings.

"What a rogue! " said the master, and he settled himself to read. "Lord above us, what a gallows-bird! " He looked extremely contented.

And after a time it was once more, "Pelle, run out, etc. "

The day was largely passed in running errands, and Pelle was not one to curtail them; he had no liking for the smelly workshop and its wooden chairs. There was so much to be fetched and carried, and Pelle considered these errands to be his especial duty; when he had nothing else to do he roved about like a young puppy, and thrust his nose into everything. Already the town had no more secrets from him.

There was in Pelle an honorable streak which subdued the whole. But hitherto he had suffered only defeat; he had again and again sacrificed his qualities and accomplishments, without so far receiving anything in return. His timidity and distrust he had stripped from him indoors, where it was of importance that he should open his defences on all sides, and his solid qualities he was on the point of sacrificing on the altar of the town as boorish. But the less protection he possessed the more he gained in intrepidity, so he went about out-of-doors undauntedly—the town should be conquered. He was enticed out of the safe refuge of his shell, and might easily be gobbled up.

The town had lured him from the security of his lair, but in other matters he was the same good little fellow—most people would have seen no difference in him, except that he had grown taller. But Father Lasse would have wept tears of blood to see his boy as he now walked along the streets, full of uncertainty and uneasy imitativeness, wearing his best coat on a workday, and yet disorderly in his dress.

Yonder he goes, sauntering along with a pair of boots, his fingers thrust through the string of the parcel, whistling with an air of bravado. Now and again he makes a grimace and moves cautiously—when his trousers rub the sensitive spots of his body. He has had a bad day. In the morning he was passing a smithy, and allowed the splendid display of energy within, half in the firelight and half in the shadow, to detain him. The flames and the clanging of the metal, the whole lively uproar of real work, fascinated him, and he had to go in and ask whether there was an opening for an apprentice. He was not so stupid as to tell them where he came from, but when he got home, Jeppe had already been told of it! But that is soon forgotten, unless, indeed, his trousers rub against his sore places. Then he remembers it; remembers that in this world everything has to be paid for; there is no getting out of things; once one begins anything one has to eat one's way through it, like the boy in the fairy-tale. And this discovery is, in the abstract, not so strikingly novel to Pelle.

He has, as always, chosen the longest way, rummaging about back yards and side streets, where there is a possibility of adventure; and all at once he is suddenly accosted by Albinus, who is now employed by a tradesman. Albinus is not amusing. He has no right to play and loiter about the warehouse in the aimless fashion that is possible out-of-doors; nor to devote himself to making a ladder stand straight up in the air while he climbs up it. Not a word can be got out of him, although Pelle does his best; so he picks up a handful of raisins and absconds.

Down at the harbor he boards a Swedish vessel, which has just arrived with a cargo of timber. "Have you anything for us to do? " he asks, holding one hand behind him, where his trousers have a hole in them.

"Klausen's apprentice has just been here and got what there was, " replied the skipper.

"That's a nuisance—you ought to have given it to us, " says Pelle. "Have you got a clay pipe? "

"Yes—just you come here! " The skipper reaches for a rope's end, but Pelle escapes and runs ashore.

"Will you give me a thrashing now? " he cries, jeering.

"You shall have a clay pipe if you'll run and get me half a krone's worth of chewing 'bacca. "

324

"What will it cost? " asks Pelle, with an air of simplicity. The skipper reaches for his rope's end again, but Pelle is off already.

"Five ore worth of chewing tobacco, the long kind, " he cries, before he gets to the door even. "But it must be the very best, because it's for an invalid. " He throws the money on the counter and puts on a cheeky expression.

Old Skipper Lau rises by the aid of his two sticks and hands Pelle the twist; his jaws are working like a mill, and all his limbs are twisted with gout. "Is it for some one lying-in? " he asks slyly.

Pelle breaks off the stem of the clay pipe, lest it should stick out of his pocket, boards the salvage steamer, and disappears forward. After a time he reappears from under the cabin hatchway, with a gigantic pair of sea-boots and a scrap of chewing tobacco. Behind the deck-house he bites a huge mouthful off the brown Cavendish, and begins to chew courageously, which makes him feel tremendously manly. But near the furnace where the ship's timbers are bent he has to unload his stomach; it seems as though all his inward parts are doing their very utmost to see how matters would be with them hanging out of his mouth. He drags himself along, sick as a cat, with thumping temples; but somewhere or other inside him a little feeling of satisfaction informs him that one has to undergo the most dreadful consequences in order to perform any really heroic deed.

In most respects the harbor, with its stacks of timber and its vessels on the slips, is just as fascinating as it was on the day when Pelle lay on the shavings and guarded Father Lasse's sack. The black man with the barking hounds still leans from the roof of the harbor warehouse, but the inexplicable thing is that one could ever have been frightened of him. But Pelle is in a hurry.

He runs a few yards, but he must of necessity stop when he comes to the old quay. There the "strong man, " the "Great Power, " is trimming some blocks of granite. He is tanned a coppery brown with wind and sun, and his thick black hair is full of splinters of granite; he wears only a shirt and canvas trousers, and the shirt is open on his powerful breast; but it lies close on his back, and reveals the play of his muscles. Every time he strikes a blow the air whistles— *whew!* —and the walls and timber-stacks echo the sound. People come hurrying by, stop short at a certain distance, and stand there looking on. A little group stands there all the time, newcomers taking the place of those that move on, like spectators in front of a cage of lions. It is as though they expect something to happen— something that will stagger everybody and give the bystanders a good fright.

Pelle goes right up to the "Great Power. " The "strong man" is the father of Jens, the second youngest apprentice. "Good-day, " he says boldly, and stands right in the giant's shadow. But the stonecutter pushes him to one side without looking to see who it is, and continues to hew at the granite: *whew! whew!*

"It is quite a long time now since he has properly used his strength, " says an old townsman. "Is he quieting down, d'you think? "

"He must have quieted down for good, " says another. "The town ought to see that he keeps quiet. " And they move on, and Pelle must move on, too—anywhere, where no one can see him.

> "Cobbler, wobbler, groats in your gruel,
> Smack on your back goes the stick—how cruel! "

It is those accursed street-urchins. Pelle is by no means in a warlike humor; he pretends not to see them. But they come up close behind him and tread on his heels, and before he knows what is happening they are upon him. The first he knows about it is that he is lying in the gutter, on his back, with all three on top of him. He has fallen alongside of the curbstone and cannot move; he is faint, too, as a result of his indiscretion; the two biggest boys spread his arms wide open on the flagstones and press them down with all their might, while the third ventures to deal with his face. It is a carefully planned outrage, and all Pelle can do is to twist his head round under the blows—and for once he is thankful for his disgracefully fat cheeks.

Then, in his need, a dazzling apparition appears before him; standing in the doorway yonder is a white baker's boy, who is royally amused. It is no other than Nilen, the wonderful little devil Nilen, of his schooldays, who was always fighting everybody like a terrier and always came out of it with a whole skin. Pelle shuts his eyes and blushes for himself, although he knows perfectly well that this is only an apparition.

But then a wonderful thing happens; the apparition leaps down into the gutter, slings the boys to one side, and helps him to his feet. Pelle recognizes the grip of those fingers—even in his schooldays they were like claws of iron.

And soon he is sitting behind the oven, on Nilen's grimy bed. "So you've become a cobbler? " says Nilen, to begin with, compassionately, for he feels a deucedly smart fellow himself in his fine white clothes, with his bare arms crossed over his naked breast. Pelle feels remarkably comfortable; he has been given a slice of bread and cream, and he decides that the world is more interesting than ever. Nilen is chewing manfully, and spitting over the end of the bed.

"Do you chew? " asks Pelle, and hastens to offer him the leaf-tobacco.

"Yes, we all do; a fellow has to when he works all night. "

Pelle cannot understand how people can keep going day and night.

"All the bakers in Copenhagen do—so that the people can get fresh bread in the morning—and our master wants to introduce it here. But it isn't every one can do it; the whole staff had to be reorganized. It's worst about midnight, when everything is turning round. Then it comes over you so that you keep on looking at the time, and the very moment the clock strikes twelve we all hold our breath, and then no one can come in or go out any more. The master himself can't stand the night shift; the 'baccy turns sour in his mouth and he has to lay it on the table. When he wakes up again he thinks it's a raisin and sticks it in the dough. What's the name of your girl? "

For a moment Pelle's thoughts caress the three daughters of old Skipper Elleby—but no, none of them shall be immolated. No, he has no girl.

"Well, you get one, then you needn't let them sit on you. I'm flirting a bit just now with the master's daughter—fine girl, she is, quite developed already—you know! But we have to look out when the old man's about! "

"Then are you going to marry her when you are a journeyman? " asks Pelle, with interest.

"And have a wife and kids on my back? You are a duffer, Pelle! No need to trouble about that! But a woman—well, that's only for when a man's bored. See? " He stretches himself, yawning.

Nilen has become quite a young man, but a little crude in his manner of expressing himself. He sits there and looks at Pelle with a curious expression in his eyes. "Cobbler's patch! " he says contemptuously, and thrusts his tongue into his cheek so as to make it bulge. Pelle says nothing; he knows he cannot thrash Nilen.

Nilen has lit his pipe and is lying on his back in bed—with his muddy shoes on—chattering. "What's your journeyman like? Ours is a conceited ass. The other day I had to fetch him a box on the ears, he was so saucy. I've learned the Copenhagen trick of doing it; it soon settles a man. Only you want to keep your head about it. " A deuce of a fellow, this Nilen, he is so grown up! Pelle feels smaller and smaller.

But suddenly Nilen jumps up in the greatest hurry. Out in the bakery a sharp voice is calling. "Out of the window—to the devil with you! " he yelps—"the journeyman! " And Pelle has to get through the window, and is so slow about it that his boots go whizzing past him. While he is jumping down he hears the well-known sound of a ringing box on the ear.

When Pelle returned from his wanderings he was tired and languid; the stuffy workshop did not seem alluring. He was dispirited, too; for the watchmaker's clock told him that he had been three hours away. He could not believe it.

The young master stood at the front door, peeping out, still in his leather jacket and apron of green baize; he was whistling softly to himself, and looked like a grown fledgling that did not dare to let itself tumble out of the nest. A whole world of amazement lay in his inquiring eyes.

"Have you been to the harbor again, you young devil? " he asked, sinking his claws into Pelle.

"Yes. " Pelle was properly ashamed.

"Well, what's going on there? What's the news? "

So Pelle had to tell it all on the stairs; how there was a Swedish timber ship whose skipper's wife was taken with childbirth out at sea, and how the cook had to deliver her; of a Russian vessel which had run into port with a mutiny on board; and anything else that might have happened. To-day there were only these boots. "They are from the salvage steamer—they want soling. "

"H'm! " The master looked at them indifferently. "Is the schooner *Andreas* ready to sail? "

But that Pelle did not know.

"What sort of a sheep's head have you got, then? Haven't you any eyes in it? Well, well, go and get me three bottles of beer! Only stick them under your blouse so that father don't see, you monster! " The master was quite good-tempered again.

Then Pelle got into his apron and buckled on the knee-strap. Everybody was bending over his work, and Master Andres was reading; no sound was to be heard but those produced by the workers, and now and again a word of reprimand from the journeyman.

Every second afternoon, about five o'clock, the workshop door would open slightly, and a naked, floury arm introduced the newspaper and laid it on the counter. This was the baker's son, Soren, who never allowed himself to be seen; he moved about from choice like a thief in the night. If the master—as he occasionally did—seized him and pulled him into the workshop, he was like a scared faun strayed from his thickets; he would stand with hanging head, concealing his eyes, and no one could get a word from him; and when he saw an opportunity, he would slip away.

The arrival of the newspaper caused quite a small commotion in the workshop. When the master felt inclined, he would read aloud—of calves with two heads and four pairs of legs; of a pumpkin that weighed fifty pounds; of the fattest man in the world; of fatalities due to the careless handling of firearms, or of snakes in Martinique. The dazzling wonder of the whole world passed like a pageant, filling the dark workshop; the political news was ignored. If the master happened to be in one of his desperate humors, he would read the most damnable nonsense: of how the Atlantic Ocean had caught fire, so that the people were living on boiled codfish; or how the heavens had got torn over America, so that angels fell right on to somebody's supper-tray. Things which one knew at once for lies—and blasphemous nonsense, too, which might at any time have got him into trouble. Rowing people was not in the master's line, he was ill the moment there was any unpleasantness; but he had his own way of making himself respected. As he went on reading some one would discover that he was getting a wigging, and would give a jump, believing that all his failings were in the paper.

When the time drew near for leaving off work, a brisker note sounded in the workshop. The long working-day was coming to an end, and the day's weariness and satiety were forgotten, and the mind looked forward—filling with thoughts of the sand-hills or the woods, wandering down a road that was bright with pleasure. Now and again a neighbor would step in, and while away the time with his gossip; something or other had happened, and Master Andres, who was so clever, must say what he thought about it. Sounds that had been confused during the day now entered the workshop, so that those within felt that they were participating in the life of the town; it was as though the walls had fallen.

About seven o'clock a peculiar sound was heard in the street without, approaching in very slowly *tempo;* there was a dull thump and then two clacking sounds; and then came the thump again, like the tread of a huge padded foot, and once more the clack-clack. This was old Bjerregrav, swinging toward the workshop on his crutches; Bjerregrav, who moved more slowly than anybody, and got forward more quickly. If Master Andres happened to be in one of his bad humors, he would limp away, in order not to remain in the same room with a cripple; at other times he was glad to see Bjerregrav.

"Well, you are a rare bird, aren't you? " he would cry, when Bjerregrav reached the landing and swung himself sideways through the door; and the old man would laugh—he had paid this visit daily now for many years. The master took no further notice of him, but went on reading; and Bjerregrav sank into his dumb pondering; his pale hands feeling one thing after another, as though the most everyday objects were unknown to him. He took hold of things just as a newborn child might have done; one had to smile at him and leave him to sit there, grubbing about like the child he really was. It was quite impossible to hold a continuous conversation with him; for even if he did actually make an observation it was sure to be quite beside the mark; Bjerregrav was given to remarking attributes which no one else noticed, or which no one would have dwelt upon.

When he sat thus, pondering over and fingering some perfectly familiar object, people used to say, "Now Bjerregrav's questioning fit is coming on! " For Bjerregrav was an inquirer; he would ask questions about the wind and the weather, and even the food that he ate. He would ask questions about the most laughable subjects—things that were self-evident to any one else—why a stone was hard, or why water extinguished fire. People did not answer him, but shrugged their shoulders compassionately. "He is quite all there, " they would say; "his head's all right. But he takes everything the wrong way round! "

The young master looked up from his book. "Now, shall I inherit Bjerregrav's money? " he asked mischievously.

"No—you've always been good to me; I don't want to cause you any misfortune. "

"Worse things than that might befall me, don't you think? "

"No, for you've got a fair competence. No one has a right to more, so long as the many suffer need. "

"Certain people have money in the bank themselves, " said Master Andres allusively.

"No, that's all over, " answered the old man cheerfully. "I'm now exactly as rich as you. "

"The devil! Have you run through the lot? " The young master turned round on his chair.

"You and your 'run through it all'! You always sit over me like a judge and accuse me of things! I'm not conscious of having done anything wrong; but it's true that the need gets worse every winter. It's a burden to have money, Andres, when men are hungry all about you; and if you help them then you learn afterward that you've done the man injury; they say it themselves, so it must be true. But now I've given the money to the Charity Organization Society, so now it will go to the right people. "

"Five thousand kroner! " said the master, musing. "Then there ought to be great rejoicing among the poor this winter. "

"Well, they won't get it direct in food and firing, " said Bjerregrav, "but it will come to them just as well in other ways. For when I'd made my offer to the Society, Shipowner Monsen—you know him— came to me, and begged me to lend him the money at one year. He would have gone bankrupt if he hadn't had it, and it was terrible to think of all the poor people who would have gone without bread if that great business of his had come to a standstill. Now the responsibility falls on me. But the money is safe enough, and in that way it does the poor twice as much good. "

Master Andres shook his head. "Suppose Bjerregrav has just sat himself down in the nettles? "

"Why? But what else could I have done? " said the old man uneasily.

"The devil knows it won't be long before he's bankrupt. He's a frothy old rogue, " murmured the master. "Has Bjerregrav got a note of hand? "

The old man nodded; he was quite proud of himself.

"And interest? Five per cent.? "

"No, no interest. For money to stand out and receive interest—I don't like that. It has to suck the interest somewhere or other, and of course it's from the poor. Interest is blood-money, Andres —and it's a new-fangled contrivance, too. When I was young we knew nothing about getting interest on our money. "

"Yes, yes:

> 'Who gives to other folks his bread
> And after suffers in their stead,
> Why club him, club him, club him dead! '"

said the master, and went on reading.

Bjerregrav sat there sunk in his own thoughts. Suddenly he looked up.

"Can you, who are so well read, tell me what keeps the moon from falling? I lay overnight puzzling over it, so as I couldn't sleep. She wanders and wanders through the sky, and you can see plainly there's nothing but air under her. "

"The devil may know, " said Master Andres thoughtfully. "She must have strength of her own, so that she holds herself up. "

"I've thought that myself—for obligation isn't enough. Now we can do that—we walk and walk where we are put down, but then we've the earth under us to support us. And you are always studying, aren't you? I suppose you have read nearly all the books in the world? " Bjerregrav took the master's book and felt it thoroughly. "That's a good book, " he said, striking his knuckles against the cover and holding the book to his ear; "good material, that. Is it a lying story or a history book? "

"It's a travel book. They go up to the North Pole, and they get frozen in, and they don't know if they'll ever get home alive again. "

"But that's terrible—that people should risk their lives so. I've often thought about that—what it's like at the end of the world—but to go and find out—no, I should never have had the courage. Never to get home again! " Bjerregrav, with an afflicted expression, looked first at one, then at another.

"And they get frost-bite in their feet—and their toes have to be amputated—in some cases, the whole foot. "

"No, be quiet! So they lose their health, poor fellows! —I don't want to hear any more! " The old man sat rocking himself to and fro, as though he felt unwell. But a few moments later he asked inquisitively: "Did the king send them up there to make war? "

"No; they went to look for the Garden of Eden. One of the people who investigate writings has discovered that it is said to lie behind the ice, " declared the master solemnly.

"The Garden of Eden—or they call it Paradise, too—but that lies where the two rivers fall into a third, in the East! That is quite plainly written. Consequently what you read there is false teaching. "

"It's at the North Pole, God's truth it is! " said the master, who was inclined to be a free-thinker; "God's truth, I tell you! The other's just a silly superstition. "

Bjerregrav maintained an angry silence. He sat for some time bending low in his chair, his eyes roaming anywhere so that they did not meet another's. "Yes, yes, " he said, in a low voice; "everybody thinks something new in order to make himself remarkable, but no one can alter the grave. "

Master Andres wriggled impatiently to and fro; he could change his mood like a woman. Bjerregrav's presence began to distress him. "Now, I've learned to conjure up spirits; will Bjerregrav make the experiment? " he said suddenly.

"No, not at any price! " said the old man, smiling uneasily.

But the master pointed, with two fingers, at his blinking eyes, and gazed at him, while he uttered the conjuration.

"In the name of the Blood, in the name of the Sap, in the name of all the Humors of the Body, the good and the bad alike, and in the name of the Ocean, " he murmured, crouching like a tom-cat.

"Stop it, I tell you! Stop it! I won't have it! " Bjerregrav was hanging helplessly between his crutches, swinging to and fro, with an eye to the door, but he could not wrest himself away from the enchantment. Then, desperately, he struck down the master's conjuring hand, and profited by the interruption of the incantation to slip away.

The master sat there blowing upon his hand. "He struck out properly, " he said, in surprise, turning his reddened hand with the palm inward.

Little Nikas did not respond. He was not superstitious, but he did not like to hear ridicule cast upon the reality of things.

"What shall I do? " asked Peter.

"Are mate Jensen's boots ready? " The master looked at the clock. "Then you can nibble your shin-bones. "

It was time to stop work. The master took his stick and hat and limped over to the beer-house to play a game of billiards; the journeyman dressed and went out; the older apprentices washed their necks in the soaking-tub. Presently they too would go out and have a proper time of it.

Pelle gazed after them. He too experienced a desperate need to shake off the oppressive day, and to escape out of doors, but his stockings were nothing but holes, and his working-blouse had to be washed so that it should be dry by the following morning. Yes, and his shirt—and he blushed up to his ears—was it a fortnight he had worn it, or was this the fourth week? The time had slipped past so.... He had meant to defer the disagreeable business of washing only for a few days—and now it had mounted up to fourteen! His body had a horrible crawling feeling; was his punishment come upon him because he had turned a deaf ear to the voice of conscience, and had ignored Father Lasse's warning, that disgrace awaited those who did not keep themselves clean?

No, thank God! But Pelle had received a thorough fright, and his ears were still burning as he scrubbed his shirt and blouse downstairs in the yard. It would be well to take it as a timely warning from on high!

And then blouse and shirt were hanging on the fence, spreading themselves abroad as though they wanted to hug the heavens for joy in their cleanliness. But Pelle sat dejectedly upstairs, at the window of the apprentices' garret, one leg outside, so that part of him at least was in the open air. The skillful darning which his father had taught him was not put into practice here; the holes were simply cobbled together, so that Father Lasse would have sunk into the earth for shame. Gradually he crept right out on to the roof; below, in the skipper's garden, the three girls were wandering idly, looking over toward the workshop, and evidently feeling bored.

Then they caught sight of him, and at once became different beings. Manna came toward him, thrust her body impatiently against the stone wall, and motioned to him with her lips. She threw her head back imperiously, and stamped with her feet—but without making a sound. The other two were bent double with suppressed laughter.

Pelle understood perfectly what this silent speech intended, but for a time he courageously stood his ground. At last, however, he could endure it no longer; he threw everything aside and next moment was with the girls.

All Pelle's dreams and unuttered longings hovered over those places where men disported themselves. To him nothing was more ridiculous than to run after petticoats. Women, for Pelle, were really rather contemptible; they had no strength, and very little intelligence; indeed, they understood nothing but the art of making themselves ornamental. But Manna and her sisters were something apart; he was still enough of a child to play, and they were excellent playmates.

Manna—the wild cat—was afraid of nothing; with her short skirts and her pigtail and her skipping movements she reminded him of a frolicsome, inquisitive young bird Skip! out of the thicket and back again! She could climb like a boy, and could carry Pelle all round the garden on her back; it was really an oversight that she should have to wear skirts. Her clothes wouldn't keep on her, and she was always tumbling into the workshop, having torn something or other off her shoes. Then she would turn everything upside down, take the master's stick away, so that he could not move, and would even get her fingers among the journeyman's American tools.

She was on good terms with Pelle the very first day.

"Whose new boy are you? " she asked him, smacking him on the back. And Pelle laughed, and returned her look frankly, with that immediate comprehension which is the secret of our early years. There was no trace of embarrassment between them; they had always known one another, and could at any time resume their play just where they had left off. In the evening Pelle used to station himself by the garden wall and wait for her; then in a moment he was over and in the middle of some game.

Manna was no ordinary cry-baby; not one who seeks to escape the consequences of her action by a display of tears. If she let herself in for a scuffle, she never sued for mercy, however hardly it went with her. But Pelle was to a certain extent restrained by the fact of her petticoats. And she, on one occasion, did not deny that she wished she could only be a little stronger!

But she had courage, and Pelle, like a good comrade, gave as good as he got, except in the workshop, where she bullied him. If she assailed him from behind, dropping something down his neck or pushing him off his wooden stool, he restrained himself, and was merely thankful that his bones were still unbroken.

All his best hours were spent in the skipper's garden, and this garden was a wonderful place, which might well hold his senses captive. The girls had strange outlandish names, which their father had brought home with him on his long voyages: Aina, Dolores, and Sjermanna! They wore heavy beads of red coral round their necks and in their ears. And about the garden lay gigantic conch-shells, in which one could hear the surging of the ocean, and tortoise-shells as big as a fifteen-pound loaf, and whole great lumps of coral.

All these things were new to Pelle, but he would not allow them to confound him; he enrolled them as quickly as possible among the things that were matters of course, and reserved himself the right to encounter, at any moment, something finer and more remarkable.

But on some evenings he would disappoint the girls, and would stroll about the town where he could see real life—or go down to the dunes or the harbor. Then they would stand dejectedly at the garden wall, bored and quarrelsome. But on Sundays, as soon as he had finished in the workshop, he would faithfully appear, and they would spin out their games, conscious of a long day in front of them. They played games innumerable, and Pelle was the center of them all; he could turn himself to anything; he became everything in turn—lawful husband, cannibal, or slave. He was like a tame bear in their hands; they would ride on him, trample all over him, and at times they would all three fall upon him and "murder" him. And he had to lie still, and allow them to bury his body and conceal all traces of it. The reality of the affair was enhanced by the fact that he was really covered with earth—all but his face, which was left bare only from necessity—they contented themselves with covering that with withered leaves. When he cried afterward over the state of his fine confirmation clothes, they brushed him with solicitous hands, and when he could scarcely be comforted they all three kissed him. With them he was always referred to as "Manna's husband. "

So Pelle's days went by. He had a certain grim humor rather than a cheerful mind; he felt gloomy, and as though things were going badly with him; and he had no one to lean upon. But he continued his campaign against the town, undaunted; he thought of it night and day, and fought, it in his sleep.

"If you're ever in a difficulty, you've always Alfred and Albinus to help you out, " Uncle Kalle had said, when Pelle was bidding him good-bye; and he did not fail to look them up. But the twins were to-day the same slippery, evasive customers as they were among the pastures; they ventured their skins neither for themselves nor for anybody else.

In other respects they had considerably improved. They had come hither from the country in order to better their positions, and to that end had accepted situations which would serve them until they had saved sufficient to allow them to commence a more distinguished career. Albinus had advanced no further, as he had no inclination to any handicraft. He was a good-tempered youth, who was willing to give up everything else if only he could practise his acrobatic feats. He always went about balancing something or other, taking pains to put all sorts of objects to the most impossible uses. He had no respect for the order of nature; he would twist his limbs into all imaginable positions, and if he threw anything into the air he expected it to stay there while he did something else. "Things must be broken in as well as animals, " he would say, and persevere indefatigably. Pelle laughed; he liked him, but he did not count on him any further.

Alfred had struck out in quite another direction. He no longer indulged in hand-springs, but walked decorously on his legs, had always much ado to pull down and straighten his collar and cuffs, and was in continual anxiety as to his clothes. He was now apprentice to a painter, but had a parting in his hair like a counter-jumper, and bought all sorts of things at the chemist's, which he smeared on his hair. If Pelle ran across him in the street, Alfred always made some excuse to shake him off; he preferred to associate with tradesmen's apprentices, and was continually greeting acquaintances right and left—people who were in a better position than himself. Alfred put on airs of importance which made Pelle long one fine day to cudgel him soundly.

The twins resembled one another in this—no one need look to them for assistance of any kind. They laughed comfortably at the very idea, and if any one made fun of Pelle they joined in the laughter.

It was not easy to get on. He had quite shaken off the farm-boy; it was his poverty that gave him trouble now. He had recklessly bound himself as apprentice for board and lodging; he had a few clothes on his body, and he had not thought other requisites necessary for one who did not stroll up and down and gad about with girls. But the town demanded that he should rig himself out. Sunday clothes were here not a bit too good for weekdays. He ought to see about getting himself a rubber collar—which had the advantage that one could wash it oneself; cuffs he regarded as a further desideratum. But that needed money, and the mighty sum of five kroner, with which he had set out to conquer the world, or, at the worst, to buy it—well, the town had enticed it out of his pocket before he was aware of it.

Hitherto Father Lasse had taken all very difficult matters upon himself; but now Pelle stood alone, and had only himself to rely on. Now he stood face to face with life, and he struggled courageously forward, like the excellent boy he was. But at times he broke down. And this struggle was a drag upon all his boyish doings and strivings.

In the workshop he made himself useful and tried to stand well with everybody. He won over little Nikas by drawing a somewhat extravagant representation of his betrothed from a photograph. The face would not come out quite right; it looked as though some one had trodden on it; but the clothes and the brooch at the throat were capital. The picture hung for a week in the workshop, and brought Pelle a wonderful piece of luck: Carlsen, who ran errands for the stone-workers, ordered two large pictures, one of himself and one of his wife, at the rate of twenty-five ore apiece. "But you must show a few curls in my hair, " he said, "for my mother's always wished I had curls. "

Pelle could not promise the pictures in less than two months' time; it was tedious work if they were to be accurate.

"Well, well; we can't spare the money sooner. This month there's the lottery, and next month the rent to pay. " Pelle could very well appreciate that, for Carlsen earned eight kroner a week and had nine children. But he felt that he could not well reduce the price. Truly, people weren't rolling in money here! And when for once he actually had a shilling in hand, then it was sure to take to its heels under his very nose, directly he began to rack his brains to decide how it could most usefully be applied: on one such occasion, for example, he had seen, in a huckster's window, a pipe in the form of a boot-leg, which was quite irresistible.

When the three girls called to him over the garden wall his childhood found companionship, and he forgot his cares and struggles. He was rather shy of anybody seeing him when he slipped across; he felt that his intercourse with the children was not to his credit; moreover, they were only "petticoats. " But he felt that he was lucky to be there, where there were curious things which were useful to play with—Chinese cups and saucers, and weapons from the South Sea Islands. Manna had a necklace of white teeth, sharp and irregular, strung together in a haphazard way, which she maintained were human teeth, and she had the courage to wear them round her bare neck. And the garden was full of wonderful plants; there were maize, and tobacco, and all sorts of other plants, which were said, in some parts of the world, to grow as thick as corn does at home.

They were finer of skin than other folk, and they were fragrant of the strange places of the world. And he played with them, and they regarded him with wonder and mended his clothes when he tore them; they made him the center of all their games—even when he was not present. There was a secret satisfaction in this—although he accepted it as a matter of course, it was a portion of all that fate and good fortune had reserved for him, a slight advance payment from the infinite fairy-tale of life. He longed to rule over them absolutely, and if they were obstinate he lectured them angrily, so that they suddenly gave in to him. He knew well enough that every proper man makes his wife behave submissively.

So passed the early summer; time was moving onward. The townsfolk had already, at Whitsuntide, provided themselves with what they needed for the summer, and out in the country people had other things to think about than trapesing into town with work for the artisans; the coming harvest occupied all their thoughts. Even in the poorest quarters, where no work was done for the peasants, one realized how utterly dependent the little town was upon the country. It was as though the town had in a moment forgotten its superiority; the manual workers no longer looked down on the peasants; they looked longingly toward the fields, spoke of the weather and the prospects of harvest, and had forgotten all their urban interests. If by exception a farmer's cart came through the streets, people ran to the window to look after it. And as the harvest stood almost at their doors, it seemed as though old memories were calling to them, and they raised their heads to listen; those who could gave up their town life and went into the country to help in the work of harvest. Both the journeyman and the two apprentices had left the workshop; Jens and Pelle could comfortably manage the work.

Pelle saw nothing of this stagnant mood; he was occupied on all sides in keeping a whole skin and getting the utmost out of life; there were thousands of impressions of good and evil which had to be assimilated, and which made a balanced whole—that remarkable thing, the town, of which Pelle never knew whether he felt inclined to bless it or curse it, —or it always held him in suspense.

And amidst all his activities, Lasse's face rose up before him and made him feel lonely in the midst of the bustle. Wherever could Father Lasse be? Would he ever hear of him again? Every day he had expected, in reliance on Karna's word, to see him blundering in at the door, and when anybody fumbled at the door-knocker he felt quite certain it was Lasse. It became a silent grief in the boy's mind, a note that sounded through all that he undertook.

V

One Sunday evening, as Pelle was running down East Street, a cart loaded with household goods came jolting in from the country. Pelle was in a great hurry, but was obliged to look at it. The driver sat in front, below the load, almost between the horses; he was tall and had ruddy cheeks, and was monstrously wrapped up, in spite of the heat. "Hallo! " Why, it was the worthy Due, Kalle's son-in-law; and above him, in the midst of all the lumber, sat Anna and the children, swaying to and fro with the motion of the cart. "Hullo! " Pelle waved his cap, and with one spring he had his foot on the shaft and was sitting next to Due, who was laughing all over his face at the encounter.

"Yes, we've had enough of the farming country, and now we've come to see if things aren't better here in town, " said Due, in his quiet manner. "And here you are, running about just like you did at home! " There was amazement in his voice.

Anna came crawling over the load, and smiled down upon him.

"Have you news of Father Lasse? " Pelle asked her. This was always his question when he met an acquaintance.

"Yes, that we have—he's just going to buy a farm up on the heath. Now, you devil, are you goin' to behave? " Anna crawled backward, and a child began to cry. Then she reappeared. "Yes, and we were to remember father to you, and mother, and all the rest. "

But Pelle had no thoughts to spare for Uncle Kalle.

"Is it up by Stone Farm? " he asked.

"No—farther to the east, by the Witch's Cell, " said Due. "It is a big piece of land, but it's not much more than stone. So long as he doesn't ruin himself over it—two have gone smash there before him. He's arranged it together with Karna. "

"Uncle Lasse will know what he's about, " said Anna. "Karna has found the money for it; she has something saved. "

Pelle couldn't sit still; his heart leaped in his body at this news. No more uncertainty—no more horrible possibilities: he had his father once more! And the dream of Lasse's life was about to be fulfilled: he could now put his feet under his own table. He had become a landowner into the bargain, if one didn't use the term too precisely; and Pelle himself—why, he was a landowner's son!

By nine o'clock in the evening he had finished everything, and was able to get off; his blood was pulsing with excitement.... Would there be horses? Why, of course; but would there be laborers, too? Had Father Lasse become one of those farmers who pay wages on a quarter-day, and come into town on a Sunday afternoon, their fur-lined collars up to their ears? Pelle could see the men quite plainly going up the stairs, one after another, taking off their wooden shoes and knocking on the door of the office—yes, they wanted to see about an advance on their wages. And Lasse scratched the back of his head, looked at them thoughtfully, and said: "Not on any account, you'd only waste it on drink. " But he gave it to them finally, for all that. "One is much too good-natured, " he said to Pelle....

For Pelle had bidden farewell to cobbling, and was living at home as a landowner's son. Really, Pelle managed the whole business—only it wouldn't do to say so. And at the Christmas feast he danced with the buxom farmer's daughters. There was whispering in the corners when Pelle made his appearance; but he went straight across the room and invited the Pastor's daughter to a dance, so that she lost her breath, and more besides, and begged him on the spot to marry her....

He hurried onward, still dreaming; longing drew him onward, and before he knew it he had travelled some miles along the high-road. The road he now turned into led him by pine woods and heath-covered hills; the houses he passed were poorer, and the distance from one to another was increasing.

Pelle took a turning a little farther on, which, to the best of his knowledge, led in the required direction, and hurried forward with awakened senses. The landscape was only half revealed by the summer night, but it was all as familiar as the mends in the back of Father Lasse's waistcoat, although he had never been here before. The poverty-stricken landscape spoke to him as with a mother's voice. Among these clay-daubed huts, the homes of poor cultivators who waged war upon the rocky ground surrounding their handful of soil, he felt safe as he had never felt before. All this had been his through many generations, down to the rags thrust into the broken window-panes and the lumber piled upon the thatch to secure it. Here was nothing for any one to rack his brains over, as elsewhere in the world; here a man could lie down at peace and rest. Yet it was not for him to till the ground and to dwell amid all these things. For he had outgrown them, as he had outgrown the shelter of his mother's skirts.

The lane gradually became a deep cart-track, which meandered between rocks and moorland. Pelle knew that he ought to keep to the east, but the track went now to the south, now to the north. He soon had enough of it, noted his direction exactly, and struck off obliquely. But it was difficult to make his way; the moonlight deceived his eyes so that he stumbled and sank into hollows, while the heather and the juniper reached as high as his waist, and hampered every movement. And then he turned obstinate, and would not turn back to the cart-track, but labored forward, so that he was soon steaming with heat; clambering over slanting ridges of rock, which were slippery with the dewfall on the moss, and letting himself tumble at hazard over the ledges. A little too late he felt a depth below him; it was as though a cold wave washed through his heart, and he clutched wildly at the air for some support. "Father Lasse! " he cried woefully; and at the same moment he was caught by brambles, and sank slowly down through their interwoven runners, which struck their myriad claws into him and reluctantly let him pass, until he was cautiously deposited, deep down among the sharp stones at the bottom of a ravine, shuddering and thanking his stars for all the thorns that had mercifully flayed his hide in order that he should not split his skull. Then he must needs grope forward, through the darkness and running water, until he found a tree and was able to climb to the surface.

Now he had lost his bearings, and when that became clear he lost his head as well. Nothing was left of the confident Pelle of a while ago; he ran blindly forward, in order to reach the summit of the hill. And as he was hastening upward, so that he might take note of the crags that lay about him, the ground rose and closed above him with a frightful clamor, and the air turned black and full of noises, and he could not see his hand before his eyes. It was like a stupendous explosion—as though released by his cheerful stamping over the rocks, the earth was hurled into the sky and dissolved in darkness, and the darkness itself cried aloud with terror and eddied round him. His heart pounded in his breast and robbed him of his last remnant of understanding; he jumped for sheer unbridled terror and bellowed like a maniac. The black mass drove over his head, so that he was forced to duck, and gleaming rifts showed and disappeared; and the darkness surged like the ocean and cried continually aloud with a hellish chaos of sounds. Then it suddenly swung to one side, drifted northward, and descended. And Pelle understood that he had stumbled upon a rookery.

He found himself behind a great rock. How he got there he did not know; but he knew that he was a terrible duffer. How easily he could have brought confusion on the fifty-odd crows by tossing a few stones into the air!

He went along the slope, very valiant in his resolve, but with shaking knees. In the far distance a fox sat upon a cliff and howled insanely at the moon, and far to the north and the south lay a transient glimmer of sea. Up here subterranean creatures had their home; when one trod upon the rock it sounded hollow.

In the southern opening the sea lay silver in the moonlight, but as Pelle looked again it disappeared, and the low-lying plain was drowned in white. In every direction the land was disappearing; Pelle watched in amazement while the sea slowly rose and filled every hollow. Then it closed above the lesser hills; one by one it swallowed them, and then it took the long ridge of hills to the east, until only the crests of the pine-trees lifted themselves above it; but Pelle did not as yet give himself up for lost; for behind all his anxiety lay a confused conception of Mount Ararat, which kept up his courage. But then it became so dreadfully cold that Pelle's breeches seemed to stick to his body. "That's the water, " he thought, and he looked round in alarm; the rock had become a little island, and he and it were floating on the ocean.

Pelle was a sturdy little realist, who had already had all manner of experiences. But now the fear had at last curdled his blood, and he accepted the supernatural without a protest. The world had evidently perished, and he himself was drifting—drifting out into space, and space was terribly cold. Father Lasse, and the workshop, Manna and the young master's shining eyes—here was an end of them all. He did not mourn them; he simply felt terribly lonely. What would be the end of it all—or was this perhaps death? Had he perhaps fallen dead a little while ago, when he tumbled over the precipice? And was he now voyaging toward the land of the blessed? Or was this the end of the world itself, of which he had heard such dreadful things said, as far back as he could remember? Perhaps he was adrift on the last scrap of earth, and was the only person still living? It did not in the least surprise Pelle that he should be left where everybody else had perished; in this moment of despair he found it quite natural.

He stood breathlessly silent and listened to the infinite; and he heard the cudgel-like blows of his pulses. Still he listened, and now he heard something more: far away in the night that surged against his ears he heard the suggestion of a sound, the vibrating note of some living creature. Infinitely remote and faint though it was, yet Pelle was so aware of it that it thrilled him all through. It was a cow feeding on the chain; he could follow the sound of her neck scrubbing up and down against the post.

He ran down over the craggy declivity, fell, and was again on his feet and running forward; the mist had swallowed him unawares. Then he was down on arable that had once been woodland; then he trod on something that felt familiar as it brushed against his feet—it was land that had once been ploughed but had now been recaptured by the heath. The sound grew louder, and changed to all those familiar sounds that one hears at night coming from an open cowshed; and now a decayed farmhouse showed through the mist. This could not of course be the farm Pelle was looking for—Father Lasse had a proper farmhouse with four wings! But he went forward.

Out in the country people do not lock everything up as carefully as they do in town; so Pelle could walk right in. Directly he opened the door of the sitting-room he was filled with an uplifting joy. The most comfortable odor he had ever known struck upon his senses —the foundation of everything fragrant—the scent of Father Lasse! It was dark in the room, and the light of the night without could not make its way through the low window. He heard the deep breathing of persons asleep, and knew that they had not awakened—the night was not nearly over yet. "Good-evening! " he said.

A hand began to grope for the matches.

"Is any one there? " said a drowsy woman's voice.

346

"Good-evening! " he cried again, and went forward into the room. "It's Pelle! " He brought out the name in a singsong voice.

"So it's you, boy! " Lasse's voice quavered, and the hands could not manage the matches; but Pelle stepped toward the voice and clasped his wrist. "And how did you find your way here in the wilderness— and at night, too? Yes, yes, I'll get up! " he continued, and he tried, with a groan, to sit up.

"No, you stop there and let me get up, " said Karna, who lay against the wall—she had kept silence while the men-folk were speaking. "He gets this lumbago, I can tell you! " she declared, jumping out of bed.

"Ay, I've been at it a bit too hard. Work comes easy when a man's his own master—it's difficult to leave off. But it'll be all right when once I've got things properly going. Work's a good embrocation for the lumbago. And how goes it with you then? I was near believing you must be dead! "

So Pelle had to sit on the edge of the bed and tell about everything in town—about the workshop, and the young master's lame leg, and everything. But he said nothing of the disagreeable things; it was not for men to dwell upon such things.

"Then you've been getting on well in foreign parts! " said Lasse, delighted. "And do they think well of you? "

"Yes! " This came a trifle slowly. In the first place, respect was just particularly what he had not won—but why trumpet forth his miseries? "The young master must like me—he often chats with me, even over the journeyman's head. "

"Now, think of that! I have often wondered, I can tell you, how you were getting on, and whether we shouldn't soon have good news of you. But everything takes time, that we know. And as you see, I'm in a very different position. "

"Yes, you've become a landowner! " said Pelle, smiling.

"The deuce, yes, so I am! " Lasse laughed, too, but then he groaned piteously with the pain in his back. "In the daytime, when I'm working hard, I get along well enough, but as soon as I lie down, then it comes on directly. And it's the devil of a pain—as though the wheels of a heavy loaded wagon were going to and fro across your back, whatever name you like to give it. Well, well! It's a fine thing, all the same, to be your own master! It's funny how it takes me—but dry bread tastes better to me at my own table than—yes, by God, I can tell you, it tastes better than cake at any other body's table! And then to be all alone on your own bit of land, and to be able to spit wherever you like to spit, without asking anybody's leave! And the soil isn't so bad; even if most of it has never been under cultivation, it has all been lying there storing up its power to produce since the beginning of the world. But about the people in the town—are they agreeable? "

Oh, Pelle had nothing to complain about. "But when were you married? " he asked suddenly.

"Well, you see, " and Lasse began to stumble over his own words, although he had been prepared for the boy to ask this very question; "in a way we aren't exactly married. That takes money, and the work here is getting forward.... But it's our intention, I needn't say, as soon as we have time and money. " It was honestly Lasse's opinion that one could just as well dispense with the ceremony; at least until children came, and demanded an honorable birth. But he could see that Pelle did not relish the idea; he was still the same pedantic little chap the moment a point of honor was in question. "As soon as we've got the harvest under shelter we'll invite people to a grand feast, " he said resolutely.

Pelle nodded eagerly. Now he was a landowner's son, and he could make the shabby-genteel boys of the town envious of him. But they mustn't be able to throw it in his face that his father was "living with a woman! "

Now Karna came in with some food. She looked at the boy with much affection. "Now, fall to, and don't despise our poor table, my son, " she said, and gave his arm a friendly pat. Pelle fell to with a good appetite. Lasse hung half out of the alcove, delighted.

"You haven't lost your appetite down there, " he said. "Do you get anything decent to eat? Karna thought the food wasn't any too good. "

"It's passable! " said Pelle obstinately. He repented of having betrayed himself to Karna that evening, when he was so depressed.

The desire to eat awoke in Lasse, so that little by little he crept out of the alcove. "You are sitting alone there, " he said, and sat down at the table in his nightcap and pants. He was wearing a knitted nightcap, one end of which fell loosely over his ear. He looked like a genuine old farmer, one that had money in his mattress. And Karna, who was moving to and fro while the menfolk ate, had a round, comfortable figure, and was carrying a big bread-knife in her hand. She inspired confidence, and she too looked a regular farmer's wife.

A place was found for Pelle on the bed. He extinguished the tallow dip before he undressed, and thrust his underclothing under the pillow.

He woke late; the sun had already left the eastern heavens. The most delicious smell of coffee filled the room. Pelle started up hastily, in order to dress himself before Karna could come in and espy his condition; he felt under the pillow—and his shirt was no longer there! And his stockings lay on a stool, and they had been darned!

"When Karna came in he lay motionless, in obstinate silence; he did not reply to her morning salutation, and kept his eyes turned toward the alcove. She ought not to have gone rummaging among his things!

"I've taken your shirt and washed it, " she said serenely, "but you can have it again this evening. After all, you can wear this until then. " She laid one of Lasse's shirts on the coverlet.

Pelle lay there for a time as though he had not heard Karna. Then he sat up, feeling very cross and got into the shirt. "No, stay there until you've drunk your coffee, " she said as he attempted to get up, and she placed a stool by him. And so Pelle had his coffee in bed, as he had dreamed it was to happen when Father Lasse remarried; and he could not go on feeling angry. But he was still burning with shame, and that made him taciturn.

During the morning Lasse and Pelle went out and inspected the property.

"It'll be best if we go round it first; then you will see plainly where the boundary lies, " said Lasse, who knew that the dimensions of the place would be a surprise to Pelle. They wandered through heather and brambles and thorns, striking across the moorland and skirting precipitous slopes. It was several hours before they had finished their round.

"It's an awfully large holding, " Pelle said again and again.

And Lasse answered proudly. "Yes, there's nearly seventy acres here—if only it were all tilled! "

It was virgin soil, but it was overrun with heather and juniper- scrub, through which brambles and honeysuckle twined their way. Halfway up a perpendicular wall of rock hung the ash and the wild cherry, gripping the bare cliff with roots that looked like crippled hands. Crab-apple trees, sloe-bushes and wild rose-briars made an impenetrable jungle, which already bore traces of Lasse's exertions. And in the midst of this luxuriant growth the rocky subsoil protruded its grim features, or came so near the surface that the sun had scorched the roots of the herbage.

"That's a proper little Paradise, " said Lasse; "you can scarcely set foot in it without treading on the berries. But it's got to be turned into arable if one is to live here.

"Isn't the soil rather middling? " said Pelle.

"Middling—when all that can grow and flourish there? " Lasse pointed to where birch and aspen stood waving their shining foliage to and fro in the breeze. "No, but it'll be a damned rough bit of work to get it ready for ploughing; I'm sorry now that you aren't at home. "

Lasse had several times made this allusion, but Pelle was deaf to it. All this was not what he had imagined; he felt no desire to play the landowner's son at home in the way Lasse had in mind.

"It'll be trouble enough here to manage about your daily bread, " he said, with remarkable precocity.

"Oh, it won't be so difficult to earn our daily bread, even if we can't hold a feast every day, " said Lasse, affronted. "And here at any rate a man can straighten his back without having a bailiff come yapping round him. Even if I were to work myself to death here, at least I've done with slavery. And you must not forget the pleasure of seeing the soil coming under one's hands, day after day, and yielding something instead of lying there useless. That is indeed the finest task a man can perform—to till the earth and make it fruitful—I can think of none better! But you—have you lost the farmer's instinct in town? "

Pelle did not reply. Although there might be something fine and splendid in working oneself to death over a bit of land, just so that something different might grow there, he himself was glad that he did not possess this farmer's instinct.

"My father, and his father, and all of our family I have ever known, we've all had something in us so that we've been driven to improve the soil, without thinking of our own comfort. But it certainly never entered the mind of one of us that we should ever hear it ill spoken of—and by one of our own people too! " Lasse spoke with his face turned away—as did the Almighty when He was wroth with His people; and Pelle felt as though he were a hateful renegade, as bad as bad could be. But nevertheless he would not give in.

"I should be no use at all here, " he said apologetically, gazing in the direction of the sea. "I don't believe in it. "

"No, you've cut yourself loose from it all, you have! " retorted Lasse bitterly. "But you'll repent it some day, in the long run. Life among the strangers there isn't all splendor and enjoyment. "

Pelle did not answer; he felt at that moment too much of a man to bandy words. He contained himself, and they went onward in silence.

"Well, of course, it isn't an estate, " said Lasse suddenly, in order to take the sting out of further criticism. Pelle was still silent.

Round the house the land was cultivated, and all round the cultivated land the luxuriant heather revealed disappearing traces of cultivation, and obliterated furrows.

"This was a cornfield once, " said Pelle.

"Well, to think of your seeing that right off! " exclaimed Lasse, half sarcastically, half in real admiration. "The deuce of an eye you've got, you truly have! I should certainly have noticed nothing particular about the heath—if I had not known. Yes, that has been under cultivation, but the heath has won it back again! That was under my predecessor, who took in more than he could work, so that it ruined him. But you can see now that something can be done with the land! " Lasse pointed to a patch of rye, and Pelle was obliged to recognize that it looked very well. But through the whole length of the field ran high ridges of broken stone, which told him what a terrible labor this soil demanded before it could be brought under cultivation. Beyond the rye lay newly-broken soil, which looked like a dammed-up ice-field; the plough had been driven through mere patches of soil. Pelle looked at it all, and it made him sad to think of his father.

Lasse himself was undismayed.

"As it is, it needs two to hold the plough. Karna is very strong, but even so it's as though one's arms would be torn from one's body every time the plough strikes. And most of it has to be broken up with pick and drill—and now and again it takes a bit of a sneeze. I use dynamite; it's more powerful than powder, and it bites down into the ground better, " he said proudly.

"How much is under cultivation here? " asked Pelle.

"With meadow and garden, almost fourteen acres; but it will be more before the year is out. "

"And two families have been ruined already by those fourteen acres, " said Karna, who had come out to call them in to dinner.

"Yes, yes; God be merciful to them—and now we get the fruit of their labors! The parish won't take the farm away again—not from us, " he said. Lasse spoke in a tone full of self-reliance. Pelle had never seen him stand so upright.

"I can never feel quite easy about it, " said Karna; "it's as though one were ploughing up churchyard soil. The first who was turned out by the parish hanged himself, so they say. "

"Yes, he had a hut on the heath there—where you see the elder-trees —but it's fallen to pieces since then. I'm so glad it didn't happen in the house. " Lasse shuddered uncomfortably. "People say he haunts the place when any misfortune is in store for those that come after him. "

"Then the house was built later? " asked Pelle, astonished, for it had such a tumble-down appearance.

"Yes, my predecessor built that. He got the land from the parish free for twenty years, provided he built a house and tilled a tonde of land a year. Those were not such bad conditions. Only he took in too much at a time; he was one of those people who rake away fiercely all the morning and have tired themselves out before midday. But he built the house well"—and Lasse kicked the thin mud-daubed wall—"and the timber-work is good. I think I shall break a lot of stone when the winter comes; the stone must be got out of the way, and it isn't so bad to earn a few hundred kroner. And in two or three years we will make the old house into a barn and build ourselves a new house—eh, Karna? With a cellar underneath and high steps outside, like they have at Stone Farm. It could be of unhewn granite, and I can manage the walls myself. "

Karna beamed with joy, but Pelle could not enter into their mood. He was disillusioned; the descent from his dream to this naked reality was too great. And a feeling rose within him of dull resentment against this endless labor, which, inexperienced though he was, was yet part of his very being by virtue of the lives of ten, nay, twenty generations. He himself had not waged the hard-fought war against the soil, but he had as a matter of course understood everything that had to do with tilling the soil ever since he could crawl, and his hands had an inborn aptitude for spade and rake and plough. But he had not inherited his father's joy in the soil; his thoughts had struck out in a new direction. Yet this endless bondage to the soil lay rooted in him, like a hatred, which gave him a survey unknown to his father. He was reasonable; he did not lose his head at the sight of seventy acres of land, but asked what they contained. He himself was not aware of it, but his whole being was quick with hostility toward the idea of spending one's strength in this useless labor; and his point of view was as experienced as though he had been Lasse's father.

"Wouldn't you have done better to buy a cottage-holding with twelve or fourteen acres of land, and that in a good state of cultivation? " he asked.

Lasse turned on him impatiently. "Yes, and then a man might stint and save all his life, and never get beyond cutting off his fly to mend his seat; he'd most likely spend twice what he made! What the deuce! I might as well have stayed where I was. Here, it's true, I do work harder and I have to use my brains more, but then there's a future before me. When I've once got the place under cultivation this will be a farm to hold its own with any of them! " Lasse gazed proudly over his holding; in his mind's eye it was waving with grain and full of prime cattle.

"It would carry six horses and a score or two of cows easily, " he said aloud. "That would bring in a nice income! What do you think, Karna? "

"I think the dinner will be cold, " said Karna, laughing. She was perfectly happy.

At dinner Lasse proposed that Pelle should send his clothes to be washed and mended at home. "You've certainly got enough to do without that, " he said indulgently. "Butcher Jensen goes to market every Saturday; he'd take it for you and put it down by the church, and it would be odd if on a Sunday no one from the heath went to church, who could bring the bundle back to us. "

But Pelle suddenly turned stubborn and made no reply.

"I just thought it would be too much for you to wash and mend for yourself, " said Lasse patiently. "In town one must have other things to think about, and then it isn't really proper work for a man! "

"I'll do it myself all right, " murmured Pelle ungraciously.

Now he would show them that he could keep himself decent. It was partly in order to revenge himself for his own neglect that he refused the offer.

"Yes, yes, " said Lasse meekly; "I just asked you. I hope you won't take it amiss. "

However strong Karna might be, and however willing to help in everything, Lasse did greatly feel the need of a man to work with him. Work of a kind that needed two had accumulated, and Pelle did not spare himself. The greater part of the day was spent in heaving great stones out of the soil and dragging them away; Lasse had knocked a sledge together, and the two moorland horses were harnessed up to it.

"Yes, you mustn't look at them too closely, " said Lasse, as he stroked the two scarecrows caressingly. "Just wait until a few months have gone by, and then you'll see! But they've plenty of spirit now. "

There was much to be done, and the sweat was soon pouring down their faces; but they were both in good spirits. Lasse was surprised at the boy's strength—with two or three such lads he could turn the whole wilderness over. Once again he sighed that Pelle was not living at home; but to this Pelle still turned a deaf ear. And before they were aware of it Karna had come out again and was calling them to supper.

"I think we'll harness the horses and drive Pelle halfway to town— as a reward for the work he's done, " said Lasse gaily. "And we've both earned a drive. " So the two screws were put into the cart.

It was amusing to watch Lasse; he was a notable driver, and one could not but be almost persuaded that he had a pair of blood horses in front of him. When they met any one he would cautiously gather up the reins in order to be prepared lest the horses should shy— "they might so easily bolt, " he said solemnly. And when he succeeded in inducing them to trot he was delighted. "They take some holding, " he would say, and to look at him you would have thought they called for a strong pair of wrists. "Damn it all, I believe I shall have to put the curb on them! " And he set both his feet against the dashboard, and sawed the reins to and fro.

When half the distance was covered Father Lasse wanted to drive just a little further, and again a little further still—oh, well, then, they might as well drive right up to the house! He had quite forgotten that the following day would be a day of hard labor both for himself and for the horses. But at last Pelle jumped out.

"Shan't we arrange that about your washing? " asked Lasse.

"No! " Pelle turned his face away—surely they might stop asking him that!

"Well, well, take care of yourself, and thanks for your help. You'll come again as soon as you can? "

Pelle smiled at them, but said nothing; he dared not open his mouth, for fear of the unmanly lump that had risen in his throat. Silently he held out his hand and ran toward the town.

VI

The other apprentices were able to provide themselves with clothes, as they worked on their own account in their own time; they got work from their friends, and at times they pirated the master's customers, by underbidding him in secret. They kept their own work under the bench; when the master was not at home they got it out and proceeded with it. "To-night I shall go out and meet my girl, " they would say, laughing. Little Nikas said nothing at all.

Pelle had no friends to give him work, and he could not have done much. If the others had much to do after work-hours or on Sundays he had to help them; but he gained nothing by so doing. And he also had Nilen's shoes to keep mended, for old acquaintances' sake.

Jeppe lectured them at great length on the subject of tips, as he had promised; for the townsfolk had been complaining of this burdensome addition to their expenditure, and in no measured terms had sworn either to abate or abolish this tax on all retail transactions. But it was only because they had read of the matter in the newspapers, and didn't want to be behind the capital! They always referred to the subject when Pelle went round with his shoes, and felt in their purses; if there was a shilling there they would hide it between their fingers, and say that he should have something next time for certain—he must remind them of it another time! At first he did remind them—they had told him to do so—but then Jeppe received a hint that his youngest apprentice must stop his attempts at swindling. Pelle could not understand it, but he conceived an increasing dislike of these people, who could resort to such a shameless trick in order to save a penny piece, which they would never have missed.

Pelle, who had been thinking that he had had enough of the world of poor folk, and must somehow contrive to get into another class, learned once again to rely on the poor, and rejoiced over every pair of poor folk's shoes which the master anathematized because they were so worn out. The poor were not afraid to pay a shilling if they had one; it made him feel really sad to see how they would search in every corner to get a few pence together, and empty their children's money-boxes, while the little ones stood by in silence, looking on with mournful eyes. And if he did not wish to accept their money they were offended. The little that he did receive he owed to people who were as poor as himself.

Money, to these folk, no longer consisted of those round, indifferent objects which people in the upper strata of human society piled up in whole heaps. Here every shilling meant so much suffering or happiness, and a grimy little copper would still the man's angry clamor and the child's despairing cry for food. Widow Hoest gave him a ten-ore piece, and he could not help reflecting that she had given him her mid-day meal for two days to come!

One day, as he was passing the miserable hovels which lay out by the northern dunes, a poor young woman came to her door and called to him; she held the remains of a pair of elastic-sided boots in her hand. "Oh, shoemaker's boy, do be so kind as to mend these a bit for me! " she pleaded. "Just sew them up anyhow, so that they'll stick on my feet for half the evening. The stone-masons are giving their feast, and I do so want to go to it! " Pelle examined the boots; there was not much to be done for them, nevertheless he took them, and mended them in his own time. He learned from Jens that the woman was the widow of a stone-cutter, who was killed by an explosion shortly after their marriage. The boots looked quite decent when he returned them.

"Well, I've no money, but I do offer you many, many thanks! " she said, looking delightedly at the boots; "and how nice you've made them look! God bless you for it. "

"Thanks killed the blacksmith's cat, " said Pelle smiling. Her pleasure was contagious.

"Yes, and God's blessing falls where two poor people share their bed, " the young woman rejoined jestingly. "Still, I wish you everything good as payment—now I can dance after all! "

Pelle was quite pleased with himself as he made off. But few doors farther on another poor woman accosted him; she had evidently heard of the success of the first, and there she stood holding a dirty pair of children's boots, which she earnestly begged him to mend. He took the boots and repaired them although it left him still poorer; he knew too well what need was to refuse. This was the first time that any one in the town had regarded him as an equal, and recognized him at the first glance as a fellow-creature. Pelle pondered over this; he did not know that poverty is cosmopolitan.

When he went out after the day's work he took a back seat; he went about with the poorest boys and behaved as unobtrusively as possible. But sometimes a desperate mood came over him, and at times he would make himself conspicuous by behavior that would have made old Lasse weep; as, for example, when he defiantly sat upon a freshly-tarred bollard. He became thereby the hero of the evening; but as soon as he was alone he went behind a fence and let down his breeches in order to ascertain the extent of the damage. He had been running his errands that day in the best clothes he possessed. This was no joke. Lasse had deeply imbued him with his own moderation, and had taught him to treat his things carefully, so that it seemed to Pelle almost a pious duty. But Pelle felt himself forsaken by all the gods, and now he defied them.

The poor women in the streets were the only people who had eyes for him. "Now look at the booby, wearing his confirmation jacket on a weekday! " they would say, and call him over in order to give him a lecture, which as a rule ended in an offer to repair the damage. But it was all one to Pelle; if he ran about out-of-doors in his best clothes he was only doing as the town did. At all events he had a shirt on, even if it was rather big! And the barber's assistant himself, who looked most important in tail-coat and top-hat, and was the ideal of every apprentice, did not always wear a shirt; Pelle had once noticed that fact as the youth was swinging some ladies. Up in the country, where a man was appraised according to the number of his shirts, such a thing would have been impossible. But here in town people did not regard such matters so strictly.

He was no longer beside himself with astonishment at the number of people—respectable folk for the most part—who had no abiding place anywhere, but all through the year drifted in the most casual manner from one spot to another. Yet the men looked contented, had wives and children, went out on Sundays, and amused themselves; and after all why should one behave as if the world was coming to an end because one hadn't a barrel of salt pork or a clamp of potatoes to see one through the winter? Recklessness was finally Pelle's refuge too; when all the lights seemed to have gone out of the future it helped him to take up the fairy-tale of life anew, and lent a glamor to naked poverty. Imagination entered even into starvation: are you or are you not going to die of it?

Pelle was poor enough for everything to be still before him, and he possessed the poor man's alert imagination; the great world and the romance of life were the motives that drew him through the void, that peculiar music of life which is never silent, but murmurs to the reckless and the careful alike. Of the world he knew well enough that it was something incomprehensibly vast—something that was always receding; yet in eighty days one could travel right round it, to the place where men walk about with their heads downward, and back again, and experience all its wonders. He himself had set out into this incomprehensible world, and here he was, stranded in this little town, where there was never a crumb to feed a hungry imagination; nothing but a teeming confusion of petty cares. One felt the cold breath of the outer winds, and the dizziness of great spaces; when the little newspaper came the small tradesmen and employers would run eagerly across the street, their spectacles on their noses, and would speak, with gestures of amazement, of the things that happened outside. "China, " they would say; "America! " and fancy that they themselves made part of the bustling world. But Pelle used to wish most ardently that something great and wonderful might wander thither and settle down among them just for once! He would have been quite contented with a little volcano underfoot, so that the houses would begin to sway and bob to one another; or a trifling inundation, so that ships would ride over the town, and have to moor themselves to the weather-cock on the church steeple. He had an irrational longing that something of this kind should happen, something to drive the blood from his heart and make his hair stand on end. But now he had enough to contend against apart from matters of this sort; the world must look after itself until times were better.

It was more difficult to renounce the old fairy-tales, for poverty itself had sung them into his heart, and they spoke to him with Father Lasse's quivering voice. "A rich child often lies in a poor mother's lap, " his father used to say, when he prophesied concerning his son's future, and the saying sank deep into the boy's mind, like the refrain of a song. But he had learned this much, that there were no elephants here, on whose necks a plucky youngster could ride astraddle, in order to ride down the tiger which was on the point of tearing the King of the Himalayas to pieces so that he would of course receive the king's daughter and half his kingdom as a reward for his heroic deed. Pelle often loitered about the harbor, but no beautifully dressed little girl ever fell into the water, so that he might rescue her, and then, when he was grown up, make her his wife.

And if such a thing did really happen he knew now that his elders would cheat him out of any tip he might receive. And he had quite given up looking for the golden coach which was to run over him, so that the two terrified ladies, who would be dressed in mourning, would take him into their carriage and carry him off to their six-storied castle! Of course, they would adopt him permanently in place of the son which they had just lost, and who, curiously enough, was exactly the same age as himself. No, there were no golden coaches here!

Out in the great world the poorest boy had the most wonderful prospects; all the great men the books had ever heard of had been poor lads like himself, who had reached their high estate through good fortune and their own valor. But all the men in town who possessed anything had attained their wealth by wearily plodding forward and sucking the blood of the poor. They were always sitting and brooding over their money, and they threw nothing away for a lucky fellow to pick up; and they left nothing lying about, lest some poor lad should come and take it. Not one of them considered it beneath him to pick up an old trouser-button off the pavement, and carry it home.

One evening Pelle was running out to fetch half a pound of canister tobacco for Jeppe. In front of the coal-merchant's house the big dog, as always, made for his legs, and he lost the twenty-five-ore piece. While he was looking for it, an elderly man came up to him. Pelle knew him very well; he was Monsen the shipowner, the richest man in the town.

"Have you lost something, my lad? " he asked, and began to assist in the search.

"Now he will question me, " thought Pelle. "And then I shall answer him boldly, and then he will look at me attentively and say—"

Pelle was always hoping for some mysterious adventure, such as happens to an able lad and raises him to fortune.

But the shipowner did nothing he was expected to do. He merely searched eagerly, and inquired: "Where were you walking? Here, weren't you? Are you quite certain of that? "

"In any case he'll give me another twenty-five ore, " thought Pelle. "Extraordinary—how eager he is! " Pelle did not really want to go on searching, but he could not very well leave off before the other.

"Well, well! " said the shipowner at last, "you may as well whistle for those twenty-five ore. But what a booby you are! " And he moved on, and Pelle looked after him for a long while before putting his hand into his own pocket.

Later, as he was returning that way, he saw a man bowed over the flagstones, striking matches as he searched. It was Monsen. The sight tickled Pelle tremendously. "Have you lost anything? " he asked mischievously, standing on the alert, lest he should get a box on the ear. "Yes, yes; twenty-five ore; " groaned the shipowner. "Can't you help me to find it, my boy? "

Well, he had long understood that Monsen was the richest man in the town, and that he had become so by provisioning ships with spoiled foodstuffs, and refitting old crank vessels, which he heavily insured. And he knew who was a thief and who a bankrupt speculator, and that Merchant Lau only did business with the little shopkeepers, because his daughter had gone to the bad. Pelle knew the secret pride of the town, the "Top-galeass, " as she was called, who in her sole self represented the allurements of the capital, and he knew the two sharpers, and the consul with the disease which was eating him up. All this was very gratifying knowledge for one of the rejected.

He had no intention of letting the town retain any trace of those splendors with which he had once endowed it. In his constant ramblings he stripped it to the buff. For instance, there stood the houses of the town, some retiring, some standing well forward, but all so neat on the side that faced the street, with their wonderful old doorways and flowers in every window. Their neatly tarred framework glistened, and they were always newly lime-washed, ochrous yellow or dazzling white, sea-green, or blue as the sky. And on Sundays there was quite a festive display of flags. But Pelle had explored the back quarters of every house; and there were sinks and traps there, with dense slimy growths, and stinking refuse-barrels, and one great dustbin with a drooping elder-tree over it. And the spaces between the cobble-stones were foul with the scales of herrings and the guts of codfish, and the lower portions of the walls were covered with patches of green moss.

The bookbinder and his wife went about hand in hand when they set out for the meeting of some religious society. But at home they fought, and in chapel, as they sat together and sang out of the same hymn-book, they would secretly pinch one another's legs. "Yes, " people used to say, "such a nice couple! " But the town couldn't throw dust in Pelle's eyes; he knew a thing or two. If only he had known just how to get himself a new blouse!

Some people didn't go without clothes so readily; they were forever making use of that fabulous thing—credit! At first it took his breath away to discover that the people here in the town got everything they wanted without paying money for it. "Will you please put it down? " they would say, when they came for their boots; and "it's to be entered, " he himself would say, when he made a purchase for his employers. All spoke the same magical formula, and Pelle was reminded of Father Lasse, who had counted his shillings over a score of times before he ventured to buy anything. He anticipated much from this discovery, and it was his intention to make good use of the magic words when his own means became exhausted.

Now, naturally, he was wiser. He had discovered that the very poor must always go marketing with their money in their hands, and even for the others there came a day of reckoning. The master already spoke with horror of the New Year; and it was very unfortunate for his business that the leather-sellers had got him in their pocket, so that he could not buy his material where it was cheapest. All the small employers made the same complaint.

But the fairy-tale of credit was not yet exhausted—there was still a manner of drawing a draft upon fortune, which could be kept waiting, and on the future, which redeems all drafts. Credit was a spark of poetry in the scramble of life; there were people going about who were poor as church mice, yet they played the lord. Alfred was such a lucky fellow; he earned not a red cent, but was always dressed like a counter-jumper, and let himself want for nothing. If he took a fancy to anything he simply went in and got it on "tick"; and he was never refused. His comrades envied him and regarded him as a child of fortune.

Pelle himself had a little flirtation with fortune. One day he went gaily into a shop, in order to procure himself some underclothing. When he asked for credit they looked at him as though he could not be quite sane, and he had to go away without effecting his object.

363

"There must be some secret about it that I don't know, " he thought; and he dimly remembered another boy, who couldn't stir the pot to cook his porridge or lay the table for himself, because he didn't know the necessary word. He sought Alfred forthwith in order to receive enlightenment.

Alfred was wearing new patent braces, and was putting on his collar. On his feet were slippers with fur edging, which looked like feeding pigeons. "I got them from a shopkeeper's daughter, " he said; and he coquetted with his legs; "she's quite gone on me. A nice girl too— only there's no money. "

Pelle explained his requirements.

"Shirts! shirts! " Alfred chortled with delight, and clapped his hands before his face. "Good Lord, he wants to gets shirts on tick! If only they had been linen shirts! " He was near bursting with laughter.

Pelle tried again. As a peasant—for he was still that—he had thought of shirts first of all; but now he wanted a summer overcoat and rubber cuffs. "Why do you want credit? " asked the shopkeeper, hesitating. "Are you expecting any money? Or is there any one who will give you a reference? "

No, Pelle didn't want to bring any one else into it; it was simply that he had no money.

"Then wait until you have, " said the shopkeeper surlily. "We don't clothe paupers! " Pelle slunk away abashed.

"You're a fool! " said Alfred shortly. "You are just like Albinus—he can never learn how to do it! "

"How do you do it then? " asked Pelle meekly.

"How do I do it—how do I do it? " Alfred could give no explanation; "it just came of itself. But naturally I don't tell them that I'm poor! No, you'd better leave it alone—it'll never succeed with you! "

"Why do you sit there and pinch your upper lip? " asked Pelle discontentedly.

"Pinch? You goat, I'm stroking my moustache! "

VII

On Saturday afternoon Pelle was busily sweeping the street. It was getting on for evening; in the little houses there was already a fire in the grate; one could hear it crackling at Builder Rasmussen's and Swedish Anders', and the smell of broiled herrings filled the street. The women were preparing something extra good in order to wheedle their husbands when they came home with the week's wages. Then they ran across to the huckster's for schnaps and beer, leaving the door wide open behind them; there was just half a minute to spare while the herring was getting cooked on the one side! And now Pelle sniffed it afar off—Madame Rasmussen was tattling away to the huckster, and a voice screeched after her: "Madame Rasmussen! Your herring is burning! " Now she came rushing back, turning her head confusedly from house to house as she scampered across the street and into her house. The blue smoke drifted down among the houses; the sun fell lower and filled the street with gold-dust.

There were people sweeping all along the street; Baker Jorgen, the washerwoman, and the Comptroller's maid-servant. The heavy boughs of the mulberry-tree across the road drooped over the wall and offered their last ripe fruits to whomsoever would pick them. On the other side of the wall the rich merchant Hans—he who married the nurse-maid—was pottering about his garden. He never came out, and the rumor ran that he was held a prisoner by his wife and her kin. But Pelle had leaned his ear against the wall, and had heard a stammering old voice repeating the same pet names, so that it sounded like one of those love-songs that never come to an end; and when in the twilight he slipped out of his attic window and climbed on to the ridge of the roof, in order to take a look at the world, he had seen a tiny little white-haired man walking down there in the garden, with his arm round the waist of a woman younger than himself. They were like a couple of young lovers, and they had to stop every other moment in order to caress one another. The most monstrous things were said of him and his money; of his fortune, that once upon a time was founded on a paper of pins, and was now so great that some curse must rest upon it.

From the baker's house the baker's son came slinking hymn-book in hand. He fled across to the shelter of the wall, and hurried off; old

Jorgen stood there gobbling with laughter as he watched him, his hands folded over his broomstick.

"O Lord, is that a man? " he cried to Jeppe, who sat at his window, shaving himself before the milk-can. "Just look how he puffs! Now he'll go in and beg God to forgive him for going courting! "

Jeppe came to the window to see and to silence him; one could hear Brother Jorgen's falsetto voice right down the street. "Has he been courting? However did you get him to venture such a leap? " he asked eagerly.

"Oh, it was while we were sitting at table. I had a tussle with my melancholy madman—because I couldn't help thinking of the little Jorgen. God knows, I told myself, no little Jorgen has come to carry on your name, and the boy's a weakling, and you've no one else to build on! It's all very well going about with your nose in the air all the days God gives you—everything will be swept away and be to no purpose. And everything of that sort—you know how I get thinking when ideas like that get the upper hand with me. I sat there and looked at the boy, and angry I felt with him, that I did; and right opposite him there was sitting a fine bit of womanhood, and he not looking at her. And with that I struck my hand on the table, and I says, 'Now, boy, just you take Marie by the hand and ask her whether she'll be your wife—I want to make an end of the matter now and see what you're good for! ' The boy all shrivels up and holds out his hand, and Marie, it don't come amiss to her. 'Yes, that I will! ' she says, and grips hold of him before he has time to think what he's doing. And we shall be having the marriage soon. "

"If you can make a boot out of that leather! " said Jeppe.

"Oh, she's a warm piece—look at the way she's built. She's thawing him already. Women, they know the way—he won't freeze in bed. "

Old Jorgen laughed contentedly, and went off to his work. "Yes, why, she'd breathe life into the dead, " he announced to the street at large.

The others went out in their finest clothes, but Pelle did not care to go. He had not been able to accomplish his constant resolution to keep himself neat and clean, and this failure weighed upon him and abashed him. And the holes in his stockings, which were now so big

366

that they could no longer be darned, were disgustingly apparent, with his skin showing through them, so that he had a loathing for himself.

Now all the young people were going out. He could see the sea in the opening at the end of the street; it was perfectly calm, and had borrowed the colors of the sunset. They would be going to the harbor or the dunes by the sea; there would be dancing on the grass, and perhaps some would get to fighting about a girl. But he wasn't going to be driven out of the pack like a mangy dog; he didn't care a hang for the whole lot of them!

He threw off his apron and established himself on a beer-barrel which stood outside before the gate. On the bench opposite sat the older inhabitants of the street, puffing at their pipes and gossiping about everything under the sun. Now the bells sounded the hour for leaving off work. Madame Rasmussen was beating her child and reviling it in time with her blows. Then suddenly all was silent; only the crying of the child continued, like a feeble evening hymn. Old Jeppe was talking about Malaga—"when I ran ashore at Malaga! "— but Baker Jorgen was still lamenting his want of an heir, and sighing: "Yes, yes; if only one could see into the future! " Then he suddenly began to talk about the Mormons. "It might really be great fun to see, some time, what they have to offer you, " he said.

"I thought you'd been a Mormon a long time, Uncle Jorgen, " said Master Andres. The old man laughed.

"Well, well; one tries all sorts of things in one's time, " he said, and looked out at the sky.

Up the street stood the watchmaker, on his stone steps, his face turned up to the zenith, while he shouted his senseless warnings: "The new time! I ask you about the new time, O God the Father! " he repeated.

Two weary stevedores were going homeward. "He'll drive all poverty out of the world and give us all a new life—that's the form his madness takes, " said one of them, with a dreary laugh.

"Then he's got the millennium on the brain? " said the other.

"No, he's just snarling at the world, " said old Jorgen, behind them. "We shall certainly get a change in the weather. "

"Things are bad with him just now, poor fellow, " said Bjerregrav, shuddering. "It was about this time of the year that he lost his wits. "

An inner voice admonished Pelle: "Don't sit there with your hands in your lap, but go in and look after your clothes! " But he could not bring himself to do so—the difficulties had become too insurmountable. On the following day Manna and the others called him, but he could not spring over the wall to join them; they had begun to turn up their noses at him and regard him critically. He did not very well understand it, but he had become an outcast, a creature who no longer cared about washing himself properly. But what was the use? He could not go on contending against the invincible! No one had warned him in time, and now the town had captured him, and he had given up everything else. He must shuffle through life as best he could.

No one had a thought for him! When washing was being done for his employers it never occurred to Madam to wash anything of his, and he was not the boy to come forward of himself. The washerwoman was more considerate; when she could she would smuggle in some of Pelle's dirty linen, although it meant more work for her. But she was poor herself; as for the rest, they only wanted to make use of him. There was no one in town who cared sufficiently for his welfare to take the trouble even to open his mouth to tell him the truth. This was a thought that made him feel quite weak about the knees, although he was fifteen years old and had courage to tackle a mad bull. More than anything else it was his loneliness that weakened his powers of resistance. He was helpless alone among all these people, a child, who had to look after himself as best he could, and be prepared for attacks from every quarter.

He sat there, making no effort to dispel the misery that had come over him, and was working its will with him, while with half an ear he listened to the life around him. But suddenly he felt something in his waistcoat pocket—money! He felt immensely relieved at once, but he did not hurry; he slipped behind the gate and counted it. One and a half kroner. He was on the point of regarding it as a gift from on high, as something which the Almighty had in His great goodness placed there, but then it occurred to him that this was his master's money. It had been given him the day before for repairs to a pair of ladies' shoes, and he had forgotten to pay it in, while the master, strangely enough, had quite forgotten to ask for it.

Pelle stood with bent back by the well outside, scrubbing himself over a bucket until his blood tingled. Then he put on his best clothes, drew his shoes on to his naked feet, to avoid the painful feeling of the ragged stockings, and buttoned his rubber collar—for the last time innocent of any tie—to his shirt. Shortly afterward he was standing outside a shop-window, contemplating some large neckties, which had just been put upon the market, and could be worn with any one of four faces outward; they filled the whole of the waistcoat, so that one did not see the shirt. Now he would be disdained no longer! For a moment he ran to and fro and breathed the air; then he got upon the scent, and ran at a breathless gallop toward the sea-dunes, where the young folk of the town played late into the summer night that lay over the wan sea.

Of course, it was only a loan. Pelle had to sole a pair of shoes for a baker's apprentice who worked with Nilen; as soon as they were finished he would repay the money. He could put the money under the cutting-out board in his master's room; the master would find it there, would gaze at it with a droll expression, and say: "What the devil is this? " And then he would knock on the wall, and would treat Pelle to a long rigmarole about his magical gifts—and then he would ask him to run out and fetch a half-bottle of port.

He did not receive the money for soling the shoes; half the sum he had to pay out for leather, and the rest was a long time coming, for the baker's apprentice was a needy wretch. But he did not doubt his own integrity; the master might be as sure of his money as if it had been in the bank. Yet now and again he forgot to give up petty sums —if some necessity or other was pressing him unexpectedly. They were, of course, all loans—until the golden time came. And that was never far away.

One day he returned home as the young master was standing at the door, staring at the driving clouds overhead. He gave Pelle's shoulder a familiar squeeze. "How was it they didn't pay you for the shoes at the Chamberlain's yesterday? "

Pelle went crimson and his hand went to his waistcoat pocket. "I forgot it, " he said in a low voice.

"Now, now! " The master shook him good-naturedly. "It's not that I mistrust you. But just to be methodical! "

Pelle's heart pounded wildly in his body; he had just decided to use the money to buy a pair of stockings, the very next time he went out —and then what would have happened? And the master's belief in him! And all at once his offence showed itself to him in all its shameful treachery; he felt as if he was on the point of being sick, so disturbed was he. Until this moment he had preserved through everything the feeling of his own worth, and now it was destroyed; there could not be any one wickeder than he in all the world. In future no one could trust him any more, and he could no longer look people straight in the face; unless he went to the master at once and cast himself and his shame unconditionally on his mercy. There was no other salvation, that he knew.

But he was not certain that the master would conceive the matter in its finer aspect, or that everything would turn out for the best; he had given up believing in fairy-tales. Then he would simply be turned away, or perhaps be sent to the courthouse, and it would be all up with him.

Pelle resolved to keep it to himself; and for many days he went about suffering from a sense of his own wickedness. But then necessity gripped him by the throat and brushed all else aside; and in order to procure himself the most necessary things he was forced to resort to the dangerous expedient of stating; when the master gave him money to buy anything, that it was to be put down. And then one day it was all up with him. The others were ready to pull down the house about his ears; they threw his things out of the garret and called him a filthy, beast. Pelle wept; he was quite convinced that not he was the guilty person, but Peter, who was always keeping company with the nastiest women, but he could get no hearing. He hurried away, with the resolves that he would never come back.

On the dunes he was captured by Emil and Peter, who had been sent out after him by old Jeppe. He did not want to go back with them, but they threw him down and dragged him back, one taking his head and one his legs. People came to the door and laughed and asked questions, and the other two gave their explanation of the matter, which was a terrible disgrace for Pelle.

And then he fell ill. He lay under the tiled roof raving with fever; they had thrown his bed into the loft. "What, isn't he up yet? " said Jeppe, astounded, when he came in to the workshop. "No? Well, he'll soon get up when he gets hungry. " It was no joke to take a sick apprentice his meals in bed. But Pelle did not come down.

Once the young master threw all considerations overboard and took some food up to him. "You're making yourself ridiculous, " sneered Jeppe; "you'll never be able to manage people like that! " And Madam scolded. But Master Andres whistled until he was out of hearing.

Poor Pelle lay there, in delirium; his little head was full of fancies, more than it would hold. But now the reaction set in, and he lay there stuffing himself with all that was brought him.

The young master sat upstairs a great deal and received enlightenment on many points. It was not his nature to do anything energetically, but he arranged that Pelle's washing should be done in the house, and he took care that Lasse should be sent for.

VIII

Jeppe was related to about half the island, but he was not greatly interested in disentangling his relationship. He could easily go right back to the founder of the family, and trace the generations through two centuries, and follow the several branches of the family from country to town and over the sea and back again, and show that Andres and the judge must be cousins twice removed. But if any insignificant person asked him: "How was it, then—weren't my father and you first cousins? " he would answer brusquely, "Maybe, but the soup grows too thin after a time. This relationship! "

"Then you and I, good Lord! are second cousins, and you are related to the judge as well, " Master Andres would say. He did not grudge people any pleasure they could derive from the facts of relationship. Poor people regarded him gratefully—they said he had kind eyes; it was a shame that he should not be allowed to live.

Jeppe was the oldest employer in the town, and among the shoemakers his workshop was the biggest. He was able, too, or rather he had been, and he still possessed the manual skill peculiar to the old days. When it came to a ticklish job he would willingly show them how to get on with it, or plan some contrivance to assist them. Elastic-sided boots and lace-up boots had superseded the old footwear, but honest skill still meant an honest reputation. And if some old fellow wanted a pair of Wellingtons or Bluchers of leather waterproofed with grease, instead of by some new-fangled devilry, he must needs go to Jeppe—no one else could shape an instep as he could. And when it came to handling the heavy dressed leathers for sea-boots there was no one like Jeppe. He was obstinate, and rigidly opposed to everything new, where everybody else was led away by novelty. In this he was peculiarly the representative of the old days, and people respected him as such.

The apprentices alone did not respect him. They did everything they could to vex him and to retaliate on him for being such a severe task-master. They all laid themselves out to mystify him, speaking of the most matter-of-fact things in dark and covert hints, in order to make old Jeppe suspicious, and if he spied upon them and caught them at something which proved to be nothing at all they had a great day of it.

"What does this mean? Where are you going without permission? " asked Jeppe, if one of them got up to go into the court; he was always forgetting that times had altered. They did not answer, and then he would fly into a passion. "I'll have you show me respect! " he would cry, stamping on the floor until the dust eddied round him. Master Andres would slowly raise his head. "What's the matter with you this time, father? " he would ask wearily. Then Jeppe would break out into fulminations against the new times.

If Master Andres and the journeyman were not present, the apprentices amused themselves by making the old man lose his temper; and this was not difficult, as he saw hostility in everything. Then he would snatch up a knee-strap and begin to rain blows upon the sinner. At the same time he would make the most extraordinary grimaces and give vent to a singular gurgling sound. "There, take that, although it grieves me to use harsh measures! " he would mew. "And that, too—and that! You've got to go through with it, if you want to enter the craft! " Then he would give the lad something that faintly resembled a kick, and would stand there struggling for breath. "You're a troublesome youngster—you'll allow that? " "Yes, my mother used to break a broomstick over my head every other day! " replied Peter, the rogue, snorting. "There, you see you are! But it may all turn out for the best even now. The foundation's not so bad! " Jeppe doddered to and fro, his hands behind his back. The rest of the day he was inclined to solemnity, and did his best to obliterate all remembrance of the punishment. "It was only for your own good! " he would say, in a propitiatory tone.

Jeppe was first cousin to the crazy Anker, but he preferred not to lay claim to the fact; the man could not help being mad, but he made his living, disgracefully enough, by selling sand in the streets—a specialist in his way. Day by day one saw Anker's long, thin figure in the streets, with a sackful of sand slung over his sloping shoulders; he wore a suit of blue twill and white woollen stockings, and his face was death-like. He was quite fleshless. "That comes of all his digging, " people said. "Look at his assistant! "

He never appeared in the workshop with his sack of sand; he was afraid of Jeppe, who was now the oldest member of the family. Elsewhere he went in and out everywhere with his clattering wooden shoes; and people bought of him, as they must have sand for their floors, and his was as good as any other. He needed next to nothing for his livelihood; people maintained that he never ate anything, but lived on his own vitals. With the money he received he bought materials for the "New Time, " and what was left he threw away, in his more exalted moments, from the top of his high stairs. The street-urchins always came running up when the word went round that the madness about the "new time" was attacking him.

He and Bjerregrav had been friends as boys. Formerly they had been inseparable, and neither of them was willing to do his duty and marry, although each was in a position to keep a wife and children. At an age when others were thinking about how to find favor with the womenfolk, these two were running about with their heads full of rubbish which enraged people. At that time a dangerous revolutionist was living with Bjerregrav's brother; he had spent many years on Christianso, but then the Government had sent him to spend the rest of his term of captivity on Bornholm. Dampe was his name; Jeppe had known him when an apprentice in Copenhagen; and his ambition was to overthrow God and king. This ambition of his did not profit him greatly; he was cast down like a second Lucifer, and only kept his head on his shoulders by virtue of an act of mercy. The two young people regarded him as then justification, and he turned their heads with his venomous talk, so that they began to ponder over things which common folk do better to leave alone. Bjerregrav came through this phase with a whole skin, but Anker paid the penalty by losing his wits. Although they both had a comfortable competence, they pondered above all things over the question of poverty—as though there was anything particular to be discovered about that!

All this was many years ago; it was about the time when the craze for freedom had broken out in the surrounding nations with fratricide and rebellion. Matters were not so bad on the island, for neither Anker nor Bjerregrav was particularly warlike; yet everybody could see that the town was not behind the rest of the world. Here the vanity of the town was quite in agreement with Master Jeppe, but for the rest he roundly condemned the whole movement. He always looked ready to fall upon Bjerregrav tooth and nail if the conversation turned on Anker's misfortune.

"Dampe! " said Jeppe scornfully, "he has turned both your heads! "

"That's a lie! " stammered Bjerregrav. "Anker went wrong later than that—after King Frederick granted us liberty. And it's only that I'm not very capable; I have my wits, thank God! " Bjerregrav solemnly

raised the fingers of his right hand to his lips, a gesture which had all
the appearance of a surviving vestige of the sign of the cross.

"You and your wits! " hissed Jeppe contemptuously. "You, who
throw your money away over the first tramp you meet! And you
defend an abominable agitator, who never goes out by daylight like
other people, but goes gallivanting about at night! "

"Yes, because he's ashamed of humanity; he wants to make the
world more beautiful! " Bjerregrav blushed with embarrassment
when he had said this.

But Jeppe was beside himself with contempt. "So gaol-birds are
ashamed of honest people! So that's why he takes his walks at night!
Well, the world would of course be a more beautiful place if it were
filled with people like you and Dampe! "

The pitiful thing about Anker was that he was such a good
craftsman. He had inherited the watchmaker's trade from his father
and grandfather, and his Bornholm striking-clocks were known all
over the world; orders came to him from Funen as well as from the
capital. But when the Constitution was granted he behaved like a
child—as though people had not always been free on Bornholm!
Now, he said, the new time had begun, and in its honor he intended,
in his insane rejoicing, to make an ingenious clock which should
show the moon and the date and the month and year. Being an
excellent craftsman, he completed it successfully, but then it entered
his head that the clock ought to show the weather as well. Like so
many whom God had endowed with His gifts, he ventured too far
and sought to rival God Himself. But here the brakes were clapped
on, and the whole project was nearly derailed. For a long time he
took it greatly to heart, but when the work was completed he
rejoiced. He was offered a large price for his masterpiece, and Jeppe
bade him close with the offer, but he answered crazily—for he was
now definitely insane—"This cannot be bought with money.
Everything I made formerly had its value in money, but not this. Can
any one buy *me*? "

For a long time he was in a dilemma as to what he should do with
his work, but then one day he came to Jeppe, saying: "Now I know;
the best ought to have the clock. I shall send it to the King. He has
given us the new time, and this clock will tell the new time. " Anker

sent the clock away, and after some time he received two hundred thalers, paid him through the Treasury.

This was a large sum of money, but Anker was not satisfied; he had expected a letter of thanks from the King's own hand. He behaved very oddly about this, and everything went wrong with him; over and over again trouble built its nest with him. The money he gave to the poor, and he lamented that the new time had not yet arrived. So he sank even deeper into his madness, and however hard Jeppe scolded him and lectured him it did no good. Finally he went so far as to fancy that he was appointed to create the new time, and then he became cheerful once more.

Three or four families of the town—very poor people, so demoralized that the sects would have nothing to do with them— gathered around Anker, and heard the voice of God in his message. "*They* lose nothing by sitting under a crazy man, " saw Jeppe scornfully. Anker himself paid no attention to them, but went his own way. Presently he was a king's son in disguise, and was betrothed to the eldest daughter of the King—and the new time was coming. Or when his mood was quieter, he would sit and work at an infallible clock which would not show the time; it would *be* the time—the new time itself.

He went to and fro in the workshop, in order to let Master Andres see the progress of his invention; he had conceived a blind affection for the young master. Every year, about the first of January, Master Andres had to write a letter for him, a love-letter to the king's daughter, and had also to take it upon him to despatch it to the proper quarter; and from time to time Anker would run in to ask whether an answer had yet arrived; and at the New Year a fresh love-letter was sent off. Master Andres had them all put away.

One evening—it was nearly time to knock off—there was a thundering knock on the workshop door, and the sound of some one humming a march drifted in from the entry. "Can you not open? " cried a solemn voice: "the Prince is here! "

"Pelle, open the door quick! " said the master. Pelle flung the door wide open, and Anker marched in. He wore a paper hat with a waving plume, and epaulettes made out of paper frills; his face was beaming, and he stood there with his hand to his hat as he allowed the march to die away. The young master rose gaily and shouldered arms with his stick.

"Your Majesty, " he said, "how goes it with the new time? "

"Not at all well! " replied Anker, becoming serious. "The pendulums that should keep the whole in motion are failing me. " He stood still, gazing at the door; his brain was working mysteriously.

"Ought they to be made of gold? " The master's eyes were twinkling, but he was earnestness personified.

"They ought to be made of eternity, " said Anker unwillingly, "and first it has got to be invented. "

For a long time he stood there, staring in front of him with his gray, empty eyes, without speaking a word. He did not move; only his temples went on working as though some worm was gnawing at them and seeking its way out.

Suddenly it became uncomfortable; his silence was sometimes like a living darkness that surrounded those about him. Pelle sat there with palpitating heart.

Then the lunatic came forward and bent over the young master's ear. "Has an answer come from the king? " he asked, in a penetrating whisper.

"No, not yet; but I expect it every day. You can be quite easy, " the master whispered back. Anker stood for a few moments in silence; he looked as though he must be meditating, but after his own fashion. Then he turned round and marched out of the workshop.

"Go after him and see he gets home all right, " said the young master. His voice sounded mournful now. Pelle followed the clockmaker up the street.

It was a Saturday evening, and the workers were on their way homeward from the great quarries and the potteries which lay about half a mile beyond the town. They passed in large groups, their dinner-boxes on their back, with a beer-bottle hung in front as a counter-weight. Their sticks struck loudly on the flagstones, and the iron heel-pieces of their wooden shoes struck out sparks as they passed. Pelle knew that weary homecoming; it was as though weariness in person had invaded the town. And he knew the sound of this taciturn procession; the snarling sound when this man or that made an unexpected and involuntary movement with his stiffened limbs, and was forced to groan with the pain of it. But to-night they gave him a different impression, and something like a smile broke through the encrusted stone-dust on their faces; it was the reflection of the bright new kroner that lay in their pockets after the exhausting labor of the week. Some of them had to visit the post-office to renew their lottery tickets or to ask for a postponement, and here and there one was about to enter a tavern, but at the last moment would be captured by his wife, leading a child by the hand.

Anker stood motionless on the sidewalk, his face turned toward the passing workers. He had bared his head, and the great plume of his hat drooped to the ground behind him; he looked agitated, as though something were fermenting within him, which could not find utterance, save in an odd, unintelligible noise. The workers shook their heads sadly as they trudged onward; one solitary young fellow threw him a playful remark. "Keep your hat on—it's not a funeral! " he cried. A few foreign seamen came strolling over the hill from the harbor; they came zigzagging down the street, peeping in at all the street doors, and laughing immoderately as they did so. One of them made straight for Anker with outstretched arms, knocked off his hat, and went on with his arm in the air as though nothing had happened. Suddenly he wheeled about. "What, are you giving yourself airs? " he cried, and therewith he attacked the lunatic, who timidly set about resisting him. Then another sailor ran up and struck Anker behind the knees, so that he fell. He lay on the ground shouting and kicking with fright, and the whole party flung itself upon him.

The boys scattered in all directions, in order to gather stones and come to Anker's assistance. Pelle stood still, his body jerking convulsively, as though the old sickness were about to attack him. Once he sprang forward toward Anker, but something within him told him that sickness had deprived him of his blind courage.

There was one pale, slender youth who was not afraid. He went right among the sailors, in order to drag them off the lunatic, who was becoming quite frantic under their treatment of him.

"He isn't in his right mind! " cried the boy, but he was hurled back with a bleeding face.

This was Morten, the brother of Jens the apprentice. He was so angry that he was sobbing.

Then a tall man came forward out of the darkness, with a rolling gait; he came forward muttering to himself. "Hurrah! " cried the boys. "Here comes the 'Great Power. '" But the man did not hear; he came to a standstill by the fighting group and stood there, still muttering. His giant figure swayed to and fro above them. "Help him, father! " cried Morten. The man laughed foolishly, and began slowly to pull his coat off. "Help him, then! " bellowed the boy, quite beside himself, shaking his father's arm. Jorgensen stretched out his hand to pat the boy's cheek, when he saw the blood on his face. "Knock them down! " cried the boy, like one possessed. Then a sudden shock ran through the giant's body—somewhat as when a heavy load is suddenly set in motion; he bowed himself a little, shook himself, and began to throw the sailors aside. One after another they stood still for a moment, feeling the place where he had seized them, and then they set off running as hard as they could toward the harbor.

Jorgensen set the madman on his legs again and escorted him home. Pelle and Morten followed them hand-in-hand. A peculiar feeling of satisfaction thrilled Pelle through; he had seen strength personified in action, and he had made a friend.

After that they were inseparable. Their friendship did not grow to full strength; it overshadowed them suddenly, magically conjured out of their hearts. In Morten's pale, handsome face there was something indescribable that made Pelle's heart throb in his breast, and a gentler note came into the voices of all who spoke to him. Pelle did not clearly understand what there could be attractive about himself; but he steeped himself in this friendship, which fell upon his ravaged soul like a beneficent rain. Morten would come up into the workshop as soon as work was over, or wait for Pelle at the corner. They always ran when they were going to meet. If Pelle had to work overtime, Morten did not go out, but sat in the workshop and amused him. He was very fond of reading, and told Pelle about the contents of many books.

Through Morten, Pelle drew nearer to Jens, and found that he had many good qualities under his warped exterior. Jens had just that broken, despondent manner which makes a child instinctively suspect a miserable home. Pelle had at first supposed that Jens and Morten must have been supported by the poor-box; he could not understand how a boy could bear his father to be a giant of whom the whole town went in terror. Jens seemed hard of hearing when any one spoke to him. "He has had so many beatings, " said Morten. "Father can't endure him, because he is stupid. " Clever he was not, but he could produce the most wonderful melodies by whistling merely with his lips, so that people would stand still and listen to him.

After his illness Pelle had a more delicate ear for everything. He no longer let the waves pass over him, careless as a child, but sent out tentacles—he was seeking for something. Everything had appeared to him as simpler than it was, and his dream of fortune had been too crudely conceived; it was easily shattered, and there was nothing behind it for him to rest on. Now he felt that he must build a better foundation, now he demanded nourishment from a wider radius, and his soul was on the alert for wider ventures; he dropped his anchors in unfamiliar seas. The goal of his desires receded into the unknown; he now overcame his aversion from the great and mysterious Beyond, where the outlines of the face of God lay hidden. The God of Bible history and the sects had for Pelle been only a man, equipped with a beard, and uprightness, and mercy, and all the rest; he was not to be despised, but the "Great Power" was certainly stronger. Hitherto Pelle had not felt the want of a God; he had only obscurely felt his membership in that all-loving God who will arise from the lowest and foulest and overshadow heaven; in that frenzied dream of the poor, who see, in a thousand bitter privations, the pilgrimage to the beloved land. But now he was seeking for that which no words can express; now the words, "the millennium, " had a peculiar sound in his ears.

Anker, of course, was crazy, because the others said so; when they laughed at him, Pelle laughed with them, but there was still something in him that filled Pelle with remorse for having laughed at him. Pelle himself would have liked to scramble money from the top of his high steps if he had been rich; and if Anker talked strangely, in curious phrases, of a time of happiness for all the poor, why, Father Lasse's lamentations had dealt with the same subject, as far back as he could remember. The foundation of the boy's nature felt a touch of the same pious awe which had forbidden Lasse and the others, out in the country, to laugh at the insane, for God's finger had touched them, so that their souls wandered in places to which no other could attain. Pelle felt the face of the unknown God gazing at him out of the mist.

He had become another being since his illness; his movements were more deliberate, and the features of his round childish face had become more marked and prominent. Those two weeks of illness had dislodged his cares, but they were imprinted on his character, to which they lent a certain gravity. He still roamed about alone, encompassing himself with solitude, and he observed the young master in his own assiduous way. He had an impression that the master was putting him to the proof, and this wounded him. He himself knew that that which lay behind his illness would never be repeated, and he writhed uneasily under suspicion.

One day he could bear it no longer. He took the ten kroner which Lasse had given him so that he might buy a much-needed winter overcoat, and went in to the master, who was in the cutting-out room, and laid them on the table. The master looked at him with a wondering expression, but there was a light in his eyes.

"What the devil is that? " he asked, drawling.

"That's master's money, " said Pelle, with averted face.

Master Andres gazed at him with dreamy eyes, and then he seemed to return, as though from another world, and Pelle all at once understood what every one said—that the young master was going to die. Then he burst into tears.

But the master himself could not understand.

"What the deuce. But that means nothing! " he cried, and he tossed the ten kroner in the air. "Lord o' me! what a lot of money! Well, you aren't poor! " He stood there, not knowing what to believe, his hand resting on Pelle's shoulder.

"It's right, " whispered Pelle. "I've reckoned it up exactly. And the master mustn't suspect me—I'll never do it again. "

Master Andres made a gesture of refusal with his hand, and wanted to speak, but at that very moment he was attacked by a paroxysm of coughing. "You young devil! " he groaned, and leaned heavily on Pelle; his face was purple. Then came a fit of sickness, and the sweat beaded his face. He stood there for a little, gasping for breath while his strength returned, and then he slipped the money into Pelle's hand and pushed him out of the room.

Pelle was greatly dejected. His uprightness was unrewarded, and what had become of his vindication? He had been so glad to think that he would shake himself free of all the disgrace. But late in the afternoon the master called him into the cutting-out room. "Here, Pelle, " he said confidentially, "I want to renew my lottery ticket; but I've no money. Can you lend me those ten kroner for a week? " So it was all as it should be; his one object was to put the whole disgrace away from him.

Jens and Morten helped him in that. There were three of them now; and Pelle had a feeling that he had a whole army at his back. The world had grown no smaller, no less attractive, by reason of the endless humiliations of the year. And Pelle knew down to the ground exactly where he stood, and that knowledge was bitter enough. Below him lay the misty void, and the bubbles which now and again rose to the surface and broke did not produce in him any feeling of mystical wonder as to the depths. But he did not feel oppressed thereby; what was, was so because it must be. And over him the other half of the round world revolved in the mystery of the blue heavens, and again and again he heard its joyous *Forward! On!*

IX

In his loneliness Pelle had often taken his way to the little house by the cemetery, where Due lived in two little rooms. It was always a sort of consolation to see familiar faces, but in other respects he did not gain much by his visits; Due was pleasant enough, but Anna thought of nothing but herself, and how she could best get on. Due had a situation as coachman at a jobmaster's, and they seemed to have a sufficiency.

"We have no intention of being satisfied with driving other people's horses, " Anna would say, "but you must crawl before you can walk. " She had no desire to return to the country.

"Out there there's no prospects for small people, who want something more than groats in their belly and a few rags on their back. You are respected about as much as the dirt you walk on, and there's no talk of any future. I shall never regret that we've come away from the country. "

Due, on the contrary, was homesick. He was quite used to knowing that there was a quarter of a mile between him and the nearest neighbor, and here he could hear, through the flimsy walls, whether his neighbors were kissing, fighting, or counting their money. "It is so close here, and then I miss the earth; the pavements are so hard. "

"He misses the manure—he can't come treading it into the room, " said Anna, in a superior way; "for that was the only thing there was plenty of in the country. Here in the town too the children can get on better; in the country poor children can't learn anything that'll help them to amount to something; they've got to work for their daily bread. It's bad to be poor in the country! "

"It's worse here in town, " said Pelle bitterly, "for here only those who dress finely amount to anything! "

"But there are all sorts of ways here by which a man can earn money, and if one way doesn't answer, he can try another. Many a man has come into town with his naked rump sticking out of his trousers, and now he's looked up to! If a man's only got the will and the energy — well, I've thought both the children ought to go to the municipal school, when they are older; knowledge is never to be despised. "

"Why not Marie as well? " asked Pelle.

"She? What? She's not fitted to learn anything. Besides, she's only a girl. "

Anna, like her brother Alfred, had set herself a lofty goal. Her eyes were quite bright when she spoke of it, and it was evidently her intention to follow it regardless of consequences. She was a loud-voiced, capable woman with an authoritative manner; Due simply sat by and smiled and kept his temper. But in his inmost heart, according to report, he knew well enough what he wanted. He never went to the public-house, but came straight home after work; and in the evening he was never happier than when all three children were scrambling over him. He made no distinction between his own two youngsters and the six-year-old Marie, whom Anna had borne before she married him.

Pelle was very fond of little Marie, who had thrived well enough so long as her child-loving grandparents had had her, but now she was thin and had stopped growing, and her eyes were too experienced. She gazed at one like a poor housewife who is always fretted and distressed, and Pelle was sorry for her. If her mother was harsh to her, he always remembered that Christmastide evening when he first visited his Uncle Kalle, and when Anna, weeping and abashed, had crept into the house, soon to be a mother. Little Anna, with the mind of a merry child, whom everybody liked. What had become of her now?

One evening, as Morten was not at liberty, he ran thither. Just as he was on the point of knocking, he heard Anna storming about indoors; suddenly the door flew open and little Marie was thrown out upon the footpath. The child was crying terribly.

"What's the matter, then? " asked Pelle, in his cheerful way.

"What's the matter? The matter is that the brat is saucy and won't eat just because she doesn't get exactly the same as the others. Here one has to slave and reckon and contrive—and for a bad girl like that! Now she's punishing herself and won't eat. Is it anything to her what the others have? Can she compare herself with them? She's a bastard brat and always will be, however you like to dress it up! "

"She can't help that! " said Pelle angrily.

"Can't help it! Perhaps I can help it? Is it my fault that she didn't come into the world a farmer's daughter, but has to put up with being a bastard? Yes, you may believe me, the neighbors' wives tell me to my face she hasn't her father's eyes, and they look at me as friendly as a lot of cats! Am I to be punished all my life, perhaps, because I looked a bit higher, and let myself be led astray in a way that didn't lead to anything? Ah, the little monster! " And she clenched her fists and shook them in the direction from which the child's crying could still be heard.

"Here one goes and wears oneself out to keep the house tidy and to be respectable, and then no one will treat me as being as good as themselves, just because once I was a bit careless! " She was quite beside herself.

"If you aren't kind to little Marie, I shall tell Uncle Kalle, " said Pelle warningly.

She spat contemptuously. "Then you can tell him. Yes, I wish to God you'd do it! Then he'd come and take her away, and delighted I should be! "

But now Due was heard stamping on the flags outside the door, and they could hear him too consoling the child. He came in holding her by the hand, and gave his wife a warning look, but said nothing. "There, there—now all that's forgotten, " he repeated, in order to check the child's sobs, and he wiped away the grimy tears from her cheeks with his great thumbs.

Anna brought him his food, sulkily enough, and out in the kitchen she muttered to herself. Due, while he ate his supper of bacon and black bread, stood the child between his knees and stared at her with round eyes. "Rider! " she said, and smiled persuasively. "Rider! " Due laid a cube of bacon on a piece of bread.

> "There came a rider riding
> On his white hoss, hoss, hoss, hoss! "

he sang, and he made the bread ride up to her mouth. "And then? "

"Then, *pop* he rode in at the gate! " said the child, and swallowed horse and rider.

While she ate she kept her eyes fixed upon him unwaveringly, with that painful earnestness which was so sad to see. But sometimes it happened that the rider rode right up to her mouth, and then, with a jerk, turned about, and disappeared, at a frantic gallop, between Due's white teeth. Then she smiled for a moment.

"There's really no sense shoving anything into her, " said Anna, who was bringing coffee in honor of the visitor. "She gets as much as she can eat, and she's not hungry. "

"She's hungry, all the same! " hummed Due.

"Then she's dainty—our poor food isn't good enough for her. She takes after her father, I can tell you! And what's more, if she isn't naughty now she soon will be when once she sees she's backed up. "

Due did not reply. "Are you quite well again now? " he asked, turning to Pelle.

"What have you been doing to-day? " asked Anna, filling her husband's long pipe.

"I had to drive a forest ranger from up yonder right across the whole of the moor. I got a krone and a half for a tip. "

"Give it to me, right away! "

Due passed her the money, and she put it into an old coffeepot. "This evening you must take the bucket to the inspector's, " she said.

Due stretched himself wearily. "I've been on the go since half-past four this morning, " he said.

"But I've promised it faithfully, so there's nothing else to be done. And then I thought you'd see to the digging for them this autumn; you can see when we've got the moonlight, and then there's Sundays. If we don't get it some one else will—and they are good payers. "

Due did not reply.

"In a year or two from now, I'm thinking, you'll have your own horses and won't need to go scraping other people's daily bread together, " she said, laying her hand on his shoulder, "Won't you go right away and take the bucket? Then it's done. And I must have some small firewood cut before you go to bed. "

Due sat there wearily blinking. After eating, fatigue came over him. He could hardly see out of his eyes, so sleepy was he. Marie handed him his cap, and at last he got on his legs. He and Pelle went out together.

The house in which Due lived lay far up the long street, which ran steeply down to the sea. It was an old watercourse, and even now when there was a violent shower the water ran down like a rushing torrent between the poor cottages.

Down on the sea-road they met a group of men who were carrying lanterns in their hands; they were armed with heavy sticks, and one of them wore an old leather hat and carried a club studded with spikes. This was the night-watch. They moved off, and behind them all went the new policeman, Pihl, in his resplendent uniform. He kept well behind the others, in order to show off his uniform, and also to ensure that none of the watch took to their heels. They were half drunk, and were taking their time; whenever they met any one they stood still and related with much detail precisely why they had taken the field. The "Great Power" was at his tricks again. He had been refractory all day, and the provost had given the order to keep an eye on him. And quite rightly, for in his cups he had met Ship-owner Monsen, on Church Hill, and had fallen upon him with blows and words of abuse: "So you take the widow's bread out of her mouth, do you? You told her the *Three Sisters* was damaged at sea, and you took over her shares for next to nothing, did you? Out of pure compassion, eh, you scoundrel? And there was nothing the matter with the ship except that she had done only too well and made a big profit, eh? So you did the poor widow a kindness, eh? " A scoundrel, he called him and at every question he struck him a blow, so that he rolled on the ground. "We are all witnesses, and now he must go to prison. A poor stone-cutter oughtn't to go about playing the judge. Come and help us catch him, Due—you are pretty strong! "

"It's nothing to do with me, " said Due.

"You do best to keep your fingers out of it, " said one of the men derisively; "you might get to know the feel of his fist. " And they went on, laughing contemptuously.

"They won't be so pleased with their errand when they've done, " said Due, laughing. "That's why they've got a nice drop stowed away— under their belts. To give them courage. The strong man's a swine, but I'd rather not be the one he goes for. "

"Suppose they don't get him at all! " said Pelle eagerly.

Due laughed. "They'll time it so that they are where he isn't. But why don't he stick to his work and leave his fool's tricks alone? He could have a good drink and sleep it off at home—he's only a poor devil, he ought to leave it to the great people to drink themselves silly! "

But Pelle took another view of the affair. The poor man of course ought to go quietly along the street and take his hat off to everybody; and if anybody greeted him in return he'd be quite proud, and tell it to his wife as quite an event, as they were going to bed. "The clerk raised his hat to me to-day—yes, that he did! " But Stonecutter Jorgensen looked neither to right nor to left when he was sober, and in his cups he trampled everybody underfoot.

Pelle by no means agreed with the pitiful opinions of the town. In the country, whence he came, strength was regarded as everything, and here was a man who could have taken strong Erik himself and put him in his pocket. He roamed about in secret, furtively measuring his wrists, and lifted objects which were much too heavy for him; he would by no means have objected to be like the "Great Power, " who, as a single individual, kept the whole town in a state of breathless excitement, whether he was in one of his raging moods or whether he lay like one dead. The thought that he was the comrade of Jens and Morten made him quite giddy, and he could not understand why they bowed themselves so completely to the judgment of the town, as no one could cast it in their teeth that they were on the parish, but only that their father was a powerful fellow.

Jens shrank from continually hearing his father's name on all lips, and avoided looking people in the eyes, but in Morten's open glance he saw no trace of this nameless grief.

One evening, when matters were quite at their worst, they took Pelle home with them. They lived in the east, by the great clay-pit, where the refuse of the town was cast away. Their mother was busy warming the supper in the oven, and in the chimney-corner sat a shrivelled old grandmother, knitting. It was a poverty-stricken home.

"I really thought that was father, " said the woman, shivering. "Has any of you heard of him? "

The boys related what they had heard; some one had seen him here, another there. "People are only too glad to keep us informed, " said Jens bitterly.

"Now it's the fourth evening that I've warmed up his supper to no purpose, " the mother continued. "Formerly he used to take care to look in at home, however much they were after him—but he may come yet. "

She tried to smile hopefully, but suddenly threw her apron in front of her eyes and burst into tears. Jens went about with hanging head, not knowing what he ought to do; Morten put his arm behind the weary back and spoke soothingly: "Come, come; it isn't worse than it has often been! " And he stroked the projecting shoulder-blades.

"No, but I did feel so glad that it was over. A whole year almost he never broke out, but took his food quietly when he came home from work, and then crawled into bed. All that time he broke nothing; he just slept and slept; at last I believed he had become weak-minded, and I was glad for him, for he had peace from those terrible ideas. I believed he had quieted down after all his disgraces, and would take life as it came; as the rest of his comrades do. And now he's broken out again as audacious as possible, and it's all begun over again! " She wept desolately.

The old woman sat by the stove, her shifting glance wandering from one to another; she was like a crafty bird of prey sitting in a cage. Then her voice began, passionless and uninflected:

"You're a great donkey; now it's the fourth evening you've made pancakes for your vagabond; you're always at him, kissing and petting him! I wouldn't sweeten my husband's sleep if he had behaved so scandalously to his wife and family; he could go to bed and get up again hungry, and dry too, for all I cared; then he'd learn manners at last. But there's no grit in you—that's the trouble; you put up with all his sauciness. "

"If I were to lay a stone in his way—why, who would be good to him, if his poor head wanted to lie soft? Grandmother ought to know how much he needs some one who believes in him. And there's nothing else I can do for him. "

"Yes, yes; work away and wear yourself out, so that there's always something for the great fellow to smash if he has a mind to! But now you go to bed and lie down; I'll wait up for Peter and give him his food, if he comes; you must be half dead with weariness, you poor worm. "

"There's an old proverb says, 'A man's mother is the devil's pother, ' but it don't apply to you, grandmother, " said the mother of the boys mildly. "You always take my part, although there's no need. But now you go to bed! It's far past your bed-time, and I'll look after Peter. It's so easy to manage him if only he knows that you mean well by him. "

The old woman behaved as though she did not hear; she went on knitting. The boys remembered that they had brought something with them; a bag of coffee-beans, some sugar-candy, and a few rolls.

"You waste all your hard-earned shillings on me, " said the mother reproachfully, and put the water to boil for the coffee, while her face beamed with gratitude.

"They've no young women to waste it on, " said the old woman dryly.

"Grandmother's out of humor this evening, " said Morten. He had taken off the old woman's glasses and looked smilingly into her gray eyes.

"Out of humor—yes, that I am! But time passes, I tell you, and here one sits on the edge of the grave, waiting for her own flesh and blood to get on and do something wonderful, but nothing ever happens! Energies are wasted—they run away like brook-water into the sea— and the years are wasted too—or is it lies I'm telling you? All want to be masters; no one wants to carry the sack; and one man seizes hold of another and clambers over him just to reach an inch higher. And there ought to be plenty in the house—but there's poverty and filth in every corner. I should think the dear God will soon have had enough of it all! Not an hour goes by but I curse the day when I let myself be wheedled away from the country; there a poor man's daily bread grows in the field, if he'll take it as it comes. But here he must go with a shilling in his fist, if it's only that he wants a scrap of cabbage for his soup. If you've money you can have it; if you haven't, you can leave it. Yes, that's how it is! But one must live in town in order to have the same luck as Peter! Everything promised splendidly, and I, stupid old woman, have always had a craving to see my own flesh and blood up at the top. And now I sit here like a beggar-princess! Oh, it has been splendid—I'm the mother of the biggest vagabond in town! "

"Grandmother shouldn't talk like that, " said the mother of the boys.

"Yes, yes; but I'm sick of it all—and yet I can't think about dying! How can I go and lay me down—who would take a stick to Peter? — the strong man! " she said contemptuously.

"Grandmother had better go quietly and lie down; I can manage Peter best if I'm alone with him, " said the wife, but the old woman did not move.

"Can't you get her to go, Morten? " whispered the mother. "You are the only one she will listen to. "

Morten lectured the old woman until he had enticed her away; he had to promise to go with her and arrange the bedclothes over her feet.

"Now, thank goodness, we've got her out of the way! " said the mother, relieved. "I'm always so afraid that father might forget what he's doing when he's like he is now; and she doesn't think of giving in to him, so it's flint against flint. But now I think you ought to go where the rest of the young folks are, instead of sitting here and hanging your heads. "

"We'll stay and see whether father comes, " declared Morten.

"But what does it matter to you—you can say good-day to father at any time. Go now—listen—father prefers to find me alone when he's like this and comes home merry. Perhaps he takes me in his arms and swings me round—he's so strong—so that I feel as giddy as a young girl. 'Ho, heigh, wench, here's the "Great Power"! ' he says, and he laughs as loud as he used to in his rowdy young days. Yes, when he's got just enough in him he gets as strong and jolly as ever he was in his very best days. I'm glad it's soon over. But that's not for you —you had better go. " She looked at them appealingly, and shrank back as some one fumbled at the door. Out-of-doors it was terrible weather.

It was only the youngest, who had come home from her day's work. She might have been ten or twelve years old and was small for her age, although she looked older; her voice was harsh and strident, and her little body seemed coarsened and worn with work. There was not a spot about her that shed or reflected a single ray of light; she was like some subterranean creature that has strayed to the surface. She went silently across the room and let herself drop into her grandmother's chair; she leaned over to one side as she sat, and now and again her features contracted.

"She's got that mischief in her back, " said the mother, stroking her thin, unlovely hair. "She got it always carrying the doctor's little boy—he's so tall and so heavy. But as long as the doctor says nothing, it can't be anything dangerous. Yes, you did really leave home too early, my child; but, after all, you get good food and you learn to be smart. And capable, that she is; she looks after the doctor's three children all by herself! The eldest is her own age, but she has to dress and undress her. Such grand children, they don't even learn how to do things for themselves! "

Pelle stared at her curiously. He himself had put up with a good deal, but to cripple himself by dragging children about, who were perhaps stronger than himself—no, no one need expect that of him! "Why do you carry the over-fed brat? " he asked.

"They must have some one to look after them, " said the mother, "and their mother, who's the nearest to them, she doesn't feel inclined to do it. And they pay her for it. "

"If it was me, I'd let the brat fall, " said Pelle boldly.

The little girl just glanced at him with her dull eyes, and a feeble interest glimmered in them. But her face retained its frozen indifference, and it was impossible to say what she was thinking, so hard and experienced was her expression.

"You mustn't teach her anything naughty, " said the mother; "she has enough to struggle against already; she's got an obstinate nature. And now you must go to bed, Karen"—she caressed her once more— "Father can't bear to see you when he's had too much. He's so fond of her, " she added helplessly.

Karen drew away from the caress without the slightest change of expression; silently she went up to the garret where she slept. Pelle had not heard her utter a sound.

"That's how she is, " said the mother, shivering. "Never a word to say 'good night'! Nothing makes any impression on her nowadays— neither good nor bad; she's grown up too soon. And I have to manage so that father doesn't see her when he's merry. He goes on like a wild beast against himself and everybody else when it comes across his mind how she's been put upon. " She looked nervously at the clock. "But go now—do listen! You'll do me a great favor if you'll go! " She was almost crying.

Morten stood up, hesitating, and the others followed his example. "Pull your collars up and run, " said the mother, and buttoned up their coats. The October gale was beating in gusts against the house, and the rain was lashing violently against the window-panes.

As they were saying good night a fresh noise was heard outside. The outer door banged against the wall, and they heard the storm burst in and fill the entry. "Ah, now it's too late! " lamented the mother reproachfully. "Why didn't you go sooner? " A monstrous breathing sounded outside, like the breathing of a gigantic beast, sniffing up and down at the crack of the door, and fumbling after the latch with its dripping paws. Jens wanted to run and open the door. "No, you mustn't do that! " cried his mother despairingly, and she pushed the bolt. She stood there, rigid, her whole body trembling. Pelle too began to shiver; he had a feeling that the storm itself was lying there in the entry like a great unwieldy being, puffing and snorting in a kind of gross content, and licking itself dry while it waited for them.

The woman bent her ear to the door, listening in frantic suspense. "What is he up to now? " she murmured; "he is so fond of teasing! " She was crying again. The boys had for the moment forgotten her.

Then the outer door was beaten in, and the monster got up on all four dripping paws, and began to call them with familiar growls. The woman turned about in her distress; waving her hands helplessly before her, and then clapping them to her face. But now the great beast became impatient; it struck the door sharply, and snarled warningly. The woman shrank back as though she herself were about to drop on all fours and answered him. "No, no! " she cried, and considered a moment. Then the door was burst in with one tremendous blow, and Master Bruin rolled over the threshold and leaped toward them in clumsy jumps, his head thrown somewhat backward as though wondering why his little comrade had not rushed to meet him, with an eager growl. "Peter, Peter, the boy! " she whispered, bending over him; but he pushed her to the floor with a snarl, and laid one heavy paw upon her. She tore herself away from him and escaped to a chair.

"Who am I? " he asked, in a stumbling, ghostly voice, confronting her.

"The great strong man! " She could not help smiling; he was ramping about in such a clumsy, comical way.

"And you? "

"The luckiest woman in all the world! " But now her voice died away in a sob.

"And where is the strong man to rest to-night? " He snatched at her breast.

She sprang up with blazing eyes. "You beast—oh, you beast! " she cried, red with shame, and she struck him in the face.

The "Great Power" wiped his face wonderingly after each blow. "We're only playing, " he said. Then, in a flash, he caught sight of the boys, who had shrunk into a corner. "There you are! " he said, and he laughed crazily; "yes, mother and I, we're having a bit of a game! Aren't we, mother? "

But the woman had run out of doors, and now stood under the eaves, sobbing.

Jorgensen moved restlessly to and fro. "She's crying, " he muttered. "There's no grit in her—she ought to have married some farmer's lad, devil take it, if the truth must be told! It catches me here and presses as though some one were shoving an iron ferrule into my brain. Come on, 'Great Power'! Come on! so that you can get some peace from it! I say every day. No, let be, I say then—you must keep a hold on yourself, or she just goes about crying! And she's never been anything but good to you! But deuce take it, if it would only come out! And then one goes to bed and says, Praise God, the day is done—and another day, and another. And they stand there and stare—and wait; but let them wait; nothing happens, for now the 'Great Power' has got control of himself! And then all at once it's there behind! Hit away! Eight in the thick of the heap! Send them all to hell, the scoundrels! 'Cause a man must drink, in order to keep his energies in check.... Well, and there she sits! Can one of you lend me a krone? "

"Not I! " said Jens.

"No, not you—he'd be a pretty duffer who'd expect anything from you! Haven't I always said 'he takes after the wrong side'? He's like his mother. He's got a heart, but he's incapable. What can you really do, Jens? Do you get fine clothes from your master, and does he treat you like a son, and will you finish up by taking over the business as his son-in-law? And why not? if I may ask the question. Your father is as much respected as Morten's. "

"Morten won't be a son-in-law, either, if his master has no daughter, " Jens muttered.

"No. But he might have had a daughter, hey? But there we've got an answer. You don't reflect. Morten, he's got something there! " He touched his forehead.

"Then you shouldn't have hit me on the head, " retorted Jens sulkily.

"On the head—well! But the understanding has its seat in the head. That's where one ought to hammer it in. For what use would it be, I ask you, supposing you commit some stupidity with your head and I smack you on the behind? You don't need any understanding there? But it has helped—you've grown much smarter. That was no fool's answer you gave me just now: 'Then you shouldn't have hit me on the head! '" He nodded in acknowledgment. "No, but here is a head that can give them some trouble—there are knots of sense in this wood, hey? " And the three boys had to feel the top of his head.

He stood there like a swaying tree, and listened with a changing expression to the less frequent sobs of his wife; she was now sitting by the fire, just facing the door. "She does nothing but cry, " he said compassionately; "that's a way the women have of amusing themselves nowadays. Life has been hard on us, and she couldn't stand hardships, poor thing! For example, if I were to say now that I'd like to smash the stove"—and here he seized a heavy chair and waved it about in the air—"then she begins to cry. She cries about everything. But if I get on I shall take another wife —one who can make a bit of a show. Because this is nonsense. Can she receive her guests and make fine conversation? Pah! What the devil is the use of my working and pulling us all out of the mud? But now I'm going out again—God knows, it ain't amusing here! "

His wife hurried across to him. "Ah, don't go out, Peter—stay here, do! " she begged.

"Am I to hang about here listening to you maundering on? " he asked sulkily, shrugging his shoulders. He was like a great, good-natured boy who gives himself airs.

"I won't maunder—I'm ever so jolly—if only you'll stay! " she cried, and she smiled through her tears. "Look at me—don't you see how glad I am? Stay with me, do, 'Great Power! '" She breathed warmly into his ear; she had shaken off her cares and pulled herself together, and was now really pretty with her glowing face.

The "Great Power" looked at her affectionately; he laughed stupidly, as though he was tickled, and allowed himself to be pulled about; he imitated her whisper to the empty air, and was overflowing with good humor. Then he slyly approached his mouth to her ear, and as she listened he trumpeted loudly, so that she started back with a little cry. "Do stay, you great baby! " she said, laughing. "I won't let you go; I can hold you! " But he shook her off, laughing, and ran out bareheaded.

For a moment it looked as though she would run after him, but then her hands fell, and she drooped her head. "Let him run off, " she said wearily; "now things must go as they will. There's nothing to be done; I've never seen him so drunk. Yes, you look at me, but you must remember that he carries his drink differently to every one else—he is quite by himself in everything! " She said this with a certain air of pride. "And he has punished the shipowner—and even the judge daren't touch him. The good God Himself can't be more upright than he is. "

X

Now the dark evenings had come when the lamp had to be lit early for the workers. The journeyman left while it was still twilight; there was little for him to do. In November the eldest apprentice had served his time. He was made to sit all alone in the master's room, and there he stayed for a whole week, working on his journeyman's task—a pair of sea-boots. No one was allowed to go in to him, and the whole affair was extremely exciting. When the boots were ready and had been inspected by some of the master-shoemakers, they were filled to the top with water and suspended in the garret; there they hung for a few days, in order to show that they were water-tight. Then Emil was solemnly appointed a journeyman, and had to treat the whole workshop. He drank brotherhood with little Nikas, and in the evening he went out and treated the other journeymen— and came home drunk as a lord. Everything passed off just as it should.

On the following day Jeppe came into the workshop. "Well, Emil, now you're a journeyman. What do you think of it? Do you mean to travel? It does a freshly baked journeyman good to go out into the world and move about and learn something. "

Emil did not reply, but began to bundle his things together. "No, no; it's not a matter of life and death to turn you out. You can come to the workshop here and share the light and the warmth until you've got something better—those are good conditions, it seems to me. Now, when I was learning, things were very different—a kick behind, and out you went! And that's for young men—it's good for them! "

He could sit in the workshop and enumerate all the masters in the whole island who had a journeyman. But that was really only a joke —it never happened that a new journeyman was engaged. On the other hand, he and the others knew well enough how many freshly-baked journeymen had been thrown on to the streets that autumn.

Emil was by no means dejected. Two evenings later they saw him off on the Copenhagen steamer. "There is work enough, " he said, beaming with delight. "You must promise me that you'll write to me in a year, " said Peter, who had finished his apprenticeship at the same time. "That I will! " said Emil.

But before a month had passed they heard that Emil was home again. He was ashamed to let himself be seen. And then one morning he came, much embarrassed, slinking into the workshop. Yes, he had got work —in several places, but had soon been sent away again. "I have learned nothing, " he said dejectedly. He loitered about for a time, to enjoy the light and warmth of the workshop, and would sit there doing some jobs of cobbling which he had got hold of. He kept himself above water until nearly Christmas-time, but then he gave in, and disgraced his handicraft by working at the harbor as an ordinary stevedore.

"I have wasted five years of my life, " he used to say when they met him; "Run away while there's time! Or it'll be the same with you as it was with me. " He did not come to the workshop any longer out of fear of Jeppe, who was extremely wroth with him for dishonoring his trade.

It was cozy in the workshop when the fire crackled in the stove and the darkness looked in at the black, uncovered window-panes. The table was moved away from the window so that all four could find place about it, the master with his book and the three apprentices each with his repairing job. The lamp hung over the table, and smoked; it managed to lessen the darkness a little. The little light it gave was gathered up by the great glass balls which focussed it and cast it upon the work. The lamp swayed slightly, and the specks of light wriggled hither and thither like tadpoles, so that the work was continually left in darkness. Then the master would curse and stare miserably at the lamp.

The others suffered with their eyes, but the master sickened in the darkness. Every moment he would stand up with a shudder. "Damn and blast it, how dark it is here; it's as dark as though one lay in the grave! Won't it give any light to-night? " Then Pelle would twist the regulator, but it was no better.

When old Jeppe came tripping in, Master Andres looked up without trying to hide his book; he was in a fighting mood.

"Who is there? " he asked, staring into the darkness. "Ah, it's father! "

"Have you got bad eyes? " asked the old man derisively. "Will you have some eye-water? "

"Father's eye-water—no thanks! But this damned light—one can't see one's hand before one's face! "

"Open your mouth, then, and your teeth will shine! " Jeppe spat the words out. This lighting was always a source of strike between them.

"No one else in the whole island works by so wretched a light, you take my word, father. "

"In my time I never heard complaints about the light, " retorted Jeppe. "And better work has been done under the glass ball than any one can do now with all their artificial discoveries. But it's disappearing now; the young people to-day know no greater pleasure than throwing their money out of the window after such modern trash. "

"Yes, in father's time—then everything was so splendid! " said Master Andres. "That was when the angels ran about with white sticks in their mouths! "

In the course of the evening now one and another would drop in to hear and tell the news. And if the young master was in a good temper they would stay. He was the fire and soul of the party, as old Bjerregrav said; he could, thanks to his reading, give explanations of so many things.

When Pelle lifted his eyes from his work he was blind. Yonder, in the workshop, where Baker Jorgen and the rest sat and gossiped, he could see nothing but dancing specks of light, and his work swam round in the midst of them; and of his comrades he saw nothing but their aprons. But in the glass ball the light was like a living fire, in whose streams a world was laboring.

"Well, this evening there's a capital light, " said Jeppe, if one of them looked to the lamp.

"You mean there's no light at all! " retorted Master Andres, twisting the regulator.

But one day the ironmonger's man brought something in a big basket —a hanging lamp with a round burner; and when it was dark the ironmonger himself came in order to light it for the first time, and to initiate Pelle into the management of the wonderful

400

contrivance. He went to work very circumstantially and with much caution. "It can explode, I needn't tell you, " he said, "but you'd have to treat the mechanism very badly first. If you only set to work with care and reason there is no danger whatever. "

Pelle stood close to him, holding the cylinder, but the others turned their heads away from the table, while the young master stood right at the back, and shuffled to and fro. "Devil knows I don't want to go to heaven in my living body! " he said, with a comical expression; "but deuce take it, where did you get the courage, Pelle? You're a saucy young spark! " And he looked at him with his wide, wondering gaze, which held in it both jest and earnest.

At last the lamp shone out; and even on the furthest shelf, high up under the ceiling, one could count every single last. "That's a regular sun! " said the young master, and he put his hand to his face; "why, good Lord, I believe it warms the room! " He was quite flushed, and his eyes were sparkling.

The old master kept well away from the lamp until the ironmonger had gone; then he came rushing over to it. "Well, aren't you blown sky-high? " he asked, in great astonishment. "It gives an ugly light —oh, a horrible light! Poof, I say! And it doesn't shine properly; it catches you in the eyes. Well, well, you can spoil your sight as far as I'm concerned! "

But for the others the lamp was a renewal of life. Master Andres sunned himself in its rays. He was like a sun-intoxicated bird; as he sat there, quite at peace, a wave of joy would suddenly come over him. And to the neighbors who gathered round the lamp in order to discover its qualities he held forth in great style, so that the light was doubled. They came often and stayed readily; the master beamed and the lamp shone; they were like insects attracted by the light—the glorious light!

Twenty times a day the master would go out to the front door, but he always came in again and sat by the window to read, his boot with the wooden heel sticking out behind him. He spat so much that Pelle had to put fresh sand every day under his place.

"Is there some sort of beast that sits in your chest and gnaws? " said Uncle Jorgen, when Andres' cough troubled him badly. "You look so well otherwise. You'll recover before we know where we are! "

"Yes, thank God! " The master laughed gaily between two attacks.

"If you only go at the beast hard enough, it'll surely die. Now, where you are, in your thirtieth year, you ought to be able to get at it. Suppose you were to give it cognac? "

Jorgen Kofod, as a rule, came clumping in with great wooden shoes, and Jeppe used to scold him. "One wouldn't believe you've got a shoemaker for a brother! " he would say crossly; "and yet we all get our black bread from you. "

"But what if I can't keep my feet warm now in those damned leather shoes? And I'm full through and through of gout—it's a real misery! " The big baker twisted himself dolefully.

"It must be dreadful with gout like that, " said Bjerregrav. "I myself have never had it. "

"Tailors don't get gout, " rejoined Baker Jorgen scornfully. "A tailor's body has no room to harbor it. So much I do know—twelve tailors go to a pound. "

Bjerregrav did not reply.

"The tailors have their own topsy-turvy world, " continued the baker. "I can't compare myself with them. A crippled tailor—well, even he has got his full strength of body. "

"A tailor is as fine a fellow as a black-bread baker! " stammered Bjerregrav nervously. "To bake black bread—why, every farmer's wife can do that! "

"Fine! I believe you! Hell and blazes! If the tailor makes a cap he has enough cloth left over to make himself a pair of breeches. That's why tailors are always dressed so fine! " The baker was talking to the empty air.

"Millers and bakers are always rogues, everybody says. " Old Bjerregrav turned to Master Andres, trembling with excitement. But the young master stood there looking gaily from one to the other, his lame leg dangling in the air.

"For the tailor nothing comes amiss—there's too much room in me! " said the baker, as though something were choking him. "Or, as another proverb says—it's of no more consequence than a tailor in hell. They are the fellows! We all know the story of the woman who brought a full-grown tailor into the world without even knowing she was with child. "

Jeppe laughed. "Now, that's enough, really; God knows neither of you will give in to the other. "

"Well, and I've no intention of trampling a tailor to death, if it can anyhow be avoided—but one can't always see them. " Baker Jorgen carefully lifted his great wooden shoes. "But they are not men. Now is there even one tailor in the town who has been overseas? No, and there were no men about while the tailor was being made. A woman stood in a draught at the front door, and there she brought forth the tailor. " The baker could not stop himself when once he began to quiz anybody; now that Soren was married, he had recovered all his good spirits.

Bjerregrav could not beat this. "You can say what you like about tailors, " he succeeded in saying at last. "But people who bake black bread are not respected as handicraftsmen—no more than the washerwoman! Tailoring and shoemaking, they are proper crafts, with craftman's tests, and all the rest. "

"Yes, shoemaking of course is another thing, " said Jeppe.

"But as many proverbs and sayings are as true of you as of us, " said Bjerregrav, desperately blinking.

"Well, it's no longer ago than last year that Master Klausen married a cabinet-maker's daughter. But whom must a tailor marry? His own serving-maid? "

"Now how can you, father! " sighed Master Andres. "One man's as good as another. "

"Yes, you turn everything upside down! But I'll have my handicraft respected. To-day all sorts of agents and wool-merchants and other trash settle in the town and talk big. But in the old days the handicraftsmen were the marrow of the land. Even the king himself had to learn a handicraft. I myself served my apprenticeship in the capital, and in the workshop where I was a prince had learned the trade. But, hang it all, I never heard of a king who learned tailoring! "

They were capable of going on forever in this way, but, as the dispute was at its worst, the door opened, and Wooden-leg Larsen stumped in, filling the workshop with fresh air. He was wearing a storm-cap and a blue pilot-coat. "Good evening, children! " he said gaily, and threw down a heap of leather ferrules and single boots on the window-bench.

His entrance put life into all. "Here's a playboy for us! Welcome home! Has it been a good summer? "

Jeppe picked up the five boots for the right foot, one after another, turned back the uppers, and held heels and soles in a straight line before his eyes. "A bungler has had these in hand, " he growled, and then he set to work on the casing for the wooden leg. "Well, did the layer of felt answer? " Larsen suffered from cold in his amputated foot.

"Yes; I've not had cold feet any more. "

"Cold feet! " The baker struck himself on the loins and laughed.

"Yes, you can say what you like, but every time my wooden leg gets wet I get a cold in the head! "

"That's the very deuce! " cried Jorgen, and his great body rolled like a hippopotamus. "A funny thing, that! "

"There are many funny things in the world, " stammered Bjerregrav. "When my brother died, my watch stopped at that very moment—it was he who gave it me. "

Wooden-leg Larsen had been through the whole kingdom with his barrel-organ, and had to tell them all about it; of the railway- trains which travelled so fast that the landscape turned round on its own axis, and of the great shops and places of amusement in the capital.

"It must be as it will, " said Master Andres. "But in the summer I shall go to the capital and work there! "

"In Jutland—that's where they have so many wrecks! " said the baker. "They say everything is sand there! I've heard that the country is shifting under their feet—moving away toward the east. Is it true that they have a post there that a man must scratch himself against before he can sit down? "

"My sister has a son who has married a Jutland woman and settled down there, " said Bjerregrav. "Have you seen anything of them? "

The baker laughed. "Tailors are so big—they've got the whole world in their waistcoat pocket. Well, and Funen? Have you been there, too? That's where the women have such a pleasant disposition. I've lain before Svendborg and taken in water, but there was no time to go ashore. " This remark sounded like a sigh.

"Can you stand it, wandering so much? " asked Bjerregrav anxiously.

Wooden-leg Larsen looked contemptuously at Bjerregrav's congenital club-foot—he had received his own injury at Heligoland, at the hands of an honorable bullet. "If one's sound of limb, " he said, spitting on the floor by the window.

Then the others had to relate what had happened in town during the course of the summer; of the Finnish barque which had stranded in the north, and how the "Great Power" had broken out again. "Now he's sitting in the dumps under lock and key. "

Bjerregrav took exception to the name they gave him; he called it blasphemy, on the ground that the Bible said that power and might belonged to God alone.

Wooden-leg Larsen said that the word, as they had used it, had nothing to do with God; it was an earthly thing; across the water people used it to drive machinery, instead of horses.

"I should think woman is the greatest power, " said Baker Jorgen, "for women rule the world, God knows they do! And God protect us if they are once let loose on us! But what do you think, Andres, you who are so book-learned? "

"The sun is the greatest power, " said Master Andres. "It rules over all life, and science has discovered that all strength and force come from the sun. When it falls into the sea and cools, then the whole world will become a lump of ice. "

"Then the sea is the greatest power! " cried Jeppe triumphantly. "Or do you know of anything else that tears everything down and washes it away? And from the sea we get everything back again. Once when I went to Malaga——"

"Yes, that really is true, " said Bjerregrav, "for most people get their living from the sea, and many their death. And the rich people we have get all their money from the sea. "

Jeppe drew himself up proudly and his glasses began to glitter. "The sea can bear what it likes, stone or iron, although it is soft itself! The heaviest loads can travel on its back. And then all at once it swallows everything down. I have seen ships which sailed right into the weather and disappeared when their time came. "

"I should very much like to know whether the different countries float on the water, or whether they stand firm on the bottom of the sea. Don't you know that, Andres? " asked Bjerregrav.

Master Andres thought they stood on the bottom of the sea, far below the surface; but Uncle Jorgen said: "Nay! Big as the sea is! "

"Yes, it's big, for I've been over the whole island, " said Bjerregrav self-consciously; "but I never got anywhere where I couldn't see the sea. Every parish in all Bornholm borders on the sea. But it has no power over the farmers and peasants—they belong to the land, don't they? "

"The sea has power over all of us, " said Larsen. "Some it refuses; they go to sea for years and years, but then in their old age they suffer from sea-sickness, and then they are warned. That is why Skipper Andersen came on shore. And others it attracts, from right away up in the country! I have been to sea with such people—they had spent their whole lives up on the island, and had seen the sea, but had never been down to the shore. And then one day the devil collared them and they left the plough and ran down to the sea and hired themselves out. And they weren't the worse seamen. "

"Yes, " said Baker Jorgen, "and all of us here have been to sea, and Bornholmers sail on all the seas, as far as a ship can go. And I have met people who had never been on the sea, and yet they were as though it was their home. When I sailed the brig *Clara* for Skipper Andersen, I had such a lad on board as ordinary seaman. He had never bathed in the sea; but one day, as we were lying at anchor, and the others were swimming around, he jumped into the water too— now this is God's truth—as though he were tumbling into his mother's arms; he thought that swimming came of its own accord. He went straight to the bottom, and was half dead before we fished him up again. "

"The devil may understand the sea! " cried Master Andres breathlessly. "It is curved like an arch everywhere, and it can get up on its hind legs and stand like a wall, although it's a fluid! And I have read in a book that there is so much silver in the sea that every man in the whole world might be rich. "

"Thou righteous God! " cried Bjerregrav, "such a thing I have never heard. Now does that come from all the ships that have gone down? Yes, the sea—that, curse it, is the greatest power! "

"It's ten o'clock, " said Jeppe. "And the lamp is going out—that devil's contrivance! " They broke up hastily, and Pelle turned the lamp out.

But long after he had laid his head on his pillow everything was going round inside it. He had swallowed everything, and imaginary pictures thronged in his brain like young birds in an over-full nest, pushing and wriggling to find a place wherein to rest. The sea was strong; now in the wintertime the surging of the billows against the cliffs was continually in his ear. Pelle was not sure whether it would stand aside for him! He had an unconscious reluctance to set himself limits, and as for the power about which they had all been disputing, it certainly had its seat in Pelle himself, like a vague consciousness that he was, despite all his defeats, invincible.

At times this feeling manifested itself visibly and helped him through the day. One afternoon they were sitting and working, after having swallowed their food in five minutes, as their custom was; the journeyman was the only one who did not grudge himself a brief mid-day rest, and he sat reading the newspaper. Suddenly he raised his head and looked wonderingly at Pelle. "Now what's this? Lasse Karlson—isn't that your father? "

"Yes, " answered Pelle, with a paralyzed tongue, and the blood rushed to his cheeks. Was Father Lasse in the news? Not among the accidents? He must have made himself remarkable in one way or another through his farming! Pelle was nearly choking with excitement, but he did not venture to ask, and Little Nikas simply sat there and looked secretive. He had assumed the expression peculiar to the young master.

But then he read aloud: "Lost! A louse with three tails has escaped, and may be left, in return for a good tip, with the landowner Lasse Karlson, Heath Farm. Broken black bread may also be brought there. "

The others burst into a shout of laughter, but Pelle turned an ashen gray. With a leap he was across the table and had pulled little Nikas to the ground underneath him; there he lay, squeezing the man's throat with his fingers, trying to throttle him, until he was overpowered. Emil and Peter had to hold him while the knee-strap put in its work.

And yet he was proud of the occurrence; what did a miserable thrashing signify as against the feat of throwing the journeyman to the ground and overcoming the slavish respect he had felt for him! Let them dare to get at him again with their lying allusions, or to make sport of Father Lasse! Pelle was not inclined to adopt circuitous methods.

And the circumstances justified him. After this he received more consideration; no one felt anxious to bring Pelle and his cobbler's tools on top of him, even although the boy could be thrashed afterward.

XI

The skipper's garden was a desert. Trees and bushes were leafless; from the workshop window one could look right through them, and over other gardens beyond, and as far as the backs of the houses in East Street. There were no more games in the garden; the paths were buried in ice and melting snow, and the blocks of coral, and the great conch-shells which, with their rosy mouths and fish-like teeth, had sung so wonderfully of the great ocean, had been taken in on account of the frost.

Manna he saw often enough. She used to come tumbling into the workshop with her school satchel or her skates; a button had got torn off, or a heel had been wrenched loose by a skate. A fresh breeze hovered about her hair and cheeks, and the cold made her face glow. "There is blood! " the young master would say, looking at her delightedly; he laughed and jested when she came in. But Manna would hold on to Pelle's shoulder and throw her foot into his lap, so that he could button her boots. Sometimes she would pinch him secretly and look angry—she was jealous of Morten. But Pelle did not understand; Morten's gentle, capable mind had entirely subjugated him and assumed the direction of their relations. Pelle was miserable if Morten was not there when he had an hour to spare. Then he would run, with his heart in his mouth, to find him; everything else was indifferent to him.

One Sunday morning, as he was sweeping the snow in the yard, the girls were in their garden; they were making a snowman.

"Hey, Pelle! " they cried, and they clapped their mittens; "come over here! You can help us to build a snow-house. We'll wall up the door and light some Christmas-tree candles: we've got some ends. Oh, do come! "

"Then Morten must come too—he'll be here directly! "

Manna turned up her nose. "No, we don't want Morten here! "

"Why not? He's so jolly! " said Pelle, wounded.

"Yes, but his father is so dreadful—everybody is afraid of him. And then he's been in prison. "

"Yes, for beating some one—that's nothing so dreadful! My father was too, when he was a young man. That's no disgrace, for it isn't for stealing. "

But Manna looked at him with an expression exactly like Jeppe's when he was criticizing somebody from his standpoint as a respectable citizen.

"But, Pelle, aren't you ashamed of it? That's how only the very poorest people think—those who haven't any feelings of shame! "

Pelle blushed for his vulgar way of looking at things. "It's no fault of Morten's that his father's like that! " he retorted lamely.

"No, we won't have Morten here. And mother won't let us. She says perhaps we can play with you, but not with anybody else. We belong to a very good family, " she said, in explanation.

"My father has a great farm—it's worth quite as much as a rotten barge, " said Pelle angrily.

"Father's ship isn't rotten! " rejoined Manna, affronted. "It's the best in the harbor here, and it has three masts! "

"All the same, you're nothing but a mean hussy! " Pelle spat over the hedge.

"Yes, and you're a Swede! " Manna blinked her eyes triumphantly, while Dolores and Aina stood behind her and put out their tongues.

Pelle felt strongly inclined to jump over the garden wall and beat them; but just then Jeppe's old woman began scolding from the kitchen, and he went on with his work.

Now, after Christmas, there was nothing at all to do. People were wearing out their old boots, or they went about in wooden shoes. Little Nikas was seldom in the workshop; he came in at meal-times and went away again, and he was always wearing his best clothes. "He earns his daily bread easily, " said Jeppe. Over on the mainland they didn't feed their people through the winter; the moment there was no more work, they kicked them out.

In the daytime Pelle was often sent on a round through the harbor in order to visit the shipping. He would find the masters standing about there in their leather aprons, talking about nautical affairs; or they would gather before their doors, to gossip, and each, from sheer habit, would carry some tool or other in his hand.

And the wolf was at the door. The "Saints" held daily meetings, and the people had time enough to attend them. Winter proved how insecurely the town was established, how feeble were its roots; it was not here as it was up in the country, where a man could enjoy himself in the knowledge that the earth was working for him. Here people made themselves as small and ate as little as possible, in order to win through the slack season.

In the workshops the apprentices sat working at cheap boots and shoes for stock; every spring the shoemakers would charter a ship in common and send a cargo to Iceland. This helped them on a little. "Fire away! " the master would repeat, over and over again; "make haste—we don't get much for it! "

The slack season gave rise to many serious questions. Many of the workers were near to destitution, and it was said that the organized charities would find it very difficult to give assistance to all who applied for it. They were busy everywhere, to their full capacity. "And I've heard it's nothing here to what it is on the mainland, " said Baker Jorgen. "There the unemployed are numbered in tens of thousands. "

"How can they live, all those thousands of poor people, if the unemployment is so great? " asked Bjerregrav. "The need is bad enough here in town, where every employer provides his people with their daily bread. "

"Here no one starves unless he wants to, " said Jeppe. "We have a well-organized system of relief. "

"You're certainly becoming a Social Democrat, Jeppe, " said Baker Jorgen; "you want to put everything on to the organized charities! "

Wooden-leg Larsen laughed; that was a new interpretation.

"Well, what do they really want? For they are not freemasons. They say they are raising their heads again over on the mainland. "

"Well, that, of course, is a thing that comes and goes with unemployment, " said Jeppe. "The people must do something. Last winter a son of the sailmaker's came home—well, he was one of them in secret. But the old folks would never admit it, and he himself was so clever that he got out of it somehow. "

"If he'd been a son of mine he would have got the stick, " said Jorgen.

"Aren't they the sort of people who are making ready for the millennium? We've got a few of their sort here, " said Bjerregrav diffidently.

"D'you mean the poor devils who believe in the watchmaker and his 'new time'? Yes, that may well be, " said Jeppe contemptuously. "I have heard they are quite wicked enough for that. I'm inclined to think they are the Antichrist the Bible foretells. "

"Ah, but what do they really want? " asked Baker Jorgen. "What is their madness really driving at? "

"What do they want? " Wooden-leg Larsen pulled himself together. "I've knocked up against a lot of people, I have, and as far as I can understand it they want to get justice; they want to take the right of coining money away from the Crown and give it to everybody. And they want to overthrow everything, that is quite certain. "

"Well, " said Master Andres, "what they want, I believe, is perfectly right, only they'll never get it. I know a little about it, on account of Garibaldi. "

"But what *do* they want, then, if they don't want to overthrow the whole world? "

"What do they want? Well, what do they want? That everybody should have exactly the same? " Master Andres was uncertain.

"Then the ship's boy would have as much as the captain! No, it would be the devil and all! " Baker Jorgen smacked his thigh and laughed.

"And they want to abolish the king, " said Wooden-leg Larsen eagerly.

"Who the devil would reign over us then? The Germans would soon come hurrying over! That's a most wicked thing, that Danish people should want to hand over their country to the enemy! All I wonder is that they don't shoot them down without trial! They'd never be admitted to Bornholm. "

"That we don't really know! " The young master smiled.

"To the devil with them—we'd all go down to the shore and shoot them: they should never land alive! "

"They are just a miserable rabble, the lot of them, " said Jeppe. "I should very much like to know whether there is a decent citizen among them. "

"Naturally, it's always the poor who complain of poverty, " said Bjerregrav. "So the thing never comes to an end. "

Baker Jorgen was the only one of them who had anything to do. Things would have to be bad indeed before the people stopped buying his black bread. He even had more to do than usual; the more people abstained from meat and cheese, the more bread they ate. He often hired Jeppe's apprentices so that they might help him in the kneading.

But he was not in a happy frame of mind. He was always shouting his abuse of Soren through the open doors, because the latter would not go near his buxom young wife. Old Jorgen had taken him and put him into bed with her with his own hands, but Soren had got out of the business by crying and trembling like a new-born calf.

"D'you think he's perhaps bewitched? " asked Master Andres.

"She's young and pretty, and there's not the least fault to be found with her—and we've fed him with eggs right through the winter. She goes about hanging her head, she gets no attention from him. 'Marie! Soren! ' I cry, just to put a little life into them—he ought to be the sort of devil I was, I can tell you! She laughs and blushes, but Soren, he simply sneaks off. It's really a shame—so dainty as she is too, in every way. Ah, it ought to have been in my young days, I can tell you! "

"You are still young enough, Uncle Jorgen! " laughed Master Andres.

"Well, a man could almost bring himself to it—when he considers what a dreadful injustice is going on under his own eyes. For, look you, Andres, I've been a dirty beast about all that sort of thing, but I've been a jolly fellow too; people were always glad to be on board with me. And I've had strength for a booze, and a girl; and for hard work in bad weather. The life I've led—it hasn't been bad; I'd live it all over again the same. But Soren—what sort of a strayed weakling is he? He can't find his own way about! Now, if only you would have a chat with him—you've got some influence over him. "

"I'll willingly try. "

"Thanks; but look here, I owe you money. " Jorgen took ten kroner and laid them on the table as he was going.

"Pelle, you devil's imp, can you run an errand for me? " The young master limped into the cutting-out room, Pelle following on his heels.

A hundred times a day the master would run to the front door, but he hurried back again directly; he could not stand the cold. His eyes were full of dreams of other countries, whose climates were kinder, and he spoke of his two brothers, of whom one was lost in South America—perhaps murdered. But the other was in Australia, herding sheep. He earned more at that than the town magistrate received as salary, and was the cleverest boxer in the neighborhood. Here the master made his bloodless hands circle one round the other, and let them fall clenched upon Pelle's back. "That, " he said, in a superior tone, "is what they call boxing. Brother Martin can cripple a man with one blow. He is paid for it, the devil! " The master shuddered. His brother had on several occasions offered to send him his steamer-ticket, but there was that damned leg. "Tell me what I should do over there, eh, Pelle? "

Pelle had to bring books from the lending library every day, and he soon learned which writers were the most exciting. He also attempted to read himself, but he could not get on with it; it was more amusing to stand about by the skating-pond and freeze and watch the others gliding over the ice. But he got Morten to tell him of exciting books, and these he brought home for the master; such was the "Flying Dutchman. " "That's a work of poetry, Lord alive! " said the master, and he related its contents to Bjerregrav, who took them all for reality.

"You should have played some part in the great world, Andres—I for my part do best to stay at home here. But you could have managed it—I'm sure of it. "

"The great world! " said the master scornfully. No, he didn't take much stock in the world—it wasn't big enough. "If I were to travel, I should like to look for the way into the interior of the earth— they say there's a way into it in Iceland. Or it would be glorious to make a voyage to the moon; but that will always be just a story. "

At the beginning of the new year the crazy Anker came to the young master and dictated a love-letter to the eldest daughter of the king. "This year he will surely answer, " he said thoughtfully. "Time is passing, and fortune disappears, and there are few that have their share of it; we need the new time very badly. "

"Yes, we certainly do, " said Master Andres. "But if such a misfortune should happen that the king should refuse, why, you are man enough to manage the matter yourself, Anker! "

It was a slack season, and, just as it was at its very worst, shoemaker Bohn returned and opened a shop on the marketplace. He had spent a year on the mainland and had learned all sorts of modern humbug. There was only one pair of boots in his window, and those were his own Sunday boots. Every Monday they were put out and exhibited again, so that there should be something to look at.

If he himself was in the shop, talking to the people, his wife would sit in the living-room behind and hammer on a boot, so that it sounded as though there were men in the workshop.

But at Shrovetide Jeppe received some orders. Master Andres came home quite cheerfully one day from Bjerhansen's cellar; there he had made the acquaintance of some of the actors of a troupe which had just arrived. "They are fellows, too! " he said, stroking his cheeks. "They travel continually from one place to another and give performances—they get to see the world! " He could not sit quiet.

The next morning they came rioting into the workshop, filling the place with their deafening gabble. "Soles and heels! " "Heels that won't come off! " "A bit of heel-work and two on the snout! " So they went on, bringing great armfuls of boots from under their cloaks, or fishing them out of bottomless pockets, and throwing them in heaps on the window-bench, each with his droll remarks. Boots and shoes they called "understandings"; they turned and twisted every word, tossing it like a ball from mouth to mouth, until not a trace of sense was left in it.

The apprentices forgot everything, and could scarcely contain themselves for laughing, and the young master overflowed with wit— he was equal to the best of them. Now one saw that he really might have luck with the women: there was no boasting or lying about it. The young actress with the hair like the lightest flax could not keep her eyes off him, although she evidently had all the others at her petticoat-tails; she made signs to her companions that they should admire the master's splendid big mustache. The master had forgotten his lame leg and thrown his stick away; he was on his knees, taking the actress's measure for a pair of high boots with patent tops and concertina-like folds in the legs. She had a hole in the heel of her stocking, but she only laughed over it; one of the actors cried "Poached egg! " and then they laughed uproariously.

Old Jeppe came tumbling into the room, attracted by the merriment. The blonde lady called him "Grandfather, " and wanted to dance with him, and Jeppe forgot his dignity and laughed with the rest. "Yes, it's to us they come when they want to have something good, " he said proudly. "And I learned my trade in Copenhagen, and I used to carry boots and shoes to more than one play-actor there. We had to work for the whole theater; Jungfer Patges, who became so famous later on, got her first dancing shoes from us. "

"Yes, those are the fellows! " said Master Andres, as at last they bustled out; "devil take me, but those are the chaps! " Jeppe could not in the least understand how they had found their way thither, and Master Andres did not explain that he had been to the tavern. "Perhaps Jungfer Patges sent them to me, " he said, gazing into the distance. "She must somehow have kept me in mind. "

Free tickets poured in on them; the young master was in the theater every evening. Pelle received a gallery ticket every time he went

416

round with a pair of boots. He was to say nothing—but the price was plainly marked on the sole with chalk.

"Did you get the money? " the master would ask eagerly; he used to stand on the stairs all the time, waiting. No, Pelle was to present their very best wishes, and to say they would come round and settle up themselves.

"Well, well, people of that sort are safe enough, " said the master.

One day Lasse came stamping into the workshop and into the midst of them all, looking the picture of a big farmer, with his fur collar drawn round his ears. He had a sack of potatoes outside; it was a present to Pelle's employers, because Pelle was learning his trade so well. Pelle was given leave and went out with his father; and he kept looking furtively at the fur collar. At last he could contain himself no longer, but turned it up inquiringly. Disillusioned, he let it fall again.

"Ah, yes—er—well—that's just tacked on to my driving-cloak. It looks well, and it keeps my ears nice and warm. You thought I'd blossomed out into a proper fur coat? No, it won't run to that just yet—but it will soon. And I could name you more than one big farmer who has nothing better than this. "

Yes, Pelle was just a trifle disappointed. But he must admit that there was no difference to be perceived between this cloak and the real bear-skin. "Are things going on all right? " he asked.

"Oh, yes; at present I am breaking stone. I've got to break twenty cords if I'm to pay everybody what's owing to him by the Devil's birthday. [Footnote: The 11th December—the general pay-day and hiring-day. —TB.] So long as we keep our health and strength, Karna and I. "

They drove to the merchant's and put up the horses. Pelle noticed that the people at the merchant's did not rush forward to Lasse quite so eagerly as they did to the real farmers; but Lasse himself behaved in quite an important manner. He stumped right into the merchant's counting-house, just like the rest, filled his pipe at the barrel, and helped himself to a drink of brandy. A cold breath of air hung about him as he went backward and forward from the cart with buttoned-up cloak, and he stamped as loudly on the sharp cobble-stones as though his boot-soles too were made of stone.

Then they went on to Due's cottage; Lasse was anxious to see how matters were prospering there. "It isn't always easy when one of the parties brings a love-child into the business. "

Pelle explained to him how matters stood. "Tell them at Uncle Kalle's that they must take little Maria back again. Anna ill-treats her. They are getting on well in other ways; now they want to buy a wagon and horses and set up as carriers. "

"Do they? Well, it's easy for those to get on who haven't any heart. " Lasse sighed.

"Look, father, " said Pelle suddenly, "there's a theater here now, and I know all the players. I take them their boots, and they give me a ticket every evening. I've seen the whole thing. "

"But, of course, that's all lies, eh? " Lasse had to pull up, in order to scrutinize Pelle's face. "So you've been in a proper theater, eh? Well, those who live in the town have got the devil to thank for it if they are cleverer than a peasant. One can have everything here! "

"Will you go with me to-night? I can get the tickets. "

Lasse was uneasy. It wasn't that he didn't want to go; but the whole thing was so unaccustomed. However, it was arranged that he should sleep the night at Due's, and in the evening they both went to the theater.

"Is it here? " asked Lasse, astounded. They had come to a great building like a barn, before which a number of people were standing. But it was fine inside. They sat right up at the top, at the back, where the seats were arranged like the side of a hill, and they had a view over the whole theater. Down below, right in front, sat some ladies who, so far as Lasse could see, were naked. "I suppose those are the performers? " he inquired.

Pelle laughed. "No, those are the grandest ladies in the town—the doctor's wife, the burgomaster's lady, and the inspector's wife, and such like. "

"What, they are so grand that they haven't enough clothes to wear! " cried Lasse. "With us we call that poverty! But where are the players, then? "

"They are the other side of the curtain. "

"Then have they begun already? "

"No, you can see they haven't—the curtain has to go up first. "

There was a hole in the curtain, and a finger came through it, and began to turn from side to side, pointing at the spectators. Lasse laughed. "That's devilish funny! " he cried, slapping his thighs, as the finger continued to point.

"It hasn't begun yet, " said Pelle.

"Is that so? " This damped Lasse's spirits a little.

But then the big crown-light began suddenly to run up through a hole in the ceiling; up in the loft some boys were kneeling round the hole, and as the light came up they blew out the lamps. Then the curtain went up, and there was a great brightly-lit hall, in which a number of pretty young girls were moving about, dressed in the most wonderful costumes—and they were speaking! Lasse was quite astonished to find that he could understand what they said; the whole thing seemed so strange and foreign to him; it was like a peep into dreamland. But there was one maiden who sat there all alone at her spinning wheel, and she was the fairest of them all.

"That's surely a fine lady? " asked Lasse.

But Pelle whispered that she was only a poor forest maiden, whom the lord of the castle had robbed, and now he wanted to force her to be his sweetheart. All the others were making a tremendous lot of her, combing her golden hair and kneeling before her; but she only looked unhappier than before. And sometimes her sadness was more than she could bear; then she opened her beautiful mouth and her wounded heart bled in song, which affected Lasse so that he had to fetch a long sighing breath.

Then a tall man with a huge red beard came stamping into the hall. Lasse saw that he was dressed like a man who has been keeping Carnival.

"That's the one we made the fine boots for, " whispered Pelle: "the lord of the castle, who wants to seduce her. "

"An ugly devil he looks too! " said Lasse, and spat. "The master at Stone Farm is a child of God compared with him! " Pelle signed to him to be quiet.

The lord of the castle drove all the other women away, and then began to tramp stormily to and fro, eyeing the forest maiden and showing the whites of his eyes. "Well, have you at last decided? " he roared, and snorted like a mad bull. And suddenly he sprang at her as if to take her by force.

"Ha! Touch me not! " she cried, "or by the living God, I will plunge this dagger into my heart! You believe you can buy my innocence because I am poor, but the honor of the poor is not to be bought with gold! "

"That's a true word! " said Lasse loudly.

But the lord of the castle gave a malicious laugh, and tugged at his red beard. He rolled his r's dreadfully.

"Is my offer not enough for you? Come, stay this night with me and you shall receive a farm with ten head of cattle, so that to-morrow you can stand at the altar with your huntsman! "

"Hold your tongue, you whoremonger! " said Lasse angrily.

Those round about him tried to calm him; one or another nudged him in the ribs. "Well, can't a man speak any longer? " Lasse turned crossly to Pelle. "I'm no clergyman, but if the girl doesn't want to, let him leave her alone; at any rate he shan't slake his lust publicly in the presence of hundreds of people with impunity! A swine like that! " Lasse was speaking loudly, and it seemed as though his words had had their effect on the lord of the castle. He stood there awhile staring in front of him, and then called a man, and bade him lead the maiden back to the forest.

Lasse breathed easily again as the curtain fell and the boys overhead by the hole in the ceiling relit the lamps and let them down again. "So far she's got out of it all right, " he told Pelle, "but I don't trust the lord—he's a scoundrel! " He was perspiring freely, and did not look entirely satisfied.

The next scene which was conjured up on the stage was a forest. It was wonderfully fine, with pelargoniums blooming on the ground, and a spring which was flowing out of something green. "That is a covered beer-barrel! " said Pelle, and now Lasse too could see the tap, but it was wonderfully natural. Right in the background one could see the lord's castle on a cliff, and in the foreground lay a fallen tree-trunk; two green-clad huntsmen sat astride of it, concocting their evil schemes. Lasse nodded—he knew something of the wickedness of the world.

Now they heard a sound, and crouched down behind the tree-trunk, each with a knife in his hand. For a moment all was silent; then came the forest maiden and her huntsman, wandering all unawares down the forest path. By the spring they took a clinging and affectionate farewell; then the man came forward, hurrying to his certain death.

This was too much. Lasse stood up. "Look out! " he cried in a choking voice: "look out! " Those behind him pulled his coat and scolded him. "No, devil take you all, I won't hold my tongue! " he cried, and laid about him. And then he leaned forward again: "Look where you're going, d'you hear! Your life is at stake! They're hiding behind the fallen tree! "

The huntsman stood where he was and stared up, and the two assassins had risen to their feet and were staring, and the actors and actresses came through from the wings and gazed upward over the auditorium. Lasse saw that the man was saved, but now he had to suffer for his services; the manager wanted to throw him out. "I can perfectly well go by myself, " he said. "An honorable man is one too many in this company! " In the street below he talked aloud to himself; he was in a blazing temper.

"It was only a play, " said Pelle dejectedly. In his heart he was ashamed of his father.

"You needn't try to teach me about that! I know very well that it all happened long ago and that I can do nothing to alter it, not if I was to stand on my head. But that such low doings should be brought to life again! If the others had felt as I did we should have taken the lord and thrashed him to death, even if it did come a hundred years too late! "

"Why—but that was Actor West, who comes to our workshop every day. "

"Is that so? Actor West, eh? Then you are Actor Codfish, to let yourself be imposed on like that! I have met people before now who had the gift of falling asleep and conjuring up long dead people in their place—but not so real as here, you understand. If you had been behind the curtain you would have seen West lying there like dead, while he, the other one—the Devil—was carrying on and ordering everybody about. It's a gift I'd rather not have; a dangerous game! If the others forget the word of command that brings him back into the body it would be all up with him, and the other would take his place. "

"But that is all superstition! When I know it's West in a play—why, I recognized him at once! "

"Oh, of course! You are always the cleverer! You'd like a dispute with the devil himself every day! So it was only a show? When he was rolling the whites of his eyes in his frantic lust! You believe me—if she hadn't had that knife he would have fallen on her and satisfied his desire in front of everybody! Because if you conjure up long bygone times the action has to have its way, however many there are to see. But that they should do it for money—for money — ugh! And now I'm going home! " Lasse would say nothing more, but had the horses harnessed.

"You had best not go there again, " he said at parting. "But if it has got hold of you already, at least put a knife in your pocket. Yes, and we'll send you your washing by Butcher Jensen, one Saturday, soon. "

Pelle went to the theater as before; he had a shrewd idea that it was only a play, but there *was* something mysterious about it; people must have a supernatural gift who evening after evening could so entirely alter their appearance and so completely enter into the people they represented. Pelle thought he would like to become an actor if he could only climb high enough.

The players created a considerable excitement when they strolled through the streets with their napping clothes and queer head-gear; people ran to their windows to see them, the old folk peeping over their shoulders. The town was as though transformed as long as they were in it.

Every mind had taken a perverse direction. The girls cried out in their sleep and dreamed of abductions; they even left their windows a little open; and every young fellow was ready to run away with the players. Those who were not theater-mad attended religious meetings in order to combat the evil.

And one day the players disappeared — as they had come — and left a cloud of debts behind them. "Devil's trash! " said the master with his despondent expression. "They've tricked us! But, all the same, they were fine fellows in their way, and they had seen the world! "

But after these happenings he could by no means get warm again. He crawled into bed and spent the best part of the month lying there.

XII

It can be very cozy on those winter evenings when everybody sits at home in the workshop and passes the time by doing nothing, because it is so dark and cold out of doors, and one has nowhere to go to. To stand about by the skating-ponds and to look on, frozen, while others go swinging past—well, Pelle has had enough of it; and as for strolling up the street toward the north, and then turning about and returning toward the south, and turning yet again, up and down the selfsame street—well, there is nothing in it unless one has good warm clothes and a girl whose waist one can hold. And Morten too is no fresh-air disciple; he is freezing, and wants to sit in the warmth.

So they slink into the workshop as soon as it begins to grow dark, and they take out the key and hang it on the nail in the entry, in order to deceive Jeppe, and then they secretly make a fire in the stove, placing a screen in front of it, so that Jeppe shall not see the light from it when he makes his rounds past the workshop windows. They crouch together on the ledge at the bottom of the stove, each with an arm round the other's shoulder, and Morten tells Pelle about the books he has read.

"Why do you do nothing but read those stupid books? " asks Pelle, when he has listened for a time.

"Because I want to know something about life and about the world, " answers Morten, out of the darkness.

"Of the world? " says Pelle, in a contemptuous tone. "I want to go out into the world and see things—what's in the books is only lies. But go on. "

And Morten goes on, good-natured as always. And in the midst of his narrative something suddenly occurs to him, and he pulls a paper packet from his breast-pocket: "That's chocolate from Bodil, " he says, and breaks the stick in two.

"Where had she put it? " asks Pelle.

"Under the sheet—I felt something hard under my back when I lay down. "

The boys laugh, while they nibble at the chocolate. Suddenly Pelle says: "Bodil, she's a child-seducer! She enticed Hans Peter away from Stone Farm—and he was only fifteen! "

Morten does not reply; but after a time his head sinks on Pelle's shoulder—his body is twitching.

"Well, you are seventeen, " says Pelle, consoling. "But it's silly all the same; she might well be your mother—apart from her age. " And they both laugh.

It can be still cozier on work-day evenings. Then the fire is burning openly in the stove, even after eight o'clock, and the lamp is shining, and Morten is there again. People come from all directions and look in for a moment's visit, and the cold, an impediment to everything else, awakens all sorts of notable reminiscences. It is as though the world itself comes creeping into the workshop. Jeppe conjures up his apprentice years in the capital, and tells of the great bankruptcy; he goes right back to the beginning of the century, to a wonderful old capital where the old people wore wigs, and the rope's-end was always at hand and the apprentices just kept body and soul together, begging on Sundays before the doors of the townsfolk. Ah, those were times! And he comes home and wants to settle down as master, but the guild won't accept him; he is too young. So he goes to sea as cook, and comes to places down south where the sun burns so fiercely that the pitch melts in the seams and the deck scorches one's feet. They are a merry band, and Jeppe, little as he is, by no means lags behind the rest. In Malaga they storm a tavern, throw all the Spaniards out of the window, and sport with the girls—until the whole town falls upon them and they have to fly to their boat. Jeppe cannot keep up with them, and the boat shoves off, so that he has to jump into the water and swim for it. Knives fall splashing about him in the water, and one sticks shivering in his shoulder-blades. When Jeppe comes to this he always begins to strip his back to show the scar, and Master Andres holds him back. Pelle and Morten have heard the story many a time, but they are willing always to hear it again.

And Baker Jorgen, who for the greater part of his life has been a seaman on the big vessels sailing the northern and southern oceans, talks about capstans and icebergs and beautiful black women from the West Indies. He sets the capstan turning, so that the great three-master makes sail out of the Havana roadstead, and all his hearers feel their hearts grow light.

> "Heave ho, the capstan,
> Waltz her well along!
> Leave the girl a-weeping,
> Strike up the song! "

So they walk round and round, twelve men with their breasts pressed against the heavy capstan-bars; the anchor is weighed, and the sail fills with the wind—and behind and through his words gleam the features of a sweetheart in every port. Bjerregrav cannot help crossing himself—he who has never accomplished anything, except to feel for the poor; but in the young master's eyes everybody travels—round and round the world, round and round the world. And Wooden-leg Larsen, who in winter is quite the well-to-do pensioner, in blue pilot-coat and fur cap, leaves his pretty, solidly-built cottage when the Spring comes, and sallies forth into the world as a poor organ-grinder—he tells them of the Zoological Gardens on the hill, and the adventurous Holm-Street, and of extraordinary beings who live upon the dustbins in the back-yards of the capital.

But Pelle's body creaks whenever he moves; his bones are growing and seeking to stretch themselves; he feels growth and restlessness in every part and corner of his being. He is the first to whom the Spring comes; one day it announces itself in him in the form of a curiosity as to what his appearance is like. Pelle has never asked himself this question before; and the scrap of looking-glass which he begged from the glazier from whom he fetches the glass scrapers tells him nothing truly. He has at bottom a feeling that he is an impossible person.

He begins to give heed to the opinions of others respecting his outward appearance; now and again a girl looks after him, and his cheeks are no longer so fat that people can chaff him about them. His fair hair is wavy; the lucky curl on his forehead is still visible as an obstinate little streak; but his ears are still terribly big, and it is of no use to pull his cap over them, in order to press them close to his head. But he is tall and well-grown for his age, and the air of the workshop has been powerless to spoil his ruddy complexion; and he is afraid of nothing in the world— particularly when he is angry. He thinks out a hundred different kinds of exercise in order to satisfy the demands of his body, but it is of no use. If he only bends over his hammer-work he feels it in every joint of his body.

And then one day the ice breaks and goes out to sea. Ships are fitted out again, and provisioned, and follow the ice, and the people of the town awake to the idea of a new life, and begin to think of green woods and summer clothing.

And one day the fishing-boats arrive! They come gliding across from Hellavik and Nogesund on the Swedish coast. They cut swiftly through the water, heeling far over under their queer lateen sails, like hungry sea-birds that sweep the waves with one wing-tip in their search for booty. A mile to seaward the fishermen of the town receive them with gunshots; they have no permission to anchor in the fishing port, but have to rent moorings for themselves in the old ship's harbor, and to spread out the gear to dry toward the north. The craftsmen of the town come flocking down to the harbor, discussing the foreign thieves who have come from a poorer country in order to take the bread out of the mouths of the townsfolk; for they are inured to all weathers, and full of courage, and are successful in their fishing. They say the same things every Spring, but when they want to buy herrings they deal with the Swedes, who sell more cheaply than the Bornholmers. "Perhaps our fishermen wear leather boots? " inquires Jeppe. "No, they wear wooden shoes week- days and Sunday alike. Let the wooden-shoe makers deal with them—I buy where the fish is cheapest! "

It is as though the Spring in person has arrived with these thin, sinewy figures, who go singing through the streets, challenging the petty envy of the town. There are women, too, on every boat, to mend and clean the gear, and they pass the workshop in crowds, searching for their old lodgings in the poor part of the town near the "Great Power's" home. Pelle's heart leaps at the sight of these young women, with pretty slippers on their feet, black shawls round their oval faces, and many fine colors in their dress. His mind is full of shadowy memories of his childhood, which have lain as quiet as though they were indeed extinguished; vague traditions of a time that he has experienced but can no longer remember; it is like a warm breath of air from another and unknown existence.

If it happens that one or another of these girls has a little child on her arm, then the town has something to talk about. Is it Merchant Lund again, as it was last year? Lund, who since then had been known only as "the Herring Merchant"? Or is it some sixteen- year-old apprentice, a scandal to his pastor and schoolmaster, whose hands he has only just left?

Then Jens goes forth with his concertina, and Pelle makes haste with his tidying up, and he and Morten hurry up to Gallows Hill, hand-in- hand, for Morten finds it difficult to run so quickly. All that the town possesses of reckless youth is there; but the Swedish girls take the lead. They dance and whirl until their slippers fly off, and little battles are fought over them. But on Saturdays the boats do not go to sea; then the men turn up, with smouldering brows, and claim their women, and then there is great slaughter.

Pelle enters into it all eagerly; here he finds an opportunity of that exercise of which his handicraft deprives his body. He hungers for heroic deeds, and presses so close to the fighters that now and again he gets a blow himself. He dances with Morten, and plucks up courage to ask one of the girls to dance with him; he is shy, and dances like a leaping kid in order to banish his shyness; and in the midst of the dance he takes to his heels and leaves the girl standing there. "Damned silly! " say the onlookers, and he hears them laughing behind him. He has a peculiar manner of entering into all this recklessness which lets the body claim its due without thought for the following day and the following year. If some man-hunting young woman tries to capture his youth he lashes out behind, and with a few wanton leaps he is off and away. But he loves to join in the singing when the men and women go homeward with closely-twined arms, and he and Morten follow them, they too with their arms about each other. Then the moon builds her bridge of light across the sea, and in the pinewood, where a white mist lies over the tree-tops, a song rises from every path, heard as a lulling music in the haunts of the wandering couples; insistently melancholy in its meaning, but issuing from the lightest hearts. It is just the kind of song to express their happiness.

"Put up, put up thy golden hair;
A son thou'lt have before a year—
No help in thy clamor and crying!
In forty weeks may'st look for me.
I come to ask how it fares with thee.
The forty weeks were left behind.
And sad she was and sick of mind,
And fell to her clamor and crying—"

And the song continues as they go through the town, couple after couple, wandering as they list. The quiet winding closes ring with songs of love and death, so that the old townsfolk lift their heads from their pillows, and, their nightcaps pushed to one side, wag gravely at all this frivolity. But youth knows nothing of this; it plunges reveling onward, with its surging blood. And one day the old people have the best of it; the blood surges no longer, but there they are, and there are the consequences, and the consequences demand paternity and maintenance. "Didn't we say so? " cry the old folk; but the young ones hang their heads, and foresee a long, crippled existence, with a hasty marriage or continual payments to a strange woman, while all through their lives a shadow of degradation and ridicule clings to them; both their wives and their company must be taken from beneath them. They talk no longer of going out into the world and making their way; they used to strut arrogantly before the old folk and demand free play for their youth, but now they go meekly in harness with hanging heads, and blink shamefacedly at the mention of their one heroic deed. And those who cannot endure their fate must leave the country secretly and by night, or swear themselves free.

The young master has his own way of enjoying himself. He takes no part in the chase after the girls; but when the sunlight is really warm, he sits before the workshop window and lets it warm his back. "Ah, that's glorious! " he says, shaking himself. Pelle has to feel his fur jacket to see how powerful the sun is. "Thank God, now we have the spring here! "

Inside the workshop they whistle and sing to the hammer-strokes; there are times when the dark room sounds like a bird-shop. "Thank God, now we have the spring! " says Master Andres over and over again, "but the messenger of spring doesn't seem to be coming this year. "

"Perhaps he is dead, " says little Nikas.

"Garibaldi dead? Good Lord! he won't die just yet. All the years I can remember he has looked just as he does now and has drunk just as hard. Lord of my body! but how he has boozed in his time, the rascal! But you won't find his equal as a shoemaker all the world over. "

One morning, soon after the arrival of the steamer, a thin, tall, sharp-shouldered man comes ducking through the workshop door. His hands and face are blue with the cold of the morning and his cheeks are rather baggy, but in his eyes burns an undying fire. "Morning, comrades! " he says, with a genial wave of the hand. "Well, how's life treating us? Master well? " He dances into the workshop, his hat pressed flat under his left arm. His coat and trousers flap against his body, revealing the fact that he is wearing nothing beneath them; his feet are thrust bare into his shoes, and he wears a thick kerchief round his neck. But such a manner and a carriage in a craftsman Pelle has never seen in all his days; and Garibaldi's voice alone is like a bell.

"Now, my son, " he says, and strikes Pelle lightly on the shoulder, "can you fetch me something to drink? Just a little, now at once, for I'm murderously thirsty. The master has credit! Pst! We'll have the bottleful—then you needn't go twice. "

Pelle runs. In half a minute he is back again. Garibaldi knows how to do things quickly; he has already tied his apron, and is on the point of passing his opinion on the work in the workshop. He takes the bottle from Pelle, throws it over his shoulder, catches it with the other hand, sets his thumb against the middle of the bottle, and drinks. Then he shows the bottle to the others. "Just to the thumbnail, eh? "

"I call that smart drinking! " says little Nikas.

"It can be done though the night is black as a crow"; Garibaldi waves his hand in a superior manner. "And old Jeppe is alive still? A smart fellow! "

Master Andres strikes on the wall. "He has come in—he is there! " he says, with his wide-opened eyes. After a time he slips into his clothes and comes out into the workshop; he hangs about gossiping, but Garibaldi is sparing of his words; he is still rusty after the night voyage.

A certain feverishness has affected them all; an anxiety lest anything should escape them. No one regards his daily work with aversion to-day; everybody exerts his capacities to the utmost. Garibaldi comes from the great world, and the spirit of adventure and the wandering life exhales from his flimsy clothes.

"If he'll only begin to tell us about it, " whispers Pelle to Jens; he cannot sit still. They hang upon his lips, gazing at him; if he is silent it is the will of Providence. Even the master does not bother him, but endures his taciturnity and little Nikas submits to being treated like an apprentice.

Garibaldi raises his head. "Well, one didn't come here to sit about and idle! " he cries gaily. "Plenty to do, master? "

"There's not much doing here, but we've always work for you, " replies Master Andres. "Besides, we've had an order for a pair of wedding-shoes, white satin with yellow stitching; but we haven't properly tackled it. " He gives little Nikas a meaning glance.

"No yellow stitching with white satin, master; white silk, of course, and white edges. "

"Is that the Paris fashion? " asks Master Andres eagerly. Garibaldi shrugs his shoulders. "Don't let us speak of Paris, Master Andres; here we have neither the leather nor the tools to make Parisian shoes; and we haven't the legs to put into them, either. "

"The deuce! Are they so fashionable? "

"Fashionable! I should say so! I can hold the foot of a well-grown Parisian woman in the hollow of my hand. And when they walk they don't touch the pavement! You could make shoes for a Parisian girl out of whipped cream, and they'd hold together! If you were to fit her with a pair of ordinary woman's beetle-crushers she'd jump straight into the sewer! "

"Well, I'm damned! " The master is hastily cutting some leather to shape. "The devil she would! "

Never did any one make himself at home more easily; Garibaldi draws a seat up to the table and is at once in full swing. No rummaging about after tools; his hand finds his way to the exact spot where the thing required lies, as though an invisible track lay between them. These hands do everything of themselves, quietly, with gentle movements, while the eyes are elsewhere; gazing out into the garden, or examining the young master, or the work of the apprentices. To Pelle and the others, who always have to look at everything from every side in turn, this is absolutely marvelous. And before they have had time to look round Garibaldi has put everything in order, and is sitting there working and looking across the room at the master, who is himself sewing to-day.

And then Jeppe comes tumbling in, annoyed that no one has told him of Garibaldi's arrival. "'Day, master—'day, craft-master! " says Garibaldi, who stands up and bows.

"Yes, " says Jeppe self-consciously, "if there were craft-masters still, I should be one. But manual work is in a wretched case to-day; there's no respect for it, and where shall a man look for respect if he doesn't respect himself? "

"That's meant for the young master, eh? " says Garibaldi laughing. "But times have altered, Master Jeppe; knee-straps and respect have given out; yes, those days are over! Begin at seven, and at six off and away! So it is in the big cities! "

"Is that this sosherlism? " says Jeppe disdainfully.

"It's all the same to me what it is—Garibaldi begins and leaves off when it pleases him! And if he wants more for his work he asks for it! And if that doesn't please them—then adieu, master, adieu! There are slaves enough, said the boy, when he got no bread. "

The others did not get very much done; they have enough to do to watch Garibaldi's manner of working. He has emptied the bottle, and now his tongue is oiled; the young master questions him, and Garibaldi talks and talks, with continual gestures. Not for a moment do his hands persist at their work; and yet the work progresses so quickly it is a revelation to watch it; it is as though it were proceeding of itself. His attention is directed upon their work, and he always interferes at the right moment; he criticizes their way of holding their tools, and works out the various fashions of cut which lend beauty to the heel and sole. It is as though he feels it when they do anything wrongly; his spirit pervades the whole workshop. "That's how one does it in Paris, " he says, or "this is Nuremberg fashion. " He speaks of Vienna and Greece in as matter-of-fact a way as though they lay yonder under Skipper Elleby's trees. In Athens he went to the castle to shake the king by the hand, for countrymen should always stand by one another in foreign parts.

"He was very nice, by the by; but he had had his breakfast already. And otherwise it's a damned bad country for traveling; there are no shoemakers there. No, there I recommend you Italy—there are shoemakers there, but no work; however, you can safely risk it and beg your way from place to place. They aren't like those industrious Germans; every time you ask them for a little present they come and say, 'Come in, please, there is some work you can do! ' And it is so warm there a man can sleep on the bare ground. Wine flows in every gutter there, but otherwise it's no joke. " Garibaldi raises the empty bottle high in the air and peeps wonderingly up at the shelves; the young master winks at Pelle, and the latter fetches another supply of drink at the gallop.

The hot blood is seething in Pelle's ears. He must go away, far away from here, and live the wandering life, like Garibaldi, who hid himself in the vineyards from the gendarmes, and stole the bacon from the chimneys while the people were in the fields. A spirit is working in him and the others; the spirit of their craft. They touch their tools and their material caressingly with their fingers; everything one handles has an inward color of its own; which tells one something. All the dustiness and familiarity of the workshop is swept away; the objects standing on the shelves glow with interest; the most tedious things contain a radiant life of their own.

The world rises before them like a cloudy wonder, traversed by endless highways deep in white dust, and Garibaldi treads them all. He has sold his journeyman's pass to a comrade for a slice of bread and butter, and is left without papers; German policemen give chase to him, and he creeps through the vineyards for fourteen days, on hands and knees, getting nothing for his pains but grapes and a shocking attack of summer cholera. Finally his clothes are so very much alive that he no longer needs to move of himself; he simply lies quiet, and lets himself be carried along until he comes to a little town. "An inn? " asks Garibaldi. Yes, there is an inn. There he tells a story to the effect that he has been robbed; and the good people put him to bed, and warm and dry his clothes. Garibaldi snores, and pushes the chair nearer the stove; snores, and pushes it a little further; and as his clothes burst into a blaze he starts up roaring and scolding and weeping, and is inconsolable. So then he is given fine new clothes and new papers, and is out on the road again, and the begging begins afresh; mountains rise and pass him by, and great cities too, cities with wide rivers. There are towns in which the wandering journeyman can get no money, but is forced to work;

damnable places, and there are German hostels where one is treated
like a prisoner; all clothes must be taken off in a long corridor, even
to one's shirt; a handful of men examine them, and then everything
is put safely away. Thirty or forty naked men are admitted, one after
another, to the great bare dormitory.

Paris—the name is like a bubble bursting in one's ear! There
Garibaldi has worked for two years, and he has been there a score of
times on passing visits. Paris is the glory of the whole world massed
together, and all the convenient contrivances of the world brought to
a state of perfection. Here in the town no respectable shoemaker will
mend the dirty shoes of the "Top-galeass"; she goes about in down-
trodden top-boots, or, if the snipping season has been poor, she
wears wooden shoes. In Paris there are women who wear shoes at
twenty guineas a pair, who carry themselves like queens, earn forty
thousand pounds a year, and are yet nothing but prostitutes. Forty
thousand! If another than Garibaldi had said it he would have had
all the lasts thrown at his head!

Pelle does not hear what the master says to him, and Jens is in a
great hurry for the cobbler's wax; he has cut the upper of the shoe he
is soling. They are quite irresponsible; as though bewitched by this
wonderful being, who goes on pouring brandy down his throat, and
turning the accursed drink into a many-colored panorama of the
whole world, and work that is like a miracle.

The news has soon spread, and people come hurrying in to see
Garibaldi, and perhaps to venture to shake him by the hand; Klausen
wants to borrow some pegs, and Marker, quite unabashed, looks in
to borrow the biggest last. The old cobbler Drejer stands modestly in
a corner and says "Yes, yes! " to the other's remarks. Garibaldi has
reached him his hand, and now he can go home to his gloomy shop
and his dirty stock and his old man's solitude. The genius of the craft
has touched him, and for the rest of his days has shed a light upon
his wretched work of patching and repairing; he has exchanged a
handshake with the man who made the cork-soled boots for the
Emperor of Germany himself when he went out to fight the French.
And the crazy Anker is there too; but does not come in, as he is shy
of strangers. He walks up and down the yard before the workshop
window, and keeps on peeping in. Garibaldi points his finger to his
forehead and nods, and Anker does the same; he is shaking with
suppressed laughter, as over some excellent joke, and runs off like a
child who must hide himself in a corner in order to savor his delight.

Baker Jorgen is there, bending down with his hands on his thighs, and his mouth wide open. "Lor' Jiminy! " he cries from time to time; "did ever one hear the like! " He watches the white silk run through the sole and form itself into glistening pearls along the edge. Pearl after pearl appears; Garibaldi's arms fly about him, and presently he touches the baker on the hip. "Am I in the way? " asks old Jorgen. "No, God forbid—stay where you are! " And his arms fly out again, and the butt of the bodkin touches the baker with a little click. "I'm certainly in the way, " says Jorgen, and moves a few inches. "Not in the least! " replies Garibaldi, stitching away. Then out fly his arms again, but this time the point of the bodkin is turned toward the baker. "Now, good Lord, I can see I'm in the way! " says Jorgen, rubbing himself behind. "Not at all! " replies Garibaldi courteously, with an inviting flourish of his hand. "Pray come nearer. " "No, thank you! No, thank you! " Old Jorgen gives a forced laugh, and hobbles away.

Otherwise Garibaldi lets them come and stare and go as they like. It does not trouble him that he is an eminent and remarkable person; quite unperturbed, he puts the brandy-bottle to his lips and drinks just as long as he is thirsty. He sits there, playing thoughtlessly with knife and leather and silk, as though he had sat on the stool all his life, instead of having just fallen from the moon. And about the middle of the afternoon the incomparable result is completed; a pair of wonderful satin shoes, slender as a neat's tongue, dazzling in their white brilliance, as though they had just walked out of the fairy-tale and were waiting for the feet of the Princess.

"Look at them, damn it all! " says the master, and passes them to little Nikas, who passes them round the circle. Garibaldi throws back his close-cropped gray head.

"You need not say who has made them—everybody can see that. Suppose now the shoes go to Jutland and are worn there and are thrown on the rubbish-heap. One day, years hence, some porridge-eater goes ploughing; a scrap of the instep comes to the surface; and a wandering journeyman, who is sitting in the ditch nibbling at his supper, rakes it toward him with his stick. That bit of instep, he says, that, or the Devil may fry me else, was part of a shoe made by Garibaldi—deuce take me, he says, but that's what it was. And in that case the journeyman must be from Paris, or Nuremberg, or Hamburg—one or the other, that's certain. Or am I talking nonsense, master? "

No; Master Andres can asseverate this is no nonsense—he who from childhood lived with Garibaldi on the highways and in great cities, who followed him so impetuously with that lame leg of his that he remembers Garibaldi's heroic feats better than Garibaldi himself. "But now you will stay here, " he says persuasively. "Now we'll work up the business—we'll get all the fine work of the whole island. " Garibaldi has nothing against this; he has had enough of toiling through the world.

Klausen will gladly make one of the company; in the eyes of all those present this proposal is a dream which will once more raise the craft to its proper level; will perhaps improve it until the little town can compete with Copenhagen. "How many medals have you really received? " says Jeppe, as he stands there with a great framed diploma in his hand. Garibaldi shrugs his shoulders. "I don't know, old master; one gets old, and one's hand gets unsteady. But what is this? Has Master Jeppe got the silver medal? "

Jeppe laughs. "For this I have to thank a tramp by the name of Garibaldi. He was here four years ago and won the silver medal for me! " Well—that is a thing Garibaldi has long forgotten! But medals are scattered about wherever he has been.

"Yes, there are a hundred masters knocking about who boast of their distinctions: first-class workshop—you can see it for yourself— 'a silver medal. ' But who did the work? Who got his day's wages and an extra drop of drink and then—good-bye, Garibaldi! What has one to show for it, master? There are plenty of trees a man can change his clothes behind—but the shirt? " For a moment he seems dejected. "Lorrain in Paris gave me two hundred francs for the golden medal I won for him; but otherwise it was always—Look in my waistcoat pocket! or—I've an old pair of trousers for you, Garibaldi! But now there's an end to that, I tell you; Garibaldi has done with bringing water to the mill for the rich townsfolk; for now he's a sosherlist! " He strikes the table so that the glass scrapers jingle. "That last was Franz in Cologne—gent's boots with cork socks. He was a stingy fellow; he annoyed Garibaldi. I'm afraid this isn't enough for the medal, master, I said; there's too much unrest in the air. Then he bid me more and yet more—but it won't run to the medal—that's all I will say. At last he sends Madame to me with coffee and Vienna bread—and she was in other respects a lady, who drove with a lackey on the box. But we were furious by that time! Well, it was a glorious distinction—to please Madame. "

"Had he many journeymen? " asks Jeppe.

"Oh, quite thirty or forty. "

"Then he must have been somebody. " Jeppe speaks in a reproving tone.

"Somebody—yes—he was a rascal! What did it matter to me that he had a lot of journeymen? I didn't cheat them out of their wages! "

Now Garibaldi is annoyed; he takes off his apron, puts his hat on sideways, and he goes into the town.

"Now he's going to look for a sweetheart! " says the young master; "he has a sweetheart in every town. "

At eight he comes sailing into the workshop again. "What, still sitting here? " he says to the apprentices. "In other parts of the world they have knocked off work two hours ago. What sort of slaves are you to sit crouching here for fourteen hours? Strike, damn it all! "

They look at one another stupidly. "Strike—what is that? "

Then comes the young master. "Now it would do one good to warm one's eyes a bit, " says Garibaldi.

"There's a bed made up for you in the cutting-out room, " says the master. But Garibaldi rolls his coat under his head and lies down on the window-bench. "If I snore, just pull my nose, " he says to Pelle, and goes to sleep. Next day he makes two pairs of kid boots with yellow stitching—for little Nikas this would be a three days' job. Master Andres has all his plans ready—Garibaldi is to be a partner. "We'll knock out a bit of wall and put in a big shop-window! " Garibaldi agrees—he really does for once feel a desire to settle down. "But we mustn't begin too big, " he says: "this isn't Paris. " He drinks a little more and does not talk much; his eyes stray to the wandering clouds outside.

On the third day Garibaldi begins to show his capacities. He does not do much more work, but he breaks a heavy stick in two with one blow as it flies through the air, and jumps over a stick which he holds in both hands. "One must have exercise, " he says restlessly.

He balances an awl on the face of a hammer and strikes it into a hole in the sole of a boot.

And suddenly he throws down his work. "Lend me ten kroner, master, " he says; "I must go and buy myself a proper suit. Now I'm settled and a partner in a business I can't go about looking like a pig. "

"It will be better for you to get that finished, " says the master quietly, pushing Garibaldi's work across to little Nikas. "We shan't see him again! "

This is really the case. He will go into the town with the honorable intentions, to buy something, and then he will be caught and whirled out into the great world, far away, quite at hazard. "He's on the way to Germany with some skipper already, " says the master.

"But he hasn't even said good-bye! " The master shrugs his shoulders.

He was like a falling star! But for Pelle and the others he signified more than that; they learned more in three days than in the whole course of their apprenticeship. And they saw brilliant prospects for the craft; it was no hole-and-corner business after all; with Garibaldi, they traveled the whole wonderful world. Pelle's blood burned with the desire to wander; he knew now what he wanted. To be capable as Garibaldi—that genius personified; and to enter the great cities with stick and knapsack as though to a flourish of trumpets.

They all retained traces of his fleeting visit. Something inside them had broken with a snap; they gripped their tools more freely, more courageously; and they had seen their handicraft pass before their eyes like a species of technical pageant. For a long time the wind of the passage of the great bird hung about the little workshop with its atmosphere of respectable citizenship.

And this fresh wind in one's ears was the spirit of handicraft itself which hovered above their heads—borne upon its two mighty pinions—genius and debauchery.

But one thing remained in Pelle's mind as a meaningless fragment— the word "strike. " What did it mean?

XIII

One could not be quite as cheerful and secure here as one could at home in the country; there was always a gnawing something in the background, which kept one from wholly surrendering oneself. Most people had wandered hither in search of fortune—poverty had destroyed their faculty of surrendering to fate; they were weary of waiting and had resolved to take matters into their own hands. And now here they were, sunk in wretchedness. They could not stir from the spot; they only labored and sunk deeper into the mire. But they continued to strive, with the strength of their bodies, until that gave way, and it was all over with them.

Pelle had often enough wondered to see how many poor people there were in the town. Why did not they go ahead with might and main until they were well off? They had all of them had intentions of that kind, but nothing came of them. Why? They themselves did not understand why, but bowed their heads as though under a curse. And if they raised them again it was only to seek that consolation of the poor—alcohol, or to attend the meetings of the home missions.

Pelle could not understand it either. He had an obscure sense of that joyous madness which arises from poverty itself, like a dim but wonderful dream of reaching the light. And he could not understand why it failed; and yet he must always follow that impetus upward which resided in him, and scramble up once more. Yet otherwise his knowledge was wide; a patched-up window-pane, or a scurfy child's head, marked an entrance to that underworld which he had known so well from birth, so that he could have found his way about it with bandaged eyes. He attached no particular importance to it, but in this direction his knowledge was continually extended; he "thee'd and thou'd" poor people from the first moment, and knew the mournful history of every cottage. And all he saw and heard was like a weary refrain—it spoke of the same eternally unalterable longing and the same defeats. He reflected no further about the matter, but it entered into his blood like an oppression, purged his mind of presumption, and vitiated his tense alertness. When he lay his head on his pillow and went to sleep the endless pulsing of his blood in his ears became the tramping of weary hordes who were for ever passing in their blind groping after the road which should lead to light and happiness. His consciousness did not grasp it, but it brooded oppressively over his days.

The middle-class society of the town was still, as far as he was concerned, a foreign world. Most of the townsfolk were as poor as church mice, but they concealed the fact skilfully, and seemed to have no other desire than to preserve appearances. "Money! " said Master Andres; "here there's only one ten-kroner note among all the employers in the town, and that goes from hand to hand. If it were to stop too long with one of them all the rest of us would stop payment! " The want of loose capital weighed on them oppressively, but they boasted of Shipowner Monsen's money—there were still rich people in the town! For the rest, each kept himself going by means of his own earnings; one had sent footwear to the West Indies, and another had made the bride-bed for the burgomaster's daughter; they maintained themselves as a caste and looked down with contempt upon the people.

Pelle himself had honestly and honorably intended to follow the same path; to keep smiles for those above him and harsh judgments for those below him; in short, like Alfred, to wriggle his way upward. But in the depths of his being his energies were working in another direction, and they continually thrust him back where he belonged. His conflict with the street-urchins stopped of itself, it was so aimless; Pelle went in and out of their houses, and the boys, so soon as they were confirmed, became his comrades.

The street boys sustained an implacable conflict with those who attended the town school and the grammar-school. They called them pigs, after the trough-like satchels which they carried on their backs. Pelle found himself between a double fire, although he accepted the disdain and the insult of those above him, as Lasse had taught him, as something that was inherent in the nature of things. "Some are born to command and some to obey, " as Lasse said.

But one day he came to blows with one of them. And having thrashed the postmaster's son until not a clean spot was left on him, he discovered that he now had a crow to pluck with the sons of all the fine folks, or else they would hold him up to ridicule. It was as though something was redeemed at his hands when he managed to plant them in the face of one of these lads, and there seemed to be a particular charm connected with the act of rolling their fine clothes in the mire. When he had thrashed a "pig" he was always in the rosiest of tempers, and he laughed to think how Father Lasse would have crossed himself!

One day he met three grammar-school students, who fell upon him then and there, beating him with their books; there was repayment in every blow. Pelle got his back against the wall, and defended himself with his belt, but could not manage the three of them; so he gave the biggest of them a terrific kick in the lower part of the body and took to his heels. The boy rolled on the ground and lay there shrieking; Pelle could see, from the other end of the street, how the other two were toiling to set him on his legs again. He himself had got off with a black eye.

"Have you been fighting again, you devil's imp? " said the young master.

No! Pelle had fallen and bruised himself.

In the evening he went round the harbor to see the steamer go out and to say good-bye to Peter. He was in a bad temper; he was oppressed by a foreboding of evil.

The steamer was swarming with people. Over the rail hung a swarm of freshly-made journeymen of that year's batch—the most courageous of them; the others had already gone into other trades, had become postmen or farm servants. "There is no employment for us in the shoe trade, " they said dejectedly as they sank. As soon as their journeyman's test-work was done they took to their heels, and new apprentices were taken all along the line. But these fellows here were crossing to the capital; they wanted to go on working at their own trade. The hundreds of apprentices of the little town were there, shouting "Hurrah! " every other moment, for those departing were the heroes who were going forth to conquer the land of promise for them all. "We are coming after you! " they cried. "Find me a place, you! Find me a place! "

Emil stood by the harbor shed, with some waterside workers, looking on. His time was long ago over. The eldest apprentice had not had the pluck to leave the island; he was now a postman in Sudland and cobbled shoes at night in order to live. Now Peter stood on the deck above, while Jens and Pelle stood below and looked up at him admiringly. "Good-bye, Pelle! " he cried. "Give Jeppe my best respects and tell him he can kiss my bootsoles! "

Some of the masters were strolling to and fro on the quay, in order to note that none of their apprentices were absconding from the town.

Jens foresaw the time when he himself would stand there penniless. "Send me your address, " he said, "and find me something over there. "

"And me too, " said Pelle.

Peter spat. "There's a bit of sour cabbage soup—take it home and give it to Jeppe with my love and I wish him good appetite! But give my very best respects to Master Andres. And when I write, then come over—there's nothing to be done in this hole. "

"Don't let the Social Democrats eat you up! " cried some one from among the spectators. The words "Social Democrat" were at this time in every mouth, although no one knew what they meant; they were used as terms of abuse.

"If they come to me with their damned rot they'll get one on the mouth! " said Peter, disdainfully. And then the steamer began to move; the last cheers were given from the outer breakwater. Pelle could have thrown himself into the sea; he was burning with desire to turn his back on it all. And then he let himself drift with the crowd from the harbor to the circus-ground. On the way he heard a few words of a conversation which made his ears burn. Two townsmen were walking ahead of him and were talking.

"They say he got such a kick that he brought up blood, " said the one.

"Yes, it's terrible, the way that scum behaves! I hope they'll arrest the ruffian. "

Pelle crept along behind the tent until he came to the opening. There he stood every evening, drinking everything in by his sense of smell. He had no money to pay his way in; but he could catch a glimpse of a whole host of magnificent things when the curtain was drawn up in order to admit a late-comer. Albinus came and went at will—as always, when jugglers were in the town. He was acquainted with them almost before he had seen them. When he had seen some clever feat of strength or skill he would come crawling out from under the canvas in order to show his companions that he could do the same thing. Then he was absolutely in his element; he would walk on his hands along the harbor railings and let his body hang over the water.

Pelle wanted to go home and sleep on the day's doings, but a happy pair came up to him—a woman who was dancing as she walked, and a timid young workman, whom she held firmly by the arm. "Here, Hans! " she said, "this is Pelle, whose doing it is that we two belong to each other! "

Then she laughed aloud for sheer delight, and Hans, smiling, held out his hand to Pelle. "I ought to thank you for it, " he said.

"Yes, it was that dance, " she said. "If my dancing-shoes hadn't been mended Hans would have run off with somebody else! " She seized Pelle's arm. And then they went on, very much pleased with one another, and Pelle's old merriment returned for a time. He too could perform all sorts of feats of strength.

On the following day Pelle was hired by Baker Jorgensen to knead some dough; the baker had received, at short notice, a large order for ship's biscuit for the *Three Sisters*.

"Keep moving properly! " he would cry every moment to the two boys, who had pulled off their stockings and were now standing up in the great kneading-trough, stamping away, with their hands gripping the battens which were firmly nailed to the rafters. The wooden ceiling between the rafters was black and greasy; a slimy paste of dust and dough and condensed vapor was running down the walls. When the boys hung too heavily on the battens the baker would cry: "Use your whole weight! Down into the dough with you—then you'll get a foot like a fine young lady! "

Soren was pottering about alone, with hanging head as always; now and again he sighed. Then old Jorgen would nudge Marie in the side, and they would both laugh. They stood close together, and as they were rolling out the dough their hands kept on meeting; they laughed and jested together. But the young man saw nothing of this.

"Don't you see? " whispered his mother, striking him sharply in the ribs; her angry eyes were constantly fixed on the pair.

"Oh, leave me alone! " the son would say, moving a little away from her. But she moved after him. "Go and put your arm round her waist— that's what she wants! Let her feel your hands on her hips! Why do you suppose she sticks out her bosom like that? Let her feel your hands on her hips! Push the old man aside! "

443

"Oh, leave me alone! " replied Soren, and he moved further away from her again.

"You are tempting your father to sin—you know what he is! And she can't properly control herself any longer, now that she claims to have a word in the matter. Are you going to put up with that? Go and take her round the waist—strike her if you can't put up with her, but make her feel that you're a man! "

"Well, are you working up there? " old Jorgen cried to the boys, turning his laughing countenance from Marie. "Tread away! The dough will draw all the rottenness out of your bodies! And you, Soren—get a move on you! "

"Yes, get a move on—don't stand there like an idiot! " continued his mother.

"Oh, leave me alone! I've done nothing to anybody; leave me in peace! "

"Pah! " The old woman spat at him. "Are you a man? Letting another handle your wife! There she is, obliged to take up with a gouty old man like that! Pah, I say! But perhaps you are a woman after all? I did once bring a girl into the world, only I always thought she was dead. But perhaps you are she? Yes, make long ears at me! " she cried to the two boys, "you've never seen anything like what's going on here! There's a son for you, who leaves his father to do all the work by himself! "

"Now then, what's the matter with you? " cried old Jorgen jollily. "Is mother turning the boys' heads? " Marie broke into a loud laugh.

Jeppe came to fetch Pelle. "Now you'll go to the Town Hall and get a thrashing, " he said, as they entered the workshop. Pelle turned an ashen gray.

"What have you been doing now? " asked Master Andres, looking sadly at him.

"Yes, and to one of our customers, too! " said Jeppe. "You've deserved that, haven't you? "

"Can't father get him let off the beating? " said Master Andres.

"I have proposed that Pelle should have a good flogging here in the workshop, in the presence of the deputy and his son. But the deputy says no. He wants justice to run its course. "

Pelle collapsed. He knew what it meant when a poor boy went to the town hall and was branded for life. His brain sought desperately for some way of escape. There was only one—death! He could secretly hide the knee-strap under his blouse and go into the little house and hang himself. He was conscious of a monotonous din; that was Jeppe, admonishing him; but the words escaped him; his soul had already began its journey toward death. As the noise ceased he rose silently.

"Well? What are you going out for? " asked Jeppe.

"I'm going to the yard. " He spoke like a sleepwalker.

"Perhaps you want to take the knee-strap out with you? "

Jeppe and the master exchanged a look of understanding. Then Master Andres came over to him. "You wouldn't be so silly? " he said, and looked deep into Pelle's eyes. Then he made himself tidy and went into the town.

"Pelle, you devil's imp, " he said, as he came home, "I've been running from Herod to Pilate, and I've arranged matters so that you can get off if you will ask for pardon. You must go to the grammar-school about one o'clock. But think it over first, as to what you are going to say, because the whole class will hear it. "

"I won't ask for pardon. " It sounded like a cry.

The master looked at Pelle hesitatingly. "But that is no disgrace— if one has done wrong. "

"I have not done wrong. They began it, and they have been making game of me for a long time. "

"But you thrashed him, Pelle, and one mustn't thrash fine folks like that; they have got a doctor's certificate that might be your ruin. Is your father a friend of the magistrate's? They can dishonor you for the rest of your life. I think you ought to choose the lesser evil. "

No, Pelle could not do that. "So let them flog me instead! " he said morosely.

"Then it will be about three o'clock at the town hall, " said the master, shortly, and he turned red about the eyes.

Suddenly Pelle felt how obstinacy must pain the young master, who, lame and sick as he was, had of his own accord gone running about the town for him. "Yes, I'll do it! " he said; "I'll do it! "

"Yes, yes! " replied Master Andres quietly; "for your own sake as well. And I believe you ought to be getting ready now. "

Pelle slunk away; it was not his intention to apologize, and he had plenty of time. He walked as though asleep; everything was dead within him. His thoughts were busy with all sorts of indifferent matters, as though he sought to delay something by chattering; Crazy Anker went by with his bag of sand on his back, his thin legs wobbling under him. "I will help him to carry it, " thought Pelle dejectedly, as he went onward; "I will help him to carry it. "

Alfred came strolling down the street; he was carrying his best walking-stick and was wearing gloves, although it was in the midst of working hours. "If he sees me now he'll turn down the corner by the coal-merchant's, " thought Pelle bitterly. "Oughtn't I to ask him to say a good word for me? He is such an important person! And he still owes me money for soling a pair of boots. "

But Alfred made straight for him. "Have you seen anything of Albinus? He has disappeared! " he said; and his pretty face seemed somehow unusually moved. He stood there chewing at his moustache, just as fine folk do when they are musing over something.

"I've got to go to the town hall, " said Pelle.

"Yes, I know—you've got to be flogged. But don't you know anything of Albinus? " Alfred had drawn him into the coal-merchant's doorway, in order not to be seen in his company.

"Yes, Albinus, Albinus—" Something was dawning in Pelle's mind. "Wait a minute—he—he—I'm sure he has run away with the circus.

446

At least, I believe he has! " Whereat Alfred turned about and ran—
ran in his best clothes!

Of course Albinus had run away with the circus. Pelle could
understand the whole affair perfectly well. The evening before he
had slipped on board Ole Hansen's yacht, which during the night
was to have taken the trick-rider across to Sweden, and now he
would live a glorious life and do what he liked. To run away—that
was the only clear opening in life. Before Pelle knew it, he was down
by the harbor, staring at a ship which was on the point of sailing. He
followed up his inspiration, and went about inquiring after a
vacancy on board some vessel, but there was none.

He sat down by the waterside, and played with a chip of wood. It
represented a three-master, and Pelle gave it a cargo; but every time
it should have gone to sea it canted over, and he had to begin the
loading all over again. All round him carpenters and stone- cutters
were working on the preparations for the new harbor; and behind
them, a little apart, stood the "Great Power, " at work, while, as
usual, a handful of people were loitering near him; they stood there
staring, in uneasy expectation that something would happen. Pelle
himself had a feeling of something ominous as he sat there and
plashed in the water to drive his ship out to sea; he would have
accepted it as a manifestation of the most sacred principle of life had
Jorgensen begun to rage before his eyes.

But the stone-cutter only laid down his hammer, in order to take his
brandy-bottle from under the stone and swallow a mouthful; with
that exception, he stood there bowed over the granite as peacefully
as though there were no other powers in the world save it and him.
He did not see the onlookers who watched him in gaping
expectation, their feet full of agility, ready to take to flight at his
slightest movement.

He struck so that the air moaned, and when he raised himself again
his glance swept over them. Gradually Pelle had concentrated all his
expectations upon this one man, who endured the hatred of the town
without moving an eyelash, and was a haunting presence in every
mind. In the boy's imagination he was like a loaded mine; one stood
there not knowing whether or not it was ignited, and in a moment
the whole might leap into the air. He was a volcano, and the town
existed from day to day by his mercy. And from time to time Pelle

allowed him to shake himself a little—just enough to make the town rock.

But now, moreover, there was a secret between them; the "Great Power" had been punished too for beating the rich folks. Pelle was not slow in deducing the consequences—was there not already a townsman standing and watching him at play? He too was the terror of the people. Perhaps he would join himself to the "Great Power"; there would be little left of the town then! In the daytime they would lie hidden among the cliffs, but at night they came down and plundered the town.

They fell upon all who had earned their living as bloodsuckers; people hid themselves in their cellars and garrets when they heard that Pelle and the "Great Power" were on the march. They hanged the rich shipowner Monsen to the church steeple, and he dangled there a terror and a warning to all. But the poor folk came to them as trustingly as lambs and ate out of their hands. They received all they desired; so poverty was banished from the world, and Pelle could proceed upon his radiant, onward way without a feeling of betrayal.

His glance fell upon the clock on the harbor guard-house; it was nearly three. He sprang up and looked irresolutely about him; he gazed out over the sea and down into the deep water of the harbor, looking for help. Manna and her sisters—they would disdainfully turn their backs upon the dishonored Pelle; they would no longer look at him. And the people would point their fingers at him, or merely look at him, and think: "Ha, there goes the boy who was flogged at the town hall! " Wherever he went in the world it would follow him like a shadow, that he had been flogged as a child; such a thing clings visibly to a man. He knew men and maids and old white-headed men who had come to Stone Farm from places where no one else had ever been. They might come as absolute strangers, but there was something in their past which in spite of all rose up behind them and went whispering from mouth to mouth.

He roamed about, desperately in his helplessness, and in the course of his wanderings came to stone-cutter Jorgensen.

"Well, " said the "Great Power, " as he laid down his hammer, "you've quarrelled nicely with the big townsfolk! Do you think you can keep a stiff upper-lip? " Then he reached for his hammer again. But Pelle took his bearings and ran despondently to the town-hall.

448

XIV

The punishment itself was nothing. It was almost laughable, those few strokes, laid on through his trousers, by the stick of the old gaoler; Pelle had known worse thrashings. But he was branded, an outcast from the society even of the very poorest; he read as much into the compassion of the people to whom he carried boots and shoes. "Good Lord, this miserable booby! Has it gone as far as that with him! " This was what he read in their eyes. Everybody would always stare at him now, and when he went down the street he saw faces in the "spy" mirrors fixed outside the windows. "There goes that shoemaker boy! "

The young master was the only one who treated him precisely as before; and Pelle repaid him for that with the most limitless devotion. He bought on credit for him and saved him from blows where only he could. If the young master in his easy-going way had promised to have something completed and had then forgotten it, Pelle would sit in his place and work overtime on it. "What's it matter to us? " Jens used to say. But Pelle would not have the customers coming to scold Master Andres, nor would he allow him to suffer the want of anything that would keep him on his feet.

He became more intimate than ever with Jens and Morten; they all suffered from the same disgrace; and he often accompanied them home, although no pleasure awaited them in their miserable cottage. They were among the very poorest, although the whole household worked. It was all of no avail.

"Nothing's any use, " the "Great Power" himself would say when he was disposed to talk; "poverty is like a sieve: everything goes straight through it, and if we stop one hole, it's running through ten others at the same time. They say I'm a swine, and why shouldn't I be? I can do the work of three men—yes, but do I get the wages of three? I get my day's wages and the rest goes into the pockets of those who employ me. Even if I wanted to keep myself decent, what should we gain by it? Can a family get decent lodging and decent food and decent clothing for nine kroner a week? Will the means of a laborer allow him to live anywhere but by the refuse-heaps, where only the pigs used to be kept? Why should I be housed like a pig and live like a pig and yet be no pig—is there any sense in that? My wife and children have to work as well as me, and how can things be decent with us when wife and children have to go out and make things decent for other people? No, look here! A peg of brandy, that makes everything seem decent, and if that doesn't do it, why, then, a bottle! " So he would sit talking, when he had been drinking a little, but otherwise he was usually silent.

Pelle knew the story of the "Great Power" now, from the daily gossip of the townsfolk, and his career seemed to him sadder than all the rest; it was as though a fairy-tale of fortune had come to a sudden end.

Among the evil reports which were continually in circulation respecting Stone-cutter Jorgensen—it seemed that there was never an end of them—it was said that in his youth he had strolled into town from across the cliffs, clad in canvas trousers, with cracked wooden shoes on his feet, but with his head in the clouds as though the whole town belonged to him. Brandy he did not touch. He had a better use for his energies, he said: he was full of great ideas of himself and would not content himself with ordinary things. And he was thoroughly capable—he was quite absurdly talented for a poor man. And at once he wanted to begin turning everything topsy-turvy. Just because he was begotten among the cliffs and crags by an old toil- worn stone-cutter, he behaved like a deity of the rocks; he brushed long-established experience aside, and introduced novel methods of work which he evolved out of his own mind. The stone was as though bewitched in his hands. If one only put a sketch before him, he would make devils' heads and subterranean monsters and sea-serpents —the sort of thing that before his time had to be ordered from the sculptors in Copenhagen. Old deserving stone-masons saw themselves suddenly set aside and had then and there to take to breaking stones; and this young fellow who had strayed into the town straightway ignored and discounted the experience of their many years. They tried, by the most ancient of all methods, to teach the young man modesty. But they gave it up. Peter Jorgensen had the strength of three men and the courage of ten. It was not good to meddle with one who had stolen his capacities from God himself, or perhaps was in league with Satan. So they resigned themselves, and avenged themselves by calling him the "Great Power"—and they put their trust in misfortune. To follow in his footsteps meant to risk a broken neck. And whenever the brave townsfolk made the journey, something of its dizzy quality remained with them.

In the night he would sit sketching and calculating, so that no one could understand when he slept; and on Sundays, when decent people went to church, he would stop at home and cut the queerest things out of stone — although he never got a penny for it.

It was at this time that the famous sculptor came from the capital of Germany to hew a great lion out of granite, in honor of Liberty. But he could not get forward with his toolbox full of butter-knives; the stone was too hard for one who was accustomed to stand scratching at marble. And when for once he really did succeed in knocking off a bit of granite, it was always in the wrong place.

Then the "Great Power" asserted himself, and undertook to hew the lion out of granite, according to a scale model of some sort which the sculptor slapped together for him! All were persuaded that he would break down in this undertaking, but he negotiated it so cleverly that he completed the work to the utmost satisfaction of those concerned. He received a good sum of money for this, but it was not enough for him; he wanted half the honor, and to be spoken of in the newspapers like the sculptor himself; and as nothing came of it he threw down his tools and refused to work any more for other people. "Why should I do the work and others have the honor of it? " he asked, and sent in a tender for a stone-cutting contract. In his unbounded arrogance he sought to push to one side those who were born to ride on the top of things. But pride comes before a fall; his doom was already hanging over him.

He had sent in the lowest tender for the work on the South Bridge. They could not disregard it; so they sought to lay every obstacle in his path; they enticed his workmen away from him and made it difficult for him to obtain materials. The district judge, who was in the conspiracy, demanded that the contract should be observed; so the "Great Power" had to work day and night with the few men left to him in order to complete the work in time. A finer bridge no one had ever seen. But he had to sell the shirt off his body in order to meet his engagements.

He lived at that time in a pretty little house that was his own property. It lay out on the eastern highway, and had a turret on the mansard — Jens and Morten had spent their early childhood there. A little garden, with tidy paths, and a grotto which was like a heap of rocks, lay in front of it. Jorgenson had planned it all himself. It was taken from him, and he had to remove to a poor quarter of the town, to live among the people to whom he rightly belonged, and to rent a house there. But he was not yet broken. He was cheerful in spite of his downfall, and more high-and-mighty than ever in his manners. It was not easy to hit him! But then he sent in a tender for the new crane-platform. They could have refused him the contract on the pretext that he had no capital at his disposal. But now he *should* be struck down! He got credit from the savings-bank, in order to get well under way, and workers and material were his to dispose of. And then, as he was in the midst of the work, the same story was repeated—only this time he was to break his neck! Rich and poor, the whole town was at one in this matter. All demanded the restoration of the old certainty, high and low, appointed by God Himself. The "Great Power" was of the humblest descent; now he could quietly go back to the class he was born in!

He failed! The legal proprietor took over a good piece of work and got it for nothing, and Stonemason Jorgensen stood up in a pair of cracked wooden shoes, with a load of debts which he would never be able to shake off. Every one rejoiced to see him return to the existence of a day-laborer. But he did not submit quietly. He took to drink. From time to time he broke out and raged like the devil himself. They could not get rid of him; he weighed upon the minds of all, like an angry rumbling; even when he was quietly going about his work they could not quite forget him. Under these conditions he squandered his last possessions, and he moved into the cottage by the refuse-heaps, where formerly no one had dwelt.

He had become another man since the grant for the great harbor project had been approved. He no longer touched any brandy; when Pelle went out to see his friends, the "Great Power" would be sitting at the window, busying himself with sketches and figures. His wife was moving about and weeping quietly to herself; the old woman was scolding. But Jorgensen turned his broad back upon them and pored silently over his own affairs. He was not to be shaken out of his self-sufficiency.

The mother received them out in the kitchen, when she heard their noisy approach. "You must move quietly—Father is calculating and calculating, poor fellow! He can get no peace in his head since the harbor plans have been seriously adopted. His ideas are always working in him. That must be so, he says, and that so! If he would only take life quietly among his equals and leave the great people to worry over their own affairs! "

He sat in the window, right in the sunlight, adding up some troublesome accounts; he whispered half to himself, and his mutilated forefinger, whose outer joint had been blown off, ran up and down the columns. Then he struck the table. "Oh, if only a man had learned something! " he groaned. The sunlight played on his dark beard; his weary labors had been powerless to stiffen his limbs or to pull him down. Drink had failed to hurt him—he sat there like strength personified; his great forehead and his throat were deeply bronzed by the sun.

"Look here, Morten! " he cried, turning to the boys. "Just look at these figures! "

Morten looked. "What is it, father? "

"What is it? Our earnings during the last week! You can see they are big figures! "

"No, father; what are they? " Morten twined his slender hand in his father's beard.

The "Great Power's" eyes grew mild under this caress.

"It's a proposed alteration—they want to keep the channel in the old place, and that is wrong; when the wind blows in from the sea, one can't get into the harbor. The channel must run out there, and the outer breakwater must curve like this"—and he pointed to his sketches. "Every fisherman and sailor will confirm what I say—but the big engineer gentlemen are so clever! "

"But are you going—again—to send in a tender? " Morten looked at his father, horrified. The man nodded.

"But you aren't good enough for them—you know you aren't! They just laugh at you! "

"This time I shall be the one to laugh, " retorted Jorgensen, his brow clouding at the thought of all the contempt he had had to endure.

"Of course they laugh at him, " said the old woman from the chimney- corner, turning her hawk-like head toward them; "but one must play at something. Peter must always play the great man! "

453

Her son did not reply.

"They say you know something about sketching, Pelle? " he said quietly. "Can't you bring this into order a bit? This here is the breakwater—supposing the water isn't there—and this is the basin —cut through the middle, you understand? But I can't get it to look right—yet the dimensions are quite correct. Here above the water-line there will be big coping-stones, and underneath it's broken stone. "

Pelle set to work, but he was too finicking.

"Not so exact! " said Jorgensen. "Only roughly! "

He was always sitting over his work when they came. From his wife they learned that he did not put in a tender, after all, but took his plans to those who had undertaken the contract and offered them his cooperation. She had now lost all faith in his schemes, and was in a state of continual anxiety. "He's so queer—he's always taken up with only this one thing, " she said, shuddering. "He never drinks — and he doesn't go raging against all the world as he used to do. "

"But that's a good thing, " said Morten consolingly.

"Yes, you may talk, but what do you know about it? If he looks after his daily bread, well, one knows what that means. But now, like this.... I'm so afraid of the reaction if he gets a set-back. Don't you believe he's changed—it's only sleeping in him. He's the same as ever about Karen; he can't endure seeing her crooked figure; she reminds him always too much of everything that isn't as it should be. She mustn't go to work, he says, but how can we do without her help? We must live! I daren't let him catch sight of her. He gets so bitter against himself, but the child has to suffer for it. And he's the only one she cares anything about. "

Karen had not grown during the last few years; she had become even more deformed; her voice was dry and shrill, as though she had passed through a frozen desert on her way to earth. She was glad when Pelle was there and she could hear him talk; if she thought he would come in the evening, she would hurry home from her situation. But she never joined in the conversation and never took part in anything. No one could guess what was going on in her mind. Her mother would suddenly break down and burst into tears if her glance by chance fell upon her.

"She really ought to leave her place at once, " said her mother over and again. "But the doctor's wife has one child after another, and then they ask so pleadingly if she can't stay yet another half-year. They think great things of her; she is so reliable with children. "

"Yes, if it was Pelle, he'd certainly let them fall. " Karen laughed —it was a creaking laugh. She said nothing more; she never asked to be allowed to go out, and she never complained. But her silence was like a silent accusation, destroying all comfort and intimacy.

But one day she came home and threw some money on the table. "Now I needn't go to Doctor's any more. "

"What's the matter? Have you done something wrong? " asked the mother, horrified.

"The doctor gave me a box on the ear because I couldn't carry Anna over the gutter—she's so heavy. "

"But you can't be sent away because he has struck you! You've certainly had a quarrel—you are so stubborn! "

"No; but I accidentally upset the perambulator with little Erik in it— so that he fell out. His head is like a mottled apple. " Her expression was unchanged.

The mother burst into tears. "But how could you do such a thing? " Karen stood there and looked at the other defiantly. Suddenly her mother seized hold of her. "You didn't do it on purpose? Did you do it on purpose? "

Karen turned away with a shrug of the shoulders and went up to the garret without saying good night. Her mother wanted to follow her.

"Let her go! " said the old woman, as though from a great distance. "You have no power over her! She was begotten in wrath. "

XV

All the winter Jens had smeared his upper lip with fowl's dung in order to grow a moustache; now it was sprouting, and he found himself a young woman; she was nurse-maid at the Consul's. "It's tremendous fun, " he said; "you ought to get one yourself. When she kisses me she sticks out her tongue like a little kid. " But Pelle wanted no young woman—in the first place, no young woman would have him, branded as he was; and then he was greatly worried.

When he raised his head from his work and looked out sideways over the manure-sheds and pigsties, he saw the green half-twilight of the heart of the apple-tree, and he could dream himself into it. It was an enchanted world of green shadows and silent movement; countless yellow caterpillars hung there, dangling to and fro, each on its slender thread; chaffinches and yellow-hammers swung themselves impetuously from bough to bough, and at every swoop snapped up a caterpillar; but these never became any fewer. Without a pause they rolled themselves down from the twigs, and hung there, so enticingly yellow, swinging to and fro in the gentle breath of the summer day, and waited to be gobbled up.

And deeper still in the green light—as though on the floor of a green sea—three brightly-clad maidens moved and played. Now and again the two younger would suddenly look over at Pelle, but they turned their eyes away again the moment he looked at them; and Manna was as grown-up and self-controlled as though he had never existed. Manna had been confirmed a long time now; her skirts were halfway to the ground, and she walked soberly along the street, arm-in-arm with her girl friends. She no longer played; she had long been conscious of a rapidly-increasing certainty that it wouldn't do to play any longer. In a few days she went over from Pelle's side to the camp of the grown-ups. She no longer turned to him in the workshop, and if he met her in the street she looked in another direction. No longer did she leap like a wild cat into the shop, tearing Pelle from his stool if she wanted something done; she went demurely up to the young master, who wrapped up her shoes in paper. But in secret she still recognized her playmate; if no one was by she would pinch his arm quite hard, and gnash her teeth together as she passed him.

But Pelle was too clumsy to understand the transition, and too much of a child to be shy of the light himself. He hung hack, lonely, and pondered, uncomprehending, over the new condition of affairs.

But now she did not know him in secret even—he simply did not exist for her any longer. And Dolores and Aina too had withdrawn their favor; when he looked out, they averted their heads and shrugged their shoulders. They were ashamed that they had ever had anything to do with such a person, and he knew very well why that was.

It had been a peculiar and voluptuous delight to be handled by those delicate and generous hands. It had been really splendid to sit there with open mouth and let all three stuff him with delicacies, so that he was in danger of choking! He wasn't allowed to swallow them down—they wanted to see how much his mouth would hold; and then they would laugh and dance round him, and their plump girlish hands would take hold of his head, one on each side, and press his jaws together. Now Pelle had gradually added quite an ell to his stature as a worldly wise citizen; he knew very well that he was of coarser clay than his companions, and that there must have been an end of it all, even without the town hall.

But it hurt him; he felt as though he had been betrayed; properly he oughtn't to touch his food. For was not Manna his betrothed? He had never thought of that! These were the pains of love! So this was what they were like! Did those who took their lives on account of unhappy love feel any different? His grief, to be sure, was not very stupendous; when the young master made a joke or cursed in his funny way he could laugh quite heartily still. That, with his disgrace, was the worst of all.

"You ought to get yourself a young woman, " said Jens. "She's as soft as a young bird, and she warms you through your clothes and everything! "

But Pelle had something else on hand. He wanted to learn to swim. He wanted to know how to do everything that the town boys did, and to win back his place among them. He no longer dreamed of leading them. So he went about with the "gang"; he drew back a little if they teased him too brutally, and then crept back again; finally they grew accustomed to him.

Every evening he ran down to the harbor. To the south of the big basin, which was now being pumped dry, there was always, in the twilight, a crowd of apprentices; they leaped naked among the rocks and swam in chattering shoals toward the west, where the sky still glowed after the sunset. A long way out a reef lay under the water, and on this they could just touch bottom; there they would rest before they swam back, their dark heads brooding on the water like chattering sea-birds.

Pelle swam out with them in order to accustom himself to deep water, although they always tried to pull him under by his legs. When the sea blushed it was as though one was swimming amid roses; and the light, slippery, shining fronds which the deep-lying weed-beds had thrown up gleamed in the evening light and slid gently across his shoulders, and far out in the west lay the land of Fortune, beyond the vast radiant portals of the sunset; or it showed its golden plains stretching out into infinity. There it lay, shining with a strange enticing radiance, so that Pelle forgot the limits of his strength, and swam out farther than his powers justified. And when he turned round, parting the floating weed with vigorous strokes, the water stared at him blackly, and the terror of the depths seized upon him.

One evening the boys had been hostile in their attitude, and one of them maintained that the marks of the whip could still be seen on Pelle's back. "Pelle has never been beaten with a whip! " cried Morten, in a rage. Pelle himself made no reply, but followed the "squadron"; his whole nature felt somehow embittered.

There was a slight swell, and this perhaps washed the swimmers out of their proper course; they could not find the reef on which they were used to rest. For a time they splashed about, trying to find it, and wasting their strength; then they turned back to the shore. Pelle looked after them with wondering eyes.

"Lie on your back and rest! " they cried, as they passed him, and then they made for the beach; a touch of panic had fallen on them. Pelle tried to rest, but he had had no practice in floating; the waves broke over his face; so he labored after the others. On the shore there was great excitement; he wondered what it meant. Morten, who had never bathed with the others, was standing on a rock and was shouting.

Some of the foremost swimmers were already in safety. "You can touch bottom here! " they shouted, standing with outstretched arms, the water up to their chins. Pelle labored on indefatigably, but he was quite convinced that it was useless. He was making hardly any progress, and he was sinking deeper and deeper. Every moment a wave washed over him and filled him with water. The stronger swimmers came out again; they swam round him and tried to help him, but they only made matters worse. He saw Morten run shouting into the water with all his clothes on, and that gave him a little strength. But then suddenly his arms became paralyzed; he went round and round in the same spot, and only his eyes were above water. Pelle had often flown in his dreams, and something had always clutched his legs and hampered his flight. But now this had become reality; he was floating in the blue sky and poised on his outspread pinions; and out of the darkness below he heard voices. "Pelle! " they cried, "little Pelle! " "Yes, Father Lasse! " he answered, and with a sense of relief he folded his weary wings; he sank in whirling haste, and a surging sounded in his ears.

Then of a sudden he felt a violent pain in his shins. His hands clutched at growing plants. He stood up with a leap, and light and air flowed over him as from a new existence. The boys were running about, frightened, one leg in their trousers, and he was standing on the submarine reef, up to the breast in the sea, vomiting salt water. Round about him swimmers were splashing, diving in every direction to fetch him up from the bottom of the sea. It was all really rather funny, and Pelle raised his arms high above his head as a greeting to life, and took the water with a long dive. Some distance farther in he appeared again, and swam to shore, parting the waves like a frolicsome porpoise. But on the beach he fell down as God had made him, in a profound sleep; he had just pulled one stocking over his big toe.

Since that day the boys recognized him again. He had certainly performed no heroic deed, but Destiny had for a moment rested upon his head—that was enough! Pelle always took the steel sharpener with him after that; and laid it on the beach with the point toward the land; he wanted after all to live a little longer. He did not allow himself to be intimidated, but plunged headlong into the water.

If the sea was so rough that they could not swim, they would lie on the brink of the water and let the waves roll them over and over.

Then the waves would come in sweeping flight from the west, as though to spring upon them; the herds of white horses drove onward, their grayish manes streaming obliquely behind them. Rearing they came, sweeping the sea with their white tails, striking out wildly with their hooves and plunging under the surface. But others sprang up and leaped over them in serried ranks. They lay flat on the water and rushed toward the land. The storm whipped the white foam out of their mouths and drove it along the beach, where it hung gleaming on the bushes, and then vanished into nothingness. Right up to the shore they dashed, and then fell dead. But fresh hordes stormed shoreward from the offing, as though the land must be over-run by them; they reared, foaming, and struck at one another; they sprang, snorting and quivering, high in the air; they broke asunder in panic; there was never an end to it all. And far out in the distance the sun went down in a flame-red mist. A streak of cloud lay across it, stretching far out into infinity. A conflagration like a glowing prairie fire surrounded the horizon, and drove the hordes before it in panic-stricken flight, and on the beach shouted the naked swarm of boys. Now and again they sprang up with outspread arms, and, shouting, chased the wild horses back into the sea.

XVI

Things were not going well in the brothers' home. Jorgensen had done nothing with his plans. He was the only person who had not known that such would be the case. The people knew, too, on very good authority, that the engineer had offered him a hundred kroner for them, and as he would not take them, but demanded a share in the undertaking and the honor of executing it, he was shown to the door.

He had never before taken anything so quietly. He did not burst out roaring with violent words; he simply betook himself to his usual day-laborer's work in the harbor, like any other worker. He did not mention his defeat, and allowed no one else to do so. He treated his wife as though she did not exist. But she had to watch him wrap himself up in silence, without knowing what was going on in his mind. She had a foreboding of something terrible, and spoke of her trouble to the boys. He made no scenes, although now and again he got drunk; he ate in silence and went to bed. When he was not working, he slept.

But as he himself had so far revealed his plans that they were known to all, it was all up with his work. The engineer had taken from Jorgensen's plans as much as he could use—every one could see that—and now the "Great Power" stood with his mouth empty, simply because he had put more in his spoon than his mouth would hold. Most people were far from envying his position, and they took plenty of time to talk about it; the town was quite accustomed to neglect its own affairs in order to throw its whole weight on his obstinate back. But now he was down in the dust all had been to the harbor to watch the "Great Power" working there—to see him, as a common laborer, carting the earth for his own wonderful scheme. They marvelled only that he took it all so quietly; it was to some extent a disappointment that he did not flinch under the weight of his burden and break out into impotent raving.

He contented himself with drinking; but that he did thoroughly. He went about it as it were in the midst of a cloud of alcoholic vapor, and worked only just enough to enable him to go on drinking. "He has never yet been like this, " said his wife, weeping. "He doesn't storm and rage, but he is angry all the time so that one can't bear him at home any longer. He breaks everything in his anger, and he scolds

461

poor Karen so that it's wretched. He has no regard for anybody, only for his old mother, and God knows how long that will last. He doesn't work, he only drinks. He steals my hard-earned money out of my dress-pocket and buys brandy with it. He has no shame left in him, although he always used to be so honorable in his way of life. And he can't stand his boozing as he used to; he's always falling about and staggering. Lately he came home all bloody—he'd knocked a hole in his head. What have we ever done to the dear God that he should punish us like this? "

The old woman said nothing, but let her glance sweep from one to the other, and thought her own thoughts.

So it went on, week after week. The boys became weary of listening to their mother's complaints, and kept away from home.

One day, when Karen had been sent on an errand for her mother, she did not return. Neither had she returned on the following day. Pelle heard of it down at the boat-harbor, where she had last been seen. They were dragging the water with nets in the hope of finding her, but no one dared tell Jorgensen. On the following afternoon they brought her to the workshop; Pelle knew what it was when he heard the many heavy footsteps out in the street. She lay on a stretcher, and two men carried her; before her the autumn wind whirled the first falling leaves, and her thin arms were hanging down to the pavement, as though she sought to find a hold there. Her disordered hair was hanging, too, and the water was dripping from her. Behind the stretcher came the "Great Power. " He was drunk. He held one hand before his eyes, and murmured as though in thought, and at every moment he raised his forefinger in the air. "She has found peace, " he said thickly, trying to look intelligent.

"Peace—the higher it is——" He could not find the word he wanted.

Jens and Pelle replaced the men at the stretcher, and bore it home. They were afraid of what was before them. But the mother stood at the door and received them silently, as though she had expected them; she was merely pale. "She couldn't bear it! " she whispered to them, and she kneeled down beside the child.

She laid her head on the little crippled body, and whispered indistinctly; now and again she pressed the child's fingers into her mouth, in order to stifle her sobs. "And you were to have run an errand for mother, " she said, and she shook her head, smilingly. "You are a nice sort of girl to me—not to be able to buy me two skeins of thread; and the money I gave you for it—have you thrown it away? " Her words came between smiles and sobs, and they sounded like a slow lament. "Did you throw the money away? It doesn't matter —it wasn't your fault. Dear child, dear little one! " Then her strength gave way. Her firmly closed mouth broke open, and closed again, and so she went on, her head rocking to and fro, while her hands felt eagerly in the child's pocket. "Didn't you run that errand for mother? " she moaned. She felt, in the midst of her grief, the need of some sort of corroboration, even if it referred to something quite indifferent. And she felt in the child's purse. There lay a few ore and a scrap of paper.

Then she suddenly stood up. Her face was terribly hard as she turned to her husband, who stood against the wall, swaying to and fro. "Peter! " she cried in agony, "Peter! Don't you know what you have done? 'Forgive me, mother, ' it says here, and she has taken four ore of the thirteen to buy sugar-candy. Look here, her hand is still quite sticky. " She opened the clenched hand, which was closed upon a scrap of sticky paper. "Ah, the poor persecuted child! She wanted to sweeten her existence with four ore worth of sugar-candy, and then into the water! A child has so much pleasure at home here! 'Forgive me, mother! ' she says, as though she had done something wrong. And everything she did was wrong; so she had to go away. Karen! Karen! I'm not angry with you—you were very welcome— what do they signify, those few ore! I didn't mean it like that when I reproached you for hanging about at home! But I didn't know what to do—we had nothing to eat. And he spent the little money there was! " She turned her face from the body to the father and pointed to him. It was the first time that the wife of the "Great Power" had ever turned upon him accusingly. But he did not understand her. "She has found peace, " he murmured, and attempted to pull himself up a little; "the peace of—" But here the old woman rose in the chimney-corner—until this moment she had not moved. "Be silent! " she said harshly, setting her stick at his breast, "or your old mother will curse the day when she brought you into the world. " Wondering, he stared at her; and a light seemed to shine through the mist as he gazed. For a time he still stood there, unable to tear his eyes from the body. He looked as though he wished to throw himself down beside his wife, who once more lay bowed above the bier, whispering. Then, with hanging head, he went upstairs and lay down.

XVII

It was after working hours when Pelle went homeward; but he did not feel inclined to run down to the harbor or to bathe. The image of the drowned child continued to follow him, and for the first time Death had met him with its mysterious "Why? ". He found no answer, and gradually he forgot it for other things. But the mystery itself continued to brood within him, and made him afraid without any sort of reason, so that he encountered the twilight even with a foreboding of evil. The secret powers which exhale from heaven and earth when light and darkness meet clutched at him with their enigmatical unrest, and he turned unquietly from one thing to another, although he must be everywhere in order to cope with this inconceivable Something that stood, threatening, behind everything. For the first time he felt, rid of all disguise, the unmercifulness which was imminent in this or that transgression of his. Never before had Life itself pressed upon him with its heavy burden.

It seemed to Pelle that something called him, but he could not clearly discover whence the call came. He crept from his window on to the roof and thence to the gable-end; perhaps it was the world that called. The hundreds of tile-covered roofs of the town lay before him, absorbing the crimson of the evening sky, and a blue smoke was rising. And voices rose out of the warm darkness that lay between the houses. He heard, too, the crazy Anker's cry; and this eternal prophecy of things irrational sounded like the complaint of a wild beast. The sea down yonder and the heavy pine-woods that lay to the north and the south—these had long been familiar to him.

But there was a singing in his ears, and out of the far distance, and something or some one stood behind him, whose warm breath struck upon his neck. He turned slowly about. He was no longer afraid in the darkness, and he knew beforehand that nothing was there. But his lucid mind had been invaded by the twilight, with its mysterious train of beings which none of the senses can confirm.

He went down into the courtyard and strolled about. Everywhere prevailed the same profound repose. Peers, the cat, was sitting on the rain-water butt, mewing peevishly at a sparrow which had perched upon the clothes-line. The young master was in his room, coughing; he had already gone to bed. Pelle bent over the edge of the well and gazed vacantly over the gardens. He was hot and dizzy, but a cool draught rose from the well and soothingly caressed his head. The bats were gliding through the air like spirits, passing so close to his face that he felt the wind of their flight, and turning about with a tiny clapping sound. He felt a most painful desire to cry.

Among the tall currant-bushes yonder something moved, and Sjermanna's head made its appearance. She was moving cautiously and peering before her. When she saw Pelle she came quickly forward.

"Good evening! " she whispered.

"Good evening! " he answered aloud, delighted to return to human society.

"Hush! You mustn't shout! " she said peremptorily.

"Why not? " Pelle himself was whispering now. He was feeling quite concerned. "Because you mustn't! Donkey! Come, I'll show you something. No, nearer still! "

Pelle pushed his head forward through the tall elder-bush, and suddenly she put her two hands about his head and kissed him violently and pushed him back. He tried gropingly to take hold of her, but she stood there laughing at him. Her face glowed in the darkness. "You haven't heard anything about it! " she whispered. "Come, I'll tell you! "

Now he was smiling all over his face. He pushed his way eagerly into the elder-bush. But at the same moment he felt her clenched fist strike his face. She laughed crazily, but he stood fixed in the same position, as though stunned, his mouth held forward as if still awaiting a kiss. "Why do you hit me? " he asked, gazing at her brokenly.

"Because I can't endure you! You're a perfect oaf, and so ugly and so common! "

"I have never done anything to you! "

"No? Anyhow, you richly deserved it! What did you want to kiss me for? "

Pelle stood there helplessly stammering. The whole world of his experience collapsed under him. "But I didn't! " he at last brought out; he looked extraordinarily foolish. Manna aped his expression. "Ugh! Bugh! Take care, or you'll freeze to the ground and turn into a lamp-post! There's nothing on the hedge here that will throw light on your understanding! "

With a leap Pelle was over the hedge. Manna took him hastily by the hand and drew him through the bushes. "Aina and Dolores will be here directly. Then we'll play, " she declared.

"I thought they couldn't come out in the evenings any more, " said Pelle, obediently allowing her to lead him. She made no reply, but looked about her as though she wanted to treat him to something as in the old days. In her need she stripped a handful of leaves off the currant-boughs, and stuffed them into his mouth. "There, take that and hold your mouth! " She was quite the old Manna once more, and Pelle laughed.

They had come to the summer-house. Manna cooled his swollen cheeks with wet earth while they waited.

"Did it hurt you much? " she asked sympathetically, putting her arm about his shoulder.

"It's nothing. What's a box on the ear? " he said manfully.

"I didn't mean it—you know that. Did *that* hurt you very much? "

Pelle gazed at her sadly. She looked at him inquisitively. "Was it here? " she said, letting her hand slide down his back. He rose silently, in order to go, but she seized him by the wrist. "Forgive me, " she whispered.

"Aren't the others coming soon? " asked Pelle harshly. He proposed to be angry with her, as in the old days.

"No! They aren't coming at all! I've deceived you. I wanted to talk to you! " Manna was gasping for breath.

"I thought you didn't want to have anything more to do with me? "

"Well, I don't! I only want—" She could not find words, and stamped angrily on the ground. Then she said slowly and solemnly, with the earnestness of a child: "Do you know what I believe? I believe—I love you! "

"Then we can get married when we are old enough! " said Pelle joyfully.

She looked at him for a moment with a measuring glance. The town-hall and the flogging! thought Pelle. He was quite resolved that he would do the beating now; but here she laughed at him. "What a glorious booby you are! " she said, and as though deep in thought, she let a handful of wet earth run down his neck.

Pelle thought for a moment of revenge; then, as though in sport, he thrust his hand into her bosom. She fell back weakly, groping submissively with her hands; a new knowledge arose in him, and impelled him to embrace her violently.

She looked at him in amazement, and tried gently to push his hand away. But it was too late. The boy had broken down her defences.

As Pelle went back into the house he was overwhelmed, but not happy. His heart hammered wildly, and a chaos reigned in his brain. Quite instinctively he trod very softly. For a long time he lay tossing to and fro without being able to sleep. His mind had resolved the enigma, and now he discovered the living blood in himself. It sang its sufferings in his ear; it welled into his cheeks and his heart; it murmured everywhere in numberless pulses, so that his whole body thrilled. Mighty and full of mystery, it surged through him like an inundation, filling him with a warm, deep astonishment. Never before had he known all this!

In the time that followed his blood was his secret confidant in everything; he felt it like a caress when it filled his limbs, causing a feeling of distension in wrists and throat. He had his secret now, and his face never betrayed the fact that he had ever known Sjermanna. His radiant days had all at once changed into radiant nights. He was still enough of a child to long for the old days, with their games in the broad light of day; but something impelled him to look forward, listening, and his questing soul bowed itself before the mysteries of life. The night had made him accomplice in her mysteries. With Manna he never spoke again. She never came into the garden, and if he met her she turned into another street. A rosy flame lay continually over her face, as though it had burned its way in. Soon afterward she went to a farm in Ostland, where an uncle of hers lived.

But Pelle felt nothing and was in no way dejected. He went about as though in a half-slumber; everything was blurred and veiled before his spiritual vision. He was quite bewildered by all that was going on within him. Something was hammering and laboring in every part and corner of him. Ideas which were too fragile were broken down and built up more strongly, so that they should bear the weight of the man in him. His limbs grew harder; his muscles became like steel, and he was conscious of a general feeling of breadth across his back, and of unapplied strength. At times he awakened out of his half-slumber into a brief amazement, when he felt himself, in one particular or another, to have become a man; as when one day he heard his own voice. It had gained a deep resonance, which was quite foreign to his ear, and forced him to listen as though it had been another that spoke.

XVIII

Pelle fought against the decline of the business. A new apprentice had been taken into the workshop, but Pelle, as before, had to do all the delicate jobs. He borrowed articles when necessary, and bought things on credit; and he had to interview impatient customers, and endeavor to pacify them. He got plenty of exercise, but he learned nothing properly. "Just run down to the harbor, " the master used to say: "Perhaps there will be some work to bring back! " But the master was much more interested in the news which he brought thence.

Pelle would also go thither without having received any orders. Everybody in the town must needs make for the harbor whenever he went from home; it was the heart through which everything came and went, money and dreams and desires and that which gratified them. Every man had been to sea, and his best memories and his hardest battles belonged to the sea. Dreams took the outward way; yonder lay the sea, and all men's thoughts were drawn to it; the thoughts of the young, who longed to go forth and seek adventure, and of the old, who lived on their memories. It was the song in all men's hearts, and the God in the inmost soul of all; the roving-ground of life's surplus, the home of all that was inexplicable and mystical. The sea had drunk the blood of thousands, but its color knew no change; the riddle of life brooded in its restless waters.

Destiny rose from the floor of the deep and with short shrift set her mark upon a man; he might escape to the land, like Baker Jorgensen, who went no more to sea when once the warning had come to him, or, like Boatman Jensen, he might rise in his sleep and walk straight over the vessel's side. Down below, where the drowned dwelt, the ships sank to bring them what they needed; and from time to time the bloodless children of the sea rose to the shore, to play with the children that were born on a Sunday, and to bring them death or happiness.

Over the sea, three times a week, came the steamer with news from Copenhagen; and vessels all wrapped in ice, and others that had sprung a heavy leak, or bore dead bodies on board; and great ships which came from warm countries and had real negroes among their crews.

Down by the harbor stood the old men who had forsaken the sea, and now all the long day through they stared out over the playground of their manhood, until Death came for them. The sea had blown gout into their limbs, had buffeted them until they were bent and bowed, and in the winter nights one could hear them roar with the pain like wild beasts. Down to the harbor drifted all the flotsam and jetsam of the land, invalids and idle men and dying men, and busy folk raced round about and up and down with fluttering coat-tails, in order to scent out possible profits.

The young sported here continually; it was as though they encountered the future when they played here by the open sea. Many never went further, but many let themselves be caught and whirled away out into the unknown. Of these was Nilen. When the ships were being fitted out he could wait no longer. He sacrificed two years' apprenticeship, and ran away on board a vessel which was starting on a long voyage. Now he was far away in the Trades, on the southern passage round America, homeward bound with a cargo of redwood. And a few left with every steamer. The girls were the most courageous when it came to cutting themselves loose; they steamed away swiftly, and the young men followed them in amorous blindness. And men fought their way outward in order to seek something more profitable than could be found at home.

Pelle had experienced all this already: he had felt this same longing, and had known the attractive force of the unknown. Up in the country districts it was the dream of all poor people to fight their way to town, and the boldest one day ventured thither, with burning cheeks, while the old people spoke warningly of the immorality of cities. And in the town here it was the dream of all to go to the capital, to Copenhagen; there fortune and happiness were to be found! He who had the courage hung one day over the ship's rail, and waved farewell, with an absent expression in his eyes, as though he had been playing a game with high stakes; over there on the mainland he would have to be a match with the best of them. But the old people shook their heads and spoke at length of the temptations and immorality of the capital.

Now and again one came back and justified their wisdom. Then they would run delightedly from door to door. "Didn't we tell you so? " But many came home at holiday seasons and were such swells that it was really the limit! And this or that girl was so extremely stylish that people had to ask the opinion of Wooden-leg Larsen about her.

The girls who got married over there—well, they were well provided for! After an interval of many years they came back to their parents' homes, travelling on deck among the cattle, and giving the stewardess a few pence to have them put in the newspaper as cabin-passengers. They were fine enough as to their clothes, but their thin haggard faces told another story. "There is certainly not enough to eat for all over there! " said the old women.

But Pelle took no interest in those that came home again. All his thoughts were with those who went away; his heart tugged painfully in his breast, so powerful was his longing to be off. The sea, whether it lay idle or seethed with anger, continually filled his head with the humming of the world "over yonder, " with a vague, mysterious song of happiness.

One day, as he was on his way to the harbor, he met old thatcher Holm from Stone Farm. Holm was going about looking at the houses from top to bottom; he was raising his feet quite high in the air from sheer astonishment, and was chattering to himself. On his arm he carried a basket loaded with bread and butter, brandy, and beer.

"Well, here's some one at last! " he said, and offered his hand. "I'm going round and wondering to myself where they all live, those that come here day after day and year after year, and whether they've done any good. Mother and I have often talked about it, that it would be splendid to know how things have turned out for this one or that. And this morning she said it would be best if I were to make a short job of it before I quite forget how to find my way about the streets here, I haven't been here for ten years. Well, according to what I've seen so far, mother and I needn't regret we've stayed at home. Nothing grows here except lamp-posts, and mother wouldn't understand anything about rearing them. Thatched roofs I've not seen here. Here in the town they'd grudge a thatcher his bread. But I'll see the harbor before I go home. "

"Then we'll go together, " said Pelle. He was glad to meet some one from his home. The country round about Stone Farm was always for him the home of his childhood. He gossiped with the old man and pointed out various objects of interest.

"Yes, I've been once, twice, three times before this to the harbor, " said Holm, "but I've never managed to see the steamer. They tell me wonderful things of it; they say all our crops are taken to Copenhagen in the steamer nowadays. "

"It's lying here to-day, " said Pelle eagerly. "This evening it goes out. "

Holm's eyes beamed. "Then I shall be able to see the beggar! I've often seen the smoke from the hill at home—drifting over the sea— and that always gave me a lot to think about. They say it eats coals and is made of iron. " He looked at Pelle uncertainly.

The great empty harbor basin, in which some hundreds of men were at work, interested him greatly. Pelle pointed out the "Great Power, " who was toiling like a madman and allowing himself to be saddled with the heaviest work.

"So that is he! " cried Holm. "I knew his father; he was a man who wanted to do things above the ordinary, but he never brought them off. And how goes it with your father? Not any too well, as I've heard? "

Pelle had been home a little while before; nothing was going well there, but as to that he was silent. "Karna isn't very well, " he said. "She tried to do too much; she's strained herself lifting things. "

"They say he'll have a difficult job to pull through. They have taken too much on themselves, " Holm continued.

Pelle made no reply; and then the steamer absorbed their whole attention. Talkative as he was, Holm quite forgot to wag his tongue.

The steamer was on the point of taking in cargo; the steam derricks were busy at both hatches, squealing each time they swung round in another direction. Holm became so light on his legs one might have thought he was treading on needles; when the derrick swung round over the quay and the chain came rattling down, he ran right back to the granary. Pelle wanted to take him on board, but he would not hear of it. "It looks a bad-tempered monster, " he said: "look how it sneezes and fusses! "

On the quay, by the forward hold, the goods of a poverty-stricken household lay all mixed together. A man stood there holding a mahogany looking-glass, the only article of value, in his arms. His expression was gloomy. By the manner in which he blew his nose—

with his knuckles instead of with his fingers—one could see that he had something unaccustomed on hand. His eyes were fixed immovably on his miserable household possessions, and they anxiously followed every breakable article as it went its airy way into the vessel's maw. His wife and children were sitting on the quay-wall, eating out of a basket of provisions. They had been sitting there for hours. The children were tired and tearful; the mother was trying to console them, and to induce them to sleep on the stone.

"Shan't we start soon? " they asked continually, in complaining tones.

"Yes, the ship starts directly, but you must be very good or I shan't take you with me. And then you'll come to the capital city, where they eat white bread and always wear leather boots. The King himself lives there, and they've got everything in the shops there. " She arranged her shawl under their heads.

"But that's Per Anker's son from Blaaholt! " cried Holm, when he had been standing a while on the quay and had caught sight of the man. "What, are you leaving the country? "

"Yes, I've decided to do so, " said the man, in an undertone, passing his hand over his face.

"And I thought you were doing so well! Didn't you go to Ostland, and didn't you take over a hotel there? "

"Yes, they enticed me out there, and now I've lost everything there. "

"You ought to have considered—considering costs nothing but a little trouble. "

"But they showed me false books, which showed a greater surplus than there really was. Shipowner Monsen was behind the whole affair, together with the brewer from the mainland, who had taken the hotel over in payment of outstanding debts. "

"But how did big folks like that manage to smell you out? " Holm scratched his head; he didn't understand the whole affair.

"Oh, they'd heard of the ten thousand, of course, which I'd inherited from my father. They throw their nets out for sums like that, and one day they sent an agent to see me. Ten thousand was just enough for the first instalment, and now they have taken the hotel over again. Out of compassion, they let me keep this trash here. " He suddenly turned his face away and wept; and then his wife came swiftly up to him.

Holm drew Pelle away. "They'd rather be rid of us, " he said quietly; and he continued to discuss the man's dismal misfortune, while they strolled out along the mole. But Pelle was not listening to him. He had caught sight of a little schooner which was cruising outside, and was every moment growing more restless.

"I believe that's the Iceland schooner! " he said at last. "So I must go back. "

"Yes, run off, " said Holm, "and many thanks for your guidance, and give my respects to Lasse and Karna. "

On the harbor hill Pelle met Master Jeppe, and farther on Drejer, Klaussen, and Blom. The Iceland boat had kept them waiting for several months; the news that she was in the roads quickly spread, and all the shoemakers of the whole town were hurrying down to the harbor, in order to hear whether good business had been done before the gangway was run out.

"The Iceland boat is there now! " said the merchants and leather-dealers, when they saw the shoemakers running by. "We must make haste and make out our bills, for now the shoemakers will be having money. "

But the skipper had most of the boots and shoes still in his hold; he returned with the terrifying news that no more boots and shoes could be disposed of in Iceland. The winter industry had been of great importance to the shoemakers.

"What does this mean? " asked Jeppe angrily. "You have been long enough about it! Have you been trying to open another agency over there? In others years you have managed to sell the whole lot. "

"I have done what I could, " replied the captain gloomily. "I offered them to the dealers in big parcels, and then I lay there and carried on a retail trade from the ship. Then I ran down the whole west coast; but there is nothing to be done. "

"Well, well, " said Jeppe, "but do the Icelanders mean to go without boots? "

"There's the factories, " replied the captain.

"The factories, the factories! " Jeppe laughed disdainfully, but with a touch of uncertainty. "You'll tell me next that they can make shoes by machinery—cut out and peg and sew and fix the treads and all? No, damn it, that can only be done by human hands directed by human intelligence. Shoemaking is work for men only. Perhaps I myself might be replaced by a machine—by a few cog-wheels that go round and round! Bah! A machine is dead, I know that, and it can't think or adapt itself to circumstances; you may have to shape the boot in a particular way for a special foot, on account of tender toes, or—here I give the sole a certain cut in the instep, so that it looks smart, or—well, one has to be careful, or one cuts into the upper! "

"There are machines which make boots, and they make them cheaper than you, too, " said the skipper brusquely.

"I should like to see them! Can you show me a boot that hasn't been made by human hands? " Jeppe laughed contemptuously. "No; there's something behind all this, by God! Some one is trying to play us a trick! " The skipper went his way, offended.

Jeppe stuck to it that there was something uncanny about it—the idea of a machine making boots was enough to haunt him. He kept on returning to it.

"They'll be making human beings by machinery too, soon! " he exclaimed angrily.

"No, " said Baker Jorgen; "there, I believe, the old method will survive! "

One day the skipper came in at the workshop door, banged a pair of shoes down on the window-bench, and went out again. They had been bought in England, and belonged to the helmsman of a bark which had just come into the harbor. The young master looked at them, turned them over in his hands, and looked at them again. Then he called Jeppe. They were sewn throughout—shoes for a grown man, yet sewn throughout! Moreover, the factory stamp was under the sole.

In Jeppe's opinion they were not worth a couple of shillings. But he could not get over the fact that they were machine-made.

"Then we are superfluous, " he said, in a quavering voice. All his old importance seemed to have fallen from him. "For if they can make the one kind on a machine, they can make another. The handicraft is condemned to death, and we shall all be without bread one fine day! Well, I, thank God, have not many years before me. " It was the first time that Jeppe had admitted that he owed his life to God.

Every time he came into the workshop he began to expatiate on the same subject. He would stand there turning the hated shoes over between his hands. Then he would criticize them. "We must take more pains next winter. "

"Father forgets it's all up with us now, " said the young master wearily.

Then the old man would be silent and hobble out. But after a time he would be back again, fingering the boots and shoes, in order to discover defects in them. His thoughts were constantly directed upon this new subject; no song of praise, no eulogy of his handicraft, passed his lips nowadays. If the young master came to him and asked his help in some difficult situation, he would refuse it; he felt no further desire to triumph over youth with his ancient dexterity, but shuffled about and shrank into himself. "And all that we have thought so highly of—what's to become of it? " he would ask. "For machines don't make masterpieces and medal work, so where will real good work come in? "

The young master did not look so far ahead; he thought principally of the money that was needed. "Devil take it, Pelle, how are we going to pay every one, Pelle? " he would ask dejectedly. Little Nikas had to look out for something else; their means would not allow them to keep a journeyman. So Nikas decided to marry, and to set up as a master shoemaker in the north. The shoemaker of the Baptist community had just died, and he could get plenty of customers by joining the sect; he was already attending their services. "But go to work carefully! " said Jeppe. "Or matters will go awry! "

It was a bad shock to all of them. Klaussen went bankrupt and had to find work on the new harbor. Blom ran away, deserting his wife and children, and they had to go home to the house of her parents. In the workshop matters had been getting worse for a long time. And now this had happened, throwing a dazzling light upon the whole question. But the young master refused to believe the worst. "I shall soon be well again now, " he said. "And then you will just see how I'll work up the business! " He lay in bed more often now, and was susceptible to every change in the weather. Pelle had to see to everything.

"Run and borrow something! " the master would say. And if Pelle returned with a refusal, he would look at the boy with his wide, wondering eyes. "They've got the souls of grocers! " he would cry. "Then we must peg those soles! "

"That won't answer with ladies' patent-leather shoes! " replied Pelle very positively.

"Damn and blast it all, it will answer! We'll black the bottom with cobbler's wax. "

But when the black was trodden off, Jungfer Lund and the others called, and were wroth. They were not accustomed to walk in pegged shoes. "It's a misunderstanding! " said the young master, the perspiration standing in clear beads on his forehead. Or he would hide and leave it to Pelle. When it was over, he would reach up to the shelf, panting with exhaustion. "Can't you do anything for me, Pelle? " he whispered.

One day Pelle plucked up courage and said it certainly wasn't healthy to take so much spirit; the master needed so much now.

"Healthy? " said the master; "no, good God, it isn't healthy! But the beasts demand it! In the beginning I couldn't get the stuff down, especially beer; but now I've accustomed myself to it. If I didn't feed them, they'd soon rush all over me and eat me up. "

"Do they swallow it, then? "

"I should think they do! As much as ever you like to give them. Or have you ever seen me tipsy? I can't get drunk; the tubercles take it all. And for them it's sheer poison. On the day when I am able to get drunk again I shall thank God, for then the beasts will be dead and the spirit will be able to attack me again. Then it'll only be a question of stopping it, otherwise it'll play the deuce with my mind! "

Since the journeyman had left, the meals had become more meager than ever. The masters had not had enough money in the spring to buy a pig. So there was no one to consume the scraps. Now they had to eat them all themselves. Master Andres was never at the table; he took scarcely any nourishment nowadays; a piece of bread-and-butter now and again, that was all. Breakfast, at half-past seven, they ate alone. It consisted of salt herrings, bread and hog's lard, and soup. The soup was made out of all sorts of odds and ends of bread and porridge, with an addition of thin beer. It was fermented and unpalatable. What was left over from breakfast was put into a great crock which stood in one corner of the kitchen, on the floor, and this was warmed up again the next morning, with the addition of a little fresh beer. So it went on all the year round. The contents were renewed only when some one kicked the crock so that it broke. The boys confined themselves to the herrings and the lard; the soup they did not use except to fish about in it. They made a jest of it, throwing all sorts of objects into it, and finding them again after half a year.

Jeppe was still lying in the alcove, asleep; his nightcap was hoved awry over one eye. Even in his sleep he still had a comical expression of self-importance. The room was thick with vapor; the old man had his own way of getting air, breathing it in with a long snort and letting it run rumbling through him. If it got too bad, the boys would make a noise; then he would wake and scold them.

They were longing for food by dinner-time; the moment Jeppe called his "Dinner! " at the door they threw everything down, ranged themselves according to age, and tumbled in behind him. They held one another tightly by the coat-tails, and made stupid grimaces. Jeppe was enthroned at the head of the table, a little cap on his head, trying to preserve seemly table-manners. No one might begin before him or continue after he had finished. They snatched at their spoons, laid them down again with a terrified glance at the old man, and nearly exploded with suppressed laughter. "Yes, I'm very hungry today, but there's no need for you to remark it! " he would say warningly, once they were in full swing. Pelle would wink at the others, and they would go on eating, emptying one dish after another. "There's no respect nowadays! " roared Jeppe, striking on the table. But when he did this discipline suddenly entered into them, and they all struck the table after him in turn. Sometimes, when matters got too bad, Master Andres had to find some reason for coming into the room.

The long working-hours, the bad food, and the foul air of the workshop left their mark on Pelle. His attachment to Master Andres was limitless; he could sit there till midnight and work without payment if a promise had been made to finish some particular job. But otherwise he was imperceptibly slipping into the general slackness, sharing the others' opinion of the day as something utterly abominable, which one must somehow endeavor to get through. To work at half pressure was a physical necessity; his rare movements wearied him, and he felt less inclined to work than to brood. The semi-darkness of the sunless workshop bleached his skin and filled him with unhealthy imaginations.

He did little work now on his own account; but he had learned to manage with very little. Whenever he contrived to get hold of a ten-ore piece, he bought a savings-stamp, so that in this way he was able to collect a few shillings, until they had grown to quite a little sum. Now and again, too, he got a little help from Lasse, but Lasse found it more and more difficult to spare anything. Moreover, he had learned to compose his mind by his work.

XIX

The crazy Anker was knocking on the workshop door. "Bjerregrav is dead! " he said solemnly. "Now there is only one who can mourn over poverty! " Then he went away and announced the news to Baker Jorgen. They heard him going from house to house, all along the street.

Bjerregrav dead! Only yesterday evening he was sitting yonder, on the chair by the window-bench, and his crutch was standing in the corner by the door; and he had offered them all his hand in his odd, ingenuous way—that unpleasantly flabby hand, at whose touch they all felt a certain aversion, so importunate was it, and almost skinless in its warmth, so that one felt as if one had involuntarily touched some one on a naked part. Pelle was always reminded of Father Lasse; he too had never learned to put on armor, but had always remained the same loyal, simple soul, unaffected by his hard experience.

The big baker had fallen foul of him as usual. Contact with this childlike, thin-skinned creature, who let his very heart burn itself out in a clasp of his hand, always made him brutal. "Now, Bjerregrav, have you tried it—you know what—since we last saw you? "

Bjerregrav turned crimson. "I am content with the experience which the dear God has chosen for me, " he answered, with blinking eyes.

"Would you believe it, he is over seventy and doesn't know yet how a woman is made! "

"Because, after all I find it suits me best to live alone, and then there's my club foot. "

"So he goes about asking questions about everything, things such as every child knows about, " said Jeppe, in a superior tone. "Bjerregrav has never rubbed off his childish innocence. "

Yet as he was going home, and Pelle was helping him over the gutter, he was still in his mood of everlasting wonder.

"What star is that? " he said; "it has quite a different light to the others. It looks so red to me—if only we don't have a severe winter, with the soil frozen and dear fuel for all the poor people. " Bjerregrav sighed.

"You mustn't look at the moon so much. Skipper Andersen came by his accident simply because he slept on deck and the moon shone right in his face; now he has gone crazy! "

Yesterday evening just the same as always—and now dead! And no one had known or guessed, so that they might have been a little kinder to him just at the last! He died in his bed, with his mind full of their last disdainful words, and now they could never go to him and say: "Don't take any notice of it, Bjerregrav; we didn't mean to be unkind. " Perhaps their behavior had embittered his last hours. At all events, there stood Jeppe and Brother Jorgen, and they could not look one another in the face; an immovable burden weighed upon them.

And it meant a void—as when the clock in a room stops ticking. The faithful sound of his crutch no longer approached the workshop about six o'clock. The young master grew restless about that time; he could not get used to the idea of Bjerregrav's absence.

"Death is a hateful thing, " he would say, when the truth came over him; "it is horribly repugnant. Why must one go away from here without leaving the least part of one behind? Now I listen for Bjerregrav's crutch, and there's a void in my ears, and after a time there won't be even that. Then he will be forgotten, and perhaps more besides, who will have followed him, and so it goes on forever. Is there anything reasonable about it all, Pelle? They talk about Heaven, but what should I care about sitting on a damp cloud and singing 'Hallelujah'? I'd much rather go about down here and get myself a drink—especially if I had a sound leg! "

The apprentices accompanied him to the grave. Jeppe wished them to do so, as a sort of atonement. Jeppe himself and Baker Jorgen, in tall hats, walked just behind the coffin. Otherwise only a few poor women and children followed, who had joined the procession out of curiosity. Coachman Due drove the hearse. He had now bought a pair of horses, and this was his first good job.

Otherwise life flowed onward, sluggish and monotonous. Winter had come again, with its commercial stagnation, and the Iceland trade was ruined. The shoemakers did no more work by artificial light; there was so little to do that it would not repay the cost of the petroleum; so the hanging lamp was put on one side and the old tin lamp was brought out again. That was good enough to sit round and to gossip by. The neighbors would come into the twilight of the workshop; if Master Andres was not there, they would slip out again, or they would sit idly there until Jeppe said it was bed-time. Pelle had begun to occupy himself with carving once more; he got as close to the lamp as possible, listening to the conversation while he worked upon a button which was to be carved like a twenty-five-ore piece. Morten was to have it for a tie-pin.

The conversation turned upon the weather, and how fortunate it was that the frost had not yet come to stop the great harbor works. Then it touched upon the "Great Power, " and from him it glanced at the crazy Anker, and poverty, and discontent. The Social Democrats "over yonder" had for a long time been occupying the public mind. All the summer through disquieting rumors had crossed the water; it was quite plain that they were increasing their power and their numbers —but what were they actually aiming at? In any case, it was nothing good. "They must be the very poorest who are revolting, " said Wooden-leg Larsen. "So their numbers must be very great! " It was as though one heard the roaring of something or other out on the horizon, but did not know what was going on there. The echo of the upheaval of the lower classes was quite distorted by the time it reached the island; people understood just so much, that the lowest classes wanted to turn God's appointed order upside down and to get to the top themselves, and involuntarily their glance fell covertly on the poor in the town. But these were going about in their customary half-slumber, working when there was work to be had and contenting themselves with that. "That would be the last straw, " said Jeppe, "here, where we have such a well-organized poor-relief! "

Baker Jorgen was the most eager—every day he came with news of some kind to discuss. Now they had threatened the life of the King himself! And now the troops were called out.

"The troops! " The young master made a disdainful gesture. "That'll help a lot! If they merely throw a handful of dynamite among the soldiers there won't be a trouser-button left whole! No, they'll conquer the capital now! " His cheeks glowed: he saw the event already in his mind's eye. "Yes, and then? Then they'll plunder the royal Mint! "

"Yes—no. Then they'll come over here—the whole party! "

"Come over here? No, by God! We'd call out all the militia and shoot them down from the shore. I've put my gun in order already! "

One day Marker came running in. "The pastrycook's got a new journeyman from over yonder—and he's a Social Democrat! " he cried breathlessly. "He came yesterday evening by the steamer. " Baker Jorgen had also heard the news.

"Yes, now they're on you! " said Jeppe, as one announcing disaster. "You've all been trifling with the new spirit of the times. This would have been something for Bjerregrav to see—him with his compassion for the poor! "

"Let the tailor rest in peace in his grave, " said Wooden-leg Larsen, in a conciliatory tone. "You mustn't blame him for the angry masses that exist to-day. He wanted nothing but people's good—and perhaps these people want to do good, too! "

"Good! " Jeppe was loud with scorn. "They want to overturn law and order, and sell the fatherland to the Germans! They say the sum is settled already, and all! "

"They say they'll be let into the capital during the night, when our own people are asleep, " said Marker.

"Yes, " said Master Andres solemnly. "They've let out that the key's hidden under the mat—the devils! " Here Baker Jorgen burst into a shout of laughter; his laughter filled the whole workshop when he once began.

They guessed what sort of a fellow the new journeyman might be. No one had seen him yet. "He certainly has red hair and a red beard, " said Baker Jorgen. "That's the good God's way of marking those who have signed themselves to the Evil One. "

"God knows what the pastrycook wants with him, " said Jeppe. "People of that sort can't do anything—they only ask. I've heard the whole lot of them are free-thinkers. "

"What a lark! " The young master shook himself contentedly. "He won't grow old here in the town! "

"Old? " The baker drew up his heavy body. "To-morrow I shall go to the pastrycook and demand that he be sent away. I am commander of the militia, and I know all the townsfolk think as I do. "

Drejer thought it might be well to pray from the pulpit—as in time of plague, and in the bad year when the field-mice infested the country.

Next morning Jorgen Kofod looked in on his way to the pastrycook's. He was wearing his old militia coat, and at his belt hung the leather wallet in which flints for the old flint-locks had been carried many years before. He filled his uniform well; but he came back without success. The pastrycook praised his new journeyman beyond all measure, and wouldn't hear a word of sending him away. He was quite besotted. "But we shall buy there no more—we must all stick to that—and no respectable family can deal with the traitor in future. "

"Did you see the journeyman, Uncle Jorgen? " asked Master Andres eagerly.

"Yes, I saw him—that is, from a distance! He had a pair of terrible, piercing eyes; but he shan't bewitch me with his serpent's glance! "

In the evening Pelle and the others were strolling about the market in order to catch a glimpse of the new journeyman—there were a number of people there, and they were all strolling to and fro with the same object in view. But he evidently kept the house.

And then one day, toward evening, the master came tumbling into the workshop. "Hurry up, damn it all! " he cried, quite out of breath; "he's passing now! " They threw down their work and stumbled along the passage into the best room, which at ordinary times they were not allowed to enter. He was a tall, powerful man, with full cheeks and a big, dashing moustache, quite as big as the master's. His nostrils were distended, and he held his chest well forward. His jacket and wasitcoat were open, as though he wanted more air. Behind him slunk a few street urchins, in the hope of seeing something; they had quite lost their accustomed insolence, and followed him in silence.

"He walks as though the whole town belonged to him! " said Jeppe scornfully. "But we'll soon finish with him here! "

XX

Out in the street some one went by, and then another, and then another; there was quite a trampling of feet. The young master knocked on the wall. "What in the world is it, Pelle? " He did not mean to get up that day.

Pelle ran out to seek information. "Jen's father has got delirium— he's cleared the whole harbor and is threatening to kill them all! "

The master raised his head a little. "By God, I believe I shall get up! " His eyes were glistening; presently he had got into his clothes, and limped out of doors; they heard him coughing terribly in the cold.

Old Jeppe put his official cap in his pocket before he ran out; perhaps the authorities would be needed. For a time the apprentices sat staring at the door like sick birds; then they, too, ran out of the house.

Outside everything was in confusion. The wildest rumors were flying about as to what Stonemason Jorgensen had done. The excitement could not have been greater had a hostile squadron come to anchor and commenced to bombard the town. Everybody dropped what he was holding and rushed down to the harbor. The smaller side-streets were one unbroken procession of children and old women and small employers in their aprons. Old gouty seamen awoke from their decrepit slumber and hobbled away, their hands dropped to the back of their loins and their faces twisted with pain.

> "Toot aroot aroot aroot.
> All the pitchy snouts! "

A few street-urchins allowed themselves this little diversion, as Pelle came running by with the other apprentices; otherwise all attention was concentrated on the one fact that the "Great Power" had broken out again! A certain festivity might have been noted on the faces of the hurrying crowd; a vivid expectation. The stonemason had been quiet for a long time now; he had labored like a giant beast of burden, to all appearance extinguished, but toiling like an elephant, and quietly taking home a couple of kroner in the evening. It was almost painful to watch him, and a disappointed silence gathered about him. And now came a sudden explosion, thrilling everybody through!

All had something to say of the "strong man" while they hastened down to the harbor. Everybody had foreseen that it must come; he had for a long time looked so strange, and had done nothing wrong, so that it was only a wonder that it hadn't come sooner! Such people ought not really to be at large; they ought to be shut up for life! They went over the events of his life for the hundredth time—from the day when he came trudging into town, young and fearless in his rags, to find a market for his energies, until the time when he drove his child into the sea and settled down as a lunatic.

Down by the harbor the people were swarming; everybody who could creep or crawl was stationed there. The crowd was good-humored, in spite of the cold and the hard times; the people stamped their feet and cracked jokes. The town had in a moment shaken off its winter sleep; the people clambered up on the blocks of stone, or hung close-packed over the rough timber frames that were to be sunk in building the breakwater. They craned their necks and started nervously, as though some one might come up suddenly and hit them over the head. Jens and Morten were there, too; they stood quite apart and were speaking to one another. They looked on mournfully, with shy, harrassed glances, and where the great slip ran obliquely down to the floor of the basin the workmen stood in crowds; they hitched up their trousers, for the sake of something to do, exchanged embarrassed glances, and swore.

But down on the floor of the great basin the "Great Power" ruled supreme. He was moving about alone, and he seemed to be as unconscious of his surroundings as a child absorbed in play; he had some purpose of his own to attend to. But what that was it was not easy to tell. In one hand he held a bundle of dynamite cartridges; with the other he was leaning on a heavy iron bar. His movements were slow and regular, not unlike those of a clumsy bear. When he stood up, his comrades shouted to him excitedly; they would come and tear him into little pieces; they would slit his belly so that he could see his own bowels; they would slash him with their knives and rub his wounds with vitriol if he didn't at once lay down his weapons and let them come down to their work.

But the "Great Power" did not deign to answer. Perhaps he never heard them. When he raised his head his glance swept the distance, laden with a mysterious burden which was not human. That face, with its deadly weariness, seemed in its sadness to be turned upon some distant place whither none could follow him. "He is mad! " they whispered; "God has taken away his wits! " Then he bent himself to his task again; he seemed to be placing the cartridges under the great breakwater which he himself had proposed. He was pulling cartridges out of every pocket; that was why they had stuck out from his body curiously.

"What the devil is he going to do now? Blow up the breakwater? " they asked, and tried to creep along behind the causeway, so as to come upon him from behind. But he had eyes all round him; at the slightest movement on their part he was there with his iron bar.

The whole works were at a standstill! Two hundred men stood idle hour after hour, growling and swearing and threatening death and the devil, but no one ventured forward. The overseer ran about irresolutely, and even the engineer had lost his head; everything was in a state of dissolution. The district judge was walking up and down in full uniform, with an impenetrable expression of face; his mere presence had a calming effect, but he did nothing.

Each proposal made was wilder than the last. Some wanted to make a gigantic screen which might be pushed toward him; others suggested capturing him with a huge pair of tongs made of long balks of timber; but no one attempted to carry out these suggestions; they were only too thankful that he allowed them to stand where they were. The "Great Power" could throw a dynamite cartridge with such force that it would explode where it struck and sweep away everything around it.

"The tip-wagons! " cried some one. Here at last was an idea! The wagons were quickly filled with armed workmen. The catch was released, but the wagons did not move. The "Great Power" with his devilish cunning, had been before them; he had spiked the endless chain so that it could not move. And now he struck away the under-pinning of a few of the supports, so that the wagons could not be launched upon him by hand.

This was no delirium; no one had ever yet seen delirium manifest itself in such a way! And he had touched no spirit since the day they had carried his daughter home. No; it was the quietest resolution imaginable; when they got up after the breakfast-hour and were strolling down to the slip, he stood there with his iron bar and quietly commanded them to keep away—the harbor belonged to him! They had received more than one sharp blow before they understood that he was in earnest; but there was no malice in him— one could see quite plainly how it hurt him to strike them. It was certainly the devil riding him—against his own will.

But where was it going to end? They had had enough of it now! For now the great harbor bell was striking midday, and there was something derisive in the sound, as though it was jeering at respectable people who only wanted to resume their work. They didn't want to waste the whole day; neither did they want to risk life and limb against the fool's tricks of a lunatic. Even the mighty Bergendal had left his contempt of death at home to-day, and was content to grumble like the rest.

"We must knock a hole in the dam, " he said, "then the brute may perish in the waves! "

They immediately picked up their tools, in order to set to work. The engineer threatened them with the law and the authorities; it would cost thousands of kroner to empty the harbor again. They would not listen to him; what use was he if he couldn't contrive for them to do their work in peace?

They strolled toward the dam, with picks and iron crowbars, in order to make the breach; the engineer and the police were thrust aside. Now it was no longer a matter of work; it was a matter of showing that two hundred men were not going to allow one crazy devil to make fools of them. Beelzebub had got to be smoked out. Either the "Great Power" would come up from the floor of the basin, or he would drown.

"You shall have a full day's wages! " cried the engineer, to hold them back. They did not listen; but when they reached the place of the intended breach, the "Great Power" was standing at the foot of the dam, swinging his pick so that the walls of the basin resounded. He beamed with helpfulness at every blow; he had posted himself at the spot where the water trickled in, and they saw with horror what an effect his blows had. It was sheer madness to do what he was doing there.

"He'll fill the harbor with water, the devil! " they cried, and they hurled stones at his head. "And such a work as it was to empty it! "

The "Great Power" took cover behind a pile and worked away.

Then there was nothing for it but to shoot him down before he had attained his object. A charge of shot in the legs, if nothing more, and he would at least be rendered harmless. The district judge was at his wits' end; but Wooden-leg Larsen was already on the way home to fetch his gun. Soon he came stumping back, surrounded by a swarm of boys.

"I've loaded it with coarse salt! " he cried, so that the judge might hear.

"Now you'll be shot dead! " they called down to him. In reply, the "Great Power" struck his pick into the foot of the dam, so that the trampled clay sighed and the moisture rose underfoot. A long crackling sound told them that the first plank was shattered.

The final resolve had been formed quite of itself; everybody was speaking of shooting him down as though the man had been long ago sentenced, and now everybody was longing for the execution. They hated the man below there with a secret hatred which needed no explanation; his defiance and unruliness affected them like a slap in the face; they would gladly have trampled him underfoot if they could.

They shouted down insults; they reminded him how in his presumption he had ruined his family, and driven his daughter to suicide; and they cast in his face his brutal attack on the rich shipowner Monsen, the benefactor of the town. For a time they roused themselves from their apathy in order to take a hand in striking him down. And now it must be done thoroughly; they must have peace from this fellow, who couldn't wear his chains quietly, but must make them grate like the voice of hatred that lay behind poverty and oppression.

The judge leaned out over the quay, in order to read his sentence over the "Great Power"—three times must it be read, so the man might have opportunity to repent. He was deathly pale, and at the second announcement he started convulsively; but the "Great Power" threw no dynamite cartridges at him; he merely lifted his hand to his head, as though in greeting, and made a few thrusting motions in the air with two of his fingers, which stood out from his forehead like a pair of horns. From where the apothecary stood in a circle of fine ladies a stifled laugh was heard. All faces were turned to where the burgomaster's wife stood tall and stately on a block of stone. But she gazed down unflinchingly at the "Great Power" as though she had never seen him before.

On the burgomaster the gesture had an effect like that of an explosion. "Shoot him down! " he roared, with purple face, stumbling excitedly along the breakwater. "Shoot him down, Larsen! "

But no one heeded his command. All were streaming toward the wagon-slip, where an old, faded little woman was in the act of groping her way along the track toward the floor of the basin. "It's the 'Great Power's' mother! " The word passed from mouth to mouth. "No! How little and old she is! One can hardly believe she could have brought such a giant into the world! "

Excitedly they followed her, while she tottered over the broken stone of the floor of the basin, which was littered with the *debris* of explosions until it resembled an ice-floe under pressure. She made her way but slowly, and it looked continually as though she must break her legs. But the old lady persevered, bent and withered though she was, with her shortsighted eyes fixed on the rocks before her feet.

Then she perceived her son, who stood with his iron bar poised in his hand. "Throw the stick away, Peter! " she cried sharply, and mechanically he let the iron rod fall. He gave way before her, slowly, until she had pinned him in a corner and attempted to seize him; then he pushed her carefully aside, as though she was something that inconvenienced him.

A sigh went through the crowd, and crept round the harbor like a wandering shudder. "He strikes his own mother—he must be mad! " they repeated, shuddering.

But the old woman was on her legs again. "Do you strike your own mother, Peter? " she cried, with sheer amazement in her voice, and reached up after his ear; she could not reach so far; but the "Great Power" bent down as though something heavy pressed upon him, and allowed her to seize his ear. Then she drew him away, over

490

stock and stone, in a slanting path to the slipway, where the people stood like a wall. And he went, bowed, across the floor of the basin, like a great beast in the little woman's hands.

Up on the quay the police stood ready to fall upon the "Great Power" with ropes; but the old woman was like pepper and salt when she saw their intention. "Get out of the way, or I'll let him loose on you! " she hissed. "Don't you see he has lost his intellect? Would you attack a man whom God has smitten? "

"Yes, he is mad! " said the people, in a conciliatory tone; "let his mother punish him—she is the nearest to him! "

XXI

Now Pelle and the youngest apprentice had to see to everything, for in November Jens had finished his term and had left at once. He had not the courage to go to Copenhagen to seek his fortune. So he rented a room in the poor quarter of the town and settled there with his young woman. They could not get married; he was only nineteen years of age. When Pelle had business in the northern portion of the town he used to look in on them. The table stood between the bed and the window, and there sat Jens, working on repairs for the poor folk of the neighborhood. When he had managed to get a job the girl would stand bending over him, waiting intently until he had finished, so that she could get something to eat. Then she would come back and cook something right away at the stove, and Jens would sit there and watch her with burning eyes until he had more work in hand. He had grown thin, and sported a sparse pointed beard; a lack of nourishment was written in both their faces. But they loved one another, and they helped one another in everything, as awkwardly as two children who are playing at "father and mother. " They had chosen the most dismal locality; the lane fell steeply to the sea, and was full of refuse; mangy cats and dogs ran about, dragging fish-offal up the steps of the houses and leaving it lying there. Dirty children were grubbing about before every door.

One Sunday morning, when Pelle had run out there to see them, he heard a shriek from one of the cottages, and the sound of chairs overturned. Startled, he stood still. "That's only one-eyed Johann beating his wife, " said an eight-year-old girl; "he does that almost every day. "

Before the door, on a chair, sat an old man, staring imperturbably at a little boy who continually circled round him.

Suddenly the child ran inward, laid his hands on the old man's knee, and said delightedly: "Father runs round the table—mother runs round the table—father beats mother—mother runs round the table and—cries. " He imitated the crying, laughed all over his little idiot's face, and dribbled. "Yes, yes, " was all the old man said. The child had no eyebrows, and the forehead was hollow over the eyes. Gleefully he ran round and round, stamping and imitating the uproar within. "Yes, yes, " said the old man imperturbably, "yes, yes! "

At the window of one of the cottages sat a woman, gazing out thoughtfully, her forehead leaning against the sash-bar. Pelle recognized her; he greeted her cheerfully. She motioned him to the door. Her bosom was still plump, but there was a shadow over her face. "Hans! " she cried uncertainly, "here is Pelle, whose doing it was that we found one another! "

The young workman replied from within the room: "Then he can clear out, and I don't care if he looks sharp about it! " He spoke threateningly.

In spite of the mild winter, Master Andres was almost always in bed now. Pelle had to receive all instructions, and replace the master as well as he could. There was no making of new boots now—only repairs. Every moment the master would knock on the wall, in order to gossip a little.

"To-morrow I shall get up, " he would say, and his eyes would shine; "yes, that I shall, Pelle! Give me sunlight tomorrow, you devil's imp! This is the turning-point—now nature is turning round in me. When that's finished I shall be quite well! I can feel how it's raging in my blood—it's war to the knife now—but the good sap is conquering! You should see me when the business is well forward— this is nothing to what it will be! And you won't forget to borrow the list of the lottery-drawings? "

He would not admit it to himself, but he was sinking. He no longer cursed the clergy, and one day Jeppe silently went for the pastor. When he had gone, Master Jeppe knocked on the wall.

"It's really devilish queer, " he said, "for suppose there should be anything in it? And then the pastor is so old, he ought rather to be thinking of himself. " The master lay there and looked thoughtful; he was staring up at the ceiling. He would lie all day like that; he did not care about reading now. "Jens was really a good boy, " he would say suddenly. "I could never endure him, but he really had a good disposition. And do you believe that I shall ever be a man again? "

"Yes, when once the warm weather comes, " said Pelle.

From time to time the crazy Anker would come to ask after Master Andres. Then the master would knock on the wall. "Let him come in, then, " he said to Pelle. "I find myself so terribly wearisome. " Anker had quite given up the marriage with the king's eldest daughter, and had now taken matters into his own hands. He was now working at a clock which would *be* the "new time" itself, and which would go in time with the happiness of the people. He brought the wheels and spring and the whole works with him, and explained them, while his gray eyes, fixed out-of-doors, wandered from one object to another. They were never on the thing he was exhibiting. He, like all the others, had a blind confidence in the young master, and explained his invention in detail. The clock would be so devised that it would show the time only when every one in the land had what he wanted. "Then one can always see and know if anybody is suffering need— there'll be no excuse then! For the time goes and goes, and they get nothing to eat; and one day their hour comes, and they go hungry into the grave. " In his temples that everlasting thing was beating which seemed to Pelle like the knocking of a restless soul imprisoned there; and his eyes skipped from one object to another with their vague, indescribable expression.

The master allowed himself to be quite carried away by Anker's talk as long as it lasted; but as soon as the watchmaker was on the other side of the door he shook it all off. "It's only the twaddle of a madman, " he said, astonished at himself.

Then Anker repeated his visit, and had something else to show. It was a cuckoo; every ten-thousandth year it would appear to the hour and cry "Cuckoo! " The time would not be shown any longer—only the long, long course of time—which never comes to an end— eternity. The master looked at Anker bewildered. "Send him away, Pelle! " he whispered, wiping the sweat from his forehead: "he makes me quite giddy; he'll turn me crazy with his nonsense! "

Pelle ought really to have spent Christmas at home, but the master would not let him leave him. "Who will chat with me all that time and look after everything? " he said. And Pelle himself was not so set on going; it was no particular pleasure nowadays to go home. Karna was ill, and Father Lasse had enough to do to keep her in good spirits. He himself was valiant enough, but it did not escape Pelle that as time went on he was sinking deeper into difficulties. He had not paid the latest instalment due, and he had not done well with the winter stone-breaking, which from year to year had helped him over the worst. He had not sufficient strength for all that fell to his lot. But he was plucky. "What does it matter if I'm a few hundred kroner in arrears when I have improved the property to the tune of several thousand? " he would say.

Pelle was obliged to admit the truth of that. "Raise a loan, " he advised.

Lasse did try to do so. Every time he was in the town he went to the lawyers and the savings-banks. But he could not raise a loan on the land, as on paper it belonged to the commune, until, in a given number of years, the whole of the sum to which Lasse had pledged himself should be paid up. On Shrove Tuesday he was again in town, and then he had lost his cheerful humor. "Now we know it, we had better give up at once, " he said despondently, "for now Ole Jensen is haunting the place—you know, he had the farm before me and hanged himself because he couldn't fulfill his engagements. Karna saw him last night. "

"Nonsense! " said Pelle. "Don't believe such a thing! " But he could not help believing in it just a little himself.

"You think so? But you see yourself that things are always getting more difficult for us—and just now, too, when we have improved the whole property so far, and ought to be enjoying the fruit of our labor. And Karna can't get well again, " he added despondently.

"Well, who knows? —perhaps it's only superstition! " he cried at last. He had courage for another attempt.

Master Andres was keeping his bed. But he was jolly enough there; the more quickly he sank, the more boldly he talked. It was quite wonderful to listen to his big words, and to see him lying there so wasted, ready to take his departure when the time should come.

At the end of February the winter was so mild that people were already beginning to look for the first heralds of spring; but then in one night came the winter from the north, blustering southward on a mighty ice-floe. Seen from the shore it looked as though all the vessels in the world had hoisted new white sails, and were on the way to Bornholm, to pay the island a visit, before they once again set out, after the winter's rest, on their distant voyages. But rejoicings over the breaking-up of the ice were brief; in four-and-twenty hours the island was hemmed in on every side by the ice-pack, so that there was not a speck of open water to be seen.

And then the snow began. "We really thought it was time to begin work on the land, " said the people; but they could put up with the cold—there was still time enough. They proceeded to snowball one another, and set their sledges in order; all through the winter there had been no toboggan-slide. Soon the snow was up to one's ankles, and the slide was made. Now it might as well stop snowing. It might lie a week or two, so that people might enjoy a few proper sleighing-parties. But the snow continued to flutter down, until it reached to the knee, and then to the waist; and by the time people were going to bed it was no longer possible to struggle through it. And those who did not need to rise before daylight were very near not getting out of bed at all, for in the night a snowstorm set in, and by the morning the snow reached to the roofs and covered all the windows. One could hear the storm raging about the chimneys, but down below it was warm enough. The apprentices had to go through the living-room to reach the workshop. The snow was deep there and had closed all outlets.

"What the devil is it? " said Master Andres, looking at Pelle in alarm. "Is the world coming to an end? "

Was the world coming to an end? Well, it might have come to an end already; they could not hear the smallest sound from without, to tell them whether their fellow-men were living still, or were already dead. They had to burn lamps all day long; but the coal was out in the snow, so they must contrive to get to the shed. They all pushed against the upper half-door of the kitchen, and succeeded in forcing it so far open that Pelle could just creep through. But once out there it was impossible to move. He disappeared in the mass of snow. They must dig a path to the well and the coal-shed; as for food, they would have to manage as best they could. At noon the sun came out, and so far the snow melted on the south side of the house that the upper edge of the window admitted a little daylight. A faint milky shimmer shone through the snow. But there was no sign of life outside.

"I believe we shall starve, like the people who go to the North Pole, " said the master, his eyes and mouth quite round with excitement. His eyes were blazing like lamps; he was deep in the world's fairy-tale.

During the evening they dug and bored halfway to Baker Jorgen's. They must at least secure their connection with the baker. Jeppe went in with a light. "Look out that it doesn't fall on you, " he said warningly. The light glistened in the snow, and the boys proceeded to amuse themselves. The young master lay in bed, and called out at every sound that came to him from outside—so loudly that his cough was terrible. He could not contain himself for curiosity. "I'll go and see the robbers' path, too, by God! " he said, over and over again. Jeppe scolded him, but he took no notice. He had his way, got into his trousers and fur jacket, and had a counterpane thrown about him. But he could not stand up, and with a despairing cry he fell back on the bed.

Pelle watched him until his heart burned within him. He took the master on his arm, and supported him carefully until they entered the tunnel. "You are strong; good Lord, you are strong! " The master held Pelle convulsively, one arm about his neck, while he waved the other in the air, as defiantly as the strong man in the circus. "Hip, hip! " He was infected by Pelle's strength. Cautiously he turned round in the glittering vault; his eyes shone like crystals of ice. But the fever was raging in his emaciated body. Pelle felt it like a devouring fire through all his clothes.

Next day the tunnel was driven farther—as far as Baker Jorgen's steps, and their connection with the outer world was secure. At Jorgen's great things had happened in the course of the last four-and-twenty hours. Marie had been so excited by the idea that the end of the world was perhaps at hand that she had hastily brought the little Jorgen into it. Old Jorgen was in the seventh heaven; he had to come over at once and tell them about it. "He's a regular devil, and he's the very image of me! "

"That I can well believe! " cried Master Andres, and laughed. "And is Uncle pleased? "

But Jeppe took the announcement very coolly; the condition of his brother's household did not please him. "Is Soren delighted with the youngster? " he asked cautiously.

"Soren? " The baker gave vent to a shout of laughter. "He can think of nothing but the last judgment—he's praying to the dear God! "

Later in the day the noise of shovels was heard. The workmen were outside; they cleared one of the pavements so that one could just get by; but the surface of the street was still on a level with the roofs.

Now one could get down to the harbor once more; it felt almost as though one were breathing again after a choking-fit. As far as the eyes could reach the ice extended, packed in high ridges and long ramparts where the waves had battled. A storm was brewing. "God be thanked! " said the old seamen, "now the ice will go! " But it did not move. And then they understood that the whole sea was frozen; there could not be one open spot as big as a soup-plate on which the storm could begin its work. But it was a wonderful sight, to see the sea lying dead and motionless as a rocky desert in the midst of this devastating storm.

And one day the first farmer came to town, with news of the country. The farms inland were snowed up; men had to dig pathways into the open fields, and lead the horses in one by one; but of accidents he knew nothing.

All activities came to a standstill. No one could do any work, and everything had to be used sparingly—especially coals and oil, both of which threatened to give out. The merchants had issued warnings as early as the beginning of the second week. Then the people began to take to all sorts of aimless doings; they built wonderful things with the snow, or wandered over the ice from town to town. And one day a dozen men made ready to go with the ice-boat to Sweden, to fetch the post; people could no longer do without news from the outside world. On Christianso they had hoisted the flag of distress; provisions were collected in small quantities, here, there, and everywhere, and preparations were made for sending an expedition thither.

And then came the famine; it grew out of the frozen earth, and became the only subject of conversation. But only those who were well provided for spoke of it; those who suffered from want were silent. People appealed to organized charity; there was Bjerregrav's five thousand kroner in the bank. But no, they were not there. Ship-owner Monsen declared that Bjerregrav had recalled the money during his lifetime. There was no statement in his will to the contrary. The people knew nothing positively; but the matter gave plenty of occasion for discussion. However things might be, Monsen was the great man, now as always—and he gave a thousand kroner out of his own pocket for the help of the needy.

Many eyes gazed out over the sea, but the men with the ice-boat did not come back; the mysterious "over yonder" had swallowed them.

It was as though the world had sunk into the sea; as if, behind the rugged ice-field which reached to the horizon, there now lay nothing but the abyss.

The "Saints" were the only people who were busy; they held overcrowded meetings, and spoke about the end of the world. All else lay as though dead. Under these conditions, who would worry himself about the future? In the workshop they sat in caps and overcoats and froze; the little coal that still remained had to be saved for the master. Pelle was in his room every moment. The master did not speak much now; he lay there and tossed to and fro, his eyes gazing up at the ceiling; but as soon as Pelle had left him he knocked for him again. "How are things going now? " he would ask wearily. "Run down to the harbor and see whether the ice isn't near breaking—it is so very cold; at this rate the whole earth will become a lump of ice. This evening they will certainly hold another meeting about the last judgment. Run and hear what they think about it. "

Pelle went, and returned with the desired information, but when he had done so the master had usually forgotten all about the matter. From time to time Pelle would announce that there seemed to be a bluish shimmer on the sea, far beyond the ice. Then the master's eyes would light up. But he was always cast down again by the next announcement. "The sea will eat up the ice yet—you'll see, " said Master Andres, as though from a great distance. "But perhaps it cannot digest so much. Then the cold will get the upper hand, and we shall all be done for! "

But one morning the ice-field drove out seaward, and a hundred men got ready to clear the channel of ice by means of dynamite. Three weeks had gone by since any post had been received from the outer world, and the steamer went out in order to fetch news from Sweden. It was caught by the ice out in the offing, and driven toward the south; from the harbor they could see it for days, drifting about in the ice-pack, now to the north and now to the south.

At last the heavy bonds were broken. But it was difficult alike for the earth and for mankind to resume the normal activities of life. Everybody's health had suffered. The young master could not stand the change from the bitter frost to the thaw; when his cough did not torment him he lay quite still. "Oh, I suffer so dreadfully, Pelle! " he complained, whispering. "I have no pain—but I suffer, Pelle. "

But then one morning he was in a good humor. "Now I am past the turning-point, " he said, in a weak but cheerful voice; "now you'll just see how quickly I shall get well. What day is it really to-day? Thursday? Death and the devil! then I must renew my lottery ticket! I am so light I was flying through the air all night long, and if I only shut my eyes I am flying again. That is the force in the new blood — by summer I shall be quite well. Then I shall go out and see the world! But one never—deuce take it! —gets to see the best—the stars and space and all that! So man must learn to fly. But I was there last night. "

Then the cough overpowered him again. Pelle had to lift him up; at every spasm there was a wet, slapping sound in his chest. He put one hand on Pelle's shoulder and leaned his forehead against the boy's body. Suddenly the cough ceased; and the white, bony hand convulsively clutched Pelle's shoulder. "Pelle, Pelle! " moaned the master, and he gazed at him, a horrible anxiety in his dying eyes.

"What does he see now? " thought Pelle, shuddering; and he laid him back on his pillow.

XXII

Often enough did Pelle regret that he had wasted five years as apprentice. During his apprenticeship he had seen a hundred, nay, two hundred youths pass into the ranks of the journeymen; and then they were forthwith turned into the streets, while new apprentices from the country filled up the ranks again. There they were, and they had to stand on their own legs. In most cases they had learned nothing properly; they had only sat earning their master's daily bread, and now they suddenly had to vindicate their calling. Emil had gone to the dogs; Peter was a postman and earned a krone a day, and had to go five miles to do that. When he got home he had to sit over the knee-strap and waxed-end, and earn the rest of his livelihood at night. Many forsook their calling altogether. They had spent the best years of their youth in useless labor.

Jens had done no better than the majority. He sat all day over repairs, and had become a small employer, but they were positively starving. The girl had recently had a miscarriage, and they had nothing to eat. When Pelle went to see them they were usually sitting still and staring at one another with red eyes; and over their heads hung the threat of the police, for they were not yet married. "If I only understood farm work! " said Jens. "Then I'd go into the country and serve with a farmer. "

Despite all his recklessness, Pelle could not help seeing his own fate in theirs; only his attachment to Master Andres had hindered him from taking to his heels and beginning something else.

Now everything suddenly came to an end; old Jeppe sold the business, with apprentices and all. Pelle did not wish to be sold. Now was his opportunity; now, by a sudden resolve, he might bring this whole chapter to an end.

"You don't go! " said Jeppe threateningly; "you have still a year of your apprenticeship before you! I shall give information to the police about you—and you've learned what that means. " But Pelle went. Afterward they could run to the police as often as they liked.

With a light and cheerful mind he rented an attic on the hill above the harbor, and removed his possessions thither. He felt as though he was stretching himself after his years of slavery; he no longer had any one over him, and he had no responsibilities, and no burdens. Year by year he had fought against a continual descent. It had by no means fortified his youthful courage vainly to pit his energies, day after day, against the decline of the workshop; he was only able to hold back the tide a little, and as for the rest, he must perforce sink with the business.

A good share of resignation and a little too much patience with regard to his eighteen years—this was for the moment his net profit from the process of going downhill.

Now it all lay at the foot of the hill, and he could stand aside and draw himself up a little. His conscience was clear, and he felt a somewhat mitigated delight in his freedom; that was all he had won He had no money for traveling, and his clothes were in a sad case; but that did not trouble him at first. He breathed deeply, and considered the times. The death of the master had left a great void within him; he missed that intelligent glance, which had given him the feeling that he was serving an idea; and the world was a terribly desolate and God-forsaken place now that this glance no longer rested on him, half lucid and half unfathomable, and now that the voice was silent which had always gone to his heart—when it was angry just as much as when it was infinitely mild or frolicsome. And where he was used to hear that voice his ear encountered only solitude.

He did nothing to arouse himself; he was for the present idle. This or that employer was after him, truly, for they all knew that he was a quick and reliable worker, and would willingly have taken him as apprentice, for a krone a week and his food. But Pelle would have none of them; he felt that his future did not lie in that direction. Beyond that he knew nothing, but only waited, with a curious apathy, for something to happen—something, anything. He had been hurried out of his settled way of life, yet he had no desire to set to work. From his window he could look out over the harbor, where the extensive alterations that had been interrupted by the winter were again in full swing. And the murmur of the work rose up to him; they were hewing, boring and blasting; the tip-wagons wandered in long rows up the slipway, threw their contents out on the shore, and returned. His limbs longed for strenuous work with pick and shovel, but his thoughts took another direction.

If he walked along the street the industrious townsfolk would turn to look after him, exchanging remarks which were loud enough to reach his ear. "There goes Master Jeppe's apprentice, loafing along, " they would tell one another; "young and strong he is, but he doesn't like work. He'll turn into a loafer if you give him time— that you can see. Yes, wasn't it he who got a beating at the town hall, for his brutal behavior? What else can you expect of him? "

So then Pelle kept the house. Now and again he got a little work from comrades, and poor people of his acquaintance; he did his best without proper implements, or if he could not manage otherwise he would go to Jens. Jens had lasts and an anvil. At other times he sat at the window, freezing, and gazed out over the harbor and the sea. He saw the ships being rigged and fitted, and with every ship that went gliding out of the harbor, to disappear below the horizon, it seemed to him that a last possibility had escaped him; but although he had such a feeling it did not stir him. He shrank from Morten, and did not mix with other people. He was ashamed to be so idle when every one else was working.

As for food, he managed fairly well; he lived on milk and bread, and needed only a few ore a day. He was able to avoid extreme hunger. As for firing, it was not to be thought of. Sitting idly in his room, he enjoyed his repose, apart from a certain feeling of shame; otherwise he was sunk in apathy.

On sunny mornings he got up early and slipped out of the town. All day long he would stroll in the great pine-woods or lie on the dunes by the shore, with the murmur of the sea sounding through his half-slumber. He ate like a dog whatever he could get that was eatable, without particularly thinking of what it consisted. The glitter of the sun on the water, and the poignant scent of the pine-trees, and the first rising of the sluggish sap which came with spring, made him dizzy, and filled his brain with half-wild imaginations. The wild animals were not afraid of him, but only stood for a moment inhaling his scent; then they would resume their daily life before his eyes. They had no power to disturb his half-slumber; but if human beings approached, he would hide himself, with a feeling of hostility, almost of hatred. He experienced a kind of well-being out in the country. The thought often occurred to him that he would give up his dwelling in the town, and creep at night under the nearest tree.

Only when the darkness hid him did he return to his room. He would throw himself, fully dressed, on his bed, and lie there until he fell asleep. As though from a remote distance he could hear his next-door neighbor, Strom the diver, moving about his room with tottering steps, and clattering with his cooking utensils close at hand. The smell of food, mingled with tobacco smoke and the odor of bedding, which crept through the thin board partition, and hovered, heavy and suffocating, above his head, became even more overpowering. His mouth watered. He shut his eyes and forced himself to think of other things, in order to deaden his hunger. Then a light, well-known step sounded on the stairs and some one knocked on the door—it was Morten. "Are you there, Pelle? " he asked. But Pelle did not move.

Pelle could hear Strom attacking his bread with great bites, and chewing it with a smacking sound; and suddenly in the intervals of mastication, another sound was audible; a curious bellowing, which was interrupted every time the man took a bite; it sounded like a child eating and crying simultaneously. That another person should cry melted something in Pelle, and filled him with a feeble sense of something living; he raised himself on his elbows and listened to Strom struggling with terror, while cold shudders chased one another down his back.

People said that Strom lived here because in his youth he had done something at home. Pelle forgot his own need and listened, rigid with terror, to this conflict with the powers of evil. Patiently, through his clenched teeth, in a voice broken by weeping, Strom attacked the throng of tiny devils with words from the Bible. "I'll do something to you at last that'll make you tuck your tails between your legs! " he cried, when he had read a little. There was a peculiar heaviness about his speech, which seemed charged with a craving for peace. "Ah! " he cried presently, "you want some more, you damned rascals, do you? Then what have you got to say to this —'I, the Lord thy God, the God of Abraham, the God of Isaac, the God of Jacob'" — Strom hurled the words at them, anger crept into his voice, and suddenly he lost patience. He took the Bible and flung it on the floor. "Satan take you, then! " he shouted, laying about him with the furniture.

Pelle lay bathed in sweat, listening to this demoniac struggle; and it was with a feeling of relief that he heard Strom open the window and drive the devils out over the roofs. The diver fought the last part of the battle with a certain humor. He addressed the corner of the room in a wheedling, flattering tone. "Come, you sweet, pretty little devil! What a white skin you have—Strom would so like to stroke you a little! No, you didn't expect that! Are we getting too clever for you? What? You'd still bite, would you, you devil's brat? There, don't scowl like that! "—Strom shut the window with an inward chuckle.

For a while he strolled about amusing himself. "Strom is still man enough to clear up Hell itself! " he said, delighted.

Pelle heard him go to bed, and he himself fell asleep. But in the night he awoke; Strom was beating time with his head against the board partition, while he lay tearfully singing "By the waters of Babylon! " But halfway through the psalm the diver stopped and stood up. Pelle heard him groping to and fro across the floor and out on the landing. Seized with alarm, he sprang out of bed and struck a light. Outside stood Strom, in the act of throwing a noose over the rafters. "What do you want here? " he said fiercely. "Can I never get any peace from you? "

"Why do you want to lay hands on yourself? " asked Pelle quietly.

"There's a woman and a little child sitting there, and she's forever and forever crying in my ear. I can't stand it any longer! " answered Strom, knotting his rope.

"Think of the little child, then! " said Pelle firmly, and he tore down the rope. Strom submitted to be led back into his room, and he crawled into bed. But Pelle must stay with him; he dared not put out the light and lie alone in the darkness.

"Is it the devils? " asked Pelle.

"What devils? " Strom knew nothing of any devils. "No, it's remorse, " he replied. "The child and its mother are continually complaining of my faithlessness. "

But next moment he would spring out of bed and stand there whistling as though he was coaxing a dog. With a sudden grip he seized something by the throat, opened the window, and threw it out. "So, that was it! " he said, relieved; "now there's none of the devil's brood left! " He reached after the bottle of brandy.

"Leave it alone! " said Pelle, and he took the bottle away from him. His will increased in strength at the sight of the other's misery.

Strom crept into bed again. He lay there tossing to and fro, and his teeth chattered. "If I could only have a mouthful! " he said pleadingly; "what harm can that do me? It's the only thing that helps me! Why should a man always torment himself and play the respectable when he can buy peace for his soul so cheaply? Give me a mouthful! " Pelle passed him the bottle. "You should take one yourself—it sets a man up! Do you think I can't see that you've suffered shipwreck, too? The poor man goes aground so easily, he has so little water under the keel. And who d'you think will help him to get off again if he's betrayed his own best friend? Take a swallow, then—it wakes the devil in us and gives us courage to live, "

No, Pelle wanted to go to bed.

"Why do you want to go now? Stay here, it is so comfortable. If you could, tell me about something, something that'll drive that damned noise out of my ears for a bit! There's a young woman and a little child, and they're always crying in my ears. "

Pelle stayed, and tried to distract the diver. He looked into his own empty soul, and he could find nothing there; so he told the man of Father Lasse and of their life at Stone Farm, with everything mixed up just as it occurred to him. But his memories rose up within him as he spoke of them, and they gazed at him so mournfully that they awakened his crippled soul to life. Suddenly he felt utterly wretched about himself, and he broke down helplessly.

"Now, now! " said Strom, raising his head. "Is it your turn now? Have you, too, something wicked to repent of, or what is it? "

"I don't know. "

"You don't know? That's almost like the women—crying is one of their pleasures. But Strom doesn't hang his head; he would like to be at peace with himself, if it weren't for a pair of child's eyes that look at him so reproachfully, day in and day out, and the crying of a girl! They're both at home there in Sweden, wringing their hands for their daily bread. And the one that should provide for them is away from them here and throws away his earnings in the beer-houses. But perhaps they're dead now because I've forsaken them. Look you, that is a real grief; there's no child's talk about that! But you must take a drink for it. "

But Pelle did not hear; he sat there gazing blindly in front of him. All at once the chair began to sail through air with him; he was almost fainting with hunger. "Give me just one drink—I've had not a mouthful of food to-day! " He smiled a shamefaced smile at the confession.

With one leap, Strom was out of bed. "No, then you shall have something to eat, " he said eagerly, and he fetched some food. "Did one ever see the like—such a desperate devil! To take brandy on an empty stomach! Eat now, and then you can drink yourself full elsewhere! Strom has enough on his conscience without that.... He can drink his brandy himself! Well, well, then, so you cried from hunger! It sounded like a child crying to me! "

Pelle often experienced such nights. They enlarged his world in the direction of the darkness. When he came home late and groped his way across the landing he always experienced a secret terror lest he should rub against Strom's lifeless body; and he only breathed freely when he heard him snoring or ramping round his room. He liked to look in on him before he went to bed.

Strom was always delighted to see him, and gave him food; but brandy he would not give him. "It's not for fellows as young as you! You'll get the taste for it early enough, perhaps. "

"You drink, yourself, " said Pelle obstinately.

"Yes, I drink to deaden remorse. But that's not necessary in your case. "

"I'm so empty inside, " said Pelle. "Really brandy might set me up a little. I feel as if I weren't human at all, but a dead thing, a table, for instance. "

"You must do something—anything—or you'll become a good-for-nothing. I've seen so many of our sort go to the dogs; we haven't enough power of resistance! "

"It's all the same to me what becomes of me! " replied Pelle drowsily. "I'm sick of the whole thing! "

XXIII

It was Sunday, and Pelle felt a longing for something unaccustomed. At first he went out to see Jens, but the young couple had had a dispute and had come to blows. The girl had let the frying-pan containing the dinner fall into the fire, and Jens had given her a box on the ears. She was still white and poorly after her miscarriage. Now they were sitting each in a corner, sulking like children. They were both penitent, but neither would say the first word. Pelle succeeded in reconciling them, and they wanted him to stay for dinner. "We've still got potatoes and salt, and I can borrow a drop of brandy from a neighbor! " But Pelle went; he could not watch them hanging on one another's necks, half weeping, and kissing and babbling, and eternally asking pardon of one another.

So he went out to Due's. They had removed to an old merchant's house where there was room for Due's horses. They seemed to be getting on well. It was said that the old consul took an interest in them and helped them on. Pelle never went into the house, but looked up Due in the stable, and if he was not at home Pelle would go away again. Anna did not treat him as though he was welcome. Due himself greeted him cordially. If he had no rounds to make he used to hang about the stable and potter round the horses; he did not care about being in the house. Pelle gave him a hand, cutting chaff for him, or helping in anything that came to hand, and then they would go into the house together. Due was at once another man if he had Pelle behind him; he was more decided in his behavior. Anna was gradually and increasingly getting the upper hand over him.

She was just as decided as ever, and kept the house in good order. She no longer had little Marie with her. She dressed her own two children well, and sent them to a school for young children, and she paid for their attendance. She was delightful to look at, and understood how to dress herself, but she would hear nothing good of any one else. Pelle was not smart enough for her; she turned up her nose at his every-day clothes, and in order to make him feel uncomfortable she was always talking about Alfred's engagement to Merchant Lau's daughter. This was a fine match for him. "*He* doesn't loaf about and sleep his time away, and sniff at other people's doors in order to get their plate of food, " she said. Pelle only laughed; nothing made any particular impression on him nowadays. The children ran about, wearying themselves in their fine clothes —they

508

must not play with the poor children out-of-doors, and must not make themselves dirty. "Oh, play with us for a bit, Uncle Pelle! " they would say, hanging on to him. "Aren't you our uncle too? Mother says you aren't our uncle. She's always wanting us to call the consul uncle, but we just run away. His nose is so horribly red. "

"Does the consul come to see you, then? " asked Pelle.

"Yes, he often comes—he's here now! "

Pelle peeped into the yard. The pretty wagon had been taken out. "Father's gone out, " said the children. Then he slipped home again. He stole a scrap of bread and a drop of brandy from Strom, who was not at home, and threw himself on his bed. As the darkness came on he strolled out and lounged, freezing, about the street corners. He had a vague desire to do something. Well-dressed people were promenading up and down the street, and many of his acquaintances were there, taking their girls for a walk; he avoided having to greet them, and to listen to whispered remarks and laughter at his expense. Lethargic as he was, he still had the acute sense of hearing that dated from the time of his disgrace at the town hall. People enjoyed finding something to say when he passed them; their laughter still had the effect of making his knees begin to jerk with a nervous movement, like the quickly-suppressed commencement of a flight.

He slipped into a side-street; he had buttoned his thin jacket tightly about him, and turned up his collar. In the half-darkness of the doorways stood young men and girls, in familiar, whispered conversation. Warmth radiated from the girls, and their bibbed aprons shone in the darkness. Pelle crept along in the cold, and knew less than ever what to do with himself; he ranged about to find a sweetheart for himself.

In the market he met Alfred, arm-in-arm with Lau's daughter. He carried a smart walking-stick, and wore brown gloves and a tall hat. "The scamp—he still owes me two and a half kroner, and I shall never get it out of him! " thought Pelle, and for a moment he felt a real desire to spring upon him and to roll all his finery in the mud. Alfred turned his head the other way. "He only knows me when he wants to do something and has no money! " said Pelle bitterly.

He ran down the street at a jog-trot, in order to keep himself warm, turning his eyes toward the windows. The bookbinder and his wife were sitting at home, singing pious songs. The man drank when at home; that one could see plainly on the blind. At the wool-merchant's they were having supper.

Farther on, at the Sow's, there was life, as always. A mist of tobacco smoke and a great deal of noise were escaping through the open window. The Sow kept a house for idle seamen, and made a great deal of money. Pelle had often been invited to visit her, but had always considered himself too good; moreover, he could not bear Rud. But this evening he seized greedily upon the memory of this invitation, and went in. Perhaps a mouthful of food would come his way.

At a round table sat a few tipsy seamen, shouting at one another, and making a deafening row. The Sow sat on a young fellow's knee; she lay half over the table and dabbled her fingers in a puddle of spilt beer; from time to time she shouted right in the face of those who were making the most noise. The last few years had not reduced her circumference.

"Now look at that! Is that you, Pelle? " she said, and she stood up to give him her hand. She was not quite sober, and had some difficulty in taking his. "That's nice of you to come, now—I really thought we weren't good enough for you! Now, sit down and have a drop; it won't cost you anything. " She motioned to him to take a seat.

The sailors were out of humor; they sat staring sleepily at Pelle. Their heavy heads wagged helplessly. "That's surely a new customer? " asked one, and the others laughed.

The Sow laughed too, but all at once became serious. "Then you can leave him out of your games, for he's far too good to be dragged into anything; one knows what you are! " She sank into a chair next to Pelle, and sat looking at him, while she rubbed her own greasy countenance. "How tall and fine you've grown—but you aren't well-off for clothes! And you don't look to be overfed.... Ah, I've known you from the time when you and your father came into the country; a little fellow you were then, and Lasse brought me my mother's hymn-book! " She was suddenly silent, and her eyes filled with tears.

One of the sailors whispered to the rest, and they began to laugh.

"Stop laughing, you swine! " she cried angrily, and she crossed over to them. "You aren't going to play any of your nonsense with him— he comes like a memory of the times when I was respectable, too. His father is the only creature living who can prove that I was once a pretty, innocent little maid, who got into bad company. He's had me on his lap and sung lullabies to me. " She looked about her defiantly, and her red face quivered.

"Didn't you weigh as much then as you do now? " asked one of the men, and embraced her.

"Don't play the fool with the little thing! " cried another. "Don't you see she's crying? Take her on your lap and sing her a lullaby— then she'll believe you are Lasse-Basse! "

Raging, she snatched up a bottle. "Will you hold your tongue with your jeering? Or you'll get this on the head! " Her greasy features seemed to run together in her excitement.

They let her be, and she sat there sobbing, her hands before her face. "Is your father still alive? " she asked. "Then give him my respects— just say the Sow sends her respects—you can safely call me the Sow! —and tell him he's the only person in the world I have to thank for anything. He thought well of me, and he brought me the news of mother's death. "

Pelle sat there listening with constraint to her tearful speech, with an empty smile. He had knives in his bowels, he was so empty, and the beer was going to his head. He remembered all the details of Stone Farm, where he had first seen and heard the Sow, just as Father Lasse had recalled her home and her childhood to her. But he did not connect any further ideas with that meeting; it was a long time ago, and—"isn't she going to give me anything to eat? " he thought, and listened unsympathetically to her heavy breathing.

The sailors sat looking at her constrainedly; a solemn silence lay on their mist-wreathed faces; they were like drunken men standing about a grave. "Give over washing the decks now—and get us something to drink! " an old fellow said suddenly. "Each of us knows what it is to have times of childish innocence come back to him, and I say it's a jolly fine thing when they will peep through the door at old devils like us! But let the water stop overboard now, I say! The more one scours an old barge the more damage comes to light! So, give us something to drink now, and then the cards, ma'am! "

She stood up and gave them what they asked for; she had mastered her emotion, but her legs were still heavy.

"That's right—and then we've got a sort of idea that to-day is Sunday! Show us your skill, ma'am, quick! "

"But that costs a krone, you know! " she said, laughing.

They collected the money and she went behind the bar and undressed. She reappeared in her chemise, with a burning candle in her hand....

Pelle slipped out. He was quite dizzy with hunger and a dull feeling of shame. He strolled on at random, not knowing what he did. He had only one feeling—that everything in the world was indifferent to him, whatever happened—whether he went on living in laborious honesty, or defiled himself with drinking, or perished—it was all one to him! What was the good of it all? No one cared what happened to him—not even he himself. Not a human soul would miss him if he went to the dogs—but yes, there was Lasse, Father Lasse! But as for going home now and allowing them to see him in all his wretchedness —when they had expected such unreasonable things of him—no, he could not do it! The last remnants of shame protested against it. And to work—what at? His dream was dead. He stood there with a vague feeling that he had come to the very edge of the abyss, which is so ominous to those in the depths.

Year in, year out, he had kept himself by his never-flagging exertions, and with the demented idea that he was mounting upward. And now he stood very near the lowest depth of life—the very bottom. And he was so tired. Why not let himself sink yet a little further; why not let destiny run its course? There would be a seductive repose in the acts, after his crazy struggle against the superior powers.

The sound of a hymn aroused him slightly. He had come down a side-street, and right in front of him stood a wide, lofty building, with the gable facing the street and a cross on the point of the gable. Hundreds of voices had sought, in the course of the years, to entice him hither; but in his arrogance he had had no use for spiritual things. What was there here for a smart youngster? And now he was stranded outside! And now he felt a longing for a little care, and he had a feeling that a hand had led him hither.

The hall was quite filled with poor families. They were packed amazingly close together on the benches, each family by itself; the men, as a rule, were asleep, and the women had all they could do to quiet their children, and to make them sit politely with their legs sticking out in front of them. These were people who had come to enjoy a little light and warmth, free of cost, in the midst of their desolate lives; on Sundays, at least, they thought, they could ask for a little of these things. They were the very poorest of the poor, and they sought refuge here, where they would not be persecuted, and where they were promised their part in the millennium. Pelle knew them all, both those whom he had seen before and those others, who wore the same expression, as of people drowned in the ocean of life. He soon found himself cozily settled among all these dishevelled nestlings, whom the pitiless wind had driven oversea, and who were now washed ashore by the waves.

A tall man with a full beard and a pair of good child-like eyes stood up among the benches, beating the time of a hymn—he was Dam, the smith. He led the singing, and as he stood there he bent his knees in time, and they all sang with him, with tremulous voices, each in his own key, of that which had passed over them. The notes forced their way through the parched, worn throats, cowering, as though afraid, now that they had flown into the light. Hesitatingly they unfurled their fragile, gauzy wings, and floated out into the room, up from the quivering lips. And under the roof they met with their hundreds of sisters, and their defilement fell from them. They became a jubilation, loud and splendid, over some unknown treasure, over the kingdom of happiness, that was close at hand. To Pelle it seemed that the air must be full of butterflies winged with sunshine:

> "O blessed, blessed shall we be
> When we, from care and mis'ry free,
> The splendor of Thy kingdom see,
> And with our Saviour come to Thee! "

"Mother, I'm hungry! " said a child's voice, as the hymn was followed by silence. The mother, herself emaciated, silenced the child with a shocked expression, and looked wonderingly about her. What a stupid idea of the child's! "You've just had your food! " she said loudly, as though she had been comfortably off. But the child went on crying: "Mother, I'm so hungry! "

Then Baker Jorgen's Soren came by, and gave the child a roll. He had a whole basket full of bread. "Are there any more children who are hungry? " he asked aloud. He looked easily in people's faces, and was quite another creature to what he was at home; here no one laughed at him, and no one whispered that he was the brother of his own son.

An old white-bearded man mounted the pulpit at the back of the hall. "That's him, " was whispered in every direction, and they all hastened to clear their throats by coughing, and to induce the children to empty their mouths of food. He took the cry of the little one as his text: "Mother, I am so hungry! " That was the voice of the world—that great, terrible cry—put into the mouth of a child. He saw no one there who had not writhed at the sound of that cry on the lips of his own flesh and blood—no one who, lest he should hear it again, had not sought to secure bread during his lifetime—no one who had not been beaten back. But they did not see God's hand when that hand, in its loving-kindness, changed that mere hunger for bread into a hunger for happiness. They were the poor, and the poor are God's chosen people. For that reason they must wander in the desert, and must blindly ask: "Where is the Promised Land? " But the gleam of which the faithful followed was not earthly happiness! God himself led them to and fro until their hunger was purged and became the true hunger—the hunger of the soul for eternal happiness!

They did not understand much of what he said; but his words set free something within them, so that they engaged in lively conversation over everyday things. But suddenly the buzz of conversation was silenced; a little hunchbacked man had clambered up on a bench and was looking them over with glittering eyes. This was Sort, the traveling shoemaker from the outer suburb.

"We want to be glad and merry, " he said, assuming a droll expression; "God's children are always glad, however much evil they have to fight against, and they can meet with no misfortune— God is Joy! " He began to laugh, as boisterously as a child, and they all laughed with him; one infected the next. They could not control themselves; it was as though an immense merriment had overwhelmed them all. The little children looked at the grown-ups and laughed, till their little throats began to cough with laughing. "He's a proper clown! " said the men to their wives, their own faces broad with laughter, "but he's got a good heart! "

On the bench next to Pelle sat a silent family, a man and wife and three children, who breathed politely through their raw little noses. The parents were little people, and there was a kind of inward deftness about them, as though they were continually striving to make themselves yet smaller. Pelle knew them a little, and entered into conversation with them. The man was a clay-worker, and they lived in one of the miserable huts near the "Great Power's" home.

"Yes, that is true—that about happiness, " said the wife. "Once we too used to dream of getting on in the world a little, so that we might be sure of our livelihood; and we scraped a little money together, that some good people lent us, and we set up in a little shop, and I kept it while father went to work. But it wouldn't answer; no one supported us, and we got poorer goods because we were poor, and who cares about dealing with very poor people? We had to give it up, and we were deeply in debt, and we're still having to pay it off— fifty ore every week, and there we shall be as long as we live, for the interest is always mounting up. But we are honorable people, thank God! " she concluded. The man took no part in the conversation.

Her last remark was perhaps evoked by a man who had quietly entered the hall, and was now crouching on a bench in the background; for he was not an honorable man. He had lived on a convict's bread and water; he was "Thieving Jacob, " who about ten years earlier had smashed in the window of Master Jeppe's best room and had stolen a pair of patent-leather shoes for his wife. He had heard of a rich man who had given his betrothed such a pair of shoes, and he wanted to see what it was like, just for once, to give a really fine present—a present worth as much as one would earn in two weeks. This he had explained before the court. "Numbskull! " said Jeppe always, when the conversation touched upon Jacob; "for such a miserable louse suddenly to get a swollen head, to want to make big presents! And if it had been for his young woman even— but for his wife! No, he paid the penalty to the very last day—in spite of Andres. "

Yes, he certainly had to pay the penalty! Even here no one would sit next to him! Pelle looked at him and wondered that his own offence should be so little regarded. The remembrance of it now only lay in people's eyes when they spoke to him. But at this moment Smith Dam went and sat next to Thieving Jacob, and they sat hand-in-hand and whispered.

And over yonder sat some one who nodded to Pelle—in such a friendly manner; it was the woman of the dancing-shoes; her young man had left her, and now she was stranded here—her dancing days were over. Yet she was grateful to Pelle; the sight of him had recalled delightful memories; one could see that by the expression of her eyes and mouth.

Pelle's own temper was softened as he sat there. Something melted within him; a quiet and humble feeling of happiness came over him. There was still one human being who believed herself in Pelle's debt, although everything had gone wrong for her.

As the meeting was breaking up, at half-past nine, she was standing in the street, in conversation with another woman. She came up to Pelle, giving him her hand. "Shall we walk a little way together? " she asked him. She evidently knew of his circumstances; he read compassion in her glance. "Come with me, " she said, as their ways parted. "I have a scrap of sausage that's got to be eaten. And we are both of us lonely. "

Hesitatingly he went with her, a little hostile, for the occasion was new and unfamiliar. But once he was seated in her little room he felt thoroughly at ease. Her white, dainty bed stood against the wall. She went to and fro about the room, cooking the sausage at the stove, while she opened her heart to him, unabashed.

It isn't everybody would take things so easily! thought Pelle, and he watched her moving figure quite happily.

They had a cheerful meal, and Pelle wanted to embrace her in his gratitude, but she pushed his hands away. "You can keep that for another time! " she said, laughing. "I'm a poor old widow, and you are nothing but a child. If you want to give me pleasure, why, just settle down and come to yourself again. It isn't right that you should be just loafing about and idling, and you so young and such a nice boy. And now go home, for I must get up early to-morrow and go to my work. "

516

Pelle visited her almost every evening. She had a disagreeable habit of shaking him out of his slumber, but her simple and unchanging manner of accepting and enduring everything was invigorating. Now and again she found a little work for him, and was always delighted when she could share her poor meal with him. "Any one like myself feels a need of seeing a man-body at the table-end once in a while, " she said. "But hands off—you don't owe me anything! "

She criticized his clothes. "They'll all fall off your body soon— why don't you put on something else and let me see to them? "

"I have nothing but these, " said Pelle, ashamed.

On Saturday evening he had to take off his rags, and creep, mother-naked, into her bed. She would take no refusal, and she took shirt and all, and put them into a bucket of water. It took her half the night to clean everything. Pelle lay in bed watching her, the coverlet up to his chin. He felt very strange. As for her, she hung the whole wash to dry over the stove, and made herself a bed on a couple of chairs. When he woke up in the middle of the morning she was sitting by the window mending his clothes.

"But what sort of a night did you have? " asked Pelle, a trifle concerned.

"Excellent! Do you know what I've thought of this morning? You ought to give up your room and stay here until you are on your feet again —you've had a good rest—for once, " she smiled teasingly. "That room is an unnecessary expense. As you see, there's room here for two. "

But Pelle would not agree. He would not hear of being supported by a woman. "Then people will believe that there's something wrong between us—and make a scandal of it, " he said.

"Let them then! " she answered, with her gay laugh. "If I've a good conscience it's indifferent to me what others think. " While she was talking she was working diligently at his linen, and she threw one article after another at his head. Then she ironed his suit. "Now you're quite a swell again! " she said, when he stood up dressed once more, and she looked at him affectionately. "It's as though you had become a new creature. If I were only ten or fifteen years younger I'd be glad to go down the street on your arm. But you shall give me a kiss—I've put you to rights again, as if you were my own child. " She kissed him heartily and turned about to the stove.

"And now I've got no better advice than that we have some cold dinner together and then go our ways, " she said, with her back still turned. "All my firing has been used overnight to dry your things, and you can't stay here in the cold. I think I can pay a visit somewhere or other, and so the day will pass; and you can find some corner to put yourself in. '

"It's all the same to me where I am, " said Pelle indifferently.

She looked at him with a peculiar smile. "Are you really always going to be a loater? " she said. "You men are extraordinary creatures! If anything at all goes wrong with you, you must start drinking right away, or plunge yourself into unhappiness in some other way—you are no better than babies! We must work quietly on, however things go with us! " She stood there hesitating in her hat and cloak. "Here's five-and-twenty ore, " she said; "that's just for a cup of coffee to warm you! "

Pelle would not accept it. "What do I want with your money? " he said. "Keep it yourself! "

"Take it, do! I know it's only a little, but I have no more, and there's no need for us to be ashamed of being helped by one another. " She put the coin in his jacket pocket and hurried off.

Pelle strolled out to the woods. He did not feel inclined to go home, to resume the aimless battle with Strom. He wandered along the deserted paths, and experienced a feeble sense of well-being when he noticed that the spring was really coming. The snow was still lying beneath the old moss-gray pinetrees, but the toadstools were already thrusting their heads up through the pine-needles, and one had a feeling, when walking over the ground, as though one trod upon rising dough.

He found himself pondering over his own affairs, and all of a sudden he awoke out of his half-slumber. Something had just occurred to him, something cozy and intimate—why, yes, it was the thought that he might go to Marie and set up for himself, like Jens and his girl. He could get hold of a few lasts and sit at home and work... he could scrape along for a bit, until better times came. She earned something too, and she was generous.

But when he thought over the matter seriously it assumed a less pleasant aspect. He had already sufficiently abused her poverty and her goodness of heart. He had taken her last scrap of firing, so that she was now forced to go out in order to get a little warmth and some supper. The idea oppressed him. Now that his eyes were opened he could not escape this feeling of shame. It went home and to bed with him, and behind all her goodness he felt her contempt for him, because he did not overcome his misery by means of work, like a respectable fellow.

On the following morning he was up early, and applied for work down at the harbor. He did not see the necessity of work in the abstract, but he would not be indebted to a woman. On Sunday evening he would repay her outlay over him and his clothes.

XXIV

Pelle stood on the floor of the basin, loading broken stone into the tip-wagons. When a wagon was full he and his comrade pushed it up to the head of the track, and came gliding back hanging to the empty wagons. Now and again the others let fall their tools, and looked across to where he stood; he was really working well for a cobbler! And he had a fine grip when it came to lifting the stone. When he had to load a great mass of rock into the wagon, he would lift it first to his knee, then he would let out an oath and put his whole body into it; he would wipe the sweat from his forehead and take a dram of brandy or a drop of beer. He was as good as any of the other men!

He did not bother himself with ideas; two and two might make five for all he cared; work and fatigue were enough for him. Hard work had made his body supple and filled him with a sense of sheer animal well-being. "Will my beer last out the afternoon to-day? " he would wonder; beyond that nothing mattered. The future did not exist, nor yet the painful feeling that it did not exist; there was no remorse in him for what he had lost, or what he had neglected; hard work swallowed up everything else. There was only this stone that had to be removed—and then the next! This wagon which had to be filled— and then the next! If the stone would not move at the first heave he clenched his teeth; he was as though possessed by his work. "He's still fresh to harness, " said the others; "he'll soon knock his horns off! " But Pelle wanted to show his strength; that was his only ambition. His mate let him work away in peace and did not fatigue himself. From time to time he praised Pelle, in order to keep his steam up.

This work down at the harbor was the hardest and lowest kind of labor; any one could get taken on for it without previous qualifications. Most of Pelle's comrades were men who had done with the world, who now let themselves go as the stream carried them, and he felt at ease among them. He stood on the solid ground, and no words had power to call the dead past to life; it had power to haunt only an empty brain. An iron curtain hung before the future; happiness lay here to his hand; the day's fatigue could straightway be banished by joyous drinking.

His free time he spent with his companions. They led an unsettled, roving life; the rumor that extensive works were to be carried out had enticed them hither. Most were unmarried; a few had wives and children somewhere, but held their tongues about them, or no longer remembered their existence, unless reminded by something outside themselves. They had no proper lodgings, but slept in Carrier Koller's forsaken barn, which was close to the harbor. They never undressed, but slept in the straw, and washed in a bucket of water that was seldom changed; their usual diet consisted of stale bread, and eggs, which they grilled over a fire made between two stones.

The life pleased Pelle, and he liked the society. On Sundays they ate and drank alternately, all day long, and lay in the smoke-filled barn; burrowing deep into the straw, they told stories, tragic stories of youngest sons who seized an axe and killed their father and mother, and all their brothers and sisters, because they thought they were being cheated of their share of their inheritance! Of children who attended confirmation class, and gave way to love, and had children themselves, and were beheaded for what they did! And of wives who did not wish to bring into the world the children it was their duty to bear, and whose wombs were closed as punishment!

Since Pelle had begun to work here he had never been out to see Marie Nielsen. "She's making a fool of you, " said the others, to whom he had spoken of Marie; "she's playing the respectable so that you shall bite. Women have always got second thoughts—it's safest to be on the lookout. They and these young widows would rather take two than one—they're the worst of all. A man must be a sturdy devil to be able to stand up against them. "

But Pelle was a man, and would allow no woman to lead him by the nose. Either you were good friends and no fuss about it, or nothing. He'd tell her that on Saturday, and throw ten kroner on the table— then they would sure enough be quits! And if she made difficulties she'd get one over the mouth! He could not forgive her for using all her firing, and having to pass Sunday in the street; the remembrance would not leave him, and it burned like an angry spark. She wanted to make herself out a martyr.

One day, about noon, Pelle was standing among the miners on the floor of the basin; Emil and he had just come from the shed, where they had swallowed a few mouthfuls of dinner. They had given up their midday sleep in order to witness the firing of a big blast during the midday pause when the harbor would be empty. The whole space was cleared, and the people in the adjacent houses had opened their windows so that they should not be shattered by the force of the explosion.

The fuse was lit, and the men took shelter behind the caissons, and stood there chatting while they waited for the explosion. The "Great Power" was there too. He was always in the neighborhood; he would stand and stare at the workers with his apathetic expression, without taking part in anything. They took no notice of him, but let him move about as he pleased. "Take better cover, Pelle, " said Emil; "it's going off directly! "

"Where are Olsen and Strom? " said some one suddenly. The men looked at one another bewildered.

"They'll be taking their midday sleep, " said Emil. "They've been drinking something chronic this morning. "

"Where are they sleeping? " roared the foreman, and he sprang from his cover. They all had a foreboding, but no one wanted to say. It flashed across them that they must do something. But no one stirred. "Lord Jesus! " said Bergendal, and he struck his fist against the stone wall. "Lord Jesus! "

The "Great Power" sprang from his shelter and ran along the side of the basin, taking long leaps from one mass of rock to the next, his mighty wooden shoes clattering as he went. "He's going to tear the fuse away! " cried Bergendal. "He'll never reach it—it must be burnt in! " There was a sound as of a cry of distress, far above the heads of those who heard it. They breathlessly followed the movements of the "Great Power"; they had come completely out of shelter. In Pelle an irrational impulse sprang into being. He made a leap forward, but was seized by the scruff of the neck. "One is enough, " said Bergendal, and he threw him back.

Now the "Great Power" had reached the goal. His hand was stretched out to seize the fuse. Suddenly he was hurled away from the fuse, as though by an invisible hand, and was swept upward and backward through the air, gently, like a human balloon, and fell on his back. Then the roar of the explosion drowned everything.

When the last fragments had fallen the men ran forward. The "Great Power" lay stretched upon his back, looking quietly up at the sky. The corners of his mouth were a little bloody and the blood trickled from a hole behind the ear. The two drunken men were scathless. They rose to their feet, bewildered, a few paces beyond the site of the explosion. The "Great Power" was borne into the shed, and while the doctor was sent for Emil tore a strip from his blouse, and soaked it in brandy, and laid it behind the ear.

The "Great Power" opened his eyes and looked about him. His glance was so intelligent that every one knew that he had not long to live.

"It smells of brandy here, " he said. "Who will stand me a drop? " Emil reached him the bottle, and he emptied it. "It tastes good, " he said easily. "Now I haven't touched brandy for I don't know how long, but what was the good? The poor man must drink brandy, or he's good for nothing; it is no joke being a poor man! There is no other salvation for him; that you have seen by Strom and Olsen—drunken men never come to any harm. Have they come to any harm? " He tried to raise his head. Strom stepped forward. "Here we are, " he said, his voice stifled with emotion. "But I'd give a good deal to have had us both blown to hell instead of this happening. None of us has wished you any good! " He held out his hand.

But the "Great Power" could not raise his; he lay there, staring up through the holes in the thatched roof. "It has been hard enough, certainly, to belong to the poor, " he said, "and it's a good thing it's all over. But you owe me no thanks. Why should I leave you in the lurch and take everything for myself—would that be like the 'Great Power'? Of course, the plan was mine! But could I have carried it out alone? No, money does everything. You've fairly deserved it! The 'Great Power' doesn't want to have more than any one else—where we have all done an equal amount of work. " He raised his hand, painfully, and made a magnanimous gesture.

"There—he believes he's the engineer of the harbor works! " said Strom. "He's wandering. Wouldn't a cold application do him good? " Emil took the bucket in order to fetch fresh water. The "Great Power" lay with closed eyes and a faint smile on his face; he was like a blind man who is listening. "Do you understand, " he said, without opening his eyes, "how we have labored and labored, and yet have been barely able to earn our daily bread? The big people sat there and ate up everything that we could produce; when we laid down our tools and wanted to still our hunger there was nothing. They stole our thoughts, and if we had a pretty sweetheart or a young daughter they could do with her too—they didn't disdain our cripple even. But now that's done with, and we will rejoice that we have lived to see it; it might have gone on for a long time. Mother wouldn't believe what I told her at all—that the bad days would soon be over. But now just see! Don't I get just as much for my work as the doctor for his? Can't I keep my wife and daughter neat and have books and get myself a piano, just as he can? Isn't it a great thing to perform manual labor too? Karen has piano lessons now, just as I've always wished, for she's weakly and can't stand any hard work. You should just come home with me and hear her play—she does it so easily too! Poor people's children have talent too, it's just that no one notices it. "

"God, how he talks! " said Strom, crying. "It's almost as if he had the delirium. "

Pelle bent down over the "Great Power. " "Now you must be good and be quiet, " he said, and laid something wet on his forehead. The blood was trickling rapidly from behind his ear.

"Let him talk, " said Olsen. "He hasn't spoken a word for months now; he must feel the need to clear his mind this once. It'll be long before he speaks again, too! "

Now the "Great Power" was only weakly moving his lips. His life was slowly bleeding away. "Have you got wet, little Karen? " he murmured. "Ah, well, it'll dry again! And now it's all well with you, now you can't complain. Is it fine to be a young lady? Only tell me everything you want. Why be modest? We've been that long enough! Gloves for the work-worn fingers, yes, yes. But you must play something for me too. Play that lovely song: 'On the joyful journey through the lands of earth.... ' That about the Eternal Kingdom! "

Gently he began to hum it; he could no longer keep time by moving his head, but he blinked his eyes in time; and now his humming broke out into words.

Something irresistibly impelled the others to sing in concert with him; perhaps the fact that it was a religious song. Pelle led them with his clear young voice; and it was he who best knew the words by heart.

> "Fair, fair is earth,
> And glorious Heaven;
> Fair is the spirit's journey long;
> Through all the lovely earthly kingdoms,
> Go we to Paradise with song. "

The "Great Power" sang with increasing strength, as though he would outsing Pelle. One of his feet was moving now, beating the time of the song. He lay with closed eyes, blindly rocking his head in time with the voices, like one who, at a drunken orgy, must put in his last word before he slips under the table. The saliva was running from the corners of his mouth.

> "The years they come,
> The years they go
> And down the road to death we throng,
> But ever sound the strains from heaven—
> The spirit's joyful pilgrim song! "

The "Great Power" ceased; his head drooped to one side, and at the same moment the others ceased to sing.

They sat in the straw and gazed at him—his last words still rang in their ears, like a crazy dream, which mingled oddly with the victorious notes of the hymn.

They were all sensible of the silent accusation of the dead, and in the solemnity of the moment they judged and condemned themselves.

"Yes, who knows what we might come to! " said one ragged fellow, thoughtfully chewing a length of straw.

"I shall never do any good, " said Emil dejectedly. "With me it's always been from bad to worse. I was apprenticed, and when I became a journeyman they gave me the sack; I had wasted five years of my life and couldn't do a thing. Pelle—he'll get on all right. "

Astonished, Pelle raised his head and gazed at Emil uncomprehendingly.

"What use is it if a poor devil tries to make his way up? He'll always be pushed down again! " said Olsen. "Just look at the 'Great Power'; could any one have had a better claim than he? No, the big folks don't allow us others to make our way up! "

"And have we allowed it ourselves? " muttered Strom. "We are always uneasy if one of our own people wants to fly over our heads! "

"I don't understand why all the poor folk don't make a stand together against the others, " said Bergendal. "We suffer the same wrongs. If we all acted together, and had nothing to do with them that mean us harm, for instance, then it would soon be seen that collective poverty is what makes the wealth of the others. And I've heard that that's what they're doing elsewhere. "

"But we shall never in this life be unanimous about anything whatever, " said an old stonemason sadly. "If one of the gentlemen only scratches our neck a bit, then we all grovel at his feet, and let ourselves be set on to one of our own chaps. If we were all like the 'Great Power, ' then things might have turned out different. "

They were silent again; they sat there and gazed at the dead man; there was something apologetic in the bearing of each and all.

"Yes, that comes late! " said Strom, with a sigh. Then he felt in the straw and pulled out a bottle.

Some of the men still sat there, trying to put into words something that ought perhaps to be said; but then came the doctor, and they drew in their horns. They picked up their beer-cans and went out to their work.

Silently Pelle gathered his possessions together and went to the foreman. He asked for his wages.

"That's sudden, " said the foreman. "You were getting on so well just now. What do you want to do now? "

"I just want my wages, " rejoined Pelle. What more he wanted, he himself did not know. And then he went home and put his room in order. It was like a pigsty; he could not understand how he could have endured such untidiness. In the meantime he thought listlessly of some way of escape. It had been very convenient to belong to the dregs of society, and to know that he could not sink any deeper; but perhaps there were still other possibilities. Emil had said a stupid thing—what did he mean by it? "Pelle, he'll get on all right! " Well, what did Emil know of the misery of others? He had enough of his own.

He went down into the street in order to buy a little milk; then he would go back and sleep. He felt a longing to deaden all the thoughts that once more began to seethe in his head.

Down in the street he ran into the arms of Sort, the wandering shoemaker. "Now we've got you! " cried Sort. "I was just coming here and wondering how best I could get to speak with you. I wanted to tell you that I begin my travelling to-morrow. Will you come with me? It is a splendid life, to be making the round of the farms now in the spring-time; and you'll go to the dogs if you stay here. Now you know all about it and you can decide. I start at six o'clock! I can't put it off any later! "

Sort had observed Pelle that evening at the prayer-meeting, and on several occasions had spoken to him in the hope of arousing him. "He can put off his travels for a fortnight as far as I'm concerned! " thought Pelle, with a touch of self-esteem. He wouldn't go! To go begging for work from farm to farm! Pelle had learned his craft in the workshop, and looked down with contempt upon the travelling cobbler, who lives from hand to mouth and goes from place to place like a beggar, working with leather and waxed-ends provided on the spot, and eating out of the same bowl as the farm servants. So much pride of craft was still left in Pelle. Since his apprentice days, he had been accustomed to regard Sort as a pitiful survival from the past, a species properly belonging to the days of serfdom.

"You'll go to the dogs! " Sort had said. And all Marie Melsen's covert allusions had meant the same thing. But what then? Perhaps he had already gone to the dogs! Suppose there was no other escape than this! But now he would sleep, and think no more of all these things.

He drank his bottle of milk and ate some bread with it, and went to bed. He heard the church clock striking—it was midnight, and glorious weather. But Pelle wanted to sleep—only to sleep! His heart was like lead.

He awoke early next morning and was out of bed with one leap. The sun filled his room, and he himself was filled with a sense of health and well-being. Quickly he slipped into his clothes—there was still so much that he wanted to do! He threw up the window, and drank in the spring morning in a breath that filled his body with a sense of profound joy. Out at sea the boats were approaching the harbor; the morning sun fell on the slack sails, and made them glow; every boat was laboring heavily forward with the aid of its tiller. He had slept like a stone, from the moment of lying down until now. Sleep lay like a gulf between yesterday and to-day. Whistling a tune to himself, he packed his belongings and set out upon his way, a little bundle under his arm. He took the direction of the church, in order to see the time. It was still not much past five. Then he made for the outermost suburb with vigorous steps, as joyful as though he were treading the road to happiness.

XXV

Two men appeared from the wood and crossed the highroad. One was little and hump-backed; he had a shoemaker's bench strapped tightly on his back; the edge rested on his hump, and a little pillow was thrust between, so that the bench should not chafe him. The other was young and strongly built; a little thin, but healthy and fresh- colored. He carried a great bundle of lasts on his back, which were held in equilibrium by another box, which he carried on his chest, and which, to judge by the sounds that proceeded from it, contained tools. At the edge of the ditch he threw down his burden and unstrapped the bench from the hunchback. They threw themselves down in the grass and gazed up into the blue sky. It was a glorious morning; the birds twittered and flew busily to and fro, and the cattle were feeding in the dewy clover, leaving long streaks behind them as they moved.

"And in spite of that, you are always happy? " said Pelle. Sort had been telling him the sad story of his childhood.

"Yes, look you, it often vexes me that I take everything so easily— but what if I can't find anything to be sad about? If I once go into the matter thoroughly, I always hit on something or other that makes me still happier—as, for instance, your society. You are young, and health beams out of your eyes. The girls become so friendly wherever we go, and it's as though I myself were the cause of their pleasure! "

"Where do you really get your knowledge of everything? " asked Pelle.

"Do you find that I know so much? " Sort laughed gaily. "I go about so much, and I see so many different households, some where man and wife are as one, and others where they live like cat and dog. I come into contact with people of every kind. And I get to know a lot, too, because I'm not like other men—more than one maiden has confided her miseries to me. And then in winter, when I sit alone, I think over everything—and the Bible is a good book, a book a man can draw wisdom from. There a man learns to look behind things; and if you once realize that everything has its other side, then you learn to use your understanding. You can go behind everything if you want to, and they all lead in the same direction—to God. And they all came from Him. He is the connection, do you see; and once a man grasps that, then he is always happy. It would be splendid to follow things up further—right up to where they divide, and then to show, in spite of all, that they finally run together in God again! But that I'm not able to do. "

"We ought to see about getting on. " Pelle yawned, and he began to bestir himself.

"Why? We're so comfortable here—and we've already done what we undertook to do. What if there should be a pair of boots yonder which Sort and Pelle won't get to sole before they're done with? Some one else will get the job! "

Pelle threw himself on his back and again pulled his cap over his eyes—he was in no hurry. He had now been travelling nearly a month with Sort, and had spent almost as much time on the road as sitting at his work. Sort could never rest when he had been a few days in one place; he must go on again! He loved the edge of the wood and the edge of the meadow, and could spend half the day there. And Pelle had many points of contact with this leisurely life in the open air; he had his whole childhood to draw upon. He could lie for hours, chewing a grass-stem, patient as a convalescent, while sun and air did their work upon him.

"Why do you never preach to me? " he said suddenly, and he peeped mischievously from tinder his cap.

"Why should I preach to you? Because I am religious? Well, so are you; every one who rejoices and is content is religious. "

"But I'm not at all content! " retorted Pelle, and he rolled on his back with all four limbs in the air. "But you—I don't understand why you don't get a congregation; you've got such a power over language. "

"Yes, if I were built as you are—fast enough. But I'm humpbacked! "

"What does that matter? You don't want to run after the women! "

"No, but one can't get on without them; they bring the men and the children after them. And it's really queer that they should—for women don't bother themselves about God! They haven't the faculty of going behind things. They choose only according to the outside—

they want to hang everything on their bodies as finery—and the men too, yes, and the dear God best of all—they've got a use for the lot! "

Pelle lay still for a time, revolving his scattered experiences. "But Marie Nielsen wasn't like that, " he said thoughtfully. "She'd willingly give the shirt off her body and ask nothing for herself. I've behaved badly to her—I didn't even say goodbye before I came away! "

"Then you must look her up when we come to town and confess your fault. There was no lovemaking between you? "

"She treated me like a child; I've told you. "

Sort was silent a while.

"If you would help me, we'd soon get a congregation! I can see it in your eyes, that you've got influence over them, if you only cared about it; for instance, the girl at Willow Farm. Thousands would come to us. "

Pelle did not answer. His thoughts were roaming back wonderingly to Willow Farm, where Sort and he had last been working; he was once more in that cold, damp room with the over-large bed, on which the pale girl's face was almost invisible. She lay there encircling her thick braids with her transparent hand, and gazed at him; and the door was gently closed behind him. "That was really a queer fancy, " he said, and he breathed deeply; "some one she'd never laid eyes on before; I could cry now when I think of it. "

"The old folks had told her we were there, and asked if she wouldn't like me to read something from God's word with her. But she'd rather see you. The father was angry and didn't want to allow it. 'She has never thought about young men before, ' he said, 'and she shall stand before the throne of God and the Lamb quite pure. ' But I said, 'Do you know so precisely that the good God cares anything for what you call purity, Ole Jensen? Let the two of them come together, if they can take any joy in it. ' Then we shut the door behind you— and how was it then? " Sort turned toward Pelle.

"You know, " replied Pelle crossly. "She just lay there and looked at me as though she was thinking: 'That's what he looks like—and he's

531

come a long way here. ' I could see by her eyes that you had spoken of me and that she knew about all my swinishness. "

Sort nodded.

"Then she held out her hand to me. How like she is to one of God's angels already—I thought—but it's a pity in one who's so young. And then I went close to her and took her hand. "

"And what then? " Sort drew nearer to Pelle. His eyes hung expectantly on Pelle's lips.

"Then she stretched out her mouth to me a little—and at that very moment I forgot what sort of a hog I'd been—and I kissed her! "

"Didn't she say anything to you—not a word? "

"She only looked at me with those eyes that you can't understand. Then I didn't know what I—what I ought to do next, so I came away. "

"Weren't you afraid that she might transfer death to you? "

"No; why should I be? I didn't think about it. But she could never think of a thing like that—so child-like as she was! "

They both lay for a time without speaking. "You have something in you that conquers them all! " said Sort at length. "If only you would help me—I'd see to the preaching! "

Pelle stretched himself indolently—he felt no desire to create a new religion. "No, I want to go away and see the world now, " he said. "There must be places in that world where they've already begun to go for the rich folks—that's where I want to go! "

"One can't achieve good by the aid of evil—you had better stay here! Here you know where you are—and if we went together—"

"No, there's nothing here for any one to do who is poor—if I go on here any longer, I shall end in the mud again. I want to have my share—even if I have to strike a bloodsucker dead to get it—and that couldn't be any very great sin! But shan't we see about getting on now? We've been a whole month now tramping round these Sudland farms. You've always promised me that we should make our way toward the heath. For months now I've heard nothing of Father Lasse and Karna. When things began to go wrong with me, it was as though I had quite forgotten them. "

Sort rose quickly. "Good! So you've still thoughts for other things than killing bloodsuckers! How far is it, then, to Heath Farm? "

"A good six miles. "

"We'll go straight there. I've no wish to begin anything to-day. "

They packed their possessions on their backs and trudged onward in cheerful gossip. Sort pictured their arrival to Pelle. "I shall go in first and ask whether they've any old boots or harness that we can mend; and then you'll come in, while we're in the middle of a conversation. "

Pelle laughed. "Shan't I carry the bench for you? I can very well strap it on the other things. "

"You shan't sweat for me as well as yourself! " rejoined Sort, laughing. "You'd want to take off even your trousers then. "

They had chattered enough, and tramped on in silence. Pelle stepped forward carelessly, drinking in the fresh air. He was conscious of a superfluity of strength and well-being; otherwise he thought of nothing, but merely rejoiced unconsciously over his visit to his home. At every moment he had to moderate his steps, so that Sort should not be left behind.

"What are you really thinking about now? " he asked suddenly. He would always have it that Sort was thinking of something the moment he fell silent. One could never know beforehand in what region he would crop up next.

"That's just what the children ask! " replied Sort, laughing. "They always want to know what's inside. "

"Tell me, then—you might as well tell me! "

"I was thinking about life. Here you walk at my side, strong and certain of victory as the young David. And yet a month ago you were part of the dregs of society! "

"Yes, that is really queer, " said Pelle, and he became thoughtful.

"But how did you get into such a mess? You could quite well have kept your head above water if you had only wanted to! "

"That I really don't know. I tell you, it's as if some one had hit you over the head; and then you run about and don't know what you're doing; and it isn't so bad if you've once got there. You work and drink and bang each other over the head with your beer-cans or bottles—"

"You say that so contentedly—you don't look behind things—that's the point! I've seen so many people shipwrecked; for the poor man it's only one little step aside, and he goes to the dogs; and he himself believes he's a devilish fine fellow. But it was a piece of luck that you got out of it all! Yes, it's a wonder remorse didn't make your life bitter. "

"If we felt remorse we had brandy, " said Pelle, with an experienced air. "That soon drives out everything else. "

"Then it certainly has its good points—it helps a man over the time of waiting! "

"Do you really believe that an eternal kingdom is coming—the 'thousand-year kingdom'—the millennium? With good times for all, for the poor and the miserable? "

Sort nodded. "God has promised it, and we must believe His Word. Something is being prepared over on the mainland, but whether it's the real millennium, I don't know. "

They tramped along. The road was stony and deserted. On either side the rocky cliffs, with their scrubby growth, were beginning to rise from the fields, and before them ranged the bluish rocky landscape of the heath or moorland. "As soon as we've been home, I shall travel; I must cross the sea and find out what they do really intend there, " said Pelle.

"I have no right to hold you back, " answered Sort quietly, "but it will be lonely travelling for me. I shall feel as if I'd lost a son. But of course you've got other things to think of than to remember a poor hunchback! The world is open to you. Once you've feathered your nest, you'll think no more of little Sort! "

"I shall think of you, right enough, " replied Pelle. "And as soon as I'm doing well I shall come back and look out for you—not before. Father will be sure to object to my idea of travelling—he would so like me to take over Heath Farm from him; but there you must back me up. I've no desire to be a farmer. "

"I'll do that. "

"Now just look at it! Nothing but stone upon stone with heather and scrubby bushes in between! That's what Heath Farm was four years ago —and now it's quite a fine property. That the two of them have done —without any outside help. "

"You must be built of good timber, " said Sort. "But what poor fellow is that up on the hill? He's got a great sack on his back and he's walking as if he'd fall down at every step. "

"That—that is Father Lasse! Hallo! " Pelle waved his cap.

Lasse came stumbling up to them; he dropped his sack and gave them his hand without looking at them.

"Are you coming this way? " cried Pelle joyfully; "we were just going on to look for you! "

"You can save yourself the trouble! You've become stingy about using your legs. Spare them altogether! " said Lasse lifelessly.

Pelle stared at him. "What's the matter? Are you leaving? "

"Yes, we're leaving! " Lasse laughed—a hollow laugh. "Leaving— yes! We've left—indeed, we've each of us gone our own way. Karna has gone where there's no more care and trouble—and here's Lasse, with all that's his! " He struck his foot against the sack, and stood there with face averted from them, his eyes fixed upon the ground.

All signs of life had vanished from Pelle's face. Horrified, he stared at his father, and his lips moved, but he could form no words.

"Here I must meet my own son by accident in the middle of the empty fields! So often as I've looked for you and asked after you! No one knew anything about you. Your own flesh and blood has turned from you, I thought—but I had to tell Karna you were ill. She fully expected to see you before she went away. Then you must give him my love, she said, and God grant all may go well with him. She thought more about you than many a mother would have done! Badly you've repaid it. It's a long time ago since you set foot in our house."

Still Pelle did not speak; he stood there swaying from side to side; every word was like the blow of a club.

"You mustn't be too hard on him!" said Sort. "He's not to blame—ill as he's been!"

"Ah, so you too have been through bad times and have got to fight your way, eh? Then, as your father, I must truly be the last to blame you." Lasse stroked his son's sleeve, and the caress gave Pelle pleasure. "Cry, too, my son—it eases the mind. In me the tears are dried up long ago. I must see how I can bear my grief; these have become hard times for me, you may well believe. Many a night have I sat by Karna and been at my wits' end—I could not leave her and go for help, and everything went wrong with us all at the same time. It almost came to my wishing you were ill. You were the one who ought to have had a kindly thought for us, and you could always have sent us news. But there's an end of it all!"

"Are you going to leave Heath Farm, father?" asked Pelle quietly.

"They have taken it away from me," replied Lasse wretchedly. "With all these troubles, I couldn't pay the last instalment, and now their patience is at an end. Out of sheer compassion they let me stay till Karna had fought out her fight and was happily buried in the earth—every one could see it wasn't a matter of many days more."

"If it is only the interest," said Sort, "I have a few hundred kroner which I've saved up for my old days."

"Now it's too late; the farm is already taken over by another man. And even if that were not the case—what should I do there without Karna? I'm no longer any use! "

"We'll go away together, father! " said Pelle, raising his head.

"No; I go nowhere now except to the churchyard. They have taken my farm away from me, and Karna has worked herself to death, and I myself have left what strength I had behind me. And then they took it away from me! "

"I will work for us both—you shall be comfortable and enjoy your old days! " Pelle saw light in the distance.

Lasse shook his head. "I can no longer put things away from me—I can no longer leave them behind and go on again! "

"I propose that we go into the town, " said Sort. "Up by the church we are sure to find some one who will drive us in. "

They collected their things and set off. Lasse walked behind the others, talking to himself; from time to time he broke out into lamentation. Then Pelle turned back to him in silence and took his hand.

"There is no one to help us and give us good advice. On the contrary, they'd gladly see us lose life and fortune if they could only earn a few shillings on that account. Even the authorities won't help the poor man. He's only there so that they can all have a cut at him and then each run off with his booty. What do they care that they bring need and misery and ruin upon us? So long as they get their taxes and their interest! I could stick them all in the throat, in cold blood! "

So he continued a while, increasing in bitterness, until he broke down like a little child.

XXVI

They lived with Sort, who had his own little house in the outermost suburb. The little travelling cobbler did not know what to do for them: Lasse was so dejected and so aimless. He could not rest; he did not recover; from time to time he broke out into lamentation. He had grown very frail, and could no longer lift his spoon to his mouth without spilling the contents. If they tried to distract him, he became obstinate.

"Now we must see about fetching your things, " they would both say repeatedly. "There is no sense in giving your furniture to the parish. "

But Lasse would not have them sent for. "They've taken everything else from me; they can take that, too, " he said. "And I won't go out there again—and let myself be pitied by every one. "

"But you'll beggar yourself, " said Sort.

"They've done that already. Let them have their way. But they'll have to answer for it in the end! "

Then Pelle procured a cart, and drove over himself to fetch them. There was quite a load to bring back. Mother Bengta's green chest he found upstairs in the attic; it was full of balls of thread. It was so strange to see it again—for many years he had not thought of his mother. "I'll have that for a travelling trunk, " he thought, and he took it with him.

Lasse was standing before the door when he returned.

"See, I've brought everything here for you, father! " he cried, lustily cracking his whip. But Lasse went in without saying a word. When they had unloaded the cart and went to look for him, he had crawled into bed. There he lay with his face to the wall, and would not speak.

Pelle told him all sorts of news of Heath Farm, in order to put a little life into him. "Now the parish has sold Heath Farm to the Hill Farm man for five thousand kroner, and they say he's got a good bargain. He wants to live there himself and to leave Hill Farm in his son's hands. "

Lasse half turned his head. "Yes, something grows there now. Now they are making thousands—and the farmer will do better still, " he said bitterly. "But it's well-manured soil. Karna overstrained herself and died and left me.... And we went so well in harness together. Her thousand kroner went into it, too... and now I'm a poor wreck. All that was put into the barren, rocky soil, so that it became good and generous soil. And then the farmer buys it, and now he wants to live there—we poor lice have prepared the way for him! What else were we there for? Fools we are to excite ourselves so over such a thing! But, how I loved the place! " Lasse suddenly burst into tears.

"Now you must be reasonable and see about becoming cheerful again, " said Sort. "The bad times for the poor man will soon be over. There is a time coming when no one will need to work himself to death for others, and when every one will reap what he himself has sown. What injury have you suffered? For you are on the right side and have thousands of kroner on which you can draw a bill. It would be still worse if you owed money to others! "

"I haven't much more time, " said Lasse, raising himself on his elbows.

"Perhaps not, you and I, for those who start on the pilgrimage must die in the desert! But for that reason we are God's chosen people, we poor folk. And Pelle, he will surely behold the Promised Land! "

"Now you ought to come in, father, and see how we have arranged it, " said Pelle.

Lasse stood up wearily and went with them. They had furnished one of Sort's empty rooms with Lasse's things. It looked quite cozy.

"We thought that you would live here until Pelle is getting on well 'over there, '" said Sort. "No, you don't need to thank me! I'm delighted to think I shall have society, as you may well understand. "

"The good God will repay it to you, " said Lasse, with a quavering voice. "We poor folk have no one but Him to rely on. "

Pelle could not rest, nor control his thoughts any longer; he must be off! "If you'll give me what the fare comes to, as I've helped you, " he told Sort, "then I'll start this evening.... "

Sort gave him thirty kroner.

"That's the half of what we took. There's not so much owing to me, " said Pelle. "You are the master and had the tools and everything. "

"I won't live by the work of other hands—only by that of my own, " said Sort, and he pushed the money across to Pelle. "Are you going to travel just as you stand? "

"No, I have plenty of money, " said Pelle gaily. "I've never before possessed so much money all at once! One can get quite a lot of clothes for that. "

"But you mustn't touch the money! Five kroner you'll need for the passage and the like, the rest you must save, so that you can face the future with confidence! "

"I shall soon earn plenty of money in Copenhagen! "

"He has always been a thoughtless lad, " said Lasse anxiously. "Once, when he came into town here to be apprenticed he had five kroner; and as for what he spent them on, he could never give any proper account! "

Sort laughed.

"Then I shall travel as I stand! " said Pelle resolutely. But that wouldn't do, either!

He could not by any means please both—they were like two anxious clucking hens.

He had no lack of linen, for Lasse had just thought of his own supply. Karna had looked after him well. "But it will be very short for your long body. It's not the same now as it was when you left Stone Farm—then we had to put a tuck in my shirt for you. "

In the matter of shoes he was not well off. It would never do for a journeyman shoemaker to look for work wearing such shoes as his. Sort and Pelle must make a pair of respectable boots. "We must leave ourselves time, " said Sort. "Think! They must be able to stand the judgment of the capital! " Pelle was impatient, and wanted to get the work quickly out of hand.

Now there was only the question of a new suit. "Then buy it ready made on credit, " said Sort. "Lasse and I will be good enough securities for a suit. "

In the evening, before he started, he and Lasse went out to look up Due. They chose the time when they were certain of meeting Due himself. They neither of them cared much for Anna. As they approached the house they saw an old richly-dressed gentleman go in at the front door.

"That is the consul, " said Pelle, "who has helped them to get on. Then Due is out with the horses, and we are certainly not welcome. "

"Is it like that with them? " said Lasse, standing still. "Then I am sorry for Due when he first finds out how his affairs really stand! He will certainly find that he has bought his independence too dearly! Yes, yes; for those who want to get on the price is hard to pay. I hope it will go well with you over there, my boy. "

They had reached the church. There stood a cart full of green plants; two men were carrying them into a dwelling-house.

"What festivity's going on here? " asked Pelle.

"There's to be a wedding to-morrow, " answered one of the men. "Merchant Lau's daughter is marrying that swaggering fellow, who's always giving himself airs—Karlsen, he's called, and he's a poor chap like ourselves. But do you suppose he'll notice us? When dirt comes to honor, there's no bearing with it! Now he's become a partner in the business! "

"Then I'll go to the wedding, " said Lasse eagerly, while they strolled on. "It is very interesting to see when one of a family comes to something. " Pelle felt that this was to some extent meant as a reproach, but he said nothing.

"Shall we have one look at the new harbor? " he said.

"No, now the sun's going down, and I'll go home and get to bed. I'm old—but you go. I shall soon find my way back. " Pelle strolled onward, but then turned aside toward the north—he would go and bid Marie Nielsen good-bye. He owed her a friendly word for all her goodness. Also, as an exception, she should for once see him in respectable clothes. She had just come home from her work, and was on the point of preparing her supper.

"No, Pelle, is that you? " she cried delightedly, "and so grand, too— you look like a prince! " Pelle had to remain to supper.

"I have really only come to thank you for all your friendliness and to say good-bye. To-morrow I go to Copenhagen. "

She looked at him earnestly. "And you are glad! "

Pelle had to tell her what he had been doing since he had last seen her. He sat there looking gratefully about the poor, clean room, with the bed set so innocently against the wall, covered with a snow-white counterpane. He had never forgotten that fragrance of soap and cleanliness and her fresh, simple nature. She had taken him in the midst of all his misery and had not thought her own white bed too good for him while she scrubbed the mire from him. When he reached the capital he would have himself photographed and send her his portrait.

"And how are you doing now? " he asked gently.

"Just as when you last saw me—only a little more lonely, " she answered earnestly.

And then he must go. "Good-bye, and may everything go well with you! " he said, and he shook her hand. "And many thanks for all your goodness! "

She stood before him silently, looking at him with an uncertain smile. "Ah, no! I'm only a human being too! " she cried suddenly, and she flung her arms about him in a passionate embrace.

And then the great day broke! Pelle awaked with the sun and had the green chest already packed before the others were up, and then he roamed about, not knowing what he should set his hand to, he was so restless and so excited. He answered at random, and his eyes were full of radiant dreams. In the morning he and Lasse carried the chest to the steamer, in order to have the evening free. Then they went to the church, in order to attend Alfred's wedding. Pelle would gladly have stayed away; he had enough to do with his own affairs, and he had no sympathy for Alfred's doings.

But Lasse pushed him along.

The sun stood high in heaven and blazed in the winding side-streets so that the tarred timberwork sweated and the gutters stank; from the harbor came the sound of the crier, with his drum, crying herrings, and announcing an auction. The people streamed to church in breathless conversation concerning this child of fortune, Alfred, who had climbed so far.

The church was full of people. It was gaily decorated, and up by the organ stood eight young women who were to sing "It is so lovely together to be! " Lasse had never seen or heard of such a wedding. "I feel quite proud! " he said.

"He's a bladder full of wind! " said Pelle. "He's taking her simply on account of the honor. "

And then the bridal pair stepped up to the altar. "It's tremendous the way Alfred has greased his head! " whispered Lasse. "It looks like a newly-licked calf's head! But she is pretty. I'm only puzzled that she's not put on her myrtle-wreath—I suppose nothing has happened? "

"Yes, she's got a child, " whispered Pelle. "Otherwise, he would never in this world have got her! "

"Oh, I see! Yes, but that's smart of him, to catch such a fine lady! "

Now the young women sang, and it sounded just as if they were angels from heaven who had come to seal the bond.

"We must take our places so that we can congratulate them, " said Lasse, and he wanted to push right through the crowd, but Pelle held him back.

"I'm afraid he won't know us to-day; but look now, there's Uncle Kalle. "

Kalle stood squeezed among the hindmost chairs, and there he had to stay until everybody had passed out. "Yes, I was very anxious to take part in this great day, " he said, "and I wanted to bring mother with me, but she thought her clothes weren't respectable enough. "

Kalle wore a new gray linsey-woolsey suit; he had grown smaller and more bent with the years.

"Why do you stand right away in the corner here, where you can see nothing? As the bridegroom's father, you must have been given your place in the first row, " said Lasse.

"I have been sitting there, too—didn't you see me sitting next to Merchant Lau? We sang out of the same hymn-book. I only got pushed here in the crowd. Now I ought to go to the wedding-feast. I was properly invited, but I don't quite know.... " He looked down at himself. Suddenly he made a movement, and laughed in his own reckless way. "Ugh—what am I doing standing here and telling lies to people who don't believe me! No, pigs don't belong in the counting-house! I might spread a bad smell, you know! People like us haven't learned to sweat scent! "

"Bah! He's too grand to know his own father! Devil take it! Then come with us so that you needn't go away hungry! " said Lasse.

"No—I've been so overfed with roast meats and wine and cakes that I can't get any more down for the present. Now I must go home and tell mother about all the splendid things. I've eighteen miles to go. "

"And you came here on foot—thirty-six miles! That's too much for your years! "

"I had really reckoned that I'd stay the night here. I didn't think... Well, an owl's been sitting there! Children can't very well climb higher than that—not to recognize their own fathers! Anna is now taking the best way to become a fine lady, too.... I shall be wondering how long I shall know myself! Devil take it, Kalle Karlsen, I'm of good family, too, look you! Well, then, ajoo! "

Wearily he set about tramping home. He looked quite pitiful in his disappointment. "He's never looked so miserable in his life! " said Lasse, gazing after him, "and it takes something, too, to make Brother Kalle chuck his gun into the ditch! "

Toward evening they went through the town to the steamer. Pelle took long strides, and a strange feeling of solemnity kept him silent. Lasse trotted along at his side; he stooped as he went. He was in a

544

doleful mood. "Now you won't forget your old father? " he said, again and again.

"There's no danger of that, " rejoined Sort. Pelle heard nothing of this; his thoughts were all set on his journey. The blue smoke of kitchen fires was drifting down among the narrow lanes. The old people were sitting out of doors on their front steps, and were gossiping over the news of the day. The evening sun fell upon round spectacles, so that great fiery eyes seemed to be staring out of their wrinkled faces. The profound peace of evening lay over the streets. But in the narrow lanes there was the breathing of that eternal, dull unrest, as of a great beast that tosses and turns and cannot sleep. Now and again it blazed up into a shout, or the crying of a child, and then began anew—like heavy, labored breathing. Pelle knew it well, that ghostly breathing, which rises always from the lair of the poor man. The cares of poverty had shepherded the evil dreams home for the night. But he was leaving this world of poverty, where life was bleeding away unnoted in the silence; in his thoughts it was fading away like a mournful song; and he gazed out over the sea, which lay glowing redly at the end of the street. Now he was going out into the world!

The crazy Anker was standing at the top of his high steps. "Goodbye! " cried Pelle, but Anker did not understand. He turned his face up to the sky and sent forth his demented cry.

Pelle threw a last glance at the workshop. "There have I spent many a good hour! " he thought; and he thought, too, of the young master. Old Jorgen was standing before his window, playing with the little Jorgen, who sat inside on the windowseat. "Peep, peep, little one! " he cried, in his shrill voice, and he hid, and bobbed up into sight again. The young wife was holding the child; she was rosy with maternal delight.

"You'll be sure to let us hear from you, " said Lasse yet again, as Pelle stood leaning over the steamer's rail. "Don't forget your old father! " He was quite helpless in his anxiety.

"I will write to you as soon as I'm getting on, " said Pelle, for the twentieth time at least. "Only don't worry! " Sure of victory, he laughed down at the old man. For the rest they stood silent and gazed at one another.

At last the steamer moved. "Good luck—take care of yourself! " he cried for the last time, as they turned the pier-head; and as long as he could see he waved his cap. Then he went right forward and sat on a coil of rope.

He had forgotten all that lay behind him. He gazed ahead as though at any moment the great world itself might rise in front of the vessel's bow. He pictured nothing to himself of what was to come and how he would meet it—he was only longing—longing!

THE END.

CPSIA information can be obtained at www.ICGtesting.com
Printed in the USA
BVOW04s1004210314

348378BV00001B/64/A